The Planet Star—Unfolding Prophecy

Bedside Books
An imprint of American Book Publishing
5442 So. 900 East, #146
Salt Lake City, UT 84117-7204
www.american-book.com
Printed in the United States of America on acid-free paper.

The Planet Star—Unfolding Prophecy

Designed by Michael Knight design@american-book.com

Publisher's Note: This is a work of fiction. Names, characters, places, and incidents either are the product of the author's imagination, or are used fictitiously, and any resemblance to actual persons, living or dead, events, or locales is entirely coincidental.

ISBN-13: 978-1-58982-454-6
ISBN-10: 1-58982-454-7

Chakrabarti, C.M., The Planet Star—Unfolding Prophecy

The Planet Star—
Unfolding Prophecy

by C. M. Chakrabarti

THE PLANET GALAN

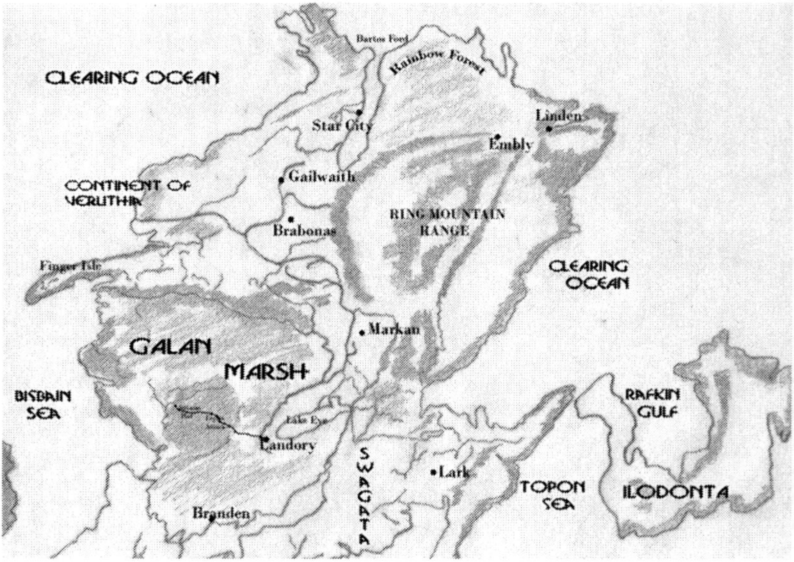

CONTENTS

PROLOGUE

The Keepers

During the ancient days of the Khalian Solar System, fifteen Keepers, super powerful creatures, came to that galactic area as mentors and guardians to the humanoid inhabitants living within a system comprised of fifteen planets. They were sent by the Keeper of the universe, to carry out his purpose to unify creatures living in that solar system. No one really knew where they came from, but the Keepers were revered and honored throughout the populace as those on a divine mission.

Upon their arrival, each Keeper possessed a unique gem from each of the fifteen Khalian planets, transferring their dominant attribute into that gemstone. The single power of each Keeper was held together by Nila, the gemstone of Unity; it's Keeper, Uzak, making him the most powerful of all the fifteen Keepers sent to the Khalian Solar System. His gemstone, Nila, a deep bluish-purple gem, emitted a force which held in subjugation, the collective attributes of all the gemstones. The unified attributes begin with Solan, Keeper of life. From him, the dominant powers form the Keepers of Knowledge, Truth, Love, and Hope were subject. Beneath these are the remaining attributes: Strength, Wisdom, Foresight, Kindness, Joy, Peace, Faith, Charity, and Health.

The Covenant

Although the Keepers were endowed with many attributes, each Keeper's dominant attribute was brought together collectively to function as a single unit. Any breach of a single Keeper would render the covenant of unification null and void, so it was not possible in this collective setting to use their other non-dominant attributes singularly. Breaching the Covenant would also separate the Keepers from one another, making it impossible for them to communicate between themselves. The Keeper of the Universe sent them as a single unit, and they were to operate as a unit until the covenant was fulfilled.

Each gem was placed in a floral star like medallion which was placed upon a pedestal. Energy from the Star emanated a shield which blanketed the entire Solar System, not only protecting it from invasion from other galaxies, but also maintain equilibrium in intellectual and technical growth.

The inhabitants were at similar cultural stages when the Keepers first appeared. Their societies were both tribal and territorial, each planet populated by less than a million beings. The Covenant of the Keepers, as demanded by the Keeper of the Universe, was the unification of the populace for the entire Khalian Solar System. The Keepers were to be both guardians and teachers, to prevent the populace from becoming warriors against one another.

In the beginning, the Keepers adopted a humanoid form and moved from planet to planet, verbally communicating with the inhabitants. As a result, intellect and technology grew rapidly and because there was so little sickness, death generally occurred at a very old age. Since most people lived between one-hundred to one-hundred-fifty years, and some beyond that, the population throughout the Khalian Solar System exploded.

The Keepers ruled for nearly seven generations, and then the time came when they would complete their mission. A ruling household was established by the Keepers, and that household would continue to govern the people as Stewards. Their stewardship would include all of the Khalian Solar System, and the fifteenth planet so named in honor of that position; *Galan*, meaning Stewards.

The Fall

Throughout the many generations, the Keepers were satisfied with the progress they made with the inhabitants in the Khalian Solar System. Seven generations after their arrival, the Keepers agreed that it was time to leave the government in the hands of the inhabitants. It was the generation of Yavik, father of Wedolan and Yashil Galan. Yavik was resourceful and wise.

Uzak, Keeper of Unity, was not in agreement with his brothers. The truth was that Uzak not only enjoyed the power he had over the people, he also relished the power he had over the Keepers since he was the unification, the glue that held together, the collective dominant attribute of each Keeper. This made him the most powerful of all Keepers, a position that might not occur in another setting, or may not happen ever again. He called his brothers foolish, for he had become vain in his imagination of power and glory. Uzak secretly planned to seize control of the entire Solar System and his brothers. During a meeting of the Council of the Keepers, Uzak closed his mind to Rendal, Keeper of Foresight, so that Rendal would not perceive his true motives, and Rendal was deceived.

"My Lords," Uzak spoke at the Council meeting, "the people still need your guidance. You know that Yashil is in line to the throne, but see how he has gone astray. He is cruel to his subjects. He rules the planet Laton with an iron fist. That planet has many hardships, and people are imprisoned for the slightest offense. Yavik is continuously interceding and overturning Yashil's decisions. Yashil is unfit to carry out all that we have accomplished. We must wait another generation."

"Rendal has foretold that the rule of government will fall to Wedolan Galan, not Yashil. You know that, Uzak," said Solan, Keeper of Life.

"But Yashil is the oldest and rightful heir of Khali," said the other. "We agreed at our first Council that when the Covenant is fulfilled, government will fall to the firstborn of the reigning Steward."

"That has happened" Solan responded. "Yavik is the firstborn and is now reigning in the place of his father. It will be Yavik's choice to select the one who will reign after him."

"I am against leaving. The time is not right," Uzak argued.

"The decision has been made, Uzak, but I warn you not to interfere with our decision to leave," Solan sharply responded.

Unable to convince the others to stay, Uzak redirected his own attributes to a second gemstone, protecting his physical body so that he could live in his body alone, after breaking the link between him and his brother, who became disembodied spirits. By breaking the Covenant, Uzak remained ageless because he was a Keeper, but lost the collective powers enjoyed as part of the unified body with the other Keepers.

1
A NEW BEGINNING

Shreela Bakra – Widow of Tima

Shreela Bakra leaned against the doorpost of her home, gazing at the purple *dorfa* tree saplings. Her long brown hair billowed in the cool gusty wind and made her shiver. Wrapping her soft gray cloak tightly around her petite frame, she again rested against the doorpost so that she could spend a few more precious moments to enjoy her last sunrise in her beloved home, gazing at the shimmering autumn scene.

Shreela's home located in the Province of Aurel on Paramon's moon, Tima, is about eight parsecs beyond the fringe of the Milky Way in the Gena Solar System. The hills and valleys of the northern most area of Aurel were clothed in the multi-colored splendor of fall. A cool intermittent wind blew in from the northwest causing the falling leaves to make a faint snipping sound as they fell upon the crisp leaves already piling up on the ground.

This gracious Bakra estate lay sequestered deep within the Acacia Forest, isolated from the nearby town of Kalinif, over five kilo-trans away. Despite the partially barren trees, the density of the forest kept Shreela's home hidden from prying eyes. Sounds of small woodland creatures skipping across the carpet of dry leaves filled the air. A well-trodden pathway leading to the mansion was covered with purple, blue, red, and orange leaves shed by the towering trees surrounding the home. Shreela looked up for a moment, watching the puffs of smoke rising from the chimney, then quickly swept away by a gentle breeze. Finally, she descended the front steps to take a short turn around the house. Stopping for a moment and shading her eyes, Shreela watched the early morning sun rays stipple through the wall of trees on the southeastern side of the mansion, revealing several large teardrop windows, recessed in the sand-colored brick structure, highlighted by three toffee-colored doors. This majestic main entrance door, standing three trans high, was magnificently covered with handcrafted wooden reliefs.

At the time of his death, Jor Bakra was a well-known astrophysicist, and Director of Research and Development for Astrofi, a large science and aerospace engineering company on Tima. Jor also ran his own private aerospace design business where he developed and produced satellite containment chambers. He was well paid for his services, both corporate and private, and Shreela lived a very comfortable life.

During the second year of their eight-year marriage, Shreela left her career job as a full-time linguist, to give birth to their only son, Soren. Since small in-home businesses were commonplace on Tima, Shreela started her own business as a language consultant contracting with several small companies. In the beginning, her business kept her quite busy, but as the price for translator equipment dropped, her business dwindled to almost nothing.

Shreela went back upstairs and began pacing the veranda. With her head bowed, eyes closed, and arms folded across her chest, she thought about the drastic changes in her life following Jor's death and argued with herself, justifying her decision to leave Tima. *I've spent almost all of the savings and credits to pay off creditors for loans secured by Jor and for supplies necessary for his research projects*, she thought. *Now I'm nearly bankrupt. Since I cannot return these supplies, I can only sell them for half the price which leaves me with just enough credits to cover payment on this house, and maintenance, for about two cycles - three at most. With one-hundred-eighty cycles left to pay, how can I carry the load without financial support?*

Shreela realized that she needed retraining before she could reenter the professional job marketplace. She had already put her home on the market, hoping there might be some credits left after expenses. Shreela soon learned that she would still not have enough left over to pay for the program on Tima, and support herself and Soren. However, there would be enough to pay for a similar program on the planet Thesbis – the planet of widows - in the Unian Solar System.

Burdened by the sadness in her heart, Shreela slowly raised her eyes and gazed wistfully into the cloudless sky. *Thesbis is so far from home*, she thought. *Still, I can't stay here and find a decent job. Being out of the mainstream for so long has created serious problems for me. With the declining need for multi-lingual skills, my options here are limited. The program on Thesbis is the best decision I can make right now*, she reassured herself on her decision to leave Tima.

Believing she had made a wise choice, Shreela looked thoughtfully around the Bakra Estate, feeling depressed by her next undertaking, how to say farewell to her best friends and closest neighbors, Kala and Machi. She was deep in thought when she was abruptly interrupted by her six-year-old, Soren, who gently tugged at her robe. She looked down at him, smiling at how handsome he was. His large brown eyes beamed brightly at her.

"Good morning, Mom."

"Good morning bright eyes," she responded, smiling. "Well,

today we finish packing for our trip to Thesbis."

"Today?"

Shreela raised her eyebrows when Soren hung his head. He hadn't done that for a few days. She was concerned that the sudden loss of his father coupled with the loss of their home might emotionally scar her young son. Stooping to Soren's eye level, she smoothed his hair with her hand to comfort him. There was no money for psychological therapy right now. Once they got to Thesbis, she would be able to afford it, but she was concerned about Soren's present state of mind, especially when he seemed withdrawn, as he had been quite often in the days following his father's death. The best she could do now is try to be sure he didn't retreat into that shell.

"Yes. We have to be there by midday tomorrow."

"We'll be alone, Mom."

"We'll be fine, you'll see," she tried to assure him. "How about going inside and washing up before eating? I'll be there in a minute."

"I'm not hungry."

"Alright, wash up and then we can just sit and talk, all right?" Soren nodded.

After Soren disappeared behind the door, Shreela stood up, taking a final look around. Another cold gust of wind chilled her to the bone. "Oooo," she muttered, shivering. As she turned to go back inside, a rustling made her turn back just in time to see a flicker of movement at the forest edge. "Hello!" she called out. The noise immediately stopped. Shreela paused on the veranda, peering into the forest. It was difficult to see, since the foliage was still very dense. A moment or two passed, but she heard nothing else. Quickly she turned, stepped inside the foyer, and closed the door.

The glitter of the six crystal shelves in the far left corner of the foyer caught her eye as she turned away from the door. The shelves, attached and appearing suspended on the wall, displayed a collection of multicolored cubes, which caught sunlight streaming in through the front window. The display was a sixth-year anniversary gift from Jor. Shreela stared at them thoughtfully for a moment.

"Mom, Mom," called Soren, looking up at his mother with alarm and tugging at her sleeve. "Are you okay?"

Shreela smiled down at him and ruffled his hair. "Yes, I'm fine. Come on, let's go and sit in the eating dome and talk."

The gray color scheme of her kitchen had always seemed cool and clean before, but now it was slightly depressing for Shreela. Even the glass-domed eating area arrayed with pewter-stained furniture resting upon a shiny, multi-colored grey, pebbled-shaped tile floor. Soren sat in the dome with his head down on the table waiting for her. Shreela sat down next to Soren, quietly observing him for a while. Despite the close bond that had been between Soren and his father, Soren seemed reluctant to grieve over Jor.

Reaching over, she gently raised Soren's head. "Soren, look at me," she said, cupping his tiny chin in her hand. "I'm glad you're here with me. I've been watching you. You are so busy trying to keep me happy that you've forgotten yourself. I know you're hurt about your father."

"But Mom, I'm takin' care of you," Soren interrupted.

"No my darling, I am taking care of you. That's my mommy job."

"But Mom...."

"Sh-h-h. I'm fine. You just worry about you."

"Then who's gonna take care of us?" Soren's eyes welled up.

"Well, we can take care of each other," she relented, smiling sadly, but feeling relieved at the same time. "We'll be all right."

Shortly after breakfast, Shreela packed a few things to carry onto the spacecraft. Except clothes and a few personal items, everything else her neighbor would ship to her later. The sun was nearing the mid-sky just as she finished.

"Soren," she called, placing a small tote bag next to the front door. As Shreela turned back down the corridor toward the kitchen, she literally scooped up Soren who was racing down the hall toward her too fast to stop without collision.

"Mom, guess what? I saw someone outside!" In his breathless excitement, he didn't even complain when she swung him up to her hip "like a baby."

"Where?"

"By the kitchen window!"

Shreela quickly walked to the kitchen and peered out the window. "There's no one there now."

"But I saw a man outside!" Soren insisted.

"I believe you, son. I just don't see anybody right now." She recalled the noise she had heard earlier. She set Soren back on his feet. "Wait here. I'll be back in a minute."

Retracing her steps through the corridor leading to the front entrance, Shreela opened the door. A man was sitting at the bottom of the outside staircase. Startled, she had to stop herself from slamming the door closed again.

"Mornin', ma'am," he said, pleasantly enough.

Shreela steadied herself and carefully studied him as he stood up to greet her. He was tall and slender, his dull reddish-brown hair was partially hidden by a tattered hat, brim folded downward, nearly covering his eyes. He was dressed like an outdoorsman, wearing hunter's boots and a weatherworn brown jacket.

"Good morning," Shreela answered, slowly descending a dozen or more stairs. Halfway down, she hesitated, looking around to see where he parked his vehicle. "I didn't hear you drive up."

"No ma'am. I'm parked way over there," the man said, waving one hand toward the transport highway.

Shreela still felt uneasy and decided not to move any closer. "How can I help you?" she asked.

"Sign on the road says this property's up for sale. Folks in town say you're widowed, so I expect you want to sell quick. Is this place still available?"

"Yes it is," Shreela answered, not in the least relieved. "It's a pretty big house, though."

"Uh-huh."

"There are twelve bedrooms and..."

"Where might you be headin', ma'am?" He didn't look or sound apologetic for the interruption.

"Thesbis."

"Uh-huh. Planet of Widows. Ten bedrooms did you say?"

"Twelve bedrooms."

"Leavin' soon, ma'am?"

"Tomorrow," Shreela responded, becoming annoyed, "but I don't see...."

"Might need to get in touch with you if there's a problem, ma'am. How big's the lot?"

"Over two-hundred-seventy geotrans."

"Thesbis. That's a good place for widows to go, ma'am."

"You're not from around here, are you?"

"No ma'am. Just moved in town a few days ago. My mate and children are lodgin' in the village."

"Well sir, this is a great place to raise children." Her desire to sell the house battled with the urge to give this man a piece of her mind.

"Uh-huh. Have children, do you?"

"A son." Shreela's face even *felt* wooden by now.

"Will you be comin' back to Tima, ma'am?"

"No." She had to work at that one word, to keep from delivering it from between clenched teeth.

"How many bathrooms?"

"Six." Shreela attempted a smile now that the property was the topic once more.

"I hear you're askin' for three-hundred-thousand credits."

"Three-hundred-*fifty*-thousand credits."

"Can't live on Thesbis forever. Where're you headin' after that?"

"I'm hoping for placement in the Khalian Solar System."

"Khali. Nice place, ma'am. I saw a stream up the way. Good place for fishin'?"

"We stock... I mean, my late spouse stocked fish in that stream."

"Uh-huh. Well, I'll be headin' back, ma'am."

"Oh, by the way, what did you say your name was?"

"Didn't ma'am. Good day, ma'am." The stranger tipped his hat and walked quickly back up the path.

Shreela stared after him until he disappeared into the woods. *What was that all about?* she wondered. At the same time, she was glad they would be leaving tomorrow. That encounter left more than a small feeling of unease behind.

As Shreela reentered the house, she found Soren standing in the entrance hallway.

"What now, Mom? Who was that guy? What did he want? Is he coming back?" Normal operating mode for Soren – a fountain of questions.

Taking each question in turn, as usual, she said, "I think we're done packing. We'll have an early lunch, and then go and say goodbye to our neighbors. Just a new guy from town. He wanted to know about the house. I don't think so."

It was late afternoon when they arrived at the home of Shreela's best friends, Kala and Machi. Unlike Shreela, whose human lineage originated on another planet, Kala and Machi were native Timanians. Kala was about Shreela's height of one-and-one-half trans, while Machi, her mate, towered over her at two trans. Although their features were situated much as Shreela's, the remarkable Timanian eyes – square shaped when fully open – with eye folds at the bottom and emerald green irises encased within a soft pink tinged cornea, added an exotic attraction much praised throughout the galaxy. Long arms, extending to their knees, ended in hands that consisted of two long wiry fingers and a thumb. Rubbery skin added protection in cold weather. Excessive body heat was removed by way of small sweat nodules behind their ears. The small, lipless mouth, topped the square chin. The Timanian nose was as varied in shape and size as the human nose.

Shreela seated herself on the floor of Machi's cozy den for an after supper chat. A large stuffed chair was placed between an oval window, and built-in shelves full of neatly arranged reading discs. An old desk sat just right of the window with three chairs nearby. Several throw rugs were scattered around the dark green tile floor. The circular room's cream-colored walls had five cleverly-recessed lights that made the light seem to come from everywhere, and nowhere in particular. Soren stood next to Machi's chair, fidgeting. "Aren't you going to sit with us, Soren?" he asked.

"Uh-oh," said Shreela. "I think he wants to play with those compu-puzzles."

"Just one last time," Soren pleaded, suddenly hanging onto Machi's arm, and gazing into his eyes with all the little-boy charm he could muster.

"It's all right, Shreela. I really don't mind," said Machi, indulgently. Soren spun to see his mother's reaction.

"Okay. I'll call you when we're ready to leave."

Soren's face lit up. "Thanks Mom," he said, rushing out of the room, then back. "Thanks Machi!" Then he was gone.

Machi chuckled as Soren scampered out. "So how are you two doing?" he asked, after Soren left.

"Quite good, considering," responded Shreela, then paused thoughtfully. "By the way, Machi, you worked with Tel Mudhar, didn't you?"

"Yes. We were good friends."

"I didn't know that he had died until last week."

"Didn't Jor tell you?" asked Kala in surprise.

"No, and that's what's so strange, since he and Jor worked together for so many years. I wonder *why* Jor didn't tell me? I checked all published death notices for information on Tel's death, but there was nothing."

"I do know Tel and Jor were working on a top secret military project. I heard there was something unusual about Tel's death, but no particulars." Machi explained. There was a moment of silence except for the sucking sound Machi made puffing on his pipe. "Maybe that's why Jor didn't say anything," he said at length.

Shreela shrugged her shoulders. "Perhaps," she responded. "His widow, Dian, left for Thesbis early last week. She called me before she left to offer her condolences on Jor's death. She was the one who told me about Tel's death."

"Dian stopped by here to say goodbye," Kala commented. "She seemed to be holding up pretty well."

"Uh-hum. I feel terrible for me," said Shreela, "but I feel worse for her. Her baby is due in five months," she said, lowering her voice, thinking back to the joy she and Jor had taken in her pregnancy.

"Have you heard from her since she left?" Machi asked.

"Yes. In fact, I received a communications disc and a few video disc brochures from her two days ago."

"What does she think about the program?"

"Well, she'd only had two sessions when she logged the disc, but she really seemed to like it."

"Looks like both of you will be relocating to the Petron Solar System after the program," said Kala. It was almost a question.

"That's what I thought, but Dian's comm-disc says she'll be going to the Khalian Solar System. She sent brochures that outline the programs available on both Khali and Petron. Honestly, I agree with her choice. I liked the job placement opportunities offered by Khali better."

"What's the difference?" asked Kala.

"One major difference is that the Petron System places you on a waiting list and subsidizes living expenses for six months if you're not placed. Khali gives you up to one year to be placed."

"That's quite a difference," said Machi.

Shreela watched Machi, for a moment or two, as he continued to puff smoke rings from his old pipe loaded with crushed Kalinif tree leaves. "You're going to Khali, aren't you?" he asked conclusively.

Shreela raised her brow in a *matter-of-fact* gesture. "Well, I am considering it," she responded. "I've already spoken to the Program Director on Thesbis about relocating to Khali instead of the Petron Solar System."

"I see." There seemed to be something that Machi was not saying.

"Tell me, Machi, what do you know about Khali?"

Machi shifted in his chair. "Hmm. I know that it is a unique solar system, with every planet in the system inhabited. It's well governed by one ruling family on the planet Galan. I've heard that young King Ewlon Galan is a good ruler."

"Do you know of any problems I might face if I decide to relocate there?"

"It used to be a popular place to live, but it has changed over the years. Still, it's a good place to go, from what I know."

Shreela still sensed a certain hesitation in Machi's voice, and he wasn't looking at her. *He's hiding something,* she thought. "Machi, everyone knows there's a conflict between Khali and Uni. What can you tell me about it? Is there something I should know?"

Machi got up from his chair and walked over to the desk. Shreela sat patiently, watching as he groped for a pipe cleaner inside the top drawer. He seemed to take his time searching, as if he were using that time to think about a response to her question. "Machi," she called out, with a question in her voice. A few more seconds passed before he finally succeeded in finding what he was looking for. He then returned to his chair and sat down.

Machi sighed and looked directly into Shreela's eyes. "I don't want to discourage you, my dear," he began, "but I have never trusted that neighboring planet, Uni. I can tell you that the Unian Solar System is always trying to create trouble between all planets in that part of the galaxy. The Khalian system is a prime target with so many inhabited planets, but the King seems able to keep things in line. I think you will be all right. Besides, you can always leave if you don't like it, can't you?"

Shreela looked up at him, searching his features for something more. His face gave no signal. "I suppose you're right," she said reluctantly. "I do have to stay in my placement job for at least two years, though."

"That time will pass quickly."

Another long interval of silence passed with only the sounds of Machi puffing on his pipe. Then, "Shreela, can I help you in settling Jor's estate?" Machi asked, changing the subject.

Shreela smiled at him. "You've done a lot already. Thank you for taking care of storing my belongings. Except for the house, Jor's estate has been settled."

"Come, my dear. Have a seat here," said Machi, patting the chair next to him. "Several days ago, you told me that the proceeds from the sale of your home would not leave enough to pay for reeducating yourself here on Tima. How can you afford to go to Thesbis? There is the matter of your journey, housing, tuition, child care for Soren, and many other things, I am sure."

"I got a small advance against my home to pay part of the tuition. Besides that, planets that participate in the relocation programs for widows, also subsidize the programs on Thesbis."

"Tima doesn't offer subsidies, then?"

"Not enough for what I need. There will be little profit from the sale of my home. Most of the proceeds will go to pay off the mortgage."

"How do you feel about relocating?" Kala asked.

"I feel sad about leaving friends, especially you and Machi, but since I don't have an extended family here on Tima, it's not as bad for me as it is for others."

"Then you must relocate," Machi commented, as if he had just then made up his mind.

Shreela smiled at that. "Uh-huh, and it has to be in a solar system that provides subsidies."

"Well then, what about your property. Have you sold it yet?" Machi asked.

"Not yet.... but earlier today, Soren said he saw someone outside, and when I looked out, I found a strange man seated on my front doorstep. He asked me about my home...actually, he asked a lot of questions – and they weren't all about the house. He wasn't from around here, and his accent was one I didn't recognize."

"New homesteaders settle on Tima all the time," Kala interjected. "Why are you bothered about this one?"

"There was something peculiar about him."

"How so?"

"He said he was in the market for a new home, but he seemed more interested in when I would be leaving Tima, and where I was going. I also wonder . . ."

"Wonder what?" Machi asked impatiently.

"I'm not sure, but for the last two or three days, I get the feeling that someone is watching me."

Machi stiffened in his chair. The smoke from his pipe flowed in an unwavering line up toward the ceiling. "What makes you think that?"

"Earlier today, I could have sworn that I heard someone moving through the forest area close to the house."

"But the forest is filled with wildlife, Shreela," said Machi, relaxing again in his chair.

"I know, but when I called out, the sounds stopped. An animal would have run away," she said.

"Maybe it was this stranger that you talked to."

"That's possible." Pouncing her head back into the soft pillows of the armchair, Shreela let out a long sigh. "I don't know. It's probably just my imagination. I'll be glad when I leave Tima. Maybe a new environment will help me to settle down." The thought of leaving her home and her friends brought moisture to her eyes.

Machi and Kala, realizing how painful her departure would be, quietly looked at each other while Shreela composed herself.

She glanced out the window at the darkening sky. "It's getting late," she said at length. "Soren and I have an early call, so we better head for home."

Shreela got up and walked toward the front door. "Soren, come on, let's go," she called. Soren thundered around the corner, playfully running into her, and pretending to be knocked senseless. She laughed as she gently grabbed him to help him into his jacket. Machi picked him up for a big hug, and then he hugged Shreela. Both she and Soren embraced Kala. "We'll miss you both," Shreela choked out tearfully, opening the door.

"And we will miss you," Machi responded gently.

Shreela and Soren stepped out into the chilly night air. "Take care of yourselves and stay in touch," Machi called out.

"We will, and you too, she shouted back. "Goodbye," she added, waving as she and Soren headed down the forest path.

The distance between Shreela's home and that of her friends was roughly one kilo-tran. Even in the rapidly waning sunlight, the golden colored leaves still on the trees stood shimmering against the darkening sky. The harvest season was Shreela's favorite time of year. As she and Soren walked along the forest path, she watched the leaves fall from the trees, equating each falling leaf to be reminiscent of some experience gone by. She giggled as she thought about the afternoon of Soren's birth. Jor raced home to be in time for the big event, but it was all over by the time he arrived. When the nurse tried to hand Soren to Jor, he didn't know what to do, so he shook Soren's hand and said, "hello." Shreela looked down at Soren, smiling to herself as she recalled the scared look on Jor's face when he first saw his son. A sudden crackling sound in the woods behind her made her jump. Shreela whirled around, half expecting to see someone following. Instead, she saw only a deserted, moonlit path in the darkening forest. Instinctively, Shreela picked Soren up and put him on her hip, quickening her pace as she headed for home.

After a long hot bath, followed by a hot cup of fruit juice, Shreela tiptoed into Soren's room. He looked peaceful as he slept with his pillow beside him rather than under his head. Satisfied, she closed the door and headed down the hall to her own bedroom.

Noise from chirping insects and other nocturnal creatures outside Shreela's window made it hard for her to rest. She finally drifted off to sleep, but it was a sleep filled with dreams of uniformed assailants dragging her off to parts unknown. She tossed and turned then jerked awake, disoriented and shaken. Her nightgown was wet from sweating, and she shivered in the cool breeze that was coming in through the window.

"I thought I closed that window," she muttered grumpily."

Shreela crawled out of bed, and walked to the open window. She glanced outside for a moment before closing it. All seemed quiet, so she closed it and reached for the lock. Just at that moment, she thought she saw someone cross the pathway just below her room. Startled, she shrank back. Since the sun was behind this part of Tima, the area around her house was shadowy. Squinting, she stared into the darkness. Except the swaying trees, the nighttime landscape remained undisturbed. After a moment, she convinced herself that her imagination and the remnants of nightmares past were playing tricks on her. Then she thought back to her encounter with the stranger earlier that day. Finally, telling herself she was being silly, she pulled down the shade, checked on Soren one more time for good measure, and went back to bed.

Ewlon Galan

As Shreela nestled under the covers and drifted back to sleep in her home on Tima, morning dawned over Raileen on Planet Thesbis. In the Widow Registration building, members of the Thesbian Placement Council gathered for a meeting called by King Ewlon Galan of the Khalian Solar System.

The large conference room, furnished with a long oval, smoked- glass table, was capable of comfortably seating up to forty adults. The gray-blue padding on the seats and backs of the chairs coordinated well with the pale gray walls. A mural of the well-known florescent floral gardens of Elgelin on planet Perican in the Khalian Solar System dominated the artwork in the room. The light of sunrise streamed in from a massive circular window bouncing off the glass topped credenza that lined the entire back wall of the room, and reflecting multi-colored prism speckles across the ceiling.

Soft, indistinguishable sounds filled the room as Chancellors from several solar systems quietly chatted with one another while waiting for King Ewlon to arrive. All sounds suddenly stopped when the conference room door opened, revealing a tall human male. He stood nearly two trans tall, with chestnut brown hair, gray-green eyes, and a hint of a cleft in his chin. King Ewlon Galan entered the room, accompanied by a tall, dark-haired man, dressed in formal dark blue military attire.

King Ewlon had ruled the fifteen planets in the Khalian Solar System for twenty years. His life as king began at twenty when his widowed mother, Mara Galan, passed him the scepter. The current situation was one of the most difficult he had faced as king, complicated by the problems created by Uzak. The recent discovery of the abductions, and even murder, of widows granted placement services in the Khalian Solar System was very unsettling.

King Ewlon, known as Ew by his friends, took his position. Though nearing forty, he maintained top physical form, and made an imposing figure at the head of the conference table.

After seating himself, Ew patiently waited for the room to quiet down before beginning his meeting. "Thank you for answering my summons to come here for an unscheduled meeting," he began. "Before I explain why we are here, I would first like to introduce you to Marty Bergon, Ambassador for Solar System Affairs on Nilar in the Petron System. I have requested Ambassador Bergon replace Ambassador Behrend, whose whereabouts after our last meeting is still a mystery. May I say that Behrend was, uh…*is* a respected ambassador whom I personally miss. Unfortunately, clues concerning his disappearance have not yet surfaced.

"Like Behrend, Bergon's background in understanding the development of solar system societies, will definitely be an asset to this Council." Ew paused as Council members nodded their heads in acknowledgement. "Ambassador Bergon," he continued, "arrived here just moments ago and has not been fully briefed on the kidnapping problem facing this Council. Today, Ambassador," Ew addressed Bergon directly, "you will learn about the hijacking of widows from Thesbis, and how Ambassador Behrend's disappearance is linked to it. Earlier you asked for clarification concerning the relationship between Uni and Khali. Since there is a connection between these solar systems and the disappearance of widows, I will tell you what I can."

"Thank you, Your Majesty," said Bergon. "I know how precious your time is."

"I am glad to be of assistance." Ew placed a small, flat, circular recording device on the table and pressed a tiny red button. A red light shown, indicating that recording of the meeting was underway. Folding his hands and laying them on the conference table, Ew leaned slightly forward and addressed Bergon directly. "I know that you have not had much time to absorb all of the documents concerning widow placement or the kidnappings, but I would like to begin, Ambassador, by asking exactly how much do you know about these kidnappings?"

Bergon sat back comfortably in his chair before addressing his audience. "Since my formal installation to this post occurred only three days ago," he began, "you are correct, Sire, in assuming that I have not had much time to review the numerous confidential documents left behind by my predecessor. However, in matters concerning the kidnapping of widows, I did learn that these abductions have been going on for several years. Ambassador Behrend's classified documents revealed a suspicion that Uzak of Uni might be responsible for this crime. It is also my understanding that this Council believes Uzak's collaborator works on Thesbis, some trade merchant, perhaps. Am I correct?"

"Widow rehabilitation and training is big business," responded Ew, nodding.

"But where are these widows going?"

"We believe Uni transports them to prison mining colonies on Uni."

"That is one of several statements in Behrend's report which confuses me," Bergon interjected. "If this Council knows what Uzak is doing, why isn't it possible to stop him, unless..."

"Unless what?" prompted Ew.

"Unless the stories about him are true," Bergon commented, lowering his voice.

"I gather you're referring to his super powers."

"Precisely, Your Majesty." Bergon sat straight up, momentarily glancing out of the window while stroking his hair back in a musing gesture. "I feel somewhat embarrassed to ask this," he commented at length, "but is this true, or is this some sort of Khalian fable?"

"No need to feel embarrassed here," Ew interjected. "There are many fascinating stories and questions surrounding the person of Uzak. Exactly, what have you heard?"

Bergon visibly relaxed back into his chair even more. "First let me say that of all the planetary and solar system societies I've studied, Uni and Khali are the most complex. To begin with, Khali is an extraordinary solar system of fifteen planets, not having a single uninhabited planet within it. That makes it unique in this galaxy. Another phenomenon is the historical documentation on Uzak and his brothers, the honored Keepers, who dwelled in the Khalian Solar System for many generations. Though I've studied the history surrounding the fall of Uzak from the body of power, there is conflicting testimony about his powers. I've examined a copy of the treatise left by your father, King Wedolan Galan, and also the chronicles of others. Your father states that Uzak is immortal. Others contend that Uzak can be wounded and possibly destroyed. I have heard arguments about his ability to read your thoughts as well as control your will power. Can you clarify some of these points?"

Ew paused for a moment, and sat back in his chair, allowing the chair to roll back just enough for him to fold his right leg, resting his foot atop his left knee. With his right forearm resting on the arm of his chair and his left hand slightly closed as it lie on the table; he turned ever so slightly in the direction of Bergon. "From what I know," he began, pensively, "Uzak's ability to read thoughts or control your will is a bogus claim. However, it is true that Uzak is immortal. He lost all other powers when he tried to destroy his brothers, but let's not forget that immortality, itself, is a superpower. Uzak has no need to eat or sleep. He can build his military might and wage war against others for countless generations."

"But there are accounts of him being wounded during the Balarai conflict. You were party to that conflict."

"I'll address that by first reminding you of an historical note," Ew responded. "Uzak's brothers, our honored Keepers, came to Khali many centuries ago when our ancestors were still living in a tribal society. We were at the beginning of our intellectual growth and unaware of other humanoids living on neighboring planets in our solar system. To work and live among us, the Keepers adopted friendly humanoid forms. At the time of his fall, Uzak maintained his humanoid form, but his flesh and body were no longer impervious to the elements of the environment, or to injury. His flesh can be torn, and he feels pain, but his body has tremendous regenerative powers."

"How do you know?"

"As you alluded to a moment ago, I faced him during the Balarai conflict." Ew paused briefly to sit back in a more formal posture but still facing Bergon. "First, Ambassador," he began, "I was only on Balarai to deliver an honorarium to one of my Interplanetary Governors. I later learned that Unians had infiltrated our security system, and that I was Uzak's personal target for assassination. That is how I came face to face with him. During the battle, I slashed Uzak's cheek with my saber. It did not bleed, and seconds after I inflicted the wound, it was gone."

"Then are you saying he can be stopped for a short time?"

"In that battle he was stopped, but I can't take full credit for it."

"But the chronicles at the Balarai...,"

Ew raised his hand, interrupting Bergon's comment. "I am aware of the documentation on that battle. It is true that Uzak was temporarily disabled during the battle with me, but not by me. Uzak is a skilled swordsman. That slice I delivered across his cheek didn't slow him down. Sure, I stunned him for a split second, but that's all. As we battled, I shoved him into the communications wall. A heavy portable monitor tipped over and crashed down on top of him. It was pure luck."

"What did you do after that?"

"There was still fighting going on in the room and also in the corridors. Uzak was on the floor, either stunned or unconscious. I don't know, and I didn't wait around to find out. My security chief rushed me out of the building and back to my shuttlecraft."

"How did Uzak get away?"

"That I cannot tell you, but I know that when that monitor fell, it hit two other soldiers fighting next to Uzak. One was killed and the other seriously wounded. The Balarai Defense Guard contained the skirmish, taking many prisoners, but Uzak was not among them."

Ew quietly watched Bergon, who stroked his well-groomed mustache. "Your personal accounting helps to make better sense of the records," Bergon said, at length. "I always believed that Uzak possessed this supernatural power of immortality. Your words, and that of others, strongly reinforce just how dangerous Uzak is to the entire galaxy. He's a fearful and fearless creature."

Ew's eyebrows shifted upwards. "Oh, but he does have fears," he said.

"How so?" Bergon asked curiously.

"His greatest fear is told in a legend well-known in the Khalian Solar System."

"That must be the *Legend of Khali*," Bergon murmured. "Yes, I've read about that. How does it go? `When the widow.....,"

"When the widow holds the treasure of the King, the end of the Unian Empire is at hand," recited Ew.

Bergon sat up and tapped the table. "That's it. To be honest with you, Your Majesty, I thought that was a fireside tale."

Ew reached over for the pitcher of water placed next to him, and poured water into his glass. "You're not alone in your thoughts, Ambassador," he said, after taking a few sips from his glass. "The Legend is only a few decades old, but some scholars dismiss this story as a childhood fantasy. The part we quoted is the prophecy."

"Do you believe it?"

"It really doesn't matter if I believe it. Uzak believes it, and that's the danger."

"So he's establishing prison colonies to gather widows with the potential to fulfill the prophecy."

"That is this Council's contention, but the Uni security is tight, making these colonies difficult to locate."

"That's another question I have. How are they able to escape the scanning devices of your satellites? Your scanners can probably pinpoint every living creature on that planet."

"True, but Uni has developed a disruptive shield around their detention camps, and they have many such prisons. We can locate the areas of disruption, but our intel indicates that, while some jails are real, others are decoys. Since we can't see past the shields, we are unable to tell which prison houses these widows, if they are there at all. They could be on another planet entirely."

"If you cannot penetrate the disruption, how do you know the prisoners are widows? Do you have any witnesses?"

Ew did not respond right away. The room seemed somber as

he looked around the table, studying the faces of other Council members. "We did have a witness," he said, at length.

"Did?"

"An escapee. It was she who was responsible for bringing about investigations into the disappearance of widows from Thesbis."

"How did she escape?"

"Nearly two years ago, a young widow from the planet Tima was somehow able to board a Unian cargo ship headed for Echlindra. You may recall that Echlindra had purchased vast quantities of *renin* for the construction of their new space rest stop. The widow was very sick, but she was able to get off the cargo ship and seek help from authorities. She told of the slave labor and deaths of other widows in the Unian renin mining colonies."

"Why do I get the feeling your only witness is dead?"

Ew stared down at the table and nodded his head. "She died two days after her arrival to Echlindra, before I or any of my staff could speak with her."

For a moment, Ew listened to the dawn creatures' soft sounds coming in through a window from the gardens below. He thought about the widow that died and was saddened, although he did not personally speak to her. Familiar frustration set in, over his inability to gain better control over the kidnapping situation.

"What was Uni's position then?" asked Bergon, interrupting Ew's thoughts.

"Uni denied claims made by the widow, and put up their disruptors shortly after those accusations were brought to light," he explained.

"Your Majesty, with this problem of widow abductions, why don't you end this placement program for widow relocation?

That might end these abductions, don't you think?"

"Maybe, but I believe it's Uzak's goal to seek and destroy the widow in the Legend. I think he would simply find another way."

"If memory serves, this prophecy has something to do with a powerful medallion held by your family. Does this thing still exist?" Bergon asked.

Ew smiled and nodded approvingly. "I see you are well-versed in legend and folklore, Ambassador. Yes, it exists."

"Then why don't you use it?"

"It is and has been in the hands of Uzak for more than three decades. Fortunately, he doesn't have the key to bring it to life."

"Who does have the key?"

Ew hesitated for a moment, unwilling to reveal more than he had to. "I don't know," he answered, "maybe the widow in the Legend."

Bergon sighed. "It's a fascinating tale, Your Majesty, but where does Ambassador Behrend fit into all of this? You said earlier that you could link his disappearance with that of the widows."

"I can, but first let me tell you how the widow's claims were actually validated by earlier research, which was completely unrelated to this problem. Twenty-two years ago," Ew continued, "I selected a commission, The Commission on Widow Rehabilitation, to become involved with providing services to young widows. It was a personal project of mine, motivated by my own experience. My mother, Queen Mara, was widowed when I was very young and my sister still an infant. Although my mother was rich and powerful, it was still difficult for her to raise two children without a father. My feelings were that if it was hard for her, it must be exponentially worse for someone with far fewer resources.

"The Commission, comprised of representatives from many planets, also included planets in the Unian Solar System."

"Excuse me, Sire," Bergon interrupted, "but knowing that Uzak controls the Unian Solar system, why would you choose Thesbis to base your operation?"

"Thesbis is on the fringe of the Unian Solar System, and ideally located between several solar systems. The Commission voted in favor of Thesbis becoming the headquarters for this program."

"And you, Sire?"

"I voted for it too." Ew noted the puzzled look on Bergon's face. "Ambassador, it's true that Uzak has been a thorn in my family's side for decades," he said, guessing Bergon's thoughts, "but his anger and fear are with Khali, not with other solar systems."

"You could have backed out of the project."

"For what reason? Backing out would not change the menace on Uni."

"And maybe these lost widows would not be lost," Bergon argued.

Ew felt a sting of guilt from Bergon's words. The atmosphere in the room became suddenly tense, and he sensed that all eyes were on him, but he was able to maintain his composure without making a single flinch. "Believe me, Ambassador, that thought has crossed my mind on more than one occasion," he responded.

Bergon squirmed in his chair, uncomfortable both with the King's admission and the fact that he had forced him there. "I don't mean to sound insensitive to your dilemma, Sire," he said at length. "I'm just highly agitated by this whole thing."

"I understand," said Ew. "Anyway, getting back to how this program works. Initially, widows came from everywhere in the galaxy. Psychological therapy, advanced education, childcare, and many other services were provided at a modest cost to the registrant. Many widows returned to their home planet and became productive in their societies. Unfortunately, the program became cost prohibitive. About ten years ago, we added restrictions, allowing only those participants willing to relocate to one of the sponsoring planets. The number of applicants decreased significantly to a more financially reasonable number. We also changed our name to The Thesbian Placement Council."

"Did the decrease in the number of widows enable you to detect these hijackings?"

"No, not at all. Four years ago, this Council began to interview widows who had been placed. We learned that many widows on the roster never finished the program, and wondered if the program might be lacking in some measure."

"But every registrant is required to complete a questionnaire before they leave."

"Most of them did, and we reorganized the basic format of the program in some areas because of that inquiry, but we had no incentive to take a closer look until after the widow of Tima escaped and revealed that there were prison mining colonies on Uni."

"According to Ambassador Behrend's records, 11,400 widows have been placed during the last four years. His notes did not give an exact accounting on the number of widows possibly kidnapped. He just noted that a little more than ten percent left the program. I would like to have a more specific number."

"For those figures, I'll turn this discussion over to Council Member Jaynt Saren who is Director of the widow program. He represents both Thesbis and Zirvag on this Council."

Ew directed attention to Saren, a tall, slender man with bulging gray eyes and thinning sandy colored hair, seated at the opposite side of the table.

"Thank you, Sire. It's good to have you here, Ambassador," Saren began. "First, when Ambassador Behrend recorded his figures, we had not completed our investigation. The final tally 1,262 widows who left the program. From that number, 720 are unaccounted for, if you count the widow, Dian Mudhar, who registered here last week."

"How do you know they're missing? Perhaps they left and relocated away from their home planet without your knowledge."

"When we learned about the accusations of the escaped widow, we immediately began a search for every widow who left without finishing," answered Ew.

"Not only that, it would be difficult for any widow to leave without a pass to board a spacecraft leaving Thesbis," Saren explained. "My office issues those passes."

"I assume you're not the only one who signs these passes."

"Correct. There are several members of my staff authorized to issue passes when I am unavailable, but that's all - not even a Council member can sign for one."

"We also noticed that the unaccounted widows were all from moon planets, such as Tima in the Gena Solar System; your own planet Nilar in the Petron System; Marshèe, and two others," commented Ew. "I don't believe it's coincidental. The Legend says that the widow would come from a moon."

"What about Behrend then?"

"I spoke to Behrend after our last meeting four months ago," said Ew. "It seems that he was on to something. He thought he knew who the inside person here on Thesbis was, but convinced me to give him more time to investigate.

Unfortunately, he never reached home after that meeting."

"Why was Council never told of this meeting between the two of you?" Saren asked, visibly annoyed.

"Behrend asked me not to reveal his suspicions. He was to bring his findings to the next council meeting."

"Why did Behrend confide in you rather than me or perhaps some others here?" he asked, in a bristling tone.

Ew looked over at Saren, angered by his accusatory tone. Ew paused a moment before speaking. "It turns out that most of those lost widows were requesting placement to the Khalian Solar System," Ew said calmly. Ew turned his attention back to Bergon. "So Bergon," he said, "you may be right after all. These missing widows might not be missing if it were not for Khali."

"And maybe they would be." Bergon sighed. "This news about Ambassador Behrend will not sit well with my government. We may very well pull out of this program. I gather that news of these missing widows is not generally known to the populace?"

"There are rumors and speculation, but they are being kept quiet for the most part," said Ew. "Other than this council, only three members of my staff along with my mother and sister are aware of this Council's findings."

"Only I and my assistant know," said Saren.

"Just me and my Vice Chancellor," said Chancellor Nical from planet Marshèe.

"Are there any others beyond you?" Ew asked the remaining Council members. All other members gave or nodded a negative reply. "Bergon," he said, facing the Ambassador, "inform your government of what you've learned here today. I'll understand if they wish to cancel their membership, but try to persuade them to stay. They can still send widows who are not from moon planets who wish to relocate to Khali."

"I will relay both the information and your request, Sire."

"Thank you. Transcripts of this meeting will be sent to you by special messenger within the next solar day."

"As I explained before we came in, Your Majesty, I am unable to stay for the entire meeting. If you will pardon me, I must leave now to catch the next diplomatic flight home."

"Council staff will inform you of the next meeting," Saren added.

"Then I will be off, but before I go, let me say that a formal response from my government concerning this problem and Ambassador Behrend's disappearance will be forthcoming."

"We will await a response from your government," said Ew. "Thank you again for coming on such short notice."

Bergon stood up. "Good day, Your Majesty, Council members."

Immediately after Bergon left the room, Ew turned to Saren. "Saren, the purpose of this meeting was to inform this Council of my knowledge of Ambassador Behrend's concerns. I made no attempts to withhold or conceal information from you or anyone else here," he stated firmly.

"I beg your pardon, Your Majesty," Saren apologized immediately. "I was just surprised to hear this news and more than a little disturbed by it."

"Does anyone else have a problem?" asked Ew.

"I agree with Bergon," said Chancellor Nical. "This news about Behrend doesn't sit well with me either. Did Behrend give the slightest hint of who the inside person is?"

"None," said Ew, "and my own source is unable to come up with anyone."

"Then what do you propose?" asked Nical.

Ew turned back to Saren. "Saren, do you get advanced information on placement for your applicants?"

"Not generally. That information is given during registration or shortly before a widow completes the program."

"But once you have the information, who has access to it?"

"Almost anyone. Those comm-discs are given to administration on Thesbis, and also a copy of all placed individuals to sponsoring planets."

"Everyone knew that Dian Mudhar was relocating to the Khalian Solar System," Ew stated rather than asked.

"Yes."

Chancellor Reeca from planet Echlindra spoke up. "Why don't we change that procedure? Information on relocation will be given to Council members only."

"That may work," said Ew. "I can arrange to have those widows transported to my solar system. For widows of Tima or Marshèe going to Khali, issue written passes to another planet, but secretly code those passes for Khali. In the meantime, I need to know if there are any current requests for placement in my realm, Saren."

"Not since Dian Mudhar. I am expecting one widow from Tima late tomorrow, but she's requesting relocation to the Petron Solar System."

"Good. Starting now, this new policy goes into effect. If there are no objections, I would like to adjourn this meeting."

It was nearly mid-morning when Ew reached the entrance to the space dock where his Director of Intelligence and friend, Pala Bhusan, met him.

Palador Bhusan was a native of Laton. He was a tall, heavy-boned human male, with a thick mustache, and well-groomed beard. He had deep brown eyes, dark curly brown hair, and rakishly good looks.

Pala walked alongside Ew. The sound of their long casual

strides bounced off the walls of the docking bay. They quietly headed toward their spacecraft, a small shuttlecraft, built for short trips in deep space. Not until they were inside did Pala break the silence between them. His voice was deep, and he spoke with a thick Latonian accent.

"How did your meeting go?" he asked.

"As expected, there was concern surrounding the reason for Behrend's disappearance," Ew said, clamping himself into one of the passenger seats. "We did implement a new policy on restricting information on widows relocating to Khali."

"Maybe Mariko has news about Behrend."

"Possibly, but I haven't been able to reach him for several days. I guess we'll find out when we meet with him tomorrow morning. He's probably out trying to auction off a few antiques."

"You can count on that," Pala said, smiling. "He never misses an opportunity to profit from his archaeological finds."

"I know, and that trait puts him in the best position to gather information inside some of those Unian military auction posts. Anyway, I can't worry about him just now. I'm already late for my next meeting on Crashellon. Come on, let's go."

A Rare Artifact Found

As King Ewlon and Pala Bhusan cruised towards Crashellon from Thesbis, a two hour flight, Milan Mariko stood behind the podium in an auction post on planet Zirvag in the Unian Solar System. A small crowd gathered to hear his auction chant and examine the artifacts Milan brought from his archaeological digs.

Milan Mariko, a likeable fellow, was a well-known archaeologist, slightly overweight, with thick, curly, black hair and deep crow's-feet in the corners of his eyes. His notoriety also included his willingness to sell certain types of artifacts not obtainable elsewhere, although some of those acquisitions were questionably authentic.

Milan's current two-fold assignment, gathering information about the missing widows, as well as news concerning Ambassador Behrend's absence, kept him on the move between Unian military auction posts. He was to report any news directly to Pala.

After auctioning off a small amount of merchandise, Milan boarded his one-man spacecraft, and headed for Uni, one-tenth parsec from Zirvag, to sell the remainder of his unusual collection. It was early afternoon when he landed at Kavic Port, a military post on Uni. The post was strictly utilitarian; a brown one-story cubicle with one window in the front. Carrying the heavy sack slung over his shoulder, Milan walked toward the post, taking a quick breather every now and then before continuing on.

"How I hate this planet," he muttered. He remembered how nasty some of the military personnel were, throwing his goods around the room, occasionally stealing both his credits and his antiques. "Still, the credits are better here than any in the galaxy -- when I can hold onto them," he added.

When Milan entered the building, another auction was already in progress. He waited on the sidelines for nearly two hours before it was over. As soon as the auctioneer began to pack up his remaining goods to leave, Milan hustled to the back and displayed his collection on the countertop.

"Ha, ha," he laughed heartily at the crowd gathered around him. "These are not only the last items up for auction, but also the finest in my collection, the first being this one-of-a-kind stone cut water urn encrusted with the rare giña gems of Tarpellis."

The gems were actually imitations, but since this crowd was not made up of antiquity experts, Milan was easily able to pass on these cheap, worthless, relics. The busy auction made for a lot of commotion. Goods were tossed back and forth, and the room was so thick with smoke that Milan constantly had to wipe his tearing eyes. But, in less than an hour, he unloaded everything he had left.

After the auction, Milan strolled outside to get a breath of the cool evening air before his departure. The auction post was close to the forest. Since it was still light outside, he decided to take a short walk just beyond the forest boundary, as he often did, before returning to the confines of his ship. Once inside the forest edge, Milan continued a parallel course away from the main pathway. It was a narrow footpath, lined on either side with large trees, wild bushes, and thick undergrowth. The foliage was dark bluish-green. He walked on bare, rocky ground since not much light penetrated the density of the trees. Woodland creatures disturbed the silence as they scampered playfully in the underbrush while birds chirped merrily from the trees.

Milan liked this particular forest and would occasionally rest under a large tree in the stone garden not far from where he entered. As he strolled toward his favorite spot, he saw the back of a forlorn individual seated against a tree. Immediately in stealth mode, he advanced, and by changing his angle of approach, Milan clearly saw who the person was. *That's Uzak of Uni*, he thought. *What's that in his hand?* Moving closer, Milan noticed that Uzak was holding aloft an unusual medallion, a beautiful signet of gem-studded leaves arranged in a circular pattern. He nearly fell when he recognized The Planet Star from pictures he had seen in the quarters of his friend, Ewlon Galan, -- pictures taken by Ew's father, Wedolan Galan.

The Planet Star, he said, mouthing his words without sound. Milan wetted his lips as one ready to dive into a tantalizing meal. *Would be nice to take that medallion home with me*, he thought. From behind a tree, he watched and listened with curiosity as Uzak argued aloud with unseen forces.

"How inventive you are, my brothers, but I control the destiny of this galaxy," Uzak said irritably. "I will find her. I am the Keeper of Unity. How dare you create this pestilent bauble to destroy me!" he spat out his anger. Suddenly, he clasped the medallion in his hand for a moment before depositing it into a secret pocket inside his jacket. He then settled back under the tree and closed his eyes.

Milan stood motionless for several minutes, debating on how to get his hands on the medallion. *Looks like he's sleep*, he thought. *Of course not, you mindless fool, Uzak never sleeps. Still, if I can get my hands on that medal... a ridiculous thought*, he argued. Milan turned to go back to his spacecraft, but was stopped by a nagging thought. *That medallion would really give Khali the upper hand*, he continued his silent deliberation. He knew the power of The Planet Star. It could mean the end of years of struggle for Khali. *I should at least try*, he argued. *Who am I trying to fool here*, he thought, *I'd love to see Khali gain the upper hand, but getting that medallion could make me a very rich man.* Milan slowly reached inside his vest and pulled out one of several small vials containing the knockout vapor blocon. *No one can resist this drug, and I only need a second -- or two. He'll never even know I was here,* he convinced himself.

Since Milan's job took him throughout the Unian Solar System, he never left his carefully concealed abode without several samples of this drug. He uncapped the vial containing the vapor, and quickly covered the top with his thumb to keep the vapor from escaping. With great stealth, he steadily moved towards the intended victim. He was within five trans of Uzak when he questioned his actions a second time. *I must be mad to think I could get away with this. He's certainly not asleep, and if I turn to leave now, I may get a saber in my back*, he thought, as he envisioned his horrible fate. Milan broke out in a sweat. *I gotta go with it now; it's too late to turn back.* Carefully watching Uzak, he stooped slightly to pass the vial beneath Uzak's nostrils. Suddenly, a strong hand grabbed him by the wrist, throwing him to the ground.

"Milan Mariko. Whatever are you doing here?"

Milan's face filled with terror as he slowly turned his head to face the villainous Lord of Uni. Thick black hair and a shaggy uni-brow amplified Uzak's callous black eyes. The scowl across his forehead sent a chilling message.

Milan stayed where he was, frozen in fear for a moment. Uzak drew his saber and brought it to within lino-trans of Milan's chest. As Uzak raised his saber for the kill strike, Milan quickly rolled away. The blade struck the ground as Milan, with the agility of a hunted creature, jumped to his feet. He began ducking and dodging the blade's edge as Uzak lunged from side to side, swinging his saber wildly.

"You sneak," Uzak sneered. Dodging a powerful slice, Milan ducked, barely in time, causing Uzak's blade to become lodged in the bow of a tree. Quickly, Milan took the momentary advantage and ran into the more dense area of the forest.

After nearly ten minutes of running, Milan came upon a large clearing with a small stream singing merrily southward. He leaned forward with his hands on his knees for a moment, trying desperately to get enough air into his tortured lungs. The sound of movement in the forest behind him spurred him to motion again. Quickly scanning the area, he noticed undergrowth of bushes several trans downstream, and rushed there for cover. Not a moment too soon. From behind the thicket, he watched as Uzak crossed the stream and headed into the forest on the other side.

Despite the security of this particular hideout, Milan put his hand over his chest as if to muffle the sound of his furiously beating heart. *Never stood a chance*, he thought. *Still, I gave it my best. Problem is, will I live to tell about it.* Milan remained in hiding a while longer before sticking his head outside the bushes. *Good, no sign of him.* Pushing his way through the thicket, he left his hiding place and headed back in the direction of his spaceship.

Several minutes passed without any sign of pursuit. Just as Milan neared the stone garden where this all began, a sound from behind spun him around just in time to see Uzak nearly on top of him. He threw his arms up and begged Uzak to reconsider. "I-I only wanted to take a look at that fine antique medallion you have. I was trying to get a closer look at it," he pleaded.

"Don't lie, junk dealer." The tone of Uzak's voice was smooth and sinister, but his advance slowed. "You know exactly what it looks like, friend of Ewlon Galan."

Milan slowly backed into a tree. With a fake, teasing, downward chop, Uzak's saber sliced the air and whacked off a large tree limb just above his head. Milan spun around behind the tree and finally drew his own saber. He knew his skills were no match for Uzak, but he used the forest trees as his shield. Swinging his saber, Uzak pursued Milan back and forth around the tree. At one point, Milan miscalculated Uzak's move and they ended up face to face.

"I grow weary of this game," Uzak said disdainfully. In a

well-poised stance, Uzak thrust his saber forward to skewer Milan through the mid-section. Frantically, Milan raised his saber to block. Unfortunately, he was unable to avoid the tip of Uzak's blade, which cut him just below the waist on the right side. He cringed at the wetness of his blood trickling from the open gash. Milan stood there for a moment, motionless, watching Uzak gloat at his discomfort. He observed the determined posture of his opponent, aware of his own mortality as he faced the immortal Keeper of Unity. His palms became clammy. The air he was dragging into his lungs seemed chalky and dry, and he felt the urge to swallow so as not to choke on the fear that gripped his heart. He shuddered at Uzak's penetrating deep-set, coal-black eyes. As Uzak moved closer, his heart quickened. The whistle of a quick slice broke the silence. Milan again frantically parried, and Uzak's blade fell short of its mark.

"I can see you want to do this the hard way, junk man," Uzak said smugly. Uzak then hacked away at Milan's saber until it shattered, leaving Milan holding the shard. He chuckled when Milan grabbed up the tree limb he had earlier chopped off. "That's good, junk dealer. We'll just take our time."

Breathing heavily from fear and exhaustion, Milan still refused to give up. With the tree limb raised to form, Milan was able to deflect the next blow downward, away from his side, but the razor-sharp saber cut into his upper thigh. As quickly as possible, he hobbled over to another tree, while Uzak calmly and arrogantly strolled behind.

The tree was low with two major offshoots from the center. Uzak raised his saber to hew Milan from the other side. Milan jumped back, just missing the blade. In his retreat from the blade, he grabbed a thick low branch and bowed it back. By that time, Uzak had come around to his side for the kill. As Uzak aimed his final sweeping slice to behead his opponent, Milan released the arched branch. THWANG! Uzak staggered from the impact, and his foot became tangled in vine-like undergrowth that grew under the shadow of the trees. He stumbled and fell backwards, hitting the ground with a thud. In desperation, Milan picked up the same tree limb he'd used earlier and moved quickly towards the stunned Unian Lord. He gathered what strength he had left, and with the thickest part of the limb, he hit the side of Uzak's skull, stunning him further.

Shakily, Milan uncapped another vial of the blocon drug and passed the small bottle beneath Uzak's nostrils. Stunned by the assault and unable to resist the effects of the vapor, Uzak succumbed to a deep sleep. Milan then removed the medallion from Uzak's inside breast pocket.

Uncertain about how long Uzak would remain unconscious, Milan limped hurriedly back to his ship. Just as he was about to enter his spacecraft, two Unian guards stopped him. Although his wounds were not bleeding profusely, the cover of night would hide his blood stained pants from inquisitive eyes.

"What's your hurry?" asked one of the guards. "We heard you did pretty good at the auction, Mariko."

The second guard began to search Milan's vest pocket before allowing him to enter his vessel. When the guard pulled Milan's credits out, the medallion fell out and onto the ground. The guard picked it up and looked at it. "What's this here?" he asked. "A pretty charm is it?"

Beads of perspiration slid down Milan's face and neck, and he tried to hide his anxiety. He managed a careless tone. "It's a small bauble from Perican. You can have it if you like."

"Other words, I kin have it 'cause nobody else wants it," the guard scoffed.

"It's truly a priceless relic," said Milan, hoping to bluff the guard.

"Ah-huh. Tell you what, I'll take these here credits, and you kin have this valuable relic." The guard shoved The Planet Star back into Milan's vest pocket, and then pushed Milan toward the door of his spacecraft. "It's good doin' business with ya. Have a good trip," he said, stuffing the credits into his pocket.

Milan entered his spacecraft and immediately plotted a course for Galan, a three-hour trip from Uni. Shortly after takeoff, he began to fear that Uzak might recover and send military craft to intercept him before he could reach his destination. With that in mind, he altered his course and headed for the nearest planet, Thesbis.

After adjusting spacecraft controls to automatic pilot, Milan removed his shirt and pants to examine his wounds. The wound on his side had stopped bleeding, but the one on his thigh still bled slightly. With his fingertips, he pinched the wound on his thigh closed, and sprayed it with an antiseptic-closure spray. He repeated the process for the injury on his side.

Turning his attention back to the cockpit, Milan tried to contact King Ewlon on an interstellar frequency to Galan. Unable to reach Ew, he transmitted a videocomm message to Ew's communications channel.

"Ew, I came across the family heirloom you have long searched for. Meet me at the Trade Post Inn in Raileen on Thesbis. Please hurry."

Nearly an hour after his departure from Uni, Milan docked at the Thesbian Spaceport. It was dusk by the time he secured a room at The Trade Post Inn, not far from the terminal building. From his bedroom window, he could see the spaceport-docking bay.

As Milan stared at the terminal building against the darkening sky over Raileen, it was night in the forest on Uni, where Uzak awakened from the drug induced sleep. Uzak slowly stood up, shook his head, and massaged his neck. He took a few steps forward. Suddenly, he patted his breast pocket and realized the medallion was gone. "MARIKO!" he bellowed, in a moment of panic and rage. Without delay, Uzak charged back to his headquarters, located next to the military auction post where Milan Mariko auctioned off his goods earlier that evening.

Uzak stood with his back to the communications-viewing monitor, facing the window and shouting orders. He knew that Milan would try to contact the Galan household, and would probably be heading that way.

"I want a copy of all intergalactic transmissions sent to Galan during the last hour," he snapped. "Set perimeter markings in all directions to within an hour's journey beyond Thesbis. Sentry ships are to scan for and stop any small vessels moving toward or beyond that point."

"Are small cargo ships included, Sire?" a voice answered over the comm line.

"No. Single-manned spacecraft only," Uzak responded. "The thief I'm looking for is Milan Mariko, the antique trader from Litathe. He is to be brought to me at once -- alive."

"I'll get on it right away, My Lord."

Uzak paced the room as he waited impatiently for a response. Minutes ticked by. Just when he felt he could wait no more, a beep sounded on the videocomm. The smiling face of Jaynt Saren covered the display monitor.

"Good evening, Sire. I have good news for you. Incoming widows from Tima have just arrived."

"Not now, Saren," Uzak interrupted.

"But my Lord," cried Saren, "there is one in particular you should see. She is thirty-eight years old and is accompanied by her six-year old son. She has also requested placement..."

"Not *now*, Saren," Uzak said firmly. "I'll meet with her before sundown tomorrow."

"But My Lord, another problem has surfaced that we should discuss. The Council is..."

Uzak abruptly snapped off the videocomm before Saren could reveal news about the early morning Council meeting. Uzak resumed his pacing for a moment or two longer before a communications officer hailed him a second time.

"What do you have?" he asked.

"My Lord, we found him.

Uzak was pleased by the quick response in locating Milan Mariko. "Where did you find him, Commander?" he asked.

"Intelligence traced him to Thesbis. He sent a message to the Galan household informing King Ewlon to meet him at The Trade Post Inn in Raileen."

"Very good, Commander. Prepare my shuttle for takeoff. Inform Admiral Pernell that I will be boarding the flagship immediately."

"Yes, My Lord. Will there be anything else?"

"Dispatch a detachment of Occupation Military Police to meet me at the Thesbian Spaceport within the hour. Inform Saren that we are to have priority landing status."

"Yes, My Lord."

2
THESBIS, PLANET OF WIDOWS

As Uzak prepared for his trip to Thesbis, Shreela and Soren sat in the reception area next to Jaynt Saren's door, in the Office of Widow Registration. The conference-style room had disc shelves lining the back wall, filled with literature on educational courses, therapy groups, day care for widows' dependent children, and other services.

Soren sat quietly, while Shreela orally answered questions into a computer log file. She thought her earlier interview with Mr. Saren went pretty well. For many days, the burden of Jor's death lay heavily on her heart, but as she hurriedly completed the log entry, she felt a little more positive about her future; that sense of moving forward with her life. Shreela was just answering the last two questions when Mr. Saren entered the reception area from his office. He had a large envelope tucked under his arm.

Shreela handed him the disc. "Here's my log, Mr. Saren."

"That's your copy," he explained. "Your log was entered onto a computer file at the same time the disc was prepared. I'll just check it over quickly."

"Thank you," Shreela responded. "I would like to thank you

for meeting us at the spaceport so late. I forgot about the time difference between Tima and Thesbis. When I made reservations to come here, I was told that my flight should arrive here by midday. I didn't check if that was midday Tima time or Thesbis time."

"That's quite alright," said Saren. "I had to work late this evening anyway."

Shreela looked directly at him as he scanned the log entry. She wondered why Saren's eyes twitched when he responded. She watched him slowly pace the room, the envelope still tucked tightly under his arm. He was tall and lanky, and the ashen color of his skin gave the impression that he spent little time in the sun.

Saren handed the disc back to her. "It seems to be in order," he commented. "As I explained to you several days ago, we had a recent opening for housing in our residential area for widows with children. Our next step is to get you into that house."

"Thank you for holding it for me a week longer. I know you have other applicants anxious to get in."

"I've also taken care of your placement request to the Khalian Solar System."

"Wonderful," Shreela responded, smiling. "There is one other thing, if I may?"

"Certainly."

"Is it possible for me to find the whereabouts of another widow?"

"It is. Who is she, and where is she from?"

"Her name is Dian Mudhar from Planet Tima. She arrived here early last week. Actually, she was a neighbor of mine."

Saren stared directly at her, seemingly surprised, causing her to feel strangely uncomfortable under his glare. *There goes that twitch again*, she thought. With his right hand, Saren gently squeezed his chin, and dropped his head. Shreela thought he looked as if he was trying to remember something.

"Dian Mudhar, Mudhar," he repeated, and then unexpectedly straightened up with a start. "Oh yes, I remember her. She's here."

Shreela smiled. "May I have her number so I can contact her?"

"Ah-h-h, unfortunately I don't know where her lodgings are. I will attempt to find out for you tomorrow. Speaking of lodgings, are you ready to see yours?" he abruptly changed the subject.

The smile on Shreela's lips faded. She looked at him with disappointment, and when her gaze crossed his, his eyes seemed cold and reserved. For a brief moment, Shreela felt anxious again, but now she felt as if she had stumbled onto something she wasn't supposed to know. Saren's eyes softened and the moment passed.

"I know you're disappointed, Mrs. Bakra," he said, smiling, "but let me see what I can come up with."

"I would appreciate that," she said, trying to pretend relief she did not feel.

"Good." Saren handed her the packet of information tucked beneath his arm, along with a green metallic card. "Here's some information you might review before you retire tonight. Go over your schedule for tomorrow, and make a note that the orientation class will be held in this building at nine-hundred hours tomorrow morning."

"What's the card for?" Shreela asked curiously.

"The card contains an encrypted code number to the house you'll lodge in while you're here. The place is fully stocked with food and other provisions, as well as a house android."

"Will there be an added cost for the android?"

"No," Saren responded. "The android is a home maintenance droid, and is included in the package. More information on how we subsidize the program is included in the packet."

"Thanks, I'll go over it tonight."

"That'll be fine. Before we leave, I need to know if you remembered to bring your biotime tablets. You'll need them to help change your biological clock."

"Yes. We took them just before we left the spacecraft. As a matter of fact, I'm beginning to feel sleepy already."

Saren laughed lightly. "Then we had better get you on your way. If you'll follow me, I'll escort you to the transport headed for your new home."

It was dark when the transport left the building, but the lights along the route let Shreela see that the tallest buildings were no more than four levels high. Lights radiated within a few shops, but most of the businesses were dark.

The transport went only a few blocks before it turned onto a residential street. Suddenly, Shreela heard the synthesized voice of the transport droid call her name:

"21 East Mallon Street, Bakra residence to the right. Transport pickup tomorrow morning at 0800 hours. Please be prompt."

The transport slowed to a stop in front of a beautiful two-level house. When the transport door opened, a long robot arm extended and lowered the Bakra baggage at the front door. Shreela laughed aloud at Soren's wide-eyed, open-mouthed expression, as he watched the transport move away.

"Come on bright eyes. Let's go inside and see if there are any more surprises."

The small box which was the front door lock was on the outside wall next to the entrance. Shreela opened the box, which contained a panel of letters and numbers, and slipped the metallic green card into a small marked slot. They heard a soft, churning noise and the door slid open.

Shreela and Soren stepped inside and looked around. The main sitting room was small and white, giving a sense of open space. The kitchen, less spacious than the one in her old home on Tima, had a small table and two chairs, which served as their dining area. Shreela headed upstairs to the second floor. In the corner opposite the stairwell, a house android silently stood at attention. She walked passed the android and peeped into the first room on her left. It was the master bedroom. She quickly dropped her bags down on the floor inside the room and then continued to escort Soren to the end of the corridor to his room. The room was furnished simply with a single bed, already made up with clean linens and a blanket. Wood-stained drawers were built into the walls for storing clothing. The dark green carpet against the soft textured ivory walls gave the room a warm look. A triangular- reddish-brown bed frame matched the drawers as well as the baseboard trim. Shreela opened the door next to the bed, and found it led to a small bath. She turned back to see that Soren was already sitting on his bed.

"I'll be back in a minute with your sleeper", she said.

"Can I have a story?"

"After your bath. Wait here. I'll be back in a minute."

Shreela headed back down the corridor to her room. Before entering, she thought to take a moment to examine the android in the corner. With the flick of a switch, the android was activated.

"Droid No. HD21 at your service. May I help you?"

Shreela laughed, noticing that only one of the android's eyes flickered as it spoke. "No," she giggled.

"Then I shall be in the parlor if you require assistance." On that note, the droid clanked down the steps and was gone.

After unpacking Soren's sleeper, Shreela headed back to Soren's room. His light was on, but he was sound asleep. Shreela removed his shoes, covered him, and turned out the light. "Good night, my little one," she whispered.

Less than one-half kilo-tran from Shreela's home, Milan Mariko stood outside the Trade Post Inn, a small two-level building, located along the main thorofare. Transient lodges, shops, recreation, and refreshment concerns lined both sides of the four-lane transport highway. It was well lit, and people were always in the streets in this area, regardless of the hour.

Milan kept his ears opened to any chatter about what happened on Uni. The memory of his battle with Uzak edged his teeth and the annoying flutter in his stomach, intensified. *With any luck, Uzak won't be able to track me down*, he thought. That hope suddenly died when a Unian military spacecraft passed overhead, landing at the Raileen Spaceport landing strip, nearly two kilo-trans from the Inn.

Milan hurried back to his room where he unlocked a small metal secure box, which he earlier hid beneath his bed mattress. He removed the medallion, slipped it into his pocket, and walked over to the window where he could see the spaceport in the distance. A trill of terror chased up his spine as armed military personnel swiftly and efficiently disembarked and headed for ground transports waiting nearby.

Without delay, Milan rushed out of his room, and charged down the back staircase to an alley behind the Inn. Despite the pain of his wounds, he ran down the alley for several blocks. He stopped at a street corner, and rested for a moment or two before heading east into the residential section of Raileen, an area reserved for widows with small children.

As Milan walked down the street trying to decide what next to do, Shreela sat at her desk and began to review some of the material given to her by Mr. Saren. She was both surprised and delighted to learn there were grade school sessions, as well as after school care services, provided in the Main Building complex. She could send Soren to school and take the necessary preparation and training classes under the same roof. She frowned and pursed her lips as she closed the book containing information about the program.

"Everything here seems too perfect," she thought aloud. She stood up to stretch her arms out, releasing the tension in her body. "I just can't seem to relax." Opening the desk drawer to store her log entry discs, she noticed a small stack of empty discs inside. She picked them up and began to sift through the pile, suddenly stopping when she came across Machi's name on a log addressed to him. "Hum…. what's this?" Without reading the contents, Shreela flipped the disc over to examine the name of the sender on the other side.

"Dian Mudhar," she whispered, aloud. "She must have been assigned to this house."

Shreela inserted the disc into the computer and began to read the letter. *That's strange*, she thought. *This letter is dated the same day as the one she sent to me. Wonder why she never sent it?*

Shreela sat down and continued to read. When she was finished, she stared blankly at the letter on her visual monitor. *There's nothing unusual in this letter*, she thought, *but why didn't Mr. Saren remember that Dian changed her lodgings, especially since she was assigned to an area for widows with children? She has no children, at least not yet.* Shreela removed the disc and held it for a moment, trying to decide what to do. "I'll digest all of this later," she said, sighing. "Right now, I can do with a breath of fresh air."

Shreela headed out of the den and down the stairs. She was

met by the house android on her way out.

"I'm going out on the front patio for a few moments before I retire."

"What about your young son, madam?" asked the android.

"He's asleep. I'll just be out front."

"Very good, madam."

"HD21, answer a question for me, will you?"

"If I can."

"Did Dian Mudhar live here before me?"

"Yes, madam."

"Why did she leave?"

"She left for class."

"I know that, but when did she pack up and leave?"

"She never returned from class, madam."

Suddenly, a sinking feeling came over Shreela. Deep lines appeared on her forehead, and a knot tightened in her stomach. "Thank you," she said, at length.

The night was cool with two full moons, and the smell of late autumn flowers heavily scented the air. Shreela observed there were several styles of homes along her street. Her residence resembled an upside-down cone. The house exteriors were made from stone that had been heated and recast into various geometric forms. Long linear-tube lights, lined each entry from the door to the intersecting walkway.

As soon as Shreela's foot crossed the threshold to step outside, the entry walkway lit up, casting a warm-blue light.

"There are trees everywhere, and each property is beautifully landscaped," Shreela whispered. "Why would someone go to such an expense for widows?" she wondered. "This program costs a good deal less than the one on Tima, but Tima doesn't offer such luxurious surroundings."

Not for the first time since her arrival did Shreela feel

troubled. Though Mr. Saren appeared to be a gracious host, Shreela had a nagging suspicion that things might not be as they appear. *Maybe I should have taken more time to consider my decision to leave home*, she thought. Her reflections became even more troublesome, as she tried to gauge the events taking place.

"Why would Mr. Saren meet me at the space dock so late? As the top administrator, I would think that sending a staff person would be more appropriate," she thought, aloud. "Not only that, I wasn't the only widow on that spacecraft, but he only interviewed me. Why?"

Shreela walked slowly toward the pedestrian walkway. She asked herself more positive questions to dispel the negative feelings she had. *Maybe I'm reading too much into all of this, and as for Dian, Mr. Saren probably wasn't involved in her leaving*, she consoled herself. *But someone removed her belongings. If not her, then who?* Suddenly, she collided with a man walking north along the pedestrian walkway. His oval face was jolly and his eyes sparkled. It was Milan Mariko.

"Your pardon," he said.

"Excuse me," Shreela apologized. Though puzzled by his presence there, Shreela gracefully nodded her head, and hurried back up the front walk. "That's peculiar," she thought, aloud. "This area is restricted to widows. What's he doing here?" she wondered.

Shreela continued to watch the man until he was out of view before entering her house.

The night was late when Shreela retired to her room. Two spaceflight hours east of Thesbis, Ewlon and Pala disembarked Ew's personal Imperial spacecraft on Galan. It was early afternoon when they docked. For Ew, it had already been a long day, beginning with his early morning meeting on Thesbis followed by another meeting on Crashellon.

"I'll check in on my messages and meet you in the recreation room in about an hour," he said to Pala. "I can use a good workout right now."

"Me too."

Ew sat at his desk in the library, adjacent to his bedroom chamber. He stared at the number of data chips neatly stacked in the automatic stacking attachment next to the video communications monitor.

"Messages," he sighed.

The twelve lino-trans high stack of data chips comprised of approximately twenty-five messages; personal messages. One by one, at the push of a button, each chip was automatically loaded into the playback slot. Instead of viewing the monitor, Ew stared outside the library window into the garden below as he listened to each message. There were messages from his mother, Mara; his sister, Megan; a few personal friends, and others. Halfway through the chips, the anxious voice of Milan Mariko came through. Ew turned to look at the monitor.

"A family heirloom," he whispered. Ew reached over to touch the replay button. He played the disc several times. Finally, he sat back in his chair with a stunned look on his face. *Milan knows that The Planet Star is the only family heirloom I'm interested in, but how could he get that from Uzak?* he questioned himself.

Excitement began to build up in Ew as he thought about the possibility of recovering The Planet Star. Quickly, he hailed Pala Bhusan. There was a sound of urgency in his voice.

"Pala, meet me in the docking bay. Milan is on Thesbis."

"Is there a problem?"

"Maybe, but I'll explain it when I see you. Prepare an unmarked spacecraft. I'll get Calo to personally clear our exit."

"On my way."

In a heartbeat, Ew contacted General Calo Laggé.

"Calo."

"My Lord, I was about to call you on a..."

"Can it wait?" he interrupted.

"I'm afraid not."

"Well, I need to see you on another matter, so break away from whatever you're doing, and meet me in my quarters in ten minutes."

Ew rushed to his bedroom chamber to change from his royal attire into street clothes. While he dressed, he thought about his long friendship with Milan Mariko. Ew became acquainted with Milan some ten years before when Ew disguised himself and ventured into the galaxy as a trader of antique goods. There were two principal reasons why Ew solicited Milan's services. One was to spy on his archenemy, Uzak, Lord of the Unian Solar System. To gain intelligence information, Ew cultivated friendships with those having easy access to Uni. Milan Mariko was such a man, a well-known archaeologist, who conducted many business transactions on Uni as well as those planets aligned with it. The other reason was that as an archaeologist, Milan Mariko would surely recognize The Planet Star if it were to surface. Though Ew believed Uzak kept it safe, he could not risk any unlooked for mishaps.

Suddenly, Ew's thoughts were abruptly intruded upon by a stiff knock at the door.

"Come on in Calo."

A medium-height gentleman with a slim build, dressed in military attire entered after invitation. He was Calo Laggé, General of the Interplanetary Defense Team, and one of Ew's closest friends.

"Good afternoon, Your Majesty."

"Good day, Calo," responded Ew. "Before I get into what I need from you, how about telling me what this crisis is that can't wait."

"Earlier today, we discovered that the security of your personal channel had been breached. Any incoming or outgoing communications, sent or received by your receiver, has been compromised."

"What! How?"

"We have been able to track the security breach to Thesbis. Your Majesty, there is someone operating from inside Thesbis or Uni. It was an expert job."

"Uzak's Security Intelligence Police?"

"Most likely."

"Have you informed Pala?"

"Yes. He's reviewing the computer output display now."

Ew walked slowly to the window and looked out into the garden below. He fastened his shirt and adjusted his clothes, while silently deliberating on several ways to handle the problem. "Continue to check on how that code was breached," he ordered. "In the meantime, I want the backup encrypted security codes put on-line. That includes not only my personal channel, but also the Shargant and Lluellyn Space Stations, Inter-Solar System Armed Forces, and the Galactic Fleet. I want people on it non-stop. The new codes should be ready no later than this evening." Ew turned back to Calo. "Can it be done?"

"It can," the other responded.

"Tell me, Calo, does this sound like we might have a security problem inside Khali?"

"We are checking that as a possibility. Do you have information, which might be suspicious?"

"Not anything concrete. Anyway, just see what you can come up with -- too many things are happening at once," he murmured to himself. Ew noticed the curious look on Calo's face. "Is there something else?" he asked.

"Pala said something about you leaving Galan shortly."

"That's what I wanted to talk to you about. I'm headed back to Thesbis."

"I see that you'll be incognito," Calo said, rather than asked. "When should I expect you be back?"

"Hopefully by tomorrow evening, at the latest."

"This will be your third trip to Thesbis this week. The situation there must be worse."

"If you mean the disappearance of widows scheduled for placement, the answer is no. That situation is still the same." Ew looked down for a moment in deep thought. His expression turned to one of concern. "As you know, the Thesbian Placement Council believes Uzak is behind these kidnappings, but until today, his contact has eluded us."

"Then you know who the contact is?" asked Calo.

"Not absolutely, but I don't believe it's a merchant."

"Who do you suspect then?"

"Jaynt Saren."

"Why do you think it's him?"

"Ambassador Behrend told me that he thought the inside person was someone on the Placement Council. Behrend thought it might be Saren, and after Saren's behavior today at the Council Meeting, I think he was right."

"Maybe he's responsible for our security breach, too."

"No," said Ew. "That sort of espionage is not his specialty, but I wouldn't be surprised to learn that he knows about it."

"Should I put someone on him?"

"Not yet. Wait until I return." Ew paced slowly toward the door. Calo likewise moved to leave. "Anyway, I'm on my way to Thesbis for another reason. Pala and I will be leaving in an unmarked vessel. You know the procedure. Clear our exit, and I'll be back in touch with you by tomorrow evening."

"Of course."

"Oh, one other thing," said Ew, "going back to our discussion on disappearing widows, see if you can locate a young widow that Council interviewed last week on Thesbis."

"Is she still on Thesbis?"

"Supposedly, but the Thesbian Placement Council staff is unable to locate her. She was scheduled to relocate to Galan after she finished the program."

Calo pulled out his log entry recorder. "What's her name?"

"Dian Mudhar. She's twenty-eight, home planet Tima, and she's pregnant."

"I'll get on it right away. Have a safe trip, My Lord."

3
NARROW ESCAPES

After closing the door behind Calo, Ew walked over to his wardrobe room to finish his disguise. He wore long blue pants, tucked inside black high-top boots. His muscular chest was partially exposed beneath the half-opened, full-sleeved, white shirt he wore under a navy blue jacket.

Ew walked directly to the back of the long rectangular closet. The back wall was a smooth, black and gray paneling, made from the hard rock, *dabernine.* When he touched one of the panels, a small, shallow, drawer extended. The drawer contained a mirror; a pair of tweezers, two plastic lenses, a triangular shaped cutout, and an irregular-shaped rubbery textured strip nearly two lino-trans in length. Ew picked up the small plastic lens discs, and inserted one in each eye. The lenses were dark brown, encircled with a narrow white band, changing his eye color from gray-green to brown. The narrow white band covered the edge of his iris, blending into the whites of his eye, making his iris appear smaller. Ew removed the triangular cutout, which was thinly padded at the tip, and pressed it against the bridge of his nose to broaden it. The rubbery textured strip was an artificial scar, which he placed at an angle along the lower left jaw. After examining himself in the mirror, Ew closed the drawer. He touched another panel, and a section of the wall moved up two trans off the floor. Ew stepped across the threshold and pressed a button on the opposite side to close it. He descended the lighted stairway leading to an underground passage.

As Ew walked along the brightly lit passage, he thought about its construction nearly ten years earlier when he first ventured out, disguised as an antique dealer. With the help of his security chief, Pala Bhusan, the location of the tunnel was virtually unknown to everyone, including his mother. Even the workers that built it weren't allowed to know where they were, or that they were working for the royal family. Ew walked for five minutes before he reached the door of his private docking bay where Pala Bhusan waited.

"Your spacecraft is ready, Sire," said Pala.

"Good. Calo should be in the control room by now. Let's go."

Ew entered a sleek ultra-modern spacecraft with light gray interior and recessed lights. He sat in one of three cockpit seats, each surrounded by a myriad of buttons and blinking lights. Through the panoramic view of the cockpit window, he stared blankly into space, wondering about Milan's message and its implication to his years of struggle with the Unian Empire.

"So, what's this news about Mariko?" asked Pala, who piloted the ship.

"He sent this log." Ew slipped the disc chip into the videocomm playback slot. "Here, I made a copy of it."

With raised eyebrows, Pala listened intently to Milan's message. "Is he referring to The Planet Star?"

"I think so, but I can't say for sure. He really sounds worried and afraid."

"Yeah, I get that, too. We better hurry."

"Um-huh. We should arrive on Thesbis within two hours." Ew stared out the cockpit window, totally oblivious to his surroundings.

"What is it, Sire?" asked Pala.

"Just thinking."

"The medallion?"

"I've waited so long to get my hands on that medallion."

"It will be the end of a long quest."

"It may also be the beginning of a new one."

"Sire?"

"It's just a feeling I get. For some reason, I feel this trip will be one of many."

It was past midnight when Ew and Pala arrived on Thesbis. They boarded a local transport going to Raileen, and disembarked two blocks from the Trade Post Inn. Ew noticed an unusually large number of Unian Military Police in the area, and the entrance to the lodge was blocked with armed soldiers checking everyone entering or leaving.

"Wait a minute, Pala," said Ew, slowing his pace. "Let's go somewhere else until we find out what's going on here."

"We can check in at the Two Moons across the street," Pala suggested. "Wonder if they're looking for Milan?"

"I wonder about that too," Ew said. "I'm even more curious about how Milan came to have The Planet Star in his possession, if that's what he has. How could he have taken it from Uzak?"

"When I spoke to him two days ago, he said he would be trading at the Garden of Stones Military Trade Auction on Uni," Pala explained. "He must have run into Uzak."

"That's a possibility, and that breach in my communications

line probably helped Uzak to track him here," Ew speculated.

A small crowd of guests gathered at the entrance of the Two Moons, absorbed in the proceedings taking place across the street. Pala and Ew pressed their way through the crowd to enter. The dark, drab lobby had two chairs against the wall next to the small registration counter where a short, balding middle-aged man stood, conversing with one of the guests. Stepping up to the counter, Ew placed several credits on the countertop and signed the guest register using an assumed name. The desk clerk quickly picked up the credits and handed Ew a magnetic room key.

While heading down the corridor, Pala and Ew were distracted by a low whistle from behind. Ew turned to see Milan with his head sticking out of one of the doors. He seemed overjoyed to see his old friends. "Come quickly," he whispered. After ushering them inside, Milan took one quick look down the corridor before closing the door.

Without conscious thought, Pala moved to his usual position of surveillance by the window, while Milan began to describe all that happened to him that day.

"I thought you were staying at the Trade Post Inn?" asked Ew.

"I was until Uzak's thugs showed up."

"What happened?"

"Well it all began after I finished selling my merchandise at the Kavic Port military post on Uni….."

Ew listened with interest as Milan explained how he had taken The Planet Star from Uzak, as well as his escape from the Unian Military Police sent to Thesbis to search for him.

Ew raised his brow. "Milan, I'm impressed," he said. "Now tell me, where is..."

"Ew," Pala suddenly interrupted.

Ew noticed the ruffle on Pala's brow. "What?"

"Soldiers are headed this way."

Ew walked over to the window to have a look, but quickly stepped back.

"What's the matter?" Milan asked nervously.

"Uzak is on his way over here. We better leave now," he said, heading toward the door. "Milan is there another way out of here?"

Milan rushed to the door behind him. "There's an escape ladder just at the end of this corridor. We can leave that way."

"Then let's go", shouted Ew.

The three men hurried down the narrow hallway, scrambling out of a side window and down the ladder. Ew and his friends raced down a side street, stopping at an old deserted junkyard three blocks north of the Two Moons. Milan, who was overweight, found it difficult to keep up with the long strides of his comrades. They entered a junkyard where Milan collapsed to his knees exhausted. "It sure isn't like our younger days," he said, gasping.

"You didn't eat as much in your younger days either," Ew chuckled. "Seriously though, how's your wound?"

Milan examined his side under the moonlight. "The bleeding has stopped. I'm a little sore, but I think I'm okay."

"You'd probably be much better if you would purchase a few updated medical supplies for that triage kit you have. Why don't you at least get a tissue regenerator?"

"That stuff is too costly."

"And that's why your wound still hurts."

Ew looked over toward Pala, who seemed to ignore the conversation taking place between him and Milan. "Pala," he called out.

"If I were searching for someone, I would definitely look

here," Pala said, surveying the area around the junkyard. "Let's get out of here."

"Come, I'll take you to where the medallion is hidden," Milan whispered.

"Hidden? What do you mean by hidden?" asked Ew. "Don't you have it on you?"

"No, I had to get rid of it."

"Of course," Ew responded sarcastically, trotting behind Milan.

Heading east for one block and continuing northward on Mallon Street, they slowed their pace as Milan neared house number twenty-one.

"Those sirens are getting close," Pala cautioned them.

"We're here anyway," said Milan.

"What does that mean?" asked Ew.

Suddenly, a military transport turned onto Mallon Street with sirens blaring. Ew and his friends immediately cut across the yard and into a wooded area behind the house. Several moments passed before the noise died down. Finally, unable to contain his anxiety any longer, Ew blurted out, "Milan, tell me why are we here, and where is The Planet Star?"

"When the Unian Military Police landed here on Thesbis," Milan began, "I was sure they would be looking for me. After I left the Trade Post Inn, I just kept running in this direction. I bumped into the young widow who lives here. She was standing outside on the walkway. That's when I slipped the medallion into her coat pocket. Sure hope she didn't find it."

Ew's mouth fell open. He stared at Milan for a moment in disbelief. "Why would you get rid of it by giving it to a stranger?"

"Well, I-I-I certainly didn't want to be caught with it on me," Milan stammered.

Frustrated, Ew slapped his hand against his forehead, sliding it downward and massaging his eyes in an attempt to release the tension. He settled back, quietly listening to the nocturnal creatures singing in the night. *At least it's not in Uzak's hand*, he thought, *but I sure wish this treasure could've come by another path. With all this business about security breaches, missing widows, legends and....* Ew suddenly perked up. "Milan, what sort of widow is she?"

"I didn't really see her too well. The ground lighting was in my face, but I remembered the address."

Maybe it was the right decision after all, he thought. Letting out an exasperated sigh and shaking his head, "Well, we can't do anything about it now," he commented. "We'll search for it in the morning after she goes to class."

Morning dawned bright and clear. Ew and his companions were awakened by a flock of birds chirping in the garden. Ew took a few moments to visually scout out his surroundings. He faced a long row of houses, each with a small backyard. The woods, where he and his companions were hiding, provided a boundary marking the end of each lot. Almost all of the houses had an elevated rear patio entrance. "As soon as the young widow leaves the house, I'll slip into that open window," he said, pointing towards the bedroom window just right of the patio door. "That balcony is low enough for me to jump up and grab onto the railing."

While Ew and his friends waited behind her house, Shreela dragged herself out of bed, seconds before the telecomm alarm sounded. Tossing and turning all night left her tired and restless.

"Soren, time to get up," she called softly, while heading towards the bathroom.

Breakfast was quiet as Shreela thought about the man she

collided with the night before. During the night, military sirens screaming up and down the streets awakened her. She wondered whether the strange man was the one being sought after. Her thoughts were interrupted by the anxious voice of her son.

"Mom, mom," Soren called. "Are you okay? You look tired. Am I goin' to school? I don't have to. I can stay here an' take care of you. Mom. Mom."

Shreela laughed softly. "So many questions during breakfast." She reached over and stroked his head. "I'm fine, little one, and yes, you will go to school today. You'll be enrolled in school this morning. It's chilly outside, so wear your jacket."

Shreela watched as Soren got up from his chair and headed toward the living room. "Okay, I'll get it now," he said.

"Comb your hair first."

From behind a tree, Ew saw the young widow and her small child, as they boarded the transport.

"She is Timanian, judging from her attire," he whispered to the others. "They have pink eyes and blue teeth, isn't that right, Milan?" he asked, still watching as the transport took off down the street.

"That's true," Milan responded. "Of course, it was pretty dark outside when I ran into her. It didn't matter what she looked like then," he explained, "I just wanted to unload that medallion. Now that Uzak knows I stole it, I won't be doing any trading for a while," he said.

Ew looked up towards the window of Shreela's bedroom. "Good, that window is still open."

"What about the house android?" Pala asked.

"I've already worked that out," said Ew. "The two of you should go around front and ring the door summons. Distract the droid while I go through that window. I'll sneak downstairs and switch the droid off from behind."

Once inside the house, Milan began to search for the medallion. "I'm sure this is the correct address!" he cried.

"Stop looking for it," Ew shouted from across the hall. "I have a pretty good idea where it is."

"Where?" Milan asked.

Ew looked at him and shook his head. "Did it ever occur to you, my friend, that she is probably wearing the same jacket she wore last night when you met her?"

Milan scratched his head thoughtfully for a moment. "Well, there's not too much we can do until she returns home," he said, sighing.

As Ew, Milan, and Pala waited around for the widow to return, Uzak paced his quarters aboard his flagship, which hovered over Thesbis. He waited anxiously for news on the search of Milan Mariko.

"Mariko is here with that medallion," he muttered, to himself. "Of that, I am certain. Galan is sure to have received Mariko's message, and if he's not here now, he will be." Uzak walked over to the videocomm and hailed the bridge commander. "Commander, what is the status of the search?"

"General Narvan hasn't reported in yet, Sire."

"When he does, I want to speak to him directly. And Commander, contact Jaynt Saren to cancel my..." Uzak suddenly stopped.

"My Lord?"

"Never mind, I'll handle it myself." Uzak abruptly ended the communication. He stared at the dark screen. "The widow from Tima," he whispered aloud, piecing together the puzzle. Uzak clenched his fist. "This may be the turning point," he cried. "I must find that widow." Alarmed that the long awaited prophecy was falling into place, Uzak immediately contacted Saren.

"Saren, the young widow you spoke of last evening, has she arrived at the complex?"

"Yes, My Lord. I spoke to her briefly just a short time ago. She was heading towards the day school where her son will attend. She must be in her class by now, though."

"Bring her to me at once."

"What should we do with her son, Sire?"

"The boy does not interest me," Uzak snapped. "Just bring me the widow!"

Uzak concluded his conversation with Saren and without delay, contacted his commander stationed on Thesbis. By then, Shreela was on her way to her first class. Enrolling Soren in school took longer than Shreela thought. She nearly tripped up the stairs in her haste to get to her classroom. Flustered and embarrassed about her tardiness, she took a seat in the back of the room, and prepared to take notes.

Shreela's first class was a full day of orientation. The orientation discussion centered around three programs. The first two, Widow Therapeutic Counseling, and Counseling with Relocation and Job Placement, were of no interest to Shreela. The third program, Counseling with Retraining, Relocation, and Job Placement, was her primary interest, but it was the last agenda item for discussion.

Shreela sat for more than an hour, listening to the detailed deliberation on the Therapy and Counseling Program. Just before the mid-morning break, a tall, humanoid male entered the room and spoke quietly to the instructor. After a few words, the instructor turned his attention back to the class.

"Mrs. Bakra," he called out, "will you please come to the

desk?" Shreela looked surprised as she walked up to the front of the class. "This escort has been sent by the Office of Widow Registration," said the instructor.

"Is there a problem?" Shreela addressed the escort.

"There's a small matter about your registration log that Mr. Saren would like to see you about."

"Does it have to be right now, or can I arrange to meet him during our break?"

"I'm afraid not. Mr. Saren will be leaving Thesbis shortly and won't be returning for a few days. Since he personally interviewed you, he wants to handle it before he leaves."

The morning already seemed to be dragging and Shreela felt relieved at having this unplanned interruption. Nodding her head, she followed the escort out of the room. Heading down the corridor, she suddenly halted in front of a restroom. "Excuse me, but I need to make one quick stop. Go on ahead and tell Mr. Saren I'll be in his office shortly."

By the time Shreela reached the reception area outside Mr. Saren's door, no one was there to show her in. She was about to knock when she heard Mr. Saren's voice from within. He sounded very angry. Shreela listened to the conversation taking place only to discover that the discussion was about her.

"I told you to bring the widow Bakra here!" Saren shouted angrily. "The Lord of Uni expects her, and if we don't deliver, we'll both be killed. Now go back to where you left her, and escort her here!"

Shreela ducked out of sight behind the reception desk. Peeping over the reception counter, she recognized the man leaving as her escort. She felt a knot tighten in her stomach. Even on the far away planet of Tima, the name of the Lord of Uni was spoken with trepidation.

Shreela carefully tiptoed outside the reception area into the corridor. Though the hallway was not crowded, it comforted her to see residents moving along the corridor. She headed towards the closest exit, seven or eight trans away. Once inside, she raced down the staircase to the first floor where the children's day school was located.

Taking a brief moment to compose herself, Shreela peered through the window of Soren's classroom. She took a deep breath, forced a smile on her face, and entered the room. The teacher, a short-thin human male, approached her.

"Is there a problem, Mrs. Bakra?" he asked.

Shreela struggled to hide the fear and panic growing inside her. "Just with my memory," she responded. "I'm sorry, Mr. Bonner, but I forgot to tell you that Soren and I have a late morning appointment," she explained. "Since it will last until late afternoon, Soren won't be returning today. We'll be here bright and early tomorrow, though."

"No need to apologize, Mrs. Bakra." Mr. Bonner turned towards Soren. "Soren, you'll be leaving with your mother now, so get your jacket. I'll see you tomorrow."

As Shreela and Soren boarded the public transport to go home, Ew walked into Shreela's kitchen and sat down next to Pala. He was reading a log entry.

"What's that you're viewing?" asked Pala.

"It's a log entry of the widow's application and a brief synopsis of her background. I'm embarrassed about snooping through her private logs, but I need more information on her."

"Who is she?"

"Her name is Shreela Bakra, from planet Tima. Seems she just arrived last night. She's traveling with her six-year old son."

"Didn't you tell me that Saren spoke about an incoming Timanian widow at the Council Meeting yesterday?"

"Uh-hum, but Saren lied. Here, look at this entry," said Ew, placing the log on the table in front of Pala. "Saren said the incoming Timanian widow made a relocation request for the Petron Solar System."

"Any staff member could have made that change," Pala commented. "Maybe Saren didn't know about this change."

"This pre-arrival interview states the contrary," said Ew. The changes appear along with Saren's signature. He knew about it alright." Ew thought about the mysterious disappearance of Ambassador Behrend. "Saren's the link," he, said at length. "Behrend suspected him for sometime, but didn't have enough proof to accuse him."

"This document ties him in with the kidnappings, then?"

"That and what Behrend learned during his investigation. Saren's behavior at yesterday's Council meeting was also suspicious."

"What did Behrend find out?"

"Behrend learned that Saren personally signed for the travel pass and release document for every widow, including the missing widows, regardless of whether or not they completed the program."

"All of them?"

"Every widow. At yesterday's meeting, Saren claimed that his staff was authorized to sign when he was unavailable. When Behrend interviewed Saren's staff, he learned that Saren didn't allow anyone other than himself to sign any travel pass or release document," Ew explained.

"What about Mrs. Bakra?"

"She's marked, Pala. She can't stay here. We'll have to get her off of Thesbis."

The conversation was cut short when Milan rushed in, his face flushed. "Two military transports just pulled up."

"Quick, upstairs," shouted Ew.

Ew stood at the door inside Shreela's bedroom, just beyond the top of the stairwell. By opening the door to a narrow slit, he could see and hear the goings on in the sitting room below. A well controlled, commanding voice rang out over all others as military personnel hustled inside.

"Our job is to wait here for the widow," the group commander explained. "Seems there was a foul up over at Administration. Lord Uzak has ordered us to straighten out this mess. As soon as this widow comes in, arrest her."

"What about the transports?" asked a member of the group. "She's sure to know somethin's up when she sees 'em parked out front."

"Yes, yes, I know," the Commander responded impatiently. "Since you asked, you can move them up and around the block. Go now."

"Yes sir."

"Burdie, stand watch at the back door."

By the time Shreela arrived at her home, the military transports had been moved out of sight. Quickly, she scanned the area around her home before she and Soren disembarked the public transport. The street was quiet and empty. Taking Soren's hand, they walked up to the front door.

"Mom, why are we coming home?"

"I need to pick up our travel permits. We can't board a spacecraft unless we have them."

"Where are we goin'?"

Shreela paused for a moment before inserting the coded card key into the slot. *That's a good question*, she thought. *I can't go home and I can't stay here.* "It'll just be a short trip."

As Shreela opened the door, she was brutally yanked inside

by one of the armed guards. Without putting up a struggle, she and Soren walked into the sitting room where the group leader was stationed. He was tall, slender, and arrogant, and Shreela felt intimidated by the way he paced the floor and slapped his baton in the palm of his hand.

"Good morning, Mrs. Bakra."

"Is there some problem here?" asked Shreela.

"You are under arrest as a foreign spy."

Shreela looked bewildered. "Wh-what? You must have me confused with someone else. I'm not a spy."

"A likely story," the Commander said coolly.

"But I'm a widow from the planet Tima in the Gena Solar System, and I'm enrolled in the rehabilitation program. Why don't you check my credentials?"

"Silence," said the Commander raising his hand. He then raised a communications device to his mouth. "Lord Uzak, we have her."

From his hiding place, Ew could see the face of the widow Bakra as she was brought before the group leader. She did not fit the formal description of a native Timanian. Her skin was soft and suntanned, not unlike his own coloring. Her face was smooth and unblemished. She had brown eyes rather than pink, and her teeth were pearl white instead of blue. Her voice, even under these conditions, was so soft he could not imagine her speaking above a whisper. Ew eased the door closed and turned to his friends.

"They're going to shuttle her to Uzak's Flagship. We've got to find a way to get her before they reach the shuttle dock. You can be sure Uzak will search her, and we cannot allow that to happen," he whispered.

"How do we get to the flagship? We have no transport, and if we do get there, how do we get inside?" asked Milan.

"I'm thinking about it," said Ew.

While the three conspirators planned their next move, Shreela and Soren boarded the military transport headed for the Thesbian spaceport. Shreela sat with Soren in her lap. There were two stops along the way, stretching the time of their journey to almost two hours. To Shreela, though, it seemed an eternity. Finally, they were ushered out of the transport. Shreela held Soren's hand, as they stood silent while orders were given to an armed guard. The guard was Ew. Abruptly, he pushed Shreela forward towards the space shuttle several hundred trans ahead. Once out of earshot, Ew spoke to her.

"When I shout GO, I want you to run as fast as you can toward that door to your right. Do you understand?" he asked, in a hushed voice.

Shreela glanced over at him. "Who are you, and why should I go with you?"

"Sh-h-h. Keep your voice down."

"Unless you tell me what you plan on doing, I'm not going anywhere except to that shuttle."

"Alright, alright," he said impatiently. "Let me put it this way, Mrs. Bakra, if you get on that shuttle, you're headed for certain death."

"And if I run, I'll die too," Shreela shot back.

"They won't kill you. You're precious cargo, but you'll die later on."

"Then who's to say you won't kill me later on?"

"Look, we can't debate this now," Ew said, annoyed. "We're almost there, so just take a chance."

"I'll think about it," Shreela responded sardonically.

As they neared the shuttle, Shreela suddenly stopped at the sound of laser discharge. Pala Bhusan, dressed in military attire, rushed out through the shuttle door. Other military personnel followed him. Before Shreela could focus on what was happening, Ew shouted and pushed her back towards the building. "GO! RUN!" he shouted.

Quickly, Shreela picked Soren up and raced for the door, three hundred trans away. Shreela was not being fired upon, but metal and concrete burned from laser blasts, which bounced off the building where she was headed. Her eyes watered from the smoke that filled the air. At last the complex door was five to six trans away. *Just a few more steps*, she thought. Shreela opened the door. Ew rushed up from behind, snatched Soren from her arms, then grabbed her hand, and together they raced down a long corridor. With a quick glance over her shoulder, Shreela saw the same military man she saw earlier at the shuttle was following them. He, too, was being pursued by a band of armed soldiers, close behind and closing. Her heart sank as she looked down the long corridor yet to be traversed. *The door is too far*, she thought. *We'll never make it.* Just as she began to feel as if they would never escape, her escort pulled her through a side exit, and abruptly pushed her into an open transport door. Both Ew and Pala jumped in next to her. The transport leaped forward. Shreela felt the craft shuddering from several laser blasts, which bounced off the sides. The laser fire dissipated quickly as the high-speed transport raced out of the Thesbian Spaceport.

Taking a moment to catch her breath, Shreela turned to the man who helped her. "Thank you. I seem to be in your debt Mister…,"

"E.G., and you are quite welcome, Mrs. Bakra," Ew nodded his head.

"I am called Shreela, and this is my son Soren. I'd like to know what is going on here, and what does Uzak want with me?" she added.

"You were in great peril Mrs. Bakra. Without knowing it, you hold in your possession a dangerous weapon. Uzak was not aware of it, but he would have discovered as much had he been successful in getting you aboard his flagship," Ew explained. "However, we'll not speak of that here."

Shreela was disturbed at his words and greatly confused about this `dangerous weapon'. "I would like to hear of it now, if you don't mind," she insisted. She paused for a response, but none was given. "Look, Mr. E., I've.."

"E.G."

"Mr. E.G., I've been pushed, shoved, and snatched from my home against my will. Some sort of explanation is not an unreasonable request."

Ew removed the Unian military guard helmet, and dropped it on the floor. "All right, Mrs. Bakra, I can tell you this much," he said. "We have reason to believe that Uzak of Uni is abducting certain widows who come to Thesbis from outside this galaxy."

"Certain widows?"

"Look, Mrs. Bakra, it's a long and complex story. Trust me one more time. I promise to give you a full accounting once we reach a safe haven."

Shreela was silent for a moment. She wanted to press the point further, but she felt weary and out of control. "Where are you taking me?" she asked.

"We're going to a defense stronghold in the mountains."

Shreela sighed for her lack of options. "Alright, I'll trust you once more."

"Thank you," said Ew. "Now, let me introduce you to my comrades. On my right is my good friend Pala Bhusan. You've already met our driver, but let me introduce you formally. Shreela Bakra, this is Milan Mariko."

Shreela's mouth fell open in surprise as she turned to look at the driver. "You're the man that nearly knocked me down last evening!" she exclaimed.

"At your service," he nodded.

"He is also our expert in the life forms on Tima. Milan told me long ago that the women of Tima have blue teeth and pink eyes," Ew commented teasingly.

"Actually, he is right. The aborigines look exactly as you have described. I was born on Tima, but my family settled there from another planet. Native Timanians are very friendly to both visitors and settlers. My two best friends are natives to that planet, and believe me, I would do almost anything to be with them now."

From the side window, Shreela watched how the landscape changed as the transport headed westward. She quickly glanced back to check on a possible pursuit. The highway was filled with transports in rapid movement up and down the thorofare. Traffic thinned as they approached the rural areas of Raileen. The transport only slightly swayed from side to side as Milan piloted through the rolling hillsides, thick with vegetation, trees, and small lakes. Wild flowers of every color garnished the hillsides in a breathtaking view. Small villages cropped up occasionally, surrounded by large estates with well-manicured grounds fenced in to keep intruders away.

Shreela turned her head to view the terrain from the front of the cab. They were quickly approaching a large mountain range. Suddenly, the transport swooped downward into a deep valley full of enormous trees and surrounded by mountains. The vegetation was so thick and mangled that no trail could be seen. Slowly, the transport sloped upward and then eventually leveled off.

Nearly thirty minutes passed before they stopped in front of a huge boulder, with large trees and shrubs growing wild on either side. Shreela saw no walking path in any direction but noticed a small bare patch caused by a transport hovering over that area. While Milan cruised to that spot, Shreela observed Pala pressing several buttons on a remote control device he kept on him. Suddenly, a large part of the mountain opened, swallowing up the transport as it quietly moved inside. The loud clang as the huge door closed was comforting, announcing they were shut in and away from the madness taking place outside. For the first time since Jor's death, Shreela felt safe.

As Ew and his companions disembarked, Uzak stood in front of the viewing monitor aboard his flagship. He contemplated his current situation, deciding among several military options available to him.

"So now they think they have out-smarted me!" he muttered. Uzak turned toward Admiral Pernell who stood nearby. "Admiral, I want Milan Mariko's spacecraft destroyed at once," he commanded. "Then, inform all military chiefs and commanders to meet me within ten minutes, in my chamber conference room."

Uzak paced the conference room waiting for his senior staff to arrive. He thought about the young widow who slipped through his hands. "She must be the one," he thought.

"Lord Uzak," the voice of Admiral Pernell called over the intercom.

Uzak walked over to the monitor. "Yes," he responded.

"My Lord, we have identified two of the widow's abductors. One was Pala Bhusan and the other Milan Mariko."

"And the third?"

"We've not been able to identify him yet, Sire."

"I believe I know who the third one is. What was their heading?"

"The Halokin Mountain Range."

"That will be all for now, Admiral."

Uzak stared at the galactic display monitor nearby. A sense of fear welled up inside him, as he glared at planet Galan. "I cannot allow Ewlon Galan to reach his home," he whispered to himself. "I know he's the third person, and he now holds The Planet Star." Uzak continued to stare at the monitor, but his momentary spate of fear dissipated, replaced by his long-held hatred of Ewlon Galan. Unconsciously, he balled his fist and clenched his jaw. "Khali belongs to me!"

Uzak seated himself at the head of the conference table as members of his senior staff entered. The caucus entered quietly and sat stiffly with their eyes turned towards their Lord.

"I am ordering an open declaration of war against the Khalian Solar System," Uzak began the meeting. "This order is effective immediately. We will carry out the offensive strategy which was finalized at our last meeting, with a few exceptions." Suddenly, Uzak's attention was drawn to Admiral Pernell who had, for a split second, conspicuously flinched at the news. "Is there a problem Admiral?" Uzak asked.

"No, My Lord."

"Speak up Admiral," Uzak commanded.

"Well, My Lord, I was wondering about the new technology on Dagmar. Since this declaration of war is six to nine weeks ahead of schedule, might I assume that technology is now in place."

"The new technology, Admiral, is not in place," Uzak replied. "Other circumstances dictate an early military offensive." Uzak again noticed that Admiral Pernell began to speak, but checked himself. "Is there something else, Admiral?"

"Yes, Sire," Pernell, answered reluctantly.

"Well, what is it?" he asked impatiently.

"My Lord, it is rumored that this technology is a new type of laser physics. Will senior military..."

"Admiral," Uzak interrupted, "we are not here to discuss the new technology," Uzak said, glaring at him, his tone collected and unwavering; firm. "You will be informed and instructed, at the proper time. Now, is there a pending question on the military strategy before us?"

"None, Sire."

Uzak turned his attention to the assembly. "Since the new laser is not available, we will implement our original plan to remove the Khalian galactic forces from the galaxy under Project Move and Refuel." Uzak looked over at his security chief. "Sezyan, where do we stand with the new information received from Intelligence on the security codes."

Sezyan, a native of Zirvag, looked at Uzak, his scarlet eyes staring across the table. "Our man on the inside says that Galan ordered new encrypted codes yesterday. He is now uploading this new schematic to our descrambler, My Lord. It will take one hour to overlay the Inter-Galactic Fleet (IGF) schematic, and another eight hours to remap the planetary shield codes."

"That's too long."

"I can change the command code string to function under our orders until the Fleet reaches the end of our disrupter field near the sentry scanner outpost off of Nilar. After that, the string will no longer be under the disruption frequency, and the current IGF code will go back on-line. By that time, the new mapping will be in place for the shield, and the Fleet will be far beyond this solar system."

Uzak thought about the plan for a moment. "I like the idea Sezyan. You have the go ahead to proceed."

"Thank you, My Lord."

"Admiral Pernell, once Chief Sezyan has completed the command string, I want you to deploy the Khalian IGF docked at the space stations, as well as those in the southwestern and northwestern quadrants, to Chimoor. With two-thirds of the IGF out of the way, our task will be easier. Both the Shargant and Lluellyn Space Stations should be under our control before twenty-two hundred hours. That gives us four hours to decoy the IGF and lower the planetary shield. Once the shield is down, begin the first round of assaults. To keep the Inter-Solar System Force (I-SS Force) inside, we will reinstate the shield with us inside. If, by chance, the IGF should return unexpectedly, they will not be able to penetrate the shield to assist I-SS Forces. The operation will begin as soon as this meeting is adjourned."

Uzak turned to speak directly to Admiral Pernell. "Admiral, you will board the battle cruiser *Crogin*, and move the fleet into the Khalian Solar System. As soon as the Khalian IGF has moved out of the area, and the shield is down, you will launch the attack. I shall join in the battle when my business here is complete." Uzak ruffled his brows at Pernell. "Are there any questions?" he asked. The room remained silent. "Then, we are adjourned."

4
A SECRET TOLD

Milan docked the transport in an area fifty trans long and fifty trans wide. Ew stepped out and looked around. It was a mammoth cave with stalagmite and stalactite formations along the perimeter. There was an open-caged elevator attached to a cable stretching to the ceiling of the cave. Ew walked over to where Shreela stood, noticing the curious look on her face as she examined the elevator and the ceiling above it.

"What are those marks on the ceiling?" she asked him.

"It's a door. Actually, the door is a moveable dome, designed for emergency exits. The outside part of the dome has been carefully camouflaged with small trees, bushes, and other foliage which grows around here."

"What and where is here?" she asked.

"Here is my home when I am away from home," Ew answered.

"And where is your home, E.G.?" she asked, her attention now drawn toward his mischievous grin. "If you have a place like this, you must have lots of secrets. Would it be unfair to ask if you are a spy?"

Ew's grin quickly evaporated, replaced by a frown across his brow. He was annoyed by her implication of underhandedness. "In answer to your first question, Mrs. Bakra, my home is on the planet Galan, and my profession is the selling of rare artifacts, the same line of work as Milan," he snapped back.

"I didn't realize that I was a rare artifact," Shreela muttered. "Don't misinterpret my next question as ingratitude," she continued, "but why did you kidnap me, and what danger am I in?"

Ew felt a pang of remorse for snapping at her. *After all, this is a strange situation to be in, and she does have the right to find out what she can,* he thought. Ew looked at Soren for a moment, reflecting on his own mother who was widowed when he was a small boy. He knew how it felt to have someone you love and depend upon suddenly snatched away. Fortunately for her, his mother had had at her disposal a complete staff to care for him and his sister. *This woman is not only far from home but appears to be totally alone.* His eyes softened, and with half a smile, he said, "Come with me. I'll tell you what I can."

Ew led them through a long and spacious, obviously man-made, corridor with doorways on either side. The lighting fixtures were simple, unadorned globes on ceiling and walls. The corridor was nearly empty; the only exception, a handful of what appeared to be maintenance personnel walking along the corridor. The sound of their footsteps echoed so that they sounded like a herd of cattle. Halfway down the hall, Ew turned to the right to open one of the doors. Flicking on the lights, he turned to face the others as they entered.

The large room was well lit, despite being underground. The blue-gray stucco back wall had been bleached in spots, creating an almost hypnotic pattern. Shelves containing color-coded documents and computer discs lined the entrance wall. The thick rust-colored carpet set off a huge, oval table with a dozen chairs. Despite the enclosed closet-like environment, the air was not at all stuffy. As she followed Ew to the conference table, Shreela turned toward the sound of falling water. She was delighted by a small, beautifully landscaped waterfall flowing through a rock bed located on the far right of the room.

After everyone seated themselves around the table, Ew spoke of all that transpired during the last solar day.

"Mrs. Bakra," he began, "Milan, Pala, and I have been trying to secure a particular artifact which has long been held by Uzak of Uni. The artifact itself has nothing to do with you directly but rather the timing of your arrival on Thesbis. It's that element of chance, which now engulfs you in what I believe to be the beginning of an intergalactic war between the two solar systems, Khali and Uni."

"War?" she asked, wide-eyed. "What is this thing, and why is it so valuable?"

"The artifact is a powerful medallion forged in Khali many decades ago," Milan interjected. "Uzak coveted it for many years and committed murder to get it. Last evening, I stole this medallion from Uzak. I planned to return it to its rightful owner, King of the Khalian Solar System, but Uzak discovered I had brought it to Thesbis. I knew that, for the simple reason that it is so powerful, Uzak should never regain possession of it… so I hid it in case I was caught."

"I'm afraid that Milan left it with you," said Ew. "If I may…" Reaching into Shreela's coat pocket, he produced the medallion. Knowing its potential power was his, and his alone, Ew's hand shook slightly as he held it up. Though he had seen pictures, its true brilliance could obviously not be captured in a photograph. Encrusted with magnificent gems, it sparkled brightly under the light. The polished, floral-pattern setting was made of the yellow metal, *pendar*.

"It's so beautiful," Shreela whispered softly. "Why did Uzak steal it in the first place? Did he use its powers for his own benefit? What are its powers?" Realizing she sounded a bit like Soren on a question spree, she clamped her mouth firmly closed on the rest of her questions and gazed at Ew expectantly.

"It's a long story, but I'll be as brief as possible." Ew turned to Pala, who stood nearby. "Have the communications officer contact Calo and send the call to me in this room," he said.

"By now, Uzak has probably guessed that you had something to do with the escape of the widow, and it is likely that the UMF is jamming all frequencies for communications outside Thesbis," Pala explained. "It may take a while to get through."

"Agreed, and with that being the case, I'll use this time to answer some of Mrs. Bakra's questions."

As Pala left the room, Ew turned his attention back to Shreela. "Mrs. Bakra," he began, "before I can answer your question, let me give you some historical background about Khali."

"First of all, the Khalian system is one of a very few systems in which every planet in the system is not only habitable, but each had its own indigenous population, all at a similar level of development. Many generations ago, when the populations of the planets of the Khalian System were in their developmental infancy, so to speak, fifteen powerful keepers came to live among us."

"Keepers?"

"Powerful beings, guardians from another dimension."

"Where did they come from?"

"Khalians never knew where they came from, but our religion teaches they were sent here by the supreme being of the universe, the Keeper of Keepers, if you will."

"Sounds like you don't believe it."

"Oh, but I do," said Ew, raising one eyebrow. "Anyway, when they arrived, each Keeper chose a rare gemstone native to the planet he guarded. They each bestowed their selected gemstones with the essence of their exalted power."

"What sort of power?"

"Powers of life, knowledge, truth, strength, wisdom, love, hope, and several others. These collective powers were used to bring unity to the Khalian Solar System. The gemstone of the Keeper of Unity was the sum and substance of all the powers."

"But there are many solar systems. Why this particular one?" Shreela asked curiously.

"Before I get into that, would anyone care for something to drink?"

"Not for me," said Milan.

"Me neither," said Shreela, "but something for Soren will be appreciated."

Ew walked over to the communications station, and hailed Pala. "When you are finished there, bring some drinks in, will you?"

"I'll be done here shortly," Pala replied.

Ew sat down again and leaned back into his chair, slightly tipping the front legs off the floor and balancing precariously on the back legs. "In answer to your question," he began, "the inhabitants of the various planets in the Khalian System were at similar cultural stages when the Keepers first arrived. The societies were tribal and each planet housed only a small number of tribes. The Keeper of the Universe set forth a covenant with his Keepers to strengthen and unify the inhabitants of this solar system."

"Why?"

"Well, for one thing, the potential for evolving into a warlike solar system was overwhelming, had we been allowed to mature on our own. The disparate tribes on each planet were typically carrying on running battles. Once we had developed to a point where we could travel to the other planets in the system, that warrior attitude would have traveled with us. For that reason, the Keepers were sent as guardians and teachers. They helped the inhabitants to live and work as one unit, and finally, to stand on their own."

"You were able to communicate with them then."

"Definitely. In the beginning, the Keepers moved from planet to planet communicating with the inhabitants. Our prosperity has resulted from both intellectual and technical growth, and there was no sickness or death as long as the Keepers were in power. The populations grew to a tremendous size."

Shreela gave Ew a puzzled look. "So, how does Uzak fit into the picture?"

"I'm coming to that," Ew said, smiling. "Most of the Keepers were satisfied with the progress of Khali throughout the many generations under their guidance. During the latter part of their rule, the Keepers established one household to be Stewards. The House of Galan was chosen, and the fifteenth planet was so named in honor of that position. In our native tongue on Galan, the solar system came to be known as the Khalian Solar System, 'Khali' meaning, 'unified body' in the common tongue.

"Now we come to Uzak. Tell me, Mrs. Bakra, what do you know about him?"

"I only know he is an evil Lord who has terrorized this part of the galaxy for decades."

"Yes, but there is something else you should know. We are up against an intractable enemy. Uzak ***is*** the Keeper of Unity."

Shreela frowned for a moment as she tried to understand what he was saying. "Oh, I see," she said at last, with comprehension.

"That makes a difference, doesn't it?"

"Yes, but if Uzak is the most powerful Keeper, how could Milan steal The Planet Star from him, and why was that necessary?"

"Good question. First let me give you a little more history.

Three generations back, Yavik Galan was Steward of Khali. Yavik had two sons, Yashil and Wedolan. Yashil was the elder son with greater rights to the throne, but because Yashil was unfit to hold that position, Uzak argued with his brothers that the covenant should remain intact for another generation. The other Keepers rejected that argument since they knew, as well as Uzak, the throne would pass to the younger son, Wedolan. They warned Uzak not to interfere with their collective decision to leave."

"And did he?"

"Oh yes. He somehow managed to redirect his own powers into another gemstone, and then destroyed Nila, the gemstone of Unity. By doing this, he was able to destroy the collective powers of the other Keepers and break the covenant. Uzak is called 'the fallen' Keeper, and although his power was diminished considerably by that act, he is still quite powerful."

"What happened after the covenant was broken?"

"Since the original gemstone of Unity no longer existed, the individual gemstones of power could not be held together, or 'unified'. There were mass graves, sickness, and fear. Khalians began to lose hope, but Yavik was a strong leader. He convinced the populace that a balance of good and bad was necessary for their survival."

"What exactly did he say to convince them of that?"

Ew leaned forward, placing the palms of his hands upon his knees, hunching his shoulders, as he thought about Shreela's question. He tried to recall Yavik's most convincing argument. Then, "Alright, let's look at the power of life," he said, leaning back into his chair. "Before the fall of Uzak, the population size was tremendous. Think of it. Eventually, the food supply would become depleted, so death was a necessary evil for survival."

"Then Uzak may have done the right thing after all."

"Not at all. You see, Shreela, death would have come anyway after the Keepers fulfilled their covenant and left the galaxy. Their commitment was made to a higher order."

"The Keeper of the Universe."

"Right, but when Uzak broke the covenant, each Keepers power became singular. They were trapped on the planet they once guarded, and unable to commune with each other or with the inhabitants except for one Keeper. With the apparent disappearance of the Keepers from the solar system, Uzak began to amass huge armies. Yavik was forced to do the same."

"That must have been a frightening time," said Shreela, shaking her head.

"Probably, but Yavik didn't live too long after the covenant was broken, and as predicted, the throne passed to Wedolan, not Yashil.

"The first year of Wedolan's reign as King of the Khalian Solar System was difficult both politically and emotionally. There were many in government who sided with Yashil, causing a split between the Interplanetary Governors. For that reason, Wedolan spent most of his first year visiting governors who were Yashil's strongest supporters. He spent hours and days trying to reunite the Governors to strengthen his administration. Near the end of his first year, Wedolan stopped on the planet Yalléon to visit with his friend, Governor Haslow.

It was there he met Solan."

"Who was Solan?"

"Who is Solan, not was."

"What?"

"Solan is the Keeper of Life. Wedolan Galan and Govenor Haslow assisted Solan in forging the new Planet Star, and reuniting the collective powers of the fifteen Keepers, including Uzak." Ew held up the medallion and put his finger on the center gemstone. "This is Nila, the gemstone of Unity," he explained. "It was artificially created by Solan. See how the other gems are joined with the center crystal through these tiny metallic-like capillaries. The gems you see here are the same kind as those originally selected by the Keepers. So you see, Shreela, the super power of the Khalian Solar System lies within this medallion," said Ew holding The Planet Star up to the light.

Ew looked up when Pala entered the room, carrying a large pitcher and drinking glasses. "The communications officer will send your call back here as soon as he can," Pala explained.

"Are the frequencies jammed as we expected?" asked Ew.

"No, but the open airwaves are at a high utilization rate. It may be slow getting through a secure frequency."

"I see." Ew focused his attention back on the medallion. He held it up towards the light and quietly studied the intricate design.

"This medallion, did it give more power to Uzak? Is that why he stole it?" asked Shreela, interrupting Ew's thoughts.

"No and yes," said Ew. "The medallion didn't give him greater power because he did not have the proper key to unlock its power. He thought the one key he had would work and that's why he stole it."

"Who has the key?"

"The rightful heir of Wedolan Galan now holds the key.

After The Planet Star was forged, it was placed upon a special pedestal, designed by Solan. The appropriate keys were given to Wedolan Galan to activate it. The Planet Star reunified the power of the Keepers, but they no longer walked and talked with the inhabitants of Khali. Instead, they draped a protective shield around the solar system, and Uzak was unable to penetrate that shield without detection."

"But that's true for anyone, isn't it?"

"Yes it is but…"

"What is so different about this shield over other planetary shields?" Shreela interrupted. "Doesn't Khali have defense shields like other planets?"

"This is not the same kind of shield. Planetary shields are meant to protect against weapons attacks. Laser and other types of energy weapons are produced by machines and can be detected by computers before they enter the orbit of a planet."

"Okay, so what would have happened to him?"

"Solan explained that because the essential being or substance of Uzak is the same as the Keepers, they would recognize another of the same substance. It's like the substance of animals is different from that of humanoids, plants, and the like. Solan also made it clear that if Uzak were to penetrate the shield, which is empowered by the Keepers, they would deliberately alter his being to that of humanoid nature. He would no longer retain any vestige of being a Keeper.

"So you see, Shreela, the shield of the Keepers was especially designed to keep Uzak, the most powerful Keeper, out of Khali. If he had the necessary keys to activate The Planet Star, he could dominate and control the collective powers of all the Keepers. This is supernatural power beyond our imagination….life, death, truth, harmony, freedom, love, and others. He would carry out all that his evil heart desires against any who oppose him."

"So how did he steal the medallion?" Shreela asked, a second time.

"He used Yashil to do his bidding. Because Yashil was his brother, Wedolan shared only one of the keys with him. Yashil frequently made trips in and out of Khali. As I understand it, ten years into Wedolan's reign, Yashil plotted with Uzak to steal The Planet Star. He thought he knew the secret code to activate or deactivate it was the same, and he gave that information to Uzak. After Yashil deactivated The Planet Star, he stole the medallion for his own personal gain, but didn't realize that Uzak planned to kill him and wield The Planet Star on his own. Deactivation of The Planet Star not only destroyed the shield around the Khalian Solar System, but also broke the unified power of the Keepers, separating them from each other, even Uzak."

"Did Yashil die?"

"He died, and so did Wedolan. Wedolan pursued Yashil to Uzak's headquarters on Uni. It was there Wedolan Galan met with an early death, leaving behind a son, daughter, and his queen. After Wedolan's body was returned to Galan in a burial tube, all necessary keys to activate The Planet Star were passed on to his son."

"If Uzak holds the power of Unity, how were the other Keepers able to unify their powers without him?" asked Shreela.

"That is a good question, Mrs. Bakra, but it would take more time than we have to explain it. "

"Okay, okay," Shreela said, impatiently, "but how do you know this thing will work?"

"We have only history to depend upon."

"What a fascinating story."

Ew quietly watched as Shreela poured a drink and placed it

before her son. He noticed a faint frown across her brow. "Is there something else you need to have cleared up?" he asked.

"I know why you kidnapped me," she said, looking directly into his eyes. "What I don't know is what does Uzak want from me?"

Ew stood up to stretch his legs. "This is a problem which gravely concerns me," he said, strolling over to the other end of the table to pour himself a drink. "Widows have been disappearing from Thesbis for many years. Most of the widows who vanished were from Tima, and there is strong evidence to suggest Uzak kidnapped them. Unfortunately, we've never been able to prove it."

Shreela thought about the strange feeling she had about being stalked. She also remembered Dian Mudhar's log to Machi that was never sent. "If what you say is true, then maybe I was right about someone following me before I left home."

Ew looked over at her with a raised brow. "How so?" he asked.

"Well, for one thing, on several occasions before I left Tima, I felt that someone was watching me. Another peculiar incident happened the day before I left. A strange man asked me all sorts of questions about where I was going and when."

"Hum-m-m. That is interesting," Ew responded. "Anything else out of the ordinary?"

"I'm not sure that this means anything, but there is something that's been bothering me. In my quarters on Thesbis, I found a log entry of one of my Timanian neighbors. The log was addressed to a mutual friend. In fact, this widow is partly responsible for me changing my decision to relocate to the Khalian Solar System instead of Petron."

"Did you ask her about the log?"

"That's just it. I never saw her, and when I asked the Director of Placement about her, he wasn't much help."

"Saren sees many widows. There's no way for him to remember all of them."

"But she wasn't on Thesbis for more than a week before her quarters were moved, or so I would guess."

"What was her name?"

"Dian Mudhar. She was scheduled for relocation to Khali in eight weeks. In fact, her relocation planet is Galan."

Ew felt a lump form in his throat. "I'll check on it when I return home," he said at length.

"I'm sorry," Shreela apologized. "I seem to have gotten off the subject. Anyway, what does Uzak want with widows?"

"It has to do with this medallion," he said, caressing The Planet Star.

Shreela frowned. "I'm still not clear on this," she said, shaking her head. "What does this medallion have to do with me?"

"Since I work so closely with the Thesbian Placement Council, I hear things that others are not privy to." Ew hesitated; uncertain as to how much Shreela should be told at this time.

"You did promise to tell me everything," Shreela reminded him.

Nodding in agreement, Ew walked back to his chair and sat down. "Several years ago," he began, "Her Royal Highness, Mara Galan, made the statement 'the power of The Planet Star lies within a distant moon planet'. That comment was made when The Thesbian Placement Council was probing the disappearance of Timanian widows, but Her Highness never elaborated on what she meant. Since then, I have reviewed the written documentation of what Her Majesty spoke of, in a treatise known as the Legend of Khali. I've already explained part of the Legend, when I spoke of the Keepers of Khali. There exists an addendum to that, written by Wedolan Galan after The Planet Star was activated. It's a prophetic revelation surrounding both the changing power of Khali and a widow from a distant moon, passed on to Wedolan by Rendal, Keeper of Foresight."

"What does it say?" Shreela prompted when he paused.

"The *prophecy* speaks of a young queen who would pass the scepter of Khali to her son before he was fully grown. In Khali, adulthood is twenty-five years. It also foretold the theft of a precious medallion and the untimely death of a king. The real thief, as we now know, is the Keeper of Unity, Uzak of Uni; the medallion is The Planet Star, and the death was that of Wedolan Galan. The prophecy does not detail but rather alludes to the destruction of Uni."

"And the widow?"

"The widow is part of that process. 'The widow will come from another star system, a moon planet. When the widow holds the treasure of the Khalian King, the end of the Unian Empire is at hand.' The Legend does go on, but this is the most crucial part, as I recall," he explained.

"Tima is the moon of Paramon in the Gena Solar System," Shreela mused aloud.

"The *prophecy* does give some clues about which moon planet. There is the description of a banner, and according to the star chart displayed on it, Tima and three other planets could fall into that category."

A creeping anxiety settled in the pit of Shreela's stomach, she shifted uneasily in her chair, uncertain about how she should respond. "I never heard of such a Legend," she said, at length, "and if I had, I would have never left home."

"It's a Legend known primarily to this galaxy so it is no

surprise that you hadn't heard of it before," Milan interjected.

"But I am not a Timanian aborigine," Shreela argued.

"The Legend never stated whether the widow was a native Timanian or if she was settled there from another planet," Milan further explained. "That's why so many different species are being kidnapped by Uzak."

A somber silence enveloped the room as each one of them became absorbed in their own thoughts. Milan thought deeply on the Legend of Khali. *The Legend stated a young widow would hold the treasure of the King. After all, I did give her the medallion. Is that what the Legend referred to? Is her part over now that Ew holds the medallion?* he asked himself.

Milan was not alone in his thoughts on the Legend of Khali. Pala, six years older than Ew, was a young boy when he heard of the Legend. Pala thought about his first meeting with Ewlon Galan. Ew had been a widower in a state of shock some eleven years before when they met. Unians who infiltrated the political system created riot conditions during a regional public forum. Ew's wife and son were among those who were stampeded to death in the panic and riot along with many others.

For several months after the death of his wife and child, Ew stayed intoxicated and refused to have guards protect his well-being. His family was greatly concerned over his lack of good judgment, or even concern, with respect to his command duties. There were whispers of government takeover as the people of the Khalian system became uncertain about Ew's fitness to rule. Ew would frequently disappear for days. It was during one of these episodes that Ew fell into a pit in the forest while stumbling home one rainy night. Hunters had prepared the pit for trapping the wild, doglike zelins. Fortunately, Pala was taking a shortcut through the forest that night to get to the spaceport where his spacecraft was docked. Enroute, Pala thought he heard a muffled cry. "Help me, help," a voice called out. Slowly and cautiously, Pala walked towards the sound. He saw a man in an animal trap, a pit, slightly more than two trans deep at the most. Pala stretched out his arm. "Grab my hand," he shouted. Pala pulled the man out, but immediately noticed the man was not stable. He dragged the man back from the edge and helped him sit on the ground. As they both sat there, Pala listened quietly as the man rambled on about his wife and child. It was then Pala learned this totally incongruous person was king of the Khalian Solar System.

Pala looked over at his old friend and remembered how desperate he was eleven years ago. He hoped Ew had learned how to separate his personal feelings from his role as king, something that he could not do before, nearly costing him his throne.

Ew's thoughts were also on the Legend. He looked at Shreela and wondered who are you? Is there really something to this Legend? Are you the one Uzak seeks? Can you really help me to remove the threat of Uzak of Uni, and by what path?

Shreela's thoughts were quite different than those of her companions. She certainly could not go back to her temporary home on Thesbis, and returning to Tima was definitely out of the question. *These men are in a hurry*, she thought. *They don't have time to be slowed down by a woman and child when the lives of millions may depend upon how quickly they move. Look at them. They're probably wondering "what are we going to do with these two,* she thought, misinterpreting the grim expression on Pala's face. "I can stay here for a while," she suggested aloud.

Ew turned to her. "No," he said. "It's too dangerous".

"What?" cried Shreela. "You can't take us with you. We'll only slow you down," she argued.

"I'm sorry, Mrs. Bakra," said Ew, "but there's no way you

can stay here."

"Wait a minute," said Shreela, "don't you think I have a say in where I should go or stay? Are you asking me to trust you again?"

Although her voice was calm and collected, Ew sensed a tinge of impatience in her tone. *She's right*, he thought. *She's in a mountain cave, alone, threatened, and trapped. Why should she trust any one of us*? "Look," he said, "I can understand how you must feel."

"Of course you don't understand how I feel."

"Okay, I don't know how you feel, but I can imagine and sympathize with how this must seem." Ew sighed. "I am asking you to trust me just one more time."

"Then explain why it's not possible for me to stay here. If this is a secret place, then I should be safe until you return, right?"

Ew glanced over at Pala. "Mrs. Bakra, this is an underground security base," Ew responded.

"What E.G. didn't tell you," Pala interrupted, "is that I am the Director of Intelligence, Security, and Operations for Khali. This is one of the secret defense bases under my jurisdiction."

"All three of you must work for the Khalian Intelligence, correct?" Ew nodded his head. "Then I was right the first time, E.G., you are a spy."

Ew just stared at her for a moment and then smiled. His earlier statement of being an antique dealer trapped him. Unwilling to reveal his true identity, he accepted her argument. "That would be my conclusion, were I in your shoes," he said.

"Then I should be safe here."

"Not necessarily," said Ew. "Uzak knows there is a secret base here in the mountains. Despite the fact that he doesn't know its exact location, he will be searching for it."

"Why would you need a security stronghold on a planet for widows?"

"This security base was constructed two years ago after suspicions surrounding the disappearance of widows began to surface. It's a long and involved story, Mrs. Bakra, so will you trust me again?"

Shreela closed her eyes and tried to absorb the lunacy of it all. "What are the chances of Uzak finding this place?" she asked.

"The possibility is great now that he is watching for signs of rescue, and he'll do whatever it takes to make it impossible for us to stay here."

"How can he do that if he doesn't know our location?"

"He can jam our communications channel so we can't transmit beyond this post, or he can torpedo blast the entire mountain range. There are many ways."

"Why didn't he just blast apart this mountain range before?"

"He wasn't in a desperate situation before. Seeking out the stronghold of an enemy and learning the secrets of his defense is considerably more satisfying and rewarding. Eventually Uzak might have been able to penetrate this secret operation and its communications code, but that takes time, a luxury he can no longer afford."

Shreela listened, and believed him. "This is all very intriguing -- as well as unsettling," she commented. "Since I apparently have few options, I agree to trust you once more, and please call me Shreela."

"Thank you, Shreela."

"So, E.G., what's our next step?"

"We'll try to get off of this planet." Ew stood up to leave. "Pala, I'm on my way to the Communications Room. Coming?"

"On my way."

"Milan, find something for our friends to eat," said Ew as he winked at Soren, "and then meet us in Communications."

"Right."

It was early evening when Ew first tried to contact his home on Galan. The communications room was small but efficient. High-tech equipment lined the back wall. Monitors displayed both galactic maps and planetary contour maps of Thesbis. An impressive array of micro discs lined a shelf beneath a giant video screen.

Ew took a moment to remove the false scar, nosepiece, and brown eye discs, before trying to make visual contact. After making several futile attempts to reach his home planet, he pounded the console in disgust.

"What's wrong?" asked Pala. "Is there still a lot of traffic on the interstellar channels?"

"No, but I can't get a line out to my security channel. The frequencies are jammed. Looks like I'll be forced to transmit on an open frequency."

"Laggé should be able to tell us what the problem is. Security may still be changing the I-SS Force codes."

"That's possible, but I'll bet this is Uzak's doing. Let's try to reach our outpost on Nilar. I'll try the secure channel first. Go and check it out on our backup system. Maybe you can get through."

Moments after Pala left the room, Ew was able to get through to Nilar, a planet in the Petron System located on the other side of Thesbis. The picture of an official came into view. It was Admiral Kryto. He appeared ruffled and weary looking.

"Your Majesty, we've been trying to track your whereabouts since early afternoon," said the Admiral. "They are scheduled to..."

Ew quickly raised his hand to halt the Admiral's explanation. "Wait a minute, hold on Admiral. First, let me ask if this channel is secure."

"According to our readings here on the bridge, we are still secure, Sire."

"Good. Now what were you about to say?"

"The IGF is already headed for Chimoor as per your instructions, Sire."

"Chimoor? What are you talking about?"

"Your Majesty, when the Khalian IGF passed through our shield barrier an hour ago, the Commander explained that the Fleet was headed to Chimoor as per your instructions. We have just reestablished contact with that flagship in light of new information coming in from our security forces."

"Admiral, I gave no such command. In fact, I'm trapped on Thesbis, which is why I'm contacting you. All channels to Galan are blocked making it impossible for me to arrange passage out of here."

"Then you are not aware of what is happening on your home planet?"

"No. I haven't been in contact with home since yesterday."

"Your Majesty, not more than an hour ago, Unian Military Forces invaded the Khalian Solar System," Kryto explained. "General Laggé has been trying to hail you on Thesbis, but all secure channels as well as open channels from Galan into Thesbis have been jammed."

For a brief moment, Ew turned away and stared blankly across the room. "Then I must get home as quickly as possible! Admiral, what is our current military status?" he asked, focusing his attention back to Kryto.

"Galan has dispatched several forces to Chimoor, no doubt a Unian ploy, which leaves Khali only partly protected. We believe forces there can hold their own, but not for an extended period."

"Are you still in contact with the Khalian Intergalactic Force?"

"Yes, Sire."

"Then, send those currently headed to Chimoor back to Galan immediately. I also want you to contact General Laggé on Galan, if you can. Tell him that I'm on my way home."

While Admiral Kryto relayed the order to his commander, Pala could see Ew was upset when he re-entered the Command Center.

"Ew, what's wrong?"

"Uzak has attacked the System."

"Your Majesty, your orders are being carried out this minute," said Kryto coming back to the telecom monitor. "Can we also assist you in some other way, Sire?"

"Yes!" Ew laughed sarcastically. "We're trapped here at the Mount Halokin Defense Center on Thesbis. Can you send a shuttle here before sundown?"

"We shall be there within the hour, Sire," Admiral Kryto assured him.

"It has started," said Ew, turning to face his old friend. "Prepare to evacuate as quickly as possible once the shuttle arrives."

"What will keep Uzak from blasting the shuttle before it lands?" asked Pala.

"It wouldn't suit his purpose. By letting the shuttle rescue us and blasting us apart when we leave, the widow, the King, and The Planet Star can no longer be a threat to him. Our warships will be there to guard our exit."

"What do we tell the widow?" asked Pala. "She's already shaky about being abducted, not once, but twice. She barely trusts us, and she's not gonna be thrilled when she notices your brown eyes are now gray."

"Uh-oh."

"Uh-oh is right," Pala grunted. "Now you have to tell her we're at war."

"I know." Ew's mood became suddenly pensive. He crossed his arms and leaned against the communication station desk. "You know, Pala, it seems as though we've been gearing up for a war with Uni for so long. Now that the war is a reality, I almost feel relieved."

"I understand the feeling."

Ew noticed the solemn expression on his old friends face. "Pala?"

"I was just thinking that Khali has never been in a major galactic war."

"Not in a physical sense, but the anxiety of waiting is a war in an emotional sense." Ew gently clapped his hand on Pala's shoulder. "I know how you feel. War is frightening. Come, we had better get ready to leave here."

From his flagship hovering over Thesbis, Uzak monitored the Galan Space Warship as it slowed to sub light speed on the other side of the planet. The warship bridge area was housed in the large open area of the elliptic-shaped bow, and the fanned tailed stern housed the shuttle bay.

A shuttle, launched from the warship, sped off to rescue the five companions stranded on Mount Halokin. Uzak watched the small spacecraft for a moment as he calculated its purpose. "Captain Bozak, send two battle cruisers to destroy the Galan warship. Then track that shuttle, pinpoint its landing site, and use mitron fusion torpedoes to destroy the entire area. I want armed pilots to move to that area in case that shuttle escapes the blast."

"My Lord," the Captain objected, "that will spread mitro rays throughout the planet. No living creature can survive in such an environment."

"So it will, Captain." Uzak continued to stare at the shuttle. "You have your orders."

"Yes, Sire."

Ew rushed to the shuttle as soon as it landed, while the others waited near the cave entrance. The multi-windowed shuttle craft had seats for up to fifteen passengers on each side. The cockpit was separated from the passenger cabin by a wall with a door. Passengers could enter through a door leading directly into the cabin or through the cockpit entrance, where Ew now stood.

As soon as Ew boarded the craft, the pilot stood at attention. "Pilot First Level Jenson reporting, Sire."

"Relax and have a seat," said Ew. "What do we have here?" he asked, training his eyes on one of the cockpit monitors.

"I'm picking up a Unian tracking signal. They've been tracking me since I left the Galan Space Warship, Solaitra."

Ew did not respond, but continued to run his eyes over the cockpit. "Wait a minute," he murmured. "Isn't this the new LT shuttle?"

"Yes, My Lord, and this is its first official run since you signed off on it last month."

"Great."

"Your Majesty, the Solaitra is under heavy attack from Unian forces. They wish to know if they should await our arrival or rendezvous with us on Nilar. What are your orders, Sire?"

"Radio the commander to return to Nilar. We'll take our chances on the speed of this shuttle." While Jenson relayed Ew's orders to the commander of the Solaitra, Ew chuckled aloud. "I would love to see the look on Uzak's face when this shuttle takes off at light speed plus ten."

Jenson turned to Ew. "The warship is leaving the area."

"Good. Let's make a run for it." Ew was just about to disembark when he suddenly stopped and turned back towards Jenson. "Incidentally, two of our passengers know me only as E.G.. You may call me E.G. or Ew, but do not refer to me as "Sire" or any title that might distinguish me from others when they are present."

"Yes, Siiiire... I mean E.G.," said Jenson.

While Jenson prepared the craft for liftoff, Ew stood by the cockpit entrance of the shuttle, impatiently waving to his companions to board. He was abruptly interrupted by a call from inside the cockpit.

"Sir, I'm picking up readings from a large Unian vessel, a battle cruiser. Their mitron defense systems have just come on-line."

"Hurry!" Ew shouted to the others. Quickly Ew hustled Shreela and Soren onto the spacecraft, followed by Milan and Pala. "Quick, get to your seats," he shouted, lowering the spacecraft door. "Jenson, let's move it."

As they headed out into space, the space shuttle was rocked by the blast from mitron torpedoes, which impacted the ground below. Above them, Ew noticed Unian Rapid Tactical Strike Fighters (RATSF). Four high speed, single pilot, disc-shaped spacecraft raced towards them. Ew blinked for a moment as high energy laser pulses bounced off the shuttle's shield. "How long before LT?" he asked.

"A second or two more," said Jenson. RATS Fighters continued to bombard the shuttle with laser blasts, causing the craft to rock from side to side. "We're ready," shouted the pilot pushing several buttons on the control panel.

As Ew looked outside the cockpit window, the galaxy stars

meshed into one continuous gray cloud. He breathed a sigh of relief, and stared into the grayness of space. Heaviness settled on his heart as he thought of the loss of those who remained behind in the cave. "This has been a costly escape," he commented at length. "How long will it take for the mitro particles to reach Raileen, Jensen?"

Jenson quickly reviewed a previous log entry. "Based on wind, temperature, and size of the blast, I would guess forty-eight hours."

"Does that take into account the change in atmospheric disturbance from the mitro wave patterns?"

"Yes, My Lord, -- I mean E.G."

Ew chewed on his lower lip for a moment. "What is our E.T.A. with the Solaitra?"

"We should rendezvous with them in… another fifteen minutes."

"Alright. Radio Admiral Atalif on our ETA, and have him meet with me in his office, not in the docking bay."

"Right away, My Lord."

"Thank you for your good work, Captain. Right now, I think I'll head back to the passenger section."

Ew entered the area where his companions sat quietly chatting to each other. "Well, we made it. Now let's hope we get there," he winked at Shreela. "We should be docking with the main spacecraft shortly."

"What will happen to my son and me?"

"You'll be sent to a safe place."

Ew quietly watched Shreela as she turned her attention back to her son. *How beautiful she is,* he thought. *To be under such a tremendous strain and yet maintain her composure is amazing.* Ew sat across from her. "Are you okay?"

"This situation is worse than you've explained, isn't it?" she asked.

"It will soon be over." He tried to make his smile reassuring, while being quietly thankful that she didn't comment on the change in his appearance.

Uzak, who had been monitoring the shuttle, was puzzled by the departure of the Galan Space Warship, shortly after the shuttle landed on Thesbis. "Very peculiar, very peculiar indeed," he mumbled. "They cannot possibly think that they're not being watched. No, there's something else going on, but what?" he asked himself. "Perhaps the shuttle was not sent on a rescue mission after all. What is Ewlon Galan up to?"

"Ground control calling flagship," called a voice over the telecom monitor. "Sire, the high-speed attack fighters are enroute to Mount Halokin. As soon as the torpedoes were launched, our scanners picked up the shuttlecraft, leaving the planet."

"Yes," Uzak responded, watching his monitor. "I see that our thieves are indeed leaving us. He sneered, watching his fighters as they approached the shuttle. *In just minutes, I'll be rid of this Galanian King and his "legendary" widow companion. At last, I will rule both Uni and Khali*, he gloated, silently congratulating himself. Suddenly, the space shuttle disappeared from the monitor. "What!" shrieked Uzak.

Captain Bozak stepped up next to Uzak and began speaking anxiously. "My Lord, I don't understand how this could be unless that was the new LT shuttle mentioned in earlier intelligence logs, but its completion is months away, according to our reports."

"Your reports are wrong, Captain." Uzak grated out the words through clenched teeth.

Bozak watched nervously as Uzak continued to scowl at the

place where the shuttle disappeared. He swallowed hard when Uzak turned his cold, menacing eyes to face him.

"I'll be in my quarters, Captain. I want the names of those officers responsible for monitoring the progress of this shuttle," Uzak said, in a deadly calm voice. The Captain couldn't control the shudder as he watched him walk off the bridge.

5
GALAN

Ewlon Races Home

Relief swept over Ew when he saw the warship *Solaitra* come into focus. He smiled when he noticed the expression on Soren's face.

"It's bigger than my house," Soren whispered, entranced.

Ew laughed aloud. "It's bigger than ten-thousand houses," he said.

Soren's awe of the massive ship reminded Ew of a trip to Brathim Zoo, on Calitholin, with his own son, Tushar. The zoo was filled with rare and exotic specimens from across the galaxy. Ew smiled to himself, likening the look on Soren's face to the look on Tushar's five-year-old face when he first saw the Dagmarian Caihab, a four-legged creature with two foot-long appendages for a mouth. Ew was saddened as he thought of the many facets of a father-son relationship: mentor, friend, father. *What a pair we make,* he thought as he watched Soren. *Here is a father without a son, and a son without a father.* He reached over, grabbed Soren, and sat him on his lap. Together they watched and talked quietly about the docking maneuver as the shuttlecraft moved slowly into the docking bay of the giant fortress.

Shreela watched Ew as he and Soren observed the docking procedure through the shuttle window. *He is quite different than what he pretends*, she thought. *Even Soren is able to sense something unique about him.* She was embarrassed when Ew unexpectedly turned and caught her staring at him. A moment of silence passed between them, his eyes folding into hers, holding her spellbound. "Did you want to say something?" she asked breaking the spell.

"It can wait," Ew replied. "Get ready to go," he said, as he stood up and headed for the exit.

Ew left the shuttle and ran off to have a private word with the ship's Admiral. Shreela and Soren stood quietly near the docking bay entrance until he returned with word on what their next move would be.

"Your rooms have already been prepared," said Ew. "I'll take you there myself, but be ready in thirty minutes for a meeting in the main conference area."

"Why am I going to a meeting?" asked Shreela curiously.

"The Admiral will be giving orders about where and how we leave this spacecraft."

"Can't he just get us to Galan?"

"Shreela, this is a warship, on its way to battle. There is no place here for civilians."

"I understand."

"A staff member will escort you to the meeting." Ew touched Shreela's shoulder, gently indicating direction. "Come, let me show you to your room."

After showing Shreela to her quarters, Ew met with Pala, Milan, and Admiral Atalif in his quarters. The Admiral, a long time friend to the Galan family, stood in a relaxed stance and carried a rolled document under his arm. His dense, frosty hair softened the deep crevices in his face; crevices that only got deeper when he smiled at Ew's entry. His wise and trustworthy presence soothed Ew. "What is the status of the rescue on Thesbis, Admiral?" he asked.

"Reports are starting to come in, Sire. Echlindra has sent eight hundred shuttles to lift and relocate survivors. The Petron Solar System has also agreed to assist in this rescue mission.

"It will be several days before the toxic dust can be neutralized. How far is the particle cloud expected to travel before then?"

"We estimate close to a five-hundred kilo-tran circumference from the point of initial contact to be the red-zone."

"How large a populace is there in the zone?"

"Almost fifteen million, My Lord. The entire area has been alerted to evacuate. The first to be relocated are those who have no means of transportation, the infirmed, and the elderly. They are all being taken to cities that are at least two-hundred kilo-trans beyond the red-zone."

"Who's overseeing this operation?"

"Chancellor Reeca from Echlindra. He is coordinating his efforts with Ina Garret in Raileen."

"Saren's assistant?" Ew asked, surprised.

"Yes Sire."

"What about Saren?"

"My understanding is that Saren has disappeared. He never returned to his home on Zirvag, and no one seems to know of his whereabouts."

Ew didn't respond but wondered whether or not Saren met with the justice he so deserved. "About our companions, Admiral," Ew said, changing the subject, "what can be done for them? Galan is in the middle of an intergalactic war so we can't send them there… Pala, don't you have some friends on Crashellon who do you favors from time to time?"

"Yes," Pala replied. "I'm sure they'd be more than willing to look out for the widow and her son until Shreela decides upon a more permanent situation. I'll contact them immediately, if you wish."

"I do, and please explain that Khali will pick up the expense for any resources they use to assist Shreela and her son."

After Pala left to send his message, Ew turned to Admiral Atalif to discuss military strategy.

"I must return home as soon as possible. What is the probability of getting beyond the Unian military blockade currently surrounding the System, Admiral?"

"That may prove to be a difficult task, Your Majesty, but we think we've come up with a plan to get you inside Galan."

"What do you propose?"

Admiral Atalif walked over and spread the document he had been holding on the conference table in front of Ew.

"Well, Sire, since there are fewer Unian battle cruisers at the southern pole of Galan, we should take that direction," he said, pointing out the logistics on the star map. "You'll be put aboard the *Fidus Achates* spacecraft, headed for home, while we hold off the cruisers."

"You can't hold off those battle cruisers alone".

"We won't be alone, My Lord. I have already arranged for two of the IGF warships returning from Chimoor to assist. That Fleet should be arriving within three hours."

"What about help from the Lluellyn Space Station?"

"That is no longer possible, My Lord. The military forces of Uni now hold that station as well as the Shargant Space Station," Atalif further explained, anticipating Ew's next question.

"When did that happen?"

"Just shortly before you boarded this vessel."

Ew sighed as he contemplated the news about the captured space stations. "Alright, Admiral, tell me about the *Achates*," he said at length.

"The *Achates* is docked in one of our lower spacebays. It's a mid-sized star cruiser with laser defense capabilities and a much greater shield tolerance than that of a shuttle. Your exposure will be limited, and landing the *Achates* will not be too difficult."

"Is there any alternative?"

"We've already ruled out two other possibilities. One would be to go in a shuttle, but it is unlikely that a shuttle launched to the planet surface can survive a military attack. Every shuttle launched to the planet surface since this battle began, has been lost."

"You mentioned another possibility."

"We could try to land this warship."

"But there are no warship landing pads on Galan. Even if we try to land this spacecraft, the heat generated from this vessel would incinerate the ground around it not to mention the certain damage to the ship."

"Then you agree that your best chance is with the Achates."

"I do. Go ahead and make the final arrangements. We should leave as soon as we come out of LT."

"Very good, Sire. I shall ready the spacecraft," said Atalif before leaving.

Ew looked over at Milan who was frowning. "Milan, you don't have to come with me. As a member of my security team, I can order you to escort Mrs. Bakra and her son to Crashellon, if you like."

"No, I'll go with you. I've come this far, I may as well go all the way," he mumbled.

"It's up to you. I'll understand if you don't join me." Ew waited a moment for some kind of response, but none was offered. "Okay," he said, "let's go and explain the plan to Pala."

The huge, circular conference room had a table with seats for fifty. Twenty or so people, primarily officers of the Galan Space Warship, gathered around. Ew noticed Shreela and Soren seated across from Admiral Atalif as he and his companions joined the group. As soon as Ew sat down, Atalif opened the meeting.

"We have two items of discussion here today," he began. "First is the matter of what to do with the passengers rescued on Thesbis. After a brief conference with Mr. E.G.," said Atalif, raising his eyebrows, "it has been decided that Mrs. Bakra and her son will be taken to Crashellon. Since Galan and her sister planets are currently involved in an intergalactic war with Uni, we believe that sending Mrs. Bakra to a planet outside the Khalian Solar System will be the best, and safest, course of action. The particulars of your journey," he addressed Shreela directly, "will be given to you before we reach that planet. The second topic of discussion," he continued, "concerns Mr. E.G. and his party. Mr. E.G. requested he be taken directly to Galan. He informed me of his need to go there, and I am in agreement with his decision. That being the case, Mr. E.G. and party will board the *Fidus Achates,* which will take them to their appointed destination."

Shreela did not hear much of the discussion that followed. She was annoyed with the Admiral's decision to send her to Crashellon. *He should have consulted me first,* she thought. *I'm tired of being shuffled around like this. Wonder whose idea this is,* she thought sarcastically, as she looked over at Ew. She continued to stare at Ew, hoping to catch his attention, but he appeared to be engrossed in what the Admiral was saying.

Ew, like Shreela, was far removed from the discussion taking place on the dais. His thoughts were on Shreela and Soren, feeling sad about their upcoming departure. *It's the only possible decision!* he tried to convince himself. *There's no sense thinking on it now. The decision has been made.*

Finally, the meeting adjourned. Shreela was about to leave the conference room when Ew tapped her on the shoulder.

"Shreela, can you wait a minute? I need to talk with you."

"I need to speak with you too," she said coolly.

They both waited patiently until the room was cleared before Ew spoke. He looked deep into her eyes. "I would have liked for you and Soren to come to Galan," he said in a husky voice. "When this is over, come and be my guest for a while. I owe you my gratitude for keeping the medallion safe until it could be returned to its rightful owner."

Shreela felt flustered. "You don't owe me anything," she said. "I didn't even know that I had the medallion."

"My appreciation is for the way you handled the situation," he explained. "You were in danger because of this treasure and endured the discomfort without complaint," he smiled. "I owe you for that." Ew bent down and lightly kissed her on her forehead. "Now, what did you want to speak with me about?"

Shreela was touched by his show of gratitude. Still, she was annoyed about the decision to send Soren and her to Crashellon. "You did it again," she said.

Ew gave her a puzzled look. "Did what?"

"You decided where I should go." Her voice, calm and collected. "E.G., you keep shuffling me around without asking me what I want." Shreela noticed the surprised look on his face as he took a step backward. "Don't look at me like that, and don't tell me it was the Admiral's decision to send me to Crashellon. It was you, right?" Ew did not respond to her question. "Right?" she asked again, more insistently.

"Shreela, I'm on my way to Galan," Ew finally responded, "and there is a war going on there. How can I suggest you go there?"

"Why suggest I go anywhere?" she shot back. "What makes you think I would want to go to Galan with you, anyway? If I want to go to Galan, that should be my decision, not yours, and if you thin..." She broke off as another thought occurred to her. "Wait a minute," she said, raising her brow. "That's why I was asked to attend this meeting. You had the Admiral explain the plan rather than you."

Ew raised his arms in surrender. "Okay, Shreela. You're right. I did it."

"Didn't we have this conversation before?" she asked sharply.

Ew glared directly into her eyes, binding her in a long, silent scrutiny. "Alright, where do you want to go?" he asked, trying to control the anger in his voice.

"I don't know yet."

Ew's eyes widened suddenly as if cold water had been thrown on him. "Then you better find out pretty quick," he responded, his brow knitted with annoyance. "This warship will be near Crashellon in a little more than an hour." Taking several long strides, he briskly walked towards the door.

"Where are you going?"

"I'll tell the Admiral you have other plans, and then I'm off to Galan."

"But we're not finished with our discussion."

"Wrong! You can inform Admiral Atalif about where you want to go," he said, and then left in a huff.

Shreela sat in her room thinking about E.G.'s last words. "I wish I hadn't lost my temper," she whispered to herself. For a second, she recalled the softness of his kiss. *I really do like him*, she thought. What was even more disconcerting was the urgent need she felt to return with him to Galan. "Atalif. Maybe I can get Atalif to let me board the Achates."

Shreela quickly walked across the room to where Soren was sitting. She grabbed both their jackets and her carryall bag. "Come on Soren."

"Are we goin' to that other place now? C-r-a-s-."

"Crashellon," she laughed. "No. I've changed my mind. Maybe we can go with Mr. E.G."

Soren smiled back at her. "I like Mr. E.G., Mom. What about you, mom? Do you like Mr. E.G. too?"

"Yes I do. Now hurry. I have to talk to the Admiral first."

"Okay."

Admiral Atalif stood up to greet Shreela as she was escorted into his small office next to the bridge area. "Mrs. Bakra," Atalif began once everyone was seated, "E.G. tells me that you have no desire to go to Crashellon."

"That's correct, Admiral."

"Mrs. Bakra, Crashellon is the closest planet we can reach that is outside the war zone. That is why it was chosen."

"Admiral, I would prefer to go to Galan. I can board.."

"That's impossible," Atalif interrupted.

"Why?"

"Madam, Galan is at war."

"I think I should be able to choose where I can go," Shreela argued.

"You can do that once you reach Crashellon."

"So can E.G. and his pals."

"That's different."

"How's that?"

"E.G. is not burdened with a child. If it were you alone, I would definitely consider it. However, I do not want to be responsible for sending a small child into a war."

"Admiral, you would not be responsible for that."

"How do you draw that conclusion, Madam?"

"You are not the child's parent."

Atalif stared at her, gently stroking his jaw with his fingers. "You will disembark on Crashellon," he said in a quiet, tranquil, but stubborn voice.

"Is this your final answer?"

"It is." Atalif got up from his chair and stood, relaxed, with his hands behind his back. After a long moment of silence, "Mrs. Bakra, there is a waiting room within the docking bay corridor. You may wait there until your shuttle is ready to leave," he offered. "One of my men will show you there."

An escort led Shreela and Soren into the docking bay corridor, a long hallway, lined with column supports. Passenger entries into the spacecraft were on the right, while the waiting room and several small military shops lined the hallway on the left.

"I can make it from here, thank you" said Shreela to her escort. "I see the waiting room sign just up ahead."

After the escort departed, Shreela slowly walked towards the waiting room. She paused when she noticed the *Fidus Achates* sign above one of the ports.

"Fidus Achates preparing for take-off," a voice came over the loudspeaker. "Will Mr. E.G. and party please board for takeoff?"

Shreela grabbed Soren's hand and got behind one of the columns, out of sight of anyone moving along the corridor. From where she stood, she could still see the *Achates* doorway.

She quietly watched as E.G., Pala, and Milan entered the vessel. After a moment or two, she and Soren walked up to the spacecraft door and slipped inside. They ducked out of sight in a small alcove to the left of the entrance. Shreela breathed a sigh of relief when the spacecraft doors closed.

As Shreela huddled next to Soren in the cramped space, preparing for takeoff as best she could, Ew and his friends sat in his quarters. The opulent room, accented with indigo-stained wood furniture and dark-cloth covered chairs, emanated wealth and power. A panoramic view of space was visible through the large windows. Ew stared thoughtfully at the view as he conversed with his friends.

"If my home has not been seized by the UMF, I should have no problem in getting to the Star Room."

"Galan Manor is probably safe, for now," Pala speculated.

"That's my hope, but Atalif said that no one's been able to reach my mother for the past six to eight hours. All communications going in or out of Galan are ...."

Ew was suddenly interrupted as the *Achates* shook violently from an external blast.

"Your Majesty," a voice summoned over the loud speaker. "Your Majesty, please come to the bridge at once."

Ew and his three companions rushed to the bridge. The huge console in the bridge area was blinking wildly. There were sirens blowing and military personnel scrambling throughout as Ew and his friends entered. A magnificent lighting display filled the bridge monitor.

"What is it?" shouted Ew.

Captain Jolique looked at Ew with a grim expression. "Your Majesty, that was the Solaitra. Three Unian battle cruisers descended upon them out of LT speed, assailing them shortly after we left. They did not stand a chance. And now the UMF is pursuing us."

Ew stared at the bridge monitor. The only movement seen on the monitor was that of UMF spacecraft.

"Ew," said Pala, distracting his thoughts.

Ew's mind snapped back to the present. "How much longer before we are able to land this thing?"

"We need at least another ten minutes," Jolique replied, as the ship rocked under heavy laser fire."

"Atalif said that two other warships would be called in to assist. They should have been here by now."

"They're on their way, My Lord. They should be here in a moment or two. I think we can hold this craft together until they arrive."

"Alright Captain. Keep me informed."

Ew turned to Pala and Milan, his face filled with sadness. His mind turned to his earlier conversation with Shreela concerning his decision to send her to Crashellon. *She would have been safer with me*, he thought. "They came so far to begin a new life," he said to Pala. "She wanted to go to Galan, but I told her it was unsafe."

"You made the right decision," Pala responded, soothingly.

Ew nodded his head. "I know."

"Come Sire," said Pala. "There's nothing we can do here."

"I need a few moments to myself. I'll meet you back on the bridge shortly."

Pala and Milan headed to their respective rooms while Ew headed back to his quarters located in the opposite direction. Pala looked worried as he looked back to see his old friend. "Ew. Are you alright?"

Ew shook his head. "I'm fine," he said, but would not turn to face his friend.

Ew exited the bridge and proceeded down the corridor to his room. His eyes passed, unseeing, over crewmembers passing up and down the hallways as they prepared for battle. Suddenly, his eyes were riveted on the Chief Security Officer escorting two captives. It was Shreela and Soren, and they were heading in his direction. Ew called out, raising his hand to stop them. "Chief, will you come with me," he commanded. Ew and the Security Chief walked a few trans away, just out of earshot.

"Where are you taking these two?"

"They were found wandering around the ship, Sire. We're heading for the detention quarters."

Ew looked over at Shreela. The tenseness of her eyes and mouth betrayed the anxiety and fear she tried to control. Ew turned back to the security officer. "It's alright. I'll take care of this. You may return to your duties."

"Yes, Sire."

Ew walked back to where Shreela and Soren were standing. Without a word, he pulled them toward him, wrapping his arms around them tightly. "I thought you two were lost on the Warship. How did you ever get aboard this ship?"

"We sneaked aboard just before takeoff," replied Shreela. "We were hiding in the small alcove near the entrance, but when laser blasts began to hit us, I tried to find another place to hide. Almost made it, too," she said wryly." A puzzled expression came over her face as she finally grasped his first question. "What did you mean when you said you thought we were lost on the Warship? What happened?"

At that moment, the ship was again rocked violently, throwing everyone off balance. Alarms sounded and uniformed personnel rushed up and down the corridor.

"I'll explain later," shouted Ew above the racket. "Come on."

The *Achates* entered the gravitational field of the planet

below. Ew grabbed Shreela's hand in an attempt to steady her as they rolled from side to side. The three of them managed to get out of the corridor, but when they finally reached the bridge, the entire area was in complete turmoil. Many officers who manned the bridge were either unconscious or dead, while those remaining were busy extinguishing electrical fires that sprang up. Captain Jolique was mortally wounded. Pala and Milan assisted in operating on manual control.

"What is our status?" shouted Ew.

"Shields are down to fifty percent, ion engines are nearing critical, communications out, scattered fires burning out of control, and life-support systems are disintegrating rapidly."

"Give the order to evacuate," Ew commanded. Ew saw two Unian Battle cruisers on the bridge view screen. "What happened to our warships!" he shouted in frustration.

"Ew, we have to jettison soon or die here," shouted Pala. "There's another thing.....," Pala began. "How did you get here!" he exclaimed noticing Shreela standing next to Ew.

"It's a long story," shouted Ew. "I hope we live to tell you about it. Come on, let's go!"

The five companions finally made their way to the jettison pod launching area where many of the pods had already been launched. With some effort, they all managed to squeeze into one of the remaining pods.

Milan struggled to free his elbow from Pala's face. "This pod's not designed to hold more than three people," he grumbled.

"It will hold up to two-thousand kino-grams," said Pala. "We'll be safe enough, just close the hatch."

Ew became irritated with Milan, as the old archaeologist tussled his way in, grumbling all the while. "Would you like to stay here, Milan? Just push the damned button!" he yelled.

Milan pushed the jettison button seconds before the *Achates* blew up. Caught in the turbulence created by the blast, the pod spun like a top as it headed towards the planet surface. Several seconds passed before the pod stabilized. By then, the face of the intrepid King of Khali turned blue. Soren, who was in Ew's arms, held Ew tightly around the neck. Milan's eyes rolled back in his head while Pala grunted with discomfort. Shreela inhaled deeply several times to keep from getting sick. "I never thought I would get to Galan like this," she said.

From his flagship quarters, Uzak watched intently as the *Fidus Achates* blew up, lighting the viewing monitor displaying the burning ash and debris. The commander of his flagship, however, abruptly interrupted his moment of glory.

"My Lord."

"Commander."

"Sire, our tracking stations are picking up several jettison pods from the destroyed spacecraft. They're headed for the planet surface."

"Destroy them all, and get me Admiral Pernell," he commanded.

"At once, My Lord."

Within seconds, the face of Admiral Pernell enveloped Uzak's viewing monitor.

"Admiral, what is the status of the Khalian I-SS Force and IGF?"

"Lord, according to our sentry ships, the IGF is still headed to Chimoor. They cannot return past our sentry scanners without detection. Since the Inter-Solar System Forces no longer control the space stations, they are forced to land their craft on the planet surface to refuel."

"Good. Send the smaller Unian Attack Destroyers docked at the Lluellyn and Shargant space stations to move in close to the ground and take out the power-cell fuel tankers. Battle cruisers from Zirvag, Dagmar, and Gundarlin, are on alert. Have them refuel at the Shargant and Lluellyn space stations, and then disperse those battle cruisers around the entire solar system over the next six hours. That should give them enough time to refuel and reach their destinations."

"Yes, My Lord."

Admiral Pernell was interrupted by a crewmember handing him a log. Uzak noticed the subtle change in Pernell's face as he reviewed it.

"Admiral?"

"My Lord, Intelligence has informed us that the shield extends across the entire Khalian Solar System except for the space station around the planet Balarai.."

"I'm aware of that, Admiral," Uzak stated coolly. "The Balarai Space Station lies in the extreme northeastern quadrant, and although it is part of that System, it lies outside the perimeter markings for the Khalian Solar System shield. Six Unian battle cruisers are already headed in that direction. Their job will be to knock out the any military defense, and to secure the space station. Since shields and armament for Balarai are not yet operational, it is no threat to us. In a few days, a crew of engineers will be dispatched to that area to begin work on the station's completion for our purposes."

"Yes, My Lord."

"How long before the Khalian Solar System shield codes are remapped with our codes?

"It is taking more time than the projected eight hours, Sire. We need at least another five or six hours at the most."

"Just get it done! Uzak glared at the blank screen. *It's only a question of time.*

Through the pod window, Ew saw other pods with military personnel inside. Unian RATS Fighters, in their relentless pursuit of those trying to escape, blasted many apart. Some of the pods were so close to one another, they collided, exploding on impact. He glanced over at Shreela and Soren, who were not aware of the danger they were in since they were not facing the small window.

"Pala," Ew whispered, "can you see what's going on out there?"

"Yeah. Looks like Unian RATS attacking the pods."

"Is there a way to maneuver this thing, or is this one of the older models?"

"This one is one of the first issued."

"Great, that means we have almost no control. Sure hope we don't bump into anyone," he said, his voice spiked with sarcasm.

"Except for speed, there is no real way to direct these older pods," Pala explained. "We are at the mercy of time and chance as to where and if we finally land."

Ew's greatest concern was where they would land. "Pala," he whispered, "I noticed that during the attack, the *Fidus Achates* was beginning its pass over the Galan Marsh. Maybe we'll fall somewhere close to the habitable regions." Peering through the pod window though, he noticed that they were falling further and deeper into the uninhabited marshlands. *Better not say anything just yet,* he thought to himself. *They'll find out soon enough.*

Pala slowly pulled the speed lever down. "Hold on everyone," he warned. "I'm about to land this thing."

The pod jerked as Pala decelerated. Finally, it landed with a thud. "Is everyone okay?" he asked.

"I think we're okay," said Ew.

Milan opened the hatch door and stepped outside. "At least

we landed on dry land," he shouted back to the others.

Ew raised his brow as he stood at the door and looked around. They had indeed landed in one of the marsh regions of Galan. There were pools of slime and mud as far as the eye could see. Insects of all types lived there, along with other creatures that Ew preferred not to think about. "We'll have a few problems getting out of here," Ew told them, "so carry whatever weapons and food discs you find on board. Pala, bring that compact communications radio. We should take that compass over there, as well as that parcel of bashi fuel sticks. We can use the sticks instead of our lasers to start a fire."

Shreela stepped outside the jettison pod and walked several trans, carefully appraising her surroundings. Ew caught the sparkle in her eye when she slowly turned to face him. She spread her arms out in a welcoming gesture. "So this is Galan."

Ew smiled back at her. "You look impressed," he said.

"I've never been in a swamp before."

"It was your decision to come with us." His mind briefly flashed back to the explosion of the warship. He smiled at her warmly. "And I'm very glad you did."

Shreela's dark brown eyes softened at the sight of him, and he noticed how the sunlight bounced off her beautiful dark brown hair. She smiled and then turned to go back to the jettison pod. Ew stood there silently, as his practiced masculine eye swept over her lovely body. Though her stride was short, her hips seemed to swivel in a slow casual side-to-side motion. Ew's eyes roamed over that one-piece pantsuit which clung to her body. He gave a sheepish grin when he noticed that Pala and Milan were watching him watch her. "She is a lovely distraction," he murmured.

Galan Under Siege

As Ew and his companions settled down for the night, nineteen-hundred kilo-trans away, the evening meal at the House of Galan was abruptly interrupted by tremors on the planet surface. Princess Megan rushed down the corridor to check on her mother, Mara, who was quite old and in poor health.

"Mother, are you alright?" Megan cried excitedly as she entered her mother's room.

"I'm fine. What's going on?" asked Mara. "We haven't had a quake on Galan in over fifty years."

A brisk knock at the door startled them both. "Your Highness, Your Highness," a voice called from without. Megan ran to open the door for General Laggé.

"Your Highness," Laggé addressed Mara, "we are under ground attack by Unian Military Forces."

"What?" Mara asked surprised. "And what happened to our galactic forces? They're supposed to keep the UMF from solar system attacks," she cried.

"We have not been able to contact the IGF," he explained.

"You should be explaining this to His Majesty, Laggé. Why are you telling me?"

"That's the problem, Your Highness. The UMF is jamming our transmitter. We cannot transmit beyond the System outposts, and because His Majesty is not within the Khalian System, we are not able to reach him. Since His Majesty is not here, we need your clearance on several military matters."

"Alright, alright," said Mara, annoyed by the absence of her son. "How do we stand militarily?"

"Our I-SS Forces are well supplied with spacecraft and munitions for about two to three weeks at the very least."

Clearly agitated by the news, Mara paced the room several times. Both Megan and General Laggé stood quietly by as she pondered her next move. Though her hair was white as snow and her back slightly bowed, Mara was a strong-willed individual with many years of political clashes and skirmishes with the Unian Solar System. With great poise she turned back to address the General.

"Laggé, I want the senior military staff to meet with me in the debriefing room in an hour, but I want Admiral Garbonst to be there for a briefing in fifteen minutes," she commanded. "Continue your efforts to make contact beyond our planetary boundary outposts."

"Yes, Your Highness." Laggé bowed and left the room.

Mara looked thoughtfully at her daughter. She could see the deep concern that Megan tried to hide behind a pair of soft green eyes. She took a few moments to quiet Megan's fears.

"When your father died," Mara began, "I was left quite alone in the decision process of this solar system. I certainly made my share of mistakes along the way, but I gave all that I could give. Ruling one planet is a chore in itself but fifteen planets is outrageous. I often wondered how your father was able to manage the multitude of problems that cropped up daily. What I learned, as supreme ruler, was that all fifteen planets work in unison. To accomplish that, you must have people in whom you can trust. The selection of such people was a long and difficult process, but I believe we have such a group in existence here today. The credit for our well-governed system really goes to Ew. Ewlon has chosen an excellent staff of advisors. They are loyal subjects who strongly support him. Most of all, they will lend their support to me," she said pausing for a moment, "or you, in his absence."

"What if something happens to you and Ew?" Megan asked

her voice filled with concern. "I'm afraid that if the command should fall to me, I may only make matters worse. My skills in military affairs have never been tested."

"My dear daughter, anyone sitting in this position is afraid. Billions of people are affected in some way, right or wrong, by any decision of this throne. If the command should befall you, always remember that, in order to survive, the Khalian Solar System must function as one unit."

"Mother, even Ew has problems getting some of these Regional Governors to agree on anything."

"That's true, but the defense of Khali is a common goal shared by all of the Governors." Mara looked at her daughter, understanding what she might have to face. "I just might surprise you and survive this ordeal," she said laughing. "Come now, you must also be present at the meeting."

Admiral Garbonst stood when Megan and Mara entered the room. Mara felt a tightening knot in her stomach as the Admiral seated her across the table from his own seat. While Garbonst assisted Megan to her chair, Mara observed him, his white hair glistening in the light, softening the deep lines of maturity in his face. She briefly reflected on their first encounter, he a young junior officer, and she, the newly installed steward of Khali. "Well Admiral, we have worked through the dawn of our lives, developing a good military posture for the defense of Khali," she reminded him. "Now we are here, in our evening years, where we will see just how effective our decisions were."

Admiral Garbonst looked over at her, his mouth slightly curved up in a subtle smile, a smile of remembrance. "Yes, Your Highness."

"What is your report?" she asked.

"Your Highness," Garbonst began, "the Lluellyn and Shargant Space Stations are now in the hands of the UMF.

Shield generator codes from both space stations have been breached, and interplanetary shield protection has been dropped. We are open to any Unian attack."

Mara settled back in her chair and then looked over at the colorless face of Megan. "And the Balarai Space Station?" she asked, turning her attention back to Garbonst.

"We are still working to bring that station back on-line, Your Highness. It will be battle-worthy within a solar day, but the shield will not be ready for another two to three weeks." Mara notably raised her brow. "The saboteurs were able to destroy better than fifty percent of the shield power source transfer conduits, which have to be rebuilt from scratch. There are six Unian battle cruisers headed towards Balarai, but that shouldn't cause a delay in our work schedule."

Mara gave him a puzzled look. "Only six? There are over thirty Khalian warships around Balarai. Those six Unian battle cruisers will be crushed as soon as they move into torpedo range." Mara rested her elbow on the table, balanced her chin and jaw in the palm of her hand, and silently deliberated possible UMF strategies. *Uzak knows those battle cruisers will be destroyed*, she thought. *What is his ploy*? Suddenly she sat up. "Admiral, Laggé earlier explained that communication frequencies were jammed by UMF disrupters, and that it was not possible for us to contact our galactic forces. Have we been able to reestablish communications with them?"

"Not yet, Madam."

"So you don't know if the galactic force comm code has been breached."

"No, Your Highness, but since I'm preparing to shuttle to the flagship, *Rotondra*, I'll check the master comm system as soon as I arrive."

"If the code is still secure, how long would it take to switch to the backup encryption?"

"Two to three hours, at the most, Madam, but His Majesty changed those codes yesterday."

"Yesterday?" she asked. "It would be impossible to unscramble the security code that fast unless..." A disquieting thought occurred to her. "...unless Uzak had help from inside Khali." A tinge of urgency filtered through her voice. "Another thing, Admiral, Uzak would not send six battleships against thirty unless he was able to decoy the Khalian IGF away from the Balarai, possibly the entire solar system. They may have already done so."

Garbonst's lip twitched involuntarily as a chill chased up his spine. "That would leave the Khalian I-SS Force to fight on their own," he expressed his thoughts. "Refueling for the UMF is not a problem, since they can use the space stations instead of returning to their power-cell crafts in deep space."

"My point exactly, Admiral."

"I'm on my way, Your Highness. If you have no objections, General Laggé has been fully briefed and will bring you up to date on all military matters in my report."

"Make it quick, Admiral, and I will wait for Laggé's report."

Following Garbonst's departure, senior military staff, along with General Laggé, began to make their way into the debriefing room where Megan and Mara sat waiting for the meeting to commence. When all were in attendance, and with a nod of Mara's head, Laggé opened the meeting.

"Your Highness," Laggé began, "we have received both good and bad news during the last hour from Admiral Kryto on Nilar."

"I thought communications were out," Mara interrupted.

"Petron patched us through their security system, Your Highness."

"I see. Go on," Mara waved her hand.

"We've received word from Admiral Kryto from our outpost station on Nilar in the Petron Solar System. He sent word that nearly two-thirds of our Intergalactic Fleet was decoyed to Chimoor."

"Chimoor?"

"Yes, Your Highness, but Admiral Kryto also said that he was contacted by His Majesty who ordered the Fleet to return to Khali."

"Where was His Majesty when he made contact?"

"His Majesty contacted Admiral Kryto from the Mount Halokin Defense Base on the planet Thesbis."

"Thesbis! What is he doing on that planet?"

"I'm not certain, Your Highness, but I do know that he and the Director of Intelligence, Pala Bhusan, were to meet someone there last evening."

"Well Laggé, where is he?"

"Admiral Kryto informed me that His Majesty was rescued and taken aboard the warship *Solaitra*."

"That's wonderful news," Megan blurted out, "when will he be here?"

General Laggé paused for a moment. "We're not sure."

"What do you mean?" Mara fired back.

"Admiral Kryto received word from Admiral Atalif that His Majesty left the warship by way of the *Fidus Achates*, headed for Galan. Kryto explained that since the Lluellyn and Shargant Space Stations had been taken over by the UMF, the plan called for the *Achates* to land on the planet surface. Admiral Atalif also sent word that two of his passengers, a widow from Tima and her son, sneaked aboard the *Achates* before takeoff. He insisted you hear this particular message."

Mara held on to her seat as she tried to maintain her

composure. "Where is Atalif now?" she asked.

"I'm sorry, Your Highness, but the UMF destroyed both the Warship and the *Achates*," Laggé said apologetically. "That is why we don't know if His Majesty will return," he said reluctantly.

The room became quiet as if everyone suddenly stopped breathing. "I suppose that's the bad news," Mara said, breaking the silence. "Tell me, General, were there any survivors?"

"Yes, Your Highness. Our monitors picked up several escape pods with markings identical to those aboard the *Achates*. Rescuers have been sent to recover the pods, but so far, His Majesty was not aboard any of them. There is one other possibility," said Laggé, hesitating.

Mara's expression became intense as hope flooded back into her eyes. "Another possibility?"

"We know that at least one jettison pod landed in the marshland region of this planet. A search in that area is already underway. Perhaps His Majesty was in that pod."

Mara recognized most of the senior staff members as she looked about the room. "These are strange tidings, indeed," she said. "Many of you already know of The Legend of Khali. A detailed accounting of the *prophecy*, surrounding the widow of Tima has never been fully disclosed to the public. Several years ago," Mara began, "Admiral Atalif asked me why I did not include the documented logs of the Legend as part of our national archives. I told Admiral Atalif what I am about to tell you now.

"My reasons at that time were as clear then as they are now. I excluded that information for the protection of this widow around whom the Legend speaks. If this Legend had been allowed to spread through the decades, Uzak would have enlisted more spies than he already has, to track down this poor creature. We have long noted the disappearance of many Timanian widows enlisting in programs offered on Thesbis. The Thesbian Placement Council has tried to trace the kidnappings to Uzak, but evidence necessary for formal indictments was never found. It is my belief that keeping a low profile on the Legend may have attributed to this widow's survival, if this is indeed the same widow. Let us hope that she is.

"Since the time grows short, I will not speak further on this subject. Copies of the treatise prepared by the late King Wedolan Galan will be distributed for your perusal, provided there is time to do so. Meanwhile, we must address the dilemma that is before us today.

"We are now facing an intergalactic war between Uni and Khali. Though I am concerned about the reason for His Majesty's absence, we as a group are forced here today to decide the fate of our homes, our children, and our future. As most of you know, it is not possible to negotiate peace with the Lord of Uni, and long have we lived under the threat of attack. An automatic counteroffensive is already underway with General Laggé in charge of Inter-Solar System Force, while Admiral Garbonst commands the Intergalactic Defense Team. Continue the current military policy, General, while I digest this new information. I will meet with you later to discuss additional battle strategies. May the Keepers of Khali keep you safe."

6
THE ERGRET

The Galan Marsh

As the shadows of eventide deepened, puffs of vapor formed over the watery bogs in the Galan Marsh, eventually creating the dense cloud cover, shielding the marsh from the starlight. The mood of the camp reflected the grim and dreary surroundings, and although there was no wind, Ew and his companions fought off the damp and chilly air, as they huddled around the campfire next to the jettison pod.

"It's a good thing you and Soren have your jackets. It gets pretty chilly in this area during the night," Ew commented.

"How cold does it get?" asked Shreela.

"Fifteen to twenty points above freezing," said Ew.

Shreela threw another bashi stick into the fire. "Shreela," called Ew, "that's enough fuel. There are only five or six bashi sticks left, and we'll have many more days out here if we're not rescued." Ew looked around on the ground.

"Milan, hand me that tree branch, will you?" While rubbing his hands together close to the flame, Ew stared thoughtfully at Pala who was standing on the fringe of the campsite. He watched as Pala silently canvassed the area, and sensed that Pala was troubled by something. After a time, Ew walked over to him. "What is it, my friend?" he asked quietly.

"I may be mistaken, Ew, but isn't this the home of the ergret?"

Ew was silent for a moment. "Yes," he answered reluctantly.

"That's a big problem, Ew. Since the ergret lives very near the innermost swamp, we are definitely far from help. It may take weeks to get out of this dismal environment, plus our journey is complicated with a mother and child to protect."

"I agree," said Ew, nodding his head. "Milan," he called out. Milan left Shreela and Soren by the fire and walked over to join his friends.

"How much do you know about the ergret?" asked Ew.

A troubled expression crossed Milan's brow. "How deep are we inside the marsh?" he asked.

"Pala thinks we're in or close to the center." Milan put his hand to his head. "Stop quaking and just tell me what you know," Ew insisted.

"Okay, okay," he said, obviously rattled and frantically straining to see out into the misty gloom. "Well, to begin with, the ergret is native to the Galan marsh; four-legged, about one to one-and one-half trans long. Their leathery hide acts as a shield against thorns and other sharp-edged vegetation common to these regions."

"What sort of artillery are we dealing with here," Ew interrupted.

"Sharp claws for ripping apart its victim," Milan explained, "and long fangs -- about seven lino-trans long."

"Doesn't this creature secrete some kind of poison?" asked Pala.

"For subduing larger prey, yes. The fangs secrete a toxin, which causes a slow paralysis to the victim. This animal also travels in pairs, male and female."

"Always?"

"Uh-huh. The ergret takes one mate during its lifetime, and they are highly protective of each other. If you kill one of them, the other will track you, for days or weeks, waiting for an opportunity to exact its revenge upon you. But Ew," he spoke frantically, "it is not possible to avoid them. They are territorial creatures, and there are many pairs scattered throughout the marshland."

"Alright, just settle down and let's not lose our focus here," said Ew. "You've confirmed pretty much what I already knew about this animal, except I didn't know they move in pairs." Ew took several paces outside the camp, staring blankly into the darkness. A sudden, chilling, thought occurred to him. "One other thing though, Milan," he said turning to face his friends, "it is my understanding that this animal has been known to stalk humans. What about that?"

"Yes, yes," he replied, nodding his head several times. "There is clear evidence and documented records that humans have been attacked by them, but human flesh is not generally part of their diet," he explained. "If they are hungry, though, they're dangerous to any living creature. We definitely have to be cautious and stay close to each other if we intend to survive," he warned.

"You, Milan and I should probably stay outside tonight and let Shreela and Soren sleep inside the pod," Pala suggested to Ew.

"Fine, but it's not tonight which worries me so much. It's the nights to follow," he said. Ew leaned against a tree and gazed up into the sky, hopelessly wishing for a peek at the stars. "We have provisions for about fourteen days, and to be honest with you, I'm not sure about which direction we should take, and what about the jettison pod. I am surprised that we have not been picked up by enemy scanners."

"Fortunately, this is one of the older pods," Pala responded. "The energy trail would not be tracked on this frequency, but rather the frequency standard set for the newer pods."

"Then we have another problem?"

"Sire?"

"Our own search craft will also be scanning for newer pods too."

"You're right," Pala said, solemnly. "Added to that problem, we can't even use the equipment we have to pinpoint our location," said Pala.

"What about the magnetic field equipment in the pod?" asked Ew.

"No good," Pala replied.

"Why?" asked Milan.

"Because of the strange magnetic fields in this region of Galan, I couldn't get a clear reading, even when I switched the polarity," Pala groaned, studying the heavily overcast sky.

"What else can happen?" Ew asked sighing.

"To make matters worse," Pala continued, "there are no stars to steer a course."

"I see that," Ew said, looking up at the sky yet again. Ew slowly walked back into the camp. "Look, don't say anything about this to the widow," he said in a low voice. "Not yet, anyway." A curious expression crossed Pala's face. "Is there something else?" he asked.

"As your friend, may I be candid?" Pala asked.

"You are my friend."

"Well my friend, you seem affected by this widow."

"Yes. She's entrancing."

"Just entrancing?"

Ew stared at Shreela for a moment. She was seated next to the fire stroking her son's head as he lay with his head in her lap. She was singing a Timanian lullaby. *By looking, no one would suspect the peril those two now face*, he thought. "She's much more," he said, "I just can't afford to think about that right now."

Nocturnal creatures moved about in search of food, filling the swamp with strange and eerie sounds. Ew felt uncomfortable as he strained to see the area around him. "Come, let's go. Pala, you can take the first watch."

Pala watched over the camp while the other two men slept next to the campfire. Halfway through his watch, he drifted off into a shallow sleep, but was awakened by a light shining in his eyes. He looked up into the sky through an opening in the clouds. Quickly, he jumped up and rushed over to where Ew was sleeping. "Ew, come on, get up. There's something you should see," he whispered.

"It can't be my turn yet! I just went to sleep," Ew groaned.

"Ew, wake up," Pala insisted, "there's a break in the clouds. We should be able to get a fix on where we are."

Reluctantly, Ew opened his eyes and with some hesitation, turned his head skyward and quietly began to study the stars. "Pala," he called after a few moments, "we are definitely in trouble. According to the position of Ranel's Belt, our location is near the center of the southwestern swamp region. At the very least, it will take us three weeks to reach the habitable regions."

"We only have enough provisions for two weeks," Pala worried.

"We might have a chance to hunt for food along the way," said Ew, raising his brow at Pala. "We're in good shape, physically that is, so we should be able to carry what we hunt. In two weeks, though, we'll be pretty tired. If we have to carry much more than ourselves, we'll move even slower. In any event, we'll have to ration the food discs."

"That's if we can find any game in these muddy, steaming, quagmires," Pala muttered.

"We won't starve," Ew assured him, "but our endurance will certainly be tested," he added. "I'm fully awake now so why don't you get some rest."

It was nearly dawn when Ew woke Milan for guard duty. Milan was walking around the camp area when Shreela opened the door to the jettison pod. She still felt tired and unrested.

"Good morning," Shreela greeted Milan who silently walked past her. "Good morning, I hope you had a good night's sleep," she repeated, thinking he did not hear her. Again Milan didn't respond but instead, turned his back to her. Shreela frowned, puzzled by the cold reception. She walked up to him. "Is there something bothering you?" she asked.

Milan stood as silent and still as the motionless trees, enduring the heat and stagnant air of the windless marsh. Only when Shreela turned to leave did he speak.

"It's not my place to tell you this, but during the last few years, I've watched E.G. recover from a terrible tragedy. He lost his wife and son in an accident, and for nearly two years, he neglected his responsibilities and himself. He is my best friend. I don't want to see him hurt again."

"In other words,..." Shreela began.

"In other words," Milan interrupted, "he is still very vulnerable."

Shreela walked towards a dead tree and leaned against the bow. Her eyes skimmed across the steaming, murky quagmires before her. Wistfully she recalled the autumn scene on Tima, the eve of her departure.

"It's obvious both you and Pala care a great deal about E.G.," she said, at length. "He is very fortunate to have such friends, but you're talking to me as if I have no understanding of the pain E.G. lives with. Maybe you've forgotten my reason for going to Thesbis," she gently reminded him. With a look of resignation, she turned and said, "My son and I are now trapped on a strange planet and forced to place our trust in people we don't know. I ask you, who here is vulnerable?"

Milan was still not satisfied with her defense. "You don't appear any worse for the wear," he responded acidly. "As a matter of fact, you look like a person who knows exactly how to take care of herself. You put on quite a flirtatious show here yesterday. No, I don't think you're vulnerable." Milan moved close to Shreela, looking directly into her eyes. "By the way, for someone who just lost a loved one, you don't appear to be the least bit upset about your loss," he said contemptuously.

Feeling the anger begin to rise inside, Shreela struggled to keep her composure. "Not everyone reacts to death the same way," her voice shook. "You don't know what I feel when I look at my child and see his father's face, a constant reminder of his absence, or when I go to sleep at night, knowing that my mate will not be with me when I get up the next day. No, Milan, it's you who does not understand."

"Oh I understand, alright."

"Do you?" she countered. "Sounds like you're jealous. Are you afraid I'll take him from you?" she asked in a low, cutting tone. Shreela felt his eyes on her as she strolled off, shaking her head in disbelief. "It was almost a good morning," she uttered a parting shot.

It was late morning when Pala and Ew got up. By then, Soren was up and about playing beside one of the many mud holes next to the campfire. Shreela sat close to him, but her thoughts were on her disturbing confrontation with Milan earlier that morning. So deep in thought was she that she did not hear Ew who walked over to where she was seated.

"Good morning, Shreela. Did you sleep well?" he asked.

"What? Oh-h, no, not really," she said, carefully avoiding his eyes.

Ew looked at her with curiosity. "Are you alright?"

"I'm fine. Just a little anxious about where we're going from here," she lied.

"Well, we need to decide what to take with us. First, let me warn you. This journey will be both long and exhausting." Ew stared at Soren as he stirred one of the many mud holes with his stick. "I'll carry Soren for you."

"That'll be a big help. Thanks."

An uneasy moment of silence passed between them. Ew sensed that something else was wrong. Without thinking, he reached over and cupped her chin in his hand. "Something is bothering you," he insisted.

A faint smile rose at the edge of her mouth. "Really, I'm fine," she pretended, "and if you'll excuse me, I need to check on something before we leave."

Ew was confused by this sudden change in attitude, but before he could go after her, Soren screamed. It was the infamous marsh andir, a massive snakelike creature nearly four trans in length with long arched fangs capable of cutting through bone. Powerful long slithery arm-like tentacles encircled Soren's waist. Quickly, Ew fired his laser at the andir. Startled by the bright light, the andir loosened its hold on Soren, enabling Ew to free the lad. Before he could move to safety, the andir wrapped another tentacle around Ew's midsection, pulling him towards its home. Milan and Pala raced to their friend's rescue while Shreela grabbed Soren from Ew's arms. Ew dropped his laser and toppled to the ground. He gasped for air as one tentacle tightened around his torso and another twisted itself around his neck. The bright light generated from the laser blasts was only a temporary deterrent, and the more Milan and Pala blasted the beast, the tighter its grip became. Ew was nearing unconsciousness when suddenly the andir let out a bloodcurdling scream, releasing Ew from its iron grip. Bubbling sounds were heard as it submerged into the mud hole.

Shreela stood near the edge of the mud hole with a lighted bashi stick in her hand. Seeing that the lasers had no effect on the beast, she grabbed the stick, and using Ew's laser to ignite it, stabbed the creature in the eye.

Ew quickly scrambled away from the mud hole. Shreela and Pala ran towards him and helped him to his feet.

Ew shuddered. His heart thumped wildly against his chest, and the sudden shock rendered him incapable of masking the fear in his eyes. "Shreela, I owe you my life." Still shaken from the ordeal, Ew stumbled over to the jettison pod and sat down in the open doorway.

"Maybe you should lie down for a while," Pala suggested.

"No, no. I just need a moment to settle down. You and Milan gather what we need for this trip."

"But we can...."

"Pala, do it now," Ew interrupted. "Really, I'm alright. I'll just rest here for a while."

While Pala and Milan moved to gather their things, Ew took a few deep breaths to calm himself. Then he turned his attention to Soren, whose eyebrows were arched and teardrops streamed down his face. Ew put his arm around him to comfort him. "It was a close call, my little friend, but we came out of it alright, didn't we?" he asked gently. "Are you alright now?"

"He's a little shaken up, but he's alright," Shreela assured him.

"Soren?"

"I'm scared."

"He'll calm down in a while," Shreela said to Ew.

"I hope so. In any event, it's time we move on from here -- the sooner the better," he added, looking back at the mud hole.

Within the hour, everyone was ready to begin the journey. The plan was to head north to Star City, home of Ewlon Galan. The distance was nearly two-thousand kilo-trans from the marsh border north of their current position. That meant picking up a transport in Landory, the closest city east of their present location, a little more than three-hundred kilo-trans away.

Pala led the way followed by Ew, Shreela, and Soren with Milan acting as rearguard. The day was sunny and mild. Though their journey was not pleasant, the sunlight kept them in good spirits. At times they waded knee deep through areas of deep muddy water, which brought to mind memories of the creature that attacked Soren and Ew earlier that day. The going was slow. They trudged through areas of dense vegetation where hanging vines and dense underbrush seemed to grab at them, reluctant to let them pass. The swamp was full of life, both seen and unseen. There were birds, biting insects, and slithering snake-like creatures living in the watery bogs. Soren had to be carried most of the way, making it difficult when they waded through deep mud or stagnant water.

The search for a campsite began in late afternoon, but it was early evening before they found a small patch of ground several trans long with a few small trees and shrubs. There were dead tree branches scattered across the opening that could be used as firewood. After unloading their gear, Milan and Ew headed out in search of game, leaving Pala to guard Shreela and Soren. Shreela collected the wood for a fire while Pala left to get water from a small pond nearby. When he returned, Shreela had already started the campfire. He walked towards the fire and placed two flausins, a metal bowl-shaped frame used to cover a crash helmet, next to the fire. They had been taken from the jettison pod.

"Use one of these for cooking and the other for washing," he said.

"Thank you," said Shreela. She then pulled a flat package from her bag and opened it.

"What's that?" asked Pala.

"It's a cleaning towel. It's been treated with a mild detergent. I only have one, so we all have to share it." She noticed a slight grin on Pala's face. "Had I known we'd be taking this extended tour of Galan, I would have brought more."

"Why were you carrying it in the first place?"

Shreela laughed. "I always carry one when I travel with my son."

At that moment, Ew and Milan returned empty handed. "No luck," said Ew.

"We can use the food discs," Shreela suggested.

"There's only enough for about fourteen days," said Pala. "We'll have to ration the discs carefully just in case we can't supplement our provisions with other food."

"I have a few discs," said Shreela. She reached into her bag and produced a small disc-shaped dispenser. "Here," she handed the dispenser to Ew.

"Thank you, Shreela," said Ew, examining the contents. "This will add a couple days to what we already have. Still, we should hunt for food whenever we can," he added. Ew winked at Shreela.

Shreela glanced over at Milan, catching his disapproving eye. "It's really nothing. Excuse me while I get Soren cleaned up before eating."

Ew jumped to his feet. "I'll help you."

Shreela hesitated for a moment. Again, she looked over at Milan. "I could use the help," she said, without losing eye contact with him.

Ew turned to look at Milan, and then back to Shreela. "Is there something going on here?" he asked.

"Not a thing," she responded, slipping her hand through the crook of Ew's arm. "Come on, let's go."

Except for the sounds of the marsh, there was almost no conversation during dinner. Everyone was absorbed in his or her own thoughts. Shreela finally pulled Soren to her lap. Within a few minutes, he was sound asleep.

While Soren slept, Ew addressed the group, voicing a few of his concerns about the journey thus far.

"Today," he began, "we were able to cover only ten kilotrans. We must be able to walk at least sixteen to twenty kilotrans a day if we are to reach Landory in three weeks. At our present speed, it will take us five to six weeks." Ew reached over and picked up a bundle lying next to him. I've figured out a way to make better time." Ew produced a knotted cloth with three holes in it. Shreela recognized her jacket that she loaned to Ew earlier that day. It was tied at the bottom and looked very much like a sack.

"What's that?" asked Pala.

"I made this carrying sack from Shreela's jacket. Each one of us can carry Soren in this. We should make better time."

"Sounds good to me," said Pala.

"Then it's settled." Ew slapped his hands on his knees and then stood up and removed his jacket. "Here," he said, handing it to Shreela, "you can use my jacket to keep warm."

"What about you?"

"I'm wearing a long-sleeved shirt. I'll be fine."

Shreela took his jacket and draped it around her shoulders. "Thank you."

"We should all turn in now," said Ew. "I'll take the first watch."

While they prepared for sleep, Ew approached Pala who was standing near the edge of the camp. "When Milan and I were hunting this evening, I could hear something following us, so keep a sharp look out, when it's your turn."

Pala nodded.

"Sleep well."

"Good night, My Liege."

The following day was sunny and a bit chilly with blotches of mist and vapor hanging low over the marsh. Continuing southeast, they could see the terrain steadily falling as they moved deeper into the heart of the marsh. Vegetation became more dense. Patches of deep, sucking mud were camouflaged by pools of stagnant water, making their passage difficult and slow. Swarming insects got into their hair and clothes, and their footing became more treacherous as they struggled through the tussocks and reed beds. There were frequent passages through areas of darkness where the sunlight could not penetrate the treetops. There were no paths to walk along so they had to be cautious of snakes and other unnamed creatures hidden among the reeds. By midday, they were miserable and exhausted, and there was no place to rest. Finally, just when the day seemed endless, they found a clearing and stopped to make camp.

"I'll keep an eye on Soren," Pala said to Shreela. "Why don't you take a short nap?"

"Call me in fifteen minutes and I'll take over," Ew volunteered.

Nearly asleep before their heads hit the ground, no one

noticed or even cared that the ground was damp. Pala sat up, but struggled to keep his eyes open until he, too, drifted off to sleep.

Soren did not feel the need to sleep since he had not walked. He climbed out of his sack and explored the clearing while the others slept. An hour or so passed when Soren abruptly awakened Pala.

"What's wrong?" he asked, in a groggy voice.

"I'm scared. Somethin's out there."

Pala sat up and looked around. There was a low growl. He stood up and pulled out his laser. Suddenly, a large four-legged creature rushed in from the right. Pala fired two times.

The rest of the camp was awakened by a loud screech. Noticing the burned body of the female ergret near the place where Milan had been sleeping, Ew quickly jumped to his feet, drew his laser, and shot in the direction of a second ergret, which ran into the bushes beyond their camp. Milan stood with a startled expression on his face. "What, where!.." he began.

"We have a real problem," said Ew, scoping out the area.

"Soren woke me, and just in time, I might add," said Pala.

"What happened?" Ew asked Soren.

"I was standing over there, when I heard a funny sound," he said, pointing towards the place where Ew fired at the second Ergret. Ew massaged his forehead and eyes. "Alright," he said, at length. "We cannot be as careless as we were today."

Milan looked over at the ergret lying dead next to where he had slept. "I'll watch over the camp," he volunteered.

"No," said Ew. "We should have a bite to eat and then move on." Ew walked over to Pala. "Since ergrets travel in pairs, we better keep an eye and ear out for the ergret that got away."

The journey during the late afternoon was slow moving as they continued to be hampered by knotted vines and slimy pools of water. Milan carried Soren followed by Pala and Shreela, with Ew acting as rearguard. The sounds of the swamp closed in on them, seemingly even more ominous than before. It was dusk when they stopped and camped. A fine mist formed over the bogs, but they were still able to see the stars in places where treetops were not mangled together.

Pala walked over to where Ew was standing. "What about a fire?" he asked. "We're running low on bashi sticks. Not only that, this whole area is soaking wet."

"How low is your laser cell?" asked Ew.

"More than half gone. That little incident at the Thesbian Spaceport took a lot of energy. What about you?"

"A little more than half full." Ew visually surveyed their surroundings. "We can use the laser to ignite dry dead tree branches," said Ew looking around -- "that's if we can find any," he added. "Milan, Shreela, listen up," he abruptly called out. "We should conserve our laser cells for any surprises up ahead," he explained. "The same goes for the bashi sticks."

"Wait a minute," Milan objected, "what about some light not to mention heat?"

"There's a full moon rising. We'll have light. As for heat, well..."

"What about the ergret?" asked Shreela.

"What about it?"

"Milan said there's another ergret tracking us." Ew shot an angry glance at Milan. "Another secret?" she asked.

"Pala, take Soren and settle him in for the night. Milan, go with them," Ew said annoyed. Ew turned back to Shreela. "Is that alright with you?" he asked sarcastically.

Shreela raised her brow. "That's fine."

Ew looked around to find a more private place to talk. "Follow me." He grabbed her hand and walked several trans away from where the others were. Shreela leaned against the bow of a tree and crossed her arms. Ew noticed how tired she looked. "How are you holding up?" he asked.

"I'm okay," she said, staring out into the muggy and dank swamp. She suddenly shuddered at the sound of creeping, crawling things hidden in the dense undergrowth. "This is a real learning experience in survival, though. Have you done this before?"

"Not in the marshlands. I'm also learning a lot from this experience."

"Since we are both learning, why would you keep silent about that second ergret?"

Ew closed his eyes and took a deep breath. "I didn't want to alarm you?" he said, in a low voice.

"Aren't you worried about what could happen if we are attacked by this animal, or any other animal?"

"Of course I am! What do you think?"

"I think that if this creature attacked us again, I'd be the only one not prepared for it."

Ew stared at her. Despite the tiredness in her eyes, he sensed her strength of determination. "I just wanted to protect you and Soren, and…"

"..and we can use your protection, E.G.," Shreela interrupted, "but part of protecting us is informing me what I'm up against."

Ew moved closer to her, resting his forearm against the tree, just above her head. He nodded his head. "Alright, Mrs. Bakra," he began, "the ergret is the fiercest animal in the Galan marsh. That ergret out there is stalking us, and will most likely attack one of us before we reach Landory. On top of that, we have only a few bashi sticks left, maybe one full cell of laser firepower, a limited food supply, and nearly nineteen days ahead of us. I hope this paints a better picture for you," he said sardonically.

"And you neglected to tell me this?" Shreela shot back.

"What's wrong with you?" Ew asked, taking a step backwards.

"What's wrong with me?" Shreela laughed sarcastically. "E.G, I'm a grown-up person. Believe it or not, I can take information and process it as well as you do. I can also take information and make decisions for myself."

"An error in judgment out here could cost you your life," he argued.

"But it will be my error!" Ew did not respond, but Shreela could see the exasperated look on his face. "E.G., there is power in information," she continued, "and you have all the information."

"What is it? Do you think I'm trying to control you?"

"Of course not. That's why you agreed to let me board the *Achates*, right?"

Ew's mouth fell open. His mind suddenly flashed back to the squabble they had in the conference room on board the warship *Solaitra.* Shreela had forced him to ponder his words with his deeds. He had made decisions for her without her consent, and he hadn't even told her that he was King, a position that would have given greater credibility to his decision making. To her, he was just a man deciding how she would proceed with her life. His eyes and tone softened. "That's not fair," he said quietly. "You really know how to cut deep -- especially when you're right," he added.

Ew felt his heart skip when he leaned with his forearm against the tree, and moved much closer to Shreela than before. A tingling sensation rippled through him as he lowered his head, moving his face close to hers. "I care about what happens to you," he said gently. Suddenly, his lips touched hers, featherlike at first, and then with urgency. For a brief moment, she did not resist his advance, but then she, seemingly reluctantly, pushed him away. An awkward moment of silence passed between them. Ew stared at her.

"We should get back to the camp," said Shreela. "Tomorrow will be another long day," she added, and walked back towards the campsite.

Ew stood there, his eyes following her until she was out of sight. "Yes, another long day," he murmured with a sigh.

Ew and his companions sat in a small circle under the moonlight. They chatted as they ate their food discs and tried to feel more positive about how far they had come.

"We walked at least thirty kilo-trans today," said Ew. "I'm pleased with our progress, and I believe we've come through the worst part. After tomorrow, the ground should begin to rise slowly, taking us away from the marsh."

"Do you think we can make the entire journey in three weeks?" Milan asked.

"Well, if the weather holds out, we might make it in another fifteen days, provided we travel at least twenty kilo-trans a day." A low rumbling sound suddenly interrupted Ew. "What's that?"

"Sounds like the engine of a spacecraft," said Pala, as the sound moved closer.

Ew jumped to his feet when he recognized the fluorescent band of red and green around a large spacecraft. "It's the Galan Searchcraft," he shouted excitedly. Ew discharged his laser two or three times, but by that time, the craft had already veered off to the southeast, away from the stranded travelers.

"They never even saw us," shouted Milan, greatly disappointed.

"They'll not pass this way again, at least not tonight, Ew," Pala commented.

"No they won't, but we have to hope their search will continue for a few more days. We just might get lucky."

Although they knew the spacecraft would not return, it was a sleepless night as they unconsciously kept their ears tuned for the sound of engines.

The third and fourth days of the journey were definitely better than the first two. Vegetation was still very dense, but the land rose slowly, away from the bogs. There were intermittent long stretches of dry ground, which enabled them to travel further, averaging between twenty-four to twenty-eight kilo-trans per day. Every now and then, Ew heard the stalking sounds of the second ergret. By the sixth day, he was certain more than one creature was stalking them. During several night watches, he cautiously slipped outside the camp to see if he could catch whoever or whatever was following them. Unfortunately, he was never able to see or determine by sound its exact location.

The weather held up with only occasional brief showers. Soaked by the rain, and dried by the sun, they continued to move southeast towards the city of Landory. After several days, the group was weary and spirits were low. The feeling that the marsh was endless hovered over them like a dark cloud. Ew tried to reassure them along the way, but as the days passed, he, like the others, fell silent and plodded along with his head bowed.

On the eve of the tenth day, it began to rain heavily. They left the reed beds and pools of stagnant water behind several days before, but the land was still very dense with vegetation, and vines became hidden traps lying in wait for them. Unable to take another step, they stopped as if called by some natural force of self-preservation. It didn't matter where they camped now since the ground was saturated. It was impossible to make a fire or hunt for game, so they sat in a huddle and quietly chewed their food discs. Shreela wondered if they would ever live to see the end of the marsh. Hope of rescue was clearly out of her thoughts since the Galan Searchcraft never returned.

Milan took the first watch while the rest of the weary band lie down on the wet ground. No one slept soundly but rather drifted in and out of sleep. It was about three hours past midnight when Milan awakened Ew. "Ew, wake up. It's your turn to watch."

"Alright, my friend, I can take over now. Try and get some rest, if you can."

It was close to the hour of dawn before the rain finally subsided. Ew sat in the dark feeling wet, cold, miserable, and tired. The moonlight could not penetrate the dense overcast sky, making it impossible to see the area around the camp. After a while, the darkness weighed heavily upon him. His eyes drooped and he shook his head vigorously to stay awake, but, despite his efforts, it was not long before he finally drifted off to sleep. A few moments later, he was jolted awake by a crackling sound in the bushes off to his left. Jumping to his feet, Ew leveled his laser in the direction of those sounds. A sense of uneasiness gripped him as he realized just how vulnerable they were. Cautiously moving towards the sound and trying to look in all directions at once, he listened for sounds of approaching animals. For one brief moment, he thought he heard a low growl and strained to determine its direction. He opened his mouth to call out to Pala, but instead, a muffled, guttural sound was all that escaped him as razor-sharp claws dug into his left shoulder. As he fought to free himself of the claws, knife-like teeth punctured his left arm causing him to drop his laser. With his free hand, Ew grabbed the ergret by the snout, wrenching its teeth from his forearm. Still struggling to get free of the excruciating claws, he felt something brush against his right side. He grit his teeth and dug his heels into the ground to maintain his balance, but almost immediately, his body gave way under the impact of a second egret attacking from behind. "Pala, Pala," he yelled, finally finding his voice. The weight and fierceness of the ergrets' attack drove him to his knees.

Several flashes of light sliced through the darkness followed by a shrill cry from one of the ergrets. Awakened by the commotion, Pala began to discharge his laser into the air in order to get a fix on what was happening. Snatching up and lighting a bashi stick, he saw the body of a dead ergret beside Ew, nearly four trans away, but his attention was quickly sidetracked by the rustling of nearby bushes. The frame of a tall figure shown in the dim light for a moment, but then disappeared into the shadow of the swamp.

Pala rushed towards Ew, pulling the dead ergret away from his prostrate body. Extensive lacerations were clearly visible on his shoulder and chest. There were teeth marks on his left wrist, and deep gashes on his forearm.. "Ew," Pala called out anxiously, gently shaking his friend. Concern and fear stabbed his heart at the weak sound of his friend's voice when he finally spoke.

Ew croaked shakily, "Pala, whatever happens to me, get me home." Without warning, his entire body shuddered violently, traumatized by the attack. Clenching the fist of his uninjured arm, he struggled to keep his eyes open. "My m-m-other knows what to do," he said, choking out his words. Unable to hold on, his body became limp as he passed into unconsciousness.

The End of an Era

Mara met with General Laggé of the Inter-Solar System

Force, as planned. By this time, her son and his companions were already on the first step of their journey to Landory.

Have the searchcraft gone out?" she asked.

"Yes, Your Highness," General Laggé responded.

"Good! They are to scour every sector of the marsh until they locate that jettison pod, and search for anyone traveling on foot. Now," she said changing the subject, "what are your recommendations for the defense of the Khalian Solar System?"

"Your Highness," Laggé began, "since we no longer control the Lluellyn and Shargant Space Stations, we have moved the I-SS Force to the surface of Tarpellis. That entire planet is on notice of evacuation."

"But Unian military forces are still firing on I-SS Forces. The UMF no longer has a need to return to Uni for refueling; they can do so on OUR space stations!" she said, sourly. "Laggé, we badly need to alter that situation. I understand that ten percent of the I-SS Force has already been destroyed."

"The main problem is there are not enough power-cell tankers to handle refueling in space," Laggé explained. "Another complication is the vulnerability of those tankers to attack by the UMF. We have to keep moving them out of range to keep them from getting blown out of the sky. The I-SS Force has no choice but to land on the planet surface in order to refuel."

"What have you learned from our Allied Defense Forces on Petron? Have they been put on alert, and is there any word from our galactic forces?"

"There has been no word from the Galactic Fleet or Admiral Garbonst, Madam. The UMF collapsed our laser shields when they cracked our program security, and bypassed our encrypted shield codes with their own. Until we are able to find their command code which bypasses our program instructions, we will not be able to overlay our own shield encryptions. At this point we are trapped. Any messages sent by the Galactic Fleet or our allies will not reach us."

Mara sighed at the news. *If ever we needed the Keepers of Khali, it's now,* she thought. "Well Laggé, it looks like we're on our own, for now, anyway. Continue working on the shield program. For lack of a better plan, we'll fight on until we can't fight any more."

"Yes, Your Highness."

"In the meantime, let's hope Admiral Garbonst can break through on his side."

Far above the planetary shields of Khali, Admiral Garbonst stood in the Officer's Conference Room aboard the Flagship *Rotondra.* "Come in, General Garren," he called out to a summons at the door."

General Garren entered the conference room. His dark brown eyes appeared weary, but he stiffened to the appropriate military posture within the presence of a superior officer."

"Relax, General, and have a seat," said the other. Garbonst watched Garren as he strode to the triangular conference table and seated himself. "What is your report on the Galactic Fleet, General?"

"We have been able to re-map the communication codes to all Fleet spacecraft, Admiral. The Fleet went back into LT speed and should join us here around Crashellon's orbit within the next hour."

"Were they able to avoid Unian sentry scanners before they went into LT?"

"Just barely. Lt. Commander Sesna delayed them for nearly an hour."

"Very good, General." Garbonst paced the side of the room

several times, the sound of his footsteps invading the silence. Finally, "General, I called this meeting to tell you about a high-risk defense protocol which is about to be taken against the Unian forces. As you know, the UMF has raised the planetary shield so we cannot communicate with Galan, nor can we go in and assist the Inter-Solar System Force." Garbonst was careful to emphasize the graveness of their situation.

"Yes," Garren nodded in agreement.

"Uzak believes the IGF is still heading for Chimoor," Garbonst continued, "and more's the better, since he has dared to move his forces closer to the Khalian System, preparing to destroy our ground defenses. Most of his big ships are inside the shield, leaving only a few Unian battle cruisers to protect the Shargant and Lluellyn space stations. Our galactic forces will move in and destroy both the space stations."

Garren's military calm fled and he stared at Garbonst with shock disbelief. "Why destroy our space stations?"

"Uzak will not expect us to reclaim those space stations, and why should he? The galactic fleet is removed, for now, and he believes that by the time they return, the battle will be over."

"I don't know, Admiral," said Garren, "that decoy was cleverly done. The actual Galactic comm code was not changed. Someone put in a command code string to decoy the Fleet while it was still inside the Unian disrupter field. Once they passed the area of disruption, the command code string collapsed. That's how Kryto was able to contact them."

"But Uzak doesn't know that the Fleet was turned back hours ago by His Majesty."

Garren thought for a moment. "Uzak expects the Fleet to come back after they reach Chimoor and realize it was a set up, is what you're saying? He doesn't know the IGF is already on its way back?"

"Precisely. He thinks he still has time to win the battle inside the shield."

"And what about the Balarai Space Station? It's only partially operational."

The UMF knows the Balarai has had problems. Their saboteurs, after all, were responsible for destroying the tractor beam transfer coils, communications tracking-base conduits, and the shield. Now there are six Unian battle cruisers guarding the station. What they don't know is that the Balarai station is battle worthy. Systems were shut down, and the crew returned to the planet surface immediately after we learned that Unian battle cruisers were headed there."

"Once we destroy the Shargant and Lluellyn stations, some of those cruisers may be drawn away from the Balarai station," Garren commented.

"Perhaps, but we will not give them that opportunity," Garbonst stated firmly.

"What do you have in mind, Admiral?"

"First of all, this strike has to be quick, since the security codes have been changed back to the original schematic. We have found their command code that bypassed our own program and implemented their schematic for the shield. We will be using the original shield code encryption. The same one we have been using for months."

"I thought the old schematic was no longer secure. Isn't that why His Majesty had the backup implemented yesterday?"

"Not true. His Majesty's personal code scheme was breached, but the I-SS and the IGF were still secure. He was, however, concerned that the Unian Intelligence code hackers might be close to breaking down I-SS and IGF codes, which brings up an interesting point. The backup codes had to be given to Unian Intelligence by someone pretending to be on our side."

"A Unian spy in the upper Khalian ranks."

"Exactly, and for that reason, Lt. Commander Sesna, you, and I are the only ones who know the IGF codes have been changed back."

"What about the return Fleet?"

"Lt. Commander Sesna has already taken care of that before they made the jump to LT."

"Which accounts for the hour delay," Garren concluded.

"Sesna has mapped the LT fallout vectors such that sixty Khalian warships will descend from LT close to the space stations. They will destroy those space stations while the bulk of the Fleet positions itself to move in and assist the Inter-Solar System Forces in driving the UMF out of the System."

"So the Fleet which is returning will not be coming to Crashellon."

"That is correct, General. Our galactic team here will move in and target Unian battle cruisers orbiting Balarai."

While Garren pondered the strategy, Garbonst touched the panel on the audio pad in front of him. "Commander Sesna."

A feminine voice came over the speaker. "Sesna here."

"What is the ETA for the return Fleet?"

"Five point four-three minutes to fall out, Sir."

"Go to Alert-One status, and set course heading two-two-one."

"Settings are locked in, Sir."

Garbonst switched off the audio panel and then looked at Garren. "Alright General, let's go."

Garbonst sat facing the visual monitor in his office quarters offside the *Rotondra* main bridge area. He watched as the Khalian IGF unleashed its violent attack against the UMF. Without taking his eyes off the screen, he moved his hand along the monitor panel. "Commander Sesna," he called, "how long before we make contact with Her Highness?"

"Any moment, Admiral..., we're on-link with her direct channel now, Sir."

Suddenly Mara's face appeared on the screen. "Your Highness," Garbonst greeted her.

"Admiral, a welcomed sight indeed," Mara responded.

"It is with regret, Madam, that I had to make a unilateral decision to destroy the Lluellyn and Shargant space stations."

"Many more would have died had you not made that decision, Admiral. As it now stands, nearly seventy-five percent of the I-SS Force is crippled or destroyed. You're arrival brings new hope."

"Thank you, Your Highness," Garbonst said relieved. "Might I assume His Majesty has not been in contact with you?"

"He has not."

Garbonst observed the subtle tightening of her jaw. "Ground communications are poor, at best, Madam. His Majesty may be trying to break through, even as we speak."

"I'm hopeful we'll hear from him soon. Thank you, Admiral."

"I'll be contacting you personally every hour to update you on the battle, and any alterations to strategy," Garbonst changed the subject.

"Then I will expect to hear from you shortly."

Garbonst bowed his head. "Your Highness," he said, and then closed communications.

The battle was well into the second day before the Unian Flagship retreated from the Khalian Solar System back to Uni, leaving behind debris from more than seven-hundred Unian battle cruisers destroyed by the forces of Khali. Several hundred badly crippled battle cruisers crept away from the solar system or were towed by other retreating Unian battle cruisers. Nearly two-thousand smaller Unian spacecraft were destroyed while many others also withdrew.

"Yes, Your Highness," Admiral Garbonst's voice came over the communications channel. "The Unian Military Force has moved out of this part of the galaxy."

"What are the estimates on damages?"

"We estimate not more than three-hundred warships, or one tenth of our Galactic Fleet is destroyed, Your Highness. Unfortunately, the I-SS Force is all but destroyed."

"How soon can we prepare for a second assault?"

Within a day or two, Your Highness, and that's if we call in the Allied Defense Force, to compensate for the loss of I-SS Forces."

"Yes, they are on notice, Garbonst," Mara commented. "Now, what is the status of the Unian Military Force?"

"The UMF was pretty battered when we escorted them out," Garbonst explained. "It will be several days before they can regroup. Many of their allies joined the battle. We were able to completely wipe out the military defenses from Gundarlin."

"Well done, Garbonst. I expect you to return for a complete debriefing."

"Thank you, Your Highness. I'm on my way."

As the defeated Unian Flagship directed its course back to Uni, Uzak sat in his quarters quietly contemplating his brief but decisive engagement with the military forces of Khali.

"I must stop Galan from returning home," he said aloud.

Jenka Danne, his long time right-hand man and co-conspirator, looked up at him. "You still believe Ewlon survived the destruction of the *Achates*, don't you, My Lord?" she asked.

Uzak stared intently into the cold, steel-gray eyes of his

accomplice, and nodded his head. "Our sources inside Galan report that Ewlon was seen getting into an escape pod."

"Many pods were destroyed, My Lord."

"Several were not, and I will not speculate, given his past record on survival. We must assume Ewlon Galan is still alive. If he is, he will definitely head for his home in Star City."

"Could he already be there or could he have engineered this battle during the last two days?" she asked.

"No. Our man inside informs me that no word has been received from Ewlon since the *Achates* was destroyed.

Jenka watched as Uzak lightly tapped his finger upon his desktop. Finally, "there is something else that bothers you," she stated rather than asked. There was no response. "Well?" she insisted.

"Yes, yes," Uzak said slightly annoyed. He studied her face, thinking on how much she resembled her father. Her coal black hair was pulled back, revealing an oval face with a straight, medium nose, -- and those eyes. She was the illegitimate daughter of Wedolan Galan, banished from Khali by her half-brother, Prince Ewlon, nearly thirty years earlier. "Jenka, why not visit her Highness, Mara Galan, and express your concerns about her family and the war?" Uzak asked, at length.

"But I can't get into the House of Galan."

"Why not?"

"Ewlon's watchdog, Pala Bhusan. Clearance goes through him now instead of Admiral Atalif."

A sinister laugh escaped Uzak's lips. "Atalif blew up with the Galan Space Warship, and Bhusan is with Ewlon, who is NOT home. Now, would Mara Galan still welcome an old friend and employee?"

Jenka thought for a moment. "Hum-m. If Ewlon kept his promise, Mara Galan does not know of my relationship to her late husband. She just might welcome me as an ex-child care employee. That secret in exchange for my life. Those were the conditions set down by Ewlon. You know, you were there."

"Then you should be welcomed as an old friend."

"Maybe, but I don't care to see...."

"But you do care," said Uzak, with an ominous tone.

"What do you mean?"

"Jenka, the new weapon is still being tested on Dagmar. It will be ready for the field in two to three months, but I cannot wait that long," he explained, clearly agitated.

"Why, My Lord?" Jenka asked cautiously.

Uzak clenched his jaw and inhaled deeply, making a horrible hissing sound as the air passed between his teeth. "Because the medallion is now in the hands of Ewlon." Uzak watched Jenka's mouth drop open and the startled look on her face. "You understand now, I see," said Uzak. "Ewlon cannot reach home. Remember the prophecy, Jenka. 'The king would be traveling with a young widow and her son.'"

"Then why are you concerned with Mara Galan?"

"Because she is at the helm right now. If I can get rid of her, the command will fall to Megan Galan."

"The same military advisors will be at her disposal. What would be different?"

"My dear Jenka," Uzak spoke condescendingly, "Megan has no command experience. Remember that the strong arm of Ewlon Galan rules all military advisors and Regional Governors. Before, it was Mara Galan. Many of those advisors and governors have their own agenda, especially the Regional Governors. Their only concern is those pathetic little regions they govern."

"Without a strong ruler, there will be chaos among the politicians," Jenka concluded.

"Exactly. After Mara dies, and she will die, that solar system will be in such chaos that anyone with just a little strategy should be able to move in and take over."

"Alright, what do you propose?"

"It appears that Ewlon and Bhusan are not in contact with the Galan household."

"Mara knows you, so I assume you have a ploy."

"I will become your uncle, the Latonian merchant, my dear."

"Uncle Kazu," Jenka smiled. "I'll make the arrangements right away."

Uzak watched as Jenka stood up and paced across the room. She stopped suddenly. "By the way, how do you propose to get rid of Mara?"

Again Uzak let out a menacing laugh. "Just watch me."

While Jenka Danne and Uzak planned their strategy to enter Galan, top ranking military staff on Galan prepared for a counteroffensive against the forces of Uni. It was the evening of the sixth day following the retreat of Unian forces from Khali, and Mara sat alone in her quarters studying several proposals on possible military strategies. It was one hour before midnight in Star City, but for Mara, it would be another sleepless night.

Several unexpected problems experienced by the Balarai Space Station's spacecraft tracking system weighed heavily on her mind. The IGF had to be put on alert to scrutinize all spacecraft before allowing entry into the Khalian Solar System, but some smaller spacecraft were able to enter undetected. Visual monitoring from the surface of Galan was difficult because of the heavy ground fog and a thick cloud cover. The torrential rains that had been falling for the last few days had made it all the more difficult. Still, Mara hoped ground control could hold fast in identifying those smaller vessels that slipped through undetected. These were just some of the problems, which made her restless and irritable.

After a while, the constant pounding of the rain further distracted Mara as she tried to study the proposals before her. Finally giving way to the distraction, she walked over to the window and peered out. The veil of night left little to see, but the sound of falling rain induced an almost hypnotic trance, stirring up memories, both old and new. Mara thought of Wedolan and how proud he was when The Planet Star was first activated. There was a feeling of security throughout the solar system unlike any in the galaxy. People would come from everywhere to enjoy the hospitality of Galan, for it became known as the garden of peace. Mara basked in those memories for a moment, but they faded as she turned to face the interior. The crackling timber and shadowy flames that danced upon the walls drew her attention to the hearth. In Mara's mind, the flames seemed to change shape and size, becoming transformed to the figure of a coffin being lowered at her feet. The crackling timbers were whispers in the night, growing louder as the storm intensified. Mara Galan, alone, rode the storm against the forces of Uni. For sixteen years, she fought back the tide until she no longer had the strength to do so. She felt depressed, old, and tired.

"Such matters should be left to the young and strong for it is now their world which they must nurture and shape for their offspring," she whispered to herself.

The chiming of the antique clock interrupted Mara's reverie. It was one hour past midnight. The old clock was a sixtieth birthday present from Ew, and Mara gazed at it with fondness. Recalling the searchcraft's return five days ago, she felt great sorrow to learn the jettison pod, which landed in the southwest marsh, could not be found, nor any travelers on foot. How she had hoped that Ew would be there.

"Perhaps he is alive," she said aloud. "Still, few have ever come through the marsh and lived to tell about it," she reminded herself. Again there was an intrusion on her thoughts, but this time it was a voice over the telecom.

"Your Highness," called General Laggé. "There is a Jenka Danne here requesting audience with you."

"Jenka Danne?" Mara asked surprised. "I haven't seen her in almost thirty years. Show her in at once."

"She brought a friend..."

"Show them both in," Mara interrupted.

Within minutes the door to Mara's quarters opened, revealing her old employee, Jenka Danne. Mara smiled fondly at her, remembering how close they were in her earlier years as Queen. "Jen Danne, it's so wonderful to see you after so many years. What brings you here?"

"Your Highness, this is my Uncle Kazu from Laton."

A tall figure stepped forward, bowing low in offering of respect to the throne. His black eyes appeared cold and threatening and there was something troubling about his posture. Mara had a peculiar feeling that this was not her first meeting with him.

"Come Jen," she said, "let me ring for refreshments and then we can talk."

After Mara ordered refreshments to be sent to her quarters, she took a few moments to study her old friend, now seated directly across from her. *She has grayed very little and her face seems not to have aged at all*, she marveled.

"How do you manage to keep your youthful face, Jenka?"

"Thank you, Your Highness. It's a family trait, so I'm told."

"We should all be so fortunate. I'll pour Oshe," Mara spoke to her personal servant who arrived with the refreshments.

"What can I do for you, Jenka?"

"Your Highness," Jenka began, "it has come to my attention that The Planet Star is no longer in the hands of Uzak, Lord of Uni. My uncle saw it no more than a month ago in the hands of another trader when he displayed his wares on Thesbis."

Mara nearly wasted the vessel of kari as she heard the words that were the salvation of her home.

"Who and where is that merchant?"

"Milan Mariko," said Uzak in a hoarse tone to disguise his voice.

Mara's expression turned to sadness as she thought of her son. She did not respond immediately but rather paused briefly to gain control of her emotions before speaking.

"Milan Mariko was with Ewlon and at least two others, when the Unian Military Force attacked the *Fidus Achates*, several days ago," Mara explained. "We fear that all are dead."

Uzak feigned a surprised look. "We were not aware of that, Your Highness. You have our sympathies, Madam."

"Thank you. For a while," Mara continued, "we hoped to find them the jettison pod which landed in the Galan marsh. Unfortunately, our searchcraft reported they could find no sign of the pod or survivors on foot when they searched the area. The search lasted five days and if you are not found in that region quickly, it is not likely you ever will be."

So I was right all along, thought Uzak. *She does not have The Planet Star and I do not agree with her about Ewlon. If he was in that jettison pod, then it is doubtful that he is dead, which means the widow and her son are with him as well*, he surmised silently. *This is a clever old woman and right now, she's the only one standing in my way. If I rid myself of her before Ewlon returns, assuming that he survived the destruction of the Fidus Achates, I can take control of Star City and Galan. Then it will be impossible for Ewlon to return The Planet Star to its original setting. For now though, I'll take my chances with Megan.*

"We're sorry to have taken up so much of your time, your Highness," said Jenka. "We hoped this might be good news for you. Now we regret our candor since it reminds you of your grief," she feigned an apology.

"I do have something that belongs to your son," said Uzak. "When he was last on Laton, he inadvertently left this behind. I believe it was to be a gift to you." Uzak pulled out a small ring made from the soft-shiny purple ore, *sechan*. The figure etched into the metal was that of Solan, Keeper of Life.

As he handed it to her, Uzak was careful to touch only the outer surface of the ring, since he had already laced the inside with a lethal dose of the sleeping drug, *janus. It should take less than an hour for the drug to be fully absorbed through her skin,* he thought. He watched as Mara studied the artisanship of the ring. "You no doubt recognize this as one of the Tulusian Empress' rings," Uzak commented. "I picked it up at an auction in Milagra on Echlindra several years ago. "Your son said you had a collection of antiques from that region."

"Not from Milagra directly," said Mara, taking the ring, "but I do own several antiques from other regions on Echlindra." Mara continued to study the design.

I must get her to wear that, thought Uzak. "Why don't you try it on, Your Highness," he suggested.

"It look's so tiny."

"Try it on your smallest finger. If it doesn't fit, I can have it enlarged," Uzak lied.

Mara slid the ring on her smallest finger. It fit like a glove.

"Wear it in good health," said Jenka, "and think of your son."

"Well at least it has brought together two old friends, and for that, I am thankful," said Mara.

"To old friends," said Uzak, *or old enemies*, he thought, while draining his vessel.

"Jen, don't be a stranger to this house. I must return to my study now, but I do hope you will come back soon." Mara finished her drink and then excused herself.

"Thank you, Your Highness. We can find our way out," said Jenka. What now?" she whispered to Uzak.

"That jettison pod which landed in the swamp concerns me. If Ewlon survived the UMF attack, and I think it possible, he will definitely head for Landory since it's the closest city to the marsh border. Let's go and prepare for his arrival to that city."

A Widow's Hand

While Jenka Danne and Uzak of Uni prepared to leave Galan Manor, deep within the southeastern marsh, Pala and his friends coped with the brutal assault on Ew by the ergret. Milan helped Pala move Ew's body back to the shelter where they had been sleeping. Because of the wet ground, Shreela laid Ew's head in her lap, draping his jacket over him to keep him as warm as possible. "We need a fire, Pala," she pleaded.

"Building a fire will be difficult." Pala surveyed the area. "We need branches or tree limbs that are dry, and everything around here is soaking wet," he said.

Shreela looked up at him. "I can bathe his wounds with hot water and use some of the salve I brought with me. Of course, it's only good for scrapes and burns, not anything this serious," she said looking at Ew's forearm.

"I'll do what I can," Pala commented. "The salve may help him for a while, but it won't solve his problem."

"What do you mean?" Shreela asked curiously.

"Ew has been mauled by one of Galan's most vicious creatures. This particular animal produces a poison through its fangs causing slow paralysis to its victim."

"Well, how long will it take to work its way through his system?"

"It takes four to five days to become completely absorbed."

"Is there a cure?"

"There is, but it's about one-hundred kilo-trans from here, in Landory. We would have reached that in another four days if this hadn't happened. We'll be fortunate if we can get there in six days." The light of dawn shown on Pala's face, reflecting the sadness in his eyes as he spoke. "In any event," he went on, "we can't leave here today."

"Look at me," said Shreela, gently drawing Pala's attention to her. "He needs us. We can't give up on him yet. We should at least try to get him to Landory before his time runs out."

"I'm not giving up, but we should at least prepare ourselves for the worst."

"What's that?"

"He could die." Almost immediately Pala felt remorse for his candor as he looked at Shreela's face. He had reminded her of her own loss. "I'll get some water. Try not to worry. We'll make it somehow," he tried to assure her as well as convince himself.

The ground was still very damp, sending a penetrating chill through Shreela's body. She tried to move Ew's arm, and as she did so, a low, nearly inaudible groan escaped his lips. She reached into her bag to retrieve a small round container of salve to spread across the wound on Ew's forearm. By this time, Pala returned empty handed, but she could see that he was excited about something. "What is it?"

"Come quickly. There's a small cave not far from here. Milan help me carry E.G. Shreela; carry as much as you can. I'll return later to gather whatever you leave behind." Having said that, Pala walked towards Ew and began to pick him up. "Milan, give me a hand, will you," he shouted.

The cave Pala spoke of was really a hollow under a hill, large enough to hold at most two people.

"What is all this?" said Shreela pointing towards the supplies inside the cave.

"I think that someone else may be staying here, most probably a woodsman or trapper," Pala said excitedly. "Look, there are two blankets and some kindling. There's also a fully charged laser gun."

"Wait a minute," said Shreela, as Milan and Pala carried Ew towards the hollow. Quickly, she moved everything outside the cave and spread one of the blankets over the cave floor.

Pala and Milan gently lowered their friend to the ground. "I'll start a fire now, Mrs. Bakra," Pala said, with half a smile. "Milan, get some water. I'll ignite this dried wood with my laser so we can hold on to that last bashi stick."

Ew began to regain consciousness. He was burning with fever and he groaned when Shreela turned his body to lie on his right side.

"This is not going to work," she said. "Even with the blanket under him, the ground is still too cold and damp. Pala, help me to put him on my lap."

Pala raised Ew into a sitting position until Shreela could get inside the cave. He then lowered Ew's head onto Shreela's lap and spread the second blanket on top of him. Again Shreela tried to examine his wounds. She could see that the blood, now dry, stuck to his shirt. She waited patiently until Milan returned with the water.

Ten to fifteen minutes passed before Milan returned with the flausins and sat them down on the ground. "How's Ew?" he quietly asked Pala.

"Not good. The widow is right. We must get him to Landory

as quickly as possible. Why don't you boil the water while I gather some timber to make a litter? We should at least try to leave here no later than dawn tomorrow."

Later that morning, Pala and Milan sat silently staring into the marshlands. Pala recounted to himself what seemed like an endless journey through this cold and wet marsh. Finally, he spoke up about the strange event just before dawn.

"Did you see anything when the ergret was killed?" he asked.

"No. I didn't even see you kill it," Milan responded, curious about the question.

"I didn't kill it, and that's where the puzzle is. Ew's laser was nearly ten trans from where he fell. He could not have killed the ergret, but someone did."

Unconsciously they both began to look about the area. Pala thought about the supplies they found and wondered if they were deliberately left in the hollow where Ew now rested. A loud sigh escaped as he began to feel the endlessness of their journey through the swamp, and the hopelessness of getting Ew to the medical attention he so desperately needed.

While Shreela bathed Ew's wounds, nearly twenty-five hundred kilo-trans northeast, in Star City, Mara Gala began to nod off to sleep while reading Admiral Garbonst's proposal. She yawned several times as the slow acting drug began to take affect. Unable to keep her eyes open, she decided to go to bed. Megan entered her mother's quarters as Mara walked towards her bedroom. "I think I'll rest for a few hours, dear," she said. "Have me paged one hour past dawn?"

"Of course. Mother, I need to talk to you."

"Yes dear?"

Megan noticed how exhausted her mother looked. "It can wait until morning," she said, changing her mind. "Good night,

Mother."

"Good night."

Mara fell into a deep sleep as soon as her head touched the pillow. Memories of Wedolan, Yavik, Yashil, the Keepers of Khali and many others, filled her dreams. Finally, she experienced the sensation of flying over the many cities of Galan, warmed by the beauty of her homeland. Passing over the marsh and heading towards a steady stream of light, Mara saw her son, Ewlon, as he lay maimed on the ground below. She was aware of his pain as she moved forward to hover near the place where he lay. She recognized the young widow of Tima, now caring for her son. Moving closer, she allowed her spirit to touch his forehead while she whispered into his ear.

"You will be alright, my son. I know now that you will live a full and happy life."

"Mo-o-ther, mo..uh..," cried Ew. His voice sounded weak and far away.

"Sh-h-h, my child. Rest now," Mara comforted him, and then she was gone.

Dawn passed to mid-morning before Ew quieted down enough for Shreela to clean the rest of his wounds. While he slept, she wet his shirt with the warm water before trying to remove it. As she slowly peeled the garment from his skin, what she saw beneath it alarmed her. The wounds had become purulent, and his entire left side felt cold and lifeless. While gently bathing the wounded areas of his forearm, Shreela noticed Ew watching her.

"Good morning," she said, smiling brightly.

"What happened?"

"While you were guarding the camp this morning, you were attacked by the ergret that had been stalking us."

"Where am I? I can't move my arm. Pala, I need to talk to Pala."

"Sh-h-h-h," Shreela quieted him. "You are in a small cave," she began, but before she could finish, Ew fell back to sleep.

Ew spent most of the day drifting in and out of sleep. His friends became anxious about him as he moaned throughout the night. There seemed little that anyone could do to make him comfortable.

The following day was sunny and dry. The extra day of rest made them feel that thirty kilo-trans was not an unreasonable distance. Pala and Milan placed Ew on the litter while Shreela picked up those supplies necessary for their journey. Dragging the litter behind him, Pala led the way followed by Shreela and Milan, who carried Soren on his shoulder at the rear.

The journey began at a good pace, but after a time, the litter became burdensome. Thick vines caused most of the problems, becoming entangled around the legs of the litter, slowing their pace considerably. By midday, the group was exhausted, but since time was short, they decided to eat the food discs as they walked. Pala began to worry about the food provisions, which had dwindled to less than a week's supply. *We must get to Landory within a week or we cannot hope to get there at all*, he thought.

Ew woke up occasionally during the day. His body ached, and he felt cold most of the time. He slept most of the day, but when he did wake, it hurt him to see the weariness so plainly molded upon the faces of his friends.

By early evening, they had walked about twelve kilo-trans. Pala and Milan exchanged places and continued on until dark. Shreela frequently stumbled from fatigue, but said nothing. The supplies had been split up among the three of them before they left that morning. Since Shreela could not carry Soren or drag the litter, she carried most of the goods.

The moon sat high in the sky when they stopped to make camp. Ew had grown progressively worse during the day, as the paralysis crept from his left shoulder down to his left foot. There was swelling and pus formation around the wounds on his shoulder and chest. Labored breathing became frequent coughing. The litter was put close to the fire, in an attempt to keep him warm, and Soren watched over him while his mother conferred with Pala and Milan, a short distance away.

"I'm worried about that cough," said Shreela. "I think he has a serious respiratory infection."

"What can we do about it?" asked Pala.

"I'm not a medical person, but I do know that if we don't treat that cough, and soon, he'll die from the respiratory infection rather than the poison from the ergret."

"There has to be something we can do," said Pala. "Milan, you're a scientist, what do you suggest?"

"Well, I do know that there are herbs we might be able to use."

"On my home planet, we have a plant known as papri, used as an antibiotic against bacterial infections," Shreela interrupted, impatiently.

"I know the plant," said Milan. "It's called *meric* on Galan, and it grows in damp places near stagnant water."

"Then it must be everywhere," she said, looking around. "Can you get some for me?"

"Yes. We should be able to find some here. Come on, Pala. We'll go together."

Pala pulled out Ew's laser that had been wedged inside his belt. "Here," he said. "We won't be long."

Shortly before midnight, Pala and Milan returned with a cloth sack filled with the *meric* plant. Pala was also holding a dead four-legged creature with a thin coat of fur, flat snout, and long, rounded, floppy ears.

"What's that?" asked Shreela.

"It's a kernet. This one is not fully grown so the meat should be sweet and tender," Pala explained.

"We can mix the meric into a broth for Ew," said Milan, using Ew's real name.

"That's a good idea," said Shreela.

"I'll get started on it," said Pala.

"I'll help," Shreela volunteered, "but I better warn you that I don't skin animals."

"I'll do that," Pala laughed.

The preparation was slow and tedious. Finally, Shreela poured the broth into one of the two flausins to cool. An hour or so later, she poured some of the broth into a drinking vessel and walked over to where Ew was sleeping.

"Ew, it's time to get up," she whispered to him.

"Shreela," Ew called out, seemingly in a dream state. His voice sounded weak, and it was difficult for him to focus on any particular thing.

Pala helped Shreela raise him into a sitting position. "Come, you must drink this. It'll help your cough." Ew swallowed about half the broth from the vessel and after a while, she could see that he was tiring. "We should try again in an hour," she whispered to Pala. Shreela looked up to see Milan standing over Pala and her.

"Since I have the first watch, why don't you and Pala get some rest," Milan offered. "I'll see to it that Ew drinks the rest of the broth before I wake you, Pala." Milan quietly watched Shreela walk over to her resting place. "Shreela," he called out, "thank you."

The sun was nearing the midday sky when Pala woke the camp on the following day. Concerned that they might have lost valuable time by sleeping in, Shreela rushed about the camp to collect those things to be carried on the day's march.

"Shreela," Pala stopped her, "you don't have to rush. Since I went out earlier to scout the area, I let everyone sleep late."

Shreela walked over to the fire where Pala was reheating the broth prepared the night before. "How is he?"

"Why don't you ask him," a voice replied.

Ew was sitting up with his eyes wide open. He was propped up by the two blankets, which had been folded to support his back. His cough was not as frequent as before and from what Shreela could see, the paralysis did not appear to go beyond his left side.

"You gave us quite a scare last night," Shreela commented.

"I feel a little better today," said Ew.

Shreela noticed a little color returning to his cheeks. She stood there silently studying him. When her gaze moved to his face, she became flustered, aware that he was staring back at her.

Shreela smiled at him. "That broth may have helped your condition."

"Well, my cough is not as bad as it was yesterday, and so far, only my left side has no feeling," he confirmed her suspicion.

Shreela looked at him thoughtfully, recalling the close call they had with him the night before. Then out of nowhere she asked, "Ew, I understand that is your first name, what does G stand for?"

"Galan."

"Come now," she responded with disbelief, "that's the name of this planet. Honestly, what does the G stand for?"

"Does it really matter?" he answered.

Again Shreela was reminded of her earlier deliberation of how unlikely it was that he was a spy. "No, I suppose not," she said with uncertainty, "and I don't believe you're a spy."

"What do you mean?"

"Well, you always seem to be in command. High ranking government official, am I right?"

Ew smiled slightly. "In a manner of speaking."

"Hum-m. I can see that you're not about to share more with me, but before this trip is over, I hope you trust me enough to tell me. I keep wondering what it is about you that's so different."

"I wonder the same about you."

Shreela blushed at his response. "Do you mind if I check on your dressing?" she asked, changing the subject.

"No, not at all."

Shreela sat down next to Ew and began to remove his shirt. Earlier, Ew's shirtsleeve had been torn off and used to wrap his arm. As Shreela slid Ew's shirt over his arm, she noticed that his left arm and shoulder felt cold and lifeless. When Shreela removed the wrapping, she could see that the external wounds were beginning to heal and there was no sign of increased wound infection. "Sure wish I had a tissue regenerator," she commented. "Anyway, the puffiness around your wounds has gone down a little," she remarked, rewrapping his arm.

"Glad to hear it," Ew commented. *It wouldn't matter one way or the other*, he thought. *I can't feel it anyway.*

Pala handed Shreela a vessel of kernet broth. When she tried to feed Ew, he took the cup with his right hand. "I can do that myself," he said annoyed.

Shreela was caught off guard, but quickly masked her feeling of surprise. She simply said "alright" and walked away.

Ew drank the broth in silence while the others shared the kernet meat. As the others conversed, Ew learned they were within twenty-five kilo-trans of Landory. "Then we should be there in about two days," he joined the conversation.

"We should,' Pala responded. "The ground is rising rapidly as we near the end of the marsh."

Shreela laughed joyfully as one seeing the light at the end of a long tunnel. "What a relief. For a while back there, I was afraid we wouldn't make it."

Ew watched her as she smiled, recalling how tired she looked the day before, stumbling under the heavy burden, which she bore in silence. The look on her face and the sound of her voice reminded him of his first meeting with her at the Mt. Halokin Defense Base on Thesbis. He remembered how warm she felt when he kissed her during the earlier part of their journey through the marsh. He realized he was falling in love with her, which added to his anxiety and depression. *I might not get the chance to explore the possibility of a relationship with her,* he thought, staring at his bandaged arm. *Maybe we won't get to Landory on time, and if we do, will I recover fully?* He asked himself. S*till, I must hold on.* "Pala," he called, "since we're so close to Landory, we should leave most of these supplies behind."

"What about the transmitter?"

"Leave it," said Ew. "We should only carry what food we have. I have already slowed our journey as it is."

"All right, Ew," Pala replied. "Since that's settled, we should break camp now and be on our way."

It was a little before midday when they headed out again. Knowing their journey was nearly over helped to raise their spirits. They broke out the dense vegetation of the marsh behind as they moved further south. The land became mossy and easier to travel. At one point, Pala glanced back over the trail, and then did a double-take. A tall slender man stood just within the trees bordering the marsh. His long dark hair stuck out from beneath an old, tattered hat. The man stared back at

Pala for a moment and with an almost imperceptible nod of his head, he turned and disappeared into the marsh. Pala, too, turned back toward his destiny with renewed strength and hope in the journey ahead.

By late evening, they had journeyed sixteen kilo-trans, putting them within a day's march of Landory. As the hour grew late, Ew became weary as the paralysis crept into his right shoulder. Fearing that his friends might continue their journey into the night without rest, he remained silent about his condition.

Pala took the first watch that night. The air was cool and although he felt comforted to be so close to their final destination, he was concerned about a new calamity facing him. He watched the sky and the stars, wondering what he would be doing a week from now. He was alarmed as he watched bright flashes racing across the skies. Smoke trails followed burning debris as it plummeted to the planet surface.

Ew was also watching the flashes. "It looks as though we are marching right into an intergalactic war, Pala."

"We expected it, Sire."

"Sire? Why so formal?"

"Just thinking?"

"What is bothering you, my friend?"

"Your attitude."

"What about it?"

Pala did not respond right away but rather stared at his friend raising a concerned eyebrow. "I look at you and know that you hold Khali in one hand, and the power to destroy Uni in the other, yet you take yourself so lightly."

"Well, I never thought I took myself lightly."

"What I mean is that you are king yet you make an effort to please your subjects. It's your subjects who should try to please you."

"What brought that on?"

"You're running out of time and you are in great pain. I think we should continue our journey into the night. Knowing you, though, it would be useless for me to even suggest as much."

Ew watched the lightening flashes of the war taking place above Galan. Every now and then, the sound of spacecraft engines came close to where they were camped, drowning out the noise of small unseen creatures that hunted in the night. He understood the term "stewardship", as it related to his position as caretaker of the Khalian Solar System. "My old and dear friend," he began, "it is true that I am your king, but understand that I'm also your servant."

"Sire?"

"The purpose of the House of Galan is not only to rule the Khalian Solar System, but also to serve the people who live there." Ew looked at Shreela who was sleeping soundly next to him. "She doesn't know, does she?"

"No, Sire. When do you plan on telling her?"

Ew closed his eyes for a moment. "Once we get to Star City, I'll have to tell her, maybe even sooner. I'm in love with her and have been so for some time," he admitted.

"I know," said Pala. "May I ask how serious you are about her?"

"I know what you're thinking. You're worried because she's from another galaxy."

"Your Majesty, the people might object. She will be considered an outsider. How do you plan to get around the issue?"

Ew stared at the angry skies as he thought about the question. "I don't intend to skirt the issue. I will face it head on," he said at length. "The people will have to accept my decision about her, and there's one other thing. If she is the widow in the Legend, and I believe she is, the people will accept her." Ew closed his eyes again.

"Sleep well, My Liege."

The night passed without incident. Just before dawn of the fourteenth day, Ew and his friends began the last stretch of their journey. By then, Ew's right shoulder was completely numb, and his right arm had that familiar tingling sensation, a sign of paralysis. Still, he chose not to speak of it. Although the litter was difficult to pull uphill, they walked a fair distance before midday. Having walked six kilo-trans by this time, Pala told them to eat and rest for an additional hour while he scouted the area north of the camp. "We should see some sign of Landory by now," he said.

While Pala was away, Shreela and Milan set up camp. Shortly thereafter, Milan took Soren for a short walk, leaving Shreela to care for Ew alone. There were a few food discs left, but she decided to heat the last of the broth for Ew. Sitting next to the litter, she began to help Ew lift himself.

"Shreela, I can't help you," he said. His voice sounded tired. "Wait 'til Milan or Pala comes back."

Shreela looked at him in surprise. "Why didn't you say something earlier?"

"Sorry."

Shreela silently watched him for a while.

"You never talk about your mate," he said, interrupting her thoughts. Shreela softly sighed but did not respond. "I understand the hurt you feel," he continued," that gnawing ache in your stomach when you think of facing each day without him. Shreela, the pain does go away in time."

Shreela stared back at him. His eyes were both warm and inviting. I don't even know your name, and yet I feel so comfortable around you, she admitted to herself. When I talk or just sit quietly with you, some of that loneliness and emptiness vanishes, leaving me with a feeling of hope. Before she realized what she was doing, she bent her head and softly kissed him. "I'm sorry," she blurted out embarrassed.

"There's no need to apologize," said Ew, "and don't feel guilty about your feelings for me."

"But.."

"Shreela," he interrupted, "this is a new life, new people, and a new planet. A new beginning."

"I know. It's hard for me to see the reality in what you're saying." Shreela paused for a moment and looked up towards the sky. She closed her eyes and took a deep breath of fresh air. "I led a very happy life on Tima with my son and husband," she said softly. "It's just that I feel as if I've betrayed the love and trust I felt only a few short weeks ago for my husband. I am sorry," she apologized again, "but right now, I feel so confused." She looked down at him, and with her hand, stroked his brow. "I'm struggling with the conflict I feel, but I need more time."

Too tired to argue, Ew did not respond to her. He closed his eyes and cherished their moment together. That time soon ended when Milan and Soren returned.

"Milan, will you help me get Ew into a sitting position?" asked Shreela.

"Of course," said Milan, who walked quickly over to where Shreela was sitting. "Here, let me do that. What's wrong with him?" Milan asked.

"It's getting real bad," Ew responded.

"We should reach Landory by late afternoon or early evening," Milan commented. "Once we get medical help, we can head for Star City."

"Thanks for trying to spare me. There's a good chance the

antidote won't work now." With great difficulty, Ew turned his head towards Milan and Shreela. "All of you are my good friends. If I die, I'm glad to spend my last hours with you."

This was an unexpected surprise to Shreela. "What are you saying?" she cried out. "I thought there was an antidote for this poison!"

"There is, but it has to be administered before the poison reaches his brain tissue," Milan explained.

"Then we can't afford to take the extra time for rest," said Shreela. "I'll go and find Pala right now."

Milan watched Shreela as she rushed off to find Pala. He sat down and looked at his old friend. "She's a good person," he admitted.

"Yes, I know," Ew said, staring directly at the other, "even if she is an 'outsider'."

Milan did not respond but was reminded of his own conflict with Shreela.

Twenty minutes passed before Shreela returned with Pala. By then, Ew had finished the broth and was lying down on the litter.

"Shreela says that your condition is much worse," Pala commented. "I agree with her about leaving this place as soon as possible. We can finish the food discs while we walk."

"Were you able to see how far we are from Landory?" asked Milan.

"Yes, and we've done better than I thought."

"How close are we?" asked Ew.

"We're within a kilo-tran of Landory. If one of us carries Soren, we can probably arrive there in a little more than an hour."

"Then let's go." Shreela urged.

Multiple Dilemmas

The late morning sun warmed the five travelers as they moved forward on the last phase of their journey to Landory. Twenty-five hundred kilo-trans northwest in Star City, the first light of dawn slowly crept through Megan Galan's bedroom window. After what seemed like hours of tossing and turning, Megan decided to get up and take a walk through the garden behind the palace. Slipping into a garden lounge dress, she stepped out into the corridor and headed towards the back steps, a long winding staircase leading to the garden entrance. As she descended the stairs, Oshe, Mara's personal servant, met her.

"May I serve you, Princess Megan?"

"I don't need anything right now, but I'll be in the garden for a while if my mother should need me."

"Yes, Your Highness," Oshe said opening the door.

While strolling through the garden, Megan inhaled deeply to catch the scent of the pink gala blossoms that heavily decorated the palace wall. There was a wide assortment of flowers, bushes, trees, and shrubs, each type separated by a triangular paved walkway on which Megan strolled. She loved this garden for it was a quiet and peaceful place to think. She walked there, trying to sort out her feelings about the war, the loss of Ewlon, her mother, as well as many other troubles, which seemed to overwhelm her in such a short time. Abruptly, her thoughts were intruded upon by a familiar voice from behind.

"Megan." She smiled as she turned to see the face of General Calo Laggé. "You're up early. Can't you sleep?" he asked.

"I've been up most of the night thinking about our situation, the war, Ewlon and mother." An anxious look crossed her brow. "Calo, what are we going to do?"

Calo pulled her into his arms and held her close to him. Finally, he sighed as the reality of the moment began to race through his thoughts. With great tenderness and sorrow, he looked into her soft green eyes. "We can't think about getting married right now," he said, "the war has taken care of that."

"I know," Megan sadly agreed.

"Sorry I didn't get to tell Ew about our plans before he left."

"Why didn't you?"

"I was so annoyed about this breach in Ew's security system. We'll tell him when he returns."

"And what if he doesn't come back?"

"I have the strangest feeling that he's out there, somewhere," Calo said, moving his head from side to side as if searching for the exact location. "I don't believe he's dead. I know him too well," he insisted.

"How can you be so sure?"

"Ew is very resourceful. I don't know when he'll return, but I believe that he will return."

Strolling along the garden path, Megan gazed at the fading stars in a dawning sky. A cool, gentle breeze caressed her face, but the chilly air reminded her of the approaching winter. "I hope you're right about Ew. This war is taking its toll on my mother."

"I agree," said Calo, and I am deeply concerned about her."

"So am I. She seemed so tired last night."

"She didn't look too well yesterday either. I was hesitant to inform her about the two guests who requested an audience with her during the very early morning hours."

Megan looked at him curiously. "What two guests?"

"Jenka Danne and her uncle from Laton."

Megan paused for a moment to think. "Are you sure it was Laton?"

"Quite sure."

"That's odd. Jenka has no relatives on Laton. She is from Uni. Do you know her uncle's name?"

"His name was Kanum. No, it was Kazu, a merchant from Laton."

Megan's voice was filled with alarm. "You're sure that's his name? Kazu?"

"Yes. Megan, what's wrong?"

"Calo, that was not her uncle. That was Uzak," she cried. "Jenka Danne was let go by Ew many years ago when he discovered that she was a Unian spy."

"Surely your mother would know that Jenka Danne was a spy. Why would she agree to see her? She did know, didn't she?"

"No. Ew promised to keep Jenka's secret, but banished her from Khali." A feeling of panic began to race through Megan's heart. She quickly headed back towards the palace. "Calo, there's no time to explain. Just hurry!" she shouted.

Not quite sure of what to expect, Megan and Calo anxiously entered Mara's quarters. The sitting room was dark and quiet except for the soft ticking of the antique clock. Megan walked to the door of Mara's sleeping chamber and pushed several buttons on the keypad next to the door jam. The door slid open.

"Calo, wait outside while I check on her," she whispered.

The dim light of dawn shown through the window, illuminating the bed and other items of furniture in the room. Megan approached her mother who seemed to be peacefully sleeping. "Mother," she called out softly. "Mother, wake up." Receiving no response, Megan picked up Mara's hand, noticing at once how cold and stiff it was. "Oh mother," she sobbed.

Memories of her life with her mother began flowing through her mind; her mother's counsel concerning her first love, Ramon Haslow, who sacrificed his life to save hers. She was only thirteen then, but her mother's patience and love helped her to live with this tragedy. She thought of her mother's strength during that period of mourning over the death of Ew's wife and her only grandchild and heir. Her sound, compassionate advice to both her and Ewlon, mixed with sympathy and love, held them all together. There were times of exhaustion for Mara, but she was never too tired to make time for them; her honesty and honor towards those she served, and so much more. Megan raised her mother's hand, kissing it and pressing it against her face, wet with tears.

As Megan mourned her mother's passing, Calo stood outside Mara's bedchamber door for what he thought was an inordinate amount of time. At long last, he opened the door and was immediately confronted with the sound of Megan crying. "Megan?" he called, as he rushed across the room to her.

Megan stood up and tearfully embraced him. "She's dead," she cried.

"What? How?"

Megan walked over to a table and picked up a small cloth to dry her face. "I don't know, she hasn't been well lately. Then again, it wouldn't surprise me to learn that Jenka Danne had something to do with this."

"Would you like me to order an autopsy right away?"

Megan nodded her head 'yes' and then slowly walked back towards her mother's bed. She continued to wipe the tears from her eyes. "Do you know what this means, Calo? The fate of Khali rests on my shoulders now. How can I hope to carry on without her or Ew? I'm no match for Uzak."

Calo put his arms around her. "Megan, listen to me," he said gently. "You have the training as well as military advisors to assist you in making the transition to Steward of Khali, or at least until Ew returns."

There was a long moment of silence as Megan composed herself. Finally, "I hope so," she said. "You go ahead with arrangements for an autopsy, and I'll begin the process for a memorial." Megan looked at her mother one last time. "Mother's at peace now," she whispered.

Calo motioned her to the exit. "Come."

Megan stared blankly at the closed door outside her mother's bedchamber. Everything seemed so dark and dreary. She inhaled deeply to drive away the weariness, and to focus more clearly on the dilemma at hand. "If this is the work of Uzak and Jenka Danne," she said to Calo, "they're probably long gone by now."

"Maybe not," the other responded. "It's pretty difficult to leave the planet surface. They may still be in Star City."

"Have transports been allowed to move throughout the City?"

"Very little. The ground fog has not lifted, and since the Balarai Space Station tracking signals were not working properly, ground tracking radar for civilian transports was put on low priority."

"I see. It'll be difficult to trail them now, but see what you can do. Also, I want you to inform military department heads of the death of Her Highness. Have them assembled in the West Wing Defense Conference Room at midday. I'm going to review the proposals Her Highness was working on yesterday. I'll let you know my decision at the meeting." Megan started to leave, but stopped for a moment and looked at him. "Thank you, Calo."

As soon as Megan entered the conference room, she began to

feel uneasy, aware that all eyes were on her. She was dressed in military attire, and her hair was neatly tucked behind her ears. Although she wore military clothing, this masculine attire could not detract from her soft feminine features or carriage. It was a strange occasion for her, and only when she noticed that Calo Laggé would be on the dais with her, did she begin to relax.

Megan addressed the staff, her voice both well controlled and command quality. "My loyal staff," she began, "by now you are aware of the passing of Her Highness, Mara Galan. Her Highness' death is a terrible blow for Khali, but we must put aside mourning and turn our energies towards securing this solar system against further outbreaks of war from Uni. Yesterday, Admiral Garbonst and General Laggé presented Her Highness with recommendations on securing the System from further infiltration of Unian military personnel until the Balarai Space Station is fully operational. I have approved those recommendations for immediate implementation, the details of which will be presented following this meeting.

"Let me caution you in saying that the Khalian Solar System, as we now know it, will survive if and only if we continue to work as a unified System. Do not let yourselves fall into Uzak's trap. It is his hope, I am certain, that we will become disorganized, thereby weakening our defenses against any Unian onslaught. Working together will minimize that problem.

"Our final order of business concerns the memorial ceremony for Her Highness. She will be laid to rest with full military honors. There will be a public viewing of her remains during the evening hours, throughout the night, and in the morning hours up until midday tomorrow. Her Highness will be laid to rest in the family sacred circle at sundown tomorrow. My assistant, Marlin Bhaten, will handle inquiries concerning this matter. Thank you." All heads bowed as Megan stepped down from the podium and exited.

For many decades, Unian spies had been able to infiltrate Galan. While Megan addressed her military staff in the West Wing, Uzak sat comfortably with Jenka Danne in a small chateau southeast of Star City's metropolitan area. Food and shelter were provided by one of Uzak's many spies. This particular Unian supporter was also acquainted with both Megan and Ewlon Galan. Boolin Daloni, Chief Engineer of the late Shargant and Lluellyn Space Stations, celebrated with Jenka and Uzak. They refreshed themselves, and basked in their participation of Mara's death. With the help of Daloni, Uzak was able to communicate with his flagship, despite the fact that the Galan Military Intelligence carefully checked all intergalactic and interplanetary communications.

"We have done well, Jenka," said Uzak, sounding pleased with himself. "Although we're not able to leave the city at this moment, my dear, I've been able to contact my flagship, and the next part of my plan is about to unfold," he added with relish.

"What's that, My Lord?"

"Since the Galan Military is having difficulty with their tracking devices in some of the substation areas, the UMF has isolated those areas, and will enter the planet where monitoring is weak. The regions of Gailwaith, Brabonas, and Landory, lie within these areas. They will fall first. The Galan interplanetary defenses are spread pretty thin, leaving these cities in the west-central part of Verlithia least protected."

"And what of Ewlon Galan? You said that you believe he will survive the marsh."

"I do. Ewlon is a resourceful man, Jenka, and remember, he is a commander, well schooled in the techniques of survival."

"What if he's already left the marsh?"

"If he was close to the border, the searchcraft would have spotted the jettison pod since vegetation along the marsh border is not very dense. No," he said confidently, "the pod landed deep inside the marsh, and it would take three to four weeks to walk through that terrain. If he has a woman and child with him, as I suspect, he could not hope to arrive in Landory any sooner than three weeks. There is time, Jenka."

"When do we invade these regions, Lord?"

"Tonight the UMF will move in under the cloud cover and attack Gailwaith by midday tomorrow," Uzak sneered. "After the invasion of Gailwaith and Brabonas, I shall personally direct the assault on Landory, and await His Majesty's exit from the marsh."

The following day proved to be both bright and clear. UMF aircraft had already entered Galan the night before, as planned. Megan was in her mother's study when Admiral Garbonst announced the first Unian military attack in the city of Gailwaith, one-thousand-sixty kilo-trans southwest of Star City.

"Your Highness," Garbonst summoned over the telecomm, "Gailwaith has been attacked and totally destroyed by the Unian Military Force. It appears that some of the larger Unian military spacecraft were able to avoid detection and slipped through to the planet surface. Since the Balarai Space Station tracking system only became fully operational earlier today, we did not detect their presence before they attacked."

"What about our counteroffensive?"

"We have one, but it is weak."

"Why?"

"The proposals which were approved by you were for the defense of intergalactic territory. Inter- planetary defenses were less urgent since the primary intent was to keep the UMF out of our galactic regions. "Unfortunately, the IGF defense procedure was continually hampered because of the...,"

"Let me guess," Megan interrupted, "the delay in the operation of the Balarai Space Station." She sharply sighed with resignation. "Well Admiral, that can't be helped, so where does that leave us now?"

"We know the UMF is headed for the city Brabonas. Twenty percent of IGF has been assigned to the solar-system defense. They are engaged in fierce combat with enemy forces forty kilo-trans north of Brabonas. Admiral Palandor is commanding that operation."

"Very good Admiral. Please continue the counteroffensive. I'll be meeting with the Regional Governors shortly, but I'll be available to you on any sudden changes in our military posture. Is there anything else?"

"One other thing, Your Highness, General Laggé has gone to Landory to prepare a defense for the invasion on that city."

Megan felt a knot form in her stomach, but she controlled her facial expression and the tone of her voice. "Thank you, Admiral. Keep me informed."

Megan sat in front of the blank monitor with fear in her eyes. *I can't lose him now. I don't want to be left alone to run this System like my mother was*, she thought anxiously. *What a nightmare.*

In one solar day, the Unian Military Force successfully seized and occupied the city of Brabonas. The civilian population was either trapped within the city limits or refugees in the mountainous areas south of the once ultra-modern metropolis. The brutality of the war left much of that city on fire, and the situation was complicated by contamination of the food and water supplies. The death toll was devastating, showing a fifty percent loss in civilian life and a thirty percent mortality rate among the IGF sent to defend that city.

After the fall of Brabonas, Uzak interrupted the Inter-Solar System communications channel to broadcast his victory speech. He informed the entire Khalian System that he was responsible not only for the death of Mara Galan, but also that of her son. It was here that Uzak broke the unity of Khali. He established the incompetence of Megan Galan, demonstrating his argument with scenes of the devastation of both Gailwaith and Brabonas. He further promised total military occupation of Galan and her sister planets, with the support of his allies, now awaiting his command. Although the Galan military was not willing to compromise with Uzak, the Regional and Interplanetary Governors were so divided that surrender was inevitable.

7
AN UNEXPECTED REUNION

Landory, a large metropolitan city situated southeast of the Galan Marsh, was surrounded by vast plains and farmlands to the south. Elevated above Lake Eye, the smoke-colored glass towers of the commerce and business center gleamed brilliantly in the sun, overshadowing the freshwater lake below. Landory's industries of crops, cattle, and fish, made it Galan's primary source for food production and processing on the continent. Its always-busy super-highway connects with the shipping port on Lake Eye. Many refer to it as the "lidless city", connoting it as the city that never sleeps. Rich in cultural events, sights and sounds, food, and entertainment, the city was always filled with visitors from all over the galaxy.

As Khali prepared to come to terms with Uzak of Uni, Ew and his friends entered Landory from the southwest. The streets were practically empty. Milan became greatly concerned that street transports were nowhere to be found. "I don't believe what I'm seeing here," he whispered to Pala.

"Yeah, I know," Pala agreed. "This is really strange. I'll bet my life the Unian Military Force is here. Keep your eyes open," he cautioned.

As a precautionary measure, Pala led them away from the main street into a back alley that would take them to the side entrance of the nearest medical building. Shreela felt confident in Pala as a guide, always certain about where he was going and how best to get there.

As soon as they entered the medical building, a security guard stationed near the front door met them. The guard immediately walked towards the litter where Ew was sleeping. He directed the group to the first examination room left of the main entrance. Milan, Shreela, and Soren entered the room only after the guard left. They had previously agreed that Pala should answer all questions.

A tall brown-skinned man entered wearing a navy-blue jacket and dark pants. Quickly walking towards Ew, he reached inside his jacket and pulled out a disc-shaped scanner. "I am Dr. Monroe," he said. "What has happened to this man?" he asked, running the scanner along Ew's arm.

"He was attacked by an ergret four days ago," Pala answered.

Dr. Monroe put the scanner back into his pocket and pulled out a small cylinder, which projected a light to examine Ew's eyes. "That certainly does explain the paralysis and shock. What were you doing in the swampland, especially during breeding season?"

"Well," Pala began, "we were headed for Gailwaith, northwest of here. The propulsion mechanism in my transport malfunctioned, forcing us to land in the marsh some one-hundred-twenty kilo-trans west of Landory."

"Alright," the doctor said, acknowledging the plausibility of Pala's story. "We need to run a few tests before we administer the antidote. What's his name?"

"Lagan."

"We will need more information on Mr. Lagan, but we can take that information at a later time."

"Can you tell us how bad he is?" Pala asked. "I mean, how far along is he?"

"The paralysis is extensive," Monroe explained, "but his respiration is good, and he's conscious. He should respond to medication, though I wouldn't guarantee as much if it were this time tomorrow."

"Thank you, Doctor."

Monroe studied their faces for a moment. "You may wait, if you like. We'll just be a minute."

Ew looked over at Shreela after Dr. Monroe left the room. "This is a new beginning," he commented. "Once we get out of here..," Ew's remark was cut short when two medical staff personnel entered the room.

"We'll be taking you to the treatment room down the hall Mr. Lagan," one of them explained. Standing at each end of the litter, they raised Ew while Pala pulled the makeshift litter from beneath him. Ew was then placed back on a levitation table and pushed out of the room.

Pala, Milan, Shreela, and Soren waited patiently for Ew's return. One hour, then two hours passed without a word. Pala reminded himself about the empty streets when they arrived. *I am almost sure that the UMF is in Landory*, he thought. *Question is, will they recognize Ewlon Galan*? After considerable debate, Pala finally decided to start searching for his old friend. The automatic doors slid open as he approached. Quickly, he stepped back, allowing the doors to snap close again.

Shreela's posture stiffened at Pala's sudden reaction. "What's the matter?" she asked.

"UMF personnel are in the hallway," he answered briskly.

"There's something going on here, I can feel it. Better stay put for a while." Pala walked over to the window, quietly contemplating their situation and deciding upon several alternatives for escape, if necessary. Another one and one-half hours passed and still Ew had not returned. Just as he was nearing the end of his patience, the door slid open. Ew stood in the doorway with his right arm draped over the doctor's shoulder for support.

"Sorry about the delay," Monroe said apologetically, "but Mr. Lagan insisted on walking here alone."

"I didn't expect him to be standing so soon," said Milan, in a surprised tone.

"If the patient gets here before the poison begins to destroy the brain tissue, the antidote works pretty fast. As a matter of fact, you should be completely recovered within the next forty-eight hours, Mr. Lagan."

"Can we take him home now?" asked Pala walking over to help Ew.

"Yes, but he should rest for the next two days. Even though he's ambulatory, his body is still traumatized from battling the toxins in his body. It would take many hours to use tissue regeneration over his entire body, so we regenerated those areas close to vital organs. The antidote and his immune system will take care of the rest." After Ew shifted his arm from the doctor to Pala, Dr. Monroe shook Ew's hand to wish him well. "Good luck Mr. Lagan, you will be alright soon, sir."

Pala sensed something different in the doctor's attitude, and he looked in askance at his friend, who had that 'I'll explain later' look in his eye. Once the doctor left, Ew conferred with his friends about the UMF personnel stationed in the hallway. "Uzak has been successful in capturing most of the small towns and villages northwest of here," he explained. "Landory is expected to fall within the next few days, and according to Dr. Monroe, Uzak himself is on his way here. I didn't find out the reason for his trip to Landory, but whatever the reason, we cannot be here when he arrives!"

"I'll agree to that," said Milan.

Ew's expression became troubled as he paused for a moment to look at his friends. "There is one other matter that greatly affects our next move. Earlier today, Uzak informed all of Galan that their king died aboard the *Fidus Achates* when it was destroyed several days ago. Uzak also bragged about the death of Her Highness, Mara Galan, and he actually took the credit for her death."

Milan's mouth dropped open in surprise. "What? How?"

"How could he get into Galan Manor?" Pala asked.

Ew closed his eyes and massaged his brow to release the tension he felt. "I don't know," he said, sighing. "Then again, maybe he said that to inject fear. One thing is certain though, Mara Galan is not running things."

"Who is?" asked Milan.

"Megan Galan."

"If the King of Khali was on the *Fidus Achates*, why didn't we know about it, Ew?" Shreela asked.

Ew hesitated for a moment, realizing that Shreela was still in the dark about his true identity. He looked over at Pala who gave him that 'you better deal with this matter soon' look. Turning back to Shreela, he noticed that she had been watching him intently, waiting for an answer to her question. "We knew that he was on board," he responded. "I will be speaking to you on that very subject, but not here. Can you wait awhile?"

"Another secret?"

"Shreela."

"Okay, okay. I'll wait until you're ready," she mumbled.

Ew walked unsteadily over to the window, his arm still draped around Pala's shoulder. Lowering his voice, he continued his conversation with Pala and Milan.

"The Governors must be having a real hard time with Megan in control," Milan commented.

"That's the problem," said Ew. "Dr. Monroe explained that the Regional and Interplanetary Governors are reluctant to work with her. They feel she is weak and unable to control some of the more aggressive members."

"But the military will back her up," Pala interjected.

"Maybe, but there is rumor that the Governors are at this very moment debating conditions for surrender."

"Then we need to get to Star City as quickly as possible. Do you have any ideas about getting a transport?"

Ew's face perked up. "As a matter of fact, I do."

"Well?"

"I had to put my trust in the hands of Dr. Monroe. I told him my real name."

Ew stumbled when Pala unexpectedly stepped back, forcing Ew's arm to fall from around his neck. "I hope the good doctor is a trustworthy fellow for your sake," he mumbled, grabbing Ew's elbow.

"Settle down, Pala," he said, lowering his voice. "To begin with, Monroe didn't believe our story about crashing in the marsh. He thought we might be running from the UMF. He also identified himself as a member of the underground military rebel force, formed in opposition to the treaty being prepared for surrender."

"He revealed that to you?" Pala asked surprised.

"Did I say I told him my real name? Fact is, he recognized me during the examination. He has agreed to let me use his trans..." Before he could finish, two UMF guards entered the room.

"We were told that you were leaving this room. Why are you still here?" one guard asked abruptly.

"My friend here became a little dizzy," Pala explained. "We thought we would wait a minute or two longer until he could steady himself."

"We were just about to leave," Milan added.

"He looks steady now," said the second guard, "so move along!"

Without hesitation, the five companions moved towards the door, proceeding out and down the long corridor, which led to the main entrance. They stood outside in front of the medical building. "We should find a place to stay until we can contact Dr. Monroe," said Ew. "How about that little lodge across the street?"

Everyone nodded in affirmation. As Ew began to move towards the flashing 'SHELTER' sign, he thought not only about the narrow escapes already experienced, but also wondered what else was in store for them.

Ew and his friends entered their suite at the lodge across the street from the medical center. During the course of three hours, they all managed to bathe the dirt and weariness from their bodies as well as take nourishment and a little rest. Both anxious and tired, Shreela and Soren rested in the bedroom while the men slept in the sitting room. The time passed without incident, and by early evening, Pala contacted Dr. Monroe, still in the medical building across the street.

"How is our patient?" Monroe asked.

"He's resting quietly at the moment. He asked me to contact you for an appointment. Right now, we are lodged in the hotel across the street from you. Would it be convenient for you to stop by, say within the hour?"

"As a matter of fact, I can see the patient right now. What is your room number?"

"One-forty-nine."

"I'll see you shortly then."

Pala walked over to the lounge chair where Ew was resting. "Ew," he whispered.

"I'm just resting my eyes," Ew responded. "I heard you talking to Dr. Monroe, and I'm thinking not to wake the widow and her son for this meeting. They both seemed so tired when we arrived. Let them rest."

"Alright," said Pala, "but I will wake Milan."

Strolling across the room, Pala abruptly halted and walked back to where Ew was sitting. "One other thing."

"Yes Pala. What is it?"

"It might be prudent to tell Shreela your true identity before someone else does."

"I need to do that, but I can't seem to find the right time."

"No time is right, my Liege. She's gonna be annoyed at any time, don't you think?"

Ew sighed loudly, shaking his head. "I know that you're right, but I'll deal with that issue when it comes to light."

"I'll wake Milan."

While Pala walked to the other side of the room to wake Milan, Ew decided it was time for him to try to stand on his own. His legs were a little wobbly but he managed quite well on his first try. Slowly making his way towards a table in the center of the room, he unconsciously stiffened his posture at the sound of a soft knock at the door.

"Who's there?" asked Pala.

"It's Monroe."

Recognizing the voice as that of Dr. Monroe, Pala pushed the button on the wall that released the lock, allowing the door to slide open.

"Good evening, gentlemen," Monroe smiled.

"Good evening, Dr. Monroe," nodded Pala. "Will you have refreshments with us?"

"Thank you, I will," Monroe answered, stepping across the threshold. He looked at Ew sitting at the table, and was quite satisfied to see his patient recovering from his injuries. "Good evening, Your Majesty," he bowed.

"Dr. Monroe," said Ew, "I am far from the halls of Galan Manor, and since I'm not attired as a king, I would prefer you call me Ew as everyone else does. Besides, I'm incognito and formal greetings are not necessary."

"If you wish, Ew. Monroe turned to Pala. "Is it possible to have the refreshment while I fill you in on the latest events?"

"Certainly."

"There are two matters I should discuss with you," Monroe began after they were all seated around the table. "The situation as it now stands is very grave indeed. Since I last spoke with you, have you heard any news of what is going on at Galan Manor?"

"No," Ew responded. "We've been resting here since we left your medical facility. We did attempt to reach my home earlier, but the frequencies are still jammed. There is no video news anywhere, so it seems."

"You're quite correct," said Monroe. "The Unian Military has taken over most of the communications station from Gailwaith to Landory." Monroe paused for a moment.

Ew frowned at the troubled look on Monroe's face. "There's something else, isn't there?" he asked.

"I don't quite know how to say this delicately, Sire, but..."

"It's alright. Just say what it is."

"I've only received information from the Khalian

underground concerning the death of your mother."

"And.."

"She was poisoned. My regrets Sire," Monroe offered an apology. The room became breathlessly still. A peculiar look spread across Ew's face as he thought of the strange dream he had of his mother while lying wounded in the swamp. For a moment or so, he quietly contemplated these sad tidings. Finally, he nodded his head for Monroe to continue. "Is there news on Princess Megan?"

"Princess Megan Galan is commanding the military forces in your absence. She is trying to resolve some of the conflicts with the Regional Governors, but all attempts have failed, thus far."

"Did your source name any of the governors?"

"One in particular stands out. Regent Brotin of Lozondra. Lozondra exports large quantities of the mineral, *chhottan*, to the Unian ally, Zirvag. Twenty-five percent of Lozondra's population works in mining that raw material. Brotin has strong support from the populace to work out an agreement between Lozondra and Uni."

"What about the other Governors?"

"The defeat of Gailwaith and Brabonas and Uzak's earlier intimidating broadcast has left the Governors divided. Nearly half of them are prepared to surrender. As a result, most of the military personnel have gone underground in opposition to the proposed treaty between Galan and Uni, and quite frankly, I agree with them. I shall do all I can to fight the UMF. I do not believe Uzak will ever be anything less than a tyrant who will reduce the Khalian System to a state of slavery."

"What else did you hear from the underground?"

"The commander of the underground awaits your arrival, Ew. I did not tell him who you were except to say that you and your friends are being sought by Uzak, and that you are in need of passage to Star City."

"Very good, Monroe," said Ew. "Will the commander aid us in our quest for Star City, and can the leader of this underground defense be trusted?"

"You can expect assistance for you and your friends through the Underground Defense Team, but the group commander is suspicious of anyone headed for the capitol of Galan. That will change once he realizes who you are." Without warning, Dr. Monroe lowered his voice to a whisper. "There is another item of concern. Uzak is expected to arrive in Landory, three hours after evening. I bribed a sentry to get this information."

"This is grim news about my mother," Ew said at length. "Unfortunately, time for mourning will have to wait. Is your transport nearby?"

"It's outside. I also have false identification tags for you and your friends, in case they are needed. I recommend a quick departure since Unian military personnel are beginning to enter Landory, their numbers increasing steadily. I fear in another hour, it may not be possible to leave the city, since blockades are being called for."

"We can leave right now," said Ew, not liking the word blockade. "Pala, wake Shreela and Soren. Tell them we will be leaving immediately. Hurry my friend! We'll wait for you outside."

As Pala went to collect Shreela and Soren, Milan helped Ew to his feet, and headed for the door.

Stopping at the desk in the lobby, Monroe paid the lodging expenses while Milan and Ew boarded a transport parked outside. Once Shreela, Soren, and Pala entered the vehicle, they quickly left and headed northeast. Shortly after their departure, some thirty kilo-trans from the medical building, they were stopped by the blockade, heavily guarded by Occupation

Military Police.

"There is a secret compartment under the floor, large enough to hide three people. I would advise that Ew, the widow and her son hide inside," Monroe said urgently.

"I thought you had identification tags for us," Pala commented.

"I do, but if they're looking for five travelers, they may not look too hard if there are only three of us."

Pala pulled the floor up. Ew, along with the widow and her son, slipped inside just as the transport in front was allowed to pass through the blockade.

"Good evening, sir," Monroe greeted the officer who approached the transport. "What seems to be the problem?" he asked.

"Step out of the transport, and surrender your identification tags," the officer commanded.

Monroe, Pala and Milan stepped outside while two military policemen began searching the inside of the transport. Since there were two pullout seats directly over the false bottom, the policemen never bothered to check the area more carefully.

"You can leave," snapped the first officer after being given the signal that all was clear.

Not to arouse suspicion, Pala and Milan casually entered the vehicle as Monroe prepared for takeoff. They rode for about four kilo-trans before Milan refolded the chairs and lifted the floor, allowing the three stowaways to exit their hiding place. Pala had been the only member of the group with reservations as to the character of Dr. Monroe. These doubts had obviously been put to rest, as he thanked the "good doctor" many times.

"Why do you have a false bottom in the back of this vehicle?" Pala asked curiously.

"This transport used to serve as a small ambulance and the

bottom was used to transport medical equipment," he explained. "When they changed to the newer models, I purchased this vehicle to haul my own equipment."

"A sound decision, my friend," Milan laughed heartily, "a sound decision indeed."

Monroe and his companions rode northeast for another half hour before stopping in the small northeastern city of Markan. It was dark as they parked at an old abandoned house on the edge of town. Monroe walked up to the Galan Military Police guarding the entrance.

"What is your business here?" asked one of the guards.

"Restoration of Galan," Monroe gave the code.

Both guards stepped aside and allowed them to enter. They walked towards what seemed to be a dead end. Suddenly, the wall opened, and everyone entered the vertical lift, which took them one-hundred trans below the planet surface to meet with the commander of the underground operation. Monroe led the way from the transport passing through one of two tunnels and stopping when the tunnel opened into a large cave filled with military personnel. All was quiet as they entered. The group commander turned to greet Monroe, but fell short of his greeting when he recognized Ew.

"Your Majesty," the commander bowed.

Ew immediately signaled him to stand and as he did, he walked over to hug him. "Calo, I'm surprised to see you here," said Ew.

"It's a long story, Sire." Calo looked at Ew's blood-stained shirtsleeve. Then his eyes caught sight of the Timanian woman standing directly behind him. He smiled and bowed to the widow. "It appears that you have a few stories of your own."

"I must speak with you privately," said Ew. "Is there a place where we can talk freely?"

"There's a room just beyond this cave. Come, I'll take you there."

Ew and his companions followed Calo as he led them back through the tunnel they had entered from and down the second tunnel. They were led to another cave furnished with a conference table and chairs. Monroe entered, shortly after they were seated, with a pot of kari and cups.

"Thank you," said Ew.

"I also have something here for the young lad," said Monroe walking over to where Soren was sitting. "This is called Ela juice. This will help him to sleep, though I dare say he needs little assistance in that department," Monroe said, smiling.

While Soren sipped his drink, Shreela and Monroe lined up several folded blankets on the floor to serve as a bed. Shreela covered Soren with another blanket when Soren laid down. She laid down alongside her son and within minutes, they were both sleep.

Calo listened with interest as Ew explained all that happened from the time he left Thesbis until Dr. Monroe at the Medical Facility treated him.

"Calo, if I can get to Star city, Uzak and his allies will be stopped by this." Ew pulled The Planet Star from his pocket and held it up before Calo's eyes.

Calo marveled at the medallion, for he had never seen it. "The Planet Star?" he asked.

Ew nodded his head.

"How did you get it from Uzak?" Calo asked.

"Milan stole it from him."

"Milan?" asked Calo, turning to look at Milan. "Really?"

"He almost lost his life in the attempt, but I'll let him tell you about that. Now, take a look at this one," said Ew, pulling out a second medallion from his other pocket. "This is a copy. Can you tell them apart?"

"No, but there must be a way to identify one from the other. The gems cannot be the same, are they?"

"Some are, but unless you have the key to unlock the power of the medallion, it is difficult to be certain which is which. I have put the real medallion on this *dabernine* chain, while the false medallion is on this gold chain."

"How did you come up with this decoy?"

"I asked Admiral Atalif to have one made when we first boarded the *Solaitra* Battle cruiser. Except for those of us who are sitting here, no one else knows of the duplication, and as you know by now, Atalif carried this knowledge to his grave."

"He'll be missed," said the other.

Ew quietly thought about his long-time relationship with the Admiral, even when he was a boy. "From this point on, I shall wear the copy, but the real medallion will remain hidden," he said. The last piece of advice given to me by Atalif was that I should remember to do this. I did not do so in the marshland, and although nothing happened to cause me to lose it, that may not be the case as we begin our journey to Star City."

"Agreed," Calo commented.

"Now, tell me, Calo, when did Uzak attack Galan?" asked Ew, changing the subject.

As evening passed into night, Calo explained all that surrounded the first attack on Galan; the failure of the searchcraft to find the jettison pod or travelers on foot in the Galan Marsh, problems with the Balarai Space Station, and the attack on Gailwaith and Brabonas.

"How did Uzak manage to murder my mother?"

"She was given an overdose of the sleeping drug, *janus*. A small ring she was wearing was laced with the drug."

"What ring?"

"We think it was given to her as a gift from an old friend who came to see her. Her name was Jenka Danne, and her supposed merchant uncle, Kazu, from Laton, accompanied her. Now we know that her uncle was Uzak."

"What?" Ew sat straight up in his chair, stunned by the news. "Of all people, why would it have to be Jenka Danne?" he whispered her name aloud.

"Megan explained that Jenka Danne was a Unian spy, and that your mother was never informed of that fact."

Reminded of his earlier argument with Shreela, the words 'information is power' rang in his ears. "No, she didn't know," he said solemnly. "I was wrong not to tell her."

"Why didn't you?"

Ew thoughtfully contemplated the reason for his silence. "I had what I thought were good reasons at the time," he said, at length, "and it cost my mother's life."

"Can you tell me?"

"Someday, perhaps, but not just yet."

"I'm sorry, Ew."

"Thank you, my friend."

Dr. Monroe entered the room, interrupting their conversation. "I must leave you now, and may the road you travel be victorious, Sire," he said.

"I will contact you when we arrive in Star City," said Calo.

"Until that time, take care and be careful of spies, Monroe," warned Ew.

"I'll keep that in mind. Good evening."

After Monroe departed, Ew asked the question closest to his heart. "How is my sister?"

Calo stood up and began to pace around the table. "She was not holding up too well when I spoke to her last," he said gravely. "Since Uzak's disturbing newscast, she's had little success in keeping the Regional and Interplanetary Governors from splitting apart." Sitting down once more, Calo looked Ew directly in the eye. "I'm afraid the UMF has taken over the palace. I haven't been able to reach Megan since early evening."

Calo turned his head away for a moment, but Ew had known Calo since they were children and although imperceptible, he could tell when things, which personally affected him, troubled Calo. "What else troubles you Calo?" he asked.

Calo sighed. "To be honest with you, Megan and I planned to marry this month."

"I got the feeling that you were withholding something when I was preparing to leave for Thesbis. Why didn't you say something then?"

"There were other more important matters."

"Maybe, but I can see there's still something else."

"In light of everything that's happening, my complaint is a small matter. Besides," he said, shrugging his shoulders, "we have more important things to discuss right now."

"Calo," Ew addressed him as a friend, "whatever the problem is, I can see that you're still annoyed, so let's have it."

"Alright, alright," Calo conceded. "It's Boolin Daloni."

A subtle grin formed around Ew's mouth. "Still trying to get Megan's attention?"

Calo nodded his head. "After you reassigned Daloni to Linden, he contacts her every chance he gets."

"That is your fault, Calo. The two of you are not formally engaged."

"We are now, but that hasn't stopped Daloni."

"Calo, by now you should know how Daloni operates," Ew said, smiling. "He's been after Megan for years, and she doesn't give him a second thought."

"And that's where the problem is, Ew. When I spoke to him

earlier today, he said that he was unable to reach Megan. I think he lied, and now is not the time for these ridiculous games. I need to contact her on military matters."

"I see your point," said Ew. "Look, contact Daloni now. Tell him I'm here, and that I need to get word on what's happening in Star City."

"I'll get on it right away."

As Calo got up to leave, Ew glanced over to where Shreela was sleeping. "Calo," he called, "one other thing before you leave."

"Yes Sire."

"Have you ever spoken to Megan concerning your feelings about Daloni's attention toward her?"

"Not yet."

"Do it. You shouldn't keep things like that from her. She's probably not even aware of how you feel about it. Besides, you shouldn't keep things from the person you love," he said, watching Shreela as she slept, holding her son close to her.

Calo looked at his friend with curiosity and then his eyes focused on Shreela. "How are things going with you?" he asked.

With a good-natured smile, "I'm not sure," he said.

"The widow seemed surprised when I bowed to you earlier. Did she know who you were before then?"

Ew shook his head.

"Does it matter?" asked Calo.

"It matters. Just take my advice and talk to Megan."

"I'll contact Daloni and then turn in. Good night My Liege."

"Alright, sleep well -- and Calo, it's good to see you again."

After Calo left the room, Ew headed over to where Soren and Shreela were sleeping. He laid down, two or three trans across from her, watching as she slept, until he too was overtaken by sleep.

8
A TRAITOR UNMASKED

Isan Monroe

Ew and his companions slept soundly within the Markan Underground Defense Base while Uzak confidently headed for Landory anticipating what he thought would be Ew's exit from the marsh. Reports that Galan military defenses were forced underground made Landory, in comparison to Brabonas, more difficult to seize and occupy. Twenty kilo-trans above the planet surface, Uzak stood silently on the bridge of his flagship, watching his ground staff on the monitor as they moved into position for the occupation of Landory. Occupation Military Police electronically erected one-way force field barriers measuring three-hundred kilo-trans in length, along the outskirts of the city. This allowed entry into the city from the marsh, but no exit without screening.

Shortly before midnight, Uzak disembarked his spacecraft. Guards and other staff officials escorted him to the main base of operations, located on the city's southwest border, not far from where Ew entered from the marsh during the early afternoon.

Uzak entered his quarters followed by General Narvan, head of the Occupation Military Police (OMP) and Military Intelligence. Narvan waited patiently as Uzak stationed himself behind his desk next to a large bay window with no covering. The desk faced a huge communications console, which covered the entire wall. The uncarpeted room, a deep gray with black trim, was oppressive to any who entered. Narvan abruptly stiffened to attention as Uzak began to fire questions at him.

"What is the status of the Galan Military?"

"According to our last report from Boolin Daloni, Sire, all remaining Galan military personnel, including those sent ahead for the defense of Landory, have gone underground," responded Narvan. "We know there is at least one base located near Markan. We are trying to pinpoint its location."

"What does Boolin report from Linden?"

"General Laggé commands the Galan Underground Defense. Laggé," he went on, "does communicate with the Linden base from Markan, but the exact location of the Markan base is closely guarded." Beads of perspiration formed across Narvan's forehead. He tried desperately to avoid Uzak's disapproving glare.

"So far, Narvan, you have given me only excuses for your failure to find that base."

"But My Lord," Narvan pleaded, "General Laggé has been careful not to share the whereabouts of the Markan base with any command personnel located in Linden. His messages are always dispatched through a secret channel code, which we have been unable to break. Messages are generally short, which does not give us enough time to do the channel search."

"Have you been able to find their connection here in Landory?"

"We are not certain, Lord, but we believe a medical doctor, Dr. Isan Monroe, works for the Galan Underground Defense."

"Has he been brought in for questioning?"

"Not yet, Sire. He..."

"Why not!"

"My Lord, he left the medical building several hours ago and has not returned," Narvan answered anxiously. "We talked to the building guard who saw Monroe go into a travelers lodge across the street from the medical building. The lodge clerk is here for questioning. He is being detained nearby."

"Bring him to me now!"

"Yes, Lord."

Within minutes of his departure, the door to Uzak's quarters opened revealing a tall thin man, hardly more than a boy.

"Lord, this is Jhun Kron, the desk clerk at the Landory Travelers Shelter," said Narvan.

Looking at Kron coldly as he picked up a log entry recorder, Uzak began the interrogation. "I understand that Dr. Monroe visited your facilities today. Why?"

The frightened desk clerk stood trembling at the threatening tone in Uzak's voice. "Yes Sire," he answered with his eyes lowered. "Dr. Monroe paid for the lodgins of five guests; three men, one woman, and a small child," Kron answered.

Unconsciously Uzak raised his eyebrows. "What did they look like?"

"There was one man who had to be helped, to and from his room. He stood slightly less than two trans tall, grayish-green eyes, medium brown hair."

"And the woman?"

"She was little, um-m-m 'bout one and one-half trans high, dark brown hair and eyes. A Timanian."

"How do you know she was Timanian?"

"She wore the wide pant-leg dress that buttons below the knee and down to the ankle, like females wear on that planet. I only guess, My Lord. She had a small boy with her, too."

Setting his log entry device down on the table, Uzak turned his back to Kron and Narvan. *I've misjudged Ewlon*, he thought, annoyed with himself. "What did they do and where did they go?" he shouted back at Kron.

"They got into a transport an' headed northeast, Sire."

Uzak paced the room several times as he thought of Ew's escape from Landory. His mood was clearly threatening to those around him. Jhun Kron stood there shaken with fear, his throat tightening in anticipation of Uzak's next command.

"You can leave!" Uzak snapped. "Guard! Guard, show this man out!" he bellowed, as one of the OMP guards entered the room. As soon as Kron was escorted out, Uzak turned back to Narvan. "General, I want all group leaders responsible for each of the barricade checkpoints brought here immediately. You will conduct an inquiry and learn who let Monroe through the blockade and bring him to me. I also want to speak with Boolin Daloni as soon as possible."

"Yes Sire," Narvan answered fearfully.

As General Narvan left the room, Uzak paced his quarters, furious with himself for assuming that Ew could not possibly get out of the marsh in less than three weeks. "I cannot allow him to reach Star City," he muttered. "He is sure to have the key necessary to activate The Planet Star. If he succeeds, the Keepers will most definitely rob me of my longevity, and I shall dwindle into oblivion. He must not win," Uzak cried out.

"My Lord," a voice came over the com. "Boolin Daloni checking in."

Uzak walked quickly to the communications console. "Daloni, I've just been informed that Ewlon Galan and a widow left Landory with Dr. Isan Monroe. Do you know anything about this doctor?" he asked irritably. "He is supposedly working with the underground and may be headed for Markan."

"I've not heard of Monroe, My Lord. Right now, I'm waiting to hear from the Markan underground base of operations, but the commander of that base has not reported in."

"When you do hear from Markan, try to find out about this Monroe. As soon as you hear anything, report it at once."

"Yes, Lord Uzak."

Uzak impatiently waited in his room for nearly an hour before Narvan returned with Lieutenant Bayonne. Uzak stared at Bayonne for a moment and then addressed Narvan.

"What have you learned?"

"Lord, this is Lieutenant Bayonne. He is stationed at the northeast barricade, east of the main transport highway. Bayonne has identified one of the men being searched for," Narvan explained.

"Lieutenant," Uzak spoke to Bayonne directly.

"Sire," he began, "we stopped Dr. Monroe about four hours ago. He was traveling with two others. These were the two men with him," he said, handing Uzak the three-dimensional rendering from an earlier log entry. It clearly pictured both Pala Bhusan and Milan Mariko.

"These renderings were taken when they passed through the barricade," Narvan interjected. "We matched them to the ones transmitted from your flagship, Sire."

"What about the woman?"

"I'm sorry, My Lord, but there was no woman with them," Bayonne responded apologetically. "Only these two men and Dr. Monroe.

"How closely was the transport checked?"

"We made everyone leave the transport, and then my men

checked the interior as well as the storage area in the back. It's standard procedure, Sire."

A deathly quiet descended on the chamber, disturbed by the heavy booted footfalls of Uzak, pacing from one end of the room to the other. Bayonne looked nervously at Narvan, uncertain as to whether or not he unwittingly committed some error. Narvan responded to Bayonne's concern by giving an assuring glance that everything was all right. Although only one or two moments passed before Uzak spoke, to Narvan and Bayonne, it seemed like hours as they stood at quiet attention waiting for a response from their leader. Finally Uzak turned and stopped directly in front of Bayonne. His glare was cold, his jaw clenched, and the tone of his voice was chilling.

"Renderings of these criminals were sent more than six hours ago. Why weren't they arrested?" asked Uzak. "You knew what they looked like."

"My Lord, we just received renderings from the flagship, three hours at most," Bayonne responded nervously.

Uzak flashed an angry glance towards Narvan. "Why is that Narvan?"

"The signal from your flagship was scattered by the Balarai Space Station disrupters, My Lord. We were told to rely on a description of the criminals until the graphic display signal could be altered. Once the signal was adjusted, the renderings were transmitted to this base."

"Who gave you those instruction?!" Uzak demanded.

"Admiral Pernell, My Lord."

"Admiral Pernell," Uzak echoed Narvan's response. Uzak paused for a moment to think. "Lieutenant, you may return to your post," he said, at length. "Expect Monroe to return at anytime. When he does, he is to be arrested and brought to me."

"Yes Lord," Bayonne said respectfully, and then quickly left the room.

"General Narvan, I want you to contact Admiral Pernell and Commander Woret, and send the call to my chamber."

"Yes, My Lord."

"I am also expecting a call from Boolin Daloni. See to it that I am notified as soon as that comes in."

Within minutes of Narvan's departure, Uzak received a summons from Admiral Pernell. "My Lord, you wanted to see me," Pernell stated, rather than asked.

"Admiral Per-nell," said Uzak, exaggerating the pronunciation of Pernell's name. "You did not inform me about transmission problems when you were with me on the flagship two hours ago."

"No, Sire. I thought the problem could be solved quickly."

"But it wasn't solved, was it?"

"Yes Sire. We fixed the problem shortly before you left."

"That was a four hour delay after my orders to dispatch the renderings of the criminals. Dispatching a courier with the renderings might have been a more acceptable solution, Admiral, don't you think?" Uzak's voice was controlled, but filled with danger. "Now, had I been properly informed of transmission problems, I would have sent a courier myself. Because of your lack of insight, the criminals have slipped through our barricade. The renderings were transmitted too late." Uzak waited for a response. When none was offered, he looked over at Commander Woret, who stood next to Admiral Pernell. "Tell me, Commander, how would you handle an incompetent?"

"Ah-h-h My Lord..."

"Let me tell you," Uzak interrupted. "You'll need to know for future reference." Standing up, Uzak put his hands behind his back, and looked intently at the Admiral. "I seem to recall, Admiral that you were greatly interested in the new technology being tested on Dagmar. I think you should have first-hand knowledge on how it works. As of now, you are reassigned to Dagmar where you will become part of that project. You will leave at once."

"Y-Y-Yes, Sire." Pernell bowed his head before leaving the area.

"Commander, I want you to have Admiral Pernell escorted to the Dagmarian Research Laboratory. Tell them that he is to be their *live specimen.* Since he will not be returning, you will take over his command.

"Yes, My Lord," Woret said, shaking.

It was dawn when General Narvan summoned Uzak, who was relaxing in a chair at the time.

"Lord, Boolin Daloni is here to see you."

"Send him in," he said to Narvan.

Within minutes, Boolin entered Uzak's quarters. "Good morning Sire," he said, greeting Uzak with a smile of accomplishment.

"I didn't expect you to come in person."

"Linden Defense has been dispatched to Star City. I was one of the last to leave so I thought I'd take the scenic route," Daloni said, grinning.

"What do you have?"

"I've received information about Monroe and his friends."

Looking up with interest, "Go on," said Uzak.

"It seems that Dr. Monroe was accompanied by five others when he arrived at the Markan Underground Defense Base; one woman and child, Pala Bhusan, Milan Mariko, and last but not least, Ewlon Galan."

Uzak sneered with delight. "I do not understand how Ewlon,

the widow, and her son managed to escape my sentries, but I had a feeling they would somehow be found together."

"All but a handful of underground troops from Markan as well as Linden were sent to Star City before dawn," Daloni continued, "but since I was sent as a special courier by General Laggé, there was enough time to deliver this message in person."

"When are they expected to leave Markan?"

"They will try to leave before midday. Laggé explained that he will be traveling to Linden with His Majesty and friends, and has requested that I return to Linden before he arrives, if at all possible. He expects to arrive in Linden by late evening," Boolin reported enthusiastically.

"Good, we will be there to greet them at Linden when they arrive. I want you with me when I declare victory to His Majesty this evening."

Calo awakened Ew and his companions shortly after dawn. They were led to another room, off to the right of the cave where they slept, and seated for their morning meal. Everyone seemed in good spirits as they sat around a large table; even Pala, who had not rested well since the night before he and Ew set out for Thesbis over nearly three weeks ago. Shreela and Soren sat quietly as Calo conversed with Ew, Pala, and Milan, about the conflict within the governorship.

"After Uzak gave his grand speech yesterday," said Calo, "I began to worry about what position the Regional and Interplanetary Governors would take after your mother's death. At first, they all supported Megan's efforts to stabilize the System. However, with the space stations obliterated and the unexpected delays in getting the Balarai Space Station operational, their attitudes began to shift towards compromise with Uni, if at all possible."

"But these Governors were handpicked by me!" exclaimed Ew. "I chose among those I considered to be the most stable during a crisis."

"And you chose well," Calo assured him. "There are, however, other conditions which have surfaced, explaining the division between the Governors."

Ew's eyebrows became furrowed. "What? What could be so drastic that the Governors would alter the policy of Khali?"

"Except for Crashellon and Nilar, our other allies are hesitant to back Khali, Ew. They are being threatened by those planets directly aligned with Uni," Calo explained. "Our Intergalactic Intelligence Agency reported that we, along with our allies, are outnumbered by Uni not only in military personnel, but also in spacecraft, weapons, and ground equipment."

"But that is no news to our allies," said Ew. "They, like Khali, have long lived under the threat of Uni, well aware of both manpower and technological deficiencies. What of the Pact Alliance between Marshèe, Grandow, and Litathe? A treaty with these planets can certainly even up the score."

"I agree, said Calo. "However, they have no desire to become involved in this intergalactic war. At this stage, they have chosen to remain non-aligned."

Ew huffed and rolled his eyes. "How ridiculous," he said. "They must certainly understand that if Uni captures Khali, it will be only a matter of time before they too, will fall into the hands of Uni." Ew gently caressed The Planet Star, suspended on a chain hanging around his neck. "We'll have to manage on our own," he said at length.

Shreela sat quietly watching Ew and the others discuss administrative and military issues concerning Khali. She thought about Machi's statement concerning the young Khalian King who seemed to have everything under control. *So this is the Khalian King that Machi spoke of*, she thought. *Such a burden he carries, and he is definitely in control yet his strength and authority is mixed with such compassion. That is some combination.* Suddenly, she blushed, realizing that Ew was staring at her.

"What's the present status of Star City?" Pala interjected.

Calo got up from the table and walked over to a makeshift counter where a pot of kari sat on a heating element. "Star City is preparing for an invasion," he reported, as he poured kari into a cup. "While you were asleep, I took the liberty of sending all but a handful of military personnel, which you saw here last eve, back to Star City. Twenty-two hundred kilo-trans northeast of here, another detachment from our underground operation in Linden, was also sent. Their primary purpose is to slow down any Unian military advance on Star City as well as to secure the House of Galan until you arrive."

"Good," said Ew. "Any word from Megan yet?"

"A courier arrived early this morning with a message. She has sent word that the House of Galan has not yet fallen to the UMF," he said, smiling.

Ew watched Calo as he drank his kari, reminded of their long friendship. "I owe you a lot," he said warmly. "This underground defense policy, which we put in place several years ago, is turning out to be one of our better military strategies. The credit is yours, Calo. You were the one who clearly saw that such a plan might be necessary if Uni ever attacked Galan. It gives us a fighting chance."

"But it was you, Your Majesty, who agreed to implement it as part of our military plan," Calo responded modestly.

"I can see you're relieved to hear from my sister," said Ew, changing the subject. "How is she?"

"She's working hard with the Governors in an attempt to

reunite Khali. I did send word you were with me, but I'm not certain about whether or not the military personnel sent from Linden ever arrived in Star City. We've not heard from them."

"Who personally took the message back to her about me being here?"

"Boolin Daloni, of all people."

Ew smiled as he rubbed his chin. "You sent him to Star City?"

"Ew, there's so much treachery and treason. I sent Boolin because I trust him to get the message to her. Besides, he was happy to know you were alive."

"I assume he'll stay in Star City," Ew said grinning.

"No way!" Calo looked sheepishly at Ew. "I mean, I asked him to return to the Linden Base before we arrive, if at all possible."

By now, it was three hours past dawn, and Soren began to grow restless. "I think Soren would probably like to go for a walk," Milan interrupted, "and I wouldn't mind stretching my legs a bit. Is it safe to walk around the base?"

"Yes," Calo assured him. "Our long range scanners are set so we'll know if anyone approaches the camp either by land or air."

"Okay, Soren. Let's go," said Milan.

"I think I'll join you," said Calo. "Perhaps the others might like to come along."

"Sure," said Ew. "Just give me a few moments alone with Shreela. We'll join you shortly."

Except for Shreela and Ew, the rest of the group headed out into the tunnel, noisily entering the vertical transport, which carried them to the surface. Ew stood up and walked towards Shreela who was standing beside the makeshift table with her back turned to him.

"I apologize for not revealing my true identity," he said quietly. "Besides," he said, looking sheepish, "I tried to tell you the G in my name stood for Galan, but you wouldn't believe me."

"Did you feel you could not trust me with your secret?" she asked, turning to face him.

"Oh no, it's not like that at all," he whispered coaxingly.

Ew cupped his hand about her chin and gently moved towards her. She felt a warm tingle under his gaze. While his hand ran up her arm, his mouth wandered up and down her neck. She wanted to resist, but her body wouldn't let her, and she moved even deeper into his arms. His lips brushed hers, a tantalizing invitation to continue their quest. Momentarily setting aside her own grief, she responded to his soft kisses, forgetting the war, Uzak, and the many other problems, which plagued them since they met. Reluctantly, she pulled away, flustered by the extended contact.

"What's wrong?" he asked, puzzled by her response.

Shreela had a worried look on her face, thinking on what just happened between them. "I'm not ready for this."

"I hope you're still not annoyed with me for keeping my identity secret, especially after the discussion we had last evening with Calo. Shreela," he pleaded, "I really didn't set out to deceive you. I planned to tell you everything once we reached Star City."

Shreela looked at him, realizing he did not understand what was going on in her mind. "No, no," she said, touching his arm. "I understand and forgive you for not telling me who you are. What I meant was....."

"What did you mean?"

"I meant that it's too soon for me to become involved with anyone, right now anyway."

"Oh," Ew said, understanding the problem. "Shreela, it's always too soon to become involved with another person after losing a spouse. Eleven days is no sooner than eleven years because you will love him until you die."

"Do you still love her?"

"I always will."

"Then, what's different?"

"The difference between then and now is the pain of her absence is gone," he said thoughtfully. "I will forever love and cherish the memory of her, but I can't continue to live my life on just memories. Trust me, it gets easier with time."

"But I feel so guilty about the way I feel about you."

"Have you ever been attracted to other men while you were married?"

"Our culture is monogamous, so much so, that a widow or widower may not have another mate after the death of a spouse."

Ew looked directly into her eyes. "That's not what I asked." Shreela looked away. "Have you ever been attracted to other men during your marriage?" Ew repeated the question.

"I guess so," she said, blushing. "I've met other men that I've liked, if that's what you mean."

Using the tips of his fingers, Ew raised her chin. "Shreela," he said gently, "that's exactly what I mean. We all meet other people that we like or even love during our lifetime. When we do settle for one person, it means that we make a commitment to that one person, at least in our culture. That doesn't mean you'll never have feelings for another. Right now, you are not committed to anyone unless you want to be committed to a memory."

"But in my society, I cannot have another relationship," she argued.

"You are not on Tima, Shreela. You are on Galan, where a widow or widower does have the right to have another mate."

Shreela stood there, pondering his words in silence. Ew moved close to her again, lifting her head until their eyes met. "Shreela, it took a long time for me to understand in my heart, that it was alright for me to have feelings for someone else. Don't feel guilty about something that's natural."

For a long moment, Shreela studied him silently, finally accepting how disturbingly attractive he was to her. "I believe what you're saying is true," she finally responded. "Remember, I'm new at this, and it's difficult to apply this logic to such an emotional situation." She put her arms around his waist, and laid her head on his chest. "You know, I knew you were special from the moment I first saw you," she said gently. "Give me a little time to adjust, alright?"

"I understand how you feel and I'll not press the issue further. If you need to talk about it, though, I'm willing to listen," he said, kissing the top of her head. "Come on, let's go for that walk."

On the same morning Ew and Shreela strolled around the Markan Defense Base, in Landory, Boolin Daloni and Uzak laid plans to capture the five travelers.

"I want a garrison sent to Linden this morning and I want that base taken over by midday," Uzak instructed.

"What about the troops sent to Star City by Laggé?"

"They were met by UMF troops just outside Star City." The smirk on Uzak's face clearly indicated his delight by this sudden change of events. "I've just received word that the Galan Underground is losing that battle, and Star City is on the brink of falling into my hands."

"And the House of Galan?"

"It's only a question of time."

Uzak and Boolin were still conversing when General Narvan's voice came over the televideocom.

"Lord, we arrested Dr. Monroe. He is here for questioning."

"Good! Bring him to my quarters at once," Uzak commanded.

Within minutes, General Narvan ushered Monroe into Uzak's quarters. There was malice in Uzak's eyes as he beheld the treasonous felon who had the audacity to refuse to accept the terms for surrender as agreed to by Galan's Governorship.

"So, you are the one responsible for committing treason against Uni. The underground military base has been declared illegal, yet you seek to align yourself with those conspirators despite the consequences."

Monroe stared at Boolin, deeply troubled about the rebellion since Boolin had access to the Khalian defense strategies. "How many others will die because of your betrayal?" Monroe questioned Boolin, directly.

"I wouldn't concern myself with 'others' if I were you," Uzak snapped. "You should worry about your own life."

"I will die anyway," said Monroe.

"You don't have to die, Monroe. Your cooperation with our forces can extend your life, and it may even prove to be rewarding," said Uzak, in an *almost* beguiling tone.

"And what must I do for this reward?" the other responded cynically.

"If we knew where the defense outposts were located, you would be doing a great service to those serving them. The war would be over quickly, and many lives would be saved."

"I would rather die than to live under the whip of a tyrant and a liar."

The room was quiet except for the long deliberate strides of

Uzak, walking across the room toward Monroe. "You will talk, Monroe," Uzak said, thumping his fingers on Monroe's shoulder. Using the back of his hand, Uzak struck Monroe across the face, hurling him across the floor. "Take him away!"

The morning sky over Landory was crystal clear. The once clean, organized, city streets and highways were overrun with UMF troops and equipment. Although Landory conceded to UMF demands for surrender, scattered sounds of laser fire split the air as Unian Military Police battled with pockets of resistance.

During the midday hour, Uzak was still conferring with Boolin Daloni when Narvan interrupted their discussions.

"Sire, we were beginning another round of interrogation with Monroe when he collapsed. We tried to revive him, but his heart could not take the strain. He is dead, Sire."

"Were you able to get any information from him?" Uzak asked.

"None, Sire."

"My Lord, I believe we have enough information to capture Galan," Daloni interjected.

Uzak paused for a moment, silently deliberating information already known by him. "I agree," he said at length. "Narvan, leave Monroe's body to rot in the street so that he may serve as an example for others who might oppose me."

"Yes, Sire. Will there be anything else?" Narvan asked, greatly relieved.

"Yes. I will be leaving for Linden shortly. Galan is not here in Landory, of that I am now certain. He is on his way to Linden. I want sentry ships to sweep the southern area along the Ring Mountain Range for any small spacecraft headed toward Linden. They are sure to try to avoid any scanning devices."

"And if we find something, My Lord?"

"Track them. I want them to reach their destination. If they deviate from a course for Linden, notify me immediately."

"Yes, My Lord."

"While I am gone," Uzak continued, "I expect you to continue your search for those who oppose the rule of Uni. I shall deal with them upon my return," he instructed.

Two hours past midday, Ew and his friends piled into the surface spacecraft destined for Linden. The trip was slow since they had to steer close to the mountains in order to avoid visual scanning. For the first nine hundred kilo-trans, they did not meet up with or even see any signs of the Unian Military Police. However, twelve-hundred kilo-trans southwest of Linden, two Unian sentry spacecraft headed directly toward them. Shreela's heart pounded furiously as she remembered her first encounter with the Unian Military Police. Soren moved close to his mother, sensing her fear.

Ew pulled them close to him. "We'll be alright," he assured them. "Calo, do you think they've spotted us?"

"No, but I'm not taking any chances. There's a small grotto in that mountain to the right, large enough for this machine to fit comfortably. We can duck in there until they pass."

Calo steered the craft toward the opening in the mountain, which was quite narrow. Maneuvering the craft was difficult, but his many years of experience enabled him to pilot the ship inside without damage. Once inside, Calo shut down all engines except the neutron levitation system necessary for suspension above the ground.

Ew and his companions sat quietly as the sentry ships moved toward their hiding place. Their slow airspeed implied that a search was in progress. The pilot of one spacecraft flew directly over them. His sensors picked up remnants of neutron particles from Calo's spacecraft. Immediately, he summoned the other craft.

"Anuj, Anuj, come in."

"Anuj here."

"I'm picking up a trail of exhaust leading to that mountain to your right. Are you picking up anything?"

"No....Wait a minute. I think I have something here."

"What is it?"

"I'm not picking up any movement over there, but I do get life form readings. I'm also getting a reading on neutron lifters exhaust."

"So am I."

"Call Defense in Landory for instructions."

"Okay, but let's not hang around here too long. Whoever's there might get wind that we're on to them."

"I'll head west," said Anuj. "You go east."

"Right."

"Anuj out."

"Defense Control, this is Darwins checking in."

"What do you have?"

"Commander, we've detected a warm aircraft hidden in a mountain cove on the fringe of Ring Mountain, twelve-hundred kilo-trans southwest of Linden. What are your orders?"

"Transmit the coordinates and leave the area. We'll take it from there."

"Yes sir. Darwins out."

Moments seemed like hours as Ew and his companions waited for the sound of engines to pass overhead and fade into the southwest. Finally, the sentry ships moved out of hearing range. Calo then fired up the engines and drove his spacecraft out of the grotto.

"Do you think they spotted us?" asked Ew.

"It's hard to tell," replied Calo.

"They did hover over us for a brief period," said Pala. "Maybe they're searching for something else."

"Possibly, but doubtful," said Ew. "Come on, let's get out of here."

The remainder of the trip was quiet, uninterrupted by sentry or any other spacecraft. Still, everyone sat anxiously watching the skies and listening for the sound of engines.

As Ew and his friends journeyed toward Linden, Uzak stepped off his Surface Spacecraft at the Linden Defense Base. An intense early morning battle between UMF and remaining Galan Underground Defense troops, left several fires ablaze in the woody area surrounding the base. The actual base structure was smoldering, but no significant damage could be seen from the outside.

The clean up of the area was already underway when Uzak arrived at the base in the early afternoon, but it was dusk before the majority of the battle debris was removed. Any remaining signs of skirmish were veiled under the darkening sky.

Linden was a small northern town located near the east coast of the continent. Most of the inhabitants, in the industrialized Linden, end their workday four hours past midday, creating the usual traffic tie-ups as people hurried home. Ew and his companions were caught up in just such a traffic jam, delaying their arrival to the Linden Underground Defense Base, located at the extreme northeastern point of Linden.

The defense base was an old factory building large enough to hold twenty surface-to-space transports, each spacecraft accommodating up to sixty people. It had been abandoned for many years before being purchased by the Galan Military Forces and secretly transformed. The people of Linden believed it to be a military prison. Since the area was fenced in with force field barriers, and staffed with military personnel surveillance, the story was an excellent camouflage.

It was dark outside when Calo pulled his spacecraft up to the space dock. As he was stepping out of the craft, Ew noticed how quiet and forlorn the base looked. The air was warm and motionless, and he opened the top of his shirt, exposing the gold chain from which The Planet Star was suspended. Even though the medallion was not visible, he refastened his shirt.

Everyone quickly walked toward the entrance, anxious to get in and settle down for the night. Calo placed his hand against the opaque screen on the wall next to the powerful two-tran thick door. When the door slid open, he was surprised to see that it was completely dark inside.

"Thought you said that Boolin would be here to meet us," said Ew.

"Only if he could make it back from Star City in time. I suppose he was delayed," Calo responded.

"Then it looks like we're on our own," said Ew, shaking his head and sighing as Calo led them inside.

Flight For Home

Calo and his companions stepped across the threshold into the dark Linden Spacecraft hold. Almost immediately, Calo switched on the lights. A look of disbelief spread across his face, and he stiffened to attention, his eyes beholding a long column of unexpected visitors.

Ew and Uzak stood face to face inside the Linden Defense Base. Everyone stood motionless, breathlessly awaiting the next move. Briefly, Uzak's eyes shifted to the party traveling with

Ew, sending a chill down Shreela's spine as Uzak's eyes met with hers. Ew was the first to address Uzak. Shreela was surprised that he seemed undaunted despite his present circumstance.

"I hear you're looking for me," Ew casually commented.

"In light of your present position, I wouldn't be so smug if I were you," Uzak snapped.

"Alright," Ew grinned. "I hear we keep missing each other."

Uzak let out a hideous sound as he drew his laser and fired. Ew immediately fell to the ground. When his friends rushed to his aid, OMP armed guards stopped them. "He's only stunned," Uzak snarled. "He won't die so easily, and he definitely won't die first. Search him!"

One of the guards yanked the gold chain from his neck. "He has only this, my Lord."

Uzak walked over to the guard, removing The Planet Star from his hand. "Take them away!"

Ew woke to find Shreela leaning over him. He readily recognized that still, quiet expression on her face, and wondered what her thoughts were. He moved to get up, but was quickly restrained by the sick feeling in his stomach. His head ached, he felt tired, and his neck and body were sore all over. "What happened?" he asked, groggily.

Pala approached Ew and spoke quietly. "We're in prison. Uzak stunned you. You've been unconscious for nearly four hours." Pala sighed. "A lot has happened."

"What's going on?" Ew asked reluctantly, studying the serious look on his friend's face.

"First of all," Pala began, "we've learned that Dr. Monroe is dead. In fact, Uzak made it a point to tell us. He has also taken The Planet Star."

Ew looked around the cell room. "Where's Milan?"

"Milan is being questioned by Uzak. No doubt the subject is his theft of The Planet Star," mumbled Pala. "Shreela is also in great danger over this medallion. She'll probably be next in line for questioning."

Ew looked at Shreela apologetically. "I should have been more...." The opening of the cell door interrupted his sentence. Milan collapsed as he was pushed inside. One sentry strode in and grabbed Shreela under the arm, yanking her to her feet. Struggling to his feet in an attempt to follow, Ew was restrained by the second sentry who leveled a laser at his head. Totally helpless, Ew silently watched Shreela being escorted through the cell door.

"I could have left her in Landory and arranged for safe passage to Crashellon for her and her son," he scolded himself. "It was my own selfishness that brought her to this place. I pray that my whim does not cost her life."

"We have to hope she'll be alright," Pala consoled his friend.

Ew shook his head and sighed. "I know, but with Uzak, I have to expect the worst," he said, looking at Milan who was still lying on the floor. Pala was attending to his wounds, but was unable to bring Milan back to consciousness. "Can you tell if he's going to be alright?" Ew asked.

"I don't know, but there's nothing we can do here. He's losing a lot of blood, and he definitely needs a doctor."

"I doubt if Uzak will agree to that," Ew said sarcastically. "All we can do now is wait."

And wait they did. It was close to dawn before Shreela was returned to the cell. Soren tearfully ran to his mother, wrapping his arms around her neck when she stooped to greet him. "I'm alright," she said, and began speaking softly to him in Timanian.

Ew looked in puzzlement at Shreela. She appeared unscratched as well as emotionally unruffled, yet there was something different about her. "What happened?" he asked.

Walking towards Ew, seemingly more concerned for him rather than herself, "are you alright?" she asked, totally unresponsive to his question.

"Shreela," cried Ew, "what happened to you?" he insisted. He noticed the strange look on her face. "Shreela, what is it?"

"I'm not sure," Shreela said truthfully. "I was standing before Uzak trying to explain my involvement with you and the others when he suddenly went into a tirade. He began screaming something about me holding some treasure or having a key that would destroy Uni. Ew, what was he talking about?"

"It's all tied to the Legend of Khali. Remember what we talked about when we were at the Mount Halokin Defense Base?"

Shreela thought for a moment, recalling the story of the Legend as Ew explained it nearly three weeks before. "Yes, I do recall that," she murmured softly to herself.

"What did Uzak say, I mean, why did he let you go?" Ew insisted.

"You were right, Ew," Shreela responded. "Uzak started out with strange comments about the Keepers of Khali, and how I was sent to destroy him. He kept asking me questions about The Planet Star, what powers I had, and on and on. When I couldn't give him the answers he wanted to hear, he became livid. For some reason, though, he suddenly let me go. He muttered something about it being too soon for me to die."

Ew watched Shreela pacing the room trying to recall the details of her strange experience. Finally, she sat down on the cot where Milan was resting. She seemed to be sorting out something in her mind. "Shreela?" he asked.

"What?"

"You look like you're in another world. What's going on with you?"

"I'm sorry. I was just trying to recall a dream I had."

Ew looked at her curiously. "Does it remind you of what happened here?"

"Yes it does."

Ew walked over to Shreela and stooped to her eye level. "Tell me about it."

"They may seem a little silly, but did you ever have a dream that you couldn't remember until the dream became a reality?"

"Many times," responded the other.

"I dreamed, not long ago, about being taken to a place where I was held prisoner. Though I had never seen the face of Uzak of Uni before today, he was the being in that dream." Shreela shivered. "As soon as I was escorted into the room where I was questioned, I recalled the dream, but in that dream, I was able to get out of that situation somehow."

Ew looked around the room. There were no windows or any other opening except for the door. "Well, that's not going to be easy. Did Uzak say anything else?"

"The Planet Star, which he now has, is important, but finding the key to unlock its power seemed to be even more important to him. What and where is this key?"

"I cannot and will not tell you that, Shreela."

"Another secret?"

"You bet."

"Why won't you tell me?"

"Uzak didn't kill you this time around, but he might do worse than that the next time."

"I would die before I told him."

"I believe you would, but what about him?" Ew looked over at Soren who stood very close to his mother.

"I understand."

It was well after dawn before three Unian sentries interrupted Ew and his companions. This time, they came for Ew. One sentry stood at the cell door with his laser gun drawn, while the other two walked toward Ew; one carrying magnetic restraint clamps to cuff Ew's arms, the other with a laser.

Ew spoke to the sentry with the clamps. "No need for those. I'll go peacefully."

"It's the rule," the sentry commented, "now raise those arms. Slowly!"

As the sentry moved to cuff him, Ew suddenly made a daring move and shoved the guard into the sentry holding the laser. The laser discharged, hitting the ceiling as the two guards toppled to the ground. Calo quickly dived onto the sentry standing at the door, but not before he fired his laser at Ew, missing Ew's head by a fraction of a lino-tran. Pala and Ew rushed the two sentries already on the ground and took their weapons. Calo rendered his victim unconscious and stood near the cell entrance with a laser in his hand.

"What now?" Calo asked Ew, while trying to look both ways down the corridor.

"Cuff these two," Ew said to Pala.

While Pala cuffed the two sentries, Ew walked to the cell door and peeped up and down the corridors. "Good, the hallways are empty. We'll lock these three in and head for that exit," he whispered and pointed out the direction to Calo. "Come on, let's go."

Calo was the first to exit. "All clear," he said.

Pala rushed over to Milan, picked him up and draped him over his shoulder. Shreela ran through the open cell door followed by Pala and Milan, and Ew, who carried Soren under his arm. There were no OMP guards posted in the corridor. Calo slammed the door shut before heading for the side exit.

Ew peered through the window in order to determine whether or not they could escape that way without being detected. "There are several surface craft, but they're at the other end of the building," he reported. Looking down the long corridor, "we can exit down there," he said, pointing to the door at the end of the long hallway, "or we can go outside from here and run along the side of the building."

"Outside is too risky," Calo cautioned.

"Inside is not much better, but we stand a better chance of not being seen."

"Let me lead the way," Calo returned.

"Okay," said Ew, "I'll take the rear."

With his laser weapon drawn, Calo led the group down the long corridor. To Shreela, the hallway seemed endless as they slowed their pace each time they neared an intersecting corridor. They were less than fifty trans from the exit when laser blasts exploded from behind. Ew turned and fired back. Carrying Soren made it difficult for him to hit a target, so he fired randomly which gave him enough time to get to the exit. Calo held the door open while Pala and Shreela scrambled through the doorway, followed by Ew. With the threat of OMP in pursuit from behind, Pala took the lead, heading for the first spacecraft, which was sitting nearly two hundred and fifty trans from the exit. By then, sirens were blaring and military personnel were rushing into the area. As they passed the halfway mark, sentries stationed on the roof open fired on them. Grabbing Soren from Ew's arms, Shreela scurried behind Pala toward the craft.

The battle filled the air with the smell of burning metal as laser blasts missed their targets and bounced off the metal plates on the ground. The moment Shreela headed up the gangplank, Calo and Ew began to run toward the spacecraft. Suddenly,

Calo dropped to the ground, wounded by a laser blast to his upper left shoulder. As Ew fled up the plank, he instinctively looked back before entering the craft. He saw his old friend lying on the ground. Without hesitation, he started back for him, firing and dodging what seemed like an endless barrage of laser fire. Calo was still firing his confiscated weapon when Ew grabbed his right forearm and helped him to his feet.

"You should have left me!" Calo shouted.

"No way," Ew shouted, firing back toward the roof of the base just above the entrance where a large number of sentries were now gathered. "Besides, I can't show up in Star City without you. She'll kill me."

"Who?" shouted Calo.

"My sister. If I don't show up with you, I had better not show up at all."

Ew and Calo headed up the gangplank. Unexpectedly, the body of a Unian Sentry came flying through the door. Pala appeared in the doorway, shouting impatiently for them to hurry. Finally the door was closed. Everyone gathered around the small bridge area, still keyed up as the spacecraft prepared for takeoff. In the midst of all the confusion, Ew's attention was drawn to the emblem on the cockpit panel. "Hey, look at this," he shouted, as he pushed a series of buttons.

"What kind of symbol is that?" asked Shreela.

"The officer in command of Unian spacecraft always marks his vessel with a personal emblem," Ew replied. "This is Uzak's personal spacecraft."

"What a strange chance this is," said Pala.

"I'm ready," said Ew. "Let's get out of here."

Although Ew and his companions knew the Unian Military Force would soon pursue them, they were amused by the irony of using Uzak's own spacecraft as they sped westward to Star

City.

Ew and his companions were hotly pursued by the UMF within minutes of their escape. Since the ship was not designed for deep space travel, they were forced to bob and weave between mountains and forest terrain. Ew was comfortable in these maneuvers since his basic training as a pilot was conducted along the northern borders of the Ring Mountain Range. In years past, the land between Linden and Star City served as a primary training course for both civilian and military pilots. Between Calo and Ew, it did not prove too difficult a task to avoid the assault from UMF spacecraft firing at them from behind.

Sitting on the edge of a small stationary chair just outside the pilot control room, grave concern lined Shreela's face as she watched over Milan who was sweating profusely and running a high fever. "We have to get help for Milan as soon as possible," she commented.

"I'm worried about him too," said Pala. "We'll be in Star City soon," he assured her. "Try not to worry."

The shortest distance between Linden and Star City was twenty-four-hundred kilo-trans. That route, however, would take them out into the open, leaving them fair game for their pursuers. Ew chose to ride the old Pilot Training course, a path that hugged mountain passages and narrow canyons. Their distance nearly doubled to forty-four-hundred kilo-trans, a thirty- minute ride at top speed, but would provide better protection.

The Pilot Training Course path zigzagged along the mountain passages of the Ring Mountain Range, so named for its shape. The first ten minutes of the trip consisted of rolling and rocking as Calo and Ew tried to avoid the laser shower from behind. At one point, they guided the ship counterclockwise around the mountain, directly into the path of a much larger surface craft traveling at moderate speed. Calo suddenly dived at a sixty-degree angle to avoid colliding with the craft, but the two sentry ships in pursuit had no time to react, crashing head on with the larger vessel. The tremendous explosion ripped large trees from their foundations as a large section of the mountainside collapsed. A huge boulder, hurled off the mountain during that explosion, perforated the hull of Ew's stolen spacecraft, creating atmospheric depressurization inside the ship. Everything not fastened down was forced toward the gaping hole. Shreela and Soren were securely strapped into stationary chairs just right of the newly formed hole while Pala and Milan were strapped in on the opposite side.

"Ew," Pala yelled over the wind tunnel sound.

"Ew shouted back through the cockpit door. "We're looking for a place to land. Hold on!"

The craft was already slowing its pace before Ew finished his sentence. He glanced over at Calo sitting next to him in the copilot seat. Although he quietly navigated the ship, Ew could see that he was in great pain.

"How's the arm?" he asked.

"It's a little sore, but I can navigate without... look over there!" Calo pointed to a hollow space on the ground, partially hidden by foliage and large trees at the mountain base.

"It looks like a decent spot to hide in," said Ew. "Can you navigate toward the innermost perimeter? We will be completely hidden from aerial view if we can land close to the innermost edge."

"The navigation computer is out so we'll have to do this manually." Between the two of them, they were able to maneuver the ship under the dense tree cover and onto the ground.

Calo shut the engines down as Ew headed toward the hull of the ship to inspect the damage. Stopping short of his destination, he noticed Soren sitting on his mother's lap. He had nearly forgotten the shock they must have experienced when the boulder perforated the hull. By the look on their faces, he thought to take a moment and calm a few frayed nerves.

"Are you alright?" he directed his question to Shreela.

"We're okay. Is it possible to repair that?" she asked, pointing toward the gaping hole in the ship's hull.

Ew stooped to address her at eye level. "I don't know. If we can't, we'll all squeeze into the cockpit before we take off," he answered, noticing the worried look on her face. Cupping his hand under Soren's chin, he smiled in an attempt to coax Soren to do the same. "Are you alright?"

"I'm good," Soren said, smiling back at Ew.

Ew briefly turned for a moment to look at the damage. *It's doubtful that we can repair this damage quickly*, he thought. "Come on, let's look at the damage," he said, turning back to Soren.

Ew pulled Soren to his feet. While they walked toward the damaged hull, Shreela sat for a moment watching as he talked with Soren about what was needed to repair the craft before they could take off again. She laughed softly when he caught her eye and winked. *This man refuses to let me mourn in peace,* she thought. *Maybe he's right about letting go. I wonder. Hum-m-m.* Shreela let out a long sigh. Finally, she got up and walked toward Pala who was helping Calo out of his shirt. "Can I help?" she asked. Poor Calo winced as Pala yanked at his shirtsleeve trying to free his arm. "Pala", she said, "would you find some kind of cutting tool and bring it here to me?' There was a slight tone of annoyance in her voice as she pulled Pala's hand off of Calo's shirtsleeve. Calo, on the other hand, looked relieved that Pala had been taken off the case. While Pala went off to look for something that might serve them, Shreela asked Calo to sit in the chair she had vacated only moments earlier. By that time, Pala returned with a triage kit he found on the bridge. The kit was well stocked, and contained a slicer and a molecular skin regenerator. Using the slicer, she cut away the shirt to expose the injured area. With the molecular skin regenerator, she scanned the device across the burned area. The damaged tissue quickly peeled away, replaced by newly regenerated tissue.

"Thank you, Shreela," said Calo.

"The laser blast only grazed your shoulder."

"Well Calo, your arm looks as good as new," said Ew, walking up to view the conditions of Calo's arm.

Calo flexed his arm. "Feels pretty good too," he responded.

Ew looked over at Shreela. "What can we do for Milan?"

"We need to bring his temperature down, it's much too high," she said. "I'm worried about him. Is it too risky for you to search for water?"

"Pala and I are going out to look for something to cover the hole in the hull." Ew looked over at Milan who was still unconscious on the bench near the entrance of the ship's bridge area. "We'll look for water too," he said. "Come on Pala, let's go now."

By the time Pala and Ew returned, Calo was resting on the floor and Shreela was sitting next to Milan. Ew handed her a container of water. "Here, we found water not far from here."

"Thank you."

"We also brought back a few large metal scraps that were scattered from the crash. We'll piece a temporary patch over the hole in the hull."

"How long will that take?" asked Calo.

"With the three of us working on it, we should be able to finish in less than an hour."

"How long do you suppose it will take us to reach Star City after we leave here?" Shreela asked.

"That all depends upon which side now controls the city." Before Ew could continue, they heard the sound of engines headed their way. Everyone held their breath, having little doubt as to whose engines they were. "Quick, everyone, into the cockpit."

Together Ew and Pala managed to get Milan inside and prop him up in the backseat behind the captain's station. After everyone was inside, Ew closed and locked the bridge door. "We cannot leave without repairing this ship," he said. "It will be impossible to maneuver this craft all the way to Star City."

"What if they spot us here?" asked Pala.

"Then we have no choice but to leave. Let's wait to see if they go away. If their stop is unusually long, I will assume they've located us and only then will we take off."

Uzak watched as his personal Surface Spacecraft sped away from the Linden Underground Defense Base carrying with it the King of the Khalian Solar System along with the keys necessary to activate his precious medallion.

"I want that ship tracked and destroyed!" he shouted angrily. "Bring me another ship!"

Within minutes, Uzak was airborne and on the path of Ew and his companions. Shortly after takeoff, the commander of the craft quickly approached Uzak who stood staring at the bridge monitor.

"My Lord, we are picking up an energy disturbance on our scanners."

Head for that disturbance," Uzak commanded.

The powerful ship engines of the Lord of Uni, rumbled as it passed over the place where Ew and his friends hid.

"Commander, I want a shuttle sent down to investigate this crash site," ordered Uzak.

"Right away, My Lord."

Uzak's ship hovered over the crash site while a shuttle went forth to examine the wreckage. Among the debris was a large badly scorched scrap of metal. Though terribly charred, the personal insignia of Uzak was scorched but clearly identifiable as part of his personal Surface Spacecraft. There being no survivors, only the large scrap of metal was placed aboard the shuttle and taken back to the main vessel.

Uzak sat at a conference table surrounded by officers ready to brief him on their findings. "Commander, what is your report on the debris from the crash site?" he questioned.

"My Lord, we retrieved part of one of the surface spacecraft with markings of your personal insignia. Most of the wreckage was mangled by the heat of an explosion."

"What caused the explosion?"

"The debris is scattered across a wide area. We conclude that there was a head-on collision between two or three ships. The shuttle crew spotted at least seven badly charred bodies in the wreckage. They also scanned the area for humanoid life forms. There were none, My Lord."

"I have reviewed the video logs of the site, Commander," said Uzak. "I am satisfied there were no survivors. Set a course for Star City."

"Yes, My Lord."

9
THE STAR ROOM

The Secret Tunnel

Ew and his friends sat quietly discussing whether or not to repair the ship's navigation system.

"There's not enough time for complete repairs on the navigation system," Pala voiced his concern.

Since we really don't know the extent of damage sustained during the explosion, it would be prudent to at least try," Calo cautioned.

"Look Calo, the hull has been repaired. That was the most important thing to be done," Pala argued. "This is not a deep space aircraft, but a low altitude transport. We can navigate without computer assist."

As the argument between Calo and Pala became heated, Ew could see that Pala's temper was about to flare, so before Calo could respond, he waved his hand to silence them both.

"Wait a minute. I agree with both of your arguments, but we must think of other factors beyond the condition of this ship. First, consider the condition of Milan. He's barely conscious now, he's weak, and he needs a doctor. Secondly, Calo, I agree with Pala about repairs. We can navigate without computer assist. At first I believed it was an hour's work, but I can see that it would take a full day to effect proper repairs, and we don't have time for that. Thirdly, Uzak is surely headed for Star City. If that city has not yet totally fallen to the UMF, I may still be able to reach the Star Room in the House of Galan and activate the real Planet Star. If this war is to end successfully for us, that fact is of paramount importance. We've wasted five minutes sitting here arguing about navigation. Now, everyone strap in, it's time to go?"

Both Pala and Calo remained silent as their leader made his decision clear. Finally Calo broke the silence as he tried to concede his position. "You're right, Ew. I'm a military strategist. It's my job to plan for minimum casualty risk. It's a difficult habit to break," he said, while gearing up the engines. Shrugging his shoulders, Calo turned his attention to the view outside the bridge window.

Shreela looked at Calo with compassion and deep understanding. "We all have a great deal to lose," she said, guessing that he was also thinking that he might not live to see Megan again. "Sometimes, we must take desperate chances if it means that many will benefit by its success. I fear that even if we leave now, our margin of success will be very narrow to attain..." Someone moving among the bushes several trans beyond the ship cut her argument short. Suddenly, they all saw a large group of OMP soldiers headed in their direction.

"Our decision is quite clear," said Ew. "Let's get out of here."

"Who are they?" Shreela asked.

"Occupation Military Police (OMP)," he explained, "ground forces responsible for controlling villages and cities during a siege. They are probably headed for the small city of Embly, several kilo-trans west of here."

The OMP troops rushed toward the ship as soon as the spacecraft engines sounded.

"They're trying to hail us," Pala said to Ew.

"Jam the frequency, and let's get out of here?"

It was nearly midday when Ew and his companions sped off toward Star City.

"I suggest we enter the city from the north," said Calo.

"The southern route is much quicker," Pala commented. "Why north?"

"The northern route is mountainous and there are forests to provide better cover. On the other hand, the countryside surrounding Star City's eastern, western, and southern borders are primarily farm or grassland," Calo explained. "We would be vulnerable for at least sixty kilo-trans before reaching the city limits. The likelihood of attack by the Galan Military is greater since our ship has Unian military markings."

"Good point," noted Pala.

"I agree," said Ew. "The underground escape passage from the house is also north of the city. Pala, make the necessary course corrections, and set coordinates to land close to where that passage exits."

It was a clear, sunny day with high visibility. Shreela quietly watched, admiring the beauty of the Galan countryside. Small purple and red shrubs burdened with bright blue berries contrasted the sand-colored grasslands that hemmed the mountain range. As the ship cruised westward, the approaching forest mesmerized Shreela. She caught her breath in wonder.

"This is the Prism Forest," said Ew. "We are within one-hundred kilo-trans of Star City."

Shreela did not respond, but sat with her mouth half-open, absorbing the magnificent display of color. Indigo tree trunks were laden with thick foliage, some with purple and pink leaves, red and blue leaves, green and orange, and many other combinations. There was the sense of a continually moving forest, as the tree color combinations shimmered and changed hue, caused by the angle of reflection of the Galanian sun. Shreela sighed at the multi-colored splendor. "So this is Galan," she whispered.

Ew glanced back for a moment to look at her face. He smiled to himself, recalling her first impression of the Galan Marsh. "Yes, this is Galan," he said softly.

It was late afternoon when Shreela caught her first glimpse of the darkened skyline of Star City as they maneuvered the ship through the mountains. She could see that inner city travelers entered by way of travel belts; clear, smoked-glass shuttle tubes connecting urban communities. Each self-contained community complex housed thousands of residents. Arc-shaped building complexes stood three to four-hundred trans high with several travel belts running between the arches.

Ew slowed the craft as they approached the northern borders of Star City, some twenty kilo-trans from the House of Galan. Flashes of laser fire exchange between Unian and Khalian spacecraft, careened across the skies. Large structures burned and belched thick black clouds of smoke and debris. Ew was saddened as he watched his home city scorch and burn under fierce Unian military attack. Suddenly, his own craft shook violently from laser fire.

"How are the shields?" Ew shouted to Calo.

"They're holding for now."

"There's a Khalian Laser Cruiser off the stern," said Pala.

"I see. They're almost on us. Let's take her down," Ew commanded.

Ew piloted the craft to an altitude several trans above the ground. Suddenly, they were hit again from behind, and the tail of the craft caught fire, making escape from the hull impossible. Ew held onto the gear and made a bumpy landing just beyond the forest boundary, outside city limits. He gritted his teeth as the craft violently careened forward, through areas of thick underbrush. The ship came to a sudden stop as it plowed into a section of trees. Quickly, Ew unfastened his seat clamp, then assisted Shreela and Soren, seated in the rear seats of the cockpit, to release their clamps. "Hurry," he cried, "We have only a few minutes before this craft explodes."

Ew pushed the emergency exit door next to his seat, outward. He helped Shreela and Soren, still dazed by the turbulent landing. Pala made his way out, and together, Ew and Pala assisted Calo in pulling Milan out of the spacecraft. Once outside, they ran nearly three hundred trans away from the craft before it blew up, hurling them to the ground.

For several minutes, the air was filled with the crackling sounds of metal burning, as well as a series of small explosions. Finally, Ew sat up breathing heavily and coughing from the smoke.

"How is everyone?" he asked, unwrapping Soren's arms from around his neck. "Shreela?"

"Few bruises, and a slight headache, but nothing that can't wait," she responded.

Ew stood up and walked thirty to forty trans back to where Pala and Calo were. They lay exhausted on the ground, still holding onto Milan, who was barely conscious. "The northern tunnel is probably five or six minutes south of here. Can he make it?" asked Ew.

"Probably not," Pala commented. "That race from the ship was too much for him. Calo and I dragged him most of the way."

"We can wait a few moments, but not too long."

"No, that's alright," said Pala. "I'll carry him over my shoulder, otherwise, it will be slow going" .

"Alright then, let's go."

Not far from where Ew and his friends scrambled from the damaged ship, Megan stood nervously in the foyer of the House of Galan while OMP forces banged at the main entrance. The door, made of strong, reinforced alloy, was not impervious to high-energy laser fire. Suddenly, she heard a Unian commander shout orders for his men to stand away from the entrance. She knew she must run or perish.

Heading for the back staircase leading to the garden behind the palace, Megan stumbled down several steps as the blast from the Unian high-energy laser cannon shook the foundations of Galan House. Composing herself, she quickly descended the remaining stairs, where she was met by Oshe who handed her a cloak and laser gun, which she carefully concealed in the inside pocket of her garment.

"Please be careful, Your Highness," Oshe cautioned.

"I'll be fine," Megan answered, slightly out of breath. Oshe opened the door that led to the garden. "I must hurry now," said Megan stepping across the threshold. "Good luck to all of you."

Megan walked quickly down the garden path, looking back once more before disappearing behind a thicket of shrubs located next to the large concrete wall, fifty trans to the right of the back door. This was the entrance to an underground passage, which exited on the northern outskirts of town. Megan exited through this door while Uzak's men stormed her home. Just as she slipped inside, she heard loud voices and rapidly moving footsteps. She shivered at the sound, and then shoved the door shut. Once inside, using the laser to ignite a large bashi stick, she made her way down a long flight of stairs and began walking northward through a long winding tunnel.

Nearly fifteen minutes passed before Megan stopped at the sound of footsteps heading toward her. The pathway curved to the right making it impossible to see more than a few trans ahead. Fear gripped her as the sound of voices echoed along the passage. There was no place for her to hide. Megan dropped the stake on the ground, and pressed her body close to the tunnel wall. With her laser gun drawn, she stood silent, awaiting the arrival of the intruders. As the voices came close, she began to sweat with fear, anxious for the encounter to be over with. Just when she felt she could wait no longer, a light shown on the pathway, silhouetting several humanoid figures against the wall. She quickly stepped out onto the path with her laser gun aimed and ready to fire. "Who dares to invade the House of Galan?" she shouted.

"Megan, it's me," the voice said in a tone, which begged for recognition.

Megan moved close to the light and dropped her weapon as she recognized the face before her. She ran into the arms of her brother, crying in disbelief, overjoyed to see him alive and well.

"Ew," she cried. "I didn't think I would ever see you again."

"I heard all about you," Ew said, smiling. "You are one tough lady, and I'm glad you were here to take care of things in my absence."

"Well, I didn't do too good a job. Galan's all but destroyed by Uni. I'm sorry Ew. I couldn't make the Governors listen to reason. Now, the House of Galan is overridden with Unian Police. It is impossible for us to return there. What are we going to do?" she asked anxiously.

"I know you did your best, and we haven't lost yet," Ew assured her, "but first, settle down for a moment and let me introduce you to some friends who have joined this little get-together between Uni and Galan." Ew reached out for Shreela's hand, gently pulling her toward the light. "Megan, this is Shreela Bakra, a widow from Tima."

Megan stared at Shreela, recalling the comments of her mother at her last military meeting. "Is this The Widow of Tima spoken of in the Legend of Khali?" she asked.

"I believe that she is," said Ew.

Megan looked wide-eyed with disbelief. "I feel as if I'm in a dream," she whispered. "I thought the Legend was another tall tale, even when mother spoke of it at the assembly shortly after Uni attacked Galan. What does this all mean, Ew?"

"It means that for good or ill, the end is in sight, but we can talk later," he said, smiling. "First, there's someone else you should talk to right now."

Megan gasped as Calo moved into the light. Tears flooded her eyes and she ran into his arms.

"Let's give them a few moments alone," Ew suggested, walking several trans ahead. Ew sat down next to Milan. "How are you feeling?" he asked, looking over at his friend.

Milan look at Ew but made no response.

"Right now, he's holding his own," Shreela interjected. "His temperature is down some, but he is still very weak."

Ew gently patted Milan's shoulder. "We're almost there," he said.

At that moment, Calo and Megan rejoined the group. "We should decide on a plan for entering the house," said Calo. "From what Megan tells me, we may find that to be the most difficult part of this entire journey. Any ideas?"

"I'm thinking about it," responded Ew. "This passage leads to the garden inside the palace grounds, but it won't help us to get into the house. If Uzak's people control the House and the grounds surrounding it, I'm afraid we'll have to wait until dark before we venture outside the tunnel."

Everyone sighed at this news. Too tired to argue the strategy, Pala just grunted his acknowledgment while Shreela flashed Ew a puzzled look. "Why does the passage lead to the garden rather than the house?" she asked.

"There is a passage that leads directly to the house, but access to that entrance is next to the space dock, which would be a direct military target," he explained. "Since the UMF has already infiltrated Galan Manor, they will search for secret passages from inside the house. The enemy could use secret passages leading directly into the house as traps. For that reason, this tunnel was constructed away from the main house, and it's northern exit is close to the mountains where one might find refuge from a hostile attack."

"That's how I planned to escape," Megan interrupted.

Ew stood up and began to pace back and forth, clearly agitated by being so close to his destination yet unable to fulfill his mission. Megan looked at him wondering what was going through his mind. "Ew," she called softly, "do you really have The Planet Star?"

"I do, but what I don't have is a way into the house without being seen," he grumbled. Ew continued to pace for a while and then plopped down on the floor next to Shreela. Everyone remained quiet, deep in thought as time ticked by.

"We should at least head toward the exit," said Ew, breaking the silence. "We may even get a chance to do a bit of snooping before dark. Megan, how long did it take you to get here?"

"Fifteen minutes at the most. It's not too far."

"Okay, let's go. Pala, I'll help Milan, and you can carry our little friend here," he said, smiling at Soren.

Pala picked up the stake, which Ew left on the ground,

walking with Soren in the lead position. The going was steady without interruption.

Finally, they arrived at the door that opened into the palace garden, which spanned the entire length of the house. Ew helped Milan to lie down on the ground while everyone else found a place to sit, propped against the wall, well inside the tunnel.

The door was made of heavy metal on the inside but camouflaged on the outside to look like a large stone. Ew walked up and put his ear against the door. Hearing no sound from the other side, he eased the door open just enough to stick his head out. The thick bushes, deliberately planted in front of the door for concealing anyone who might enter or exit that way, obstructed most of his view. At that moment, there was the sound of light footsteps, followed by heavy footfalls of booted soldiers. Through a small opening in the bushes, Ew saw the backs of some of his house servants. A fierce command shattered the silence of the garden, and then the sound of lasers followed by the terrible thudding sound of bodies falling to the ground. One of those bodies fell through the bushes. It was Oshe, Mara's personal servant. She quickly scrambled inside the thicket as the sound of lasers continued. Ew let out a low whistle. Oshe turned around, startled by the sound but even more surprised to see Ew, whom she recognized immediately. He was standing at the entrance with his hand extended. She grabbed his hand and was pulled quickly inside.

Everyone remained silent for a few moments as another wave of laser fire rang out. Occasional laser blasts hit the door creating a terrible series of echoes as the door reverberated under the force. Megan moved close to Calo, Soren hugged his mother tightly, and Oshe stood trembling near the door. Pala sat silent next to Milan while Ew stood close to Oshe near the entrance, holding Megan's laser gun ready to fire at the slightest provocation. Finally the sound of explosive weapons stopped. For a long moment, all was quiet outside. The silence was broken by a muffled command followed by the sound of dragging bodies. Shreela shuddered as the sound of heavy boots disturbed the deathly silence on the other side of the door.

Assuming the murders were over, Ew relaxed his stance and walked over to Oshe who began to cry. Ew put his arm around her to quiet her.

"I'm sorry, Your Majesty," Oshe apologized.

"There's no need for apologies," Ew softly responded. "Can you tell us what has just happened here?"

"Yes...yes," she stammered, trying to gain control of herself. "After her Highness left the house," she began, "the Unian Military broke down the doors and arrested everyone inside. They asked us where Her Highness was, and we told them Her Highness didn't come home since last evening."

"Did they believe you?"

"No, Sire. It didn't matter anyway, Your Majesty. The soldiers were ordered to kill every living thing in the house. At least that's what I heard the guard say." Oshe paused for a moment, unable to continue.

Sensing her reluctance, Ew tried to coax her into continuing her story. "Oshe, I need to know what happened. Come on, you're safe now," he said. Oshe looked into his eyes. "Don't be frightened."

Oshe inhaled deeply. "Yes, My Lord." Oshe leaned against the tunnel wall with her eyes closed and began to unwind the most horrible part of her story.

"We were all pushed into the recreation room and put into little groups, ... house servants, grounds servants, staff, and others. We just stood and waited for a very long time. Then he came, his eyes black as coals and filled with such hate. I remember how much I wanted to hide from those terrible eyes."

"Who came?" asked Ew.

"It was the Lord of Uni, powerful and fierce he was, My Lord," she half whispered to herself. "In all my life, I've never been so afraid as I was when he walked in. He ordered each group be taken to the garden and eliminated. I was in group four. They know how many servants there were in each group, Sire. They're lookin' for me now."

"Why would they be looking for you? A Pala blurted.

"I was the first one they questioned. Surely they'll remember me," don't you think?"

"How did you escape the laser fire?"

Ew looked curiously at the faint smile on Oshe's face. "I tricked them," she said.

"Tricked them?"

"You see, My Lord, there were about fifteen in my group, but there were only three soldiers firing. We were lined against the wall, but there they stood, a great ways across the courtyard next to the house. I hoped I wouldn't be one of the first three shot. When the leader shouted 'fire', I tried to fall back at the same time."

"And while they continued to fire, you slid behind the bushes, right?" Ew interjected.

"Not right away, because they were bringing in the next group and the group after that. I inched my way back, hoping that while the firing was going on, I could finally make my way to the opening in the bushes. I had nothing to lose, My Lord. I am happy to escape with a few cuts and scratches." Oshe sighed as she concluded her story. "What are we to do now, my Lord?"

"Well first, I need to get inside the house without being seen."

"Very difficult, Sire, but at least no one's looking for you."

Ew looked at Oshe. "What's that?"

"Begging your pardon, My Lord, but it's a good thing Uzak thinks you're dead."

"How do you know Uzak believes His Majesty is dead?" asked Pala.

"He said so, Sir," Oshe replied. "When he came to the room where we were standing, our commander asked if the King's quarters would be heavily guarded. Uzak said it wasn't necessary. 'His Majesty Galan wouldn't be coming back, as he was dead,' Oshe explained.

"Then why are they overrunning my home?" Ew wondered aloud.

"A heavy guard was ordered around the palace grounds to capture Her Highness, Megan Galan, when she returned, My Lord."

Ew walked back to the door and opened it. He stood in the doorway for a moment or two before he closed it and walked back toward his friends.

"It's nearly dark outside," he said. "If we are to win this war, I must get inside the house."

"What is your plan?" asked Calo.

"I'll try to scale the wall to my bedroom window just above the garden, and get to the Star Room from there," he explained. "Pala, I want you to remain here while I try to get into my room."

"But Ew," Pala cried, "I can help you get inside. Calo can guard the others."

"No!" Ew commanded. Ew rarely raised his voice in a commanding tone to Pala, except when he tended to be stubborn, and he could see this was just such an occasion. "Pala", he said, softening the tone of his voice. "I need you here. If anything goes wrong, you'll have to help Calo inside the star Room."

"Calo?" Megan asked surprised.

Ew turned to his sister. "Yes, Calo", he replied. "If I do not return, Calo knows where to find the key to The Planet Star. In that case he will need your help," he said turning back to Pala.

Pala nodded his head. "I'll check to see if the coast is clear," he said, trudging off.

As Pala opened the door to investigate the garden, Ew walked over to Shreela, seated furthest from the door, and sat down next to her.

"You've been very quiet lately, he said softly in her ear. "Are you alright?"

"I'm fine. It's you I'm concerned about." Shreela pulled his hand into hers and looked into his eyes. "I wish I could go with you."

Cradling her chin in his hands, Ew slowly moved his face close to hers. "You have fulfilled your role as spoken in the Legend. You were with me when I needed you most, beginning with the andir in the swamp, and after the attack on me by the ergret. I must now do my part and finish this quest for good or ill, and I must do it alone."

Shreela could see in his eyes there was no room to argue. It was clear that his mind was made up. "Be careful," she cautioned. "Uzak is a dangerous being, and he'll stop at nothing short of your death."

"I love you, Shreela Bakra," he whispered. "I'll be back for you." Ending with those words, Ew gently drew her to him and kissed her. Then he was gone.

Though torn between Ew and her old life with Jor on the

planet Tima, Shreela finally allowed herself to acknowledge her love for him. Still, she was hesitant to say those precious words to him. *He hides his loneliness, this Khalian King,* she thought. *Would it hurt if he knew that I love him?* she asked herself, watching Ew hug Megan and start for the door. *I admit that I do care for him and not saying it to him does not change how I feel.* As Ew stepped across the threshold and closed the door, Shreela jumped up and called his name as she rushed to catch him. She slipped outside quietly closing the door behind.

"What are you doing here?" Ew asked, startled by Shreela's tap on his shoulder from behind.

"I want to speak with you before you leave."

"Shreela, I can't talk to you right now."

"Just for a moment," she pleaded.

"All right, but make it quick," he whispered. "Pala, keep an eye out for anyone entering the garden." Ew moved a few trans to the left of the door, pulling Shreela toward him. Though concealed by the bushes, there was still an uneasiness felt by both of them as they stared at each other under the star-filled sky.

"Now, what is so important that it can't wait until my return?" he asked in a low voice.

Putting her arms around him and looking lovingly into his eyes, "I didn't want you to go without knowing how much I love you," she said softly. "I know that saying I love you does not detract from the love I felt for Jor. I still feel a little guilty, but I am learning to handle that," she said, moving close into his embrace, kissing him on the lips, softly, but with great passion. Ew had to force himself to break away in order to concentrate on completing his quest.

"Well," he said surprised, but pleased, about this change in attitude. "I'm certainly glad it couldn't wait."

Shreela smiled at him, whispering "May you find victory in your quest," and then tiptoed back to the door. Ew watched her as she quickly slid back inside, continuing to stare in that direction until Pala interrupted him.

"Ew, you can go now. I should warn you that a sentry is posted on the roof. He passes on this side of the palace every four to five minutes."

Ew looked at his old friend for a moment before speaking. They had been through much together. Indeed, his very life was saved by this big, tough, and at times, very stubborn Latonian. "Well my good friend, Pala Bhusan, for good or ill, the time is now. Take care of yourself and the others," he said hugging his friend.

"Be careful, my Liege."

"You must go inside now, Pala."

Pala watched as Ew turned, cautiously sneaking through the garden and disappearing into the night.

"Take care, my friend," Pala whispered again.

Upon entering the tunnel, Pala looked over at Milan who rested with his head on Shreela's lap. "How is he?" he asked.

He's still in pretty bad shape, but at least he's remaining conscious," she responded. "He complained earlier that his head and chest hurt. Maybe he has cracked a few ribs, but the swelling on the back of his head has gone down. He must have a doctor, and soon."

"Yes, soon."

The Star Crystal

All was quiet in the tunnel as Ew's companions thought of him, wondering what would be the outcome of his quest. Ew, on the other hand, thought of his friends hidden away in the tunnel as he scaled along a vertical pipe attached to a corner wall leading to his bedroom window, ten trans from the ground.

Recalling some of the risks taken during this quest, he vowed to be more cautious than before. His journey through the marsh was nearly disastrous as well as his carelessness in not checking Linden more carefully before walking into a trap.

"This is the last stage of my journey, and I must assume discovery lay ahead for every step taken toward the Star Room," he whispered to himself.

Most of the exterior wall was sheathed with light-gray, textured dabernine block, measuring ten lino-trans lengthwise, and ten lino-trans thick. Every third block was a smooth, polished surface, which protruded nearly one-tenth tran beyond the textured blocks. Blocks were held in place with a strong bonding adhesive, but with a life expectancy of two centuries. The one-and-one-half century old mansion already showed signs of aging. There were cracks and some chipping away of blocks on the southern side that received the most weather wear. The vertical pipe lined up along one of the four inner structural indentations. The pipe, also made of rough-cut dabernine, was hollow, and only served as part of the geometric design of the structure.

Raising his foot, Ew braced it against protruding dabernine blocks, and hoisted himself upwards along the vertical pipe. Slowly and cautiously, he continued his climb, stopping every now and then to survey the ground below. *Three more steps and I'll be at my window,* he thought. With his next step, three or four trans from his window ledge, several pieces of loosened stone fell to the ground with a loud clattering sound. Immediately, he stopped and pressed his body as close as possible to the wall directly under his bedroom window. He remained there, a statue, as the sentry on duty rushed toward the disturbance.

Directing the light of a large lamp onto the ground, the sentry could see the debris on the walkway below. He aimed the light slowly up the wall until a small flock of birds, which had been nesting in the tree close to the mansion, flew wildly about the court, startled by the light. He was joined by another sentry who rushed up to see what the commotion was.

"What happened?" he asked, looking over the side.

"There are loose stones on the side of this old building. Some of them fell onto the walkway. When I came here to have a look, the birds nesting in this tree went crazy."

"Did you check to see if someone is trying to scale the wall?"

"Nah. Why would someone scale this old wall with its loose stones? It's easier to climb that tree, over there," he pointed. "No, one of those birds tried to perch on that ledge over there, see," he said, focusing the lamp upon the broken ledge beneath Ew's bedroom window. "Just look at the size of them creatures. Yep, them birds made this mess," he explained.

"Maybe," said the other, not at all convinced by his friend's argument.

"Look," said the first sentry. Skimming his hand lightly across the crowned edging of the room some of the loose stones crashed to the ground. However, the other guard still seemed skeptical about the whole thing. "Alright," said the first sentry, "let's go down and have a look."

Ew remained where he was for a few moments, listening to the sound of footsteps as they moved out of hearing range. Careful to adjust his footing around the unstable area, he continued his climb until he was above the window ledge. With a quick push, the window opened and he slipped in. After entering, Ew carefully closed the window and stopped the swaying of the window treatment, only seconds before a searchlight from outside penetrated the opaque curtains, lighting up the room. Assuming the two sentries were now investigating the area below his window, he sat down, laying low until things settled down.

While looking about his room, Ew felt comforted by the familiar surroundings. *It seems as if I've been away for ages*, he thought. Pulling down the pocket zipper of his left boot, he slid the real Planet Star from its hiding place. Suddenly, the light from outside his window went out. Ew stood up and peeped through the window. He saw the sentinels walking toward the entrance leading back into the house.

Ew turned, skulking through his bedchamber, down a short hallway, and through his library to a door leading to the main corridor outside his suite. He put his ear to the door and listened for sounds outside, then opened the door, cautiously looking up and down the corridor. The hallway was empty. Breathing a sigh of relief, he closed the door. The sound of his blood rushed through his ears, and his heart pounded with excitement as he leaned against the library door. It was difficult to believe after thirty-six years, his quest was about to come to an end.

In a single moment, a lifetime of painful memories resurfaced, flooding his mind. The muscles in his jaw tightened as he clenched his teeth, recalling the deaths of his wife, mother, servants, and many others. His anger was kindled even more when he thought of the widows who suffered and died at the hands of Uzak... *and then there is Shreela,* he thought aloud. His jaw relaxed as he thought of her, this strong yet loving and compassionate soul who touched his life in a way that he hadn't experienced since the death of his wife. With lingering thoughts of Shreela, he took control of his angry emotions and focused on the task before him.

Ew opened the door again and looked about. Sounds of

voices drifted down the corridor from the floor below, but the hallway leading to the staircase was clear. Quickly, stepping across the threshold, he silently moved toward the staircase at the end of the corridor. The hallway seemed longer than he remembered, and his footsteps sounded like a stampede of some large game animal. Just as he reached the stairwell, he heard voices from below. Someone was coming up the steps. Quickly, he ducked out of sight through the door on his left, next to the staircase. From inside, he heard the voices of the two sentries who debated about the loose brick that earlier fell onto the garden path. Ew listened intently to their conversation.

"Look, you check on that room at the end o the hall. I guarantee no one's in there," said one sentry.

"I'll check it, you can be sure," said the other. "We can't afford any slip ups, you know."

"Fine, but I'm headin' back to my post on the roof."

"I'll be there in a bit. Better make your report."

"Why? There's nothin' to report."

"He always finds out. He knows everything."

"Aw, I'm not startin' nothin. I'll see you back on the roof after you check out that room."

Cautiously opening the door and surveying the corridor, Ew saw no signs of either sentry. Taking three steps at a time, he made a quick ascent to the next floor, quietly pacing down the hallway to the Star Room door.

All was quiet in the garden as Pala stepped outside the tunnel to have a look around the palace grounds. Ew had been gone for nearly an hour and still there was no sign of disturbance or disruption. Looking up to Ew's bedroom window, Pala could see the closed window. The room was dark as before. Since he did not watch Ew's ascent to the window and was not aware of the debate which had taken place moments earlier, Pala stood at the secret door wondering whether or not Ew got inside the room unnoticed or perhaps he had been captured.

Shreela saw the worried look on Pala's face when he returned to the tunnel, careful to close the door behind him. "What is it?" she asked.

"Something should have happened by now. It's been nearly an hour since Ew left here. Something is wrong, I can feel it."

They all looked at each other, quietly concerned as to the fate of Ew. Finally, Shreela spoke up, more positive than the others, in an attempt to change the cloud of doom hovering over their thoughts.

"Look," she said, "Ew has been gone for almost an hour and already we have given up on him. We cannot allow ourselves to imagine the worst. He may be sitting in his room right now thinking of a way into the Star Room. There may be police in the corridor making it unsafe to leave his room. There are many possibilities," she argued convincingly. "Let's just wait and see."

Pala knew she was right. He smiled at her, nodded his head in agreement, and silently thanked her for reminding him that it was necessary to think logically during a time of crisis, such as this.

The Star Room door had no outstanding features that might call attention to any who might pass by. Like all other doors, the hand painted motif fused with the cloth-textured wall covering. Briefly, Ew paused to insert his ring into the key-lock panel. The door quietly slid open.

Once inside, Ew's attention was immediately drawn to the mural on the wall opposite the doorway. It was filled with cracks and chipped paint, and in some areas, the exterior dabernine sheathing and mortar were exposed. Despite the evidence of gradual decay, the room maintained an aura of magnificent grandeur, which elevated it to the level of that which was sacred. The mural itself was a depiction of The Planet Star. Each of the fifteen petals clearly identified the planet name, Keeper, and Keeper's gem found on that planet. Unlike the lifeless medallion, which Ew held in his hand, the gemstones painted on the mural were still bright and intense, eclipsed only by the scarlet coloring of the crystalline center, which seemed to pulsate with life. To the right of the mural sat the dust-covered mounting altar for The Planet Star. The one-by-one trans flare base curved inward into a long, slender, circular post. At the top, the post split, forming an enclosed circle with a small gap at the top. It was the resting place for The Planet Star.

Ew recalled his mother's explanation of how The Planet Star worked.

"You must polarize the final key, the Star Crystal, with the center of The Planet Star, and speak the sacred words to bring life to the medallion," she explained. Ew unconsciously rubbed the back of his left hand where the crystalline disc lay beneath the surface of his skin. "Once contact is made, the entire crystalline pedestal will reverberate in a strobe like fashion, flashing several hues of red during activation. An almost imperceptible, narrow beam of energy, given off by The Planet Star, will shoot directly up toward the crystalline bubble-shaped dome in the ceiling. Upon penetration of the crystal dome, the narrow beam will split into thousands of directions, shielding the entire Khalian Solar System."

At times Ew felt uncertain of this power for he had never seen The Planet Star in its active state. Unconsciously caressing the medallion's crystalline center, Ew slowly moved toward the pedestal. He inserted the medallion into the circular loop. The medallion did not touch the loop, but was held in place by a magnetic force, exerting equal pressure on all sides. Ew silently stood before the crystalline pedestal, deciding the moment of activation had arrived. He had only to initiate the operation, and Khali would once again become a haven of peace and joy. As he attempted to line up the disc from his hand to the crystalline center of the medallion, he was startled by a soft, insidious chuckle. The quiet manner in which the laughter was emitted in no way deprived it of its fiendishness and impending danger. The sound of ominous laughter caused Ew to spin around just in time to evade the point of Uzak's sword as it swished by him within lino-trans of his body.

"A duplicate. Did you think I would not know?"

Ew did not respond. The many harrowing, life-endangering situations experienced by Ew, instilled within him an ability to think quickly and clearly when his life was threatened. With incredible speed, he drew his sword in time to parry a vicious and well aimed attack by Uzak. He was forced to use all the agility of which he was capable, as he made a strategic retreat, which came to an end when he backed into a wall. Uzak, being fully assured that his immortality would once again render him invulnerable, decided to execute Ew, not by mortal wounding, but by gruesome decapitation.

Ewlon, the only creature alive who could destroy Uzak's immutability of immortality, stood before the dreaded Lord of Uni with his back against the wall. Escape seemed nearly impossible. Carefully aiming his sword, Uzak swung with all his strength, maneuvering his blade so that with one powerful stroke; he could sever his opponent's head from his body. Ew quickly stooped down in a low crouch as the edge of Uzak's blade passed over his head with a whistling sound, the point digging deeply into a crevice in the wall. Ew perceived how vulnerable the invulnerable one had become. From his crouched position, Ew lunged with great impetus, and drove his saber, up to its hilt, into Uzak's body. Uzak lost his balance, stumbled and fell to the floor with Ew's saber still in his body.

Ew understood that once Uzak removed the saber from his body, his body's regenerative powers would make him once again a formidable foe. With only seconds to activate The Planet Star, he again focused the Star Crystal disc upon the crystalline center of the medallion, and uttered the words that would bring from without, the energy field emitted by the Star Crystal.

"Le plu nastra losai"

The Planet Star was silent. As Ew waited for a response, beads of perspiration formed across his brow. Suddenly, the crystalline center began to flicker bright red. A narrow beam of light formed between the center of The Planet Star and the Star Crystal disc, located beneath the surface skin on the back of Ew's hand. The contact was complete. By this time, Uzak had recovered.

Uzak cried aloud as he saw the energy beam emission from Ew's left hand. At long last he understood that when he sent Wedolan home thirty-six years before, he also sent the key for which he had long searched. It was now too late for him to continue his battle with Ew. Once the energy beam from the Star Crystal made contact with The Planet Star, his fate would be sealed. *If I can escape in my vessel before the membrane shield envelopes the Khalian System, I can retain my longevity*, he thought. *I'll fight again in another age.*

Scrambling to his feet, Uzak rushed out the door and down the corridor that led to the back staircase. The sight of the great Lord of Uni fleeing Galan manor panicked military personnel who followed their dreaded Lord out of Galan Manor.

Ew watched Uzak as he barged out of the Star Room in great haste. He knew he must trap Uzak within the membrane shield before Uzak could leave the Khalian System. He could not kill Uzak, but his power of unity and longevity would be diminished, forcing him to live out the remainder of his life as a mortal. As the energy beam from the Star Crystal polarized with The Planet Star, Ew's body became fixed to the place where he stood. The face of the medallion slowly turned upward. Suddenly, a beam of light shot up to the dome. The crystalline dome flashed various hues of red in sync with the strobe effect given off by the crystalline pedestal. There was a high pitched, whistling sound and the beam of light split as it penetrated the dome.

As the membrane shield spread outward, the magnet-like attraction that kept Ew fixed in one place, as well as the glow which surrounded his person, slowly diminished. Exhausted by the ordeal, he collapsed on the Star Room floor.

Pala opened the tunnel door to look out. He saw OMP, UMF, and other Unian officials running through the garden and vaulting over the large concrete wall toward military shuttlecraft stationed behind the palace. "Calo," he shouted excitedly, "come and look!"

Calo walked briskly to the door. "What's going on?"

"Unians. Look at them. They're leaving in a big hurry."

Calo looked up toward the dome directly over the Star Room. "Pala, look at the dome," he shouted, pointing upwards. "See how the light throbs."

"I see it."

"What now?" Calo asked.

"I'm heading for the Star Room. You stay here with Milan and the others."

Shreela went to the tunnel door and stepped outside with Calo. Together they watched as Pala rushed out into the night. She observed the panic in the courtyard, noticing how no one seemed to care about Pala as he headed toward the door leading into the palace. For a brief moment, her mind went out to Ew. *How I wish I could be with him, now at the moment of his triumph*, she thought. She looked over at Calo whose attention was focused on the fleeing soldiers and the dome. She watched him for a moment and then quietly slipped through an opening in the bushes several trans away.

The panic continued as Unian Police stampeding out of the Galan mansion, through the garden, and over the wall. Uzak collided with Shreela as she raced toward the mansion. "The widower's widow," he snarled.

Terror gripped at Shreela's heart as Uzak grabbed her by the hand and yanked her toward the garden wall. Struggling to free herself only intensified his grip. "What do you want with me?" she cried.

"Ewlon has my life in his hands, I shall hold yours," he growled. "An inequitable exchange, and am sure, but an exchange nonetheless."

Uzak was nearing the wall when from out of nowhere, he noticed Calo Laggé running toward him with his saber drawn. Undaunted, Uzak continued his forward approach. Calo lunged forward to cut him off. Still holding Shreela's hand, Uzak used his free hand, grabbing Calo's blade and yanking it out of his grasp. Quickly, he threw the saber, flipping the blade back toward Calo. Calo jumped to the side, but not quick enough as the blade plunged deep into his upper thigh. Calo let out a cry of pain and fell to the ground. Uzak rushed past him, and with great strength, he crossed over the two trans-high wall pulling Shreela with him. Again Shreela offered some resistance, but

Uzak was too powerful, a madman, dragging her when she stumbled. Her flesh scraped and burned, making contact with the pavement. Finally, they reached a small four-seat space cruiser.

"Pilot, take to space at the highest possible sped, and set course for Dagmar," Uzak shouted.

"Yes, My Lord."

Uzak threw Shreela inside and locked her into the magnetic torso clamps. He looked at her malevolently. "If this spacecraft is destroyed, you will die with it."

Many Unians and their allies still on the ground, disintegrated inside the membrane shield. Spaceship crews inside the System also disintegrated, causing many a collision between empty ships controlled by no one. Several minutes passed and still Uzak's spacecraft had not cleared the outskirts of the Khalian Solar System. Uzak looked back toward the House of Galan. He could not see the mansion or the dome of the Star Room, but he perceived the membrane shield as it enveloped his body. The body of his pilot vanished like many others, and Uzak understood that he was also lost. He did not escape the effects of the membrane shield. A lonely space cruiser bound for Dagmar, cruised through the solar system with one mortal female, and one newly born mortal male.

10
THE RESTORATION OF GALAN

The shouting of Pala standing outside the Star Room door aroused Ew. Staggering to his feet, he stumbled to the door and pressed the button on the wall. Pala rushed inside.

Ew mumbled in a low almost inaudible voice as he tried to recover from the strain during his contact with The Planet Star. "The shield is activated," he said.

"I know," said Pala, anxious to hear Ew's story, "and I saw Uzak leave in a big hurry. What happened? Are you alright?"

"I'll be fine in a few minutes. Just let me sit down here for a moment or two." Ew sat on the floor next to the pedestal, which was still energized with light. He looked around noticing that Pala was alone. "Where are the others?"

"They're in the tunnel. We should probably go back soon. They must be pretty worried by now."

"Alright, I'm ready when you are," Ew said untruthfully. When he stood up, the Star Crystal fell off of his hand and onto the floor. He reached down to pick it up, but before he could grab the crystal, it disappeared before his eyes. As a reflex action, Ew yanked his hand back, staring at the spot where the Star Crystal had lain only seconds before. "Did you see that?" he asked. They stared at each other not quite knowing what to think or do. There was a long moment of silence as Ew wondered if this was a sign of something new to come. "There's nothing more to do here," he said at length. "Say nothing of this to the others. We will speak of it later."

Ew and Pala walked down the empty corridor and descended the back staircase leading to the garden. As they stepped out into the garden, Ew quickly surveyed the area, taking note of the damage. He sighed deeply and frowned.

"There's not much damage considering the animals who created it," Pala grunted.

"It's not the garden that hurts me, Pala, but the innocent blood that was spilled here," he said sadly, recalling how Uzak exacted his punishment on the House of Galan by murdering his servants.

Looking in the direction of the hidden door located in the concrete wall, the full moon enabled him to see the opening in the thicket, just beyond the secret door. Oshe was peering out at them from afar. As they walked toward the secret tunnel, Megan rushed out to greet them.

"How is everyone?" asked Ew. He raised his eyebrow when Megan's slow response peaked his curiosity.

"Milan seems to be a lot better now, but I think we should start looking for a doctor," she said, avoiding her brother's eyes. "I trust that all has gone well with you."

Ew sensed that Megan was not being totally honest with him. "Something has happened, hasn't it?" he asked. "Megan, look at me." Gently raising her chin in order to read her eyes, "I can hear it in your voice and see it in your eyes. What is it Megan, and where is Shreela?"

Megan paused for a moment. "After Pala left," she began, "Shreela must have decided to follow him to the house."

"Where is she?" Ew asked for the second time.

"She's gone, Ew. We tried to help her but..."

"Where is she!" Ew demanded, cutting her off.

"We heard screams near the wall. When we went outside, we saw Uzak struggling with her.

"Where was Calo?"

"Calo went after Uzak with his saber, but he wasn't able to get Shreela back. Uzak hurt Calo really bad before he dragged Shreela out of the courtyard. I'm sorry," she cried.

Ew stood there, looking first at Pala, and then back to Megan. There was a stunned look on his face.

"Why would she leave the tunnel anyway?" he asked, shaking his head in disbelief. Quickly walking to the door, he looked inside the tunnel, half expecting to see Shreela smiling back at him. Instead, he found Oshe, Calo, Milan, and Soren. Soren, unaware of what had happened, smiled enthusiastically at Ew, standing at the tunnel entrance. Without a word, Ew walked over and picked Soren off the ground. "Pala, get Milan and Calo into the house and find medical help," he ordered, and then left to go back to the house.

It was two hours before dawn. Ew sat in a chair next to a small bed where Soren lay sleeping. He spent a long time sitting and thinking of alternative ways in which his mission could have been accomplished without endangering or at least reducing the risk for both Soren and Shreela. *This person has already lost his father, how can I tell him about his mother,* he thought watching Soren as he slept. *He has been running for so long, and for one so young, he has met the challenge with the strength of an adult. Much of his strength is due to the influence of his mother. Indeed, my own success would not have been possible without her.* There were so many questions with so few answers. Ew stood up and began pacing the room as he tried to unlock some of the mystery concerning the Star Crystal and Shreela. Without warning, a low rumbling sound interrupted his thoughts. The ground shook beneath his feet and then it stopped. Just as he headed for the door, he heard Megan call his name. He opened the door to find her outside. She looked frightened, her voice filled with alarm.

"What was that rumbling? It felt like a quake," said Ew.

"Go to the Star Room," she pleaded. "Something is going on in there. Quick! I'll stay here with Soren."

Ew responded to the urgency in her voice. "I'm on my way."

When Ew reached the Star Room, Calo and Pala met him there. Again the floor began to tremble and shake.

"Do you think this has something to do with the Star Crystal?" asked Pala.

"Let's find out," said Ew inserting his Ring into the key-lock.

As soon as the door opened, the tremors stopped. Ew entered the room, followed by Pala and then Calo. He slowly moved toward the crystalline pedestal. He was halfway there when the floor began to shake again, but this time, the tremors were more violent. Pala ran back to the door and pressed the button to open it. Nothing happened. He tried several times without success.

"Ew," he shouted over the noise, "the door won't open."

"Here let me try." Stumbling toward the door, Ew also pressed the button several times but was unable to get the door to open.

"We're trapped," cried Pala.

"I think you're right." Ew shouted, heading back to the pedestal. As suddenly as they started, the tremors stopped. Looking up at the dome, Ew noticed the energy beam outside the dome was no longer split. Beyond the crystalline dome, the beam was concentrated in a narrow linear configuration, at an angle directly in the path of a distant star. They covered their ears as a high-pitched whistling sound filled the air. Through the dome ceiling, they watched the beam. There was a sudden flash of light, and the star was gone. At that moment, all three of them fell to the floor as the room shook violently. The crystalline dome shattered, scattering fragments of the gemstone throughout the Star Room. Before anyone could react to the situation, things quieted down almost as quickly as they flared up.

"Look," Pala shouted, his attention now drawn toward the beam.

"I see it," said Ew, watching as the energy beam began to fade before their eyes. "The membrane shield is no longer active. The Star Crystal is gone and without it, The Planet Star will never again be activated," he remarked sadly.

"You no longer need The Planet Star," a voice called out.

Ew looked about trying to pinpoint the location of the voice. From the center of the room, a filmy outline of a humanoid form came into focus. The image of Rendal, Keeper of Foresight, appeared before them, and spoke to them from some other dimension of time and space. "I am Rendal, Keeper of Foresight. It is with pleasure that I have verbal communication with a member of the House of Galan. Ewlon, there is much for you to learn and I know of the many questions which burden your heart. I shall answer them using the foresight that has been given to me."

Sitting on the floor with the others, Ew watched intently as the specter crossed the room and stood directly in front of the crystalline pedestal, now silent, and the light that burned within only moments before was gone.

"I shall speak now for all the Keepers of Khali," said Rendal. "We the Keepers of the Khalian Solar System relied on The Planet Star to reunite our powers. Since Uzak disobeyed the sacred covenant and broke the unity of the Keepers, we needed a method through which our collective powers would render him powerless. That, as you have been told, would be accomplished by way of The Planet Star. Many years ago when Wedolan Galan first activated The Planet Star, our powers were intended to secure only the Khalian Solar System. We could not extend our powers as far as Uni. When The Planet Star was stolen from this room nearly four decades ago, the Keepers of Khali slept for many years and could not be awakened until The Planet Star was again activated. This time, Uzak was trapped within the membrane shield and robbed of his power, thereby extending our capabilities beyond Khali to Uni. As witnessed by you, that planet no longer exists."

"What happened to Uzak, and what will he do to Shreela," asked Ew.

"Uzak is not dead but he is diminished. He is no longer a Keeper and he will live out his life as a mortal," Rendal explained. "Now he will know and understand the length of a day, the emptiness of the belly, the heat of the desert and the cold of winter, the pain of illness, and the silence of death."

"But what of Khali?" Milan interjected.

"Galan has a good King, but his task is not yet complete. Uzak can no longer threaten the Khalian Solar System as an immortal being. The King and the Keeper of Unity now stand on equal footing. The task of the Keepers of Khali is now complete."

"And Shreela?" Ew asked again. Rendal moved back to the center of the room. Jumping to his feet, Ew moved toward the fading figure of Rendal. "Will I ever see her again? Please tell me of Shreela," he begged.

"You will see her again. She now holds the Star Crystal. You must find her with your Star Ring, but do so before the power of your Ring diminishes. Search for the place in the Treatise in the Legend of Khali, which was left to you by your father," he advised, and then he was gone.

Ew stared into space for a moment without uttering a word. Then he turned to look at his friends with hope in his eyes. "It looks as if we are on our own now. Come, let us begin rebuilding our homes and our hearts."

For several days following Galan's liberation from the tyranny of Uni, scouts were sent out to find and help bring refugees back home. With the restoration of Galan already underway, Megan and Calo made wedding plans. Milan was up and about, and there was celebration in the air as many soldiers and refugees returned to their homes.

On a cool evening, two weeks following the destruction of Uni, Ew stood in the garden with Soren in his arms, looking up into the sky. He tried to comfort himself. *At last the Khalian Solar System is at peace, at least for now, but time is running out for Shreela,* he thought anxiously. Sensing Soren's concern over the absence of his mother, he was careful not to worry him further with his own sadness.

"Will we find my mom soon?" Soren asked, staring into the sky.

Ew looked at Soren, reminded of the expression on his face when he first saw the Galan Battle cruiser. *That seems like ages ago*, he thought. He knew of Soren's worries and he felt honored by Soren's trust. *He's lost his father. I must find his mother*, he insisted. Slowly walking back toward Galan Mansion. "Yes," he said at length, "we'll find her."

EPILOGUE
The Reign of Wedolan Galan

The Revelation of Solan

After the fall of Uzak, Yavik Galan, Steward of the Khalian Solar System, held firm in his administration. Despite the calamity of mass sickness and death, he continued his rule of the Khalian Solar System, committed to the laws and teachings given by the Keepers. He responded to these forces as "part of the balance of nature." Although Yavik, like all Khalians, was surprised by the sudden disappearance of fourteen Keepers, he restructured his administration by appointing one single governor for each planet, replacing each of the missing Keepers. His greatest curiosity and concern focused on why Uzak moved out of Galan and set up his domain on planet Uni, as well as why Uzak had not gone with the other Keepers. Though Uzak was a frequent visitor to the planet Galan, he was unable to convince Yavik that it was the will of his brothers that he, Uzak, remain. There was no way for Yavik to disprove Uzak's claim, but throughout his reign, Yavik remained respectful but distrustful of him.

During his stewardship, Yavik noticed a gradual and

continual buildup of military strength on the planet Uni and those planets aligned with it. The number of military spacecraft policing the solar system around Uni increased, and military personnel moving between Uni and her legion planets grew at an alarming rate. As a precaution, the Khalian Solar System began to develop armaments capable of defending itself against any possible attack from Uni. On his deathbed, Yavik pleaded with his youngest son, Wedolan, to find a way to remove the threat of war from the galaxy. "Wedolan, my son, the stewardship of the Khalian Solar System, I leave to you as my heir. It will be difficult, my son, but my advice to you is that you find a way to work with Uni and bring peace back to this part of the galaxy."

The first year of Wedolan's reign as King of the Khalian Solar System was politically and emotionally difficult. There were many who sided with his brother, Yashil, causing a split between the Interplanetary Governors. For that reason, Wedolan spent most of the first year of his rule strengthening his administration by working to reunite those Governors who were Yashil's strongest supporters. Near the end of his first year, Wedolan made a brief stop over on the planet Yalléon, to meet with his old friend and Governor, Haslow. On the evening of Wedolan's arrival, both Haslow and Wedolan strolled around Haslow's estate. Wedolan noticed a light burning in the main guest house. "I see you have company", he commented.

"My wife's parents were supposed to arrive for a short visit. I expected them tomorrow, but it seems they arrived early. They are great folks. Come and I will introduce you to them", said Haslow.

Together, Wedolan and Haslow walked up the narrow winding path leading to the front door. Once inside the house, Haslow led the way down the long corridor illuminated by a light from the sitting room. As soon as Haslow crossed the threshold, the room became dark. Wedolan jumped, startled by the slamming of the front door. "Let's get out of here," said Wedolan. Before he could leave the room, he stopped at the sight of a faint glowing of a specter in the middle of the room.

"Wedolan Galan," a voice spoke out, "I am Solan, Keeper of Life. I have long awaited your arrival to Yalléon."

Both men stared intently at the filmy figure. Wedolan was a young boy when he last heard the voice or even saw a Keeper. Puzzled and afraid, he turned towards the doorway to leave.

"Do not fear, Wedolan," said Solan. "Come and sit with me, and I will explain. Wedolan looked at his friend, Haslow, and after a moment or two, he reluctantly sat down.

"What do you mean that you have been waiting for my arrival here on Yalléon?" Wedolan asked at length.

"Many years ago," Solan began, "the Keepers came here for the express purpose of uniting what you now call the Khalian Solar System. Although it is not unusual to find fifteen planets revolving around the same sun, it is a phenomenon to find advanced life forms existing on all the planets in a solar system. We chose Khali for that reason, knowing that during the evolutionary process as you would mature and move out into the galaxy, the possibility of warlike tendencies would also evolve. For several generations, the Khalian Solar System has been at peace, but the ironic twist is that the war we worked to prevent is being perpetrated by one of our own."

"Uzak", Wedolan blurted out, and then was embarrassed.

"Yes, that is true," Solan said sadly. "In order for us to act as guardians to the entire Solar System, each of us selected a rare gem from the planet to which we were assigned. Our most dominant attribute, or power as you might call it, was transferred to that gem."

"Why did you transfer power to a gem? Could you not simply carry out your work without such a mechanism?"

"We all have many of the same attributes, but each of us has been given one particular dominant attribute which is to be used for this particular work. Our instruction comes from a higher authority."

"The Keeper of the Universe."

"Yes. Each gem was encased in a floral medallion which sat on a pedestal. Uzak was the guardian of that medallion, and the power generated from the gem was directed to one focal point, which was Nila, a rare gem from the planet Uni. Uzak held within his gemstone the collective powers of the other fourteen Keepers."

"Doesn't that make him the most powerful Keeper?" Wedolan asked.

"Yes and no. When we were all united, Uzak enjoyed great power, but when he breached the covenant, he too was diminished."

"But why did he do this?"

"He did not want to leave the Khalian Solar System. When Uzak learned that we were planning to leave, since our task was complete, he destroyed Nila, which, in turn, destroyed the gemstones of all Keepers. We did not lose our individual powers, but with one exception, we did lose our ability to commune with each other. Only I can communicate with the other Keepers, but on an individual basis."

"So that is why we thought the Keepers left the Solar System."

"Our leaving the Solar System together would signify that the terms of the Covenant, as given by the Keeper of the Universe, was satisfied. Uzak destroyed Nila before that could happen, and it forced us to roam the planet once guarded by us. The

Covenant is still not complete".

"Why is Uzak not disembodied like you?"

"That is a good question. I will try to frame my answer in a way that you will understand. Because he is a Keeper, Uzak cannot be diminished in his power except by us. At the time he broke the Covenant, Uzak transferred his power to second gemstone. You must understand, Wedolan, that by transferring power to a gem, we empty ourselves. Any one of us could have breached the Covenant by removing our attribute. When Uzak did that, our individual dominant attribute was restored, but we were no longer unified."

"If that is so, then Uzak's power of unity means nothing since he no longer unifies anything."

"True enough, but we cannot return to the Keeper of the Universe since we did not disband our union collectively. There was never an opportunity to do so since Uzak deceived us of his true purpose. From Uni, he opened his mind and declared war against his brothers. By the time he acted on his plan, it was too late."

Solan fell silent. In that moment, Wedolan experienced a sense of loneliness from the Keeper. "A hollow grave; not dead yet not alive," he thought. "Wedolan, you and Haslow must help me to end this reign of Uzak", said Solan, intruding his thoughts. Wedolan could not hide the shocked look on his face. He looked at his friend, Haslow, and then turning back to Solan "What,...how can we help?"

"Do not fear Uzak, Wedolan. He has weaknesses that can be exploited," replied Solan. "The power of the Keepers will be reunited again, but first, I need you to bring a crystalline gemstone from each planet in the Khalian Solar System, and Nila from Uni. I will give you the names of each, and where they can be found."

Several moments passed as Wedolan logged both the gemstone and its location into his voice recorder. Once he completed his recording, Wedolan felt a cool breeze on his face. "What was that?" he asked.

"As the Keeper and preserver of Life, I have endowed both of you with certain powers that will protect you against wild beasts living in or around areas where certain gemstones are located. These powers will continue until your task is complete. I will wait here for your return."

Search for the Gemstones

Wedolan rose early the next day, feeling that the entire event with Solan was merely a dream. He pondered Solan's final words as he studied the landscapes where the gems were to be found. The gemstone, Salaitra, on Planet Laton, would be the most difficult to retrieve since its location was the middle of the Ebony jungle. It was late afternoon when he met with Haslow to discuss their journey.

"We should begin no later than seven days from now," said Wedolan. I will return to Galan this evening to make arrangements for my absence. While I am there, search Yalléon for Iléd. If possible, meet me at the House of Galan in five days. Together we will search the remaining planets for the remaining fourteen gemstones."

"The Jalon Mountain Range is an hour from here, but I expect it to take at least a day to reach the area where the Iléd crystals are located. That country is hilly with very few paths. The vegetation is very dense, in the search area, so it will be difficult to steer a surface spacecraft. I will have to go on foot, at least within the last two or three kilo-trans. The entire trip should take no more than three days."

"Good. Then I will leave you now, and expect to see you within five days. Good luck, my friend," said Wedolan, as he left the room.

Several weeks passed before they completed their task. Together they traveled to the planet Perican in search of the gemstone *Valle*. This crystal could only be found in a cave at the bottom of the Curon Ocean. In a small sub-oceanic vessel, they were able to get close to the cave, but they had to dress in life support gear and swim to the cave in order to find the gems. Using a sharp pick, Wedolan dug out portions of the cave wall where the crystals were embedded in the cave rock. He thought about Solan's shroud of protection since they were not bothered by any of the large ocean creatures, either to or from the cave. From Perican they journeyed to Balarai to recover the gemstone *Dercon* and from there to Farande to search for the crystal *Quelque*. This proved to be a most difficult trip since the location of this gem was in the rocky wilderness. The bright and hot sun exposed the land which had very little vegetation or water. One rock formation looked very much like the next, and for a while, they found themselves going in circles. They began their search, using the surface hovercraft, which was stored in the hull of their spaceship. Wedolan was so anxious to begin that he neglected to recalibrate the compass, causing them to go in circles. After circling twice, he realized his error, corrected all of the settings, and then headed out one final time. Several hours passed before they returned to the ship with the crystalline rock to add to their collection. From the planet Hanilov, they secured the gemstone *Apin*, and from there, they journeyed to Balor to find the crystalline pebblestone *Shinalin*.

After twelve weeks, Wedolan and Haslow finally reached the planet Laton to search for the gem *Salaitra*. It was dark when they landed so they decided to camp on the outskirts of the

Ebony jungle. Despite the posted guards around the camp, Wedolan felt a little skittish about the echoing growling sounds of game animals and predators that seemed to lurk near the jungle border. At day break, both he and Haslow began the final part of their journey on foot. Since they were shrouded in the protection of Solan, they left the guard behind and headed into the jungle alone. For several hours they cut their way through areas of dense vegetation. By midday, they reached a small water hole, but there were several wild species of animals to meet them. The cooper-colored rocky soil was an indication that there was a significant deposit of salaitra.

"This will definitely be a test of the protective cover given by Solan," commented Haslow.

"We've been protected this far," said Wedolan. "Come on, friend, let's go."

As they moved close to the water's edge, the wild creatures began to slowly move away. Quickly, Wedolan unpacked a soil sifter and a hand shovel. Together, they dug out soil and sifted it but with no result. "Let's move close to the water, and scoop out the mud at the water edge", said Wedolan. Almost immediately Haslow scooped several irregularly shaped reddish-brown rocks. "The color fits the description Solan gave," said Wedolan.

"This could be just a rock," Haslow commented. "How can we be sure?"

Wedolan laid the sample on the ground, and with his hand held pick, chipped away at the stone. "See here, Haslow," he said, pointing at one particular area. "There is a black vein of ore embedded within this rock, just as Solan described it. Let's get a few more like this before we head back."

It was nearly dark before the two men returned to their spacecraft. Wedolan felt weary but satisfied that their journey was nearly over. "We should continue our journey back to Yalléon," he said.

"I'll be glad to get home," said the other.

Forging of The Planet Star

Solan was pleased when Wedolan and Haslow returned with all of the gemstones. "The most difficult task has been accomplished," he said.

"What is our next step?" asked Wedolan.

"We shall create a floral leaf circular medallion, cast in solid gold," Solan responded. "It will be a replication of the original. There will be fourteen leaves, and upon each leaf will be placed one of the crystalline gemstones secured by you. The center stone will be the gem Nila."

"How does it work?"

"I will energize my own gem, as well as Nila. I have the attribute of unity, but it is not as powerful as Uzak's power. However, it will suffice. Then I shall reach each of the remaining Keepers who will energize the remaining thirteen stones. A protective shield will envelope the entire Khalian Solar System."

"How will you get rid of Uzak?"

"That has yet to be decided by all the Keepers. For now, though, he will not be able to enter the Khalian Solar System. Should he try to do so, the shield will diminish him, and he will become whatever life form he has chosen to take."

"Then he would be reduced to a humanoid."

"Yes, and with powers no greater than any other humanoid."

Twenty-five days passed before Solan summoned Wedolan to come alone to the guest hour on Yalléon. He presented Wedolan with a *star ring*, and a *star crystal*. "The ring," he began, "is used to levitate the medallion in the middle of the mounting circle of at the top of the pedestal. The star crystal is the final key that will activate *The Planet Star*, as I have named it."

"How does it work?"

"Your craftsmen designed this metal tube that shoots out a laser beam. This beam will change the molecular structure of the star crystal into an energy field which can be absorbed into the skin of your hand. Once the beam is turned off, the state of the crystal will return to its original solid form. It will not damage your hand. Once The Planet Star is suspended within the circular loop, place the back of your hand close to the center stone, Nila. This will energize the medallion, and unify the Keepers of Khali."

"You cannot do that here?"

"No, Wedolan. I have prepared the pedestal in addition to these items. Return to your home on Galan, and begin the process there. I caution you not to share this information except with the Consulate and your wife, Queen Mara, who will be able to assist you in implanting the Star Crystal."

"Then I should go at once."

"Yes, and remember that the reunification of the Keepers now rests with you."

Several days after returning to Galan, Wedolan met with both the Consulate and Mara, explaining the reason for his absence.

"During the last few months, I have spent a great deal of time with Solan, the Keeper of Life."

"What do you mean?" Mara asked, stunned. "We thought the Keepers left Khali many years ago."

"I know, my dear, but they did not leave. Instead, they were scattered by an evil act of Uzak. I cannot go into great detail at this moment, but I will record a formal document, detailing all that I have learned. Right now, I need your assistance in another matter concerning the Keepers."

After he explained what he was about to do, Wedolan led them to what he named the *Star Room* which had been locked, after the crystal pedestal, dome, and setting were placed inside several days earlier. As soon as *The Planet Star* was activated, a linear stream of light shot up toward the crystal dome in the ceiling. Once the light hit the dome, it was split into thousands of directions, spreading across the Solar System and creating a shield as the Keepers were once again united.

The Legend of Khali

After the activation of The Planet Star, Solan appeared with Rendal to greet both Wedolan and Mara Galan, but Wedolan was surprised to see that Solan still appeared as a specter. "I expected you to appear with flesh and bone," he said.

"We will not return in the same form as we did when we first arrived in Khali, and our purpose has changed."

"What is this new purpose you speak of?"

"Since Uni falls outside the Khalian Solar System, Uzak could not be trapped within the shield. You might recall, Wedolan, our conversation concerning energizing the Nila gemstone. Since unity is not my dominant power, the scope of the shield is limited. He is aware of the shield around Khali. Our goal now is to diminish Uzak, but we must wait for him to make a fatal mistake."

"Will it be soon?"

"Not in your lifetime, Wedolan. Some of what lies ahead will be difficult for you to accept, but it may prove advantageous to have knowledge of it. For this reason, I am accompanied by Rendal, Keeper of Foresight, and it is he who will speak on such matters," Solan concluded.

"Wedolan", Rendal began, "as I touch your mind, you will see images of what is to come. I encourage you to record what you see, so that those who follow you will have a record of what will come."

Later that evening, Wedolan sequestered himself in his study, and recorded his visions.

"I saw The Planet Star, as it was taken from the Star Room in the House of Galan. The face of the thief was not visible and yet I understood that it was someone close to me. That vision faded. Then, there was the image of a woman passing the scepter of Khali from her hand to that of a young man, I would judge to be no more than twenty years old. My attention was drawn to him, for he looked very much like me. In his other hand, he held the banner of Uni. It became more difficult to interpret the visions, as they rapidly faded in and out. Technology within the visions was greatly advanced, compared to the present day.

There were puzzling scenes of people dressed in attire unfamiliar to me. In one vision, I saw a woman crying. Her face looked tired and worn. I saw that she was holding the hand of a small child, perhaps five or six years at most. They stood before the coffin of a man, perhaps a husband and father. The foot of the coffin was draped with a banner, its insignia, that of the small moon Tima in the Gena Galaxy, according to our star charts. Suddenly, the woman approached the same young man from the previous vision. With a long slender saber, she hewed the banner of Uni in half. Then I saw the young man standing behind the widow, holding aloft The Planet Star, while the widow fought with her saber against the dark outline of a figure, which fell before her feet. Suddenly scenes rapidly flashed before my eyes. I saw a labor camp filled with women, followed by a scene of the Galan marshland. While trying to determine how these two scenes were related, a vision of The Planet Star mounted on its setting in the Star Room, came into view. The young man holding the scepter stood in front of the mount. The vision faded and then refocused on the planet Uni. A beam of light from out of the vastness of space was aimed directly at the center of that planet. I heard a cataclysmic explosion, and as the beam of light faded, I saw that the planet Uni was gone.

Next I saw The Planet Star, which now seemed to pulsate like the flame of fire. Then, without warning, it too was gone. Suddenly, there appeared two figures standing alone. It was the young man and woman, but there was another male figure in the shadows. The Star Crystal was now in the hands of the woman. Then the vision ended".

For many years Wedolan reviewed and interpreted these visions, and wrote commentaries on each.

READER'S DESCRIPTION OF TERMS

APIN ***(A'-pin);*** Gemstone for the planet Hanilov; Keeper is Lien; Power of kindness.

ASTROPHI ***(As-tro-fi);*** A high tech aerospace design company where Jor Bakra worked as an astrophysicists. Astrofi's prestige grew because of Jor's innovativeness in space propulsion systems, which yielded many lucrative government contracts from several solar systems.

BAKRA, JOR ***Bak'ra, Jor);*** Shreela Bakra's recently deceased husband..

BAKRA, SHREELA ***(Bak'-ra, Shree'-la);*** Shreela Bakra is the Widow from Tima and the widow described in the Legend of Khali.

BAKRA, SOREN ***(Bak'-ra, Sor'en);*** Soren Bakra is Shreela's six-year old son.

BALARAI ***(Bal'-a'ra');*** Space station located outside the Khalian Solar System

BAYONNE ***(Bay-own');*** Lieutenant Bayonne of the Occupation Military Police. He allowed Ewlon and his friends to leave Landory.

BEHREND ***(Bear-end);*** Ambassador from the Petron Solar System; expert in solar system societal development; member of the Thesbian Placement Council. Behrend mysteriously disappeared before he could reveal the inside person working with Uzak in the abduction of widows from Thesbis.

BERGON ***(Ber'-gun);*** Bergon replaced Ambassador Behrend on the Thesbian Placement Council. Bergon was an expert in solar system development as well as a scholar on the Khalian Solar System and the Keepers of Khali. Bergon was also from the Petron Solar System.

BHUSAN, PALADOR ***(Bhu-shan', Pal-a-door);*** Native Latonian. One of King Ewlon's best friends.

BLOCON, ***(co'-con);*** An extinct carnivore living on the planet Perican in ancient times. This creature would sting its prey with venom to subdue them to a sleeplike state. The venomous drug was delivered in liquid form. Milan was able to collect the liquid from one of his archaeological finds. He changed the liquid to a potent gas vapor and stored it in small vials.

CALITHOLIN ***(Cal-ith-o-lin);*** Familiar name for the planet ROTHOR, a planet in the Khalian Solar System; the gemstone of Rothor is Calitholin; Keeper is *Ilata* – endowed with the power of *strength.*

CETRA, ***(set-ra');*** Khalian word for soap

CHHOTTAN ***(Chō-tan);*** Red rock imported to Zirvag as a fertilizer for exotic plants, purchased throughout the galaxy.

DABERNINE ***(Dab'-ber-neen);*** Hard marbleized ore; black in color; used in exterior building blocks, walkways, interior counters, cabinets, wall décor; polished to a high gloss; highly durable; wears slowly

DAGMAR ***(Dag'mar);*** Dagmar was the planet aligned with

Uni. The research for the M.E.P. beam (Molecular Exchange Processor) was conducted on this planet. The Dagmarian Science and Research Team was made up of those engineers (including Jenka Danne) responsible for the development of the beam. This technology was also the new technology which Uzak would not reveal to Admiral Pernell before the first Unian strike against Khali.

DALONI, BOOLIN ***(Dal-on'-ee, Boo-lin);*** Chief Engineer of the Lluellyn and Shargant Space Stations. Boolin was also a traitor; Uzak's "inside man".

DANNE JENKA ***(Dawn, Jen-ka);*** Ewlon and Megan's half-sister and illegitimate daughter of Wedolan Galan. Co-conspirator to Uzak.

DORFA TREE SAPLING - this is a small bush like tree with soft violet circular leaves. When fully mature, the leaves are leathery-textured, and the leaf color changes from violet to concord. Such saplings are planted in late summer, but generally mature between six to eight weeks. The leather textured leaves are a protection against the cold and frost of winter.

DELLO ***(Del-lo);*** Keeper of Joy; gemstone Ininston and planet of guardianship, Windon

ECHLINDRA ***(Etch-lin'-dra);*** Planet located on the fringe of the Petron Solar System. Echlindra had representation on the Thesbian Placement Council on Thesbis and was a short stopover between the planets Dagmar and Calith.

ENA ***(E'-na);*** Keeper of Peace; gemstone Valle; Guardianship, Perican.

ERGRET ***(Er-gret);*** Four-legged beast which lives in the Galan marsh. Can emit toxins to paralyze prey but uses fangs and sharp claws to subdue victims.

FARANDE ***(Far-ăn'-de);*** One of the fifteen planets in the

Khalian Solar System; gemstone is *quelque*; Keeper is *Rendal* – endowed with the power of *foresight.*

FERBINN *(Fer-binn);* Keeper of Truth; gemstone Burzan; planet of guardianship, Lozondra.

FIDAS ACHATES *(Fee'-dus Ak-ā-tees);* Mid sized space cruiser that is capable of short trips in deep space; Ew and his companions boarded this ship to take them from the battle cruiser to the planet surface on Galan; ship was destroyed by Unian Military Force.

FINDRAE *(Fin-dray);* The Township where Bakra mansion was located on planet Tima.

GALAN EWLON *(Ga-lan', You'-lon);* Ewlon Galan is the King of the Khalian Solar System and Uzak's arch foe.

GALAN, MARA *(Ga-lon', Mar'-a);* Mother of Ewlon and his sister Megan Galan. Mara ruled alone for sixteen years after the death of her husband. She passed the scepter to Ew when he was twenty years old.

GALAN MEGAN *(Ga-lon', Mej-an);* Ew's younger sister.

GENA SOLAR SYSTEM; Solar System in which Tima was one of the moon planets. Tima was also the home planet of Shreela Bakra.

GEO TRAN; a geo tran is a measurement comparable to an acre.

HANILOV *(Han-ĭ-lov);* Hanilov is one of the fifteen planets in the Khalian Solar System; gemstone is *Apin*; Keeper is *Lien* – endowed with the power of *kindness.*

HASLOW *(Has-lo);* Governor of the planet Yalléon, one of the fifteen planets in the Khalian Solar System.

ILATA *(I-la-ta);* see *CALITHOLIN*

JAINEN (Jay'-nen); - see MELAN

JANUS *(Jan-us);* a sleeping drug which is absorbed through the pores of the skin. Due to its absorption nature, the drug is usually administered through a high pressurized, non-percutaneous syringe. Uzak used the drug in its clear and fine, powdery state to lace the Tulusian ring which he gave to Mara Galan. An overdose of this drug destroys the brain tissue, ending in death.

JYOTI ***(Jo-tee);*** Keeper of Faith; gemstone Giña; planet of guardianship, Tarpellis.

KALA ***(Ka-la);*** One of Shreela's closest friends from her home planet Tima.

KARI, ***(car-ee);*** a stimulating drink; very much like coffee on Earth.

KHALIAN SOLAR SYSTEM ***(Ka-lee'-an);*** Sixteen planets created by the Keeper of the Universe and guarded by the fifteen Keepers sent by him. The Galan family later ruled this solar system.

KILO-TRAN; A kilo-tran is a little more than a half mile.

LANDORY ***(Lan'-door-ee);*** A large city bordering the southeastern Galan Marsh on the continent Verlithia

LIEN ***(Lee-en);*** Keeper of Kindness; gemstone Apin; planet of guardianship, Hanilov

LINO-TRAN; A lino-tran is equal to .38 inches

LITATHE, ***(Lit-ath');*** Home planet of Milan Mariko

LLER ***(Lair);*** Keeper of Knowledge; gem Shinalin; planet of guardianship, Balor.

LT Speed – LT = Light Speed + .10(Light Speed). Speed of light plus ten percent of light speed.

MACHI ***(Ma'-key');*** Husband of Kala. A native Timanian and Shreela Bakra's good friend and neighbor.

MARIKO, MILAN ***(Mar-i-ko', Mee-lan');*** Archeologist. Close friend and confidant to King Ewlon Galan.

MELAN ***(Mee-lan);*** Planet in the Khalian Solar System;

gemstone is *Lieatra*; Keeper *Jainen* – Power is *hope and joy.*

MARSHÈE ***(Mar-shey);*** Planet in the neighboring solar system close to Khali. Marshèe's Chancellor, Nical, was a member of the Thesbian Placement Council working with Ewlon to investigate the disappearance of widows, as well as a new strategy to counteract Uzak's intelligence sources from identifying widows coming from moon planets (such as Tima), being trained and then placed in the Khalian Solar System for the required two years of employment.

MERIC ***(Mer-ik);*** Plant on Galan used as an antibiotic for bacterial infections.

MONROE, ISAN ***(Mon-ro, I-zan);*** Medical Doctor in Landory who saved the life of Ewlon Galan from the deadly poison of the Ergret. Escorted Ew and his comrades to the secret defense base in Markan. Later murdered by Uzak's Occupation Military Police when questioned about his role in Galan's underground defense.

MT. HALOKIN ***(Hal-o'-kin);*** Mt. Halokin housed a secret Galanian Military Defense Base on planet Thesbis.

MUDHAR, DIAN ***(Mud-har, Dee-an');*** widow friend and neighbor of Shreela Bakra. Her journey to Thesbis preceded Shreela's by two weeks. Tel Mudhar, Dian's husband, died mysteriously, leaving behind his pregnant wife.

NARVAN ***(Nar-van);*** General Narvan was responsible for the Occupation Military Police. He was the General responsible for the capture and death of Dr. Isan Monroe.

NILAR ***(Nil-ar);*** The second moon in the Petron Solar System. Since it was a habitable moon, widows from Nilar planning to relocate in the Khalian Planetary System were also potential victims for kidnapping by Uzak. Nilar was militarily aligned with Galan, and Marty Bergon was the ambassador sent to Thesbis to replace Ambassador Behrend on the Thesbis Placement Council.

OSHE ***(O'-shay);*** Mara's personal maidservant.

PAPRI ***(Pa'-pree);*** Name for Meric on the Planet Tima.

PARAMON ***(Par'–ă-mon);*** a planet in the Gena Solar System; Tima is the moon of Paramon.

PENDAR ***(Pen-dar);*** an orange-yellow ore;

PENNAT ***(Pen-not);*** Keeper of Wisdom; gemstone Ampurn; planet of guardianship, Mangen.

PERTH; Keeper of Health; gemstone Dercon; planet of guardianship, Balarai.

PETRON *(Pet-ron);* see NILAR.

RAILEEN ***(Ray-leen');*** city on the planet Thesbis where Shreela was registered for counseling and rehabilitation.

RATSF ***(Rapid Tactical Strike Fighters);*** Small disc-shaped Unian fighter spacecraft accommodating up to one pilot. These spacecraft are capable of great speed, and are housed on spacecraft carriers. They are primarily used in quick and dirty tactical strikes.

RENDAL (Ren-dal); see FARANDE

ROTONDRA ***(Ro-tawn-dră);*** – Galan's flagship, commanded by Admiral Garbonst.

SATELLITE CONTAINMENT CHAMBERS were used to molecularly alter and dispose of debris left behind by spacecraft garbage dumping. These containment chambers were developed and designed by Jor Bakra, and became part of his own private business.

SHECHAN ***(say-chan);*** a rare metallic ore used to fashion expensive jewelry. Highly malleable and temperature sensitive; purple in color; found only on the planet Echlindra.

SOLAN ***(So-lan);*** see *YALLÉON*

SOLAITRA ***(So-lā-trŭ)*** – One of Galan's main battle cruisers. The Solaitra was sent to send a rescue shuttle for Ewlon and his friends, trapped at the Mt. Halokin Defense Base. It was later blown up by the Unian Military Force, just after Ewlon and his companions left on the Fidus Achates to land on Galan.

STAR CRYSTAL an elliptical disc which energized The Planet Star by verbal command. It was the actual key to The Planet Star's operation. They key itself was forged by Solan, Keeper of Life, and placed in the hand of Wedolan Galan. When Uzak killed Wedolan Galan, he unknowingly sent him back home in a burial tube with the Star Crystal still intact. It was removed from Wedolan and placed beneath the surface of Ewlon's left hand.

STUBEN ***(Stu-ben);*** Keeper of Charity; gem Dartolj; planet of guardianship, Telpagari.

SURFACE SPACECRAFT; Spacecraft used for short range interplanetary travel. Cannot be used for deep space travel.

THESBIS ***(Thez'-bis);*** Thesbis, Planet of Widows; This was the place where widows went to rehabilitation and training. It is one of the planets in the Unian Solar System.

TIMA ***(Tee'-ma);*** Small moon in the Gena Solar System and home of Shreela and Suman Bakra.

TRAN; A tran is equal to 3.2 feet or 38 inches.

TSA Keeper of Love; gemstone Salaitra; planet of guardianship, Laton.

THE PLANET STAR a medallion of fifteen leafed petals connected to a round, crystalline stone. Each petal is adorned with a single oval-cut gem. Each gem is different in color; one from each planet in the Khalian Solar System. Each gem is bestowed with the power of the guardian Keeper of the planet where the gem originated. The center crystal is the Nila stone, the gem of unity. This gem unified all of the powers and its Keeper was Uzak of Uni.

TUSHAR ***(Tū-shar);*** King Ewlon's deceased son, killed in a stampede with his mother.

UZAK ***(U'-zak);*** Keeper of Unity; gemstone Nila; Planet of guardianship Galan, but later ruled Uni which was outside the Khalian Solar System. Before The Planet Star was forged, each Keeper possessed their own gem of power. Uzak directed his power of unification into a new Nila gemstone before he destroyed the original gem, which was already in sync with those of the other Keepers. By doing this, he broke the covenant and the unified power of his brothers. The Keepers became disembodied and could not communicate with each other or with the inhabitants who lived on the planet they guarded, except for Solan, Keeper of Life. Uzak was not disembodied but retained his power of immortality. Solan was able to reconstruct the body of power. He communed with each Keeper separately and was able to reunite their powers through the forging of The Planet Star.

WEDOLAN ***(Wed'-o-lan);*** Wedolan Galan was father to Ewlon and Megan Galan, and Jenka Danne.

YALLÉON ***(Yăl-ā'-on);*** Planet in the Khalian Solar System; its gemston *Ilĕd,* was found in the Jalon Mountains; Keeper is *Solan* – endowed with the power of *life*, and responsible for the forging of The Planet Star that would ultimately defeat Uzak.

YASHIL ***(Yash'-ill);*** Yashil was Wedolan's only brother. He was responsible for stealing The Planet Star from the home of Wedolan Galan. It was his hope to claim the throne of Galan as his birthright and use the power of The Planet Star to gain that power.

YAVIK GALAN ***(Yav'-ik Ga-lan');*** Yavik was the father to both Wedolan and Yashil Galan. It was during his reign that Uzak broke the covenant, and fell from the body of power.

VERLITHIA ***(Ver-lith'-e-a);*** One of six continents on the planet Galan. Continent of Star City which is the capitol of Galan and of the Khalian Solar System. Star City was also the home of the ruling Stewards, the Galan family, appointed by Solan, Keeper of Life.

ACKNOWLEDGMENTS

I would like to thank my husband, Satyananda, and my sons, Suman and Amitabha, for the many hours of patience with me while I compiled this work. I would also like to acknowledge my gratitude to my father, Robert Conaway (who has passed on), my brother, Gregory Morris, and my good friend, Kathleen Marusko, for the tremendous number of hours dedicated to editing the original manuscript and many hours of consultation and support.

I would also like to extend my deepest gratitude to Charmain Grigowsky, my editor, and American Book Publishing for the amazing work done to bring this work to fruition.

ABOUT THE AUTHOR

C. M. Chakrabarti was born Cheryll M. Conaway in Pittsburgh, Pennsylvania. She was the youngest daughter of Robert Conaway, a U.S. Steelworker, and Georgia Strayhorn Conaway (both deceased). Cheryll spent her elementary years in Pittsburgh, but moved with her family to New York City where she attended junior high and high school. Several years after graduation, Cheryll returned to Pittsburgh where she graduated with a B. S. degree from the University of Pittsburgh.

C. M. Chakrabarti has been a mother, a secretary, a research and health systems analyst, and served as an appointed member of the Governor's Committee on Health Data Systems. Her avocation to authorship started as a diversion to her work as a trained mathematician

Recently, C.M. Chakrabarti attended a small college to study opera and has worked for the last three years as an administrator of a budding opera company. C.M. Chakrabarti is also active with Billy Strayhorn Songs, Inc., a family corporation, working to promote the music and legacy of Billy Strayhorn, her mother's brother and her uncle.

About This Book

Teach Yours[illegible] w you can combine the Int[illegible] needs—all while exploring th[illegible] world.

Over the co[illegible] tools—and more importantly, y[illegible] et's truly staggering amount of information [illegible] ing you need to make the Internet your own.

Who Should Read This Book

Anyone interested in learning more about the Internet should read this book. Beginners will find the basics they need to get started on the Internet, learning its tools, its resources, and its rules. More advanced Internetters will find advice on how to combine the tools at their disposal to pursue their interests or needs in specific areas.

How the Book Is Structured

Teach Yourself the Internet consists of 21 chapters, each representing a *day* of activities. On Day 1, you'll go on an all-too-brief tour of the Internet, then you'll spend the rest of the first week learning the fundamental Internet tools. It's after Week 1, however, that *Teach Yourself the Internet* diverges from the other Internet guides. Starting with Day 8, you'll spend your days putting your first week's knowledge to the test by following a broad range of excursions. Each scenario helps you combine the various tools for the purpose of finding, retrieving, and working with information related to a specific topic. Week 2 offers scenarios of personal interest, while those of Week 3 are oriented toward professional topics.

Conventions

Note: A Note box presents interesting pieces of information related to the surrounding discussion.

Tip: A Tip box offers advice or teaches an easier way to do something.

Warning: A Warning box warns you about potential problems and helps you steer clear of disaster.

Excursion

And throughout the course of each day's lesson, we'll take you on numerous Excursions to places on the Internet. Think of these as field trips designed to show you first-hand a particular Internet tool or techni[illegible] in action.

Teach Yourself the Internet

Around the World in 21 Days

Teach Yourself the Internet: Around the World in 21 Days

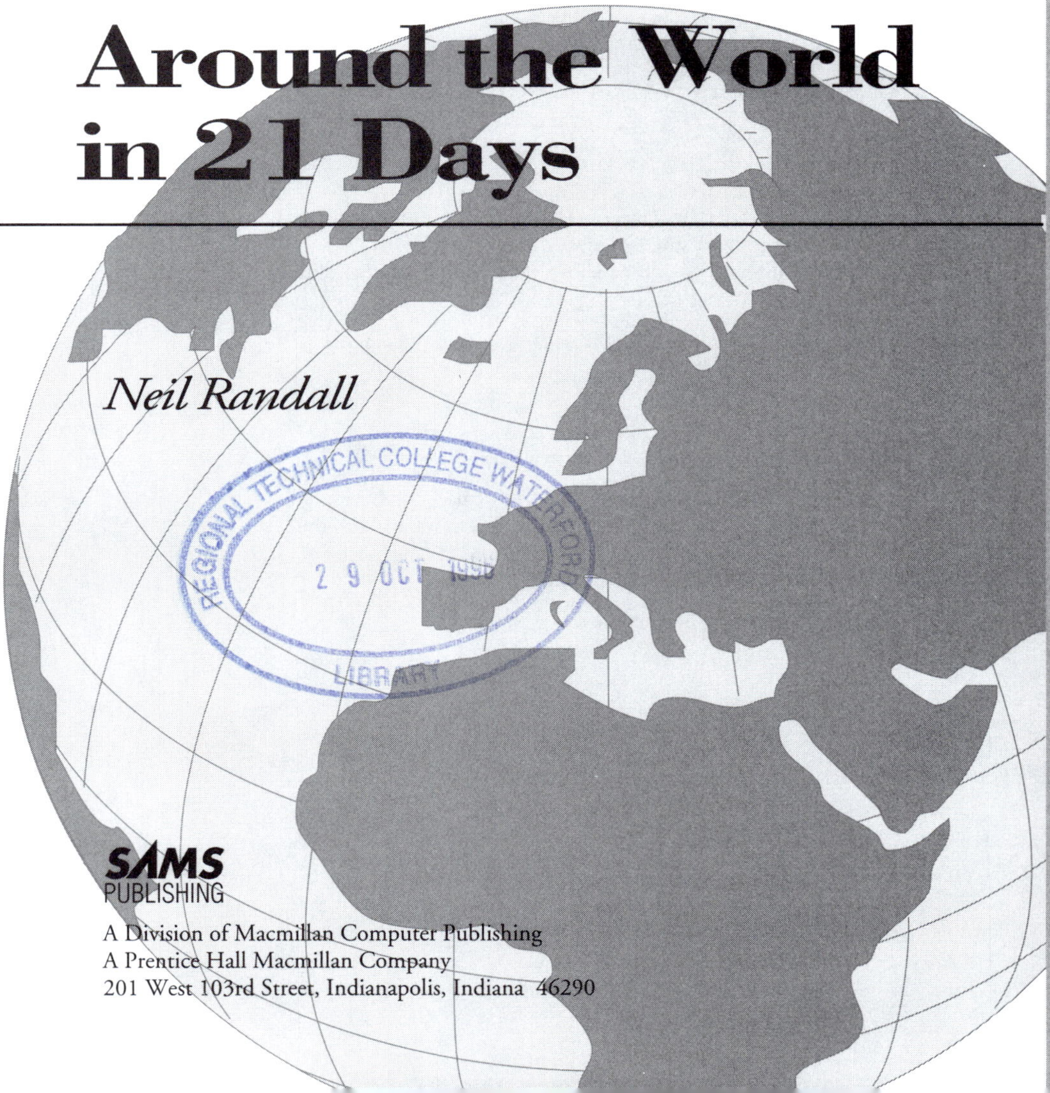

Neil Randall

SAMS PUBLISHING

A Division of Macmillan Computer Publishing
A Prentice Hall Macmillan Company
201 West 103rd Street, Indianapolis, Indiana 46290

This book is dedicated to Selby Bateman.

International Standard Book Number: 0-672-30519-4

Library of Congress Catalog Card Number: 94-65777

97 96 95 4 3

Interpretation of the printing code: the rightmost double-digit number is the year of the book's printing; the rightmost single-digit, the number of the book's printing. For example, a printing code of 94-1 shows that the first printing of the book occurred in 1994.

Composed in AGaramond and MCPdigital by Macmillan Computer Publishing

Printed in the United States of America

Trademarks

Publisher
Richard K. Swadley

Associate Publisher
Jordan Gold

Acquisitions Manager
Stacy Hiquet

Managing Editor
Cindy Morrow

Acquisitions Editor
Mark Taber

Development Editor
Mark Taber

Production Editors
David Bradford
Mitzi Foster Gianakos

Copy Editors
Jill Bond
Mary Inderstrodt
Matthew Usher
Joe Williams
Kitty Wilson

Editorial Coordinator
Bill Whitmer

Editorial Assistants
Carol Ackerman
Sharon Cox
Lynette Quinn

Technical Reviewers
James C. Armstrong, Jr.
David F. Randall

Marketing Manager
Gregg Bushyeager

Cover Designer
Dan Armstrong

Book Designer
Alyssa Yesh

Director of Production and Manufacturing
Jeff Valler

Imprint Manager
Juli Cook

Manufacturing Coordinator
Paul Gilchrist

Production Analysts
Dennis Clay Hager
Mary Beth Wakefield

Graphics Image Specialists
Tim Montgomery
Dennis Sheehan
Susan VandeWalle

Production
Nick Anderson
Elaine Brush
Amanda Byus
Jenny Chung
Kim Cofer
Lisa Daugherty
Terri Edwards
Kimberly K. Hannel
Angela P. Judy
Greg Kemp
Ayanna Lacey
Stephanie J. McComb
Jamie Milazzo
Wendy Ott
Shelly Palma
Casey Price
Chad Poore
Kim Scott
Michelle Self
Susan Shepard
Tonya R. Simpson
SA Springer
Marcella Thompson
Suzanne Tully
Dennis Wesner

Indexer
Jeanne Clark

Overview

Contents

Dear Readers:

Thank you for purchasing Sams Publishing's *Teach Yourself the Internet: Around the World in 21 Days*, another in our growing line of Internet books. This title is an expansion of our best-selling *Teach Yourself in 21 Days* series, which has more than one million books in print in less than two years.

The Internet is exploding at a rate that dwarfs other online services. CompuServe, with a membership of approximately 1.5 million, is growing at 60,000 users per month. America Online doubled in size over the last few months to 600,000 users. Prodigy, because it comes bundled with many computers, is larger than America Online and CompuServe combined. But the Internet is adding as many as 1 million users *each month* to its 25 million user base—and there is no sign of this slowing.

Our goal at Sams is to help you gain more knowledge about the Internet and maximize your use of this vast information resource. We want to be your Internet information resource. In addition to the title you currently have in your hands, Sams has also published such best-sellers as *Navigating the Internet, Deluxe Edition* and *The Internet Unleashed. Navigating* serves as a perfect introduction to the Internet with lots of tips, important information, and a great guide to the Internet called the Gazetteer. *The Internet Unleashed* brings together more than 30 Internet experts, who share their knowledge with you in a comprehensive 1,400-page book. Both books include a disk with enough utilities and software to help you connect to the Internet.

Other Sams books due out this month include *Your Internet Consultant*, by well-known Internet expert Kevin Savetz, which answers all the frequently asked questions (FAQs) about the Internet, and *The Internet Business Guide*, by Rosalind Resnick and Dave Taylor, which offers tips for using the Internet for business purposes, such as online seminars, electronic mail, and direct marketing. *Tricks of the Internet Gurus*, slated for fall release, will provide tips and tricks from a variety of Internet experts, including some surprise Internet "legends." *The Waite Group's UNIX Communications and the Internet, 3E*, is a guide to the Internet specifically intended for UNIX users. *Education on the Internet* is a practical guide aimed at helping students, educators, and others use the Internet to aid in learning. *The Usenet Guidebook* combines an interesting, lively discussion of Usenet's unique history and culture with practical and detailed advice for getting the most out of Usenet newsgroups, including how to start and moderate a newsgroup. *A Programmer's Guide to the Internet* is a guidebook that helps programmers find information on the Internet to make their jobs easier, including code snippets, tidbits about the latest software releases, bug information, programming utilities, coding techniques, and more.

In addition, this fall, Sams will be a major part of the Macmillan Computer Publishing Internet site. This site will enable Web, Gopher, FTP, and Telnet access and will be a hub for computer-related information, including lots of information about our books and others, seminars taught by our best-selling authors, the most popular shareware and software, source code from our books, special offers and discounts, mailing lists, and a wide variety of other information. We'll be publishing access information in future editions of our books. I hope to see you there!

If you have any questions or concerns, don't hesitate to drop me a line. I can be reached at (317) 581-3670 or via e-mail at `samspub@netcom.com`.

Sincerely,

Richard Swadley
President and Publisher

Acknowledgments

My thank you list is huge, so I won't even try to include everyone. But here are the people without whom this book simply wouldn't have happened:

- David Wade, whose idea it was in the first place, and who remains its true coauthor.
- Celine Latulipe, whose timely and superb contributions kept me from despairing.
- David Randall, who came through when it mattered with first-rate work.
- Jim Hartling, who guided others through more thoroughly than I could have ever asked.
- Stewart Lindsay, Marion Muirhead, Angela Pollock, Neil Humphrey, Christa Ptatschek, Laurie Pearce, Carol DeVrieze, Craig Miller, and Charlotte Montenegro, whose excellent contributions gave this book its real strength.
- My mother and father, Kay and Lloyd Randall, who always encouraged.
- And—mostly—Heather, Catherine, and Michelle, who put up with a great deal of neglect but never once complained.

About the Author

Neil Randall

Neil Randall teaches English at the University of Waterloo in Waterloo, Ontario. He offers courses in professional writing and rhetorical theory, and he conducts research in issues surrounding the Internet, Computer-Mediated Communications, and other technological issues. He has published articles and reviews in several computer magazines, including *Windows*, *Compute*, *Amiga World*, and *Computing Canada*, and is currently a columnist for *PC Gamer* and a contributing editor for *CD-ROM Today* and *Computer Entertainment News*. He writes a weekly newspaper column dealing with computers and has published several related newspaper features.

Introduction

Let's face it—this isn't the first Internet guide on the market. There are others, and some are excellent. In fact, I've used a number of them myself, and I continue to recommend them to my friends.

Their strengths are clear. They guide you, step-by-step, through the sometimes bewildering variety of tools you need to know if you want to become Internet-savvy. They explain them in varying degrees of thoroughness, and they make it possible to work through the Internet at all. What they don't do—nor are they meant to—is show you how you can combine the tools to satisfy your own interests and research needs.

Teach Yourself the Internet: Around the World in 21 Days attempts to do just that. Over the course of its 21 chapters, you'll learn the major Internet tools, and more importantly you'll combine these tools to sift through the Internet's truly staggering amount of information. By the time you finish, you'll have everything you need to make the Internet your own.

And that's the point—making it *your* Internet, using it for *your* purposes, getting it to satisfy *your* needs and *your* curiosity. Like any technology, the Internet will be valuable to you only if you—and any people you care about—can put it to good use. If you're interested in technologies for their own sake, the Internet has lots to offer. If you want your technologies to somehow make your life better (and what else are technologies for?), well, that's where the Internet shines. That's what this book helps you do.

Two other points about this book. First, I designed it so that you can get a great deal out of it without actually being on the Internet. Read it in a coffee shop, or on a plane, or in front of the TV, and you'll get a good idea of what the Internet has to offer. Second, I wanted users of Microsoft Windows or the Macintosh to feel at home. While the text examples are taken from UNIX accounts, all of the screen captures are from my own Windows machine in my study, and Mac screens look similar. This was important to me, because these two groups of Internet users are growing very, very quickly.

How the Book Is Structured

Teach Yourself the Internet consists of 21 chapters, each representing a day of activities. On Day 1, you'll go on an all-too-brief tour of the Internet, then you'll spend the rest of the first week learning the fundamental Internet tools. Day 2 takes you through the basics of the Internet, including tools like Telnet, while Day 3 looks at e-mail and Day 4 explores newsgroups and mailing lists. On Day 5, you'll move on to Gopher, then Day 6 looks at retrieving files through FTP, Archie, and WAIS. The last day of Week 1 puts you face to face with the World Wide Web.

It's after Week 1, however, that *Teach Yourself the Internet* diverges from the other Internet guides. Starting with Day 8, you'll spend your days putting your first week's knowledge to the test by following a broad range of excursions. Each excursion helps you combine the various tools for the purpose of finding, retrieving, and working with information related to a specific topic. Week 2 offers scenarios of personal interest, while those of Week 3 are focused on professional topics.

In Week 2, for instance, you'll use the Internet to gather information about searching for a job, choosing a university, putting together an art collection, and publishing your own Internet magazines (plus three others). By comparison, the topics in Week 3 are more professionally focused and include gathering business information, plugging into the growing community of education professionals, exploring the Internet for social issues, and learning of the activities of governments, the courts, and scientific research organizations.

When you've completed all 14 scenarios, you'll be more than ready to branch out on your own, combining the Internet tools to track down information about topics of your own particular interest. In fact, by that time you'll probably already have started. Once you get going, and you see items on a Gopher menu or a World Wide Web site that interest you, you'll be so tempted to explore them that you'll almost certainly set this book aside and do some "surfing" on your own. I encourage you to do so, but I also encourage you to pick the book back up. There's more to learn in each succeeding chapter, and you can put all of it to use in your own detailed searches and retrievals.

The Role of the Contributors

Not only will you explore the Internet through a variety of topics, you'll also do so from a number of different viewpoints. To demonstrate first-hand that the Internet is a collaborative venture, I enlisted a number of contributors to write the basis of many of the scenarios (and even two of the Week 1 chapters). A high school teacher, for example, leads you through the K-12 education scenario, while an art enthusiast examines the Internet's archives of digital art. A woman committed to gender studies explores women's issues on the Internet, a technical communications professional looks at job-related education from that professional vantage point, and so on.

In each chapter that features a contributor, the structure is as follows: I introduce the chapter, then the contributor takes over, then I come back in with additional material and summary information. There are two exceptions to this rule—Days 13 and 19—but in all cases it will be made clear who's doing the actual writing.

My Internet Address

At various points in this book, you'll see my Internet address revealed in its full, multipart glory. Here's an invitation to use it. If you have any comments about *Teach Yourself the Internet*, send me a message. If you have a question, I'll try to answer it. A small warning, though; the answers will be brief, and I may not get back to you immediately (I have a day job).

After You're Finished Reading

This book isn't a one-time item. It will continue to evolve along with the Internet itself, and I invite you to be part of that evolution. By the time you read this, a World Wide Web and Gopher site will be in place, designed specifically for readers of *Teach Yourself the Internet: Around the World in 21 Days*. Here you'll find links to additional resources, comments and frequently asked questions from readers, and whatever other information becomes important. Please join us, and please let us know your Internetting needs.

The URL address for the Web site is `http://watarts.uwaterloo.ca/TYI/tyi.html`. See Day 7 for how to access the Web. If you're having trouble doing so, e-mail me at `nrandall@watserv1.uwaterloo.ca`.

WEEK 1

Learning the Internet Tools

AT A GLANCE

1
2
3
4
5
6
7

WEEK

1

The Internet: A World Tour from Your Armchair

On Day 1, we'll take a quick tour of the Internet. Beginning with a brief discussion of what the Internet actually consists of, we'll then move from location to location around the globe to get a sense of how broad-reaching the Net has become. Along the way we'll meet a few people, find some good reading material, and see how Internetters are presenting themselves. All this is in preparation for Day 2, when the real excursions begin.

Today you'll do the following:

- ☐ Get an idea of what the Internet consists of.
- ☐ Visit Internet locations around the globe.
- ☐ Find out what people are using the Internet for.

Note: You don't need an Internet account to complete Day 1. In fact, you don't even need a computer. Think of this as a slide show or a set of overhead transparencies: your task for this chapter—unlike the rest —is to observe rather than to do. Of course, if you have a computer and an Internet account, by all means follow along.

Your Introductory Class

One of the great traditions of higher education is the introductory class. Usually it's shorter than the rest will be, and it's almost always more immediately enjoyable. Instructors make use of audio-visual equipment to give broad overviews of the material, and emphasis is placed on familiarizing rather than learning. There's no pressure, the term stretches out before you, and except for the fact that there aren't enough chairs in the room, everything's pretty much right with the world.

Day 1 is this book's version of that time-honored event. Essentially, you're being asked to sit back and watch the world go by, and in the process to get an idea of what the Internet is and how truly global it has become. The fact that you've bought this book means that you've already heard of the Net, and you're either on it or thinking about getting your own account. Day 1 offers a glimpse of what that account can offer you.

So enjoy. The real work's just ahead.

Putting the Net in Perspective

The Internet is big. So big, in fact, that it's hard to get a handle on it. You've probably read things about how many computers are hooked up to how many networks, with how many users in how many countries. Doesn't mean much, though, does it? The whole thing is just too huge.

So let's knock it down a bit.

Inside your computer is a hard drive. Most likely, the drive contains several hundred files; if you run Microsoft Windows 3.1, for instance, you've got a couple hundred right there. How do you keep track of all these files? Usually, you don't have to, because your programs know where to find things themselves. When you need to find a specific file, though, you can laboriously do so yourself, or you can get some software to do it for you.

As long as you have only one moderately-sized hard drive—80-120 megabytes, say—finding files isn't much of a problem. Upgrade to 240 or 340 megabytes, however, and locating that one elusive file gets a bit dicier. Looking through directory after directory gets tedious very fast, so you'll start to make use of the file-search programs provided with any number of new software packages.

Even so, it's no big deal. You've got a hard drive, and you can find what's on it. Everything's fine.

Now add a second hard drive. Start filling it with program files, graphics files, multimedia files, all the stuff you can find. Suddenly, it's no longer even an option to search for a specific file on your own. You need that file-search program, and you want one with enough features to help you narrow down your search.

As soon as you have those two drives under control, add a few more. A hard-card, for example, and a couple of daisy-chained SCSI drives. Ridiculous? Hardly. That's what I have, and I'm not alone. But forget about realism for a bit. Picture your computer with five hard drives, together totaling over two gigabytes of storage space. Any guesses how long it would take to find one single, solitary text file? Especially on a DOS machine, with its dopey file-naming convention? You need that file-search program more than ever. In fact, you can hardly operate without it.

Now let's get really adventurous. Imagine a system with not just five hard drives, but five million. Imagine that every ten minutes, another hundred or so are being added on. Imagine that you have no control over who puts them there, nor what files are loaded onto them. All you know is that you have access to most of them.

Welcome to the Internet.

The Internet is nothing more than a bunch of computers all joined together. These computers have three major functions:

- First, they let people on one computer send messages to people on another.
- Second, they store files that people might want access to.
- Third, they let people on one computer connect to a remote one to do things as if they were actually at that site.

That's it. That's primarily what the Internet is.

So why is everybody from the United States government to the British Broadcasting Corporation jumping onto it? Because, quite simply, they want to send messages and access those files. Or, to reverse this, they want to receive messages and provide files that can be accessed by others.

But the Internet's popularity can be even more easily explained. It's huge, and it's global. Get on the Net (as it's called), and you can suddenly exchange messages and files with over a million computers in dozens of countries. Every ten minutes or so, another computer network attaches itself to the Net, which means that those million-plus computers are getting company very quickly. Think about all the users, and think about all the hard drives. Every one of those computers has files you might be interested in, and every one of them also has users you might want to contact.

The only trouble is finding them. To help you, some inventive programmers have developed some equally inventive software.

- *Archie*, for instance, is a program that goes out and searches the Net for files, then builds a huge database of the files that are out there. When you do an Archie search, you're actually accessing this database. The program tells you where to find it; that is, it tells you which computer—or computers—holds that file. (See Day 6 for more details on Archie.)
- *Gopher*, the most popular Internet program of all next to your mailer, provides links from computer to computer. There are always other ways of making these links, but Gopher makes it easy by replacing the Internet's rather arcane commands with numbered lists (or pictured lists if you're working in Windows or on a Macintosh). You may not be comfortable typing `ftp ftp.reston.va.us`, but choosing number 5 in a list is easy enough for anyone. (Day 5 deals extensively with Gopher.)
- The *World Wide Web* (WWW) is even easier, as long as you're working in a graphical environment like Windows, the Mac, or UNIX's X Window. Each WWW screen looks like a well-designed page in a document, with some words

or phrases highlighted or underlined. Click on one of these, and you'll be taken somewhere else. Through the WWW you can get into Gophers, download files, and all sorts of other Internet activities. (For more on the World Wide Web, see Day 7.)

And that's just three. Over the course of this book you'll learn about others, many with exotic and more or less impenetrable names. WAIS, Veronica, ERIC, CARL—all of them are designed to help you find things. The fact that there are so many is testament enough to how big the Net is. Keep in mind that most Internet programs are designed just to help you find whatever you want to find.

The other side of the Net, of course, is the phenomenon known as electronic mail. I can't even imagine the days—not too long ago—when I had no recourse to e-mail at all. A few months on the Internet, and you won't either. Every day I receive at least fifty messages, and sometimes nearly two hundred. Many of them simply tell me about new stuff on the Net, to be sure, but there's lots of the person-to-person kind as well. Join the Net, and e-mail can quickly become your life.

Is that a good thing? That's probably not the point. Good or bad, it happens. I personally think it can be very good indeed. While it's true that e-mail can become a time-consuming monster, and as a result can be (and is) used as a crutch, it can also be the most important link you have to people with similar personal or professional interests. Reading your e-mail in the morning can be one the most thought-provoking and even inspiring events of the day, and writing a few quick replies can get you going quickly. It can also bog you down, but that's just a matter of self-management.

I've seen e-mail transform people. I've seen it expand their intellectual and even social horizons. I've helped people use it to propose, negotiate, and submit entire projects. I've also seen it destroy people's carefully planned schedules, but that's been the much rarer event.

The point is that e-mail exists, and it's not about to disappear. It can be used as a tool for sending everything from sticky notes to lengthy documentation, and its sheer flexibility makes it indispensable.

That's what the Internet is: a carefully developed collection of communication and file access technologies. What's so amazing about it is that it exists at all. Try to network three PCs together in the same room, and you'll quickly learn how complex and unforgiving networking technology can be. Extend those problems across oceans and a huge array of operating systems and communications incompatibilities, and you begin to see how Internet researchers have been spending their time. Right at this moment, I'm sitting in front of a 486 PC that is networked through complex transmission scheme to a Cray supercomputer in Illinois, a Macintosh in British Columbia, an IBM mainframe in

Australia, and who knows what pieces of old and new technology in Peru, Brazil, the Netherlands, Norway, the U.K., Poland, Italy, Turkey, Singapore, Malaysia, Japan… .

You get the idea. It's all pretty impressive.

So let's tour. We'll visit a number of locations near and far, meet a few interesting people, and start to skim the surface of the information ocean.

Welcome to the Internet.

A World Tour via the Internet, with Greetings from Abroad

For the remainder of this chapter, we're going to use the Internet to tour the world. You can either join in by signing on to your Internet account, or you can simply read along and see what the Internet has to offer. In fact, this chapter is designed for anyone who is curious about the Net but who hasn't actually been on it, or who has done a few things on the Internet and is wondering what else there is to know.

What will happen during this tour is known as *Net surfing*. We're going to do nothing more than "surf" from one "site" to another to see what the new site contains. The important thing to keep in mind is that each site is another computer physically located somewhere else in the world. We'll be using the Internet to connect to a computer in the United States, then from there to a computer in Canada, then Mexico. Then we'll link back to the U.S., where we'll connect to computers in Europe, the Middle East, Asia, and so on.

When we connect to the remote computer, we'll be looking at a screen that contains information and points to other sources of information. Someone at that location has set up a Gopher directory or a World Wide Web page that anybody on the Internet can access, and this directory or page will display on our monitors. We'll temporarily become part of that remote computer, able to examine whatever its owners have given us permission to see.

Ready? Okay, we're off.

This tour is structured quite simply, and unlike most tour buses this one stops whenever you want it to, and for however long you wish. In fact, you can even skip entire continents and return to them later.

Here's what we'll do. We'll start from the United States, visit a few countries on each continent—unless of course the continent has only one, or even none—and end up back in the United States. We'll visit primarily Gopher and World Wide Web sites, because through them we can do pretty much anything else (except send e-mail). Along the way...well, let's just see what happens.

Note: To access Gopher sites, I'll use two programs designed for Microsoft Windows: Winsock Gopher and WinGopher (see Day 2 for how to get them). I could use the more familiar text-based Gopher programs, which are available on UNIX-based Internet accounts, but then you wouldn't actually know if we were visiting the site or if I'd just typed the text by myself. In this book, we don't do tourism scams.

The World Wide Web browsers you'll see here are NCSA Mosaic and LII Cello, both of which you'll see a lot of throughout this book. See Day 2 for where to find these programs, and Day 7 for a more extensive look at them. Both programs are designed to display files coded in what's called Hypertext Markup Language (HTML). They're designed to make Internet resources easy to access, and to add graphics and other multimedia features to these resources.

Special Note to Macintosh Users: This book uses Microsoft Windows as the platform for all graphical examples. The only reason for this is that Windows is what I primarily use. I'm asking you, as a personal favor, not to feel slighted by this decision. GUI-based Gopher programs are available for Macs, of course, as is the famous Mosaic (in fact, the Mac version was available first, as you know). I've used the Mac version of Mosaic, and I've used Eudora and other Mac programs, and I'm aware of the relative strengths of each. I'm also aware of Microsoft Windows's many weaknesses. But the Windows machine I use is newer and faster than the Macintosh I own, which is the main reason why you see Windows screens rather than Mac screens throughout this book.

Special Note to UNIX Users: See my note to Mac users for why the graphical screens throughout this chapter and this entire book are taken from Microsoft Windows. I'm aware of the UNIX-based graphical environments and that the UNIX version of Mosaic is richer than either the Windows or the Mac version. I'm also aware that the Internet is essentially UNIX-driven and that software for other platforms is largely written to allow them to interact with UNIX environments. My decision to use Windows was simply one of convenience.

Enough with the notes and explanations. Let's get rolling.

North America

The Internet started in the United States, and this is where most of the activity is taking place. You'd probably expect Japan to be next, but that's not the case. Because of a wide range of concerns and issues, Japan got a late start, but they're picking up steam. Second to North America is Europe, in fact, and we'll go there next.

Excursion 1.1. U.S.A.

For now, though, let's start with the United States. This is the Internet's birthplace, and with recent Presidential initiatives, it's where the Net will expand most quickly. We'll begin with a significant location, the University of Minnesota, the home of the important browsing program called Gopher.

Figure 1.1 shows the result of Gophering to the following address: `gopher.tc.umn.edu`. (See Day 5 for details on how to do this.) At the top left of the screen is the main Gopher. We could choose any item from the menu, but let's opt for University of Minnesota Campus Information, the last item listed. This leads us to the long listing on the right half of the screen, with all sorts of interesting choices available. Because this is only the introductory session, let's forgo the more serious-looking stuff, and head right for Campus Events. The result is the listing on the lower left, each of which has additional information. The obvious choice here is WOW! What's on Wednesdays, but let's go someplace else instead.

Tip: Whenever you encounter a Gopher listing, you'll have these kinds of choices. Each listing leads to another, with the only ending point being an actual document that you can read or download. As you can already see, Gopher browsing can be time-consuming, instructive, and quite addicting.

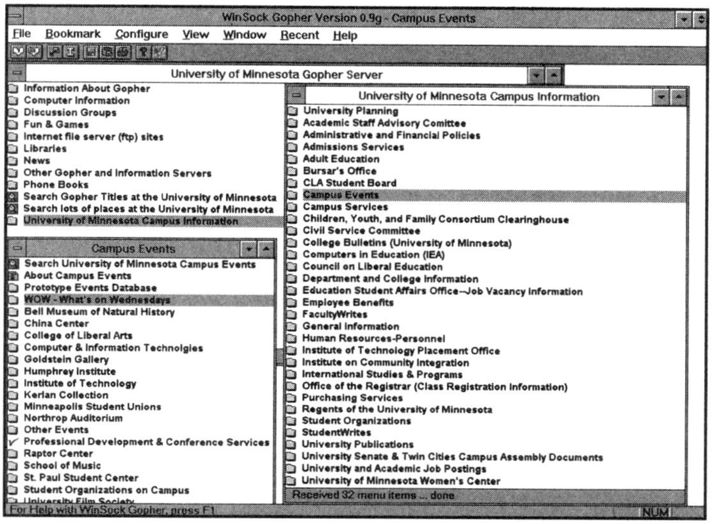

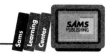

Figure 1.1. *University of Minnesota Gopher servers.*

Excursion 1.2. Canada

The United States's largest trading partner and all that, Canada began developing its internetworking capabilities soon after the Internet became a reality. So let's go east of Minnesota and into New Brunswick, where we find a World Wide Web site and the University of New Brunswick (address: `http://degaulle.hil.unb.ca:80/UNB.html`—see Day 7 for information about how to access WWW sites). Figure 1.2 demonstrates the Web's potential for incorporating graphics and even sound—the little Speaker icon beside the Welcome line is a sound file that we can play if we have the necessary hardware and software. See Day 2 for details on WWW audio, video, and viewers.

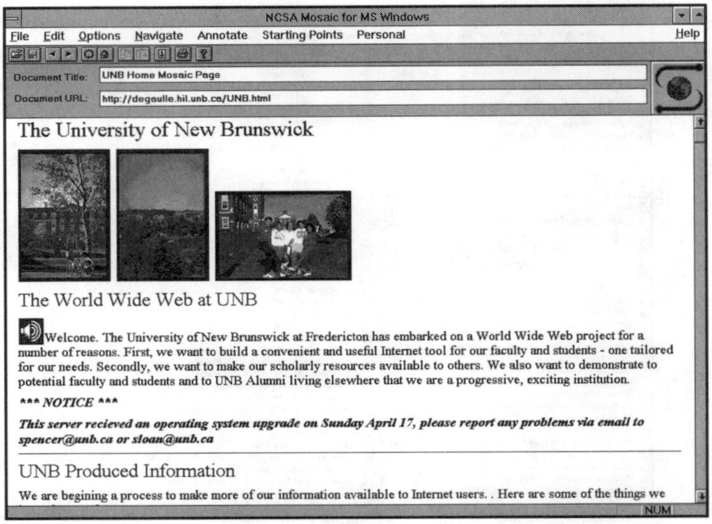

Figure 1.2. *The University of New Brunswick home page.*

Excursion 1.3. Mexico

Far to the southwest of New Brunswick lies Mexico (the third of the NAFTA partners), and that's where we head next. Mexican information is accessible primarily through Gophers, so we return to our Gopher program and see what we find. From the Other Gopher and Information Servers line of the University of Minnesota Gopher we arrive, eventually, at Figure 1.3. Here we see a collection of Mexican Gophers in the middle of the screen, with two additional selections, PROFMEXIS and the Monterey Institute of Technology, displayed to the left and right respectively.

Note: As you might expect, most of the Mexican information is in Spanish. As you'll also discover, however, a great many Gopher and WWW sites offer English versions. For better or for worse, English has established itself as the *lingua franca* of the Internet, although other languages are starting to appear.

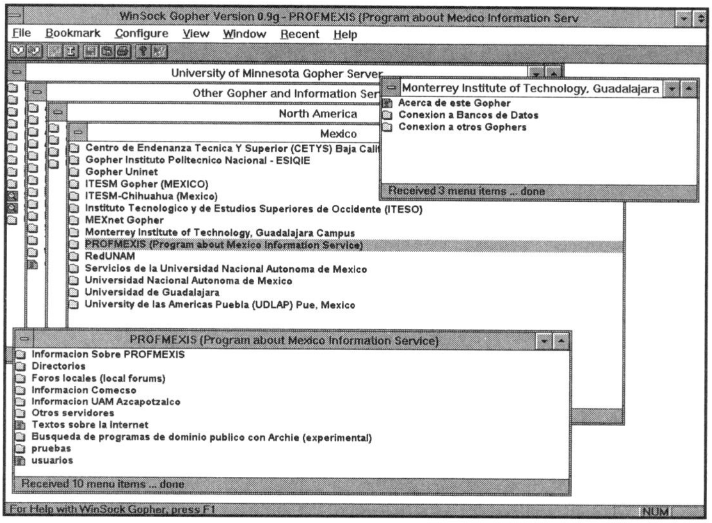

Figure 1.3. *Mexican Gopher servers.*

Excursion 1.4. The Virtual Tourist

Back to the U.S.A., and this time to Buffalo, New York. Here we find an extremely useful bit of Internet technology, the *clickable map.* The Virtual Tourist, shown in Figure 1.4, is a World Wide Web page (`http://wings.buffalo.edu/world`) that lets you click your mouse pointer on whatever section of the world you'd like; in turn, you'll receive another clickable map. We'll be returning to the Virtual Tourist frequently throughout this book. It's an exceptionally useful guide to the world's Internet resources.

At this point, let me pause the tour to meet our first new contact. Brandon Plewe is Assistant Coordinator, Campus-Wide Information Services, for the State University of New York at Buffalo. He'd like to say hello:

> Welcome to the Virtual Tourist. This service has been provided to you by many people around the world who want you to know more about themselves, their lands, and their resources on the Internet. We hope you find it a valuable trailmap as you backpack around cyberspace.
>
> The Virtual Tourist is really two guides in one. The first is a catalog of information about the real world, and the second is a guide to the services in the

virtual world of the Internet. You can use the first kind of service to learn more about another country or region, or perhaps even plan a trip there. The second will be useful to you in your travels in cyberspace, by showing you what resources each area has to offer.

Unfortunately, this volunteer effort is far from complete. Perhaps, down the road, you too can contribute to the Virtual Tourist.

Brandon Plewe

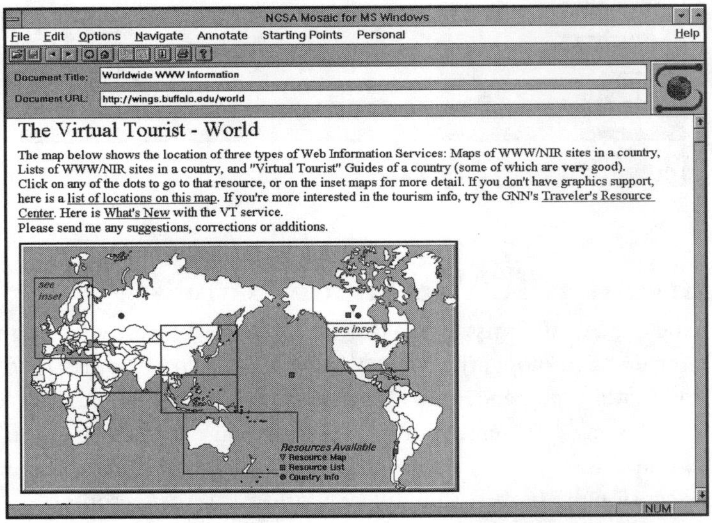

Figure 1.4. *The Virtual Tourist top-level page.*

Note: This is the first of several greetings from around the world you'll find in this chapter. I located all these people through the World Wide Web, then e-mailed them and asked if they'd provide a short welcome note to put in the book. It's a testament to the sheer power and cooperativeness of the Internet that the messages all arrived within a few days of my request, and that, of all the people I asked, only one turned my request down. I don't know about you, but I find this kind of amazing.

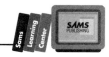

Europe

As far as the Internet is concerned, Europe is already highly developed, with an increasing number of sites appearing almost daily. Figure 1.5 shows the European inset of the Virtual Tourist map, along with the clickable map of Germany that appears if you select that country. As you can see from the map's key, a large number of sites are available, including several that include city information.

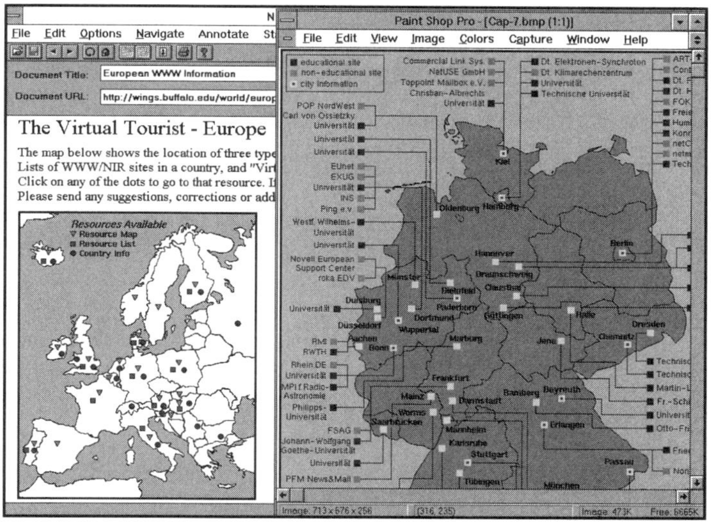

Figure 1.5. *The Virtual Tourist page for Europe.*

We won't visit Germany right now, however. Instead, we'll take a quick swing through the U.K. on our way to three smaller places: Switzerland, Hungary, and Sardinia.

Excursion 1.5. The United Kingdom

The U.K. is the dominant European nation from an Internet perspective, as one glance at the multi-item Gopher menu in Figure 1.6 demonstrates (UK Gopher Servers item from `ukoln.bath.ac.uk`). The left half of Figure 1.6 shows a small portion of the 89 items in the list, from which we'll choose the venerable University of Cambridge. Once again we'll bypass the serious details, skipping right to information about the Cambridge area (Cambridge area information item from `gopher.cam.ac.uk`). This appears at the bottom right of the screen, which consists primarily of documents. A quick click on the Theatres in Cambridge item would give us information about what's happening there in the world of theater, but again let's just skip on through.

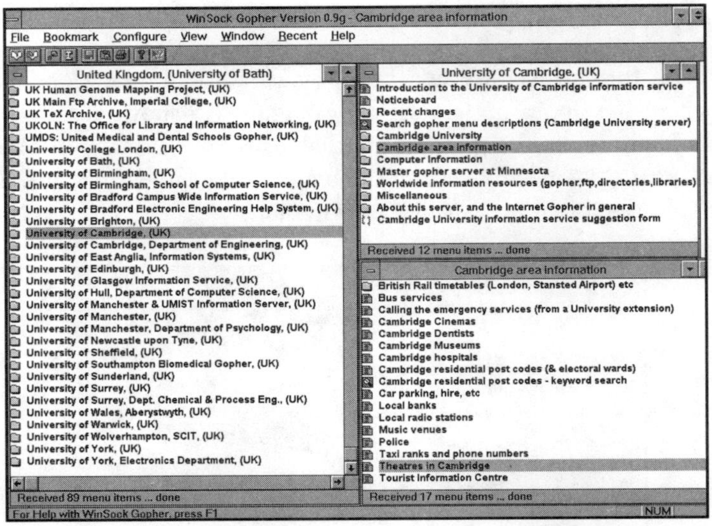

Figure 1.6. *Gopher servers in the U.K.*

Excursion 1.6. Switzerland

Among the more impressive Internet sites in Switzerland is TECFA, Technologies de Formation et Apprentisage, based at the University of Geneva. Figure 1.7 shows TECFA's colorful home page (`http://tecfa.unige.ch`), including links to other educational technology sites.

Once again, let's stop the tour for a quick meeting. Here is Daniel Schneider, "webslave" as he calls himself, from the Faculte de Psychologie et des Sciences de l'Education at Geneva, again with a message written specifically for this book.

> TECFA is an academic team active in the field of Educational Technology. It belongs to the School of Education and Psychology of the University of Geneva and includes about 10 collaborators. TECFA's main research interests are the applications of artificial intelligence to education, the cognitive effects of educational software, and the communication issues with new technologies (distance education, multimedia systems, multimedia courseware, and so on).

> The Internet is very important to us. Swiss academia is small and in most fields we lack "critical mass" and therefore we depend very much on international cooperation.
>
> We have access to fairly fast lines (2 mbps). In the near future, we will participate in experimental ATM networks that would enable us, for instance, to do full-motion video and 3-D animations over long distances and therefore bring the world still closer.
>
> *Daniel Schneider*

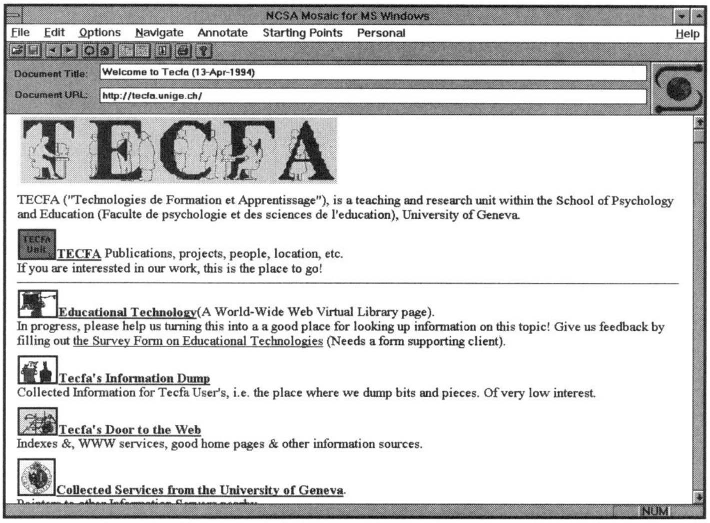

Figure 1.7. *TECFA home page—Switzerland.*

Excursion 1.7. Hungary

From Switzerland it's eastward across Austria and into Hungary, where we find another clickable map in Figure 1.8 (`http://www.fsz.bme.hu/hungary/homepage.html`).

We also find the home page for the Department of Process Control at the Technical University of Budapest (shown in Figure 1.9) at `http://www.fsz.bme.hu/welcome.html`.

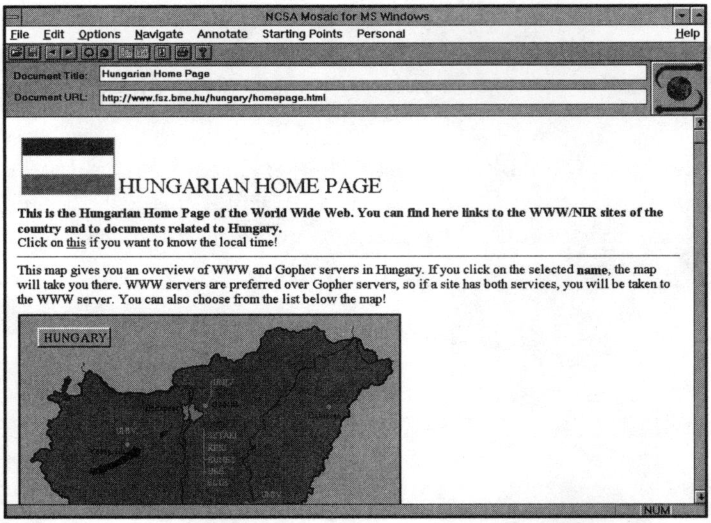

Figure 1.8. *Clickable map for Hungary.*

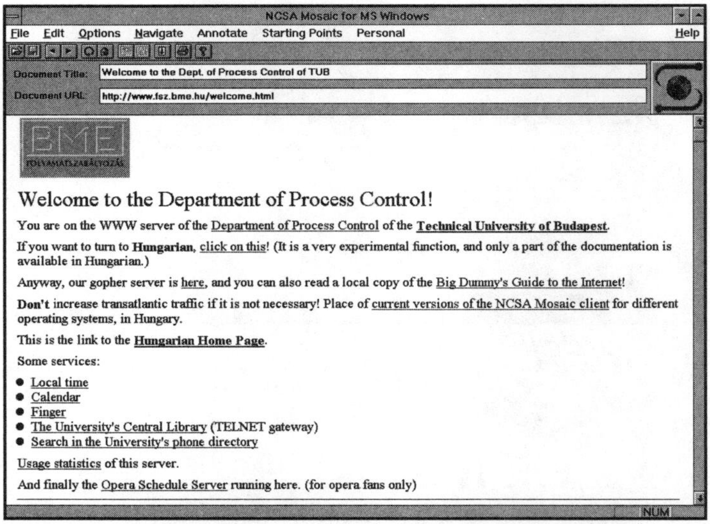

Figure 1.9. *Department of Process Control home page.*

These pages are the work, in part at least, of Tamas Maray, who greets you now from his home country.

Welcome to Hungary!

This small East European country has been connected to the Internet since 1991, and the first few Hungarian WWW servers are already available to you! So, welcome to the Hungarian Home Page of the World Wide Web, which is carried by the WWW server of the Process Control Department of the Technical University of Budapest (`http://www.fsz.bme.hu/welcome.html`). This server was set up at the end of 1993, among the first in Hungary.

At present, there are almost 4,000 computers connected to the Internet in Hungary. Most of the users are from the academic field—researchers, professors, students, and so on—though commercial users have also started to appear. With the required infrastructure in place, the popularity and use of Internet is growing fast. At the moment, WWW technology is very new on the Hungarian Net. The first two WWW servers were launched in 1993, though some new servers have appeared since then.

On the Hungarian Home Page (`http://www.fsz.bme.hu/hungary/homepage.html`) you will find the (probably) complete list of all the important Hungarian public services available through Internet, such as the WWW and Gopher servers, databases through Telnet, and so on. Beyond that, you can retrieve information and data about Hungary, Budapest, and the Technical University of Budapest, and you can reach the "Opera Schedule Server" (`http://www.fsz.bme.hu/opera/main.html`), which is very popular among classical music lover users of the Internet.

In the future, we would like to improve the database of our server to increase the multimedia information about Hungary and Budapest. We also want to create pages for the Budapest World Expo in 1996. Spreading the WWW culture in Hungary is something we consider to be very important.

Our Web project—supported by the Process Control Department of the Technical University of Budapest—is based on the work of three persons, though we want to draw more people into the project and we want to apply for external support as well. All three of us—Janos Mohacsi, Imre Szeberenyi and I—as young researchers and professors of the University's Faculty of Electrical Engineering and Informatics, are among the first keen users of the Internet in Hungary, and we are doing our best to initiate and spread the wonderful WWW technology in this country.

See you on our server,

Tamas Maray

Excursion 1.8. Sardinia

Finally in Europe, somewhat out of our way geographically but certainly not on the Net, we come to the island of Sardinia. Here is another burst of somewhat unexpected Internet activity, including some graphically gorgeous work such as the Sardinian history page shown in Figure 1.10 (`http://www.crs4.it/~zip/sardegna.html`).

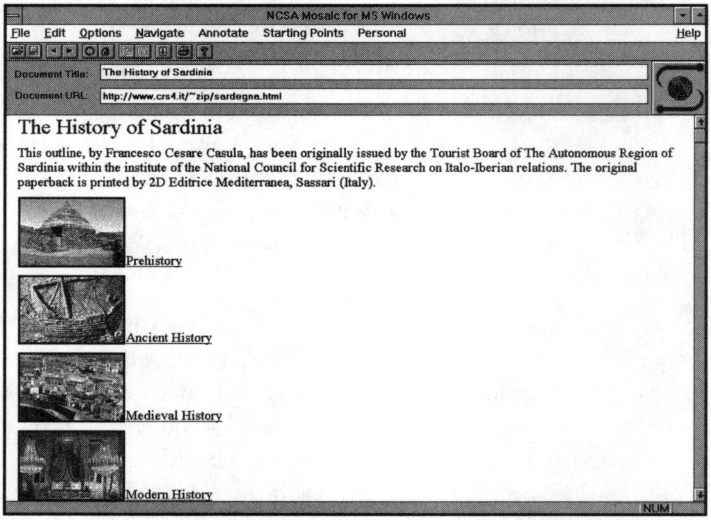

Figure 1.10. *Sardinia—information page on Sardinian history.*

Now for something *extra* special. Pietro Zanarini, Head of Scientific Visualization Group at the Centre for Advanced Studies, Research and Development in Sardinia (CRS4), has prepared not just a welcome message, but an entire welcome page on the World Wide Web! The page is located at `http://www.crs4.it/~zip/sardinia/welcome.html`, and it offers links to all kinds of other Sardinian information. Figure 1.11 shows this page, but only the text. There's also some very strong graphical work, but I'll let you find that out on your own. See Day 7 for details on how to get to an `http:` address.

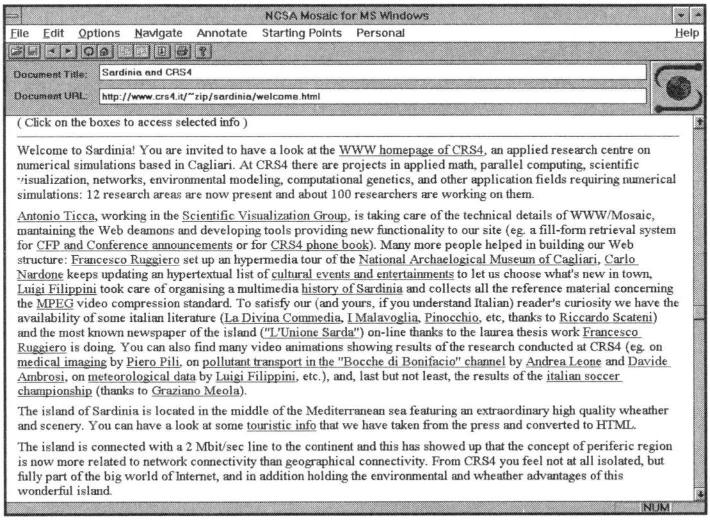
NCSA Mosaic for MS Windows
File Edit Options Navigate Annotate Starting Points Personal Help
Document Title: Sardinia and CRS4
Document URL: http://www.crs4.it/~zip/sardinia/welcome.html

(Click on the boxes to access selected info)

Welcome to Sardinia! You are invited to have a look at the WWW homepage of CRS4, an applied research centre on numerical simulations based in Cagliari. At CRS4 there are projects in applied math, parallel computing, scientific visualization, networks, environmental modeling, computational genetics, and other application fields requiring numerical simulations: 12 research areas are now present and about 100 researchers are working on them.

Antonio Ticca, working in the Scientific Visualization Group, is taking care of the technical details of WWW/Mosaic, mantaining the Web deamons and developing tools providing new functionality to our site (eg. a fill-form retrieval system for CFP and Conference announcements or for CRS4 phone book). Many more people helped in building our Web structure: Francesco Ruggiero set up an hypermedia tour of the National Archaelogical Museum of Cagliari, Carlo Nardone keeps updating an hypertextual list of cultural events and entertainments to let us choose what's new in town, Luigi Filippini took care of organising a multimedia history of Sardinia and collects all the reference material concerning the MPEG video compression standard. To satisfy our (and yours, if you understand Italian) reader's curiosity we have the availability of some italian literature (La Divina Commedia, I Malavoglia, Pinocchio, etc, thanks to Riccardo Scateni) and the most known newspaper of the island ("L'Unione Sarda") on-line thanks to the laurea thesis work Francesco Ruggiero is doing. You can also find many video animations showing results of the research conducted at CRS4 (eg. on medical imaging by Piero Pili, on pollutant transport in the "Bocche di Bonifacio" channel by Andrea Leone and Davide Ambrosi, on meteorological data by Luigi Filippini, etc.), and, last but not least, the results of the italian soccer championship (thanks to Graziano Meola).

The island of Sardinia is located in the middle of the Mediterranean sea featuring an extraordinary high quality wheather and scenery. You can have a look at some touristic info that we have taken from the press and converted to HTML.

The island is connected with a 2 Mbit/sec line to the continent and this has showed up that the concept of periferic region is now more related to network connectivity than geographical connectivity. From CRS4 you feel not at all isolated, but fully part of the big world of Internet, and in addition holding the environmental and wheather advantages of this wonderful island.

NUM

Figure 1.11. *Pietro Zanarini's special welcome page.*

Here's the message that informed me of the page's existence:

> Hi Neil,
>
> I apologize for giving you the CRS4 "Welcome message" after a week, but I worked on it a while...and now I'm quite satisfied. But, of course, you (and your readers) have to like it, so please don't hesitate to give me any kind of feedback.
>
> *Pietro*

Not much problem there, I'd venture to say.

The Middle East

Yeah, I know the Middle East is part of Asia, and not a separate continent on its own, but it seems only natural to treat it separately. Partly that's because of the seemingly constant world focus on the area, and partly it's because Internet sites have begun to appear with some frequency. In either case, the Middle East is well worth paying attention to. The other reason is that we'll touch down in Australia later in this book, so that continent won't be featured here.

Excursion 1.9. Israel

First stop, Israel. Among the more interesting sites here are the Gopher servers shown in Figure 1.12 (israel-info.gov.il or jerusalem1.datasrv.co.il). From these selections we could get detailed information about the Arab-Israeli peace process, the Hebron tragedy, and almost anything else we want to know. There are also links to Jewish Internet sites in other parts of the world.

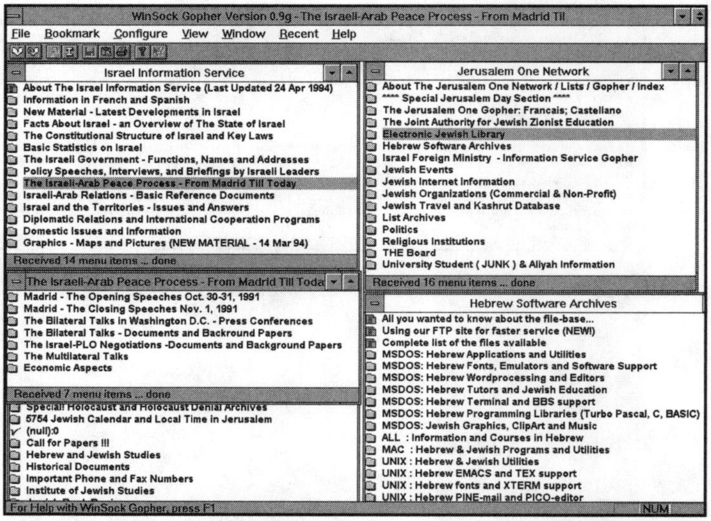

Figure 1.12. *Several Israeli Gopher menus.*

Also in Israel we find the Weizmann Institute of Science World Wide Web site (Figure 1.13). WISDOM, as this site is creatively called, offers information about the Institute and links to other Israeli Internet locations. Its World Wide Web address is `http://eris.wisdom.weizmann.ac.il`.

Time for another pause, this time to meet Shimon Edelman. Dr. Edelman is Senior Researcher in the Department of Applied Mathematics and Computer Science at the Weizmann Institute, and he has prepared the following greeting.

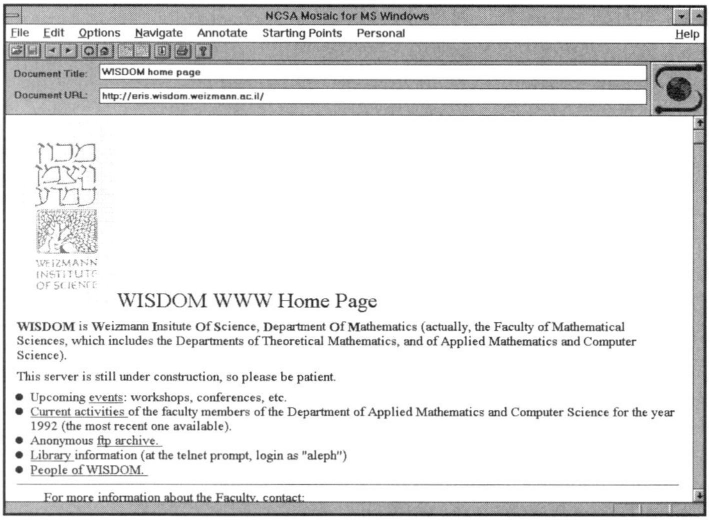

Figure 1.13. *Weizmann Institute of Science page.*

My home page represents a minimal attempt to facilitate access to the information I have to offer over the Net (mainly my FTP archive, and some teaching-related material), by making it both easy and fun. Serious improvements to the looks and to the contents are expected when I finally have the time for this (following my retirement, in a few decades).

My home organization, the Weizmann Institute of Science, was founded in 1934 by Dr. Chaim Weizmann, a distinguished researcher in organic chemistry, and a brilliant politician, who made important contributions to the Zionist cause, and later became the first president of the newly established State of Israel. The Weizmann Institute is devoted to basic research in a wide range of disciplines, from molecular biology and biochemistry to mathematics and environmental sciences. The Institute, along with the six other Israeli universities and a rapidly increasing number of hi-tech industrial enterprises, benefits from the instant global communications service provided by the Internet. All my colleagues here use e-mail, and many of us rely on the Net for regular exchange of data with collaborators all over the world.

As to my home country, you may be able to find information on Israel on the Net, but you have to come over and see it to believe it.

Shimon Edelman

Excursion 1.10. Turkey

Leaving Israel, we head northward to Turkey. Ankara, specifically, or at least nearby. This time it's the Middle East Technical University, whose home page, shown in Figure 1.14 (`http://www.metu.edu.tr/METU/MetuHome.html`), points to a substantial archive of material about the institution and its programs.

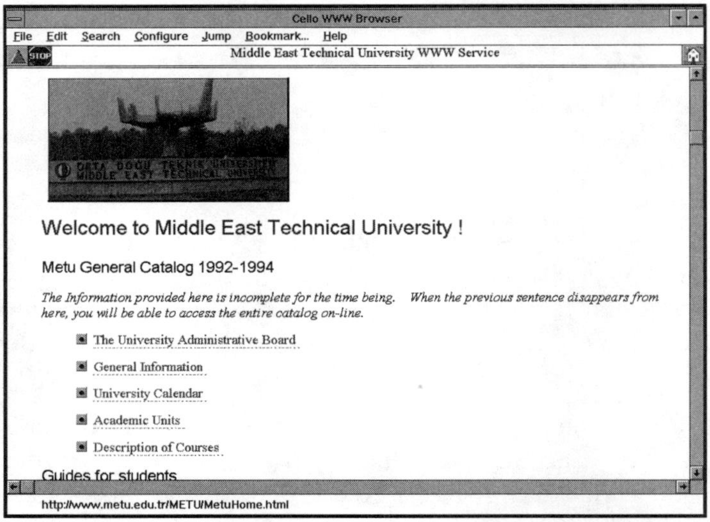

Figure 1.14. *Middle East Technical University, Turkey.*

Another hello, this time from Erdal Taner, Information Service Manager at METU. As the Internet would have it, this message appeared exactly as I was finishing off this chapter. Excellent timing, wouldn't you say?

Founded in 1956, Middle East Technical University (METU) is a university campus located 7 km west of Ankara. The Campus, located on 11,000 acres of forested land that includes Lake Eymir, has 350,000 square meters of floor space. The campus has been forested entirely throught the efforts of University employees and students since the early 1960s. METU has more than 43,000 graduates and now serves about 20,000 students from all parts of the world.

METU Campus Network (METU-NET) is composed of a fiber-optic 16 Mbit Campus backbone network with departmental LANs tied to the backbone. The METU Computer Center operates both the METU-NET and the national/international connections. It is, in fact, the Internet international gateway for Turkey. The TCP/IP protocol is the common protocol on the METU-NET, making it possible for Internet to be accessed throughout the Campus. For student use, there are 5 fully LANed PC labs—PCs equipped with necessary software to use all the possible Internet services (Telnet, FTP, SMTP, FSP, Gopher, WWW, WAIS, and so forth).

As Internet services have become quite common on the campus, some information services have been initiated. The main services for METU (like METU Archive, METU Home Gopher, and METU WWW Home) are maintained by The Computer Center. The idea of having a Campus Wide Information System in METU-NET has resulted in building such a system on the popular Internet Information Retrieval tools. WWW is the core of the METU-CWIS, and a Gopher server is also being used to facilitate a number of Gopher gateways. In addition, WAIS is used to create a searchable index over some parts of information in the METU WWW Server.

If you wish to find more information about METU, point your URL to the `http://www.metu.edu.tr/`.

As the home page shows, it also looks like an excellent campus to visit for real.

Asia

Excursion 1.11. Sri Lanka

Next it's off to Asia, with a first stop at Sri Lanka (Figure 1.15). This is a very recent site, and it's actually situated at Stanford University, not on the island at all (`http://suif.stanford.edu/~saman/lanka/sri_lanka.html`). But it offers a look at what the Internet promises for the future in Sri Lanka, and even at this stage it contains a solid amount of information about life in that part of the world.

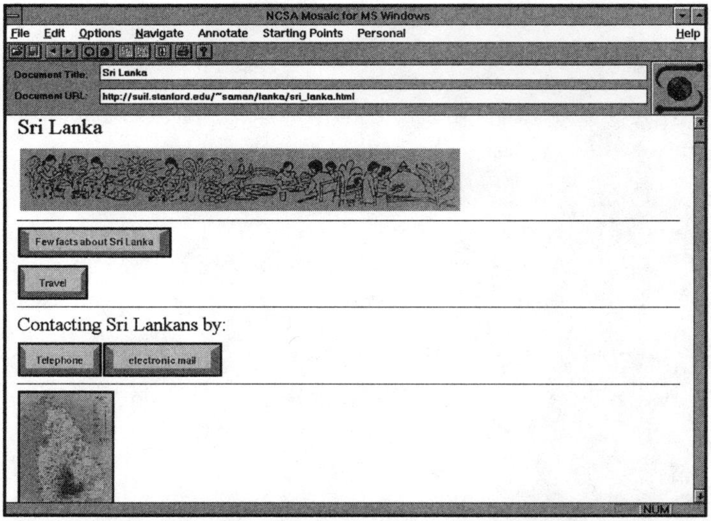

Figure 1.15. *Sri Lanka home page, with information on reaching Sri Lankans.*

Excursion 1.12. Malaysia

Almost due east of Sri Lanka is Malaysia, the long, thin land mass jutting into Indonesia. Here we find the WWW home page for the Universiti Sains Malaysia (Figure 1.16), which offers links to information about Penang Island, where this university stands (`http://www.cs.usm.my`).

And, once again, we have a welcome message, this time from the truly lovely Penang Island. Let's hear what Vincent Gregory, Systems Analyst in the Computer Aided Translation Unit, has to say to us.

> Welcome to Universiti Sains Malaysia (USM), Penang WWW server. The web server project at USM was initiated by Vincent Gregory and put together by staff at the Computer Aided Translation Unit. The server provides information about the university (details of history, administration, research, and so on), about Penang Island (ideal for tourists), and also links to other web servers in Malaysia.
>
> Malaysians enjoy Internet connectivity via the local JARING (Joint Advanced Research Integrated Networking) network. The original name of JARING was "Rangkom"—a pilot.

the UUCP-based computer networking project was started by MIMOS (Malaysian Institute of Microelectronic Systems), a government R&D body, at the end of 1986. Full Internet connectivity was established in 1990 with a 64K satellite link to NSFnet in USA. Within the country 64K lines link the various states together with plans for future upgrade to 128K lines.

Internet connectivity is provided to both private and public organizations plus home users. All universities and major organizations are connected to the network.

Penang Island (The Pearl of the Orient) is located on the northwest of Malaysia and is a popular tourist destination. Information on the Island, tourist attractions, food, culture, languages, maps, pictures, etc. can be found on the Web server. The information on this server is updated regularly and any comments, feedback, or requests are appreciated.

N. Vincent Gregory

If you ask me, it sounds like a must-visit—both virtually and, someday, physically.

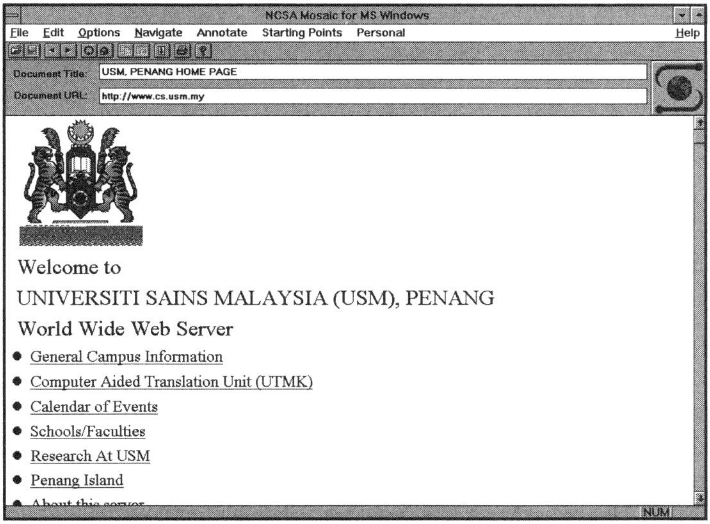

Figure 1.16. *USM Penang home page.*

Excursion 1.12. Japan

Our last stop in Asia is Japan. First we'll take a look at the Japanese clickable map (Figure 1.17) as a demonstration of how far Internet access has come in this nation, despite a very late start (`http://www.ntt.jp/japan/map/`).

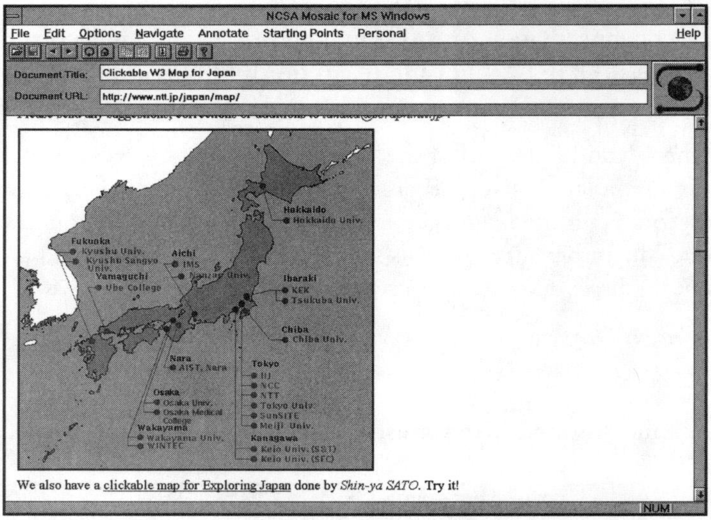

Figure 1.17. *Clickable map of the Japanese islands.*

We'll visit Japan a few times during the course of this book. For now, let's head to Tokyo, where Figure 1.18 shows the Tokyo Netsurfing Association's main page (`http://iikk.inter.net`). One of those responsible for the creation of this page is Joichi Ito, who has also stopped by to say hello.

> Hi!
>
> Thank you for accessing Tomigaya. Tomigaya is the name of the district in Tokyo where my http server and I live. Tomigaya is run by the Tokyo Netsurfing Association, a loosely organized group of hackers, musicians, artists, night club promoters, and video gamers. The Tokyo Netsurfing Association is sponsored by Eccosys, Ltd., a virtual company that focuses on Internet evangelical work helping companies set up systems based on ideas that emerge as we hack Tomigaya.

Tomigaya is one of the few sites in Japan where artists and young people not working in a research environment can hack Web pages and develop Internet software. Hopefully the number of cottage IPs will increase over the next year and we'll have more company.

The Internet is just beginning to emerge in Japan. Currently only ATT JENS and IIJ provide commercial Internet service. This number should increase dramatically over the next year. There is still no CIX equivalent in Japan, so University and non-commercial research traffic has to travel all the way to the CIX in the United States to get through to commercial Japanese sites. Bad news for Japanese academics trying to access Tomigaya.

We get our service from PSI Japan, which is setting up in Japan as I write this message.

Hopefully the penetration of the Internet will be another black ship to open the doors of the Japanese information and entertainment industry, as Admiral Perry's black ship opened trade to Japan. Expect to see a lot more stuff from Japan on the Internet soon!

Joi

Figure 1.18. *Tomigaya home page.*

South America

Across the Pacific lies South America, where Internet access has started slowly but is now well on its way. The continent's largest country, Brazil, also boasts the strongest Net access, but we'll bypass this center in favor of two smaller nations.

Excursion 1.13. Chile

Entering South America from the southwest, we arrive first in Chile. Figure 1.19 (`http://www.dcc.uchile.cl`) gives us a glimpse of the colorful home page of the Universidad de Chile, particularly its Computer Science department. Here we have links to other Chilean servers, the vast majority of which, at this stage, are Gopher sites.

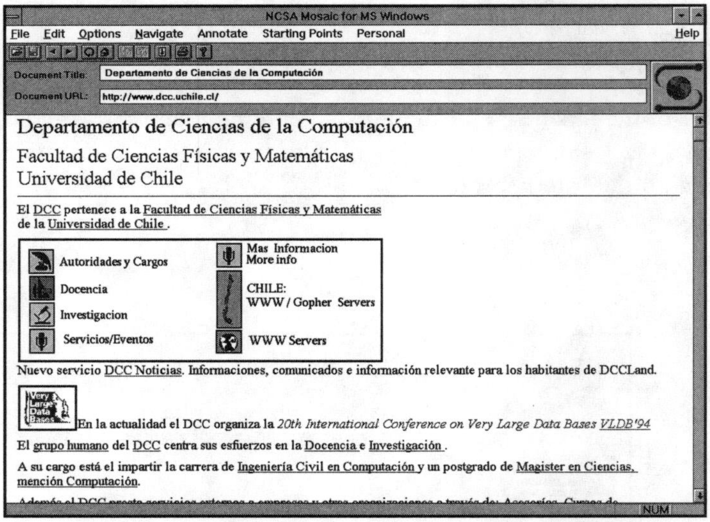

Figure 1.19. *Universidad de Chile WWW page.*

Excursion 1.14. Peru

Added very recently to the Net, the Peruvian Web site shown in Figure 1.20 (`http://www.rcp.net/pe/rcp.html`) provides links to the small but growing number of other Internet sites in Peru.

Figure 1.20. *The first Peruvian WWW site.*

Back in North America

We're back where we started, in the U.S.A. What better place to end our tour than a Web page featuring the country's two most visible officials? Figure 1.21 (`http://sunsite.unc.edu/npr/nptoc.html`) offers information about the National Performance Review, part of which is directly related to technologies such as those we'll use during the course of this book.

With the right audio equipment, we could even listen to what they have to say, but what's important is that the page is there at all. With even governments and courts (as we'll see) turning to the Net for dissemination of information, it's very clear that the Internet's time has come.

That's it. The tour's over. Starting tomorrow, bring your curiosity.

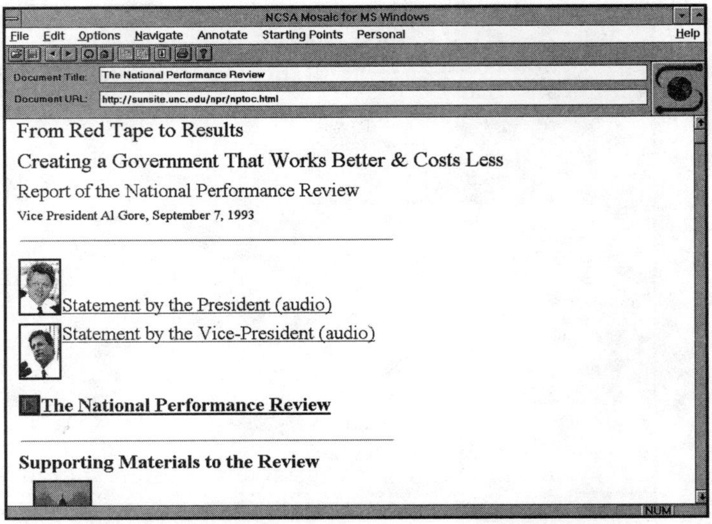

Figure 1.21. *The National Performance Review information page.*

Summary

Day 1 has introduced you to a very small portion of the Internet sites available throughout the world. By joining this brief tour, you've seen Gopher and World Wide Web sites in places as diverse and Hungary and Sri Lanka, and you've met some of the people who put these sites together. All this was by way of introducing you to the Internet's sheer scope, in preparation for the kinds of exploring the next 20 days will bring.

Task Review

On Day 1, an introductory tour of the Internet, you did the following:

- ☐ Learned what the Internet consists of.
- ☐ Visited Internet locations around the globe.
- ☐ Found out how people in these locations are making use of the Net.
- ☐ Met some of the people who make these locations accessible.

Q&A

Q Is that all there is to the Internet? Clicking from place to place and seeing what's there?

A No, far from it. But surfing, as it's called, is an extremely important part nevertheless. If you don't spend at least some of your time touring, you won't know the locations that are worth visiting for other reasons.

Still, as the next chapters will show, surfing is only a small part of the Internet. The real interest begins when you see the information available from within these sites. At any one of the locations we visited, there was far more to see than we examined. Links to files, other locations, submenus, and data of all kinds, with even more as these link to still other sites. Keep in mind that some of the locations visited on Day 1 were very much under construction; the best-developed locations can boast an enormous amount of information.

You've toured the Net. Now you'll see what it has to offer you.

WEEK 1

2

Into the Breach: Getting Started on the Net

With your world tour of the Internet completed, it's time to find out where it came from and how to work with it. Day 2 is a compendium of several items of interest, and our goal is to help you get started exploring the Net. Once you've finished, you'll be more than ready to move on to a more detailed look at the specific tools.

On Day 2, you will:

- ☐ Learn about the Internet's history.
- ☐ Understand the equipment needed for Internet access.
- ☐ Assess the type of Internet access required.
- ☐ Recognize a variety of Internet do's and don'ts.
- ☐ Log on to your account.
- ☐ Learn a basic set of UNIX commands.
- ☐ Telnet to remote computers.

Welcome to the Net

On Day 1, all you had to do was sit back and enjoy. Starting with Day 2, you'll sit back no longer. That doesn't mean in any way that the enjoyment is gone as well. In fact, as any Internetter can tell you, the excitement is in the doing. The Internet is anything but a passive medium.

Day 2 covers a wide range of details. First, we'll look (albeit very briefly) at the history of the global network. We'll then examine the hardware and software needed to gain access, as well as the different types of access available. We'll look at some things you should and shouldn't do, including a quick discussion of what's come to be called *netiquette.*

Then, it's on to the Net itself. You'll log on to your account, change your password, and spend a short period of time learning as little about UNIX as you can realistically get away with. Next, it's a look at perhaps the most basic Internet program, Telnet, through which you can connect to any Internet computer, anywhere.

Note: Every item in this chapter is presented briefly. A full description of the Internet's history, the necessary equipment, how to sign on, and all the other topics would require a separate book on its own. Throughout this book, I make one basic assumption: You want to *use* the Internet, not learn its technical complexities. That's why I deal with each separate tool only to the degree that you can begin using it and finding out more on your own. It's also why I don't give space to every single tool available. There are others, and as you become more interested and involved you'll discover them and learn how to use them.

By the end of Day 2, you'll be ready to move on to the intricacies of electronic mail (Day 3), mailing lists and newsgroups (Day 4), and the rest of the major Internet tools.

So Where Did the Internet Come From, Anyway?

Although the Internet has only recently been making headlines, it's been in existence—in one form or another—for over two decades. The following short history offers a bit of background that will help you understand some of its strengths, weaknesses, and idiosyncrasies.

ARPANET: There's This Nuclear Problem, See...

The Internet began as the ARPANET, back in early 1969. Funded by the U.S. Advanced Research Projects Agency (ARPA, hence the name), ARPANET was designed to let researchers communicate and share information with each other. Also high in the design goals was this: The network should be able to survive even if part of it was physically destroyed. This was 1969, remember, and the threat of nuclear attack was still on everyone's mind.

Basically, then, the idea was this: Build a network for researchers around the United States to use in their day-to-day activities and, in the process, make sure that blowing up a machine in one location doesn't stop the network from functioning.

Four ARPANET sites were established as test locations: the University of Utah, the Stanford Research Institute, and two University of California sites, Santa Barbara and Los Angeles. In September 1969, the ARPANET was switched on. Compared with the coverage of Woodstock and the first moon landing only a few weeks before this, the new network didn't get a whole lot of press. Who cared?

A few years later, many people did. Over a thousand watched ARPANET's first public demonstration in the fall of 1972, and that, effectively, is when the whole idea of a national—even international—network began to take hold. Everyone started developing reasons why they needed to be part of it, and what such a network could do for them. This isn't to say, mind you, that ARPANET was ever implemented with this goal in mind. From its beginnings, it was apparently designed to be small, with only a few key research sites participating.

Two Major Technologies: Breaking Up is Easy To Do

If there were two single technical decisions that allowed the network to function at all, it was the development of packet-switching technology and the design of TCP/IP.

Packet-switching makes it possible for data from different machines to share common transmission lines. Without it, dedicated lines linking one computer directly to another would be necessary, or at least preferred. With it in place, the network could be built with lines linking node to node (that is, one machine or network to another machine or network), with data routed through the nodes depending on its origin and destination.

Essentially, packet-switching technology breaks data down into little *packets*, each with a code showing its destination and instructions for putting the packets back together again. The packets move individually through the network, joining up again when they all reach the destination. It's a bit like the days when hitchhiking was still considered a safe practice. If four of you were trying to hitchhike somewhere, it wasn't likely you'd get a ride. Instead, you'd split up, each find your own ride, and agree to meet at a specific place. In effect, you were being packet-switched without knowing it.

TCP/IP means Transmission Control Protocol/Internet Protocol, but it's doubtful you'll ever need to know that. You'll need to remember the initials, though, because any computer that hooks onto the Internet must make use of TCP/IP. This technology, developed in the mid-70s, provides the standard means by which computers can talk to each other. Just like social protocol with its rules that everyone adheres to (you don't tell your boss's husband that his suit would look better on someone who weighed considerably less), computer protocol establishes procedures to allow effective communication to take place. TCP/IP became and remains the standard, and it allows the Internet's connectivity to happen.

NSFNET and NREN: A Plot for Breeding Acronyms?

The ARPANET lasted until 1990. In the meantime, it had been split into two networks. MILNET handled military affairs, while ARPANET carried data for research into networking and other fields. Universities scrambled to join, and the networks began to attract non-scientists and non-technologists as well. In the mid-80s, the National Science Foundation linked six U.S. supercomputer centers in a network called (not surprisingly) NSFNET, with data speeds increased from 56,000 bits per second (your modem probably runs at 9600 bps or 14.4 kbps, by comparison) to 1.5 mbps. This type of connection, called T-1, remains in place, but in 1990, the T-3 specification was introduced, allowing connection speeds of 45 mbps. (Anyone still working with a 2400 bps modem may wish to stop reading for a few minutes and calmly smash the thing to bits.)

In the late '80s, the NSF turned the funding and management of NSFNET over to the a nonprofit group of universities called the Michigan Educational Research Information Triad (MERIT). MERIT worked with MCI and IBM on expanding and improving high-speed national access, and eventually the three organizations formed Advanced Network Services (ANS), created to run NSFNET. This was important: The NSF had established an *acceptable-use policy* (called AUP, naturally) that allowed no commercial access to NSFNET, but now corporations were beginning to get involved. The look of the network was starting to change.

By 1990, NSFNET had taken over from ARPANET, and the latter was discontinued. In 1991, U.S. President George Bush signed the High Performance Computing Act, which essentially established a new network, the National Research and Education Network (NREN). NREN was to use NSFNET as its basis (initials getting to you yet?), and ironically enough has some research goals similar to those of the original ARPANET. Importantly, though, NREN was specifically established to join governmental and commercial organizations, which means that NSFNET's non-commercial policy is, for the most part, gone.

Other Networks: Because It Was Time

While all this was going on, there were other organizations interested in global networking. The Computer Science Network (CSNET) was established by the NSF to help universities that couldn't access NSFNET get onto what was slowly coming to be called the Internet. The only tool this new network could use, however, was electronic mail, so it had its limitations. Enter another new network, this one created "because it's time" and therefore called BITNET (really, it's true), offering e-mail, mailing lists, file transfer capabilities, and other options. Unfortunately, BITNET didn't use TCP/IP, so it had to develop another way of sharing information with NSFNET.

Eventually, BITNET and CSNET realized they were trying to do much the same thing (that is, connect to NSFNET), so they formed the Corporation for Research and Educational Networking (CREN). As they complete their merge—the technical difficulties are considerable—they also will be working to integrate more completely with NREN. Now, if CREN and NREN ever get together completely, we can only assume they'll change the name to WREN. Then it'll really fly (sorry).

Not to be outdone, of course, other parts of the world decided to hook into the emerging network. Canada established CA*NET and NETNORTH, the former corresponding roughly with NSFNET and the latter with BITNET. European networks began to form as well, with EARN and EUNet being the primary examples. With South America, the Middle East, Australia, and the Pacific Rim taking an active interest in the Internet, it's only a matter of time until more nationally- and continentally-based networks join in. The term *Internet* originally referred to ARPA's experiments in internetworking, but it's quickly becoming the abbreviation for international networking (popularly, at least, if not officially).

Statistics: The Facts, Just Give Us the Facts

I really don't want to provide real numbers here, because between the time I finish writing this book and the time it hits the shelves they'll be wrong. Here are a few guidelines, just so you have some figures you can pass around at a dinner party. The Internet began with four host computers in 1969. Now, it incorporates about 15,000 sub-networks in over 60 countries, and these networks consist in turn of roughly 1.5 million host computers. Interestingly, the number of commercially-based computers has practically overtaken the number of research- and education-based computers on the Net. The future has begun.

How many users are on the Internet? Nobody knows. Each host, remember, can have a number of individual users. You and your PC or Mac may be an individual host with one user, but a university will typically have several hosts, each with many users. It would be possible to figure it out, I suppose, but at the rate the Internet is growing, it would be futile. As soon as the numbers were in, they'd be wrong and uninteresting. Instead, let's just say that the Internet has millions of users. Good enough?

Now, What Do I Need to Get Started?

To connect to the Internet, you need three major items:

- A computer
- A service provider
- The right software

Depending on the type of connection, you might also need:

- A modem
- A dedicated line

That's it, really. As you might expect, however, there's more to it than just that. Let's get into a few of the details, without launching into a full-blown explanation. I'm going to proceed by addressing primarily the needs of the PC or Mac user dialing through a modem for reasons of complexity that will become reasonably obvious.

Types of Access

There are two essential types of Internet access. They go by a variety of names, but let's cut through everything and call them the following (even though there are variations of each):

- *Indirect Access*—This is the most common type of access. Your machine is essentially a terminal attached to a main computer (sometimes via a modem), which in turn has direct access to the Internet. Often, services and capabilities are restricted by the owner of the main computer.
- *Direct Access*—This is the most desirable type of access. Your computer is an individual node on the Internet, capable of doing whatever it's possible to do on the Net. Your machine has its own IP (Internet protocol) number, and you can establish it as an FTP, World Wide Web, Gopher or Telnet site if you wish.

Note: As mentioned, there are other terms for type of access. Among the most common are *dial-up access*, in which you dial into a server through a modem, and *dedicated access*, in which your machine is hooked up to the Net through dedicated connection such as a separate high-speed line. The problem is that the terms overlap. Some providers offer dial-up access that, through SLIP or PPP, essentially gives you dedicated access. Furthermore, your firm can have dedicated access, but through its local network you have what's sometimes called *terminal access*, meaning your computer is just a terminal on the machine that's hooked up directly. I've used direct and indirect because they distinguish between being a node on the Net and being connected to a machine that is, in turn, a node on the Net.

Indirect Access

If you're connecting to the Internet through a commercial, governmental, or educational institution, you likely already have indirect access. You'll know this as soon as you try to access a favorite newsgroup (newsgroups are covered in Day 4), which suddenly isn't available to you any more even though you know it's still operating.

Note: In many cases, this is reasonable: The owners of the main computer want you to work, not read irrelevant news or play addictive games, so they simply remove the temptation (it's their computer, remember). In other cases—many of them covered in the press—such restrictions are tantamount to blatant censorship; these are often referred to by euphemisms such as institutional responsibility.

You may already have indirect access. If you're working for a large company, or if you're a student, staff, or faculty member at a university (or, increasingly, a K-12 school), check with your systems people to see what kind of access you have. Be persistent; sometimes systems people come up a bit short on the information-giving process, often because they're too busy putting out high-tech fires.

When you hook up to a host UNIX machine, you'll be effecting a *shell* connection. This means, basically, that your computer is a terminal on that machine, and that you're using a UNIX shell as your main interface.

Shell connections are the most common of all. Most Internet users either link to the Net through shell connections at work, or they dial in to a UNIX machine and enter the shell that way. With this type of connection, you'll have an account on the host machine, and you'll be allocated a limited amount of that system's resources (typically, a megabyte or so of hard disk space). That machine will normally be part of a local network (often through Ethernet), which in turn will be connected to the Internet.

You can also get indirect access through electronic bulletin boards (BBSs) and commercial online services. Check out the local BBS scene by heading down to good computer store, or find a locally produced computer newspaper. If you know college students, have them check the bulletin boards (the real ones, with all the thumbtacks and sublet notices, not the electronic ones); information is available here as well.

Warning: Access through these services is often partial. A BBS might offer e-mail capabilities, for instance, or a combination of e-mail, newsgroups, and FTP. Rarely do they offer the full range of possibilities. Still, it's a good way to get started.

Commercial online services such as CompuServe, GEnie, Delphi, Prodigy, America Online, and MCI Mail offer Internet access to varying degrees. Delphi has long been offering access to all or at least most Internet services, and is well worth checking out. CompuServe and America Online are implementing Internet access in stages, as are the others. To find out who has what, either call them (they have toll-free 800 numbers), or follow the computer magazines at your local magazine stand.

Warning: Internet access through commercial online services often results in unexpected charges. Even though these are clearly explained up-front, it's entirely possible to get a credit card charge triple or quadruple what you were expecting (each service has a base monthly fee, with additions for various services). Sending an e-mail message to the Internet from CompuServe, for instance, costs extra, even though e-mailing someone on CompuServe itself is included in the basic cost. Another service charges only a dime or so per Internet message sent or received, but join a few mailing lists and you'll soon be getting 20-50 messages per day. Start slowly, and see how it goes.

Direct Access

Direct Internet access means that your computer has access to all available Internet functions. Instead of being a terminal on a host, your computer is an individual node on the Internet. That means that you can establish yourself as an FTP, Gopher, World Wide Web, or Archie site, or anything else you want to be. Whether or not you want to do that depends on your needs, your computer's power, and the speed of your connection.

If your organization is directly connected to the Internet through a high-speed, dedicated line, you might be able to arrange direct access. This will be handled through your systems people. In most cases, your computer will already be part of an internal network (usually an Ethernet system), that in turn connects via high-speed line to the Internet.

Note that this is different from being simply a terminal on the main computer. Here, you're a separate machine, dependent on the main computers for such things as shared software and shared files, but fully capable of existing on your own. In the terminal-only type of connection, your machine is entirely dependent on the main computer's software (which is why these connections are often referred to as dumb terminals).

Warning: Even though you may have all the tools in place for a direct Internet connection, don't think for a minute that it's an inalienable right. Many firms simply don't allow it, for all kinds of reasons. Sometimes it's security, sometimes it's lack of knowledge and/or lack of systems support (these connections consume technical resources), sometimes it's a matter of them not knowing the benefits. In the latter case, see Day 15 for a discussion of how to make them aware.

Another form of direct access is through SLIP or PPP connections. *SLIP* (Serial Line Internet Protocol) is the most common PC or Microsoft Windows connection, while *PPP* (Point to Point Protocol) is common to the Macintosh (but they're not respectively restricted).

SLIP and PPP let you essentially directly access the Internet through a modem. You're still dependent on a host computer, however, which itself has direct, high-speed Internet access.

> **Note:** In any type of direct Internet access, TCP/IP software is required. In the case of the Ethernet connection, your networking software will take care of TCP/IP protocols. For SLIP/PPP connections, the TCP/IP software must be present on the host computer, while your PC/Mac must have software that lets your modem make a TCP/IP connection. These are available on the Internet itself (for the most part), but also from whoever is providing the Internet service in the first place—either your organization or a commercial Internet service provider—and you should work with them on establishing the correct software suite. In the case of commercial providers, for example, this software will be made readily available when you sign on the dotted line (and your first check clears the bank).

SLIP/PPP connections have two major disadvantages:

- They're slow, because they rely completely on the speed of your modem. Don't even bother connecting at less than 9600 bps; 14.4 kbps should be your minimum consideration.
- You're not always connected to the Internet. When you shut down the modem connection, you're off the Net. So make sure you don't establish yourself as an important Gopher, FTP, or WWW site, because unless you leave your modem on all the time (and remember that costs are usually associated with the number of connect-time hours), you won't be accessible.

On the other hand, SLIP/PPP connections have one huge advantage:

- They're cheaper, by a long shot, than dedicated direct access. I pay my commercial service provider $300 per year for full Internet access, which gives me 50 hours per month (and 50 cents per hour after the first 50 hours). By comparison, a direct line would cost thousands of dollars per year.

> **Warning:** SLIP and PPP software must be present on *both* your computer and the host computer. Just because your Mac has PPP software on its hard drive, or your Windows machine has the necessary SLIP software, doesn't mean you can dial in to a host computer and get onto the Net. The other machine has to run software to make the connection happen. As before, SLIP/PPP connections are dependent on systems resources (including systems personnel) at the host computer site.

Where To Get the Software

The nice thing about Internet software is that much of it is free. As soon as you get your Internet account, you can download it from an FTP site. Then it's a matter of installing it on your system, just as if you'd bought it commercially.

An excellent source of software for DOS and Windows machines is accessible via anonymous FTP (see Day 6 for how to do this) at `sunsite.unc.edu`, in the directory `/pub/micro/pc-stuff/ms-windows/winsock`. Once here, you have a number of directories to access.

First is `/winsock 1.1`, in which you'll find `winsock.zip`. Winsock is the software Microsoft Windows needs for SLIP connections; when you decompress this program (you'll need the program `pkunzip.exe` to do so, which is also available at `sunsite.unc.edu`) and install it, you'll end up with two essential files in the `c:\windows` directory on your hard drive: `tcpman.exe` and `winsock.dll`. With these, you can't go any further, and you must have SLIP software running on the computer you dial in to.

In the `/apps` directory, you'll find a huge assortment of programs that run under Winsock:

- **Eudora 1.4** (`eudora14.exe`) is the major Windows mailer (see Day 3).
- **Winsock Gopher** (`wsg-10.exe`) is an excellent Gopher program shown throughout this book (see Day 8, for example).
- **Winsock FTP** (`ws-ftp.zip`) is a very strong FTP package.
- **Winsock Archie** (`wsarchie.zip`) allows graphical searches.
- **Trumpet News Reader** (`wtwsk10a.zip`) is the most popular Windows-based news reader.
- **QVTNet** (`qvtnet394.zip`) is an excellent terminal program.

You'll also want the two World Wide Web browsers, Cello and Mosaic.

Cello (`cello.zip`) is available via anonymous FTP at `ftp.law.cornell.edu`, in the directory `/pub/LII/Cello`. Also here are the graphics viewers `lview31.zip` and `gswin.zip`, and the sound player `wplny09b.zip`.

To get Mosaic, anonymous FTP to `ftp.NCSA.uiuc.edu` and enter the directory `/PC/Mosaic`. Here you'll find `wmos20a4.zip`, which is the main program, and `win32s.zip`, the Windows 32 software you'll need to run it. You can get a (perfectly good) older version of Mosaic, `wmos20a3.zip`, in the `/old` directory. In the `/viewers` directory are `lview` and `gswin` again, but also an MPEG (video) player, `mpegw32e.zip`.

In the /mac directory of ftp.NCSA.uiuc.edu (accessible once again via anonymous FTP), you'll find everything you need to run Mosaic on your Macintosh. Included here are the compressed Mosaic itself (NCSAMosaicMac.103.sit.hqx, along with the decompresser Stuffit_Expander_3.0.7.sea.hqx. In the /Helpers directory you'll find the sound player SoundMachine.sit.hqx, as well as the graphics viewer JPEGView3.0.sit.hqx.

To make your Mac connection work, you'll need to buy the software package MacTCP, distributed by Apple. Once it's installed and you have your Internet connection, a wide range of software is available to you.

An excellent site for Mac Internet software is in Finland, at the anonymous FTP address garbo.uwasa.fi, in the directory /mac/tcp. Here you'll find the mailer Eudora (eudora142.cpt), MacPPP (for PPP connections—macppp201.sit), Mosaic (ncsamosaic103.sit), NCSA's Telnet program (ncsatelnet26te.cpt), along with news readers, Talk programs, FTP programs, an Archie program, and a Gopher package (turbogopher107g.cpt).

Equipment

Almost any type of computer can connect to the Internet. The most common types are the following:

- UNIX machines (Sun, HP, Silicon Graphics, DEC, IBM, many others)
- IBM-compatibles (IBM, Compaq, Dell, DEC, Zeos, DTK, Gateway, zillions others)
- Apple Macintosh (Apple, no others)

If you're running a UNIX machine, you're probably already part of an organization, because UNIX has never been known as a home computer. In fact, one of UNIX's great strengths is networking, which is why the Internet itself is pretty well based on it. I'll forego any discussions of UNIX hardware here.

For direct connections via IBM-compatibles, you'll need Microsoft Windows. If you want to do any serious Internet work, you'll want 8MB of memory, a 240+MB hard drive, and a 14,400+ bps modem. An increasing number of Internet software packages are coming available, and it's probably safe to say that, as with all other software areas, Windows will become the main developmental platform for new Net interfaces within the next year or so. Already, for example, the strong World Wide Web browser Cello is available only on Windows.

For Macintoshes, you'll need the best Mac you can get, again with 8MB of memory (although 4MB will do in a pinch). Try for a 200+MB hard drive, and a 14,400+ bps modem. Several Internet programs are already available as freeware for the Mac.

Access Providers

These are many and varied. You can get full access, partial access, or time-limited access in a variety of speeds and for a variety of costs. Check your local newspapers and bulletin boards for details, or just start asking around.

An excellent online source for information about access providers is a listing called PDIAL. If you're on the Internet, you can obtain this listing by sending e-mail to `info-deli-server@netcom.com`; your message should read `send pdial` (nothing more). You can also get it through FTP at `nic.merit.edu`, in the directory `/internet/providers/pdial`; look for the file `pdial`. (See Day 6 for FTP issues.) Of course, these methods already assume you're on the Internet, which you're probably not (because you want the file). It's also available for download from most commercial online services as well as from local BBSs. You'll also find it on a variety of CD-ROMs (including those that come with magazines such as *CD-ROM Today,* and your local computer store should be able to help you as well.

Okay, I'm Ready: Anything I Should Know Before Firing Up?

Yes. A few things.

First, Internet access isn't a right, at least not yet. You can be kicked off by the local access provider if you start offending people or doing stupid things. In other words, there's such a thing as Internet etiquette, which has become, in Internet terminology, *netiquette.*

Netiquette is based on several important assumptions:

- The Internet is a cooperative venture.
- The Internet is open.
- Nobody owns or polices the Internet.
- Nobody wants people around who don't play nice.

It's also based on two crucial technological facts:

- The Internet is a collection of hundreds of thousands of computers linked via a complex series of expensive high-speed connections that handle an almost staggering amount of important data.
- Your flame (See Day 3) isn't important data.

As a result of all this, here are a few important rules of netiquette:

- Don't access remote computers for intensive operations such as FTP or MUDs during that machine's business hours. Keep a time-zone chart on the wall above your monitor, and pay attention to it. Sometimes you won't be allowed in; other times, you'll simply slow everything down.
- When accessing an Archie, WWW, or other site, try to find the computer with the most direct connection to your own (usually the closest geographically). If you have a choice between doing an Archie search on the computer down the road or the one half-way across the globe, don't choose the latter because it's so cool to be getting stuff from so far away. This needlessly consumes huge gobs of bandwidth—the finite capacity of the Internet's wires to carry networking traffic. On the other hand, it's often a *very* good idea to access overseas sites, if doing so avoids clogging up local computers during business hours. Again, keep that time chart handy.
- Don't post messages to newsgroups, or send e-mail to mailing lists, that the entire list doesn't need to see. If you're just saying, "Liked your message, Joe," and nothing else, send the thing to Joe, not to everyone on `alt.internet.overkill` or whatever group it was. Messages like this are infuriating to readers, and they quickly destroy your credibility.
- Don't send three messages when one will do. All of this uses up bandwidth, and more importantly, from a personal point of view, it clogs mailboxes. If people start seeing your name eight times per day, they'll quickly learn to dread you.
- Don't hide behind your anonymity. Nobody on the Net knows who you are, where you are, what you look like, or anything else about you, but that doesn't mean you can send offensive, degrading, harassing, threatening, demeaning, or just plain idiotic messages.
- Don't send junk mail to entire lists. If you do, prepare to get 50 times as much mail in return, usually in the form of very long messages that will tie up your mailbox forever. This kind of thing can be automated by people who know how.

I could go on, but I won't. Some of this is covered in other chapters. The point is the Internet is available, it's exciting, it's even fun, but it's not a plaything designed expressly for your or my personal enjoyment. Treat it with respect, okay?

Okay, I'll Be Good: Now Let's Get Going!

Unless you have specific instructions from your organization's systems administrator for connecting to the Internet, the process is essentially as follows:

1. Get the login prompt on your screen. This will look like one of the following:

```
login:
username:
login name:
```

2. Type your user name at this prompt, then press Enter.

> **Note:** You don't have to use your full Internet address here, just the user name for the system you've logged into.

```
login: nrandall
```

3. When the password prompt appears (it does so automatically), type your password.

```
login: nrandall
Password: not4U2knoW
```

4. Wait for system confirmation. You'll either receive another request for your name and password, or you'll be shown a series of login messages (which are useful only because they show you've succeeded), or you'll just receive the UNIX command prompt, which means you're successful.

> **Note:** The UNIX command prompt is usually a dollar sign (`$`) or a percent sign (`%`), but if you want to change it, you can usually do so. Check with your systems administrator, or pick up a good UNIX book, if you want to change it.

5. You may be asked for a terminal type. The most common seems to be DEC VT100, but there are many other possibilities. You can set up your communications software to emulate specific terminals, in which case you choose the one you've emulated.

```
TERM (unknown): vt100
```

Note: If you want to know what terminals are available to you, press a couple nonsense characters (for example, ddd) and press Enter. On most systems, this will generate an error message and a list of available terminal types.

6. You may also be given a choice of protocols. When logging into one of my accounts, I'm given the following protocol list to choose from:

```
Choose Protocol:
1.  Shell
2.  SLIP
3.  PPP
```

Here, if I want a standard UNIX shell account, I type 1 and press Enter. If I want to use my Macintosh (see the preceding account types), I choose Point-to-Point Protocol (PPP). Because I'm primarily a Microsoft Windows user, and most Windows software to date uses Serial Line Internet Protocol (SLIP) connections, I choose #2.

7. Following is what a login looks like on my main Internet account:

```
SunOS UNIX (watserv1)

watserv1 login: nrandall
Password: xxxxxxxxxxxxxxx
Last login: cn-ts1 (ttys9) Tue Apr 19 13:42:30 1994
You have new mail.
TERM = (vt100) vt100

[51]%
```

(At this point, I know I'm on.)

8. Once you're logged in, you can do whatever you want to do. To check your mail, type `mail`, `elm`, or `pine`. To start an FTP session, type `ftp`. (See Day 6 for details.) To begin a Talk session, type `talk username@full.address`. (See Day 5 for details.) To do a Telnet or browse a Gopher, see the following sections.

Hey, Why Doesn't DIR Do Anything?

My guess is that you don't actually want to know UNIX. Or you have plans to learn it, but maybe a bit later. For now, your real goal is to learn only what you have to in order to get Internetting.

Why do I guess that? Because that's the way I started with UNIX. I'd heard all the horror stories—UNIX is even uglier than DOS, the only good UNIX command is a changed UNIX command, all of them—and I really had no interest. No, I shouldn't say that. I had interest, just as I have interest in all operating systems, but there was that lack-of-time problem to consider.

So I floundered about, learning only what I needed to know. I learned enough about the vi editor to use the e-mail program Elm, and enough about Telnet to let me get from one of my accounts to the other. Inevitably, I ran into trouble. Someone attached a WordPerfect file to an Elm message one day, but when I detached it I had no idea where it went. A local program called Files let me see it, but I had no idea what to do from there.

Eventually I learned Kermit, to help me solve that problem and, slowly but surely, a few more UNIX details. Still, I didn't know the most basic stuff, the sort of commands I used with DOS every day of my life. As I found out early, DOS's famous `DIR` didn't do a thing.

Later in this chapter, we'll deal with Telnet. Next chapter, we'll look at Mail, Elm, and Pine. By the time you reach the end of Day 6, you'll know FTP, Archie, XModem, and Kermit as well. For now, though, here are the very basic essentials. UNIX is huge, and extremely customizable as well, but I'm still willing to bet you want to know the absolutely minimal amount.

Note: No matter how much you think you don't want to know UNIX, keep firmly in mind that UNIX is an extremely powerful, extremely capable operating system. I've talked to all kinds of people who don't like it, or who guffaw at its almost cryptic nature, but most of them simply haven't worked with it very much. Once you work your way into UNIX, and you realize its amazing flexibility and customizability, as well as its multiuser stability and its networking capabilities, you'll come to realize why it's the workhorse of the Internet.

2

Excursion 2.1. The *ls* and *cd* Commands

The first great UNIX mystery for anyone coming over from DOS is how to get a directory listing. Simple, as it turns out, but don't expect UNIX to volunteer the information. The command is `ls`, short for list; like `DIR`, it comes in a variety of flavors.

The basic `ls` command is simply `ls`. Just type **`ls`** at the command prompt, and you'll get a list of files. On my main account, the procedure looks like this:

```
[56]% ls
Mail                interview_andrews   shopping.txt
News                mail                interview_johnson
README              mbox                whodat
bin                 me                  xmodem.log
catherine.memo      propos.txt
```

A couple things to note here. First, the listing is in columns (this can be changed if you wish), and no file information is provided. Second, UNIX filenames have far different conventions than DOS's anemic 11-character rule. Knowing this is important primarily when you're FTPing from another site. You will find some incredibly long filenames, and you have to remember to type them exactly as they appear, *including* the exact same case. The file named `README`, preceding, cannot be entered as `readme`. In UNIX, the two aren't the same thing at all.

Note: The basic requirements for a UNIX filename are as follows:

- UNIX filenames are case sensitive; this means you can have several files named readme, all using different case combinations—for example, README, Readme, ReadMe, readme, readMe, and so on.
- UNIX filenames can consist of almost any combination of characters, digits, dashes, plus signs, underline characters, or dots.
- UNIX filenames cannot begin with dashes or plus signs.

Often, you'll need information about file sizes and dates. No problem. This time, use the -l switch with your command. The same directory with this switch looks like this:

```
[57]% ls -l
total 51
drwx------  2 nrandall      512 Apr 12 12:45 Mail
drwxr-x--x  7 nrandall      512 Feb 13 21:40 News
-rw-r----  1 nrandall      757 Mar 24 18:47 README
drwx--s--x  2 nrandall      512 Mar 26  1990 bin
-rw------  1 nrandall        4 Feb 23 12:00 catherine.memo
-rw-r----  1 nrandall     3038 Mar 22 14:02 interview_andrews
drwx------  2 nrandall     1024 Apr 19 09:32 mail
-rw------  1 nrandall    10741 Feb 23 12:03 mbox
-rw-r----  1 nrandall       90 Jan  8 21:09 me
-rw-r----  1 nrandall     5267 Apr  7 20:57 propos.txt
-rw-r----  1 nrandall    15935 Mar 31 14:41 shopping.txt
-rw-r----  1 nrandall     2771 Mar 22 13:54 interview_johnson
-rw-r----  1 nrandall      186 Nov 11  1990 whodat
-rw-r----  1 nrandall     3242 Apr  7 20:59 xmodem.log
```

The file size, in bytes, is shown to the left of the date. Also of importance is the first column, which lists the attributes. It all has to do with who can do what to which file, but for your immediate purposes, only the first character really matters. The rule is if the first character is a hyphen (-), the item is a file; if the first character is a letter d, the item is a directory.

Before going back to ls, here's another command: cd. Like the DOS version, this command changes your current directory. Because the preceding item mail is a directory (its attribute column begins with d), you can use cd to get into that directory, and then ls gives a different result.

```
[59]% cd mail
[60]% ls
amato          courses        infobits       net-happenings  sent-mail
bnr            deutsch        inktank        nii             strangelove
business       education      interesting    oha-list        stuff
```

The new items in the directory are actually the folders I created in the Pine mailer. (See Day 3 for details.) The point, for now, is that I'm in a different directory. Not that UNIX was about to volunteer that information. I didn't actually get a response to the cd mail command. I had to do something further to determine where I was.

Actually, there's another way, and this command, too, is useful. The pwd command will tell you what directory you're currently in (for example, your working directory).

```
[66]% pwd
/home/watserv1/nrandall/mail
[67]%
```

Warning: The UNIX directory structure uses the slash character (/), not DOS's infamous backslash (\) to separate directories. This usually confuses converted DOS users for about a year after starting to use the Net.

How do you get back to the first directory? Several ways actually, but just using `cd ..` will do for most purposes.

```
[62]% cd ..
```

Back to `ls`. One last `ls` switch worth knowing is `-a`. This one shows you all files in your directory, even those that are hidden. In UNIX, a hidden file is simply one whose filename starts with a period (.), and they aren't displayed with the normal `ls` command. Note the difference in the directories with the `-a` switch, however:

```
[58]% ls -a
.                    .oldnewsrc           Mail
..                   .pine-debug1         News
.Xauthority          .pine-debug2         README
.addressbook         .pine-debug3         bin
.cshrc               .pine-debug4         catherine.memo
.elm                 .pinerc              interview_andrews
.files               .pinerc.save         mail
.forware             .pinercbu            mbox
.gopherrc            .profile             me
.gopherrc~           .rnlast              propos.txt
.history             .rnsoft              shopping.txt
.letter              .signature           interview_johnson
.login               .signature.save      whodat
.newsrc              .xsession            xmodem.log
```

Files like `.pinerc`, `.elm`, `.gopherrc`, or `.newsrc` are configuration files. You can change them manually, but it's usually better to let the software do it for you.

Excursion 2.2. Deleting, Copying, and Renaming Files

To delete a file in UNIX, type **`rm`** ***`filename`*** at the prompt (`rm` means remove). For example, the following will delete the file `interview_andrews`:

```
[59]% rm interview_andrews
```

Warning: You won't be asked for confirmation, and there are no undelete utilities. The file is gone, done like dinner, history, outta here. Don't use `rm` unless you mean it.

To copy a file, type **`cp`** ***`filename`*** **`new.`*****`filename`***. For instance, you could have copied the previous file like this, resulting in two identical files:

```
[60]% cp interview_andrews really-fascination-interview.cool
```

However, you can't, because you already deleted it.

Finally, to rename a file, use the `mv` (move) command:

```
[61]% mv interview_andrews old-andrews.interview
```

This way, you'd have one file only, with a different name than before.

That's it. UNIX for minimalists. Anything else you truly need will be covered in its respective section, beginning with Telnet and `rlogin` immediately following.

Note: Eventually, you'll want to know more about UNIX, because UNIX is the basis for the Internet. Several good UNIX primers are available, but why not start with Dave Taylor's *Teach Yourself UNIX in a Week*, which is in the same series as the book you're reading right now. I realize it sounds like I'm sucking up to my publisher by recommending a book in the same series as my own, but Taylor's book really is excellent. I've been using it to learn UNIX in greater detail as I find the time.

Any Way of Getting onto All Those Other Machines Out There?

Yes, lots of ways. You can Gopher to them (see the following), you can FTP to them (see Day 6), or you can use the World Wide Web (see Day 7), but the most direct way is to Telnet into the site, or to use the similar but lesser-featured `rlogin`.

2

Excursion 2.3. Telnetting to a Machine on which You Have an Account

The most common use of Telnet is through Gopher or the World Wide Web, but it's also fairly common from the UNIX command line. Here, its primary function is to log into a remote computer on which you have an account. This will happen, for instance, if you're traveling and you find yourself sitting in front of a machine connected to the Internet. You want to check your mail, of course, because about two days after finishing this book you'll already be an e-mail addict (much like food or drug addiction, except that society looks more favorably on it).

In my case, the remote login through Telnet would look like this:

```
$ telnet watserv1.uwaterloo.ca
Trying 129.97.129.140...
Connected to watserv1.uwaterloo.ca.
Escape character is '^]'.

SunOS UNIX (watserv1)

watserv1 login: nrandall
Password: NotTelling
Last login: cn-ts1 (ttyp1) Tue Apr 19 19:41:19 1994
You have new mail.

[56]% logout
```

There are a few things worth noting here:

- The `telnet` command is followed by the name of the host machine, not my own Internet address. My address is `nrandall@watserv1.uwaterloo.ca`; the stuff after the `@` sign is the host name.
- The digits on the second line comprise the host computer's *IP* (Internet Protocol) address. Computers don't do names, they do numbers, which means this is the computer's real name.

- The fourth line says that the escape character is `^]`. This means, "hold the Ctrl key down and press the closing square bracket (]) key." This is the standard method of canceling a Telnet session, and it's extremely valuable. Often a Telnet will take many minutes, and there's no point waiting.
- Once in the remote system, you enter the login name and password for that system, not the one you're currently in. These will likely be different.
- Once you've logged in completely, you can do whatever you normally do, including read your mail, transfer files via FTP, enter Gophers, and so on. You can even use your remote system to Telnet back to the machine you're currently using. In fact, you can Telnet several places in a series of Telnet subsessions, but make sure you log out of each in succession.

Just for fun, let's Telnet into a computer on which I have no account.

```
[53]% telnet ai.mit.edu
Trying 128.52.32.80 ...
Connected to ai.mit.edu.
Escape character is '^]'.

SunOS UNIX (life)

login: nrandall
Password: NoThingWorKs
Login incorrect
login: nrandall
Password: TRYsomethingFAST
login: nrandall
Password: iFeelUnWanTed
login: Connection closed by foreign host.
```

Typically, you get three tries to get your login name and password right, then you're booted out. Oh well....

It's not actually necessary to include a host name with a Telnet command. By just typing **telnet** by itself, you start a Telnet session, at which point you can get a list of Telnet options by typing **help**. Then, to connect to a remote machine, you use the `open` command with the desired host name. All this is shown in the following:

```
$ telnet
telnet> help
Commands may be abbreviated.  Commands are:

close           close current connection
```

```
logout          forcibly logout remote user and close the connection
display         display operating parameters
mode            try to enter line or character mode ('mode ?' for more)
open            connect to a site
quit            exit telnet
send            transmit special characters ('send ?' for more)
set             set operating parameters ('set ?' for more)
unset           unset operating parameters ('unset ?' for more)
status          print status information
toggle          toggle operating parameters ('toggle ?' for more)
slc             change state of special charaters ('slc ?' for more)
z               suspend telnet
!               invoke a subshell
environ         change environment variables ('environ ?' for more)
?               print help information
telnet>open watserv1.uwaterloo.ca
```

To end a Telnet session, type **quit** (or the Ctrl+] combination).

In many situations on the Internet, you can use Telnet to connect to a system, then a series of special login names or passwords to enter permissible areas. Connecting to World Wide Web (see Day 7) or Archie sites (see Day 6) through a UNIX shell account is like this, where you normally type **www** or **archie** as the login name (which will bypass the password).

One such site (among a great many) is NISS, the National Information on Software and Services, located in the United Kingdom. Following is the Telnet session that will take you into the site. Notice that the Telnet address is `sun.nsf.ac.uk`, and that your login name is `janet`. Once you're in, you need another access name, `uk.acc.niss`, to complete the connection and receive the menu of commands.

```
$ telnet sun.nsf.ac.uk
Trying 128.86.8.7...
Connected to sun.nsfnet-relay.ac.uk.
Escape character is '^]'.


SunOS UNIX (sun.nsfnet-relay.ac.uk)

login: janet
Password: [no password, just press Enter]

Welcome to the JANET X.25 PAD Service.

Enter a JANET hostname (i.e uk.ac.janet.news) 'h' for help or 'q' to quit.
hostname: uk.ac.niss
SunLink X.25 PAD V7.0. Type ^P<cr> for Executive, ^Pb for break
Calling... connected...
```

```
Welcome to the NISS Gateway

Checking your terminal type...

    ****  N I S S   G A T E W A Y  ********  M A I N  M E N U  ****


  AA) NISS Bulletin Board               (NISSBB - Traditional access)
  AB) NISS Bulletin Board               (NISSBB - Gopher access)
  B)  NISS Public Access Collections    (NISSPAC)
  C)  NISSWAIS Service  - free text searching of selected databases
  D)  NISS Newspapers and Journals Services
  E)  NISS Gopher Services
```

Excursion 2.4. The *rlogin* Command

The `rlogin` command is much like Telnet, except that it has fewer options. Still, if you have accounts with identical login names on two separate computers, `rlogin` is often more convenient. Here's how I move from one account to another using `rlogin`:

```
$ rlogin watserv1.uwaterloo.ca
Password:
Last login: nic.hookup.net (ttyp3) Tue Apr 19 21:11:25 1994
You have new mail.

[51]% logout
```

Note: If you make a mistake on your password, you'll be asked for a new login name as well, which makes the session very much like Telnet.

Warning: `Logout` is the proper exit command for `rlogin`. The Ctrl+] combination does not work.

Summary

Day 2 has introduced the Internet itself, its history, and types of access. You've also covered issues of netiquette, and you've learned the basics of logging on. Also covered was one of the most basic Internet activities, Telnet. With these in place, you're ready to move onto the more complex Internet topics, but even at this stage you can work your way around the world. Didn't take long, did it?

2

Task Review

On Day 2, you did the following:

- ☐ Learned about the Internet's history.
- ☐ Assessed the type of Internet access required.
- ☐ Learned the basic of netiquette.
- ☐ Logged on to your account.
- ☐ Learned a basic set of UNIX commands.
- ☐ Telnetted to remote computers.

Q&A

Q My friend told me that setting up SLIP or PPP access was extremely complex. How do I find out about this?

A Your service provider can help you. To set up your SLIP or PPP software, you'll need to know such items as your IP number, your mail and news server names, various domain names, and often some other information. All of this is exclusive to the service you're receiving, and you can get this information only from your provider.

Usually, the service provider will give you software on disk or via download that will include all this information (as well as your password); or you'll receive it by phone or in a letter. Then you'll be guided through the initial setup. Yes, it's complex, but a good service provider will make sure you get up and running as quickly as possible.

Q Shouldn't I change my password as soon as I log on?

A Well, that's the general rule, but part of it depends on whether or not your account has anything worth stealing (that's why I never locked my '83 T-Bird). For the most part, though, you should change your password every few months or so, much more frequently if you've been alerted to security problems.

To do so, enter the UNIX command `passwd` and follow the prompts. You'll be asked to type the old password, then the new one, then the new one again to confirm. Your systems people will have regulations or guidelines about what your password should consist of. The rule of thumb is to keep it as *complex* as you possibly can. Don't, for heaven's sake, use your name, or your username, or your spouse's or dog's name, or anything else that could be easily traced.

3

WEEK 1

Electronic Mail: The Fundamental Internet Tool

Nothing is more essential to using the Internet than mastering electronic mail. Through e-mail you can exchange ideas, concerns, agendas, memos, documents, and files with anyone on the Internet in any part of the world. The Internet was originally designed as a communications tool, and the spread of e-mail has proven the design to be an enormous success. This chapter outlines this flexible and ubiquitous tool, demonstrating its capabilities and offering some important guidelines.

On Day 3, you will:

- ☐ Focus a reader's attention through effective use of the Subject line.
- ☐ Create a useful signature.
- ☐ Consider the different forms of accepted e-mail etiquette.
- ☐ Decide among the three major UNIX mailers.
- ☐ Decide if you need a graphical mailer such as Eudora.
- ☐ Attach documents or other files to a message.
- ☐ Determine a message's recipients.

Using E-Mail

Even if you've never been on the Internet, you already know about e-mail. Research and military personnel have been sending e-mail messages over the phone lines for decades now, and in the past half-dozen years or so e-mail has become a staple of online services like CompuServe, GEnie, America Online, and MCI Mail. Over the same period of time, business computers have become more and more networked, and for many business employees, e-mail now is an everyday way of life.

It's an everyday way of life on the Internet, too, but the stakes are a whole lot higher.

There's no real difference between Internet e-mail and CompuServe e-mail. There isn't even a significant difference between Internet e-mail and the e-mail that flows through a local business office. Basically, you send messages to other people and groups, and you wait for the answers to arrive. Then you reply to the answers, wait for more responses, and so on. An endless cycle, and in many ways pretty mundane.

Here's the difference, though. If you're on your company's local network, or even its nationwide or multinational network, you're writing mainly to others in your company (no matter where they are). If you're an MCI Mail user, you're writing mainly to other MCI Mail users. Essentially, the messages go to MCI Mail's computer, or to your company's computer or network. Once you're on the Internet, however, you can start sending messages to any user on any computer anywhere in the world.

Anyone, that is, who's also on the Internet.

Note: It is, in fact, quite possible to reach a user of MCI Mail, CompuServe, GEnie, America Online, or other commercial online services through Internet mail. See the Extra Credit section at the end of this chapter for details.

Feel like e-mailing your friend who works at a university on the West Coast? No sweat; just type in the full address and let fly. Need to set up a product demonstration with a client in New Zealand? As long as you have the Internet address, you don't even have to worry about whether you'll be getting him out of bed. Trying to organize a frequent research exchange with colleagues in Venezuela, Colombia, Brazil, and three other South American countries? Go into your e-mail program, set them up as a group called `samerica`, and then start sending messages with attached files to all of them at once.

It's easy, it's enjoyable, it's fast, and it's effective. What else could you ask for?

Electronic mail is the most fundamental of Internet applications. It's the one that everyone learns first, and usually the one that draws people to the Internet in the first place. I'm a fairly typical example. For the first three years of my Internet life, I didn't know you could do anything *except* e-mail. Nobody told me about FTPs or Gophers, and the World Wide Web didn't even exist yet. As a matter of fact, I didn't even know that the Internet was the thing I was on.

What I *did* know was that I could keep in contact with a few colleagues who'd managed to scatter themselves around the world, and with some who hid in their offices down the hall. That's what I wanted, and that's what I got. I e-mailed infrequently at first, but slowly things started to pick up.

The turning point for me was realizing how fast it all was. I'd send a message to an associate in the morning, and often he'd reply in less than an hour. When I sent a message late at night (I worked late, he started early), an answer would almost always be waiting for me first thing in the morning. Then I began to realize something else. There's simply no way those exchanges would have happened at all, if we'd been depending on the good old mail services. Not only is snail-mail (as it's called) too slow, it's also a completely different activity.

Writing a letter takes time. I'm not about to send a one-sentence response through the mail, so I wait until I have more important things to say. That means a delay. Once I have them, though, there's even more delay. Find a pen, find some paper, do the writing, find an envelope, find a stamp. Then—this one has always been tough for me—remember to actually put the envelope in a mailbox. It isn't unusual at all for a stamped envelope to sit on the front seat of my car for a couple days, and I suspect I'm not alone. More time lost, more delays to deal with.

With e-mail, things have changed. I log in every morning, read my messages, and respond immediately to those that want an answer (delinquency is really noticed in e-mail). Four or five times per day I log in and check again, and usually there's something else to answer. In total, reading and answering e-mail will take you anywhere from a few minutes to a couple of hours a day, and after a short time you get really good at recognizing and deleting the stuff that isn't of any interest to you. However long it takes you, it's almost invariably time well spent.

Immediacy, conciseness, global connections. What more could e-mail do?

A lot, actually. You can join mailing lists, have files sent to you, all sorts of things. But those are issues for Day 4. Right now, let's just deal with e-mail proper.

Sending Messages

If you want to send someone a message, you need two things.

First, you need the person's address. Not the street address (123 Front St., Realtown, Virginia, USA), but rather the Internet address (`darien@darkroad.fionavar.net`). As soon as you get an Internet account, call your friends and find out their Internet addresses. That's the way your e-mail network gets started.

Next, you need an e-mail program. There are three types, depending on the type of Internet access you have (see Day 2 for details on the different types of Internet access). If you have Internet shell access only, you're normally restricted to the e-mail programs that already exist on the UNIX computer you've hooked to. If you have direct Internet access and a Macintosh or a PC, you probably can use the more attractive e-mail programs designed for graphical environments like the Macintosh or Microsoft Windows. Finally, if you're hooked into the Net through your company's network, you'll just use the mailer you normally use.

> **Tip:** As always, check with your network administrator to find out what type of Internet access you have. Sometimes, however, there are other possibilities, even though you may not be told about them. Keeping political protocol firmly in mind, explore a bit further with your systems people.

Eudora: A Graphical Mailer

The best-known graphical e-mail program for Windows and the Mac is Eudora. It's out there as freeware and is included with the sign-on fee with many Internet service providers (see Day 2 for details on how to get it via FTP). Lately, though, it's been taken over (some would say rescued) by a company called QUALCOMM in San Diego, which now offers a commercial version in addition to the freeware package. Eudora is easy to use, and it looks a lot better than the programs available with standard UNIX shells—just as you'd expect from a GUI-based mailer.

The Three Major UNIX Mailers

A considerable number of e-mail programs have been designed for UNIX systems, but three of them are the best known:

- *Mail*, which like so many UNIX programs is full-featured but comes with an interface that can best be described as brutal. There's actually more than one version of Mail, but the interfaces remain brutal.
- *Elm*, equally full-featured and quite a bit easier to use, although its editor, like Mail's, is anything but intuitive and requires considerable practice. Elm's default editor is vi, a standard UNIX editor, and if you decide you don't like it, you can tell Elm to load an alternative by typing **o** (for options) from Elm's main screen and making the change in configuration. But first-time users of Elm will almost invariably encounter vi, and while extremely powerful, it's hardly a walk in the park.
- *Pine*, a somewhat simplified program but far and away the best one for novices to start with, and maybe for many people to stay with. Pine greatly simplifies such everyday procedures as typing text, saving messages in separate folders, and creating address books with aliases.

Address Books and Aliases

Address books and aliases (also known as nicknames) are crucial if you e-mail frequently. As you've seen, Internet addresses often are long and complex, and it's hard enough to remember your own, let alone someone you only infrequently send messages to. All e-mail programs enable you to create and save aliases ; when you want to send a message to your friend Joseph Worthington at the University of Chicago, for example, you just type the alias (**joe**, for example), and the program fills in the full address (jaworthi@dragon.uchicago.edu, or whatever).

A good mail program also will enable you to capture the address from an incoming message and assign an alias to it. When you're reading a message in Pine, for example, and you want to capture the sender's address, you just enter **T**. You're then asked for an alias, and then to confirm the person's full name and full address. Pine then tucks the address nicely in your address book, and you no longer have to type the full version again.

You also can use your e-mail program to create groups. Groups combine the names of recipients, and when you want to send a message to the entire group, you address it to the group name only. You might have a project team scattered in different locations, for example. Put all the individual addresses into a group called team, and then address the messages to team. The message will go out to every member of the group.

The Elements of an E-Mail Message

No matter which e-mail program you use, sending a message is done basically the same way. You address the message, fill in the subject line, type in the message, and then send it. Other options include sending to multiple recipients or groups, and attaching files for the recipient to download.

The *TO:* Line

In the TO: line, you type the recipient's address. Either that, or you type the alias you've created for the recipient. If you want to send the message to more than one recipient, separate the addresses (or the aliases) with a comma (or simply a space with some mailers). You also can include a group name in the same line.

For example, to send a message to Donna Johns (dcjohns@entropy.cmu.edu), for whom you have no alias, Suzanne Pelletier (whose alias is set up as "sue"), and all the members of your research team (which you've set up as "research"), your TO: line will look as follows:

```
TO: dcjohns@entropy.cmu.edu,sue,research
```

The *CC:* Line

`CC:` means *carbon copy*, a holdover term from the days of, well, carbon paper. By including an address on the `CC:` line, you're copying the message to someone else's e-mail address.

Tip: Why use the `CC:` line when you could just include the address in the `TO:` line? Essentially, for the same reason you'd do so if you were sending a business memo. The `TO:` line contains the addresses of the people you want to alert directly to the message contents. The `CC:` line contains the addresses of people who should see the message, but whose responses—and attention—you're not really requesting. You might even include it for simple filing purposes. Technically, addresses in the `CC:` line can often be given a lower delivery priority, a consideration for network efficiency.

The *ATTACHMENTS:* Line

Just as in a paper letter or memo, you may have some documents you want to include as an attachment. In an e-mail message, this means you want to attach a file to the message, one the recipient will detach, download, and work with. You might, for example, be e-mailing a coworker about a problem with budget figures, so you attach the Lotus 1-2-3 file you're working on (you know that she works with 1-2-3 as well). She receives the message, which automatically tells her a file is attached. She then detaches it, downloads it, and opens it in her 1-2-3 program.

Attaching a file differs depending on your type of Internet access. The idea is the same, though. When you get to this line, you tell the e-mail program to attach a file that's present on your hard drive. The only question is where the file is actually located.

Warning: The `ATTACHMENTS:` line may not actually be called "Attachments," depending on your mailer. Sometimes it's abbreviated, while on mailers operating on your organization's network you might have an entirely different term. The idea is the same, though: to let you send a file through e-mail. However, attaching a file depends on standards for allowing this to transpire—the proposed standard is called MIME—and as yet this isn't fully implemented. Check with your systems people to see if you can actually transmit a file through e-mail.

If you have direct Internet access, the file is probably on the hard drive of your PC or Mac (or your UNIX station), or on your company's network drive. In Eudora, for example, you select Attach Document from the Message menu, and Eudora presents you with the Windows or Mac file selection box. Double-click the file you want, and then finish your message. Eudora will upload it from your hard drive when you actually send the message. When you receive a message containing an attached file, the reverse procedure takes place.

Tip: You can configure Eudora in a number of different ways through the Configuration dialog box in the Special menu. Among other options, you can tell Eudora to download attached files automatically to a specific directory. If you choose this option, it's best to create a separate directory for these downloads, and if you receive your e-mail automatically, be sure to check this directory regularly for downloaded attachments.

If you're working from a standalone PC or Mac, however, and you access the Internet through a UNIX shell account, an extra step often is necessary. In these cases, you can't attach a file directly from your own computer's drive. Instead, you have to place it on the host system's drive. To do so, you'll have to upload the file from your PC or Mac to the host, using the host's XModem or Kermit programs (see Day 6 for details on using them) There may be others on your system, but these two are the most common.

After the file is uploaded to the host computer, you can attach it to your message. In Pine, for example, you place the cursor on the `ATTACHMENTS:` line and press Ctrl+T, as the menu on the bottom of the screen tells you. You'll be given a list of files on your drive, which you can choose by cursoring to the one you want. You also can change directories from here.

The *SUBJECT:* Line

The `SUBJECT:` line is the first element of the message that's completely up to you. Make a mistake on the other three lines, and you'll get error messages. On the `SUBJECT:` line, you're on your own.

Warning: Don't overlook the `SUBJECT:` line's importance. Many Internet users receive dozens—even hundreds!—of messages every day. They can't possibly read them all. So they rely on two message elements to guide them through.

The first, of course, is the address line: if they recognize the name of the sender, they'll read that message. The second is the subject line.

When readers are faced with several screens of messages in their in boxes, the subject lines are often the only way of determining what's worth reading. So it's very important to give them a subject line that will stop them from pressing Delete. Remember, you may be new to sending e-mail across the Internet, but your recipients probably aren't. They're likely busy, and swamped with stuff to read.

Above all, be sure not to leave the subject line blank. I'm one of many readers who routinely delete—before reading—any message that doesn't have a subject line. Unless, of course, I recognize the sender's name.

Doing something with the `SUBJECT:` line is especially important since it's not required on an e-mail message. You can leave it blank, or you can simply re-send the existing line. It's voluntary, but it's important.

The Message Area

There are no rules—you can type whatever you want. There are, however, some guidelines. Simple ones, and not much different from the ones you know about sending memos. Remember, the idea is to get your point across.

- Write clearly. If you have something to say, write it so the reader will understand.
- Write concisely. You have no interest in receiving a 4-page memo, and your reader doesn't want a 4-screen message. A good rule of thumb is this: if the message is more than one screen in length (say, 25 lines or so), it's too long. Trim it, unless you can fully justify not doing so.
- Write civilly. Back to office memo. You wouldn't send a memo swearing at the recipient, or suggesting a questionable parentage, so don't do so here. AND DON'T SCREAM. Words typed in uppercase usually are read as anger rather than enthusiasm, and you'll be seen as an impolite and unsophisticated "flamer."
- Don't send three messages where one will do. This happens especially in mailing lists (see Day 4), where one person will get caught up in the discussion and reply to just about everything. If you see four or five messages in one day

from the same address, you'll instantly lower your opinion of that person, no matter how thoughtful the messages themselves might be.

- Ask for a response if you want a response. Don't assume that the addressee will read between the lines and figure out what you want. Nobody has time.

All these guidelines, of course, go out the window when you're dealing with personal messages to friends. But not long after getting on the Internet, such messages probably will be the minority.

Receiving Messages

Knowing how to send well-constructed and useful messages is crucial, but you'll be spending far more of your e-mail time receiving messages that others send your way. If you get only a few, there's not much to do other than read them, but unless you're an unusual Internetter, you'll quickly find yourself deluged with them. Suddenly it becomes important to know how to store them, reply to them, or delete them before even seeing them, to maintain some sense of order.

Reading New Messages

When you fire up your e-mail program, the first thing you're likely to see is how many messages are waiting for you. In some programs, you have to actually request a check for messages, but usually the program does it for you by default. Find your message index or your in box, and start reading your mail.

To do this, cursor down to the message and press Enter (or the spacebar, in some mailers). In Eudora, double-click the message you want to read. Then settle back and read away.

> **Tip:** Actually, you don't even have to go that far if you don't want. The first thing to do is to go through the message index and pick out which ones you simply want to delete. Do that, and the list gets much shorter. Deleting, by the way, is a matter of either pressing the D key, as in Elm or Pine, or clicking the message and then the Delete button (or using Ctrl+D) in Eudora.

Deleting and Undeleting Messages

When you have a message on the screen in front of you, a number of options are open. You can delete it, save it, reply to it, forward it, print it, or export it. Or you can just leave it where it is.

> **Warning:** If you receive a large number of messages, you won't want to leave any in your in box for long. These things pile up at an unbelievable rate, and soon you won't even know why you wanted to keep it.

If you delete a message, you won't immediately lose it. In almost all e-mail programs, you can undelete a deleted message, as long as you do so before exiting the program. In Pine, for example, cursor up to the deleted message (it's marked with a "D"), and type **U**. If you exit the program before remembering to undelete it, however, it's gone.

> **Tip:** In Eudora, you can set your preferences to leave deleted messages in the trash folder or to have them deleted when you exit the program. Watch out, though, that your trash folder doesn't get too full. Usually it's best to let the program delete them.

Saving Messages

Apart from deleting the message, the action you'll most likely take with an e-mail message is to save it. This is especially true as you start receiving messages from mailing lists, most of which you either can't or don't want to reply to, but which you want to keep for their valuable contents.

> **Note:** You can print messages (this varies widely from system to system and program to program—check with your systems administrator), but it's often a better idea to keep selected messages available to you on your disk rather than printing them out. That way, you know where they are, and you reply directly from the saved message. Many people, though, prefer hard copy. I'm one of the ones who doesn't.

The easiest of the four mailers for saving messages are Eudora, in which you can create storage folders on your own hard drive, and Pine, which offers a superbly easy-to-use folder system.

When reading a message in Pine, just type **B** to save, and then type the desired folder name at the prompt. If the folder doesn't exist, Pine will tell you, and will let you create it on the spot. It then will save the message in the folder and delete it from the in box.

Tip: The saved-message folders in the mailers are simply files to which you continually append new text. You can FTP one of these files from one account to another if you want to work with the whole folder at once (see Day 6 for details on FTP). This especially is useful if you work on a PC or Mac at home and a UNIX machine at work. Simply FTP the folder to your home computer, then load it into a word processor and take the details you want. Sometimes this is necessary when you're running out of disk space on your office machine.

Replying to Messages

Replying to a message is much the same as sending one. You type **R** (in Elm or Pine, for example), or click the Reply button or menu item (in Eudora).

Then it's time to make two decisions:

- Decide if you want to send the reply to everyone who received the original. Often this is unnecessary, so don't automatically do so (the e-mail program usually will give you a choice).
- Determine whether you want to include the original message in your reply. Be careful with this one. While it's useful to include certain lines from the original to refresh the sender's memory, nothing is as infuriating as getting the full text of a long message sent back to you (or across a mailing list). Be selective.

After you decide, type your message, paying attention to the points of etiquette outlined later in Excursion 3.1.

Forwarding a Message

Often you'll get a message that you want someone else to read. Forwarding a message is like sending an original message, except that the forwarded message is attached to the end. Simply use the forwarding command (it's the F key in the UNIX mailers) and fill in the message. Then send it, as if it were a reply or a new message.

You can do three useful things to a forwarded message before sending it:

- Alter the subject line, to make the message's contents clear.
- Include an introductory sentence or paragraph explaining why you're forwarding it.
- Edit the message, cutting out extraneous information such as the original header and whatever material isn't important to the recipient.

Printing a Message

You can always print a message you want to keep. Printing differs on individual systems, but you usually can set it up to appear on the printer that sits on your desk. This is, without a doubt, the most convenient way to store messages, but unless you're adept at filing paper (I'm not), you'll end up with tons of them scattered all around before too long.

Warning: Before printing a message from inside a network, check with your systems administrator. With the Print command staring you in the face, it's tempting to just press the appropriate key and trudge over to the printer, but often the printer destination has to be properly set up. Don't make assumptions about where your message will print out. This especially is important if the message is something you don't want other people to read—it could end up in an entirely different building.

Exporting a Message

Exporting a message means sending the message as a text file out of your UNIX mailing program and onto your hard drive. The standard procedure is to choose the Export command (Pine's is `e`, for example), and then give the file a name. You then can delete the mail message itself if you want.

When you export a message, it becomes a fully editable text file that you can load into a word processor on UNIX, download to your home system, FTP to another account, or do whatever else you do with text files. See Day 6 for details on getting directory listings and downloading and FTPing files.

Other E-Mail Considerations

Signature

At the end of some messages, you'll notice a clever "sign-off" message. This often includes the sender's full name and address, and possibly a phone or fax number, an alternate e-mail address, and even a quote or witty saying. Your own messages, you'll instantly notice, don't have this interesting and appealing feature. Naturally, you'd like to change that.

What you've seen is called a *signature*. It's created by the user in a separate text editor, and then saved to disk and brought in by the e-mail program.

Warning: When subscribing to a mailing list (see Day 4), be sure to erase your Signature before sending the subscription message. The Listserv software can't process the request if there's anything more than the standard one-line message.

Creating a Signature

In Eudora, select Signature from the Window menu. Then type in whatever you want (but see the following Warning box). Close the Signature window. Next time you send a new message or reply to or forward an existing one, choose Signature from the middle box on the toolbar. The signature won't display on your screen as you're typing the message, but it will appear on the recipient's screen.

Tip: You can configure Eudora, using the Switches command on the Special menu, to use your Signature by default. If you don't want it to appear, you'll have to use the Signature box on the toolbar to turn it off. Also note that users of the commercial version of Eudora can have two separate signature files with which they can work.

For UNIX mailers, you need to create a separate file that your mailer will look for each time you begin composing a message. In Pine's case, for example, this file is called `.signature` (note the preceding dot); whenever you choose the Compose command from Pine's main menu, the contents of this file will appear in the message area (you can edit or delete it, as with any other message text). You can configure each mailer to look for a specific signature file, but configuring mailers is beyond the scope of this book.

The best-known UNIX editor is vi. An easier and less powerful alternative is pico, which is the default editor used by Pine. Either enables you to produce your signature file.

Warning: Keep your signature civil, by the way. That means not too long, and not filled with nifty line pictures. And if you include a funny message, remember that most things are funny only once, so change such a signature regularly. In other words, treat your signature file like your answering machine message. Short, informative, and not too cutesy.

Emoticons (a.k.a. Smileys) and Other Questionable Conventions

You've likely heard about emoticons. They're the little symbols you type into an e-mail message to convey a subtle emotion or suggestion. The best known are the smiling face (hence the name smileys), `:-)` and the winking face, `;-)`. The first shows that you're trying to convey a happy or good thought, the second that you're letting the reader know that what you just wrote was a bit wink-wink humorous. The idea is that your readers tilt their heads to the left so the symbol actually looks like a face. These things have become so numerous that there's even a smiley dictionary available.

Warning: I hate smileys. I really do. So I'm not going to waste any pages of this book dealing with them. There's already an entire book devoted to them that you can find at your local bookstore, so if you're determined to use them go ahead and buy it. But if you ever send me a message, please don't use them. At best, I'll ignore them. At worst, I'll reply with a *flame* (see Flaming).

Emoticons aren't the only e-mail convention I—and a bunch of other people—find annoying. Often in a message, you'll see a humorous or ironic statement followed with something like this: <grin> The idea, of course, is that not everyone understands irony, so sometimes it's necessary to do this to prevent misunderstanding, in the same way you'd actually grin in face-to-face conversation. My point is a bit different than this; if your writing isn't good enough to get the idea of irony, humor, or sarcasm across, don't use it. As far as I'm concerned, the <grin> symbol is equivalent to the way 5-year olds tell jokes and then keep asking, "Get it? Get it?" It does nothing for your credibility as a writer.

But then, maybe I'm just uncool.

Flaming

Flaming is the practice of sounding off in e-mail messages or on newsgroups. In other words, the practice of yelling and screaming as if you were standing in front of the person you want to tell off.

It's so tempting. You read a message that drives you up a wall, so you fire up your e-mail program and blast away. The sender was stupid, after all, and he deserves to be denounced. And you're the best person to do it.

The only problem is, once you've sent the message, you can't easily get it back. If you write an angry letter, you can wait for a while before dropping it in the mailbox, then change your mind before it actually goes. Sending a flame is a lot like picking up the phone and screaming in someone's ear—except that most of us back down when we actually hear the person's voice. It's even worse when you're flaming in public, across a mailing list or a newsgroup. It's rarely impressive, and you usually come across as a prize jerk.

> **Note:** E-mail at its best combines letters and phone calls. Like the latter, it's almost immediate, but like the former you have a chance to formulate an intelligent question or response. At its worst, e-mail combines them badly. As with phone calls, you can scream at someone immediately, but as with letters you can hide behind the fact that you don't see the recipient.

So don't flame. Stop yourself. Believe me, you'll feel better about doing so. And remember that, if someone has written something stupid in public, you won't be the only one who realizes it. The Internet is crammed with intelligent people.

E-Mail Examples

This section features a number of e-mail examples. Each makes a particular point or demonstrates a particular concept. Your own e-mail experiences, of course, will be different than mine, but the ideas essentially are the same. Keep in mind that e-mail is a communication device, something that people use willingly but also seriously, and you'll avoid the problems many beginning e-mailers make. Among the most important is this: Don't assume that people are waiting breathlessly for you to send them something.

Excursion 3.1. Brevity and Informality

One of the strengths of e-mail is its informality and its brevity. In the following message, I'm using the UNIX e-mail program Pine to send a message to an associate who's asked me how to use UNIX's XModem program to download files to her hard drive.

```
To      : Celine Latulipe <clatulip@ccs.carleton.ca>
Cc      :
Attchmnt:
Subject : Instructions for xmodeming files
---- Message Text ----

Using xmodem isn't easy, but it's not that bad. First, type "ls" at the
unix prompt to see what your files are called. Next, type "xmodem sb
filename" (sb means send binary - use st if it's a text file). You'll get
a prompt telling you to download the file. Now use your communications
software to do the download, making sure you're using xmodem protocol.

That's about it. Le me know if it works.

Neil Randall                          Department of English
nrandall@watserv1.uwaterloo.ca        University of Waterloo
```

Unlike a formal answer to the question, there's no need for numbered lists or lengthy commentary, and the message can be tailored quickly and precisely to the specific recipient. In this case, I've assumed an understanding of the difference between text and binary files and of the process of choosing a download protocol.

Three other things worth noting:

- I've used lots of contractions, something you probably wouldn't do in formal correspondence. A good e-mail message combines conversational informality with written precision, with the only goal being instant communication. If I'd phoned this person, I'd have used lots of contractions as well; that's why they're in the message.

- There's an error in the message. The first word of the last sentence should be "Let", not "Le". No matter, even though it's coming from someone in a department of English. E-mail messages almost always contain typos. They're typed quickly, after all, and the recipient knows that.
- The bottom of the message shows my name, e-mail address, and other facts. This is the "signature" that accompanies all my messages. For messages to friends or well-known colleagues I usually delete the signature, but it's handy to have.

Excursion 3.2. In Box #1: Pine

As you can see in the example below, Pine's folder index lets you see how many messages are in that particular folder.

```
Pine 3.87    FOLDER INDEX       Folder: INBOX  Message 4 of 29

     1   Feb 10  John Williamson    (7,556) New granting program for research in
     2   Feb 16  Gleason Sackman    (3,268) Virginia Etext Centre via WWW (fwd)
     3   Feb 16  Eric Smith        (14,786) Computers and Composing Conference
     4   Feb 17  Gleason Sackman    (9,447) Internet-on-a-disk: a new newsletter
+    5   Feb 17  DAVIDSON J - RE      (611) hiig
     6   Feb 17  Gleason Sackman    (1,747) Commerce page, Live Video Demos
     7   Feb 17  H-RHETOR           (2,742) New Book: Landmark essays on
     8   Feb 17  Gleason Sackman    (5,143) Cello v1 released (fwd)
+    9   Feb 18  Annette Paulson    (1,456) Re: U of T dial instr
    10   Feb 18  Gleason Sackman    (3,963) Hunt Helpers (fwd)
    11   Feb 18  Gleason Sackman    (4,514) Update: the Internet and Mediated
    12   Feb 18  Gleason Sackman    (3,881) Update of Internet Tools Summary
    13   Feb 19  Deborah Johnson    (6,490) Business and the Internet Conference
+   14   Feb 20  patrick (p.t) s    (2,256) course project #7
    15   Feb 21  David Randall      (1,747) Where's that *?#(*@ bike gopher??!!!
+   16   Feb 21  John Jacob Ande    (4,785) computers and sociological change+
```

Actually, this list is standard for most UNIX mailers. You can cursor down to the message you want, press Enter, and read what the sender had to say. Or, as happens more frequently, you can just cursor to the message line and delete it, without reading it at all. This is particularly useful if you belong to several mailing lists, as you almost inevitably will.

One important feature of e-mail programs is that they show you how large the message is. On this screen, the number in parentheses shows the size of the message in bytes (some mailers show the number of lines in the message). If you're using an account through a UNIX server rather than your own personal computer, you probably have a limited amount of disk space on which to store messages. Be sure to handle the large ones before they take command of your system. Either print them or export them as text files for downloading. Then delete them, to make room for more.

One of Pine's nicer features (at least, beginning with version 3.87) is the plus sign at the far left of some messages. This indicates that the message is being sent to me, not to a list. I usually read these first, because they require personal attention. If you reply to a message, the symbol changes to an "A" (for "answered"), a similarly nice touch.

Excursion 3.3. The Back-and-Forth Reply

I got into an interesting exchange with a colleague about a conference we'd both been to. Over the course of the two weeks following the conference, we exchanged about 40 messages. Some were detailed and lengthy, but most consisted of only one or two sentences. E-mail discussions are good at allowing an ongoing exchange of compact ideas, with each person responding only when they have a bit of time to do so.

```
To      : "Alex J. Thompson" <ajthomps@math.ncsu.edu>
Cc      :
Attchmnt:
Subject : Re: Yesterday's forum
---- Message Text ----
>
> But couldn't that be said to represent a rather narrow interpretation
> of "language"?  8-)
>
> Alex

I suppose. But isn't it just as possible that the interpretation was
simply wrong? I mean, didn't sound all that sure of himself.

Neil
```

The screen shows a reply, using Pine. Notice that the subject line begins with `Re:`. Pine adds this automatically, indicating that it's a reply to an ongoing thread (a *thread* is a continuing e-mail topic). Also, the text from the original message is set apart with the > symbol; I included part of that message to remind the recipient of what he said, and Pine added the symbols.

Tip: The secret to a good reply is to actually reply, and not to go off in an entirely new direction. If you want to start a new discussion, indicate that in the subject line.

One other thing: Notice the emoticon (smiley) at the end of the second line of the original. Tilt your head to the left, and you can see the smiling face. I hate smileys.

Excursion 3.4. In Box #2: Elm

The following is the mailbox index in the UNIX e-mail program Elm:

```
Mailbox is '/usr/spool/mail/nrandall' with 29 messages  [Elm 2.3 PL11]


     1   Feb 23 Gleason Sackman    (83)   Gopher jewels list (fwd)
     2   Feb 22 Elaine Brennan     (52)   7.0510  New List: TECHEVAL  (1/29)
     3   Feb 22 Guy Keller         (26)   Re: Lots o' stuff
     4   Feb 22 David Randall      (63)   Finally found that *&)^%%$& gopher
     5   Feb 22 Steven Mendelsoh   (142)  Re: CyConf. Update
     6   Feb 21 Phil Agre          (107)  privacy and prescriptions in Germany
     7   Feb 21 hartling           (38)   Need that chapter asap!!
     8   Feb 21 Gleason Sackman    (154)  5th International CONFERENCE
     9   Feb 20 ralph              (45)   paper on the way
    10   Feb 20 Donald Carroll     (21)   Re: FYI Alan Emerson


  You can use any of the following commands by pressing the first character:
d)elete or u)ndelete mail,  m)ail a message,  r)eply or f)orward mail,  q)uit
   To read a message, press <return>.  J = move down, k = move up, ? = help

Command: _
```

It's similar to Pine's, except that it shows the actual directory and gives a menu of options (Pine gives menus elsewhere that Elm doesn't, though). One of the things Elm doesn't do, which Pine does, is distinguish between messages addressed specifically to you and those sent to you as a group message. There's nothing on the far left side of this list to indicate six of these messages aren't specifically for me.

Take note of the subject line (the far right column). At a glance, I can tell which messages contain a subject I'm interested in. That's why it's so vitally important to include a useful subject line with each message. The last message says, "paper on the way," and since I'm waiting for one, I know I'll need to see that message. Many of the rest are messages from discussion groups, informing me of newly available information. I may or may not wish to read these, and if I don't, I can simply delete them.

Remember, if you don't offer a subject line, don't expect the recipient to read your message.

Excursion 3.5. Message Headers

Welcome to the world of Internet headers (see Day 2 for a fuller explanation of them).

```
Date:  Tue, 22 Feb 1994 07:55:36 -0800
Errors-To: sackman@plains.nodak.edu
Reply-To: net-happenings@is.internic.net
Originator: net-happenings@is.internic.net
Sender: net-happenings@is.internic.net
Precedence: bulk
To: Multiple recipients of list <net-happenings@is.internic.net>
Subject: Health Care Reform Bookshelf Available on Global Internet (fwd)
X-Listserver-Version: 6.0 -- UNIX ListServer by Anastasios Kotsikonas
X-Comment: InterNIC Net Happenings
X-Status:

Forwarded by Gleason Sackman - InterNIC net-happenings moderator
()()()()()()()()()()()()()()()()()()()()()()()()()()()()()()()()

---------- Text of forwarded message ----------
Date: Mon, 21 Feb 1994 21:40:29 -0800 (PST)
From: "Rob Raisch, The Internet Company" <raisch@internet.com>
To: com-priv@psi.com
Subject: Health Care Reform Bookshelf Available on Global Internet
 There are 50 lines left (35%). Press <space> for more, or 'i' to return.
```

Here, I'm reading a message about the Health Care Reform Bookshelf. The entire screen shows nothing except where the original messages all came from, and rarely is this information useful unless you're trying to figure out why a message went astray or got "bounced" back to you (even then, it's a matter for the system specialists). Still, if you do a great deal with e-mail, and you fully understand the routings that have taken place, you will frequently have need of this material. Most users won't, though.

Let's face it, though. It all looks pretty ugly. This is, in fact, the major problem with the UNIX mailers. In order of ugliness, Mail wins hands down (with earlier mailers even worse), and while Elm improves on it somewhat, Pine is somewhat more aesthetically pleasing. Combine a UNIX mailer with the intimidating, ugly information presented in these headers, and you understand instantly why the Macintosh became so popular. The good news is that UNIX graphical environments, like the Windows and Macintosh e-mail programs, don't force you to look at this stuff.

Tip: Another point. When you're replying to a message, make sure your reply actually is going where you want it to. If you belong to a mailing list, you might want to reply to the sender of the message without forcing everyone on the list to read it. Study the routing information to see where your message will end up.

Excursion 3.6. In Box #3: Mail

And speaking of ugly, this is the mailbox index from Mail:

```
Mail version 4.3a 88/05/27.   Type ? for help.
"/Usr/spool/mail/nrandall": 29 messages
>   1 joan@monde.uwaterloo.ca  "New granting program fo" Thu Feb 10 11:32
    2 sackman@plains.nodak.edu  "Virginia Etext Centre " Wed Feb 16 11:36
    3 LCARL@MIZZOU2.BITNET@uga.cl.uga  "Computers & Wr " Wed Feb 16 22:11
    4 sackman@plains.nodak.edu  "Internet-on-a-Disk: a " Thu Feb 17 04:44
    5 snrensse@watserv2.uwaterloo.ca                "hiig" Thu Feb 17 11:39
    6 sackman@plains.nodak.edu  "Commerce page, Live Vi" Thu Feb 17 11:40
    7 HATCHL@jkhbcrs.byu.edu  "New Book: Landmark essay" Thu Feb 17 11:42
    8 sackman@plains.nodak.edu  "Cello v1 released (fwd" Thu Feb 17 18:56
    9 apresley@relay.tkcds.waterloo.on  "Re: U of T dia" Fri Feb 18 10:39
   10 sackman@plains.nodak.edu      "Hunt Helpers (fwd)" Fri Feb 18 12:45
   11 sackman@plains.nodak.edu  "update: the Internet a" Sat Feb 19 00:32
   12 sackman@plains.nodak.edu  "Update of Internet Too" Sat Feb 19 16:05
   13 sackman@plains.nodak.edu  "List of Dedicated Line" Sat Feb 19 16:35
   14 Deborah_+d_RKG_+3Deborah+_Brown+  "Business and t" Sat Feb 19 19:47
   15 sackman@plains.nodak.edu  "UPLOADED: Internet Tra" Sun Feb 20 13:00
   16 acc651rsmit@artslp.wastar.uwaterloo.ca            Sun Feb 20 16:56
```

For whatever reasons, the subject lines aren't lined up properly, even though the dates are (because I don't usually care about the date, nor about the full return address—which is also given precedence—I think the priority's wrong). The sender's address and the subject line meld into one another, and the user-hostile "&" prompt does nothing to convince me I can actually do anything (pre-Windows users will remember the equally disgusting C:> prompt in DOS). The thing about Mail, though, is that it's available everywhere, so you should spend some time at least learning how to get by with it.

But not too long. If your system doesn't offer either Elm or Pine, start a petition to make it happen. E-mail is supposed to be interesting, informative, and easy to use, and the Mail program works against all three.

Excursion 3.7. Help Screens for Mail and Elm

All three UNIX e-mail programs offer useful help screens. These two are from Mail and Elm, the two that need the most. Pay particular attention to the escape commands. Especially when you're first beginning, you'll want to be able to back out of sending a message, and in neither program is doing so exactly intuitive. The first is from Mail, the second from Pine.

```
Mail Commands   (Condensed list; see "man mail" for full details)
t <message list>            type messages
n                           goto and type next message
e <message list>            edit messages
f <message list>            give head lines of messages
d <message list>            delete messages
s <message list> file       append messages to file
u <message list>            undelete messages
R <message list>            reply to senders of messages
r <message list>            reply to all original recipients of the message
pre <message lest>          make messages go back to /usr/spool/mail
m <user list>               nmail to specific users
q                           quit, saving unresolved messages in mbox
x                           quit, do not remove system mailbox
h                           print out active message headers
!                           shell escape
c [directory]               chdir to directory or home if none given
A <message list> can contain any of the following, separated by spaces:
  integers or rangers         1 4-7
  names of people who sent you mail      jclark ptrudeau jturner bmulroney
  subjects                     /hockey/
  keywords in a header line or the text  /uucp/from   /Jun/date /midterm/text
$ _
-------------------------------------------------------------------------------------
     Command                          Elm 2.3 Action

     <RETURN>, <SPACE>          Display current message
      |                         Pipe current message or tagged messages to
                                a system command.
      !                         Shell escape
      $                         Resynchronize folder
      ?                         This screen of information
      +, <RIGHT>                Display next index page
      -, <LEFT>                 Display previous index page
      =                         Set current message to first message
      *                         Set current message to last message
     <NUMBER><RETURN>           Set current message to <NUMBER>
      /                         Search from/subjects for pattern
      //                        Search entire message texts for pattern
      >                         Save current message or tagged messages
                                to a folder
 <                          Scan current message for calendar entries
      a                         Alias, change to 'alial' mode
      b                         Bounder (re-mail) current message

Press <space> to continue, 'q' to return._
```

As the help screens show, there's a number of things you can do with your messages. If you're like most users, though, you won't actually know that you can do them, nor perhaps even what they mean. Don't worry about it. I wasn't sure about three-quarters of the possibilities for the first year I used Elm, and I know several Elm users who just aren't interested in anything beyond sending, replying, and printing. But if you're going to make e-mail a strong part of your day, you should try out the various possibilities. Or get someone to show you.

Note: Believe me, these help screens live up to their name. The help screens in Pine aren't as necessary because of Pine's built-in menu system, but for things like moving the cursor around the screen and exporting files, they're still extremely useful.

Excursion 3.8. A Reply in Elm

This screen shows a reply in Elm. There's no real difference between replying in Elm and replying in Pine, except that Pine's screen is nicer looking and somewhat more intuitive. Also, Pine makes file attachment considerably easier. But the idea is the same.

```
To register for the conference, please send this registration form along
with a check payable to the RGT Foundation for the $200 registration fee.
Mail completed form to the Internet Conference c/o the RGT Foundation at
the address given above.

Name:    (Prof., Dr., Mr., Ms., Mrs.):
         First:
         Middle Initial:
         Last:
Title:
Organization:
Address:
City, State, Zip Code:
-----------------------------------------------------------------------------
Command: Reply to message               To: Deborah_Brown
Subject of message: Re: Business and the Internet Conference Registration
Copies to: _
```

Warning: Although it's not shown here, Elm's default editor—where you actually write your message—takes a fair bit of getting used to. It's based on UNIX's famous vi editor, which takes for granted a considerable amount of UNIX know-how. I remember the first time I used Elm: I had no idea that to start typing you had to type `i` (for "input"). I'd start typing a line, but nothing would appear (usually) until I'd typed an `i`. It was a little disconcerting.

Another thing Elm doesn't do automatically is allow word wrap. Now, given that I could use word wrap on my Commodore 64 ten years ago, this struck me as odd. Pine, by contrast, assumes word wrap, as well as such things as full-screen editing.

So do I prefer Pine? Yes, as must be obvious from what I've said throughout this chapter. But I know several people who swear up and down that Elm is the more capable program, and indeed it is more feature-rich. If you mention Pine to these people, they readily offer a 10-paragraph lecture on why it's not worth using. My advice? Try them all, then take your pick.

Excursion 3.9. The Graphical Mailer: Eudora

On to Eudora, the most popular Windows and Macintosh e-mail program. As Figure 3.1 shows, the idea isn't the numbered list, but rather what looks like a database screen containing information about sender, time and date of message, length, and subject. You double-click the message to read it, single-click one of the icons to reply, forward, redirect, or print it. Or simply send it to the trash.

Notice the three folders: In, Out, and Trash. All incoming messages (naturally) appear in the In folder. When you send a message, it is still available in the Out folder. Delete one, and it goes into the Trash folder. You can instruct Eudora to delete the Trash folder whenever you exit the program, or you can leave the messages there until you delete them yourself. You also can set Eudora up so that it doesn't save your outgoing messages. This isn't a bad idea if you always remember to copy important messages to yourself, but usually it's best to let them all be saved. That way you can go back and read what you wrote, and you also can double-check to make sure you sent the messages you were supposed to. And every once in a while, you can highlight a bunch and delete them.

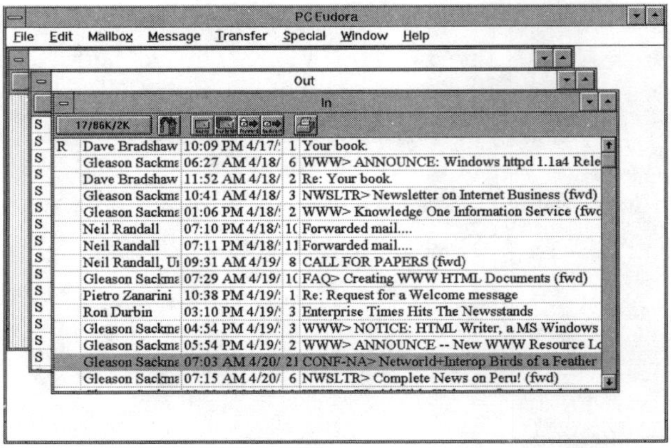

Figure 3.1. *Eudora for Windows.*

Tip: Eudora also works well as an offline mailer. Configure it so that it doesn't automatically check for messages, and then boot it up whether online or off. You can read your mail, transfer it into folders, delete it, or print it, and if you compose a new message or a reply, Eudora will queue it rather than send it. Next time you log on, the queued messages automatically will be sent.

Excursion 3.10. Sending a Message in Eudora

When you send a message in Eudora, you get another window (see Figure 3.2). In this one, you can enter the recipient's address or alias, copy it to other users, type in a subject line, and attach a file. File attachment (shown here) is actually done through the pull-down menus, and it works well. You also can create a signature from within Eudora (plus an alternate signature in the commercial version), then from the toolboxes above the message tell Eudora to include it. A number of other buttons allow different and various functions. Eudora is quite full-featured.

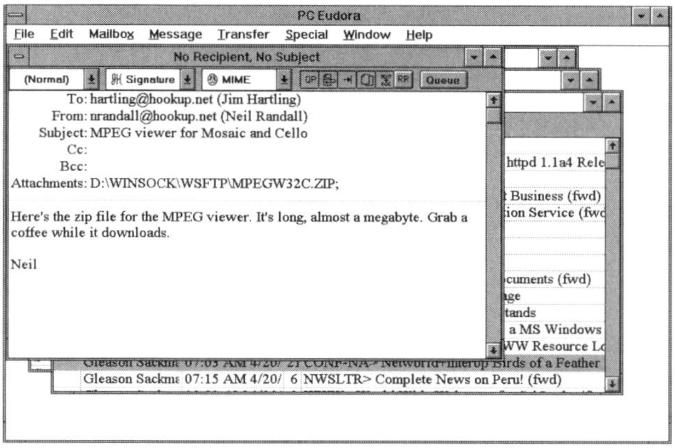

Figure 3.2. *Sending a message in Eudora.*

Warning: It's not as easy as it should be, though—at least not yet. Creating nicknames is no problem as long as you're looking at a message from which you want to take the address, but creating them from scratch is far too difficult. Creating and saving messages in different folders also could use some work. Maybe this will change, now that Eudora has been taken on by a commercial software house. The bad news is that now we'll have to pay for it.

Excursion 3.11. Eudora's Finger Command

From inside Eudora you can execute the Finger command, as shown in Figure 3.3. Now, despite its name, fingering has nothing to do with the actual digits on your hand. Instead, it has to do with finding out whether a specific user currently is online. If you know an Internet address, you can "finger" that address to find out who the address belongs to, when they last received mail, when they last read their mail, and whether they're online. This is useful when you've sent a message and you want to find out if they've received and read it.

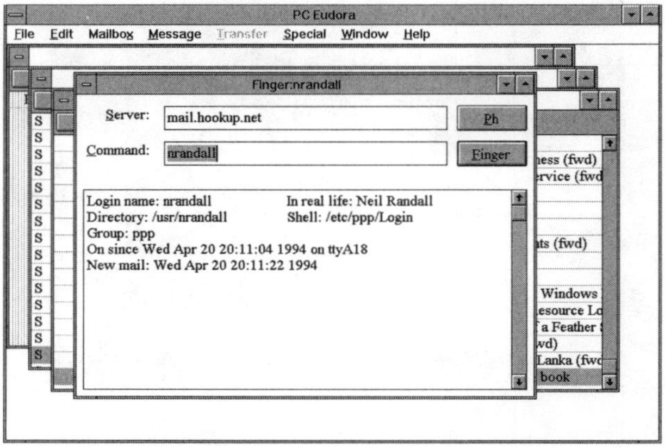

Figure 3.3. *Executing Finger from inside Eudora.*

Note: Finger isn't unique to Eudora by any means. You can finger users from any UNIX system. The problem is that finger usually doesn't help you discover a person's address. One important capability is using finger to determine who's currently online. To find out if I'm currently online, for instance, type `finger watserv1@uwaterloo` and read the list of names. Finger is also shown in Excursion 3.12.

Excursion 3.12. Fingering from Mosaic

As shown in Figure 3.4, you also can do a finger command from inside Mosaic, perhaps the most famous graphical Internet program. Mosaic (discussed fully in Day 7) is a program designed to help you navigate through the growing World Wide Web, but you can use it for a wide range of other purposes as well, including Gophering and FTPing. Here, I've used it to do a finger command, and while the information is no different from Eudora's, it looks a little better. It's nice to see your address in many-point typeface, and the Canadian flag strikes me as a spiffy extra.

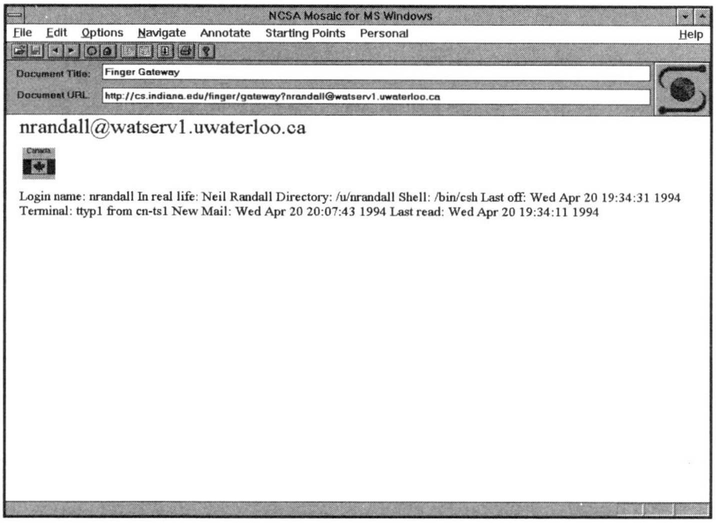

Figure 3.4. *Example of finger from Mosaic.*

Note: Mosaic, by the way, is reason alone to get the type of Internet account that allows you to use graphical programs. As soon as you have this kind of access you can use Eudora, Mosaic, and other gems such as WinGopher, H-Gopher, Winsock Gopher, WAIS Manager, and another strong World Wide Web browser, Cello. These programs are shown elsewhere in this book.

Excursion 3.13. File Attachments in Pine

These screens show what happens when you attach a file using Pine. When sending the file, you cursor into the Attachments line, then press Ctrl+T to go to the file menu to select the file you want to attach. When the message is received, it shows that a file is attached, and gives an instruction for viewing or saving it. Type **v**, and you're prompted through the viewing or saving. Because of UNIX's speed, and especially the high-speed connections across the Net, sending files this way is extremely efficient.

The first message shows the file being sent; the second shows what the recipient sees:

```
To      : Jim Amoretti <jamorett@vx9.cso.uiuc.edu>
Cc      : Neil Randall <nrandall@watserv1.uwaterloo.ca>
Attchmnt: 1. /U/nrandall/internet.txt (4.1 KB) ""
Subject : Instructions re Internet access
---- Message Text ----
Jim,

Here's the file. I've copied it to myself as well.


Neil Randall                          Department of English
nrandall@watserv1.uwaterloo.ca       University of Waterloo




^G Get Help  ^C Cancel   ^R Read File  ^Y Prev Pg   ^K Cut Text   ^O Postpone
^X Send      ^J Justify  ^W Where is   ^V Next Pg   ^U UnCut Text ^T To Spell


--------------
Cc: Neil Randall <nrandall@watserv1.uwaterloo.ca>
Subject: Instructions re Internet access
Parts/attachments:
   1 Shown    8 lines   Text
   2   OK    90 lines   Text
-----------------------------------------

Jim,

Here's the file. I've copied it to myself as well.


Neil Randall                          Department of English
nrandall@watserv1.uwaterloo.ca       University of Waterloo


  [Part 2, ""  Text  90 lines]
  [Not Shown. Use the "V" command to view or save this part}

Enter attachment number to view or save (1 - 2) : _
```

Summary

Electronic mail is the Internet's most obvious and most instantly useful function. You can send messages to anyone in the world, as long as you know that person's e-mail address—and unlike some commercial online services, the message won't carry a fee. You can create groups of recipients who receive the same message at the same time, you can attach files for downloading, you can forward messages, and you can keep a message stream going indefinitely.

You also can use e-mail to join special interest mailing lists generated by listserv software. These lists tend to be more specific and more disciplined than newsgroups, and many have an academic focus. Through these lists you can find out about current research and upcoming conferences and gatherings, and the lists often lead you to other Internet resources in your topic area.

Many who use e-mail find it the single most effective means of communicating with peers, friends, colleagues, and even clients. E-mail offers the benefits of both letter-writing (considered responses, depth of thought) and telephone conversation (immediacy, brevity, informality), without the inconviences of either. But it can be—and often is—abused. If you find yourself sending out five messages a day to the same person and only getting one in response, ask yourself if you shouldn't step back a bit and reconsider. And if you start seeing 10 messages over three days from the same person on a mailing list, ask yourself if you haven't been doing the same thing. It can be annoying, distracting, and counter-productive.

Task Review

This chapter has concentrated on the things to consider when using e-mail, rather than on how to send and receive messages. You now are fully qualified to do the following:

- Include a useful, readable, and sensible subject line with each message.
- Avoid flaming.
- Think carefully before cluttering your message with smileys.
- Create a sensible, intelligent, and useful signature.
- Decide among the three UNIX mailers Mail, Elm, and Pine.
- Decide if you want access to a graphical mailer like Eudora.
- Attach documents or other files to a message.
- Determine whether you should reply to a full mailing list or just the originator of the message.
- Create address books with aliases for easier use.
- Find the important information in a message header.

Q&A

Q How do I go about creating a signature file? The help menus don't help me.

A In Eudora, it's simple. Just go into the Windows menu and select Signature, and then type what you want. Then, when you're typing a new message, make sure Signature is turned on in the small box above the message. The only problem with Eudora is that the signature doesn't appear as you're typing your message; rest assured, however, that the recipient will see it.

For a UNIX mailer, the procedure is a bit more difficult. Essentially, you have to create a separate text file called `.signature` (note the dot in front of the filename). Do so using a UNIX editor such as vi or pico. After the file is created, your mailer will pick it up and include it automatically. If you know how, you can alter the mailer's configuration file to include a different file as its signature, but if you can do that, you already know about signature files.

Q How do I include two or more names in the `TO:` field?

A The first way is to type all the addresses, separating each with a comma. Note that you can combine aliases and full addresses in the following way:

```
TO: nrandall@watserv1.uwaterloo.ca,tom,carole@office
```

(my full address, the address you've nicknamed "tom," and Carole next door)

If you have a group of two or more people you frequently e-mail, set them up as a group name. In any of the mailers, you can do so as part of the address book (or as part of the Nicknames feature in Eudora). Create the group and include the individual addresses inside it. Note that you can use aliases when creating a group, so that after you've nicknamed a long address as "tom" you can simply specify "tom" in the group.

Q Do I have to read a message before I delete it?

A Not in any of the UNIX mailers, nor in Eudora. Just press Delete and get rid of it. In older systems, however (I'm thinking of VMS, where I began my e-mail career), you may not always have this option. If that's the case, reading mail becomes an incredible pain, unless you have few correspondents. Try to upgrade if at all possible.

Q Can I send a message to myself?

A Yes. Just fill in the appropriate address.

Q How do I show emphasis in an e-mail message?

A Good question. Don't count on using things like underlining or italics, unless you know that your recipient's system will display them. If you absolutely must emphasize, consider using ALL CAPS, but this practice is heavily frowned on throughout the Net. The best approach simply is to write forcefully, relying on none of these tactics.

Q Is it true that systems administrators can read my e-mail?

A Usually, yes, if they really want to. In fact, there's a series of enormous debates going on as to whether or not e-mail is considered official correspondence (internal or external) for the sake of organizational policy. The best bet is this: If you wouldn't send a memo saying it, don't use e-mail to say it. If you want to communicate personally with someone, phone them in your off-hours, or send them an old-fashioned letter.

Q If I can attach files to an e-mail message, why don't I just type them up using my word processor and attach them, rather than typing directly into the e-mail program?

A With long messages, that's actually a good idea. When you type using a word processor, you usually spend more time organizing and thinking about your writing. But for everyday correspondence, it's just too inconvenient, not only for you but for your recipient. Remember that the person who gets your file has to download it and open it in a word processor. Unless you know your message merits that kind of extra effort, don't count on it being read.

Extra Credit: Sending E-mail Messages to Commercial Online Services

Internet users and those on the commercial online services—CompuServe, GEnie, Prodigy, America Online, Delphi, MCI Mail, and so forth—can exchange electronic mail. Everything is the same as sending to another Internet address, except that the `TO:` address itself has a few different elements (both from the Net and from inside the commercial service).

Excursion 3.14. Sending E-mail to Virgil

Table 3.1 summarizes the address patterns for each service.

Note: Our fictional user for these examples is the poet Virgil, who has an Internet address of `virgil@aeneid.rome.it`.

Table 3.1. Address patterns for commercial online services.

If user is on:	With username:	Address from Net as follows:
America Online	VirgilR	`virgilr@aol.com` (capitals removed)
BIX	virgilr	`virgilr@bix.com`
CompuServe	73859,1788	`73859.1788@Compuserve.com` (comma replaced by period)
GEnie	virgilr2	`virgilr2@genie.geis.com`
MCI Mail	Virgil (256-4985)	`Virgil@mcimail.com` (if there's only one Virgil)
		`256-4985@mcimail.com` (to guarantee no duplicate Virgils)
Prodigy	virgil3	`virgil3@prodigy.com`

These are the major services. For others, one of the simplest things to do is have the recipient send you a message first, then store the return address as an alias for later use.

4

WEEK 1

Birds of a Feather: Newsgroups and Mailing Lists

Day 4 is devoted to one of the Internet's most appealing features, the capability of finding and exchanging ideas with people who share your personal or professional interests. No matter what your area of interest, there is probably a newsgroup or mailing list already in place with participants from just about anywhere. Finding them can be difficult, though, and active participation has its rules and protocols. These are the kinds of issues Day 4 deals with.

On Day 4, you will learn how to do the following:

- ☐ Locate mailing lists.
- ☐ Subscribe to mailing lists.
- ☐ Post to a mailing list.
- ☐ Access newsgroups using the rn and trn programs.
- ☐ Read posts on selected newsgroups.
- ☐ Post to a newsgroup—contributing to the conversation.

Interacting with People Who Share Your Interests

In the past few days you've had a tour of the Internet, a look at several of the issues, and a chance to work with the fundamental tools. You've sent and received e-mail, and you've explored Gopher sites until your eyes hurt. The sense of the Net's enormous connectivity is becoming clear, and it's time to see what else it can do for you.

Despite its obvious strengths, e-mail by itself is not enough. It's excellent as long as you know someone's Internet address, but eventually you'll run out of people you know and things to discuss. Those whose addresses you've managed to gather aren't necessarily interested in the same things you are, at least not to the same degree. Somewhere in the world, someone must share your passion for medieval architecture, or training Cocker Spaniels, or which Australian wine goes best with tripe, or theories of consciousness, or global marketing, or *Gilligan's Island*....

The question is, now that you want more, where do you find it? Where can you find/meet people on the Net who share your interests? Where do you go with questions you might have, to discuss your world and its ongoing development, as well as discover new worlds and opinions you hadn't thought existed? In short, where is all this global interaction you've heard so much about in the press?

The answer lies in newsgroups (Usenet) and in mailing lists (also called discussion lists—or, in many cases, *Listservs*), and that's what this chapter is about. Today you'll learn how to choose from the myriad of newsgroups and mailing lists available, how to access and read them, and how to participate in their conversations.

I'll begin the journey with a look at mailing lists. After that, I'll bring in Stewart Lindsay, a newsgroup aficionado, to discuss the wonders of Usenet.

Mailing Lists

Where newsgroups combine personal, professional, and all other topics, mailing lists (also called discussion lists and Listservs, among other names) are designed primarily to be professionally oriented. Many, in fact, are based on academic topics, offering scholars from a wide range of disciplines a place to meet, discuss, and occasionally even socialize. Mailing lists have been established to be used for collaborative classrooms, and even as the distribution method for conferences.

Most mailing lists are moderated. This means that someone is watching over them, to some degree or another. The moderator's function is to keep the list more or less on the topic and to prevent idiocy. Usually, however, moderators have little time to worry a great deal about such things, so the lists tend to moderate themselves. Still, the existence of the moderator is what generally distinguishes mailing lists from newgroups.

Working with mailing lists is easier than working with newgroups, mainly because you don't have to master new software. While effective newgroup participation practically requires you to learn rn or trn, or one of the graphical newgroup readers, mailing lists are handled exclusively via e-mail. As soon as you know how to send and receive e-mail messages, you're ready to subscribe to mailing lists.

Excursion 4.1. Discovering Mailing Lists

You can find out about the existence of mailing lists in a number of ways. The easiest way is to talk to other Internetters in your office, who probably will be on one or two lists already and who can help you subscribe.

Next easiest is to use Gopher. By connecting to any good Gopher (see Day 5 for examples and instructions), you usually can maneuver your way into an item called Internet Resources, or something similar to that. In here, look for a directory or file called Mailing Lists or Discussion Lists. This will give you all you need to get started.

Excursion 4.2. Subscribing to Mailing Lists

Most mailing lists are available through Listserv software in BITNET sites, rather than on the Internet itself. To subscribe, you send a subscription message to the Listserv's address.

To subscribe to a BITNET mailing list, do the following:

1. Open your mail program (Mail, Elm, Pine, Eudora, and so on) and prepare to send a message.
2. In the `TO:` line, type **`LISTSERV@`*`ADDRESS`*`.BITNET`** (where *`ADDRESS`* is the list's address as shown in the information file).
3. Leave the subject line completely blank.
4. In the first line of the message area, type **`subscribe`** ***`LISTNAME Your_Name`***. (Use your real first and last name for *`Your_Name`*, such as Jane Smith.)
5. Be sure not to include a signature in your message (See Day 3 for information on signature files).
6. Send the message.

Figures 4.1 shows the subscription messages to our two chosen lists.

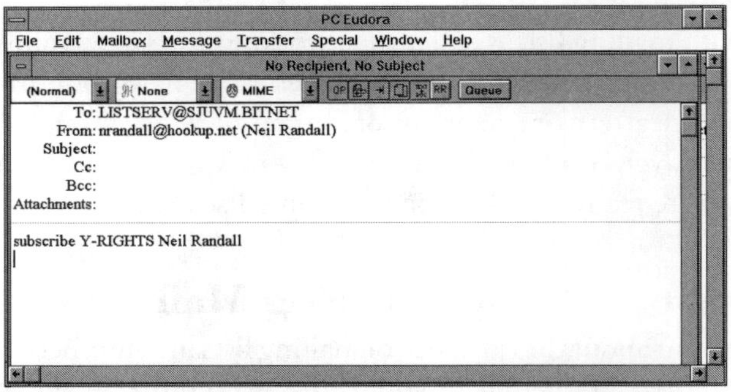

Figure 4.1. *A subscription message through Eudora to the Youth Rights list.*

Shortly, you'll receive confirmation of your subscription. This usually consists of two messages, one telling you about computer time used (which you can erase), and another introducing you to the list and explaining other details.

Warning: Save the introductory message! If you don't, you will find it difficult to unsubscribe to the list, or to set it for other functions or any other activities. Print it if you don't want to store it, but don't just delete it. There's nothing more annoying to list members than seeing ten people in a row trying to unsubscribe who don't know how to do so because they deleted this message.

In our example the confirmation came back within seconds:

```
Return-Path: <@stjohns.edu:LISTSERV@SJUVM.STJOHNS.EDU>
Date:        Fri, 22 Apr 1994 11:35:19 -0400
From: BITNET list server at SJUVM (1.7f) <LISTSERV@stjohns.edu>
Subject:     Your subscription to list Y-RIGHTS
To: Neil Randall <nrandall@HOOKUP.NET>
X-LSV-ListID: Y-RIGHTS

Dear networker,

  Your  subscription to  list  Y-RIGHTS (Y-Rights:  Kid/Teen Rights  Discussion
Group) has been accepted.

  (Yeah! - another subscriber! Welcome! —Ken, listowner)

  Y-RIGHTS is an open discussion group on the subject of the rights of kids and
teenagers. Everyone is welcome here, no matter who or what you are. You could
be a faculty member, a teenager, a parent, a manual laborer, a student working
in a class about rights, or whatever. You are welcome here.

  One thing that I would like from you is a little auto-biography. Just a few
words about what you are in life, what you were, what you will be... and even
maybe what your interest is in this subject.

  There aren't too many things to remember on this list. Try to keep "Flaming"
to a minimum, and remember that there's a human being out there on the other
end of this thing. Try to respect other people's opinions (in other words....
saying "You're WRONG, buster! This is the way that it is..... " isn't the way
two respectful individuals should treat each other). Thanks :)

  You may leave the list at any time by sending a "SIGNOFF Y-RIGHTS" command to
LISTSERV@SJUVM. Please note that this command must NOT be sent to the list
address (Y-RIGHTS@SJUVM) but to the LISTSERV address (LISTSERV@SJUVM).
  The amount of acknowledgement you wish to receive from this list upon
completion of a mailing operation can be changed by means of a "SET Y-RIGHTS
option" command, where "option" may be either "ACK" (mail acknowledgement),
"MSGACK" (interactive messages only) or "NOACK".
```

```
  Contributions sent to this list are automatically archived. You can obtain a
list of the available archive files by sending an "INDEX Y-RIGHTS" command to
LISTSERV@SJUVM. These files can then be retrieved by means of a "GET Y-RIGHTS
filetype" command, or using the database search facilities of LISTSERV. Send an
"INFO DATABASE" command for more information on the latter.

  I will try to set it up so that there is a "Digest format" available for
Y-RIGHTS. This will probably be something to the effect of receiving the
Archives automatically each week. I will have to check into this furthur. More
on this later.

  Please note that it is presently possible for other people to determine that
you are signed up to the list through the use of the "REVIEW" command, which
returns the network address and name of all the subscribers. If you do not wish
your name to be available to others in this fashion, just issue a "SET Y-RIGHTS
CONCEAL" command.

  More information on LISTSERV commands  can be found in the "General
Introduction guide", which you can retrieve by sending an "INFO GENINTRO"
command to LISTSERV@SJUVM.
```

The introductory message tells about the list and shows you how to do the following:

- ☐ Unsubscribe.
- ☐ Stop your mail temporarily.
- ☐ Restart your mail.
- ☐ Acknowledge your postings.
- ☐ Receive once-a-day or once-a week-digest postings rather than each one as it's posted. This especially is useful if you're getting 10 to 20 messages per day (which is hardly uncommon).

Now it's just a matter of sitting back and waiting, and checking your mail every so often for postings.

Excursion 4.3. Posting to a Mailing List

You can post to a mailing list according to the instructions in the introductory message, but the usual way simply is to reply to the message. It's nothing but an ordinary e-mail message, after all, with the exception that it's been sent to a group rather than just you. Following is the procedure:

1. Having read the message, start a Reply sequence (in Elm or Pine, for example, type **r**).
2. If your mailing software prompts you, decide whether to include the original message in the reply, and whether to post to the entire list. Press **y** or **n** as desired.
3. Send the message. Depending on how the list is set up, you may get a copy of your own message as it's posted to the list.

Before posting your first message, read the following guidelines regarding posting to a mailing list:

- Don't just automatically resend the original message. In fact, don't send it in its complete original form *at all.* If you want to include part of it, include that part and delete the rest. Show that you've actually thought about what you're doing; it enhances your credibility immensely with the rest of the group.
- If you have something personal to say to the sender of the last message, e-mail that person and *not* the entire group (your mail program will prompt you for this option).

4

Note: This is extremely important! Mailing lists are designed to be more professional than newsgroups; often they're accessed by people at work. Nobody wants to read a message that says, "Nice work, Barb!", or—much worse—"Glad to hear about Chelsea's sax recital, Bill. Best to Hillary, okay?" Even worse, some people completely forget that the messages are broadcast all over the place, and include *extremely* personal information. I have been hugely embarrassed for people who have outlined their marital problems, their legal problems, and even their prison experiences in what should have been a personal e-mail.

- If you have four things to say, say them in one message, not four separate ones. Nobody wants to see your name appear in their mailer six times a day.
- Be brief, unless you can justify not being brief. One screen of text is more than enough for most people to read.

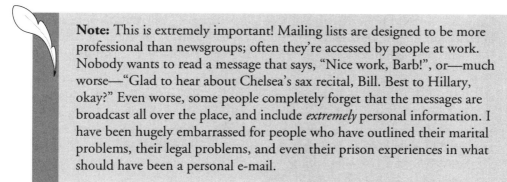

Usenet Newsgroups

by Stewart Lindsay

About the Contributor

Stewart Lindsay is completing his Master's degree at the University of Waterloo. His fascination with newgroups goes back a few years, and he's spent a huge number of hours subscribing to them, reading them, posting to them, and acquiring all sorts of e-friends in the process. He will guide you through the newgroups section of this chapter.

Introduction to Usenet

Although it is a prominent and much-hyped feature of the Internet, Usenet started out as a separate network. It was put into place in the late '70s by a couple of students at Duke University, and its first connection was to the nearby Chapel Hill campus of the University of North Carolina. As its potential became clear the network expanded quickly, sites on the Internet began to carry it and many users got their first Internet experience through it.

The idea behind Usenet is that people have topics they want to discuss, and they want to involve others from anywhere in the world in the discussion. Once you find a newsgroup you're interested in joining, you subscribe to it, then load a program called a *news reader* in order to read new messages. With these readers you can read every message in succession, or you can follow message *threads* (sub-topics) that you're especially interested in. At any point, you can post a reply to a message you've read, or you can start an entirely new discussion.

Usenet newsgroups are classified according to a grouping called hierarchies. In general, the hierarchies help you locate groups you're interested in. Some of the major categories are:

- `alt`: Topics about...well, you name it—UFOs, sex, TV, dogs...
- `bionet`: Topics appealing to biologists
- `bit`: BITNET mailing lists (usually mirrors of the Listserv versions)
- `biz`: Topics dealing with business, some on specific companies or products
- `clari`: Topics from ClariNet through the UPI wire service

- de: Newsgroups from Germany, often in German
- fr: Newsgroups from France, often in French
- k12: Topics appealing to users involved in K-12 education
- comp: Topics appealing to computer hobbyists and professionals
- misc: Topics not fitting into the other categories
- news: Topics regarding new Internet information and events
- rec: Topics appealing to hobbyists of all kinds
- sci: Science topics
- soc: Cultural and social topics
- talk: Topics lending themselves to debates

Usenet isn't carried by all Internet sites—and even where it is, some sites restrict access to certain hierarchies. It's not uncommon, for instance, to have Usenet access but no way of getting the alt groups. Talk with your systems people if you want hierarchies or newsgroups added for potential subscription.

Okay, so the Usenet is the means by which I can interact. How do I get there? This part is quite straightforward. Most Net providers use a newsreader program called *rn* or *trn*. Because of the popularity of these programs (they are available at a large percentage of sites), this chapter deals with them exclusively. Other readers are available for UNIX, Macs, PCs, and other platforms, but rn and trn are dominant.

The name rn stands for "Read News," while trn is "Threaded Read News." They are, in fact, the same program, but they differ in the way they present the various groups for your viewing.

The rn program is the bare-bones version that presents articles within each group as they are received. That is, in a newsgroup discussing American culture, article 231 could be about the growing problem of gun-based violence, while the next article, 232, could be a request for information on the annual Peach Festival in Georgia. Both articles have to do with American culture, and rn serves them up in chronological order. As explained later in this chapter, you can thread the groups, but you have to do so yourself.

On the other hand, trn offers threading, a very simple way to filter what you want to read from what you have no interest in. It lets you choose articles, based on their subject line, before you read and without having to wade through several (sometimes hundreds) of articles to find something of interest.

Warning: One thing you always have to remember about Usenet is that, for the most part, it is an unmoderated forum (especially in the `alt` groups; several `soc`, `comp`, and other groups are moderated). Unlike a newspaper or magazine, there is no editor to filter anything; anyone can (and, believe me, usually does) say what they like. You are your own editor on the Net, and using threading is one way to quickly learn to filter out the noise. Kill files (see later in this chapter) are another good way.

Excursion 4.4. Getting onto Newsgroups

Note: In this chapter, trn is used for all examples, but if your server has only rn, don't worry: First, bug your Systems Administrator for trn, and if that doesn't work, just get onto the groups as shown here. Things will be pretty much the same, except that you won't have automatic threading from the beginning.

To start, type **`trn`** at the UNIX prompt:

```
% trn
```

Because this is your first time, you probably won't be subscribed to any newsgroups, although some servers automatically subscribe you to local newsgroups of interest. Even if you have been pre-subscribed to a newsgroup, just follow along as if you get the following message:

```
No unread news in subscribed-to newsgroups.
To subscribe to a new newsgroup use the g<newsgroup> command.
****** End of newsgroups -- what next? [qnp]
```

Tip: At any time, if you forget what commands are available at any point, just press `h` for help. Also, trn usually will give you a choice of three or four of the most likely commands in square brackets: `[qnp]` means quit, next, or previous. Always remember that besides pressing the appropriate key, you can press the space bar to select the first item (in the preceding case, quit).

After pressing **h**, you'll get the following:

```
Newsgroup Selection commands:
t        Toggle the newsgroup between threaded and unthreaded reading.
c        Catch up (mark all articles as read).
A        Abandon read/unread changes to this newsgroup since you started trn.
n        Go to the next newsgroup with unread news.
N        Go to the next newsgroup.
p        Go to the previous newsgroup with unread news.
P        Go to the previous newsgroup.
-        Go to the previously displayed newsgroup.
1        Go to the first newsgroup.
^        Go to the first newsgroup with unread news.
$        Go to the last newsgroup.
g name   Go to the named newsgroup. Subscribe to new newsgroups this way too.
/pat     Search forward for newsgroup matching pattern.
?pat     Search backward for newsgroup matching pattern.
         (Use * and ? style patterns. Append r to include read newsgroups.)
l pat    List unsubscribed newsgroups containing pattern.
m name   Move named newsgroup elsewhere (no name moves current newsgroup).
o pat    Only display newsgroups matching pattern. Omit pat to unrestrict.
O pat    Like o, but skip empty groups.
a pat    Like o, but also scans for unsubscribed newsgroups matching pattern.
L        List current .newsrc.
&        Print current command-line switch settings.
         Set (or unset) more command-line switches.
&&       Print current macro definitions.
&&def    Define a new macro.
!cmd     Shell escape.
q        Quit trn.
x        Quit, restoring .newsrc to its state at startup of trn.
^K       Edit the global KILL file. Use commands like /pattern/j to suppress
         pattern in every newsgroup.
v        Print version and the address for reporting bugs.
```

Tip: This list is extremely useful, so it's probably a good idea to mark this page for future reference, but for now we need to find what's out there.

Press **l** to get a master list of all available newsgroups at your site. This list is extremely long, however, and contains several thousand groups from which to choose. If, at any time, you want to stop reading the list, Press Ctrl+C to escape back to the Newsgroups prompt.

Pressing **l** generates something looking like the following: (I have edited out most, but tried to keep a broad section of a variety of newsgroups types to give you an idea what's available.)

```
****** End of newsgroups -- what next? [qnp] l
Completely unsubscribed newsgroups:

ab.politics
advocacy
air.unix
alt.abortion.inequity
alt.activism
alt.activism.d
alt.activism.death-penalty
alt.adoption
alt.aldus.freehand
alt.aldus.misc
alt.aldus.pagemaker
alt.alien.visitors
alt.angst
alt.barney.dinosaur.die.die.die
alt.bbs
alt.bbs.ads
alt.binaries.pictures.cartoons
alt.binaries.pictures.d
alt.binaries.clip-art
alt.coffee
alt.current-events.bosnia
alt.current-events.clinton.whitewater
alt.current-events.flood-of-93
alt.current-events.la-quake
alt.current-events.somalia
alt.fan.dan-quayle
alt.fan.dave_barry
alt.fan.rush-limbaugh
alt.fishing
alt.sex
alt.tv.ren-n-stimpy
alt.tv.simpsons
bionet.genome.chromosomes
bionet.immunology
bionet.info-theory
bionet.jobs
bionet.journals.contents
bionet.neuroscience
bit.listserv.catholic
bit.listserv.cdromlan
bit.listserv.pagemakr
bit.listserv.tech-l
```

```
bit.listserv.tecmat-l
bit.listserv.tesl-l
bit.listserv.test
biz.books.technical
de.sci.electronics
de.soc.jugendarbeit
de.soc.weltanschauung
fr.news.distribution
fr.news.divers
k12.chat.elementary
k12.chat.junior
k12.chat.senior
k12.chat.teacher
misc.invest.real-estate
misc.invest.stocks
misc.jobs.contract
misc.jobs.misc
rec.arts.startrek.current
rec.aviation
rec.food.veg.cooking
rec.gambling
rec.humor.d
sci.med.dentistry
sci.med.nursing
soc.culture.burma
soc.culture.canada
soc.culture.jewish
soc.culture.usa

****** End of newsgroups -- what next? [qnp]
```

As you can see, there are newsgroups for pretty much every topic under the sun.

The first part of the newsgroup name gives an indication of the general category into which that newsgroup belongs (see the preceding list). By far the most diverse category (or *hierarchy*, in Usenet lingo) is the `alt` (alternative) hierarchy. This is the one you read about in *Time* and *Newsweek*. This is where you find the comical (`alt.humor`), the bizarre (`alt.barney.die.die.die`), and a mixture of both (`alt.jokes.tasteless`). This also is where you find the sexually oriented topics that cause frequent protests.

So, to avoid being offended, stick with groups you know are to your liking. `alt.fan.letterman` most likely will be about David Letterman (and rumors abound that he, himself, sometimes "lurks"—reads, but doesn't contribute); `alt.sex` probably is going to be discussions of a sexual nature. The ones that may surprise you are those with ambiguous names: `alt.motss` isn't about a brand of Clamato juice, but rather is an acronym for "members of the same sex."

After you decide on a couple of groups (best to start out with a few, as you always can add more later), just use the go command by typing **g** (see the preceding command list).

To subscribe to the group `alt.coffee` (presumably general discussions about the nectar of the gods), for example, type the following at the UNIX command prompt:

```
****** End of newsgroups -- what next? [qnp] g alt.coffee
```

Because you have never accessed the group before, you'll get the message

```
Newsgroup alt.coffee not in .newsrc—subscribe? [ynYN]
```

Don't worry about the capital letters just now, just press **y** and you'll get

```
====== 1068 unread articles in alt.coffee -- read now? [+ynq]
```

This means that you now are in the newsgroup `alt.coffee`. There are 1,068 articles that you personally have not read. You now have a choice. Press **q** to quit, **n** go to the next Newsgroup (but there aren't any yet) without reading this one, **y** start reading in chronological order, or **+** to see a threaded list of Subject lines.

Tip: For those without trn, rn will look exactly the same except there is no automatic threading. If you still want to view using subject threads, just press y to go to the first article, and then type **_t** to thread the group.

If you forget the commands, just press **h** to display the help list of commands within a Newsgroup.

So now, you want to display the threads available for viewing. Press **+** or the spacebar (since that's the first choice given in brackets).

```
====== 1068 unread articles in alt.coffee -- read now? [+ynq] +

Getting overview file..

alt.coffee          196 articles

a Alex Loukes        1  Caffeine's Frequently Asked Questions
b Alwyn Perland      3  >Essentials for Great Coffee!
  Tom Bridgeman
  Jonathan Linden
  John Calling       1  >Essentials for Great Coffee!(porcelain mellita)
d Sarah Rostern      1  >the enviro/social implications
e Matthew Murts      1  favorite bean
f Matthew Murts      1  >DUNKIN' DONUTS
g Matthew Murts      1  CNN & Coffee
i R B Whiteman       7  >Good cheep Coffee
```

```
  Cob
  Robert McDonald
  Tom Bridgeman
  Rosie
  Bob Banks
  Bob Banks
j Jaclyn Rand       3  >Starbuck's Rules!
  Jeanette Skeller
  David Feinstein

-- Select threads (date order) -- Top 9% [>Z] --
```

This screen means that within the newsgroup `alt.coffee`, 196 articles are available for viewing. Note that this is less than the 1,068 unread articles shown at the beginning. The reason for the difference is that most sites periodically purge older messages because of space considerations. Because the `alt.` groups tend to be thought of as being not as "serious" as some of the others, they tend to be purged more frequently. Some sites purge `alt.` messages more than two days old, others every week.

Of the articles available for you to read, this screen shows the first 9 percent (bottom right) according to the date in which the first article of the thread occurred. Thus, threads (which essentially are discussion lines) that have been ongoing for sometime will be shown first, with newer threads coming later.

The first article is a very important one. It is what is known as a *FAQ* (Frequently Asked Questions), and many newsgroups are set up to have their particular FAQ as the first article newcomers get (that is, it never gets purged). It's a good idea to read this post to get an idea of what the group is all about, as well as answer most questions you might have. The David Letterman FAQ, for example, gives details such as his birthday (12 April 1947), his route to stardom, and details of the woman who apparently thinks he's her husband and keeps breaking into his house.

Warning: Before doing anything else, be sure to read the FAQ! It will save you from asking a question that gets asked of the group every week (which is a good way to get flamed).

Notice that some of the thread subjects have a greater than sign > in front of them. This means that this is an older thread, and all the articles shown refer to a previous posting. Alwyn Perland (I've changed the names, although the group and all article subjects are genuine) didn't start the discussion on Essentials for Great Coffee, but he and the other two contributors to that thread are continuing the conversation.

New threads, such as CNN & Coffee, are not preceded by a >.

To view a particular thread, press the letter preceding it, or move the cursor down to it using the arrow keys and press **+**. To select the CNN & Coffee thread (here just a single article), press **g**. A + will appear next to it. If you change your mind and don't want to read that thread, deselect it by pressing the letter again. In this example, pressing **g** removes the +.

To get to more articles, press the space bar or the right arrow key.

```
alt.coffee           196 articles

a Stephen Jakes      1  >*** chemicals in flavored coffee?? ***
b Michael Shogan     1  >music with coffee
d Barry Jartolli     2  >Tanzania Peaberry Rules!
  Bob Barrie
e Barry Jartolli     3  >Where do you buy unroasted coffee (re:home roasting)
  Lawrence Graham
  Chris Pearl
f Barry Jartolli     2  >Iowa City coffee
  Sheila Mcdonald
g Barry Jartolli     1  >organic coffee
l John Arnold        1  >The Perfect Coffee House
o John Cherry        2  >Green Card Lottery- Final One?
  William Kolb

-- Select threads (date order) -- 15% [>Z] --
```

You now can see more of the 196 articles available (you've now viewed the first 15 percent). To select articles for viewing, type the appropriate letter.

> **Note:** You can't just select individual articles; you must select the thread. Thus you can't just view Sheila Mcdonald's post concerning Iowa City coffee, you have to look at Barry Jartolli's as well. But that's not a big problem: It's easy to skip through articles you want only to skim.

To view the articles in the selected threads press Enter at any time. I selected the Essentials for Great Coffee and CNN & Coffee threads, and came up with the following:

```
alt.coffee #938 (4 + 192 more)
From: aperland@kevin.seas.Berkeley.EDU (Alwyn Perland)
```

```
Re: Essentials for Great Coffee!
Organization: University of Berkeley
Date: Sun Mar 10 19:28:20 EDT 1994
Lines: 5
Anyone know where you can get a cone filter holder that's NOT made of
PLASTIC? My parents used to have a porcelain one, but glass would also be
OK.
alwyn
End of article 938 (of 1068) -- what next? [npq]
```

On this screen, I see the first article of the first thread is article 938 (in case I want to find it again). I have selected four articles and there are 192 more articles that I haven't selected yet.

On the last line I see that there have been 1,068 articles since the inception of the group. I'm also asked what I want to do next. Pressing `n` or the space bar will take me to the next selected article (the one by Todd Bridgeman). After that thread is finished, I will get to the next selected topic, CNN & Coffee.

Using trn enables you to concentrate on a single topic line (although, often there is some "topic drift" within a thread) without having to always think back, "now what was she referring to?". But sometimes, it still is hard to figure out what someone is referring to. That's why responses often have "included text" from the prior post:

```
alt.coffee #1037 (1 + 191 more)
From: jlinden@bill.com (Jonathan Linden)          Re: Essentials for Great Coffee!
Followup-To: alt.coffee

Date: Sat Mar 16 12:54:20 EDT 1994
Lines: 33

In article <CoB6vI.55L@ihs.com>, Alwyn Perland (aperland@kevin.seas.Berkeley.EDU)
wrote:

>  Anyone know where you can get a cone filter holder that's NOT
>made of PLASTIC? My parents used to have a porcelain one, but
>glass would also be OK.
I can think of two - Melitta (king of the plastic manual-fill drip maker)
makes a porcelain (is that spelled right?!) carafe/cone setup.  Very pretty
looking, I suspect they work great.
I suggest that, aesthetics aside, the plastic cone is superior. Problem with
the ceramic version is that it's quite massive, and is going to cool your hot
water much more than the plastic cone. It's prettier, sure, but more
functional? I think not.
--MORE--(66%)
```

This shows that Jonathan Linden is responding to Alwyn's request, and, to refresh people's memories (especially as this is five days after the original post), he includes part of Alwyn's post (lines preceded by >). Some readers, use a colon instead.

Because there is some included text, the post doesn't fit on a single screen. The `--MORE--(66%)` tells you that there is more to the post and that you have already seen 66 percent of it. If you want to view the rest of the post, press the space bar; if you don't want to view anymore, press `n` to go to the next article.

Tip: Press **n** to go to the next article; you don't need to scroll through an entire post before going on. This especially is useful as with some groups, whole programs and magazine texts can be posted.

Note also in the preceding articles that the author of the article (as well as the author of any included text) is shown in one of the *headers*. A header is shown at the top of the article and gives subject, author, date and, usually, the number of lines in the post. These can be used to send mail directly to an author (especially useful if you're shy about posting to the group).

After you have read all selected articles, you'll be returned to the list of threads. If you want to read more, select threads as before and continue. If nothing strikes your fancy, and you want to discard the remaining threads (who wants to wade through old stuff every time?), press **c** to "catch up"; this tells trn that you don't want to see those postings again.

```
alt.coffee          191 articles

a Fred Duckman      1  There's still a city without Starbuck's (thank goodness)
b Fred Duckman      1  SEND US YOUR FAVORITE CAFES!
d K.R.              1  Chickory (sp?)
e Steven Munk       2  Yet Another Mail-Order Coffee place
  Bobby Bittman

-- Select threads (date order) -- Bot [Z>] --
```

Press **c**.

```
Do you really want to mark everything as read? [yn]  y

****** End of newsgroups -- what next? [npq]
```

Now, let's go back to the newsgroup list and get another group. This time, however, you don't want to scroll through thousands of groups, you just want to get those groups having to do with culture. To do this, type **l culture**.

```
****** End of newsgroups -- what next? [npq] l culture
```

And up comes any group with the string "culture" in it (including such things as "agriculture"):

```
Completely unsubscribed newsgroups:
alt.culture.hawaii
alt.culture.indonesia
alt.culture.kerala
alt.culture.ny-upstate
alt.culture.oregon
alt.culture.tamil
alt.culture.us.asian-indian
resif.culture
sci.agriculture
soc.culture.afghanistan
soc.culture.burma
soc.culture.canada
soc.culture.caribbean
soc.culture.celtic
soc.culture.german
soc.culture.greek
soc.culture.hongkong.entertainment
soc.culture.indian
soc.culture.indian.american
soc.culture.soviet
soc.culture.uruguay
soc.culture.usa
soc.culture.venezuela
soc.culture.vietnamese
soc.culture.yugoslavia
trial.soc.culture.czechoslovak
trial.soc.culture.italian
```

A lot of groups have to do with culture (I've edited the list for space), but the one that strikes me as interesting right now is `soc.culture.usa`, presumably about American culture.

To get there, type **g soc.culture.usa**, and press **y** (yes) when asked if you want to subscribe:

```
****** End of newsgroups -- what next? [npq] g soc.culture.usa
Newsgroup soc.culture.usa not in .newsrc -- subscribe? [ynYN]  y
```

Now, because this is not my first newsgroup, I'm asked where I want to put this new group:

```
Put newsgroup where? [$^Lq]
```

What this means is that I am being given the choice of where in my list of subscribed groups I want to put `soc.culture.usa`. Do I want to read this group first whenever I invoke trn? Last? Somewhere in the middle (assuming I am on several groups)?

Since I (honestly) can never remember what my choices are, I'll press **h** for help:

```
Type ^ to put the newsgroup first (position 0).
Type $ to put the newsgroup last (position 2).
Type . to put it before the current newsgroup (position 2).
Type -newsgroup name to put it before that newsgroup.
Type +newsgroup name to put it after that newsgroup.
Type a number between 0 and 2 to put it at that position.
Type L for a listing of newsgroups and their positions.
Type q to abort the current action.
```

In my case I have about 15 groups I subscribe to, so I can place any new group near other similar groups (I keep all my science groups together, all my investment groups, and so on). Really, though, it doesn't matter much, so let's put this group last.

```
Put newsgroup where? [$^Lq] $
===== 25634 unread articles in soc.culture.usa -- read now? [+ynq]
```

I now see that there are a total of 25,634 articles in the group. Remember, however, that this is a total number, and groups usually get purged, leaving probably a few hundred articles).

Pressing the spacebar or **+** displays the now familiar thread list:

```
Getting overview file.....
soc.culture.usa          486 articles

a Michael Peters    1  >what tourist crime victims can expect in Texas
b Steven Rose       1  Gun deaths scoreboard, latest score??
d jlam@salty.nbc    3  >Whack the Whole Family, Not Just the Boy
  Karen Flute
  Catherine T Beck
e Steven Shoup      1  >NYT Mag: "The History of a Hoax"

-- Select threads (date order) -- Top 1% [>Z] --
```

You now can select threads as before by pressing the letter next to the thread, catch up all articles by pressing **c**, or press **q** to quit and leave the list intact.

Excursion 4.5. International Newsgroups

Like many other things on the Internet, most newsgroups originate in the U.S. Increasingly, however, other nations are offering their own. The following is a partial listing of a variety of international newsgroups that you may wish to take part in. Note, however, that your local site may not carry all these groups.

Australia:

```
aus.acs
aus.ads.commercial
aus.ads.forsale
aus.ads.jobs
aus.ads.wanted
aus.aswec
aus.cdrom
aus.comms.fps
aus.comms.videocon
aus.computers.ai
aus.computers.amiga
aus.computers.cdrom
aus.computers.linux
aus.education.rpl
aus.flame
```

Chile:

```
chile.anuncios
chile.chile-l
chile.chilenet
chile.ciencia-ficcion
chile.comp.mac
chile.comp.pc
chile.comp.sun
chile.compraventas
chile.consultas
chile.economia
chile.futbol
chile.grupos
chile.humor
chile.trabajos
chile.uucp
chile.varios
```

Germany:

```
de.admin.archiv
de.admin.news.groups
de.admin.news.misc
de.alt.buecher
de.alt.comm.mgetty
de.comp.sys.amiga.advocacy
de.comp.sys.amiga.archive
de.comp.sys.amiga.chat
de.comp.sys.amiga.misc
de.markt
de.markt.jobs
de.markt.misc
```

Finland:

```
finet.atk.kielet
finet.koti.tee-se-itse
finet.koulutus.opintotuki
finet.kulttuurit.venaja
finet.kulttuurit.viro
finet.markkinat.kaupalliset
finet.markkinat.pc
finet.politiikka.yk
finet.uutiset.baltia
finet.viestinta.bbs
finet.viestinta.freenet
finet.yhteiskunta.anarkismi
```

France:

```
fr.announce.divers
fr.announce.important
fr.announce.newgroups
fr.announce.newusers
fr.announce.seminaires
fr.bio.biolmol
fr.bio.general
fr.bio.genome
fr.bio.logiciel
fr.network.modems
fr.news.8bits
fr.news.distribution
```

```
fr.news.divers
fr.news.groups
fr.rec.cuisine
fr.rec.divers
fr.rec.genealogie
fr.rec.humour
fr.rec.oracle
fr.rec.sport
fr.res-doct.archi
fr.sci.automatique
fr.sci.cogni.outil
```

The Netherlands:

```
nlnet.comp
nlnet.culinair
nlnet.misc
nlnet.sport
nlnet.taal
nlnet.tv
```

Excursion 4.6. Unsubscribing to a Newsgroup

If, after looking at a group, you decide that it's not for you, you can unsubscribe very easily. Just press `u` when in the group. To unsubscribe to `soc.culture.usa`, for example:

```
===== 486 unread articles in soc.culture.usa -- read now? [+ynq] u
Unsubscribed to newsgroup soc.culture.usa
```

And if you want to go back to it, you can always resubscribe:

```
****** End of newsgroups -- what next? [npq] g soc.culture.usa

Newsgroup soc.culture.usa is unsubscribed -- resubscribe? [yn]  y

====== 486 unread articles in soc.culture.usa -- read now? [+ynq]
```

Notice that you don't see the 25,000 articles you did when you first subscribed. This is because the system remembers that you have already been there once (it asked if you wanted to resubscribe, right?), and has already "caught up" any purged articles, as well as any articles you may have read the first time.

Excursion 4.7. Saving an Article

Sometimes you may read a post you want to save for later, either to print or to keep on file for future reference. To do this, press s (for save) at anytime while viewing an article (you don't have to be at the end of the post). If you press Enter immediately after pressing s, the post will be saved to a file in your News directory with the name of the newsgroup. Thus, if you wanted to save an article you liked on the `alt.coffee` newsgroup, press **s** and Enter while viewing the article and you will be prompted as follows:

```
From: Keber@freenet.Waterloo.ON.CA (James Keber)

Subject: thoughts...
Date: Mon Mar 18 11:57:55 EDT 1994
Lines: 13


The sound of birds outside my window,
My love is grinding the beans,
That first refreshing cup of Starbucks,
The first Sunday of Spring

--
End of article 1068 (of 1068) -- what next? [npq] s
```

trn then tells you that the file doesn't exist, and asks in what form ("mailbox" or "file") you want it created. Press **n**. (Mailbox format just has more information in the headers it saves and isn't very useful.)

```
File /u2/slindsay/News/alt.coffee doesn't exist--
use mailbox format? [ynq] n

Saved to file /u2/slindsay/News/alt.coffee
```

The next time you want to save an article on the `alt.coffee` newsgroup and press **s** and Enter, trn will automatically append the post to the end of the file `alt.coffee`. This is a good way to keep an archive of useful information from a particular group. If, however, you wanted to save the post to a file of its own, rather than pressing **s** and then Enter, type **s *filename*** and then press Enter. This saves the post to a file of that name.

```
End of article 1068 (of 1068) -- what next? [npq] s coffee.poem

File /u2/slindsay/News/coffee.poem doesn't exist--
```

```
use mailbox format? [ynq] n

Saved to file /u2/slindsay/News/coffee.poem
```

You can find the file in the News directory. You also can append other poems to this file by typing **s coffee.poem**. I use this to save interesting FTP sites (see Day 6) that people occasionally post to a newsgroup. If you type **s site**, the post is appended to your site file. Note that this works from any newsgroup—you can save a post from alt.coffee in coffee.poem and then append a post from soc.culture.usa automatically by typing **s coffee.poem**.

Saving and Using Binary Files

Most posts on newsgroups are text files (such as those you have looked at up to now). But program and other executable files also can be posted to the Net. Such groups as comp.lang.c++ have a lot of C++ programming language files.

Binary files, however, cannot be posted as is to the Net, because newsgroups can handle only text or ASCII type files. In order to be posted to a newsgroup, a binary file first must be coded into a text file. In order to use such a post, you save it to a file as usual and then decode it.

Most UNIX systems have the capability to code and decode files using UUencode/ UUdecode. These programs also are available for DOS PCs and can be found by doing an Archie search (see Day 6).

I subscribe to the newsgroup alt.binaries.clip-art. UUencoded files of various types of clip art (line drawings that can be used in desktop publishing) are posted daily. I also can post a request for a particular type of picture that I need and someone will usually post it within a short time.

To view a binary picture, first go to the newsgroup as before by typing **g alt.binaries.clip-art.**

```
====== 25 unread articles in alt.binaries.clip-art read now? [+ynq]  y


Article 479 of alt.binaries.clip-art:
Xref: watserv2.uwaterloo.ca alt.binaries.clip-art:479
Newsgroups: alt.binaries.clip-art
From: jeffc@pcu.teary.com (Jeff Cantor)
Subject: PCX Clip Art: giraffe 1/1
Date: Mon, 18 Mar 1994 03:45:24 GMT
Lines: 509
```

```
This is a hi-quality PCX of a giraffe

section 1 of uuencode 5.22 of file big_neck.pcx    by R.E.M.

begin 644 big_neck.pcx
M"@(!'0""'_'L\""""""""""""""""""""""""
M"""""""""""""""'!2"!""""""""""""""""
M""""""""""""""""""""""""""""""#__\C_P?__
M_\C_P?___\C_P?___\C_P?___\C_P?___\C_P?___\C_P?___\C_P?___\C_
MP?___\C_P?___\C_P?___\C_P?___\C_P?___\C_P?___\C_P?___\C_P?__
M_\C_P?___\C_P?___\C_P?___\C_P?___\C_P?___\C_P?___\C_P?___\C_
MP?___\C_P?___\C_P?___\C_P?___\C_P?___\C_P?___\C_P?___\C_P?__
M_\C_P?___\C_P?___\C_P?___\C_P?___\C_P?___\C_P?___\C_P?___\C_
MP?___\C_P?___\C_P?_0_\'_P=_U_\'_T/_!_Y?U_\'_T/_!_Y?U_\'_T/_!
M_YGU_\'_T/_!_Y'"_\'_P</Q_\'_T/_!_YS"_\'_!O'_P?_0_\'_A,+_P?\&
M\?_!_]#_P?_!UG_!_\'^'#_P_\'_T/_!_\'6?\'_P?X'/_#_P?_0_\'_P<(?
MP?_!_@!\?^__P?_0_\'_P=H?P?_!_0!\/^__P?_0_\'_P<+!S\'_P?@'P?@'
M[__!_]#_P?_!PT?!_\'X'<'X'^__P?_0_\'_P<!#P?_!^''!\''O_\'_T/_!
M_\'(8<'_P?@!P?`![__!_]#_P?_!P'#!_\'X`\'@`^__P?_0_\'_P<"PP?_!
M^'?!X@?O_\'_T/_!_\'(DG_!X'?!P'?O_\'_T/_!_\'MFC_!X'?!P'_O_\'_
MT/_!_\'@'!_!P'^''^__P?_0_\'_P>"'X'?@!_O_\'_T/_!_\'P3@^"'P@_
—MORE—01%
```

Believe it or not, that is a picture of a giraffe! It is a UUencoded version (you can tell if a file is UUencoded by looking for the M at the beginning of each line) of a file called `big_neck.pcx`. (Look after the `begin 644`—this is a UUdecode command line). So I know that this is a picture of a giraffe in .pcx format. There are several graphics formats, the most common being `.jpg` (JPEG), `.gif` (GIF), `.tif` (TIFF) and `.pcx` (PCX). You need a special viewer for each type (although some viewers can handle several types), but PCX files are pretty easy to view, as the Windows Paintbrush can use them. (TIFF files, by the way, are used by several fax programs, such as Eclipse Fax.)

To save this post to a file, type **`s giraffe`**.

> **Tip:** You may not have to do all this work. Your version of trn or rn may well support the `e` command, which means *extract*. Extract will look for a uuencoded binary within the posting, then automatically uudecode it and save it to your disk. In some cases you'll get binary files that are sent in several parts, and extract can handle these as well. Try it.

```
End of article 479 (of 504) -- what next? [npq] s giraffe

File /u2/slindsay/News/giraffe doesn't exist--
```

```
use mailbox format? [ynq] n

Saved to file /u2/slindsay/News/giraffe
```

Then exit trn by pressing **q**, and change to your News directory.

```
@watarts[102]% cd News
```

To show the files in that directory, type **ls**.

```
@watarts[103]% ls

alt.coffee  coffee.poem  giraffe  site
```

The list includes all your saved posts (the two coffee posts from earlier in the chapter), as well as your *site* file of good FTP sites posted in newsgroups.

To decode the giraffe file—reconvert it from a text file into a binary—type **uudecode giraffe**.

```
@watarts[104]% uudecode giraffe
@watarts[105]%
```

Notice that, unlike DOS, UNIX doesn't tell you if the procedure was successful. It will tell you if there is a problem, so, with UNIX, no news is good news.

Typing `ls` again shows the new addition to your directory:

```
@watarts[105]% ls

alt.coffee  big_neck.pcx  coffee.poem  giraffe  site
```

The `.pcx` file already is there to download to your PC using XModem or Kermit (see Day 6). But what about the `giraffe` text file? Because I've decoded it, I have no real use for it anymore. To delete it, type **rm giraffe**. (`rm`, for "remove," performs the same action as does the DOS `DEL` command).

```
@watarts[106]%rm giraffe
```

It's now gone, but you have the binary picture to enjoy and use.

Excursion 4.8. Posting to a Newsgroup

You now can access newsgroups, save messages, and even act as a sort of editor, filtering through the seemingly unending posts to what interests you. Now you want to get in on the action, to contribute to the conversation, or, to use Net-speak, "exit lurker mode."

There are two ways to post to a newsgroup, either by using the program Postnews, or by responding to a post while reading a newsgroup. Both ways are quite straightforward.

Reading the posts I selected earlier from the `alt.coffee` newsgroup, I noticed one I wanted to respond to:

```
alt.coffee #990
From: mmurts@clear.norman.edu (Matthew Murts)

Date: Mon Mar 11 13:41:04 EDT 1994
Lines: 10

        Today (March 11) CNN ran a story on the rebirth (or so they say) of
coffee drinking. They had the owner/ Pres./ head of Coffee Connection on
the story talking about business and a bunch of people explaining their
addiction. Check it out if you wish...it'll probably be on during the day.
```

To respond to this article while reading it, press **F** (Shift+F—press **h** for a list of commands if you forget):

```
End of article 990 (of 1068) -- what next? [npq] F
```

Be sure to double-check the attribution against the signature and trim the quoted article down as much as possible.

```
(leaving cbreak mode; cwd=/u2/slindsay/News)
Invoking command: QUOTECHARS='>' Pnews -h /u2/slindsay/.rnhead



This program posts news to thousands of machines throughout the entire
civilized world. Your message will cost the net hundreds if not thousands
of dollars to send everywhere. Please be sure you know what you are doing.

Are you absolutely sure that you want to do this? [ny] y

Prepared file to include [none]:
```

If you have composed a response in your word processor and saved it as a text or ASCII file, you can include it by typing the filename here. Otherwise, press Enter.

```
"/u2/slindsay/.article" 26 lines, 633 characters
Newsgroups: alt.coffee
Subject: Re: CNN & Coffee
Summary:
Expires:
Sender:
Followup-To:
Distribution:
Organization: University of Waterloo
Keywords:
Cc:

In article <1994Mar11.174104.28707@orlith.norman.edu>,
From: mmurts@clear.norman.edu (Matthew Murts) wrote:
>
>
>Today (April 11) CNN ran a story on the rebirth (or so they say) of
>coffee drinking. They had the owner/ Pres./ head of Coffee Connection on
>the story talking about business and a bunch of people explaining their
>addiction. Check it out if you wish...it'll probably be on during the day.
>
```

Just like when creating a kill file, trn brings you to vi editor to work. (You can ask your systems administrator for a list of vi commands—most will be able to provide one.)

The vi editor is loaded with a copy of the post I want to respond to. If the post is long, it's always a good idea to trim excessive included text (as the editor asked you to do previously). To do this, move the cursor to a line you want to delete and press `d` twice. This will delete that line. To create space after the current line, press `o` (or `O` if you want the open line before the current line).

Trimming included text is an important part of netiquette. Including a hundred lines of a previous post and then adding a one line response uses up considerable resources, and is a quick way to get yourself "flamed" (see later in this chapter for other "flame-bait").

Moving the cursor below the included text, press **`i`** to enter Insert mode and start typing a message.

Note: It is very important to remember that vi, although powerful and useful, is much more primitive than word processors such as Microsoft Word and WordPerfect. Unlike other word processors, in vi, you have to press Enter at the end of each line (just like using a typewriter—remember those?).

```
"/u2/slindsay/.article" 26 lines, 633 characters
Newsgroups: alt.coffee
Subject: Re: CNN & Coffee
Summary:
Expires:
Sender:
Followup-To:
Distribution:
Organization: University of Waterloo
Keywords:
Cc:

In article <1994Mar11.174104.28707@norman.edu>,
From: mmurts@clear.norman.edu (Matthew Murts) wrote:
>
>
>  Today (April 11) CNN ran a story on the rebirth (or so they say) of
>coffee drinking. They had the owner/ Pres./ head of Coffee Connection on
>the story talking about business and a bunch of people explaining their
>addiction. Check it out if you wish...it'll probably be on during the day.


I really enjoyed the story, but am unfamiliar with Coffee Connection - Is
it a national Chain or localized? And is the "rebirth" of coffee a West
Coast thing as many say, or is it as strong in the East (where I am in the
East, coffee houses are booming, but is it as strong as out West?)

Cheers,
Stew
******************************
```

To exit Insert mode, press Esc and then press **Z** twice. vi answers with

```
What now?  [send, edit, list, quit, write]
```

You now can choose any of the choices by typing it and pressing Enter. I usually list my posts to review them before posting.

When you're ready, type **send** to post your response.

```
What now?  [send, edit, list, quit, write] send
```

You now are returned to trn at the point from which you left.

The other way to post an article, either starting a new thread or responding to a previous article, is to type **postnews** at the UNIX prompt:

```
@watarts[101]% postnews
Is this message in response to some other message? y
```

If you are starting a new thread, press n for no. Because you are responding to an article, however, press **y**.

Postnews asks for the newsgroup to post to:

```
In what newsgroup was the article posted? alt.coffee
```

Remember that articles are purged periodically. Postnews tells you what article numbers are valid and then asks for the article number to which you want to respond:

```
Valid article numbers are from 873 to 1068

What was the article number? 990

article /usr/spool/news/alt/coffee/990
From: mmurts@abacus.bates.edu (Matthew Murts)
Subject: CNN & Coffee
Is this the one you want? y
```

This is the one I want, so I press **y** for yes.

```
Do you want to include a copy of the article? y
```

If you answer yes to this question, Postnews will include the entire article you are responding to and asks you to trim the text:

```
OK, but please edit it to suppress unnecessary verbiage, signatures, etc.
```

You now are taken into vi in the same way as when you responded while reading the newsgroup. Posting proceeds in the same way, except that when finished, you return to the UNIX prompt.

Summary

Newsgroups and mailing lists enable you to communicate with people who share your interests and concerns, on both a personal and a professional level. Using mailing lists requires little more than a knowledge of your e-mail program, but newgroup participation means learning some new software. Still, they're well worth the effort if you want to see the Internet at its best, as a global communications tool with thousands of interested participants.

Task Review

On Day 4, you learned to perform the following tasks:

- ☐ Locate mailing lists.
- ☐ Subscribe to mailing lists.
- ☐ Post to a mailing list.
- ☐ Understand mailing list etiquette.
- ☐ Access newsgroups using rn and trn.
- ☐ Read posts on selected newsgroups.
- ☐ Post to a newsgroup—contributing to the conversation.

Q&A

Q I'm ready to post to a newsgroup but am still a little unsure of myself. What sort of things should I avoid when posting? Are there any big no-nos?

A Good question, and one that far too few people ask. Yes, there are definitely several things to watch out for when posting. In order to avoid being "flamed" (or insulted), try to remember that you are talking to *people.* Many people on the Net get caught up with themselves being (often) alone in the safety of their home, and they think they can say just about anything with impunity. While this is largely true (flames won't actually hurt if you are thick-skinned), but you must remember that you aren't completely anonymous, and are still subject to laws of libel, slander, and copyright. Other than these legal caveats, there are things you can do to ensure relatively smooth posting. On the other hand, speaking from personal experience, there are several things you can do that will get you flamed.

Q When reading a particular article in trn or rn, I find that I want to go to another article. How do I get there?

A If you currently are reading article 2768, for example, and you remember from a previous session an interesting post (that you forgot to save, shame on you). To get to it, you can press `P` (Shift+P) to move backward one article (by number, not thread), or, if you know the article number (2699, for example), type the number and press Enter. You'll see the following:

```
End of article 2768 (of 3019)—what next? [npq] 2699
```

This takes you to article 2699. Moving forward, without losing intervening articles, also is possible.

Q Can I start my own mailing list?

A Yes, but it takes planning. You'll need to work with your Systems Administrator, who can establish a location for the list and ensure that the Listserv software is available and working. You'll also need to set aside a few hours a week for administrative functions; as "listowner," you'll have to moderate, deal with glitches and irate (or just confused) subscribers, and keep on top of cross-postings and other good and bad possibilities. I've never been a listowner; others, however, tell me it's interesting and enjoyable, but occasionally it can be intrusive and thankless.

5

WEEK 1

A Rodent to the Rescue: The Indispensable Gopher

Day 5 introduces you to Gopher, the multi-purpose browsing and searching system that has quickly become one of the Internet's most important and versatile tools. Through Gopher you can move quickly from computer to computer across the entire Net, viewing and downloading information as you discover it. The resources available via Gopher are many, and more significantly, they're extremely easy to access.

On Day 5 you'll:

- Enter and explore a sample Gopher site.
- Download, save, and mail files from Gophers.
- Bookmark your favorite Gopher sites.
- Explore a number of specific sites in the United States and beyond.

Let Gopher Lead the Way

The Internet is a big place. So big, in fact, that a variety of software has been developed to help you find your way around. One of the foremost programs, and the one with which you should become familiar before anything else, is Gopher.

Gopher isn't really a tool. Instead, it's a combination of tools. Gopher provides links to files and directories at local and remote machines alike, and it essentially hides all the details from you (unless you specifically request them). That's what makes Gopher so effortless to use. Instead of using FTP commands to retrieve a file (see Day 6), you can simply Gopher to the site, select the file, and download it to your hard drive.

One of the nicest things about using Gopher is that you don't have to remember Internet addresses and the like. As soon as you find a local Gopher, you can usually work your way all around the Internet from that original site. In this chapter, we'll start at the University of Chicago's main Gopher, then move from there to a variety of different Gophers.

Excursion 5.1. Entering a Gopher Site

To get to a Gopher site, type **`gopher`** and the Internet address of a Gopher site. In the following example, the specified host was the University of Chicago, `uic.edu`.

> **Tip:** On many systems, it's not even necessary to go this far. When you log in, try typing **`gopher`** by itself (followed by Enter, of course). If the system has a local Gopher set up, and a great many do, you'll be presented with its menu.

```
$ gopher uic.edu
```

It's as simple as that. A few seconds later, we get the following menu:

```
1.  Gopher at UIC/ADN/
2.  What's New (18 Apr 1994).
3.  Search the UIC Campus and Beyond/
4.  The Administrator/
5.  The Campus/
6.  The Classroom/
7.  The Community/
8.  The Computer/
9.  The Library/
10. The Researcher/
11. The World/
```

Excursion 5.2. Selecting a Menu Item

This is what all Gophers basically look like. It's a list with each item pointing to a file or another site. In this case, let's select item 11, The World. We can do so either by cursoring down to the item and pressing Enter, or by typing the item number and pressing Enter. (On some graphical Gophers, you can double-click on the item with your mouse.)

Note: On a Gopher menu, you'll see a variety of line endings. The main ones are the following:

/	A directory; selecting this item will take you to another menu of choices.
.	A file available for viewing or downloading.
<?>	A database; prompts with a search box.
<TEL>	A Telnet site; you will exit Gopher and start a Telnet session.
<CSO>	An Internet phone book; enables searches for specific users.

An item like The World exists on practically every Gopher server. Its purpose is to move you beyond the local Gopher and into links with Gophers in other places. This one following offers a number of choices, including subject, location, and phonebook directories. Note that item 5 is a text file we could read by selecting, while the rest point to other directories. We'll see what else is available in Illinois by choosing item 1.

```
1.  Other Illinois Gophers/
2.  University of Minnesota/
3.  CICnet Gopher/
4.  Library of Congress (LC MARVEL)/
5.  The Internet Mall.
6.  Netnews: Usenet, news services, etc (local access only)/
7.  United States Government gophers/
8.  Veronica - Netwide Gopher Title Index/
9.  Gopher Jewels/
10. The World By Subject (from Rice)/
11. The World by Location (from Minnesota)/
12. The World By Phonebook (from Notre Dame)/
```

Excursion 5.3. Moving Back up to the Previous Menu

```
                       Other Illinois Gophers

  1.  Administrative Information Systems and Services (AISS)/
  2.  Bradley University/
  3.  Board of Governors Universities (CSU, EIU, GSU, NEIU, WIU)/
  4.  Illinois State University/
  5.  Loyola University Chicago/
  6.  Northern Illinois University/
  7.  Northwestern University/
  8.  University of Chicago/
  9.  University of Illinois College of Medicine at Peoria Gopher/
 10.  University of Illinois at Urbana-Champaign/

Press ? for Help, q to Quit, u to go up a menu           Page: 1/1
```

Here's the result of the Illinois Gopher selection. Interesting later, maybe, but there were so many other tempting items on the previous menu. Note the line below the Gopher (bolded here). We could press **?** to get help (this is easy—why bother?), or **q** to quit Gopher completely, or **u** to move back to the previous menu. Let's do the latter.

Excursion 5.4. Paging Through Long Gopher Lists

It took us back to the previous menu (shown in Excursion 5.2). The next interesting item is United States Government Gophers. Nice to know the government is taking part in all of this.

```
     United States Government gophers

 1.  Call for assistance....
 2.  POLITICS and GOVERNMENT/
 3.  Definition of a "United States Government Gopher".
 4.  Federal Government Information (via Library of Congress)/
 5.  LEGI-SLATE Gopher Service (via UMN)/ /
 6.  AVES: Bird Related Information/
 7.  Americans Communicating Electronically/
 8.  Arkansas-Red River Forecast Center (NOAA)/
 9.  AskERIC - (Educational Resources Information Center)/
10.  CYFERNet  USDA Children Youth Family Education Research Network/
11.  Co-operative Human Linkage Center (CHLC) Gopher/
12.  Comprehensive Epidemiological Data Resource (CEDR) Gopher/
13.  Defense Technical Information Center Public Gopher/
14.  ERIC Clearinghouse for Science, Math, Environmental (OSU)/
15.  ERIC Clearinghouse on Assessment and Evaluation/
16.  ESnet Information Services Gopher/
17.  Electronic Government Information Service/
18.  Environment, Safety & Health (USDE) Gopher/

Press ? for Help, q to Quit, u to go up a menu               Page: 1/7
```

Ah-ha! Our first full screen of choices. Not only is the government involved, but there are 18 choices here, most of which point to other sites. No, wait, there are more than 18. This list only goes alphabetically as far as E.

Notice the bottom line again. At the far right is a page reference, showing the page number you're currently on and the total number of pages in this menu. Hmmm...there's over a hundred items here, so why not browse before choosing one?

Although it doesn't say so on the menu, pressing the spacebar takes you to the next screen, and pressing the hyphen key (-) takes you back up a screen.

Warning: Don't confuse the hyphen key with the **u** (up) key. Often—very often, in fact—you'll wait a minute or so for a long Gopher menu to appear, spacebar down a few pages, then press the u key when you meant to press the hyphen to move up a page. The result? You're back to the previous menu, completely out of the list you spent so long retrieving. It's enough to drive you to Gophercide.

Excursion 5.5. Working with Files

Back to The World menu again (by using the **u** key). This time, we'll select item 9, the fascinatingly named Gopher Jewels.

> **Note:** Gopher Jewels is listed on many, many Gophers, and it's well worth visiting regularly. It's continually being updated, and it's the best source of complete Gopher information.

The second page of Gopher Jewels looks (in part) like this:

```
                    Gopher Jewels

19. Environment/
20. Federal Agency and Related Gopher Sites/
21. Free-Nets And Other Community Or State Gophers/
22. Fun Stuff & Multimedia/
23. General Reference Resources/
24. Geography/
25. Geology and Oceanography/
26. Global or World-Wide Topics/
27. Grants/
28. History/
29. Internet Cyberspace related/
30. Internet Resources by Type (Gopher, Phone, USENET, WAIS, Other)//
```

Having already become entranced by the Internet, why not see what's available in item 29, Internet Cyberspace related. At the very least, it sounds interesting. Here's a portion of what we get.

```
            Internet Cyberspace related

19. InterNIC: Internet Network Information Center/
20. International Telecommunication Union (ITU) Gopher/
21. Internet Society (includes IETF)/
22. Internet Wiretap (Cyberspace)/
23. MFJ Task Force/
24. MIT, Digital Information Infrastructure Guide/
25. Matrix Information and Directory Services, Inc. (MIDS), Austin, TX/
```

No question here. Internet Wiretap (Cyberspace) sounds irresistible, so let's resist no longer.

```
    Internet Wiretap (Cyberspace)

1.  A Cynic Looks at Moo.
2.  Cardozo Law Forum Article on Neidorf.
3.  Case for Telecommunications Deregulation.
4.  Common BBS Acronyms.
5.  Computer Underground (Meyer & Thomas).
6.  Concerning Hackers who Break into Systems.
7.  Crypto Anarchist Manifesto.
8.  Cyberpunk From Subculture To Mainstream.
```

Fascinating stuff. All of them are text files, so let's pick one to read. Following is a short paragraph from Concerning Hackers who Break into Systems.

```
From such a profile I expect to be able to construct a picture of
the discourses in which hacking takes place. By a discourse I mean
the invisible background of assumptions that transcends individuals
—More— (5%) [Hit space to continue, Del to abort]
```

Notice the last line on the screen. We've seen only 5 percent of the article (that is, there are 20 more screens to read), and we have no time to read it now. The instructions say we can use the spacebar to get the next screen, or the Delete key to abort.

Once again, Gopher's little help menus aren't fully helpful. In fact, there's another important option. By pressing the **q** key (for Quit), we receive the following menu at the bottom of the screen:

```
Press <RETURN> to continue,
   <m> to mail, <D> to download, <s> to save, or <p> to print:
```

Warning: This menu is confusing in one important regard. Pressing **<RETURN>** (or Enter) doesn't actually do what it says. You'd expect to be able to continue reading the article, but in fact pressing Enter takes you back to menu where you found the article title in the first place. In the case of long files, this can be an extremely frustrating choice. There is, in fact, no way of continuing to read the article at this point.

This menu offers us the following choices:

<RETURN>	Go back to previous menu.
<m>	Mail the document to an account (your own, for example).
<D>	Download the file (Note: This is Shift+D, not just d).
<s>	Save the file to your account's hard disk.
<p>	Print the file to the specified printer.

The first file option is to mail it to an account. This is especially useful if you want someone else to have a copy, or if you're accustomed to working with files on a particular account of your own. The following example shows the file being mailed to my main account, accomplished by typing the *full* address into the box.

```
      1.  A Cynic Looks at Moo.
      2.  Cardozo Law Forum Article on Neidorf.
      3.  Case for Telecommunications Deregulation.
      4.  Common BBS Acronyms.
 +------------------------------------------------------------------------------+
 |                                                                              |
 | Mail current document to:  nrandall@watserv1.uwaterloo.ca                    |
 |                                                                              |
 |                                              [Cancel ^G] [Accept - Enter]    |
 |                                                                              |
 |                                                                              |
 +------------------------------------------------------------------------------+
      12. GAO report on Computer Security.
      13. Internet Connectivity in Eastern Europe.
      14. JP Barlow: Crime and Puzzlement.
```

Another choice is save the account on your hard drive. This means, in almost all cases, that it will be saved as a file on the machine holding the UNIX account itself, not on your own home computer (if you're working from home). You can accomplish the latter through the download feature. The following example shows the filename suggested by the save feature; you can edit it to say whatever you want (within the UNIX filename restrictions).

```
      1.  A Cynic Looks at Moo.
      2.  Cardozo Law Forum Article on Neidorf.
      3.  Case for Telecommunications Deregulation.
      4.  Common BBS Acronyms.
 +------------------------------------------------------------------------------+
 |                                                                              |
 | Save in file:   Concerning-Hackers-who-Break-into-Systems                    |
 |                                                                              |
 |                                              [Cancel ^G] [Accept - Enter]    |
 |                                                                              |
 +------------------------------------------------------------------------------+
```

```
        12. GAO report on Computer Security.
        13. Internet Connectivity in Eastern Europe.
        14. JP Barlow: Crime and Puzzlement.
        15. James Joyce and the Prehistory of Cyberspace.
```

Because printing varies so much from machine to machine, I won't deal with that option (check with your systems people). Instead, let's move to the option popular for those who log in from PCs or Macs (or Amigas or anything else, for that matter). The download feature lets us place the file on our PC's hard drive, using one of the protocols listed in the box. In order to use this, you must know how to use your communications software to download files.

```
        1.  A Cynic Looks at Moo.
        2.  Cardozo Law Forum Article on Neidorf.
        3.  Case|------------------------------------------|
        4.  Comm|                                           |
        5.  Comp|  1. Zmodem                                |
 -->    6.  Conc|  2. Ymodem                                |
        7.  Cryp|  3. Xmodem-1K                             |
        8.  Cybe|  4. Xmodem-CRC                            |
        9.  Defa|  5. Kermit                                |
        10. Elec|  6. Text                                  |
        11. Figh|                                           |
        12. GAO |  Choose a download method:                |
        13. Inte|                                           |
        14. JP B|  [Cancel ^G]  [Choose 1-6]                |
        15. Jame|                                           |
        16. Laws|------------------------------------------|
        17. MUD as a Psychological Model.
        18. Mindvox: Voices In My Head, Patrick Kroupa.
```

Once you've chosen your download protocol, you can then instruct the communications software to save the file in whatever directory on your hard drive you wish.

Excursion 5.6. Bookmarks

It would be extremely tedious to keep working your way back to a particularly interesting gopher site, so Gopher quite nicely offers a bookmarking feature. Essentially, your list of bookmarks creates a personal Gopher menu, which you can access at any point in a Gopher session by pressing the **v** (for view) key.

To create a bookmark, cursor to the desired item and then press the **a** (for add) key. In the following example, item 22 from the Internet Cyberspace related menu has been chosen, because we've found Internet Wiretap (Cyberspace) worth returning to in the future.

```
19. InterNIC: Internet Network Information Center/
20. International Telecommunication Union (ITU) Gopher/
21. Internet Society (includes IETF)/
22. Internet Wiretap (Cyberspace)/
+-----------------------------------------------------------------+
|                                                                 |
| Name for this bookmark?   Internet Wiretap (Cyberspace)         |
|                                                                 |
|                             [Cancel ^G] [Accept - Enter]        |
|                                                      e          |
+-----------------------------------------------------------------+
30. Northwestern Univ, Infrastructure Technology Institute/
31. Open Source Solutions, Inc., OSSgopher/
32. PSGnet/RAINet: low-cost and international networking/
```

Gopher suggests a bookmark name, the same as the item name. You can change this if you wish.

Warning: When you bookmark an item, keep in mind that you are bookmarking only that item, not the entire menu on which the item appears. In the preceding example, the bookmark is to the Internet Wiretap item, and when I select that item from my bookmark's menu I will go straight there, not back to the Internet Cyberspace related menu. Nor can I choose the **u** key from the bookmark menu to go back to the Internet Cyberspace related menu. This is especially frustrating when you Gopher directly into a site from the command line, and you want to capture the full first menu. You simply can't do it.

With the bookmark chosen, we can see our bookmark menu by pressing **v**. Mine looks like this.

```
        Bookmarks

    1.  A List Of Gophers With Subject Trees/
    2.  Federal Agency and Related Gopher Sites/
    3.  Legal or Law related/
    4.  Patents and Copy Rights/
    5.  Limit search to jobs in the Northeast <?>
    6.  SEARCH using any word or words of your choosing/
    7.  SEARCH using The Chronicle's list of job titles/
    8.  Employment Opportunities and Resume Postings/
```

```
9. Gopher-Jewels/
10. Internet Wiretap (Cyberspace)/
```

Notice item 10, the site we've just bookmarked.

Excursion 5.7. Getting Technical Information and Searching for Titles

Bookmarking is one way of making a Gopher item easy to get to. Another is to request technical information, which you can use to Gopher directly to the site. You can receive technical information by cursoring to any menu item and pressing the equals sign (=). Here is the technical information for the Gopher Jewels menu item on the University of Chicago menu.

```
Type=1
Name=Gopher Jewels
Path=1/Other_Gophers_and_Information_Resources/Gophers_by_Subject/Gopher_Jewels
Host=cwis.usc.edu
Port=70

Press <RETURN> to continue,
   <m> to mail, <D> to download, <s> to save, or <p> to print:
```

From now on, we could reach Gopher Jewels by typing `gopher cwis.usc.edu` at the command line and selecting `Other Gophers and Information Resources`, then `Gophers by Subject`, then `Gopher Jewels`. In this case, the path is no shorter.

The last major Gopher feature worth knowing about is searching titles. If you've encountered a multi-page Gopher list, you don't have to keep hitting the spacebar to find a specific item. Instead, pressing the slash key (/) will yield a search box, as shown in the following seven-page list.

```
United States Government gophers

     1.   Call for assistance....
     2.   POLITICS and GOVERNMENT/
     3.   Definition of a "United States Government Gopher".
     4.   Federal Government Information (via Library of Congress)/
```

```
|------------------------------------------------------------------------|
|                                                                        |
| Search directory titles for  NASA                                      |
|                                                                        |
|                                    [Cancel ^G] [Accept - Enter]        |
|                                                                        |
|------------------------------------------------------------------------|
     12. Comprehensive Epidemiological Data Resource (CEDR) Gopher/
     13. Defense Technical Information Center Public Gopher/
     14. ERIC Clearinghouse for Science, Math, Environmental (OSU)/
     15. ERIC Clearinghouse on Assessment and Evaluation/
     16. ESnet Information Services Gopher/
     17. Electronic Government Information Service/
     18. Environment, Safety & Health (USDE) Gopher/

Press ? for Help, q to Quit, u to go up a menu                Page: 1/7
```

If the search locates a title, you'll be taken directly to the first item containing the search string. Here, our search for NASA leads us to item 40, three screens down:

```
     37. Lawrence Berkeley Laboratory (LBL)/
     38. Library of Congress MARVEL Information System/
     39. Los Alamos National Laboratory/
-->  40. NASA Ames Research Center K-12 Gopher/
     41. NASA Center for Aerospace Information/
     42. NASA Center for Computational Sciences/
     43. NASA Goddard Space Flight Center/
```

Note: After your search has been successful, you can request the next item with the same search string by pressing the **n** (for *next*) key.

That's it for the Gopher basics. From this point on in your Internet explorations, you'll encounter Gopher repeatedly, daily, inevitably. Set up your bookmarks, surf to your heart's content, and find the information you need.

The remainder of this chapter is devoted to interesting Gopher sites. There's a wealth of them in every Internet-connected country in the world, and we'll explore only a few of them. They'll lead to many, many others, which is, after all, the whole point. Enjoy.

Exceptional Gophers from Around the World

There are Gophers and there are Gophers. Some offer only one or two menu items, and usually a link to other larger Gophers. Others, however, are complete in themselves, with hordes of subdirectories, files, and all sorts of well-designed links. Here we'll look at some of the best and most established, to get a sense of what's available on a Gopher tour of the world.

Excursion 5.8. Gopher Jewels (*cwis.usc.edu*)

We've already encountered Gopher Jewels, back in Excursion 5.5. However, it's such an extensive resource that we'll take another quick look at it now.

Gopher Jewels, as its name suggests, is a fully-organized listing of many of the best Gophers on the Internet. It is under development primarily by David Riggins at the Texas Department of Commerce in Austin, Texas, who also maintains a mailing list to let you know regularly about new Gopher offerings.

To subscribe to the Gopher Jewels mailing list, send an e-mail message to `LISTPROC@EINET.NET`, leaving the subject line blank and, in the message area, typing **`SUBSCRIBE GOPHERJEWELS`** ***`FIRSTNAME LASTNAME`*** (remember *not* to include your signature file). Shortly after, you'll start to see Riggins' name appear in your mailer almost daily, each time with another worthwhile Gopher site to visit.

Every so often, you'll also receive a message summarizing what's new on Gopher Jewels, what's to come, and how the Gophers are currently arranged.

Gopher Jewels is available from a large number of Gophers. Enjoy it; it's exceptional.

Excursion 5.9. The University of Minnesota Gopher (*gopher.tc.umn.edu*)

Like Gopher Jewels, this site is also accessible from any number of Gophers worldwide. Because it's the original home of the Gopher, why not take a look? It's at `gopher.tc.umn.edu`.

```
1. Information About Gopher
2. Computer Information
3. Discussion Groups
4. Fun & Games
5. Internet file server (ftp) sites
6. Libraries
7. News
```

```
8.  Other Gopher and Information Servers
9.  Phone Books
10. Search Gopher Titles at the University of Minnesota
11. Search lots of places at the University of Minnesota
12. University of Minnesota Campus Information
```

There's nothing really sensationally noteworthy here, until you select Other Gopher and Information Servers. This yields the following menu, which has practically become a commonplace link on Gophers around the world:

```
1.  All the Gopher Servers in the World
2.  Search titles in Gopherspace using veronica
3.  Africa
4.  Asia
5.  Europe
6.  International Organizations
7.  Middle East
8.  North America
9.  Pacific
10. Russia
11. South America
12. Terminal Based Information
13. WAIS Based Information
14. Gopher Server Registration
```

From here you can link to a huge variety of Gophers in just about any nation you can think of. The only thing missing from this list is the extremely useful item called New Gophers, from `liberty.uc.wlu.edu`, in the path Finding Gopher Resources, then All Gopher Sites, then New Gophers.

Excursion 5.10. The Rice University Gopher (*riceinfo.rice.edu*)

For an example of an extremely well-developed campus Gopher, try RiceInfo (`riceinfo.rice.edu`). Here you'll find directories pointing to Rice itself, to Houston, and to a range of other Gophers.

```
1.  About RiceInfo
2.  More About RiceInfo and Gopher
3.  Calendars and Campus Events
4.  Campus Life at Rice
5.  Computer Information
6.  Health and Safety at Rice
```

```
7.  Houston Information
8.  Information by Subject Area
9.  Library Services
10. Other Gopher and Information Servers
11. Research Interests and Opportunities
12. Rice Campus Directory
13. Rice Course Schedules and Admissions Information
14. Rice University and Departmental Policies
15. Search all of RiceInfo by title
16. Weather
```

Surf through this Gopher and you'll find a huge number of resources organized similarly to Gopher Jewels. Under Information by Subject Area, you're also presented with a range of search tools, as shown by the following partial menu:

```
1.  About the RiceInfo collection of "Information by Subject Area"
2.   More about "Information by Subject Area"
3.   Clearinghouse of Subject-Oriented Internet Resource Guides (UMich)
4.   Search all of Gopherspace by title: Jughead (from WLU)
5.   Search all of Gopherspace by title: Veronica
6.   Search all of RiceInfo by title: Jughead
7.  Aerospace
8.  Agriculture and Forestry
9.  Anthropology and Culture
10. Architecture
```

Excursion 5.11. The Electronic Frontier Foundation Gopher (*gopher.eff.org*)

The Electronic Frontier Foundation specializes in issues dealing with freedom in cyberspace. As the following list shows, many of the directories on the main Gopher menu here demonstrate this commitment:

```
1.  About the Electronic Frontier Foundation's Gopher Service
2.  ALERTS! - Action alerts on important and impending issues
3.  Electronic Frontier Foundation files & information
4.  Computers & Academic Freedom archives & info
5.  Other Similar Organizations and Groups
6.  Net Info (Big Dummy's Guide to the Internet, FAQs, etc.)
7.  Publications (CuD, Bruce Sterling, Mike Godwin, etc.)
8.  Search all of Gopherspace using Veronica - 4800+ servers
9.  Other Gopher and Information Servers around the World
```

Note, for example, the Publications item, which offers directories for several well-known organizations and people all concerned with similar issues. Part of the menu is as follows:

```
11. Bruce_Sterling
12. CuD
13. E-journals
14. EFF_Net_Guide
15. EFF_misc_authors
16. EFF_newsletters
17. EFF_papers
18. FAQ_RFC_FYI_IEN
19. Jerry_Berman
20. John_Gilmore
21. John_Perry_Barlow
22. Mike_Godwin
23. Misc
24. Mitch_Kapor
25. README.more
26. Shari_Steele
27. William_Gibson
```

Sterling, Gibson, Kapor, and lots of other stuff as well. Excellent reading, and highly provocative.

Excursion 5.12. The Nova Scotia Technology Network Gopher (*nstn.ns.ca*)

Another strong site is the Nova Scotia Technology Network Gopher, located at `nstn.ns.ca`. The main menu demonstrates some of the directories being developed here, some of which simply cry out to be explored:

```
1.  Canadian Educational Network Coalition
2.  Canadian Weather Forecasts
3.  Education and Schools
4.  Experimental Things
5.  Internet Resources
6.  NSTN Information
7.  NSTN's CyberMall
8.  New Stuff
9.  Nova Scotia Associations
10. Online Bulletin Board Systems and Catalogs
```

Aside from the CyberMall and Experimental Things, of highest interest is the Internet Resources item, which yields the following menu:

```
1.  Definitions of Internet Terms
2.  FTP Sites Search
3.  Gopher-Jewels
4.  Guides to the Internet via SunSite, UNC
5.  Internet Services List
6.  Internet Services List Search
7.  Mail Lists
8.  Oakland SIMTEL mirror
9.  RFCs
10. Search SIMTEL for software
11. Search Usenet Newsgroup Descriptions
12. Search the DDN Network Information Center database
```

With links to the Internet Services List and Gopher Jewels, as well as the software resources at SIMTEL, this Gopher can keep you browsing for a good long time.

Excursion 5.13. The U.K. Office for Library and Information Networking Gopher (*ukoln.bath.ac.uk*)

Directly across the Atlantic from Nova Scotia (well, more or less) is the Jolly Old U.K., and a very strong Gopher site at UKOLN (`ukoln.bath.ac.uk`). The main menu is short, but it leads to a range of very useful sites.

```
1.  Information about this Service
2.  UK Gopher Servers
3.  Other Gopher Servers
4.  BUBL Information Service
5.  Miscellaneous
6.  Hytelnet
7.  Information by Subject
8.  Publications
9.  UK Directory Services
10. UK Library Gopher Servers
```

Among the best here are the BUBL Information Service and UK Gopher Servers items, the latter of which yields a huge menu looking, in part, like this:

```
1.  About this list of gopher servers
2.  ALMAC BBS, (UK)
3.  Action for Blind People, (UK)
4.  Aston University, (UK)
5.  BUBL Information Service, (UK)
6.  Bristol Maths and Stats Gopher Service, (UK)
7.  Brunel University, (UK)
```

```
8.  Colloid Group, Department of Chemistry, University of Surrey, (UK)
9.  Communications Research Group, Nottingham University, (UK)
10. Cranfield Institute of Technology, (UK)
11. Daresbury Laboratory, (UK)
12. De Montfort University Gopher Server, (UK)
13. Decanter Magazine, (UK)
14. Dundee University Library, (UK)
15. Oxford University Computing Laboratory, (UK)
```

This is the first 15 of almost 100 items, and each is a directory to another Gopher. If you want to know what's happening on the Internet in the U.K., there's no better place to start.

Excursion 5.14. The Australian National University Gopher (*info.anu.edu.au*)

Because we entered the U.K. from one former British colony, Canada, it's only natural that we exit by heading to another former colony. At the Australian National University we find a very carefully developed Gopher, with a main menu that looks like this:

```
1.  About ELISA (Electronic Library Information Service at ANU)
2.  What's New on ELISA
3.  -------------------- LIBRARY SERVICES --------------------
4.  ANU Library Services
5.  Other ACT Library Services & Catalogues
6.  Australian Library Catalogues
7.  Worldwide Library Catalogues
8.  ------------ NETWORKED INFORMATION SERVICES --------------
9.  The Electronic Library - Internet Resources by Subject
10. ANU Networked Information Servers
11. Australian Networked Information Servers
12. Worldwide Networked Information Servers
13. ------------------ INDEXES & DIRECTORIES -----------------
14. Phone and Email Directories
15. Internet Information
16. Search Gopherspace: Jughead & Veronica
```

From the Worldwide Networked Information Servers item we get the following menu, showing the (quite natural) Asian focus of ANU's efforts:

```
1.  Search for Gophers by Name or Internet Address
2.  All the Gophers in the World via ANU
3.  Australia
4.  Gopher Jewels
```

```
5.  Gophers of Scholarly Societies
6.  Hong Kong
7.  India
8.  Japan
9.  Korea
10. Library Gophers
11. Malaysia
12. New Zealand
13. Search titles in GopherSpace: Veronica (AARNet,Australia)
14. Services in the Pacific Region
15. Singapore
16. Taiwan
17. Thailand
```

One link along, Japan, will show how much information is to be gained by exploring these sites. Here is the Japanese portion of the ANU Gopher, with, of course, additional links to other sources:

```
1.  DNA Data Bank of Japan, Natl. Inst. of Genetics, Mishima
2.  Dept. of Applied Molecular Sci., IMS, ONRI, [Okazaki, Aichi]
3.  JPNIC (Japan Network Information Center), Tokyo, Japan
4.  Japan Organized InterNetwork (JOIN)
5.  Keio University, Science and Technology campus gopher (Japan)
6.  Matsushita Electric Group, Japan (gopher.mei.co.jp)
7.  National Cancer Center, Tokyo JAPAN
8.  National Institute for Physiological Sciences [Okazaki, Aichi]
9.  Reitaku-University(Computer System Center) Chiba, JAPAN
10. Saitama University
11. TRON Project Information, Univ. of Tokyo, Japan
12. University of Electro-Communications(UEC)
13. World Data Center on Microorganisms (WDC), RIKEN, Japan
```

It's pretty clear by now that the amount of information to be obtained through Gopher surfing alone is enormous. Go to any of these Gophers and start choosing menu items. I guarantee you'll never exhaust the possibilities.

Summary

Gopher is the easiest and the most accessible Internet browsing tool available. Furthermore, hundreds of sites have constructed hundreds of Gophers filled with thousands of documents all available for retrieval, so Gopher isn't just easy, it's also both highly useful and extremely exciting. Its only downside is that it's both overwhelming and addictive. If you can resist the urge to just surf, and actually sit back and explore one or two sites completely, you'll have a much better start at taming information overload. And that, in a nutshell, is what Gopher is trying to do.

Task Review

On Day 5, you:

- ☐ Entered and explored a sample Gopher site.
- ☐ Downloaded, saved, and mailed files from Gophers.
- ☐ Bookmarked your favorite Gopher sites.
- ☐ Explored a number of specific sites in the U.S. and beyond.
- ☐ Entered the huge world of Gopher.

Q&A

Q How are Gophers constructed?

A See Day 13 for more information about this, but essentially here's what happens. First, the host computer must run the appropriate Gopher software, available from the University of Minnesota (you can find this information through from Minnesota's Boombox Gopher, at `boombox.micro.umn.edu`). Basically (and oversimplified), Gopher is told to look for a specific directory on the local network. When that directory is linked to Gopher, Gopher then displays its contents as a menu. Depending on the Gopher software you're running, it will be a numbered list or will display icons beside the entries. Directories appear differently than do files, and so on. As a Gopher maintainer, your job is to set up the directories, sub-directories, and files within those directories so that they're in the order you want and so that they will display the names you want them to display. And, of course, you can specify links to other Gophers as well. It's not difficult, but if you want to build a useful Gopher the process can be time-consuming.

Q If Gopher is so powerful, why bother with anything else?

A Gopher is extremely powerful, but it's not the be-all and end-all of Internet access. For one thing, a Gopher menu is just that, a menu. Menus aren't always nearly as well designed as they might be, and often they obscure their own contents. That's how the World Wide Web can help, at least in part. Another point is that, while Gopher does Telnet and FTP commands (and others), if you already know how to do these tasks, there's no reason to dig through Gopher menus to accomplish them. In fact, advances in individual pieces of software aren't necessarily reflected in Gopher automatically. Still, the advantages of Gopher are so strong that, to many users, these are minor concerns. For a number of people I know, in fact, Gopher and e-mail represent everything they need on the Internet.

6

WEEK 1

All the Tools That Fit: FTP, XModem, Archie, and WAIS

In the introduction to this book, I mentioned that the Internet consists of countless computers with countless accessible data files. Because this is indeed the case, two problems suggest themselves immediately. First, how do you find them? Second, how do you get them?

In fact, the second is much easier than the first. Once you know where a file resides, and as long as you're allowed access to it, getting a copy of it for your own machine isn't difficult at all. Finding a file in the first place is anything but obvious. What the Internet has always needed is software to help locate files, and fortunately it's a need that the software developers have worked overtime at satisfying.

By the time you've finished Day 6, the Internet will seem a bit more unified. That's how powerful the software it uses has become.

Today you will learn to use:

- FTP to transfer a file from another computer to your own account.
- XModem and Kermit to transfer a file from a UNIX machine to your PC.
- Archie to search for files scattered around the Internet.
- WAIS to learn where information on many topics is stored.

FTP: File Transfer Protocol

FTP has been around a long time. About as long, in fact, as the Internet itself. It's essentially the most basic command you can perform on the Net, because its only function is to let you exchange files with another computer. To use FTP fully, you need an account on both machines, but to just get into another machine and retrieve a file you can perform a special function called *anonymous FTP*.

If you've been on the Internet performing the tasks from the previous chapters, you've probably already heard about anonymous FTP. On mailing lists, in newsgroups, even in MUDs and in Gophers, the term appears more than just occasionally. That's because anonymous FTP is considered as fundamental as e-mail to productive Internet use, and it's a function others on the Net expect you to be able to handle. So you'll see a number of messages with a line that goes something like, *"You can get a copy of this document for yourself via anonymous FTP at* `cs.andrew.ncsu.edu` *in the* `pub/law` *directory. It's called* `kramer_vs_kramer.ps`*."*

What does this statement mean? Basically, it's no different from a co-worker who uses a 486 telling you that you can find a copy of her memo called `kramer.doc` in the `c:\data\docs\memos` directory of the network drive. As long as you can get into that directory, and as long as the directory hasn't been restricted from your access, you can copy the file to your own system, load it into your word processor, and read it.

In the case of the FTP message, however, you're being told the following: A file named `Kramer_vs_Kramer.ps` is stored on a computer at North Carolina State University. The system is identified as `cs.andrew.ncsu.edu`, and the file is located in the directory called `law`, which is a subdirectory of the directory called `pub`. You can get into the machine using anonymous FTP and retrieve it. Here's how:

1. To get this hypothetical file, you'd enter your Internet account, exit all Gopher or Mail programs, and type the following command:

   ```
   ftp cs.andrew.ncsu.edu
   ```

2. Soon, NCSU's computer would respond with any one of a variety of messages, but the most important would be a request for a login name, at which point you'd type the word `anonymous`.

   ```
   login: anonymous
   ```

> **Note:** Anonymous FTP means just what it says. You log in with the username `anonymous`. Don't type your actual Internet name here, or the remote computer will treat you as if you have a real account on that system. Later in this chapter you'll discover that there are other commands you can enter at the `login:` or `Name:` prompt as well.

3. Next, you'd be asked for a password, just as if you were logging into your own Internet account. Here, though, instead of typing your regular password, you type your full Internet address.

   ```
   password: nrandall@watserv1.uwaterloo.ca
   ```

4. In a few seconds, NCSU's computer would respond with a message telling you you're in, and an `ftp>` prompt would appear. At this point, you'd change into the directory you want by using the `cd`—change directory—command (sometimes it's `cwd`).

   ```
   ftp> cd pub/law
   ```

5. Again you'd be told you've been successful, and finally you'd be able to transfer the actual file.

   ```
   ftp> get Kramer_VS_Kramer.ps
   ```

Warning: If you're not used to working with UNIX filenames, there are a few things to keep in mind. First, they can be much longer than MS-DOS filenames, which must use the annoying 11-character (8.3) convention. Second, they can include underscores and other characters, including multiple dots (periods). Finally—and this is crucial—case matters. If you want to edit, rename, erase, download, or otherwise deal with a file named `README-Before-TRYing`, you must type all upper- and lowercase characters exactly as they appear. Otherwise, the system will respond that it can't find the file.

That's it. The file is now being transferred to your account.

Excursion 6.1. FTP: An Online Example

The previous hypothetical example shows how FTP is supposed to happen. In practice, it's never quite this smooth for many reasons. First, the destination computer might not let you log on, usually because it's temporarily busy or because anonymous FTP is discouraged or disallowed during peak computing hours. Second, names of directories often change, and you have to search for the file. Third, there's the problem of actually using an FTP'd file: If it transfers to your Internet account, but you want to use it on your home computer, you may need a further download.

In this example, I was searching for a Finger utility for my Macintosh. Knowing that `nstn.ns.ca` maintains reasonably good software archives, I decided to give it a try.

```
$ ftp nstn.ns.ca
Connected to nstn.ns.ca.
220 owl FTP server (SunOS 4.1) ready.
Name (nstn.ns.ca:nrandall): anonymous
331 Guest login ok, send ident as password.
Password: nrandall@watserv1.uwaterloo.ca
230 Guest login ok, access restrictions apply.
```

The first part of the FTP session simply told FTP which computer to link up to and then the username and password to use. Note that the password, which is my full user address, didn't actually display when typed. In fact, it's extremely easy to make a mistake here, so it's a good idea to assign this string to a hotkey or macro button if your communications program has such a feature (which most do).

> **Warning:** Assigning a password to a hot key is a good idea *only* for anonymous FTPs, in which a password isn't really a password. Do not *ever* assign regular passwords to hotkeys or macro buttons; they can easily be discovered, and your account will no longer be secure.

Because I had no idea what file I was looking for, or even if this computer had Macintosh files available, my next step was to ask for a list of files and directories. The standard FTP command for this is `dir`, which is the same as the MS-DOS command. I could also have used the UNIX equivalent, `ls`, with the same results.

```
ftp> dir
200 PORT command successful.
150 ASCII data connection for /bin/ls (198.133.162.1,1371) (0 bytes).
total 31
-rw------   1 root     ftp         1102 Jun 18  1993 .gnomelog
-rw------   1 wheel    ftp          119 Jun 18  1993 README
drwxr-xr-x  3 wheel    ftp          512 Jul 23  1991 associations
drwxr-xr-x  2 root     ftp          512 Jun 28  1990 bin
drwxr-xr-x  2 wheel    6            512 Apr 28  1992 ca-domain
drwxr-xr-x  3 wheel    ftp          512 Nov  5  1991 cadcam-exec
dr-xr-xr-x  2 wheel    ftp          512 Jan 14  1993 canoc-l
dr-xr-xr-x  2 wheel    ftp          512 Oct  2  1992 charlottetown-accord
drwxr-xr-x  2 root     ftp          512 Mar 31  1992 dev
d--x--x--x  4 wheel    ftp          512 Mar  8  1993 dnd-anon
drwxr-xr-x  2 root     ftp          512 May 28  1990 etc
drwxrwxrwx  4 40       ftp         1024 Mar 26 19:51 in.coming
dr-xr-xr-x  3 wheel    ftp          512 May  7  1993 learning-connection
drwxr-xr-x 37 60       ftp         1024 Feb 15 15:24 listserv
drwxr-xr-x  2 root     root        8192 Dec 10 10:28 lost+found
drwxr-xr-x  2 wheel    ftp          512 Jan  2  1992 marketing-wg
drwxr-xr-x  2 wheel    ftp          512 Mar  2 16:56 nstn-documentation
drwxr-xr-x  3 wheel    ftp          512 Dec  2  1991 planning-l
d--x--x--x  5 wheel    ftp          512 Oct 26 19:05 private
drwxr-xr-x 13 wheel    ftp          512 Dec 20 15:47 pub
dr-xr-xr-x  3 wheel    ftp          512 Jul 23  1991 sians-exec
dr-xr-xr-x  3 wheel    ftp          512 Jul 23  1991 sqg-exec
dr-xr-xr-x  4 root     ftp          512 May 28  1990 usr
226 ASCII Transfer complete.
```

When you're doing FTPs, it's important to understand how to read the `dir` result (if you're familiar with UNIX, you already know how to do so). This looks a bit confusing, but it's actually quite simple. The only columns you need to pay strict attention to are the first and last, with the date being sometimes useful, and the file size, immediately to the left of the date, more useful still.

The first character in the first column tells you whether or not the item is a file or a directory. If this character is a `d`, it's a directory; otherwise, it's a file. In this listing, most of the items were obviously directories, and I had to figure out which directory I wanted to enter.

In many anonymous FTP situations, the directory with the most interesting and useful material is called `pub` (short for public). The list I received displayed `pub` fourth from the bottom. The command to change directories is `cd`, again exactly like MS-DOS. The next step was to change to the appropriate directory, then type another `dir` command to get a listing there as well.

```
ftp> cd pub
250 CWD command successful.
ftp> dir
200 PORT command successful.
150 ASCII data connection for /bin/ls (198.133.162.1,1376) (0 bytes).
total 13
dr-xr-xr-x  2 wheel    ftp          512 Jun  7  1993 cansig
drwxr-xr-x  2 1324     30           512 Jan  4 14:17 internet-business-journal
drwxr-xr-x  2 wheel    ftp          512 Oct 17 16:33 interview
dr-xr-xr-x  4 1377     ftp          512 Sep 21  1993 irtool
drwxr-xr-x  2 wheel    ftp         1024 Mar 24 16:05 mac-stuff
drwxr-xr-x  4 wheel    ftp         1024 Oct 24 21:46 netinfo
dr-xr-xr-x  2 wheel    ftp          512 Jun  7  1993 novaknowledge
drwxr-xr-x 12 wheel    ftp          512 Mar  8 23:34 pc-stuff
drwxr-xr-x  2 daniel   ftp         3072 Mar 27 03:30 talk-radio
drwxr-xr-x  5 wheel    ftp          512 Jul  2  1993 unix-stuff
drwxr-xr-x  3 wheel    ftp          512 Dec 21 14:47 windows-stuff
226 ASCII Transfer complete.
```

There were a number of directories here I'd love to have explored—internet-business-journal and talk-radio in particular, but I forced myself to remember that the goal was to find a Macintosh Finger utility. The appropriate directory, quite obviously, was the fifth one on the list, mac-stuff.

Note: Once again, be sure to pay attention to hyphens, underscores, spaces, and capitalizations in UNIX directory names.

```
ftp> cd mac-stuff
250 CWD command successful.
ftp> dir
200 PORT command successful.
150 ASCII data connection for /bin/ls (198.133.162.1,1403) (0 bytes).
total 5004
-r--r--r--  1 wheel    ftp         168366 Feb 22 18:52 Anarchie110.hqx
-r--r--r--  1 wheel    ftp          40320 Mar  5  1993 Archie_0.9.cpt.bin
-r--r--r--  1 wheel    ftp         103552 Mar 22  1993 Compact_Pro.bin
-r--r--r--  1 wheel    ftp           3405 Mar 22  1993 Disinfectant_3.0_intro.txt
-r--r--r--  1 wheel    ftp          97152 Mar  5  1993 Fetch_2.1b2.cpt.bin
-r--r--r--  1 wheel    ftp           1281 Mar 22  1993 Gatekeeper_1.2.7_intro.txt
-r--r--r--  1 wheel    ftp         128256 Mar  5  1993 Gopher_1.0.5.cpt.bin
-r--r--r--  1 wheel    ftp         832640 Feb 16 17:38 Homer_0.93.sit.bin
-r--r--r--  1 wheel    ftp           5958 Mar 11  1993 MacSLIP.script.1.0
-r--r--r--  1 wheel    ftp         677783 Mar 23 19:58 NCSAMosaicMac.1.0.3.sit.hqx
-r--r--r--  1 wheel    ftp         663696 Nov 12 13:29 NCSAMosaicMac.10.sit.hqx
-r--r--r--  1 wheel    ftp         172928 Mar  5  1993 NCSA_Telnet_2.5.cpt.bin
-r--r--r--  1 wheel    ftp         822528 Mar  5  1993 NSTN.sea.bin
-r--r--r--  1 wheel    ftp         173568 Mar 22  1993 disinfectant30.sea.bin
-r--r--r--  1 wheel    ftp         331077 Mar 24 16:10 eudora142.hqx
-r--r--r--  1 wheel    ftp         142530 Oct  6 17:59 finger.hqx
-r--r--r--  1 wheel    ftp         223872 Mar 22  1993 gatekeeper-127.cpt.bin
-r--r--r--  1 wheel    ftp          74624 Mar  5  1993 ircle-1.0.cpt.bin
-r--r--r--  1 wheel    ftp         287354 Nov 12 17:03 newswatcher2.0d17.sea.hqx
226 ASCII Transfer complete.
```

It looked like there was some great stuff here: Eudora, Mosaic, Gopher, Archie—everything a Mac Internet user could want. Sure enough, there was even a Finger utility, or so the filename `finger.hqx`, fourth from the bottom, led me to believe. Double-checking the first digit on that line to ensure that this was a file rather than a directory (which the opening dash confirmed), I decided to transfer the file but, suddenly, I couldn't remember how. I thought I'd just type **help** to remind myself.

```
ftp> help
Commands may be abbreviated.  Commands are:

!          debug        mget       pwd        status
$          dir          mkdir      quit       struct
account    disconnect   mls        quote      system
append     form         mode       recv       sunique
ascii      get          modtime    reget      tenex
bell       glob         mput       rstatus    trace
binary     hash         newer      rhelp      type
bye        help         nmap       rename     user
case       idle         nlist      reset      umask
cd         image        ntrans     restart    verbose
cdup       lcd          open       rmdir      ?
chmod      ls           prompt     runique
```

```
close      macdef       proxy       send
cr         mdelete      sendport    site
delete     mdir         put         size
```

Note: The command `help` often works from inside UNIX commands, such as FTP, Telnet, and, as you'll see later in this chapter, XModem, Kermit, and Archie. At the main UNIX prompt itself, however, you can usually get help only through the `man` command (short for *manual*). A typical example would be `man ls`, which will give you help for the `ls` (list) command.

Scanning the list, I encountered the command `get`, and recalled that it was the command I wanted. A few other commands are worth noting here as well, though. First, if you want to move back a directory, choose the command `cdup`, or type, as in DOS, `cd ..` to do the same thing (not shown in the help list). Second, `put` is the opposite of `get`. Although you'll rarely be allowed to upload a file in anonymous FTP, the `put` command is worth keeping in mind for non-anonymous sessions (those where you have an actual account on the remote computer). Third, if the `ftp>` prompt is showing and you want to connect to a different machine, type `open` and the other computer's address. Finally, if you want to change the username or password, the `user` command makes it possible.

One other command is extremely important. Files can be transferred in ASCII or binary format. Essentially, ASCII files are unformatted (such as plain text files), while binary files contain formatting codes—these include graphics files (.GIF, .JPG, .PCX), sound or video files (.WAV, .AU, .MID), word processor files (.DOC, .WP5, .SAM), and a host of others (.PS, .DBF, .WK1, and so forth). Usually, a description or "readme" file is ASCII, while program or compressed files (or graphics files) are binary. After a bit of practice, you'll know which files are which.

FTP contains ASCII and binary commands, as shown previously, and you should always specify which you want to use. In this case, the file was in .HQX format, a file using Macintosh compression, which meant it was binary. I set the type to `binary`, used `get` to retrieve the file, then completed the FTP session by typing the `quit` command.

```
ftp> binary
200 Type set to I.
ftp> get finger.hqx
local: finger.hqx remote: finger.hqx
200 PORT command successful.
```

```
150 Binary data connection for finger.hqx (198.133.162.1,1425) (142530 bytes).
226 Binary Transfer complete.
142530 bytes received in 46 seconds (3.1 Kbytes/s)
ftp> quit
221 Goodbye.
```

That was it. I had my file. The only problem was that it was on the UNIX machine where my Internet account resided, not on my Mac where I wanted it. I needed to download it from one computer to the other, and for that I used the ubiquitous program XModem.

There's more to FTP than the commands shown in the previous examples. While the `ftp>` prompt is displayed, any of the commands in Table 6.1 may be useful to you.

Table 6.1. Other FTP commands.

Command	Description
`ascii`	Switches to ASCII mode, the mode to be used for copying text files
`binary`	Switches to binary mode, the mode to be used for copying binary files (ZIP files, .GIF, .HEX, and so forth)
`cd`	Changes the current directory on the remote computer
`close`	Ends the current FTP session without quitting FTP entirely
`dir/ls`	Lists the files in the current directory on the remote computer
`get`	Copies a file from the remote to the local computer
`hash`	Displays a `#` on the screen for every 1KB transferred
`help`	Gets help regarding FTP commands
`lcd`	Changes the directory on the local computer
`lpwd`	Displays the current directory name on the local computer
`mget`	Copies multiple files from the remote to the local computer
`mput`	Copies multiple files from the local to the remote computer
`open`	Starts a new FTP session from within FTP
`put`	Copies a file from the local to the remote computer

continues

6

Table 6.1. continued

Command	Description
pwd	Shows the present working directory (pwd) on the remote computer
user	Restarts the user/password process

Soon after you start using FTP regularly, you'll discover a wide range of file types available for download. Many will be compressed—that is, reduced in size to save disk space and transfer time—and you'll need the appropriate software on your system to uncompress them so you can use them. You can find uncompression utilities on the Internet, or as shareware or freeware on BBS or commercial online services, or on floppy- or CD-ROM-based shareware collections for your computer.

Here are the major files types you'll encounter (but there are many, many others). If you're familiar with the types of files you find on your computer, you'll be able to instantly recognize most of those listed in Table 6.2.

Table 6.2. File types.

File Suffix	FTP Mode	File Type
.arc	binary	ARChive (compressed, rare)
.arj	binary	Arj (compressed, usually DOS)
.asc	ASCII	ASCII (text-based) files
.doc	binary	Document (word processor)
.gif	binary	Graphics
.gz	binary	GNU Zip; not compatible with Zip
.hqx	binary	HQX (Macintosh)
.jpg	binary	JPEG Graphics
.lzh	binary	LHa, LHarc, Larc (compressed)
.mpg	binary	MPEG (video standard)
.ps	binary	Postscript (formatted text)
.sit	binary	Stuffit (Macintosh)

File Suffix	FTP Mode	File Type
`.tar`	binary	Tape ARchive (Unix)
`.txt`	ASCII	Text file (very common)
`.uu`	ASCII	uuencode/uudecode, also `.uue` (compressed)
`.Z`	binary	Unix, often seen in combination with `.tar`
`.zip`	binary	Zip (compressed; extremely common)
`.zoo`	binary	Zoo (compressed)

Note: You will also find files that require specific programs. For example, `.ppt` files require Microsoft PowerPoint, while `.wp5` files need WordPerfect 5.0 or 5.1.

Downloading Files Using XModem and Kermit

Once you've used FTP to transfer a file from a remote computer to your account, you aren't necessarily finished. Everything's fine as long as the computer that now contains the file is the one you use regularly, but sometimes this isn't the case. You might, for example, have an Internet on your UNIX machine at work, but you need the file on your PC or Macintosh at home. At some point in your Internet life, you'll almost certainly have to download from one to the other.

6

Note: As more and more people gain direct access to the Internet from their personal computers, this kind of downloading will all but disappear. Even now, a PC or Mac hooked directly to the Net can have a file FTPed directly to its hard drive, as shown in Figure 6.1. Until this happens, the more common scenario is an Internet account on a UNIX-based server, for which your PC at work or home acts only as an attached terminal. In this scenario, the FTP session brings the file to the server but not to the PC. Thus the need for further downloading.

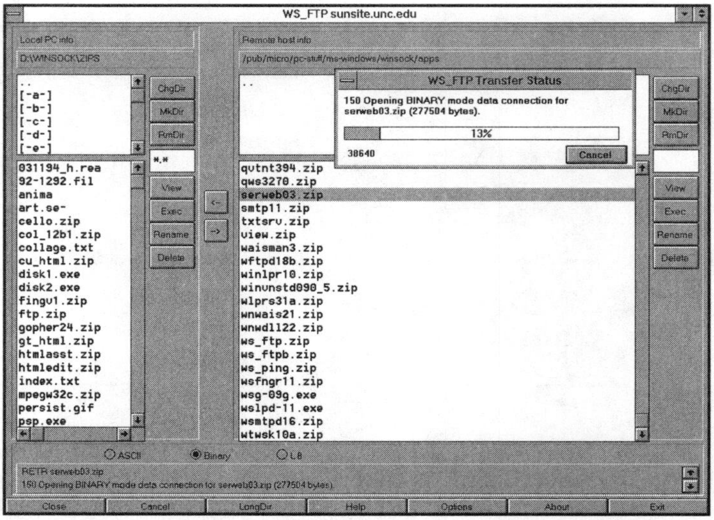

Figure 6.1. *FTPing directly to your PC.*

A huge range of software is available for uploading and downloading files. Two, however, are extremely common: XModem and Kermit. All communications packages for PCs and Macs allow XModem file transfer, and practically all allow Kermit transfer. Check the configuration menus in your particular package.

Note: This section takes you step-by-step through the download process, but only as far as the UNIX machine is concerned. That's because there are far too many communications packages for PCs and Macs to make specific procedures worth specifying. The thing to keep in mind is this: At one point in the download procedure, you'll be told to proceed from your own computer. Do what has to be done locally—either press a keystroke combination or access the appropriate menu—to finish the process.

Excursion 6.2. The First Download: XModem

In this example, I wanted to get a text file and a binary file that I had FTPed to my UNIX account. After logging in, I checked the files available in my local directory by using the simplest version of the `ls` command.

```
% ls
Mail          ftpfaq.txt      porusch.txt
News          gopher1.bin     tribal-interviews
README        interview       whodat
agre.txt      mail            xmodem.log
bin           mbox            xmodemsc.txt
dead.letter   me
```

Usually, this is enough. In many cases, however, a more complete listing is preferable, one that shows file sizes and dates. For this, the `ls -l` version of the command is necessary.

```
% ls -l
total 151drwx---  2 nrandall       512 Nov 14 15:27 Mail
drwxr-x--x   7 nrandall      512 Feb 13 21:40 News
-rw-r-----   1 nrandall      757 Mar 24 18:47 README
-rw-r-----   1 nrandall    63638 Mar  6 00:09 agre.txt
drwx--s--x   2 nrandall      512 Mar 26  1990 bin
-rw-------   1 nrandall        4 Feb 23 12:00 dead.letter
-rw-r-----   1 nrandall    28487 Mar 24 09:02 ftpfaq.txt
-rw-r-----   1 nrandall    51810 Mar 24 18:53 gopher1.bin
-rw-r-----   1 nrandall     3038 Mar 22 14:02 interview
drwx------   2 nrandall     1024 Mar 27 09:48 mail
-rw-------   1 nrandall    10741 Feb 23 12:03 mbox
-rw-r-----   1 nrandall       90 Jan  8 21:09 me
-rw-r-----   1 nrandall    15021 Mar  8 09:58 porusch.txt
-rw-r-----   1 nrandall     2771 Mar 22 13:54 tribal-interviews
-rw-r-----   1 nrandall      186 Nov 11  1990 whodat
-rw-r-----   1 nrandall    18113 Mar 25 11:01 xmodem.log
-rw-r-----   1 nrandall        0 Mar 27 09:50 xmodemsc.txt
```

Because I was using a 14,400 bps modem to download, I wasn't all that worried about file size. However, if I'd only managed a 2400 bps connection (because the host computer was extremely busy), I would have thought twice before fetching that 63KB file displayed fourth from the top. I knew, however, that the one I needed was `ftpfaq.txt`, and at 28KB, it wasn't going to take an inordinate amount of time.

6

As usually happens, though, I couldn't quite remember the exact syntax of the XModem command. By typing **`xmodem`** by itself, and then hitting Enter, I got the following screen:

```
% xmodem
Xmodem Version 3.10 (04 Jan. 1991) — UNIX-Microcomputer File Transfer Facility
Usage:        xmodem -[rb!rt!ra!sb!st!sa][options] filename
Major Commands —
```

```
        rb <-- Receive Binary
        rt <-- Receive Text
        ra <-- Receive Apple macintosh text
        sb <-- Send Binary
        st <-- Send Text
        sa <-- Send Apple macintosh text
Options --
        y  <-- Use YMODEM Batch Mode on transmit
        g  <-- Select YMODEM-G Mode on receive
        m  <-- Use MODEM7 Batch Mode on transmit
        k  <-- Use 1K packets on transmit
        c  <-- Select CRC mode on receive
        t  <-- Indicate a TOO BUSY Unix system
        d  <-- Delete xmodem.log file before starting
        l  <-- (ell) Turn OFF Log File Entries
        x  <-- Include copious debugging information in log file
        p  <-- Use with SunOS tip ~C command
        w  <-- Wait before initial handshake
        e  <-- Supress EOT confirmation
        n  <-- Allow mid-transfer CAN-CAN aborts
```

My options were to send or receive `ftpfaq.txt` as a binary file, a text file, or a Macintosh-specific text file, and I had the choice of several additional options. To keep it simple, and knowing that the file was simple text, I opted for the `st` (send text) command.

Note: Even though the final destination for a file downloaded from your UNIX account is your own PC, you have to use the command `send` rather than `receive`. Think of the UNIX machine as being egocentric and you'll have no problem. You have to look at everything from its perspective, not your own. This can be confusing, though, because in the case of FTP, the reverse is the case; there, you get the file *from* the remote machine, while here you `send` the file *to* your home machine.

```
% xmodem st ftpfaq.txt
Xmodem Version 3.10 (04 Jan. 1991) — UNIX-Microcomputer File Transfer Facility
File ftpfaq.txt Ready to SEND in text mode
Estimated File Size 28K, 223 Sectors, 28487 Bytes
Estimated transmission time 4 minutes 25 seconds
Send several Control-X characters to cancel
```

That did it. The file was ready to be downloaded to my trusty 486. I told my communications software to receive a text file using XModem protocol, specified a directory and filename (which I didn't actually bother changing) and within a couple minutes, it was where it belonged.

Excursion 6.3. The Second Download: Kermit

For the next file, I decided to use Kermit. If anything, it's probably even more common than XModem, and it's well worth knowing. It's also a wee bit more user-friendly.

Unlike XModem, Kermit offers an interactive environment. That is, you actually enter Kermit the way you enter FTP, then work from there.

```
% kermit
C-Kermit 5A(189), 30 June 93, SunOS 4.1 (BSD)
Type ? or HELP for help
```

Kermit offers its own internal help system, although learning about the program's actual command takes a bit of further digging.

```
C-Kermit> help
C-Kermit 5A(189), 30 June 93, Copyright (C) 1985, 1993,
Trustees of Columbia University in the City of New York.

Type INTRO for an introduction to C-Kermit, press ? for a list of commands.
Type HELP followed by a command name for help about a specific command.
Type NEWS for news about new features.
While typing commands, you may use the following special characters:
 DEL, RUBOUT, BACKSPACE, CTRL-H: Delete the most recent character typed.
 CTRL-W:  Delete the most recent word typed.
 CTRL-U:  Delete the current line.
 CTRL-R:  Redisplay the current line.
 ?        (question mark) Display a menu for the current command field.
 ESC      (or TAB) Attempt to complete the current field.
 \        (backslash) include the following character literally
          or introduce a backslash code, variable, or function.
Command words other than filenames can be abbreviated in most contexts.
From system level, type "kermit -h" for help about command-line options.

DOCUMENTATION: "Using C-Kermit" by Frank da Cruz and Christine M. Gianone,
Digital Press.  DP ISBN: 1-55558-108-0; Prentice-Hall ISBN: 0-13-037490-3.
DECdirect: +1-800-344-4825, Order Number EY-J896E-DP, US $34.95.
```

The most important finding here was the first line, which tells how to get further help on specific commands. First, I needed a list of available commands.

```
C-Kermit> ?
 apc                 ask                 askq                assign
 bug                 bye                 cd                  check
 clear               close               comment             connect
 declare             decrement           define              delete
 dial                directory           disable             do
 echo                enable              end                 exit
 finish              for                 get                 getok
 goto                hangup              help                if
 increment           input               introduction        log
 mail                msend               msleep              news
 open                output              pause               ping
 print               push                pwd                 quit
 read                receive             redial              reinput
 remote              rename              return              run
 script              send                server              set
 show                space               statistics          stop
 suspend             take                telnet              translate
 transmit            type                version             wait
 while               who                 write               xif
```

Hmmm…lots of choices. While I could scarcely restrain myself from finding out what `msleep` was all about, I decided to stick to efficiency and learn how to use `send`.

Tip: While Kermit offers a number of commands, only a few are necessary for simple uploading or downloading. Learn `send`, `receive`, `dir`, `connect`, and `exit`, and you'll be off and running. The rest are for more complex sessions, including those where one computer or the other acts as a host machine for communications purposes.

```
C-Kermit> help send

Syntax: SEND (or S) filespec [name]
Send the file or files specified by filespec.
filespec may contain wildcard characters '*' or '?'. If no wildcards,
then 'name' may be used to specify the name 'filespec' is sent under; if
'name' is omitted, the file is sent under its own name.
```

Okay, now I knew how to do it. Next, I needed another directory listing, to get the precise name of the file. Looking at the commands menu, I saw that `dir` was once again available.

```
C-Kermit> dir
total 184
drwx------  2 nrandall     512 Nov 14 15:27 Mail
drwxr-x--x  7 nrandall     512 Feb 13 21:40 News
-rw-r-----  1 nrandall     757 Mar 24 18:47 README
-rw-r-----  1 nrandall   63638 Mar  6 00:09 agre.txt
drwx--s--x  2 nrandall     512 Mar 26  1990 bin
-rw-------  1 nrandall       4 Feb 23 12:00 dead.letter
-rw-r-----  1 nrandall   28487 Mar 24 09:02 ftpfaq.txt
-rw-r-----  1 nrandall   51810 Mar 24 18:53 gopher1.bin
-rw-r-----  1 nrandall    3038 Mar 22 14:02 interview
drwx------  2 nrandall    1024 Mar 27 09:48 mail
-rw-------  1 nrandall   10741 Feb 23 12:03 mbox
-rw-r-----  1 nrandall      90 Jan  8 21:09 me
-rw-r-----  1 nrandall   15021 Mar  8 09:58 porusch.txt
-rw-r-----  1 nrandall    2771 Mar 22 13:54 tribal-interviews
-rw-r-----  1 nrandall     186 Nov 11  1990 whodat
-rw-r-----  1 nrandall   18592 Mar 27 09:53 xmodem.log
-rw-r-----  1 nrandall   32768 Mar 27 09:53 xmodemsc.txt
```

The file I wanted was called gopher1.bin. At only 51,810 bytes, it would take a few minutes to download, but that wasn't too bad. Unlike XModem, Kermit didn't need to be told whether it was a binary or a text file, so the command was very simple.

```
C-Kermit> send gopher1.bin
Return to your local Kermit and give a RECEIVE command.
```

As with XModem, the rest was up to me. I told my communications package to download a file using Kermit protocol, chose the directory and filename, and in a short while it was there. Finally, it was time to end the Kermit session.

6

```
C-Kermit> quit
```

Searching the Internet for Files

With FTP, you can copy any file you can find from a remote computer to your own account. Then, using XModem or Kermit, you can download that file to your personal machine. How do you go about finding files in the first place? The Internet is vast, after all, with thousands upon thousands of computers containing quite literally millions of available files. Even with an army of helpers, you'd be hard-pressed to find a particular file that's important to your needs.

Fortunately, you don't need the army of helpers. Instead, you can make use of several important Internet search tools. Among these are Gopher (see Day 2) and the World Wide Web (see Day 7). Gopher and the Web rely entirely on the existence of several lower level tools, and we'll look at these here. These are tools that keep track of FTP sites and create lists of what they hold, reporting those findings when we search what they've found. Quite simply, they're invaluable.

Option One: Archie

Archie was the first of the important Internet search tools. It was designed, essentially, to keep a database of directories and files in FTP sites on the Internet. Archie sites hold copies of the database, and you enter these sites to search it.

Note: When you do an Archie search, it's important to realize that you're not actually scanning the Internet or files. Instead, you're searching through the Archie database at the Archie site. This database is updated frequently, but—with the exception of the moment of updating—it is never completely current. If you enter a specific FTP site frequently, it's quite possible that you'll be more up-to-date for that particular site than the Archie database will be. Archie's value is that it keeps tabs on a whole host of FTP sites.

Warning: Several locations hold the Archie database. One of the best-known is Rutgers University. Because Archie is so commonly accessed, however, this site frequently gets jammed with users. As soon as you can, find an Archie site near you (your own host might be such a site) and use it instead. In the first example, following, I was able to connect to the Rutgers site, but my searches kept timing out.

Table 6.3 is a partial list of Archie sites, as retrieved by typing `servers` while engaged in an Archie search. Note the country address; it's important to choose the site nearest you.

Table 6.3. Archie sites.

Host Name	IP Address	Country
archie.au	139.130.4.6	Australia
archie.edvz.uni-linz.ac.at	140.78.3.8	Austria
archie.univie.ac.at	131.130.1.23	Austria
archie.uqam.ca	132.208.250.10	Canada
archie.funet.fi	128.214.6.100	Finland
archie.th-darmstadt.de	130.83.22.60	Germany
archie.ac.il	132.65.6.15	Israel
archie.unipi.it	131.114.21.10	Italy
archie.wide.ad.jp	133.4.3.6	Japan
archie.kr	128.134.1.1	Korea
archie.sogang.ac.kr	163.239.1.11	Korea
archie.rediris.es	130.206.1.2	Spain
archie.luth.se	130.240.18.4	Sweden
archie.switch.ch	130.59.1.40	Switzerland
archie.ncu.edu.tw	140.115.19.24	Taiwan
archie.doc.ic.ac.uk	146.169.11.3	United Kingdom
archie.unl.edu	129.93.1.14	USA (NE)
archie.internic.net	198.48.45.10	USA (NJ)
archie.rutgers.edu	128.6.18.15	USA (NJ)
archie.ans.net	147.225.1.10	USA (NY)
archie.sura.net	128.167.254.179	USA (MD)

Excursion 6.4. Finding Info on NAFTA Using Archie

For a research project at a local company, I needed some information about the North American Free Trade Agreement. Here, I thought, was a perfect opportunity to do an Archie search. I logged into the UNIX account at my university and went from there.

The first step in an Archie search is to Telnet to the Archie host. Here, I chose the well-known Rutgers site, logging in by using the username `archie`.

```
% telnet archie.rutgers.edu
Trying 128.6.18.15 ...
Connected to dorm.Rutgers.EDU.
Escape character is '^]'.

SunOS UNIX (dorm.rutgers.edu) (ttyq4)

login: archie
Last login: Sun Mar 27 09:59:37 from danno.cs.bris.ac

SunOS Release 4.1.3 (TDSERVER-SUN4C) #2: Mon Jul 19 18:37:02 EDT 1993
telnet-client: error getting motd from 'archie.rutgers.edu'.
Timed out (ardp)
# Bunyip Information Systems, 1993
# Terminal type set to 'vt100 24 80'.
# 'erase' character is '^?'.
# 'search' (type string) has the value 'sub'.
```

No problem. I was in, and the search type was listed as `sub`. This means that the search string I type will try to find filenames that contain that string, and that upper- or lowercase doesn't matter. Other search types include `exact`, where the search string must match the filename exactly, and `subcase`, which is the same as `sub` except that it will match case as well. You can use the `set search` command from the `archie>` prompt to set the type to your liking.

Before performing the actual search, I decided to ask for help. As with Kermit, typing **`help`** itself actually led me to the real help, the question mark. Typing **`?`** gave me the list of possibilities I was after.

```
archie> help
  These are the commands you can use in help:
              .    drop down one level in the hierarchy
              ?    display a list of valid subtopics at the current level
       done, ^D, ^C    quit from help entirely
           <string>    help on a topic or subtopic
```

```
help> ?

# Subtopics:
#
#       about
#       autologout
#       bugs
#       bye
#       done
#       email
#       exit
#       find
#       general
#       help
#       list
#       mail
#       motd
#       nopager
#       pager
#       prog
#       quit
#       regex
#       servers
#       set
#       show
#       site
#       term
#       unset
#       version
#       whatis
#       whats_new
```

I knew from using Archie previously that the command for doing searches was `prog`. From the `help>` prompt, I typed **`prog`** to remind myself of what to do.

```
help> prog

 The 'find' command (also known as the 'prog' command)
 allows you to search the database for a specified pattern.

 The usage is:

    find <expression>

 where the interpretation of <expression> depends on the
 current value of the 'search' variable. Searches may be
 performed in a number of different ways. See the help
 section on the 'search' variable for a full explanation.

 The output of find can be sorted in different ways,
 depending on the value of the 'sortby' variable. See help
 for the 'sortby' variable for a full explanation.
```

Here's a clear case of software designers listening to users. With this version of Archie, the `prog` command still exists, but it could now be replaced by find. Sure enough, asking for help on find yielded exactly the same instructions, so obviously it worked. It was time to leave the help system. But as with Kermit, this was easier said than done. Quit didn't work, so I asked for help with help itself. This told me to use done instead. I should've guessed.

Now for a search.

I left the Rutgers server by typing **`quit`** and logged into the server at the University of Quebec in Montreal (`archie.uqam.ca`). The menus are in French, but they're relatively easy to decipher, and it's a little closer to home. Once again, I used `archie` as a username and `nafta` as my search word.

```
%telnet archie.uqam.ca
Trying...
Connected to paprika.telecom.uqam.ca.
Escape character is '^]'.


SunOS UNIX (paprika)

login: archie
Last login: Wed May 18 12:18:30 from gate1.SRP.GOV
SunOS Release 4.1.3 (GENERIC_SMALL) #3: Mon Jul 27 16:45:05 PDT 1992

# Version frangaise rialisie en collaboration avec le
# Service des Tilicommunications, Universiti du Quibec ' Montrial.


                        Bienvenue sur archie.uqam.ca !

                        Service des Telecomunications

# Bunyip Information Systems, 1993
# Type de terminal rigli ' 'vt100 24 80'.
# caracthre 'erase' est '^?'.
uqam archie> find nafta
en cours... =
```

In a few short seconds I had a staggering amount of information. The following is only a small portion, but enough to give you an idea of what you're likely to find if you do a fairly general search on a well-studied topic:

```
Ordinateur central cs.columbia.edu    (128.59.1.2)
Dernihre mise ' jour 09:14 20 Feb 1994

    Endroit: /archives/mirror1/lpf
      FICHIER    -rw-rw-r-- 18261 bytes 14:10  9 Nov 1993  nafta.objs-sugg.gz


Ordinateur central cs.columbia.edu    (128.59.1.2)
Dernihre mise ' jour 09:14 20 Feb 1994

    Endroit: /archives/mirror1/lpf
      FICHIER    -rw-rw-r-- 415521 bytes 12:22  9 Nov 1993  nafta.tar.gz

Ordinateur central ftp.cco.caltech.edu    (131.215.48.151)
Dernihre mise ' jour 09:11 20 Feb 1994

    Endroit: /pub/bjmccall/Clinton/Campaign2
      FICHIER    -rw-r--r-- 21050 bytes 02:55 15 Sep 1993  nafta.txt.Z

Ordinateur central ftp.cco.caltech.edu    (131.215.48.151)
Dernihre mise ' jour 09:11 20 Feb 1994

    Endroit: /pub/bjmccall/Clinton/dec92
      FICHIER    -rw-r--r-- 2260 bytes 00:00 18 Dec 1992  nafta.stat.Z
```

Clearly, there were lots of NAFTA files available, and Archie had told me where I could find them. At this point, I quit Archie, went back into my own account, and did an FTP into `ftp.cco.caltech.edu`. From the `ftp>` prompt I went into the `/pub/bjmccall/Clinton/dec92` directory (using `cd`, of course), and retrieved the file using the `get` command.

That's what Archie does. It tells you exactly where to find the files you need. Once you have this information, you can use FTP to transfer them to your own account.

Enough with the NAFTA material. Clearly, if I started doing FTPs at 11:00 a.m., I wouldn't be finished until suppertime. However, NAFTA wasn't the only thing on my mind. I was busily configuring my word processor, Microsoft Word for Windows (nicknamed WinWord), and I wondered what might be out there to help me make the program work better than it does. Since I had to sign on to an Archie server again, this time I thought I'd try the University of Nebraska in Lincoln (`archie.unl.edu`). Once signed on, I simply typed **`find winword`**.

```
unl-archie> find winword

# Search type: sub.
# Your queue position: 1
# Estimated time for completion: 00:03
working...  \


Host ftp.cic.net    (192.131.22.5)
Last updated 14:30 22 Jan 1994

   Location: /pub/great-lakes/gopher/partners/.GLNPO
      FILE    -rw-r--r--   31087 bytes  17:55  4 Oct 1993  Ecosystem-Charter-for-the-
Great-Lakes-(DRAFT--WinWord-version)q

Host mvb.saic.com    (139.121.19.1)
Last updated 10:09 13 Mar 1994

    Location: /LT92A.DIR;1/NCSA.DIR;1/PC.DIR;1/CONTRIBUTIONS.DIR;1
      FILE    -rw-r-x-w-     304 bytes  10:03 30 May 1992  TEL23DOC_WINWORD.ZIP;1

Host pyrite.rutgers.edu    (128.6.4.15)
Last updated 14:13 10 Mar 1994

    Location: /gong/incoming/..  /.nib/3dStudi0
      FILE    -rw-r----      0 bytes  09:12  9 Mar 1994  #I wouldn't mind a good
winword 6 disk 9 or excel 5 disks 3-5

Host calypso-2.oit.unc.edu    (198.86.40.81)
Last updated 15:02 10 Mar 1994

    Location: /pub/packages/infosystems/WWW/tools/editing/macros
      DIRECTORY    drwxr-xr-x     512 bytes  08:15  5 Feb 1994  ms-winword
```

Again, the Archie search gave me more than I expected. The last of the directories—macros—interested me more than others because I was about to construct some complex macros and I wondered if they'd already been done. I used another of Archie's features, `whatis`, to determine if there might be any specific files I could use.

```
unl-archie> whatis macros

capp                     Cut and paste processor
dbug                     Debugging macros for C programs
indexmac                 Troff(1) macros to create an index
macro65.dot              New global formatting macros for Winword 6.0
mti.roff                 Travel itinerary macros for *roff
mx-macros                Troff macros for "ACM Transactions"
parmacs                  Parallel programmming macros  (argonne)
plum-ansi-macros         Plum-Hall X3J11 macro explainer
prep                     FORTRAN Preprocessor which supports macros, flow
```

```
                              control extensions, vector statement shorthand, and
                              automatic loop unrolling for certain classes of loops
tmac.ti                       Travel-itinerary macros for nroff
travel-macros                 Troff(1) macros for producing itineraries and expense
                              reports
ue3.9-macros                  Interactive speller and other MicroEMACS macros
```

Obviously, the `macro65.dot` file was the one I wanted. The next step was to find out where it was, and `find macro65.dot` answered this question. All that was left was to FTP to the site, `cd` into the appropriate directory, and `get` the file. In the meantime, though, it was time to leave Nebraska's Archie site.

```
unl-archie> bye
# Bye.
Connection closed by foreign host.
```

Archie has both strengths and weaknesses. Its strengths are that it's easy to use and extremely informative. Its weakness is that it tells you where the files are, but you still have to go out and retrieve them for yourself. All in all, the strengths outweigh the weaknesses, and Archie remains one of the Internet's most important tools.

Option Two: WAIS

Pronounced *ways*, WAIS stands for Wide Area Information Servers. Unlike Archie, WAIS depends for its completeness on more than one supplier of databases. Essentially, anyone can add a database to the WAIS world by creating and maintaining an index of material on a particular server, and these can be free or for profit. Several indexed servers exist, each containing its own database of documents, graphics files, and any other kind of digital information. A company called Thinking Machines in Massachusetts maintains a directory of WAIS servers. The best way to think of WAIS servers is as collections or libraries, and when you do a WAIS search you're asking for files in a specific collection relevant to what you want to see.

You can reach the WAIS servers directly, but more frequently you'll access them through Gopher. Most Gopher lists contain a reference to other resources, which lead to a menu with WAIS as one of its options.

Excursion 6.5. Collecting Internet Information with WAIS

For a course I was teaching, I needed a great deal of Internet material. Knowing WAIS's power, as well as the likelihood that someone, somewhere must have an indexed collection of Internet information, I decided to enter my local Gopher and see what I could find.

```
% gopher uwinfo.uwaterloo.ca

      7.  UWdir ... faculty, staff, students (name, dept, email, etc)/
      8.  Events, news, weather/
-->  9.  Electronic Resources Around the World/
     10. DAILY BULLETIN (latest: Friday, March 25)/
     11. What's New on UWinfo? (Student Information Systems Project)/
     12. {Index of Menu Items, all UWinfo servers}
```

Selecting #9 from the first menu yielded the menu following, with WAIS appearing as the last of a number of useful items. By selecting #12, the subsequent WAIS menu itself appeared.

```
      8.  FTP (file transfer protocol) services/
       9.  WWW (World Wide Web) servers via telnet/
     10. Finding Someone on the Internet/
     11. University of Waterloo gophers/
-->  12. WAIS (Wide Area Information Servers) databases


      1.  About Wide Area Information Servers (WAIS)/
      2.  Subject sorted WAIS databases from Sweden/
-->  3.  WAIS (through Think Com) <TEL>
      4.  WAIS (through University of Minnesota)/
      5.  WAIS Sources from Arizona State University
```

Then it was on to WAIS itself. Where better to start than `think.com` itself, where Thinking Machines keeps the directory of servers? I selected #3, and was told that I was about to Telnet into `quake.think.com`. Once there, the login name `wais` took me where I wanted to be.

```
-->  +-------------WAIS (through Think Com)--------------------+
     |                                                        |
     |  Warning!!!!!, you are about to leave the Internet     |
```

```
      |  Gopher program and connect to another host. If   |
      |  you get stuck press the control key and the      |
      |  ] key, and then type quit                        |
      |                                                   |
      |  Connecting to quake.think.com using telnet.      |
      |                                                   |
      |  Use the account name "wais" to log in            |
      |                                                   |
      |                     [Cancel: ^G] [OK: Enter]      |
      |                                                   |
      +---------------------------------------------------+

Trying 192.31.181.1 ...
Connected to quake.think.com.
Escape character is '^]'.

SunOS UNIX (quake.think.com)

login: wais
Last login: Sun Mar 27 15:54:56 from psulias.psu.edu
SunOS Release 4.1.3 (SUN4C-STANDARD) #9: Wed Oct 27 18:18:30 EDT 1993
Welcome to swais.
Please type user identifier (optional, i.e user@host): nrandall@watserv1.uwaterloo.ca

TERM = (vt100) vt100
Starting swais (this may take a little while)...

This is the new experimental "wais" login on Quake.Think.COM
```

Using WAIS's keyword feature, I asked, very simply, for material related to the string `internet`. I wasn't surprised to receive quite a number of possibilities.

```
  #    Score   Source                   Title                     Lines
001:   [1000] (directory-of-se)    internet_info                   37
002:   [ 957] (directory-of-se)    ANU-Internet-Voyager-Guide      79
003:   [ 913] (directory-of-se)    internet_services               24
004:   [ 870] (directory-of-se)    internet-mail                  131
005:   [ 826] (directory-of-se)    Internet-user-glossary          29
006:   [ 783] (directory-of-se)    internic-internet-drafts        63
007:   [ 783] (directory-of-se)    ripe-internet-drafts            16
008:   [ 739] (directory-of-se)    comp.internet.library           14
009:   [ 739] (directory-of-se)    internet-intros                 13
010:   [ 739] (directory-of-se)    internet-standards-merit        15
011:   [ 696] (directory-of-se)    internet-rfcs-europe            13
012:   [ 696] (directory-of-se)    internet-standards              64
013:   [ 522] (directory-of-se)    AskERIC-Helpsheets              17
014:   [ 522] (directory-of-se)    AskERIC-Infoguides              17
015:   [ 435] (directory-of-se)    fidonet-nodelist                74
016:   [ 391] (directory-of-se)    SURAnetGuide-All                23
017:   [ 304] (directory-of-se)    IAT-Documents                   33
```

> **Note:** The number under the heading `Score` shows how high a score WAIS has given the document it has located. This score is a reflection of how well the document fits your search criteria. What this means is that the document `internet-info` contained the text string `internet` (which is what I asked for) more often than any of the other documents. Obviously, this is far from a foolproof system, but at least it's something to go by.

Third on the list of documents was something called internet_services. It seemed interesting, and especially relevant, so I selected it and received the following sublist:

```
002:   [ 957] (directory-of-se)    ANU-Internet-Voyager-Guide           79
003:   [ 913] (directory-of-se)    internet_services                    24
004:   [ 870] (directory-of-se)    internet-mail                       131
005:   [ 826] (directory-of-se)    Internet-user-glossary               29
006:   [ 783] (directory-of-se)    internic-internet-drafts             63
007:   [ 783] (directory-of-se)    ripe-internet-drafts                 16
008:   [ 739] (directory-of-se)    comp.internet.library                14
009:   [ 739] (directory-of-se)    internet-intros                      13
010:   [ 739] (directory-of-se)    internet-standards-merit             15
011:   [ 696] (directory-of-se)    internet-rfcs-europe                 13
012:   [ 696] (directory-of-se)    internet-standards                   64
013:   [ 522] (directory-of-se)    AskERIC-Helpsheets                   17
014:   [ 522] (directory-of-se)    AskERIC-Infoguides                   17
015:   [ 435] (directory-of-se)    fidonet-nodelist                     74
016:   [ 391] (directory-of-se)    SURAnetGuide-All                     23
017:   [ 304] (directory-of-se)    rfcs                                 65
```

Because I was interested in many of the technical aspects of the Internet, I elected to see what was available in the last item on the list, rfcs. What I discovered was a database of RFCs available for perusal at the address `ds.internic.net`, and a long keyword list that I've only partially reproduced here. Exiting WAIS, I did an FTP to that address and began downloading the files I needed.

> **Note:** RFC is short for *Request for Comment.* These are document types that have been around since the Internet's earliest days. As new ideas were considered for use across the Net, designers would make the technical details available and ask other designers, programmers, and technicians for comments about these details. RFCs remain an important part of the Internet's development today, and they reflect the continuing cooperation among its technicians.

```
Retrieving: rfcs
"rfcs.src" from directory-of-servers.src...

SWAIS                    Document Display              Page:  1
(:source
 :version  3
 :ip-address "198.49.45.10"
 :ip-name "ds.internic.net"
 :tcp-port 210
 :database-name "rfcs"
 :cost 0.00
 :cost-unit :free
 :maintainer "admin@ds.internic.net"
 :keyword-list (
      10
      192
      accepted
      address
      bit
      command
      connection
      control
      data
      domain
      file
      group
      host
      information
      internet
      ip
      mail
      may
      message
      name
      net
      network
```

Other Methods of Accessing WAIS

You can get into the WAIS databases directly or through Gophers, but there are other ways as well.

Recently, WAIS access has been made available on the World Wide Web. Figure 6.2 shows the form for a WAIS search in the Microsoft Windows version of NCSA Mosaic.

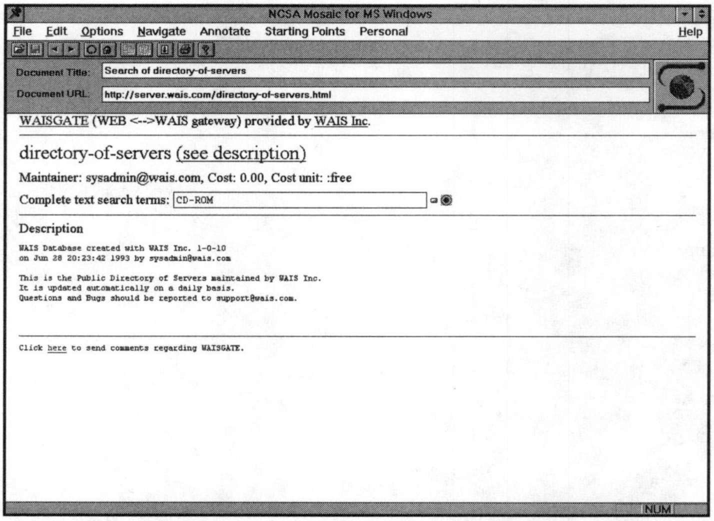

Figure 6.2. *A WAIS search using NCSA Mosaic.*

Here I was searching for files dealing with CD-ROM technology; I typed **`CD-ROM`** in the "complete text search terms" box and clicked the small search button immediately to its right. The result was Figure 6.3 (note that I turned off Mosaic's graphics, which is why the icons simply display the word *Image*), which gives me a clearly displayed list complete with scores and file sizes. I can click from here to access.

This is WAIS Manager, again for Microsoft Windows (similar programs are available for the Macintosh and graphical UNIX systems). Several existing servers ship with the program, and they can be updated through FTP. You choose a database to search, then wait as the program connects you to the appropriate site and retrieves the list of resources complete with scores and file sizes. You can then double-click the desired file to retrieve and display it, or you can use it to perform subsequent WAIS searches.

In fact, one of WAIS's strengths is its capability to let you keep refining a search. By starting broadly and then using the acquired material to narrow things down, you can eventually find a limited amount of excellent information rather than a large number of only potentially useful files. All WAIS software lets you perform this kind of focus-narrowing, and as you become increasingly adept at WAIS searches, you'll find the techniques easier and easier to master. Best of all, it's well worth the effort.

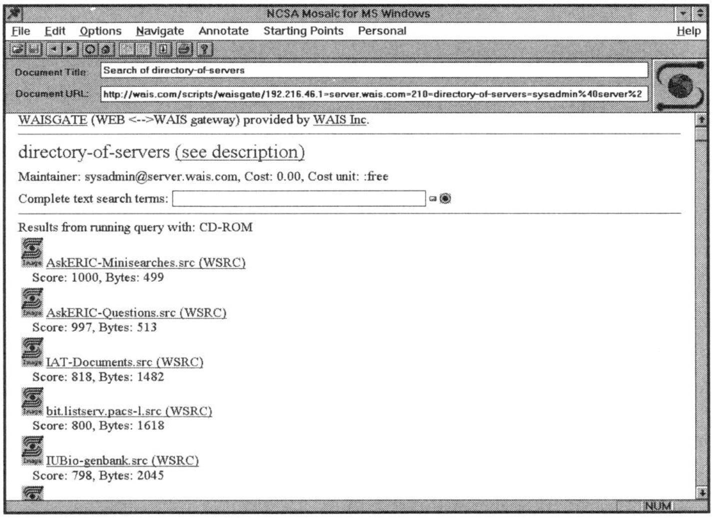

Figure 6.3. *WAIS results through World Wide Web.*

Another highly usable WAIS search program is shown in Figure 6.4.

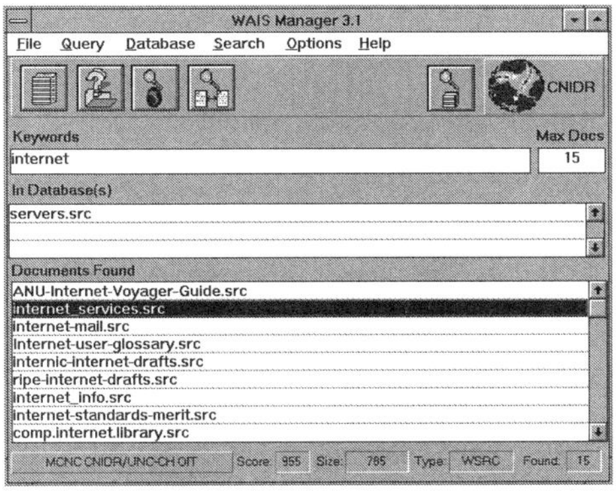

Figure 6.4. *WAIS Manager for Microsoft Windows.*

Summary

The Internet contains an enormous amount of information, but without help it's almost impossible to find. Fortunately, powerful search tools exist to assist you in your searches, and once you find the files you want, another set of tools lets you retrieve them and download them to your home machine. FTP, XModem, Kermit, Archie, and WAIS will become your nearly constant companions as you do the kind of detailed research the Internet lets you perform.

Task Review

On Day 6 you performed the following tasks:

- ☐ Used FTP to transfer a file from another computer to your own account.
- ☐ Learned how to use XModem and Kermit to transfer a file from a UNIX machine to your PC.
- ☐ Worked with Archie to search for files scattered around the Internet.
- ☐ Used WAIS to learn where information on many topics is stored.

Q&A

Q When I try to do a WAIS search, I can't seem to get connected to the remote machine. What's the problem?

A As with any Internet activity, pay attention to time zones. If you're on the U.S. West Coast and you're trying a WAIS search on a machine in the Eastern time zone, remember the three-hour difference. It may be the crack of dawn where you are, but across the continent computers are in full swing with daily business activity, and your search is probably set at minimal priority. Another issue, however, is that computers shut down from time to time, either for maintenance, software or hardware installation, or just because they crashed. Finally, it may be your own host computer that's causing the problem by not sending the request in the first place. My advice is to try again later.

Q FTP works great, but sometimes when I get a list of files in the directory, the output scrolls way off the top of the screen. Is there any way I can stop it?

A Try the command `ls ¦more` (`¦` is the pipe symbol, two vertical dashes, usually located above the backslash key on standard PC keyboards). This should deliver one screen of details at a time, then wait for you to hit the space bar. Most systems support this feature.

There are a couple other ways, however. First, select a communications package that has what's called a *screen buffer* or *backscroll buffer* or something similar. These will let you see what's gone off the top of the screen (although activating them isn't always as easy as it might be). Second, if you're working on a pure character-based terminal, use UNIX's `script` command. Type **`script`** ***`filename`*** (call the file whatever you want), then do your directory listings. Type **`exit`** to get out of **`script`**, then load the file into a standard editor (or word processor). `Script` captures the session in an ASCII file, and you can use it whenever you want to track what you're doing and where you've been.

Q I've tried to download to my PC using XModem, but nothing seems to happen. Should I buy a new communications program?

A If you're using an especially old communications package, you might want to consider upgrading anyway, because the new ones take advantage of faster modems and additional transfer protocols. There are excellent shareware packages available for every computer type, so there's really no excuse for using an old version. One of the things continually tested in upgraded programs is compatibility, and this may well be the problem here.

But not necessarily. Before doing anything, double-check that you've selected the right download protocol in the program on your own computer. There are several varieties of XModem, and while some are faster than others you should start with the most basic, XModem itself (not XModem-1K or something with a similar extension). Also, make sure that you told the remote computer to send the file rather than receive it (that is, use xmodem st or sb). Finally, make sure that you in fact activate the download. I used to think it just happened automatically, which it often does with other protocols, but XModem needs elbow grease.

Q I did an Archie search for some Internet tools for my Macintosh, and I found the same programs in many different sites. Should I just use the first one I find?

A No. Make sure to examine the dates, and select the most recent one. A program like Eudora, for instance, is scattered all over the Net, which is good for accessibility but bad for ensuring the latest upgrade. There are old versions of just about every program in largely forgotten directories, and the last thing you want to do is retrieve an old version. You might even wind up with an old alpha or beta version (that is, an incomplete test version). Be on guard against this.

Q I keep hearing (and seeing on my local Gopher server) references to Hytelnet, ERIC, CARL, Veronica, and other tools that seem to be for searching. What are they?

A Excellent question. In the interest of space, this chapter covered only the most significant and best-known search programs, Archie and WAIS, but there are plenty of others. Hytelnet is essentially a feature-rich version of the standard Telnet, letting you select from menus in a manner somewhat similar to Gopher. ERIC and CARL are especially interesting to educators (at every level); both are extensive databases offering a wide range of material. Veronica is a search program that many prefer to Archie, because instead of just giving you a list of documents it also lets you FTP them from that list.

While all of these programs can be launched from the UNIX prompt, it's far easier to use them from within a Gopher. Practically every Gopher contains a menu line for Veronica searches, and if you find the line that reads something like Other Information Sources (I've seen few Gophers without such a line), you'll almost invariably see a menu item for ERIC, CARL, and Hytelnet. Usually these screens offer small how-to files as well, to help get you started.

Q Wait a minute! A search program called Veronica. Any relation to Archie?

A Actually, yes. One of computing's more enjoyable contributions to our culture is its variety of naming systems, and Internet tools are no different. Archie originally was a shortened version of Archive, which is what the program reflects. This name, of course, suggested the famous comic book character to another designer, who promptly selected the name Veronica, one of Archie Andrew's two girlfriends. Whether or not the idea that the character Veronica was richer and prettier than Archie had anything to do with the naming is impossible to say, but Veronica searches, which can also be done through most Gophers, in fact take Archie searches one step further. Archie shows you where the document resides, but Veronica lets you FTP from the search screen (Note: upcoming versions of Archie will let you do this and more). To carry the comic book thing further, there is currently a Jughead search program available; if anyone ever does a Miss Grundy, I suggest it's time we quit and start over.

Extra Credit: ArchiePlex

The preceding Archie instructions represent the most common way of accessing and using this popular search program, but recently a more interactive method has appeared. ArchiePlex makes use of the capabilities of the World Wide Web and, in particular, software that supports HTML Forms (*HTML* means *hypertext mark-up language*, the system used to create the WWW pages you'll see in Day 7). One such program is NCSA Mosaic, in its most recent versions at least, and for Extra Credit let's use Mosaic to perform a new style of Archie search.

Excursion 6.6. Using ArchiePlex To Search for NII Information

Figure 6.5 shows the ArchiePlex form. The URL line at the top of the screen shows its location: `http://www.lerc.nasa.gov/Doc/archieplex.html`.

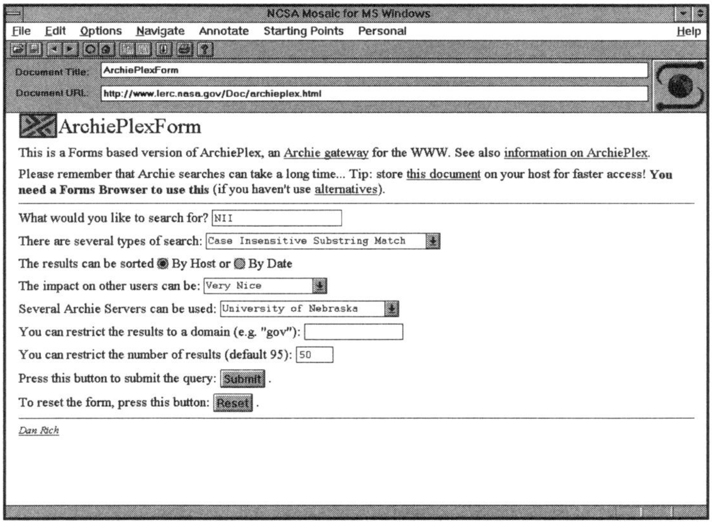

Figure 6.5. *The ArchiePlex form.*

You can download this form to your own system so you don't have to search for it each time; because it sends an Archie request to the computer you select, you don't have to start from the NASA site.

On this form, I've filled in several of the boxes. First, I've decided to search for material about the Clinton administration's proposed information superhighway, which goes by the official name *National Information Infrastructure*, mercifully shortened to *NII*. So NII goes in the first box.

Second, I've opted for the default search type: Case Insensitive Substring Match. This is the subcase from the standard Archie, as described previously. Next, I've clicked on the button to have the search sorted by Host rather than Date, although the latter is often more useful. The *impact on other users* box I've left at the default Very Nice. Essentially, this lets you decide how important your search is, and how much you're willing to inconvenience other users of the site where the search is taking place.

In the next box, I've selected the University of Nebraska from the list of search sites (which you receive by clicking on the down arrow beside the box), because I did this early in the morning when most Nebraskans were still in bed. I decided not to restrict my search by Internet *domain*, even though the suggested `.gov` seemed in order. I wanted comments beyond official government versions. Last, I restricted the results to include 50 documents, and I clicked on the *Submit* button.

Figure 6.6 shows a portion of the search results.

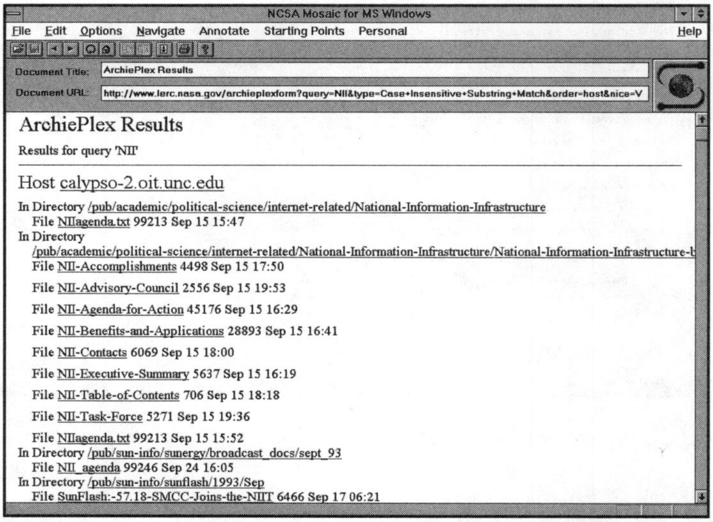

Figure 6.6. *Results of ArchiPlex search.*

As I requested, they were sorted by Host, and each of the underscored blue phrases offers me a location or document to select. By clicking any one of them, Mosaic will launch an FTP command, which will either take me to the FTP site for further searching (in the case of site or directory highlight), or retrieve the program automatically (in the case of actual document name).

Scrolling down the list, I decided to FTP to a specific site and look around from there. Figure 6.7 shows the result of that move, an FTP directory containing the same documents I was told about on the Mosaic search results screen.

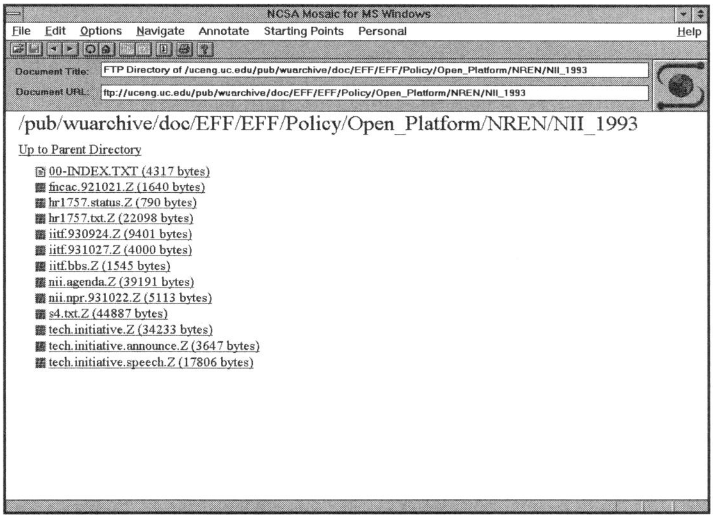

Figure 6.7. *FTP directory resulting from ArchiePlex search.*

The benefit to going into the actual site is that there may be documents there that the Archie search didn't pick out but which may be tangentially related anyway. At this point, it was simply a matter of selecting Load to Disk from Mosaic's Options menu, then clicking the desired document. A few seconds later, the document was on my hard drive, ready for reading and use in my research.

7

WEEK 1

Click and Ye Shall Receive: The World Wide Web and Mosaic

The World Wide Web (WWW) offers a hypermedia environment for accessing the Internet. It is the first Internet tool—or perhaps better termed a toolkit—that takes advantage of the graphical user interface standards of X Window, Microsoft Windows, and the Macintosh. Unlike other Net tools, it displays graphics, plays sound, and even runs movies, as long as you have the equipment to support it. Creators of WWW pages are taking advantage of the Web's multimedia nature to design fully interactive materials across a huge range of subjects.

Today you will learn:

- ☐ The benefits of the World Wide Web as a medium of information presentation.
- ☐ The differences between the Web and other Internet tools.
- ☐ How the Web incorporates Gopher, FTP, Telnet, Archie, WAIS, and so on.
- ☐ How to access the Web in a nongraphical environment.
- ☐ The differences between the two primary WWW browsers, Mosaic and Cello.
- ☐ The appearance, content, and location of dozens of WWW pages.

The Web and the Net: Made for Each Other?

If you're still wondering what all the fuss is about the Internet, your wondering is about to end. As long as you can get into the Net directly and make use of a program called Mosaic or another called Cello, you're about to discover how even the Internet can be user-friendly. Mosaic and Cello let you point and click your way around what's called the World Wide Web, a Net interface based on screens with hypertext links. Unlike most of the Internet, the WWW is colorful, and because of that it offers excitement beyond the fact that the Net houses hordes of information. What you find is entirely dependent on the people who designed the screens, but a good Web page can take you all over the world.

What Exactly Is the World Wide Web?

Unlike FTP and Telnet, the Web is not a program. Unlike Archie and Veronica, it's not a search tool. Unlike Gopher, it's not a specific information browser. Instead, the Web refers both to the way in which we can access information and to the network of information itself. In other words, the Web is in the position of becoming almost synonymous with the Internet itself.

Which makes some sense, after all. William Gibson and other cyberpunk authors have given us terms like the matrix to work with, and when we think of the matrix we think of all the linked electronic information that's out there. The World Wide Web's name evokes the same kind of information morass. Somehow, incredible amounts of available data have been linked one piece to another, in an almost web-like structure. It's a great name, mysterious and yet familiar, probably the best name of all the Internet tools.

Actually, calling the WWW a tool isn't right, either, because the Web provides access to all the other major tools. Once on a Web page, you easily can Gopher or FTP, and in fact most Web pages provide automatic links to a number of Gopher and FTP sites. You also can use the Web to Telnet to other machines, and search tools like Archie and WAIS are extremely Web-friendly as well. If you have access to a graphical version of the Web, you'll quickly find it at the center of your Internet activities. It's that intuitive, and it's that powerful.

What makes it so strong? Simply put, presentation. Gophers are fine; they're usable, unintimidating, and easy to understand. Anyone can look at a list and figure out which item they want to choose. But lists are ultimately quite boring. They all look pretty much alike, and they all do much the same thing.

A WWW page takes advantage of the fact that all our lives we've been interacting with the printed page. A Web page looks like a page from a book or magazine; rather than lists you have paragraphs, and graphics often are dispersed throughout. Some pages are tasteful, others quite garish; some are clearly professional, others bear the stamp of the amateur.

The only difference—and it's a huge one—is that a Web page contains links to other Web pages, Gopher servers, FTP sites, and so on. When you're reading a book and you see an interesting reference to another book, your only option is to head to the library and hunt the book down. Which means that most of the time, of course, you don't bother. On a Web page, referenced information areas are highlighted; the reference is underlined and usually a different color than the standard text. Move the mouse to the highlight until the cursor changes shape, then click. Presto! You're taken to the referenced site.

Note: This is hypertext, maybe the most powerful demonstration to date of that concept. If you've ever used the help system of a GUI environment like the Mac or Windows, using the Web will be instantly familiar. Those systems also use hypertext: from the Contents page you just click the topic you want, and a new page will pop up, usually with other hypertext links. The Web is precisely the same idea, except that instead of just making the link on your hard drive or CD-ROM, it can fire its link request half-way around the world. No matter how jaded you get about all this global network stuff, watching the WWW do its thing remains pretty awesome for a long time after you've started using it.

The nice thing about a Web page is that the linked reference can be placed anywhere on the page. Some Web pages are designed like the Contents pages on a GUI help screen, but others are simply free-flowing prose with highlighted words or phrases, and with graphics that may themselves be links to other locations. It's not uncommon, for example, to see a single paragraph with three or four separate highlights and illustrated with two or three small graphics, all the features working together in a comfortably readable design. Like printed prose, you can simply read past the links if you want, getting a good sense of what's available before branching out into the great digital unknown.

And the operative word is *unknown.* While you'll get to know some Web pages like the back of your hand, you'll never get to know them all. Like Gophers, Web pages are proliferating at an almost unbelievable rate, because they're fairly easy to design and implement. Commercial Internet providers often provide their own Web page, and dedicated Webbers quickly will become familiar with the pages at the National Center for Supercomputing Applications (NCSA), home of the famous WWW software Mosaic. The NCSA maintains a What's New page that gives you at least some idea of what's been added recently, and one look at it is a rather sobering experience. Just when you think you might be on top of the information world, along comes another dollop of new WWW pages, each of which points to all kinds of other stuff to know.

Note: This is a major point. The World Wide Web may have begun more or less as a small brochure with only a few pages, but it quickly grew to the size of a magazine. As I'm writing this, it already contains enough pages for a good-sized book, and by this time next year it'll have taken on the size of a substantial book collection. Not long from now, it'll be a library all its own, and we'll see more and more pages guiding you to different Web pages. And given that any Web page can easily point to dozens, even hundreds, of other information sources, it doesn't take long to feel overwhelmed by the sheer amount of material that's out there.

But that's the bad news. The good news is that the Web makes that material more manageable than does any other current Internet tool. You may not be able to access everything, but at least you have a sense of what's being made available—which is something that not even Gopher can do.

Excursion 7.1. WWW Tour, Stop 1: The NCSA Demo Page, and the EXPO Ticket Office

Time for a tour. If you have access to Mosaic, fire it up and follow along. If not, just keep reading. You don't actually have to travel to places to find a travelogue informative, and for the next few pages that's what this chapter will become.

Where to start? How about the beginning. No, not the well-constructed tutorials about the Web itself—those are fine, but you'd like to get moving. So how about going to NCSA's Demo Page? Once there, we can start finding our own way around.

In other words, forget the lessons. Let's just jump in and fly.

Warning: Actually, there's one lesson we simply can't ignore. Once again, it's the primary rule of Netiquette. Try to avoid Webbing during business hours, because that's when computers around the world are busiest doing real things. If you fire up Mosaic at noon, try to select a location somewhere in the world that will no longer be fulfilling its daily computational needs. Eastern Europe, for example, or maybe the Far East. By the same token, if you're Webbing at 3 a.m., remember that those European computers you're accessing are experiencing their morning backlogs. In many cases, in fact, you won't have a choice: the machine you're trying to reach simply won't let you in.

Figure 7.1 shows a very small portion of NCSA's Demo Page (`http://www.ncsa.uiuc.edu/demoweb/demo.html`). This page offers a wide range of WWW browsing points, and if your computer is set up with the appropriate audio equipment and drivers you can even hear audio clips narrating the topic.

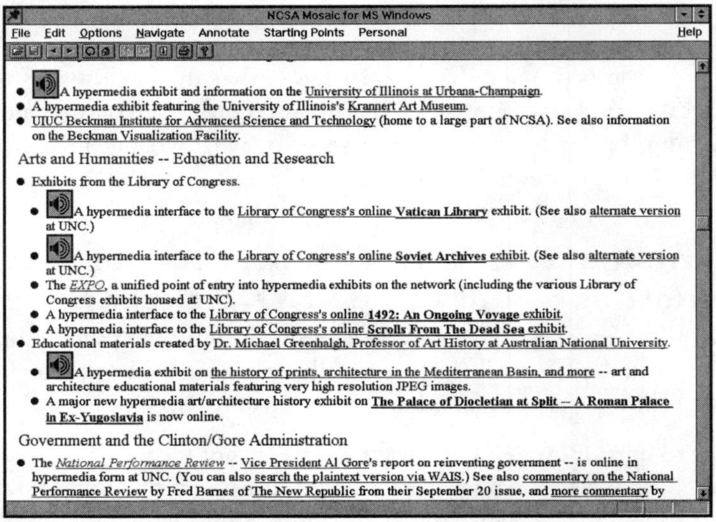

Figure 7.1. *NCSA Mosaic Demo Document.*

There's a fair bit of interesting stuff here, but let's start somewhere. Let's also assume that we feel like both enjoying ourselves and learning something (yes, it's possible to do both). Scrolling down the page, you'll notice a section called Arts and Humanities—Education and Research. Here, the Vatican Library, Soviet Archives, 1492: An Ongoing Voyage, and Scrolls From the Dead Sea exhibits and 1492 exhibits look fascinating, so we'll choose the EXPO highlight to give us access to all four. Moving the cursor over this highlight, you'll notice that Mosaic shows the target address on the status bar at the bottom of the screen. Fine, click.

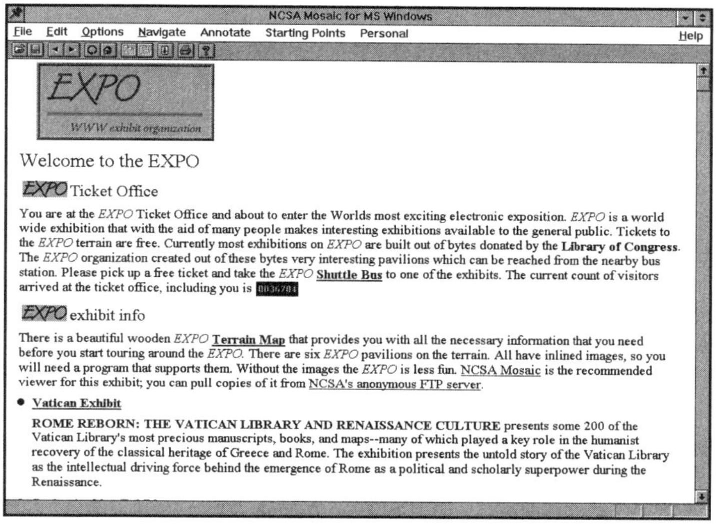

Figure 7.2. *The EXPO Ticket Office.*

Here we are: Figure 7.2, the Expo Ticket Office (`http://sunsite.unc.edu/expo/ticket_office.html`). Notice the way this page is set up: readable text with just a few clickable highlights. One of them is a shuttle bus, a nice touch for a page that's built on the metaphor of the tour exhibit. Scrolling down the page, we come to Figure 7.3, which gives us hypertext jumps to the four exhibits we're interested in. If we scroll a bit further we'll find more, but four is sufficient for now (so much to see, so little time ...). Columbus and the discovery/devastation of America—depending on your point of view—has always been a fascination, so let's see what the 1492 exhibit has to offer.

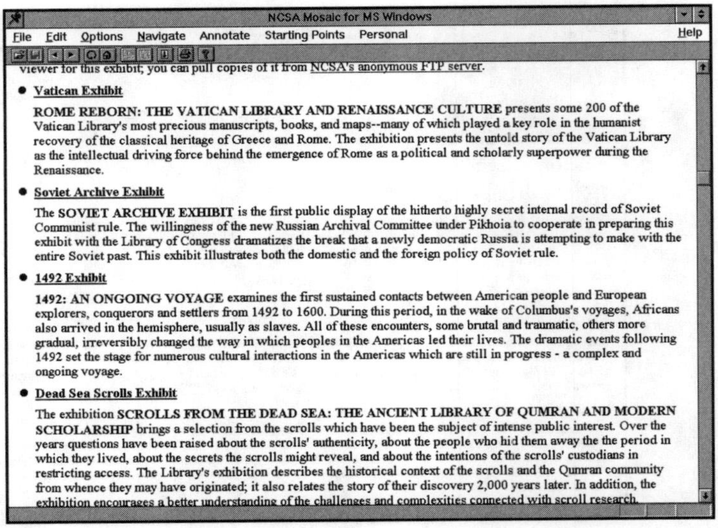

Figure 7.3. *Links to four exhibits from EXPO.*

Excursion 7.2. WWW Tour, Stop 2: 1492

Figure 7.4 shows one of the Web's most consistently strong features—pleasant graphics. The text of the piece sounds sophisticated enough to warrant further investigation, so scroll down and see the possible links. In Figure 7.5, a number of choices are possible, including a bibliography of readings and return to the Shuttle Bus. Of the six sections of the exhibit, one of the more interesting-sounding is What Came To Be Called "America".

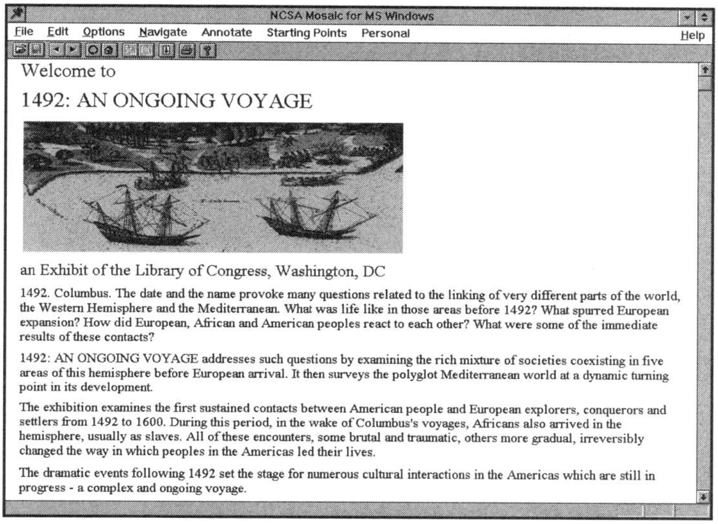

Figure 7.4. *1492 page demonstrating the WWW's graphics.*

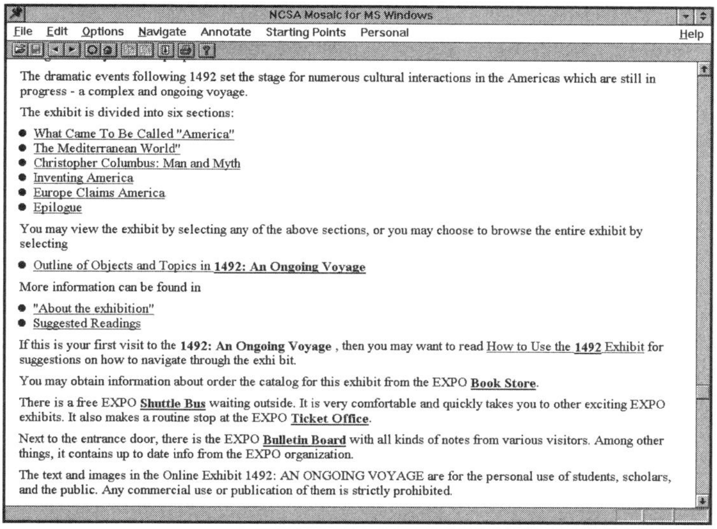

Figure 7.5. *Choices available on the 1492 page.*

Following this section three screens in, we arrive at Figure 7.6.

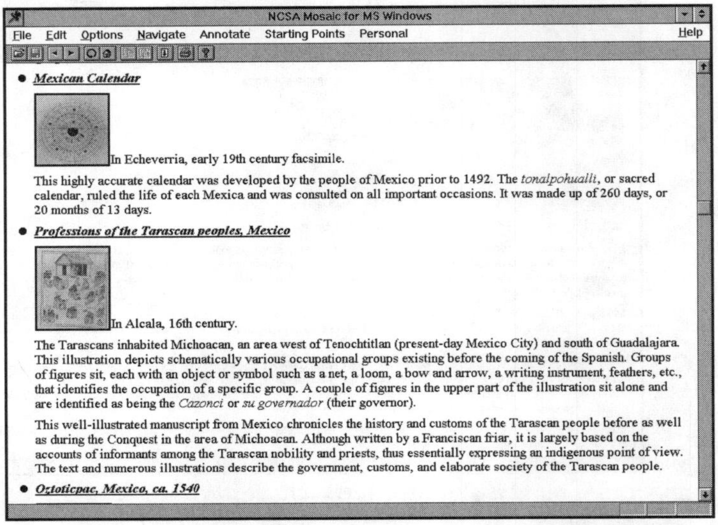

Figure 7.6. *Page showing links to information about the "new world."*

On this page are three major links, one dealing with the Mexican calendar, a second with the professions of the Tarascan peoples, and the third with the estate of Oztoticpac. Moving the pointer over any of these reveals—by looking at Mosaic's status bar—that none of the three is a link to another page at all. Instead, they all have the file extension .GIF, which means that if you click them (either the picture or the highlighted title), you'll download a .GIF file. Whether you download it for viewing or directly to your hard drive depends on whether or not you select Load to Disk from the options menu. If you don't have a viewer set up but you want the file anyway, download it to your drive.

> **Note:** Often a Web page will give you two options in cases like this. If you click the graphic, you'll download it, but if you click the highlighted title you'll link to another page. In this case, there's only one choice.

Tip: The World Wide Web contains numerous pages with downloadable graphics, sound, text, or video files. In almost every case, there'll be a note somewhere on the page or on a linked page explaining that you're free to download the files for personal or research use, but not for commercial use. Commercial use, incidentally, includes such things as business presentations, so take care not to abuse this privilege. If you want to use them otherwise, write for permission; often you'll find a contact name on the page itself.

Tip: If you're using a modem (no matter what speed), you might want to consider turning off the graphics when retrieving Web pages. In Mosaic, you can do so by going to the Options menu and toggling off the command Display Inline Images. In Cello, the command is in the Configuration menu; go down to Graphics and over to Fetch Automatically, and toggle it off. When you get to a screen whose graphics you want to see, toggle the graphics display back on and reload the document (Reload is in Mosaic's Navigate menu and Cello's File menu).

Excursion 7.3. WWW Tour, Stop 3: The Vatican Library

Okay, so we know a bit more about 1492 than we did before we started. That Vatican exhibit keeps calling, though, so let's hop on the Shuttle Bus and head back to the Ticket Office. This time, it's off to the Vatican section, where, two clicks later, we find ourselves in the Main Hall. (See Figure 7.7.)

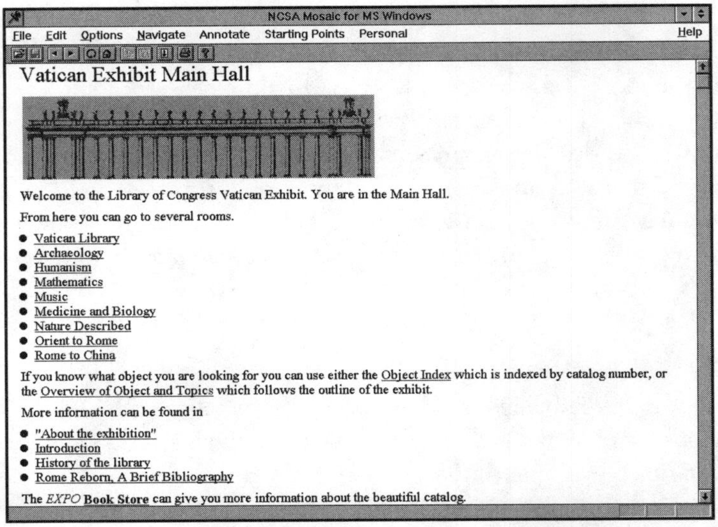

Figure 7.7. *The Vatican Exhibit's main hall page.*

From here, a click on the Vatican Library and then on the City Recovers brings us to Figure 7.8, a long page that offers everything from views of the nearly deserted city of Rome in the fourteenth century to information about other artifacts in the library from that time. Most of these are .JPG files, which means that, like .GIFs, they're downloadable graphics. Beware, though: these files can get extremely large, especially as you move to the illuminated manuscripts available elsewhere.

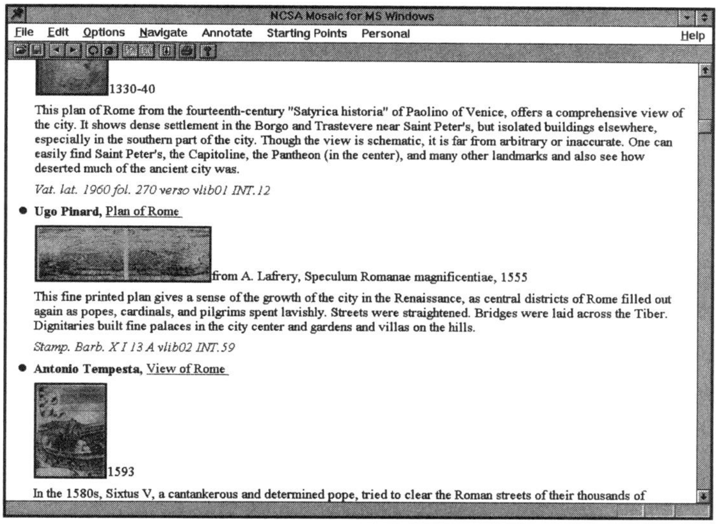

Figure 7.8. *Page about the history of Rome, from Vatican Exhibit.*

One more stop before we leave the Library of Congress Expo. Hopping aboard the Shuttle Bus, we bypass the Restaurant (real recipes here, folks) and head to the Soviet exhibit. A guided tour leads us to all sorts of fascinating information, provided not by political speculation but rather by the new Russian authorities themselves. Among them is a discussion of Chernobyl, with a separate page pointing out the plant's design flaws (see Figure 7.9).

There's lots more to do here, but this is only one tiny portion of the World Wide Web. So let's move away from the Library of Congress exhibit and, using the same point-and-click techniques, find other entertaining, informative, or just plain interesting locations.

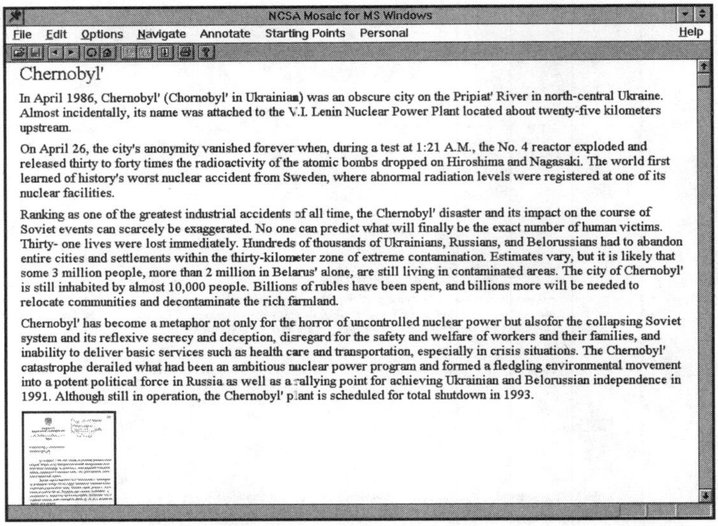

Figure 7.9. *Chernobyl page from Soviet exhibit.*

Tip: We've seen how to download graphics files, but in some of the locations, we'll find sound and video files as well. All such files can be downloaded to your drive, but Mosaic (and Cello) works best when you can view or listen from within the program itself. In order to do so, you have to specify in the configuration files what graphics, sound, and video "viewers" are to be used. If you don't have viewers readily available, you can download them from the Web itself. From Mosaic's Starting Points menu, select Home Pages and then NCSA's (`http://www.ncsa.uiuc.edu/General/NCSAhome.html`). You'll encounter Figure 7.10, which includes an item called NCSA developed-software. You can click your way from here right into the NCSA FTP site, then use the Load to Disk feature and download the viewers you need. Each comes with installation instructions.

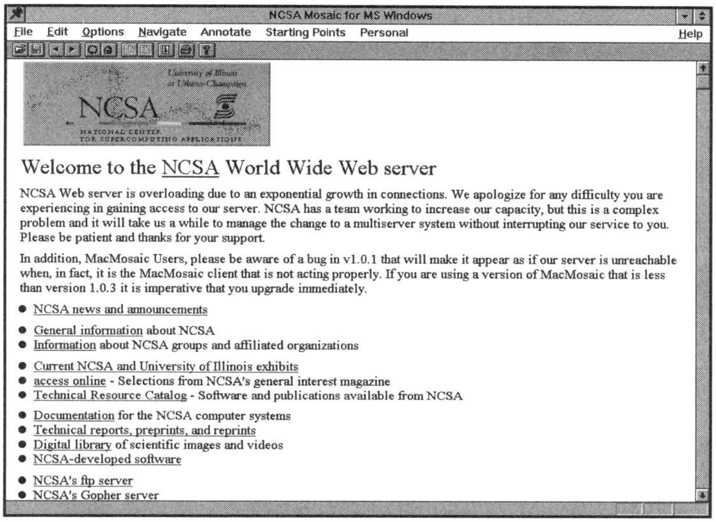

Figure 7.10. *NCSA World Wide Web main page.*

Excursion 7.4. WWW Tour, Stop 4: The NCSA What's New Page and a Quick Check on the Coffee Machine

Back to the Starting Points menu, and this time to the What's New page (see Figure 7.11—`http://www.ncsa.uiuc.edu/SDG/Software/Mosaic/Docs/whats-new.html`).

One of the most amazing pages on the Web, this one is updated two to three times per week, and as the entry from March 18 shows, more and more is being added all the time. Scrolling down this page, we discover that *Mother Jones* magazine is not only on the WWW, but has just released a new issue, so we click there and then into the current issue (`http://www.mojones.com/motherjones.html`). Figure 7.12 shows what's available from this exceptionally interesting magazine, several links pointing to a number of strong articles.

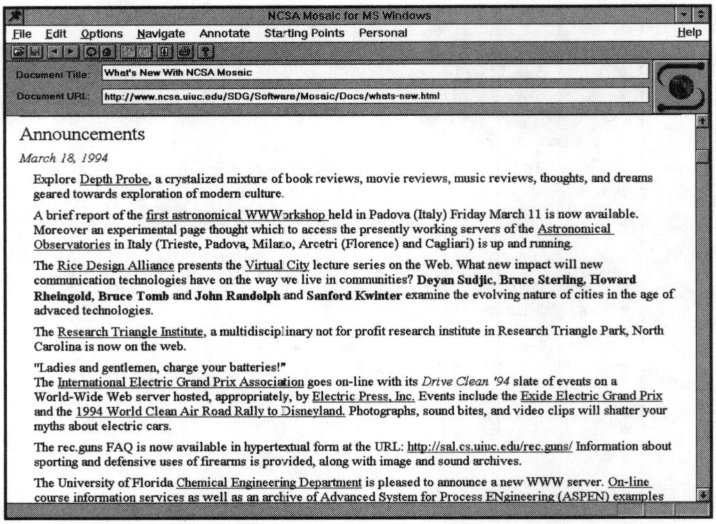

Figure 7.11. *NCSA's What's New page.*

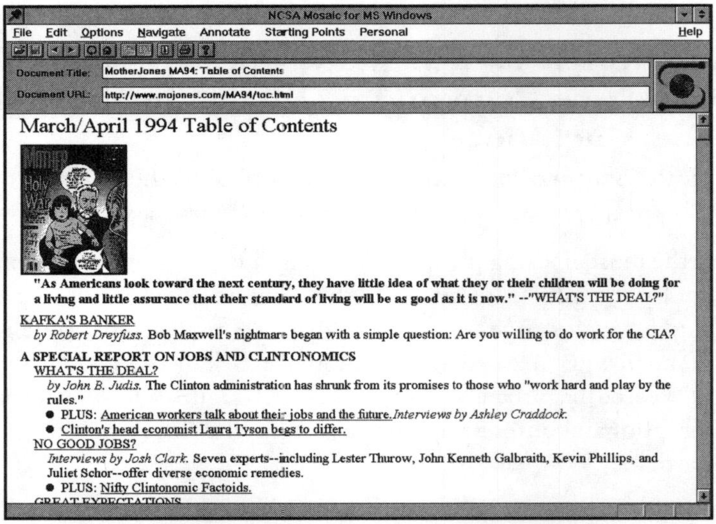

Figure 7.12. Mother Jones *magazine WWW page.*

Coffee time! We've spent a good chunk of time touring and reading, so some refreshment is in order. To demonstrate that not everything on the World Wide Web is serious, let's look at Cambridge University's Trojan Room Coffee Machine page (see Figure 7.13—`http://www.cl.cam.ac.uk/coffee/coffee.html`). Essentially, there's a camera trained on the coffee machine, and by clicking on the Click Here link you get an updated picture to let you know if it's worth going upstairs to get one. Frivolous, sure—and useful only for those in the building—but it demonstrates even more of the Web's enormous potential.

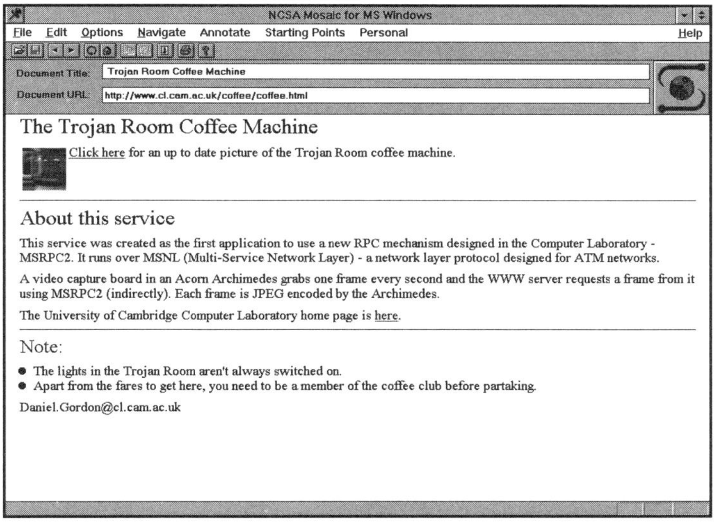

Figure 7.13. *Trojan Room Coffee Machine page from Cambridge.*

That's it for the tour. We've visited exhibits on 1492, the Vatican, and the Soviet archives, we've downloaded images and learned where to find viewers for graphics, sound, and video, we've found and curled up with the most recent issue of *Mother Jones* magazine, and we've even found out if there's fresh coffee at Cambridge University. All of this, by the way, through pointing and clicking on some very attractive pages.

Browsing the Web: The Major Software Packages

Let's take a short break from actually touring the World Wide Web, and look instead at the various ways of doing so. These ways are called *browsers.*

Note: Nowhere is the relationship between the World Wide Web and our ability to read more apparent than in the fact that its tools are called browsers. When you fire up Archie, Veronica, or WAIS, you know you're about to do a search, and if you've ever done serious work in a library you know that searching is precise, task-specific, and often quite tiring. Browsing, on the other hand, is a pleasure. You browse to get a feel for what's going on and to locate material that might be of interest to you. Browsing in an unpressured, thoroughly enjoyable activity, something you do on a rainy Sunday afternoon.

Warning: That's the good news, of course. The bad news is that, from the standpoint of efficiency and actually getting work done, browsing can be disastrous. If you're trying to find something specific, use WWW software carefully and with exact goals in mind. Otherwise, it's like opening an encyclopedia with no particular subject in mind. You might learn a lot, but you're not likely to accomplish anything you can look back to with satisfaction.

Several browsers are available. On a nongraphical screen, the easiest to use is Lynx, a UNIX browser that you'll find when you log in via Telnet to several WWW sites. If you're a Microsoft Windows user with direct Internet access, be sure to check out Cello, a graphical Web browser developed by the Legal Information Institute at Cornell University's law school. But by far the best-known of the browsers is NCSA Mosaic, with versions for a variety of UNIX platforms and for Microsoft Windows, the Macintosh, and the Commodore Amiga.

Lynx: Character-Based Browsing

First, a quick look at the most usable character-based browser, UNIX's Lynx. I'll say only a few words about it, because I can't imagine anyone using it if they have access to either Mosaic or Cello (discussed in the next two sections). It's okay, but only just.

You enter a Lynx browser through the Telnet command, and you can access most Lynx WWW hosts through Gopher. Telnet, as you know by now, tends to produce slow displays and results, and Lynx suffers greatly as a result. Once logged in, Lynx's options appear on the bottom of the screen, as shown in Figure 7.14.

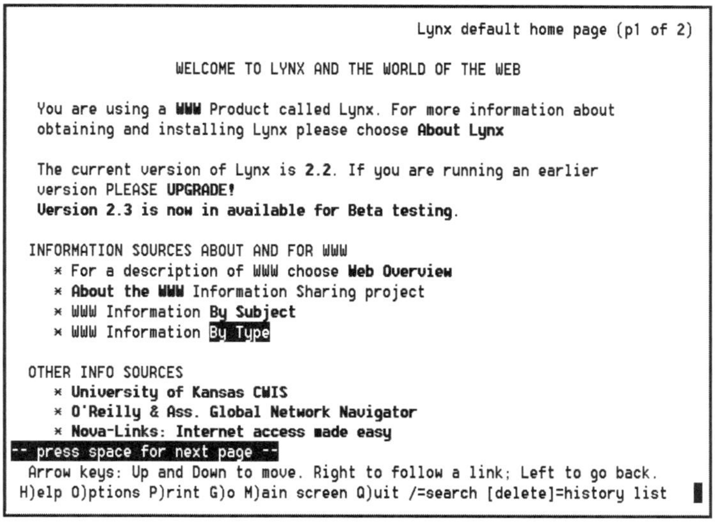

Figure 7.14. *Lynx introductory screen.*

As this figure shows, you can move to the next page by pressing the spacebar, or you can use the arrow keys to browse. The hypertext links are in boldface. Pressing the up or down arrows moves you to the next or previous link on the screen. When you've reached the desired link, you follow it by pressing the right arrow, and you can move back up a link by pressing the left arrow.

It's all fairly straightforward, but the results are nowhere near as intuitive or graphically compelling as the Mosaic or Cello screens. Figure 7.15, for example, displays a small portion of the NCSA What's New Page, and it just doesn't do what the Web was designed to do.

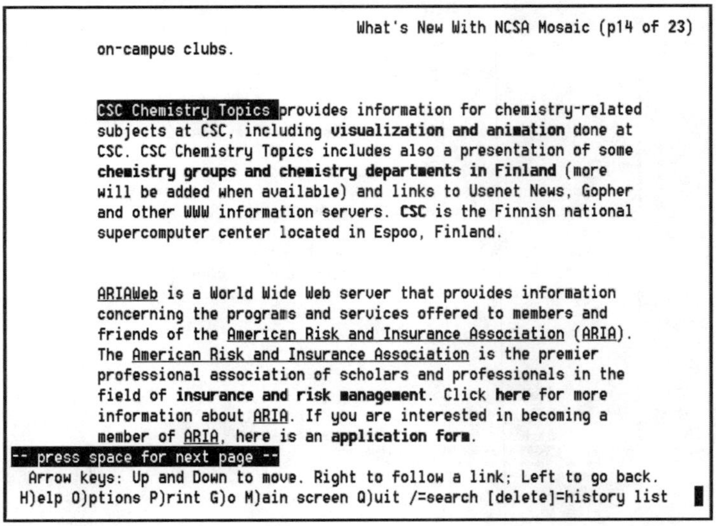

What's New With NCSA Mosaic (p14 of 23)
on-campus clubs.
CSC Chemistry Topics provides information for chemistry-related subjects at CSC, including visualization and animation done at CSC. CSC Chemistry Topics includes also a presentation of some chemistry groups and chemistry departments in Finland (more will be added when available) and links to Usenet News, Gopher and other WWW information servers. CSC is the Finnish national supercomputer center located in Espoo, Finland.
ARIAWeb is a World Wide Web server that provides information concerning the programs and services offered to members and friends of the American Risk and Insurance Association (ARIA). The American Risk and Insurance Association is the premier professional association of scholars and professionals in the field of insurance and risk management. Click here for more information about ARIA. If you are interested in becoming a member of ARIA, here is an application form.
-- press space for next page --
Arrow keys: Up and Down to move. Right to follow a link; Left to go back.
H)elp O)ptions P)rint G)o M)ain screen Q)uit /=search [delete]=history list

Figure 7.15. *NCSA What's New Page through Lynx.*

There's also the problem of displaying graphics, which simply can't be done on most UNIX terminal screens. And forget about sound, video, and the like.

Note: So why use Lynx? Because, for a number of users, it's the only option. Not everyone has the equipment or the type of Internet connection needed to use Mosaic or Cello. But I really can't recommend the Web as a strong feature of the Internet if Lynx is all you have to work with. In such a case, you're better to stick with Gophers and the other independent tools.

NCSA Mosaic: The Best-Known Graphical Browser

Tip: See Day 2 for download locations of the Mosaic software.

Developed by the National Center of Supercomputing Applications at the University of Illinois at Urbana-Champaign, Mosaic has become the most admired piece of Internet software available. In fact, Mosaic is seen as synonymous with the World Wide Web in the same way that, until recently, spreadsheeting meant Lotus 1-2-3. As more and more Internet users get direct access accounts, it's entirely possible that people will start to equate Mosaic with not just the Web, but with the Internet itself. It's that powerful a piece of software.

Note: This is a contentious issue among dedicated Cello users (see the following section on LII Cello). All too often on Web pages and in the press, references to the World Wide Web are equated with references to Mosaic. But Mosaic was first, and it runs on multiple platforms; that's why it has this reputation. Other Web browsers besides Mosaic and Cello will follow, but they'll have an uphill fight. Still, the perfect browser has yet to appear.

Mosaic seems magical. Instead of lists, you have a page with formatted text, clear highlights, and colorful graphics. Instead of typing arcane FTP commands, you just click the file you want and wait for it to download. Instead of mastering the syntax of an Archie search, you fill in a form. A couple of days ago, I even used a Mosaic form to order flowers for my wife! (And, yep, they arrived.)

When you first boot up Mosaic, a number of choices already await you. From the Starting Points menu you can select a number of *home pages.* Home pages are at the first page of any institution's (or person's) WWW section; usually the home page contains links to sub-pages, but the home page itself is a kind of introductory document. Although it's not a home page, a great place to start is NCSA's Mosaic What's New Page, because from here you can click your way all around the world. Under the menu item Other Documents are several other interesting places to visit, but you'll find out soon enough that you can reach all of them from pages scattered throughout the Web.

A few other interesting areas appear in the Starting Points menu. First, there's a list of Gopher servers. Select any one of them, and you'll see that Mosaic operates just fine as Gopher software, certainly more colorfully than character-based Gopher lists (but not as well as dedicated Gopher programs). Also available is a list of FTP sites, and here you'll discover that Mosaic also lets you do anonymous FTPs with little fuss (again, though, a dedicated FTP program has stronger features). There's a Finger gateway, and Whois gateway, and a specific link to the InterNIC Information Source Gopher as well, so you know right away that Mosaic is almost a one-stop Internet resource tool.

For now, though, let's stick with the WWW itself. At some point, you'll find yourself staring at a Web page you just know you'll want to come back to. Mosaic lets you do this, but it's probably the least intuitive part of the package. In the Navigate menu is an item called Menu Editor, which, as its name implies, enables you to edit the menus. What it's best at, though, is letting you save Web locations. Click Menu Editor, and then in the Menus box choose the menu in which you want the page to appear. Click Insert, and the Add Item box will appear, showing the Title of the page and its URL address. You can change the title to suit yourself, but often you won't need to. You also can use the Menu editor to create new sub-menu items, thereby creating cascading menus of your own.

Why is the menu editor necessary? First, because you'll find hordes of locations you want to keep track of. Second, because the World Wide Web locates items by pointing to their Uniform Resource Locator (URL) address, and I'm convinced that no human being can possibly remember these things. As an example, the URL for the main FTP page reads `http://hoohoo.ncsa.uiuc.edu:80/ftp.interface.html`. Another, this one from Mosaic's World Wide Web Info menu item, shows the following URL: `http://info.cern.ch/hypertext/WWW/LineMode/Defaults/default.html`. Now, I realize that someone reading this book right now is thinking, "What's so tough about that?", but given the well-known psychological fact that seven items is pretty well the upper limit for instant recall, I suspect most of us have neither the interest nor the ability to remember these URLs. Mosaic's menu editor makes it unnecessary.

Tip: Don't ignore the URLs. Somewhere along the line—in a mailing list or a news group, for example—you'll find out about a Web page you haven't seen anywhere. Inevitably, you'll be told something like, "There's a new WWW home page devoted exclusively to fans of *Charlie's Angels*. Its URL is `http://nostalgia.popculture.com/TV/seventies/hair/fawcettjacksonsmith.html`. Enjoy." In order to get there, you'll have to use the Open URL feature in Mosaic's File menu, and then laboriously enter the URL address. Once you're there, of course, you can fire up the menu editor and bookmark the location so you can return much more easily.

There's another thing you can do with Web pages. You can save them to your hard disk and call them up from there, using the Open Local File item from the File menu. For a favorite or long Web page, this is a good idea, because if it's on your hard drive you have access to it even if you can't get into the server it came from. Any time you find something you want to download to your drive, you have to decide in advance that you want to do so, and then select the horribly named Load to Disk command from the Options menu. Then click the item you want to download, and you'll see your system's usual dialog box.

There are only a couple of other issues to address in Mosaic. First, you can annotate any page you find, in order to make it more personal. Second, you'll want to download some viewers. *Viewers* are programs that automatically load whenever Mosaic brings in a file, letting you see it or hear it (or, in the case of video, both). You'll need a good viewer for .GIF and .JPG graphics files, another for .AU sound files, and a third for .MPG video files. You'll also find other sorts of files out there (.WAV, .MID, .VOC, .AVI, and so on), so you'll need viewers for these as well. Then, in order to make them work with Mosaic, you must tell Mosaic where to find them. In the case of the Windows version of Mosaic, this means extensive editing of the `mosaic.ini` file that came with Mosaic in the first place. Mosaic comes with a text file available to help you, but it would be much better if you could specify these things through a menu item in Mosaic itself.

LII Cello: Competition for Mosaic in Microsoft Windows

Tip: See Day 2 for download locations for Cello.

Cello is the product of the Legal Information Institute at the Law School of Cornell University. It was designed for Microsoft Windows users (only) as a competitor to Mosaic, but in fact I recommend having both. Some of Mosaic's shortcomings are addressed very capably by Cello, and in a few important ways Cello is the easier program to use.

Note: Most of the features discussed about Mosaic also are fully implemented in Cello. In this section, I'll simply touch on the differences.

To me, Cello doesn't look quite as nice as Mosaic, although that's merely personal opinion (and hotly contested in LII's mailing list, Cello-L). Cello's nonsolid underlining scheme isn't as immediately striking as Mosaic's, and if you choose not to display graphics (a choice modem users frequently will make), a graphic-dominated page can look quite ugly. Cello's sculpted bullets are sharper than Mosaic's, however, and its easy method of choosing font colors enables you to customize the page the way you want it. More importantly, Cello's ease-of-use features outweigh its minor esthetic deficiencies, and once you've worked with it you'll go back to it repeatedly.

When you're browsing the WWW, bookmarking features are crucial; Cello's are much easier to use than Mosaic's, albeit less complete. Rather than burying the feature inside another menu, Cello offers a Bookmark menu and a dialog box that make the process quick and simple. Simply click the Mark Current Document button, change the name of the bookmark if you want, and you've done it.

You can use the Jump menu to go to other WWW, Gopher, and FTP sites. This is one of Cello's strongest features. Where Mosaic asks you to go to the File menu, select Open URL, and then type in the address complete with prefixes like `gopher://`, Cello lets you open the appropriate dialog box from the Jump menu and type fewer characters.

Cello also makes downloading somewhat easier. You select your download directory from the Configure menu (this becomes the default for all downloads, although you can change it), and then click the item you want to download. Cello will put it in that directory and tell you when it's done (Mosaic doesn't tell you anything).

Other features also outdo Mosaic. You can, for example, set up your e-mail address, mail server, and other pointers directly through Cello's Configure menu, and you can specify your own Telnet client and Editor here as well. You also can mail files directly from Cello to other Internet addresses through a simple but useful mail program included in the package. Unlike Mosaic, Cello includes a strong help system (Mosaic has none at all as of this writing), and this offers extremely useful assistance in writing your own Web pages (see the Extra Credit section at the end of this chapter).

Cello doesn't make use of Windows' status bar (the gray bar at the bottom of the screen) as usefully as Mosaic, however. While Mosaic displays the link address when you pass the cursor over the hyperlink, Cello does not. Nor does Cello tell you the progress of a download, as Mosaic does. Cello does, however, offer what's called a *peek* mode, extremely useful for modem users. Peek loads only the first 4096 bytes of the destination page, letting you see if you really want to be there or not (select File/Reload Document to fetch the whole page if you decide you do).

Tip: For new Internet users, I'd recommend Cello over Mosaic. Eventually, though, you'll want to have both. And since both are available through FTP sites, the price certainly is right.

Excursion 7.5. More WWW Sites to Visit and Explore

In the first excursions in this chapter, we visited only a very tiny fraction of the WWW sites available for browsing. It's time to take a look at a number of others, but keep in mind that even these barely scratch the Web's expanding surface.

> **Tip:** Given the speed at which the Web is expanding (at least 20 important new locations per week, often more), this entire chapter is in danger of being out of date by the time you read it. It's not so much that what's shown here won't be around any longer (it will be, although it might look different), but rather that so much more will be available to you. Treat this as a starting point, then explore on your own.

Figure 7.16 shows a portion of the Webbed Information System from North Carolina State University (`http://dewey.lib.ncsu.edu`). Of note here are the icons in the colorful graphics. Clicking on any one of them will take you to that location. It's yet another way of navigating through cyberspace. One of the places this home page takes you to appears in Figure 7.17, and operates as a guide to a number of Internet resources.

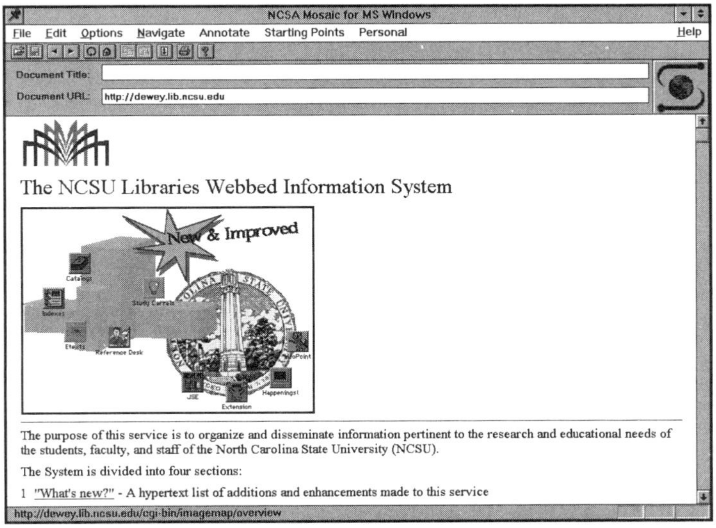

Figure 7.16. *The NCSU Libraries Webbed Information System.*

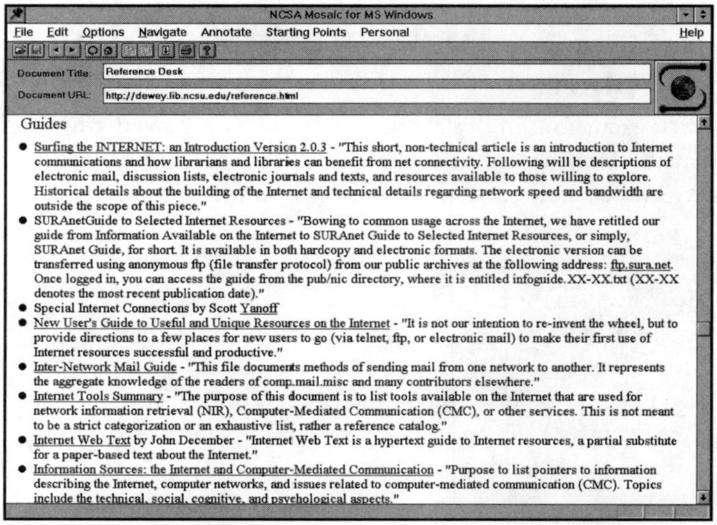

Figure 7.17. *NCSU guide to Internet resources.*

Surfing the Internet is a very useful guide, and anything by Internet collector Scott Yanoff (the third bullet) is worth investigating. The work of another Internet collector, John December, appears in the last three items on the screen, with the Internet Tools Summary especially useful if you want to know more about what's available (see Day 12 for a closer look at December's work).

In Figure 7.18, you see the commercial potential of the Web beginning to appear. Here is the subscription information for a U.K.-based magazine about the World Wide Web, *3W* (`http://marketplace.com:70/0/3W/subsinfo.html`). And speaking of commercial potential, how about Figure 7.19? Grant's Florist and Greenhouse maintains an order-over-the-Web service for delivery anywhere within the United States or Canada. After choosing from a selection of arrangements on the home page, you jump to this order page (`http://florist.com:1080/flowers/order-flowers.html`) and fill in the blanks. There's even a note on the safety of sending credit card information over the Internet, and for those with no sense of what day it happens to be the company provides an online reminder service as well. And, oh yeah, it works.

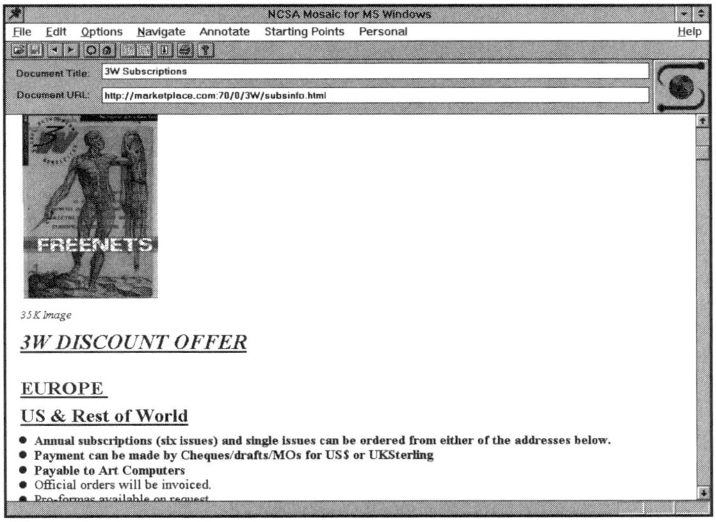

Figure 7.18. *Subscription information for* 3W *Magazine.*

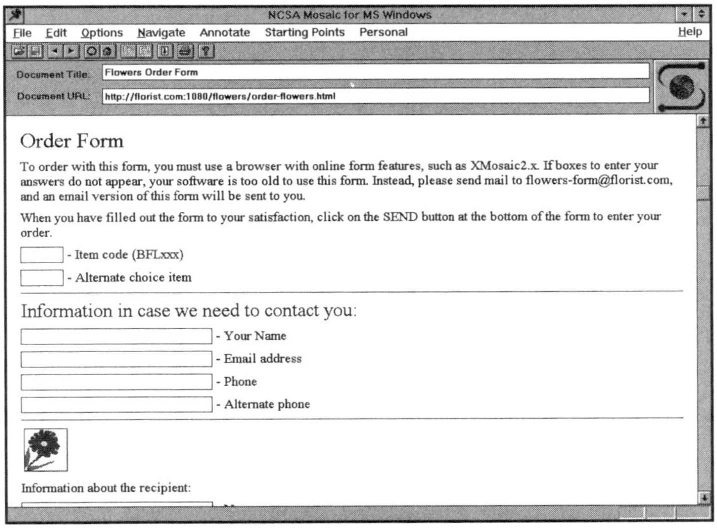

Figure 7.19. *WWW page for ordering flowers from the Net.*

Looking for a house? The Web can help here as well (see Figure 7.20).

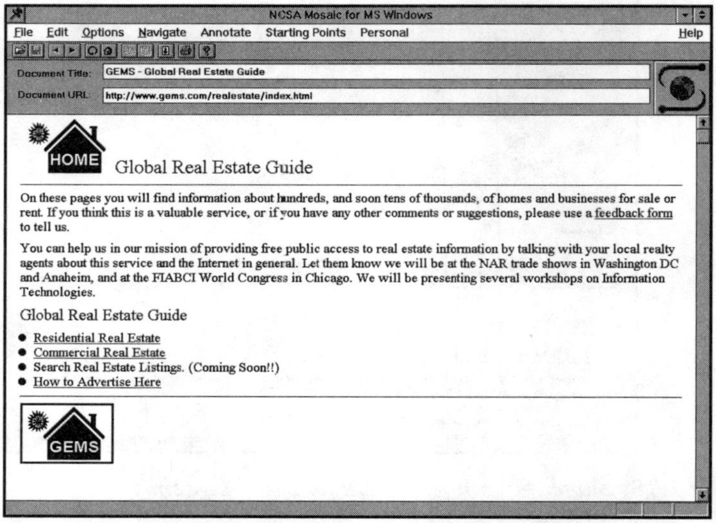

Figure 7.20. *Global Real Estate Guide home page.*

Although the listings on the Global Real Estate Guide (`http://www.gems.com/realestate/index.html`) aren't yet anywhere near as extensive as those in the average newspaper, this page shows the power of the Web as a marketing tool. Perhaps one of the Web's most exciting commercial prospects lies in its potential usefulness for stores who might usually rely on mail order to get the word out. The Communion Clothing Company (California) has established an online catalog (`http://www.internex.com/communion/commp2.html`) to serve this function (see Figure 7.21).

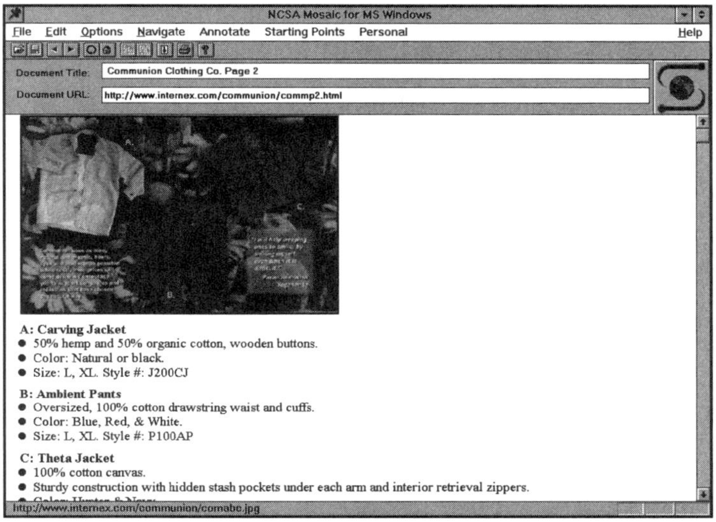

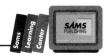

Figure 7.21. *Catalog page from Communion Clothing Company.*

Not surprisingly, publishers were among the first to realize the Internet's potential. Far from the stodgy paper-based Luddites we sometimes imagine them to be, publishers constantly are searching for new ways of getting their products to the public (which is, after all, what the word *publishing* means). Early in the World Wide Web's history, O'Reilly and Associates put together the *Global Network Navigator* (`http://nearnet.gnn.com/news/home/news.html`), an online magazine with considerable appeal (see Figure 7.22).

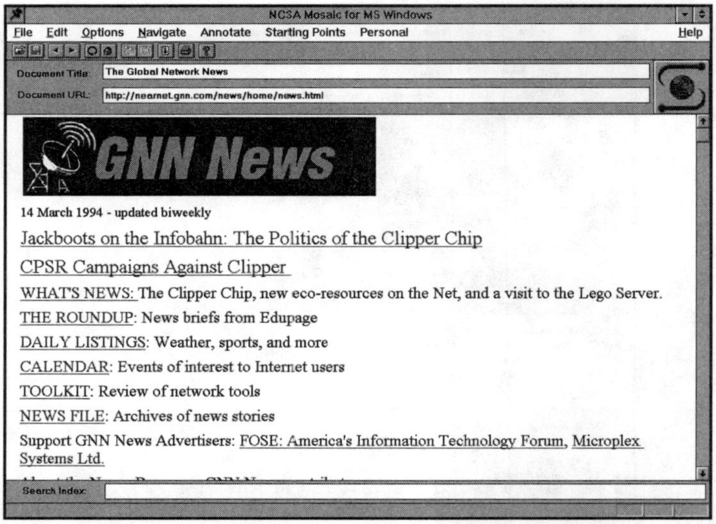

Figure 7.22. The Global Network Navigator.

A little less graphically ambitious, the *Palo Alto Weekly* newspaper has also gone online (in fact, the entire town is moving its way onto the Net), and anyone with a Web browser has access to some very interesting reading on a weekly basis (see Figure 7.23—`http://www.service.com/PAW/home.html`). And while you might expect a magazine like *Wired* to have its own Web page (`http://wired.com`), it's actually more exciting to see publications like Vancouver's *International Teletimes* (`http://www.wimsey.com/teletimes.root/teletimes_home_page.html`) finding a new electronic audience (see Figure 7.24).

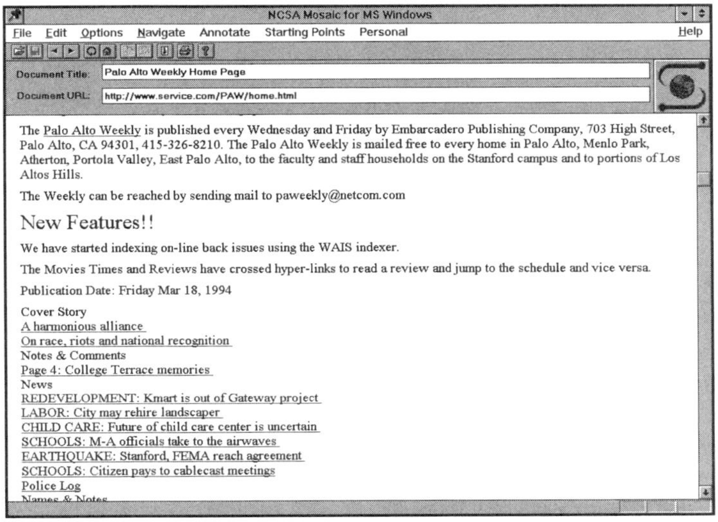

Figure 7.23. *WWW page for the* Palo Alto Weekly *newspaper.*

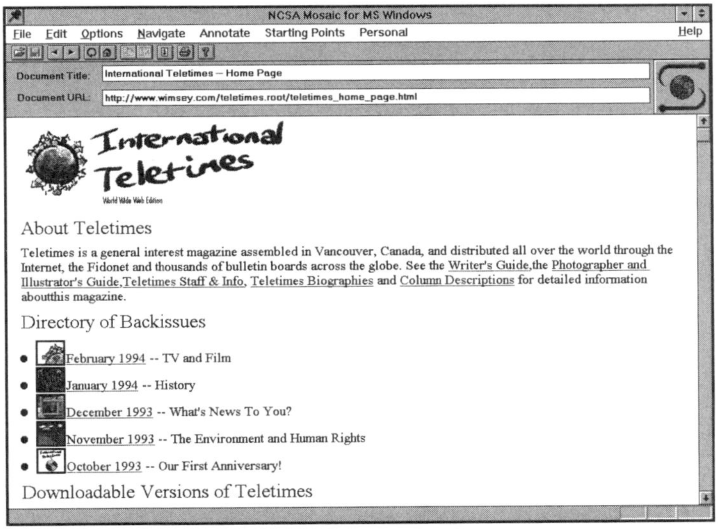

Figure 7.24. International Teletimes *home page.*

One of the Web's underdeveloped potentials is that of public service. Part of the reason, of course, is that the majority of the public still doesn't have access to it. But if the Missing

Children Database is any indication (`http://www.scubed.com:8001/public_service/mc_db.html`), there's every reason for wide public access to become the norm (see Figure 7.25). Several Web sites mirror this CompuServe-based archive, and when you access it you get photos and other information about the children. As is sensibly requested by the sites themselves, however, I won't show any of the actual files here, in case the parents are reading this. The access page is sufficient to get the point across.

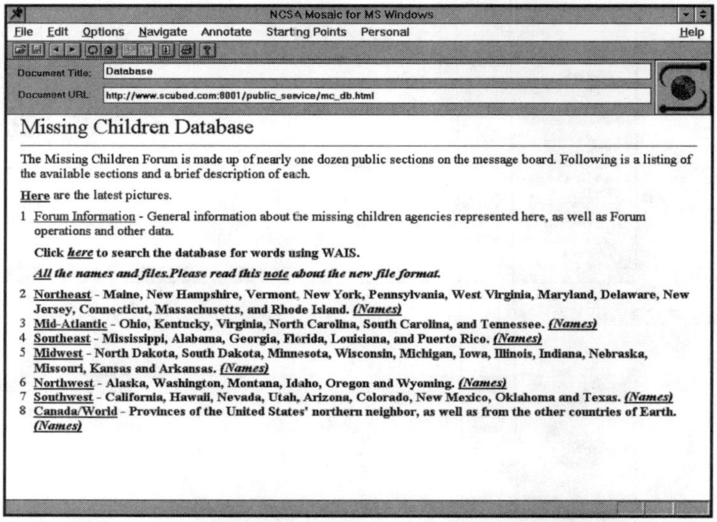

Figure 7.25. *WWW page showing Missing Children Database.*

Despite all the commercial and public service activity beginning to emerge, however, it's still worth noting that the Internet began as a research tool, and a great deal of the WWW's activity stems from universities. Figure 7.26 shows the home page of the Electronic Visualization Laboratory at the University of Illinois at Chicago. From this page you can access several truly fascinating topics, many with their own multimedia displays and downloads.

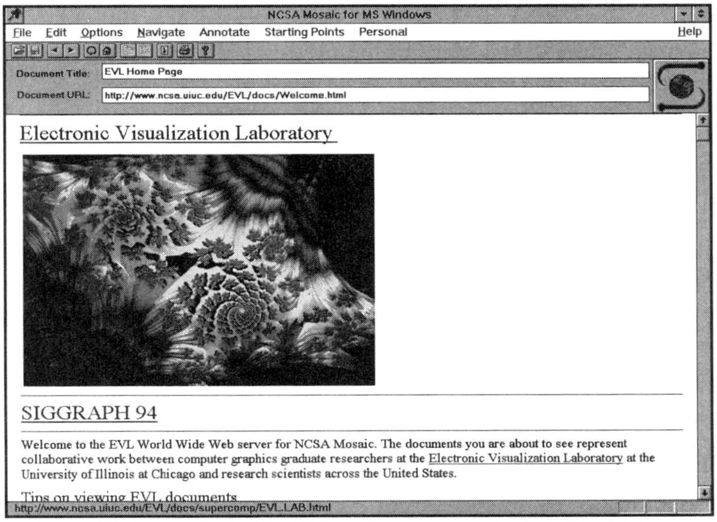

Figure 7.26. *Electronic Visualization Laboratory at Illinois.*

Of similar scientific interest is the National Center for Atmospheric Research in Boulder, Colorado, whose main page (`http://http.ucar.edu/metapage.html`) offers an audio introduction and, at the top, a composite image from which you can gain access to the Center's different divisions (see Figure 7.27).

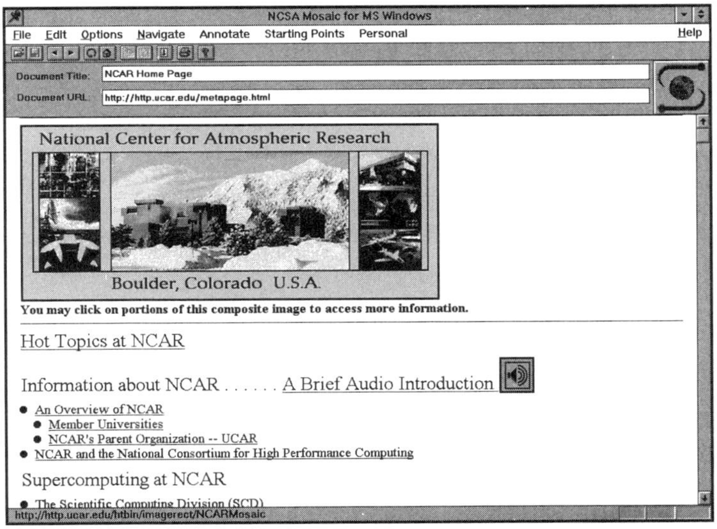

Figure 7.27. *National Center for Atmospheric Research home page.*

And while you might expect the scientists and computer professionals to make extensive use of the Web's hypertext capabilities, you'll find scads of new material appearing for the nonscientific and nontechnical disciplines. The English Department at Carnegie Mellon University in Pittsburgh maintains The English Server (`http://english-server.hss.cmu.edu`), with a wide range of humanities subjects. Among them is one called Bad Subjects, which, as you might expect, offers substantial food for thought (see Figure 7.28).

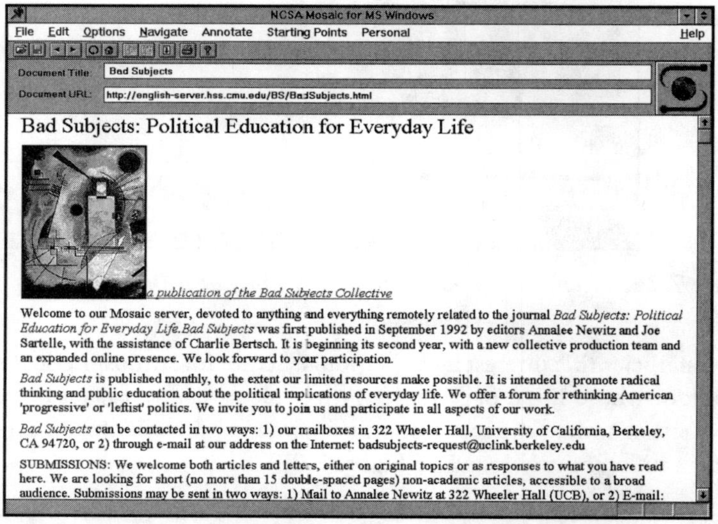

Figure 7.28. *The English Server at Carnegie Mellon University.*

Also from Carnegie Mellon comes a particularly engrossing Fun Page (`http://www.cs.cmu.edu:8001/Web/funstuff.html`), and from this page you can do all sorts of enjoyable things. If you like experimental art, for example, click one of the International Interactive Genetic Art exhibits, and then cast your vote on the resulting page (see Figure 7.29).

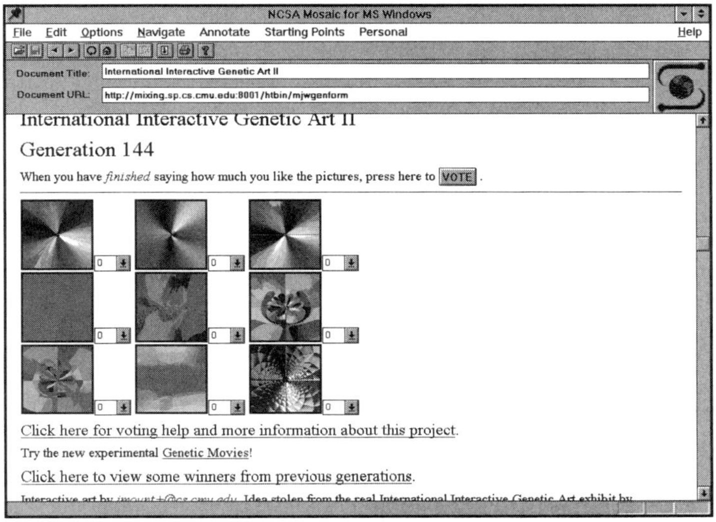

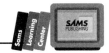

Figure 7.29. *Interactive Genetic Art exhibit at CMU.*

How long, we might wonder, until a voting system like this becomes the standard for, say, the Neilson ratings on TV? Or even local politics? The CMU Fun Page takes you to President Clinton's Saturday radio addresses, a Grateful Dead information site, the home page for the Canadian Broadcasting Corporation, some interactive WWW games, and into extra-curricular areas like the Backcountry Home Page.

An especially interesting type of WWW activity is represented by The Virtual Tourist (see Figure 7.30—`http://wings.buffalo.edu/world`). By clicking any area of the world (or on the insets), you can get increasingly detailed information about what's available electronically from that region. A few clicks in, you see the large map of the U.K. with all the Internet resources, and then it's simply a matter of picking the place you want to visit (see Figure 7.31).

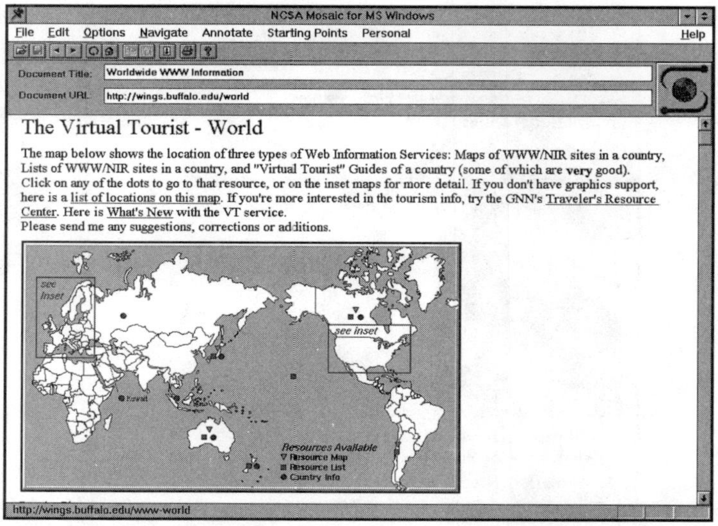

Figure 7.30. *The Virtual Tourist main page.*

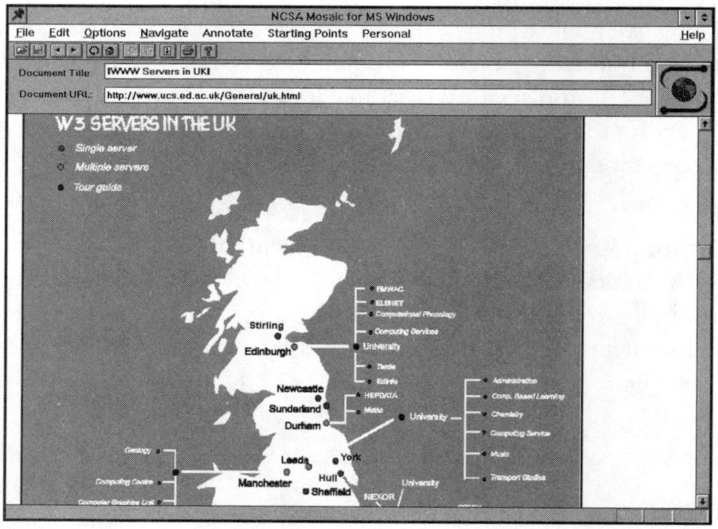

Figure 7.31. *Clickable map of the U.K.*

We'll choose the city tour of Cardiff, and Figure 7.32 shows several additional links. One is to the local castle, but I'll let you discover that for yourself.

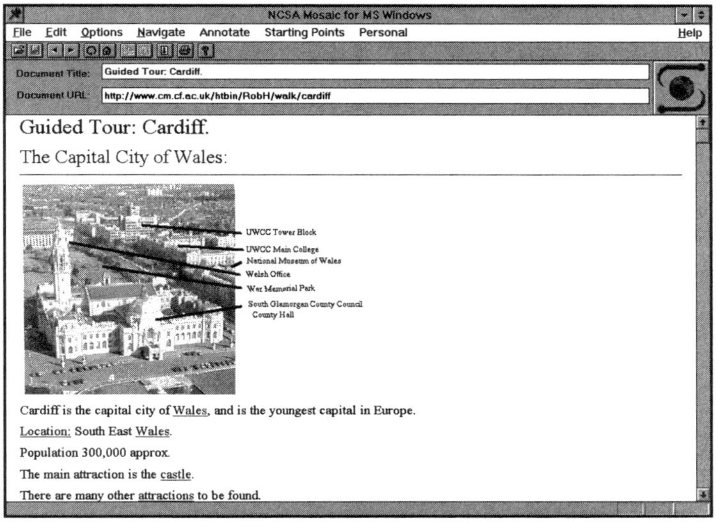

Figure 7.32. *WWW City tour of Cardiff, Wales.*

Summary

The World Wide Web provides Internet access in the form of hypertext documents. Each *page* on the Web provides links to other pages, to Gopher servers, to FTP sites, and to Internet search sites. Graphical software browsers such as Mosaic and Cello are quickly becoming the standard for interacting with the Web, because they allow graphics, sound, and video files to be included with the page. The WWW is growing at a nearly unbelievable pace.

Task Review

The tasks you've completed in this chapter have had less to do with learning a new system and more with figuring out how to explore the Internet. In a way, you haven't done much besides point and click. But you've actually performed more complex tasks than that, even though they may well have seemed quite intuitive. At this point in your WWW life, you're very much able to:

- ☐ Recognize and use a hypertext link.
- ☐ Choose a Home Page from Mosaic's menu.

- ☐ Bookmark pages you want to revisit.
- ☐ Go directly to a Web page by way of a URL.
- ☐ Use the WWW to download a graphics, sound, or video file to your hard drive.
- ☐ Order flowers for your mother.
- ☐ Find a tour of Cardiff, Wales.
- ☐ Spend many hours having an unusually good time.

Q&A

Q Why do I get so many messages telling me the hypertext link couldn't be opened?

A Keep in mind that a link in the World Wide Web usually hooks you up to another computer in another place. Not every computer is available at all times. Some of them shut down for periods of time, usually because of maintenance or (more recently) cost issues. Most of them are busy at certain times of the day handling extensive local computing issues, and in the case of universities they may well be overloaded late in the term when assignments are due. Always consider the time of day where the physical machine actually resides. If you stick to Webbing in after-hours (for the destination computer, not for you), you'll run into very few problems. There's always the chance, though, that the systems people have simply cut off outside access.

Q Can I access Gophers through Mosaic or Cello?

A Sure can. In fact, the Gophers look better in both cases (but especially in Cello) than they do in character-based Gopher software. And not just Gophers. You can FTP and Telnet through the Web as well, and you can conduct WAIS and Archie searches. It's almost an all-purpose tool.

Q Does anybody really know how to read URLs?

A Apparently, yes. If you think about a URL as a kind of extended directory path, it might be easier. In fact, that's more or less what it is. DOS users have little trouble with a command like `copy c:\wp51\docs\memos\october\project.rpt`, and one glance at a URL will tell you it isn't much different. The problem is that there's no easy equivalent to a DIR command to find out which URLs are available. You just have to start clicking around and bookmarking the pages (which means storing their URLs) you find most intriguing.

Q I access the Web through a modem, and the graphics take forever to appear. Anything I can do about this?

A Yes. The graphics that appear automatically with Web pages are called inline graphics. Graphical browsers enable you to turn off this feature. In Mosaic, uncheck Display Inline Images in the Options menu. In Cello, uncheck Graphics/Fetch Automatically in the Configure menu. A placeholder will show up in place of inline graphics until you check these items again. Cello, incidentally, offers an additional feature specifically for modem use: Peek mode. By holding down the Control key when you click the highlighted link, you receive only the first 4KB of the target file. This enables you to see if the link is worth exploring before you commit yourself to the full page (some of these pages are 60-120KB in size). If you decide you'd like to see the entire page, select Reload Document from the File menu.

The modem point is worth examining further, however. It takes only a few minutes with the Web to realize that it works best (by far) over a dedicated line at very high speeds. Even a 14.4 kbps modem, the fastest modem in common use, transfers graphics and sound files far too slowly to demonstrate the Web's true multimedia capabilities. But for many users, the modem approach is the only way available or practical. If you're one of these (as I am, for the most part), just be more selective in what you explore, and be prepared to wait.

Q Can I create my own World Wide Web pages?

A Sure. See the final section of Day 13 for some basic instructions in doing so. WWW pages are written in a fairly simple code called HTML, which stands for Hypertext Markup Language. You can either create these pages from scratch, or more simply you can download your favorite page, load the downloaded file into a word processor that supports pure ASCII (most do), and edit to your heart's content.

WEEK

2

Using the Internet Personally

AT A GLANCE

8

9

10

11

12

13

14

WEEK 2

8

Teach Yourself the Internet... on the Internet

No matter how many instructions, examples, or guidelines you read, learning the Internet really begins when you start sending e-mail, joining newsgroups, browsing Gophers, and doing Archie searches. So why not carry this one step further and learn the Internet from the Internet itself? This is what Day 8 helps you do, by exploring online tutorials, downloading guides and instruction manuals, and finding what the experts have to say.

On Day 8, you will do the following:

- ☐ Use Gopher and the World Wide Web to learn about the Internet's Resources.
- ☐ Join newsgroups dealing with Internet tools and issues.
- ☐ Subscribe to mailing lists about the Internet and its tools.
- ☐ Download Internet guides from FTP sites.

The Internet as an Information Source about Itself

Like most technologies, the Internet is learned best in a hands-on manner. Admittedly, this book has been designed so that you don't actually have to be *on* the Internet to *learn* the Internet, but if you've read this far you've already become interested enough to spring for an account and follow along. In this chapter, you'll use that account to help learn the Internet and its tools even better.

The richest source of Internet information is the Internet itself. If you want facts, statistics, suggestions, or software, turn to the Net for your needs. But it doesn't stop there. The Internet is also a rich resource for *learning* about the Internet. And that makes it a bit unusual in the world of computing. If you buy a new computer, it's unlikely that the computer itself will teach you how to use it effectively; if you buy a CD-ROM drive, you'll need all kinds of information external to the CD-ROM to get it running at all. But the Internet teaches its own, you might say, and as long as you're willing to search, there isn't a lot you can't find.

> **Warning:** "Search" is the operative word here. It's true that the Net holds all kinds of useful information about how to use itself, but the help is anything but easy to find. When you know a site or two, things get considerably simpler, but getting there is much less than half the fun. Still, it's often very much worth the effort.

Mailing Lists

As you might expect, those who spend their hours keeping track of what's available on the Internet use the Net's capabilities to make their findings public. One such method is the mailing list—as it turns out, this is the most practical way of all.

Excursion 8.1. The Net-happenings List

Get used to the name Gleason Sackman. If you've any interest at all in hearing about new Internet activity (and who doesn't?), you're going to read that name several times daily. That's because, starting right now, you're going to subscribe to Sackman's *net-happenings* mailing list, which is the Net's most indispensable source of new information.

To subscribe to net-happenings, send an e-mail message to the following address, entering the following on the first line of the message area:

```
To      : majordomo@is.internic.net
Cc      :
Attchmnt:
Subject :
---- Message Text ----
subscribe net-happenings firstname lastname
```

Warning: As always, when subscribing to a mailing list (see Day 4), leave the `subject:` line empty, and remember to *exclude* your signature file.

In a few minutes or so, you'll receive a confirmation message, which looks somewhat like this:

```
Date: Fri, 22 Apr 1994 17:45:04 -0700
From: listserv@is.internic.net
To: nrandall@watserv1.uwaterloo.ca
Cc: sackman@plains.nodak.edu
Subject: SUBSCRIBE NET-HAPPENINGS NEIL RANDALL
The net-happenings list is a service of InterNIC Information Services. The
purpose of the list is to distribute to the community announcements of
interest to network staffers and end users. This includes conference
announcements, call for papers, publications, newsletters, network tools
updates, and network resources. Net-happenings is a moderated,
announcements-only mailing list which gathers announcements from many
Internet sources and concentrates them onto one list. Traffic is
around 10-15 messages per day, and is archived daily.
```

From this point on, you'll start to see messages in your mailbox that let you know what's happening on the Internet. There are other such lists—the Gopher Jewels list, for example—but net-happenings often cross-posts the information from those lists anyway. In fact, most of net-happenings's information comes from other lists and newsgroups. Here's an example of what net-happenings offers:

```
Forwarded by Gleason Sackman - InterNIC net-happenings moderator
****************************************************************

---------- Forwarded message ----------
Date: Sun, 17 Apr 1994 23:17:43 EDT
From: Roger R. Espinosa <roger@trillium.soe.umich.edu>
To: Multiple recipients of list EDTECH <EDTECH@msu.bitnet>
Subject: DeweyWeb: A World Wide Web Experiment in Education...

                       THE DEWEYWEB:JOURNEY NORTH

     An experiment in using the WWW for the support of education.
--------------------------------------------------------------------------------

If you've been curious about how the World Wide Web could be used in
classrooms, and have been bugged by its one-way nature, I'm hoping you'll
take a look at:

                http://ics.soe.umich.edu/

(Or, for those who cut and paste these things:
<A HREF="http://ics.soe.umich.edu/" The DeweyWeb Experiment</A>

The DeweyWeb:Journey North is an experiment in building an web
environment that students can expand. Based on the World School's
Journey North activity, the primary feature of the experiment is a
series of maps which can be altered by students, as they enter in
observations of wildlife migration.
```

Tip: When you see a message such as this one, and you're interested in seeing the site mentioned, the best idea is to launch your Web, Gopher, or FTP program immediately and check it out, placing a bookmark in it if you find it useful. If you simply store or even print these pages, you'll soon find newer stuff that pushes the previous addresses into the background.

Excursion 8.2. Other Mailing Lists

Other useful mailing lists include the following:

- NEW-LIST (announcements of new mailing lists) at `LISTSERV@VM1.NODAK.EDU`
- NEWJOURN-L (announcements of new electronic journals) at `listserv@E-MATH.ams.com`
- GOPHERJEWELS (announcements of new Gophers) at `listproc@einet.net`

Newsgroups

A number of newsgroups have the Internet as their subject matter. One, in fact—`alt.internet.services`—contains many of the same announcements found in the net-happenings list from Excursion 8.1. An important feature of the Internet newsgroups is that, obviously, they prompt considerable discussion.

Excursion 8.3. Finding Newsgroups Dealing with the Internet

The following is a list of Internet-oriented newsgroups, obtained by entering **`l internet`** at `trn`'s prompt (see Day 4 for details on finding and subscribing to newsgroups):

```
alt.bbs.internet
alt.best.of.internet
alt.horror.shub-internet
alt.internet.access.wanted
alt.internet.talk-radio
ba.internet
comp.internet.library
de.comm.internet
info.big-internet
tnn.internet.firewall
```

Another list, showing newsgroups for the Internet Emergency Task Force (IETF), is shown in Figure 8.1. It is taken from the considerably more user-friendly Trumpet Newsreader (a Microsoft Windows program).

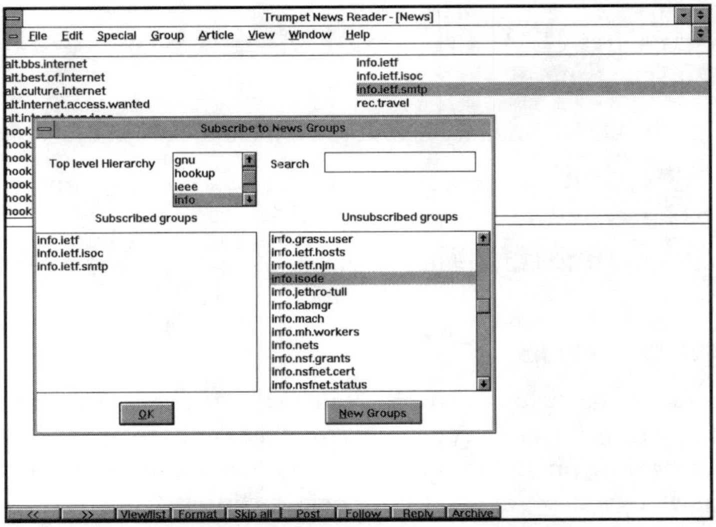

Figure 8.1. *A list of unsubscribed Internet newsgroups on Trumpet Newsreader.*

Excursion 8.4. Examining and Reading New Messages on *alt.internet.services*

One of the groups not listed in Excursion 8.3 is the extremely popular `alt.internet.services`. The reason is simple: I was already a subscriber. This is a must-read newsgroup for anyone wanting to find out more about the Internet, even if you're already a subscriber to the net-happenings mailing list. Figure 8.2 shows a very small portion of the messages posted to this group after two weeks of my not reading it, and it shows equally well the range of discussions taking place.

Newsgroups provide both news about the Internet and a place to discuss that news. If you're serious about keeping in touch with Net events, by all means join a few newsgroups. Be prepared, however, to read them frequently, or you'll end up with far too many to deal with at any given time.

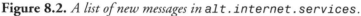

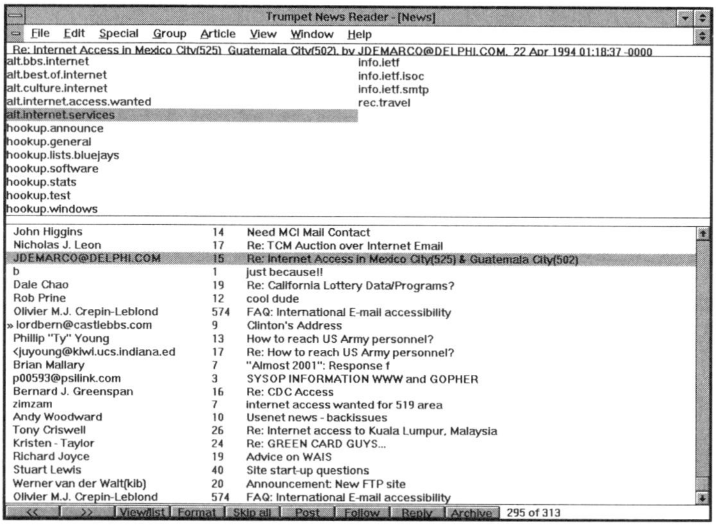

Figure 8.2. *A list of new messages in* `alt.internet.services`.

Gopher Sites

Newsgroups and mailing lists are excellent places to start your self-education about the Internet and its resources, but inevitably they end up pointing you toward Gopher sites. In fact, you don't even need to access the lists to find Gopher-based information. As you've known since Day 5, you can browse Gophers in search of whatever you like, and finding Internet information is anything but difficult.

Essentially, you're searching for any Gopher item with a title such as Internet Resources. Alternatively, you can just find the ubiquitously available Gopher Jewels items. From these items you can browse for large amounts of Internet information, entering FTP sites and obtaining training guides, text files, and even software to help you along.

Excursion 8.5. The Merit Gopher: Information About the Internet

If you remember your Internet history from Day 2, you'll recall the importance of the consortium named Merit. As you might expect, Merit has its own Gopher site, which contains a wealth of data about the Net. To access this site, Gopher to `nic.merit.edu`.

Figure 8.3 shows the resulting list, including some items leading directly to Internet information.

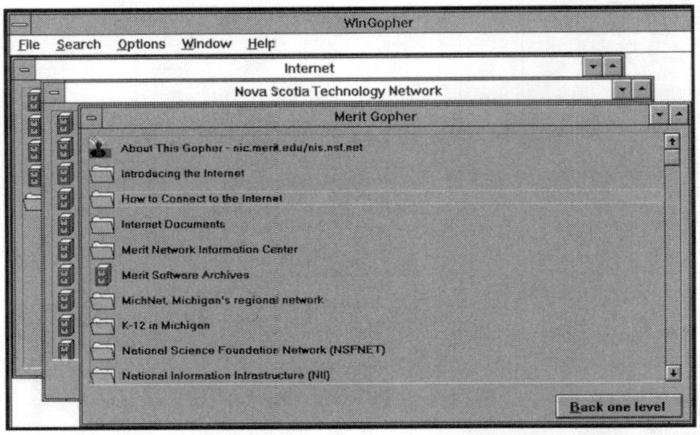

Figure 8.3. *Merit Gopher at* `nic.merit.edu`.

If your purpose is to teach yourself details about the Internet itself, rather than just about Internet tools available for use, the Merit site is well worth exploring.

Excursion 8.6. The SunSite Gopher: Information About Internet Tools

Another extremely useful site is the SunSite Gopher at the University of North Carolina. Here you'll find a wealth of files with information about how to use the various Internet tools. The main Gopher list is shown in Figure 8.4. To reach this Gopher to `dewey.lib.ncsu.edu`, then follow the path NCSU's "Library Without Walls," Reference Desk, and finally Guides (to subject literature, to Internet resources, and so on). Here you'll find the collection of documents.

> **Note:** This is the first place you should consider when Gophering to find tutorial material, but keep in mind that not everything archived here is completely up-to-date. Some materials date from 1993 and even 1994, but earlier guides from 1990 and before are still available. Nevertheless, you can't go wrong downloading any number of these files.

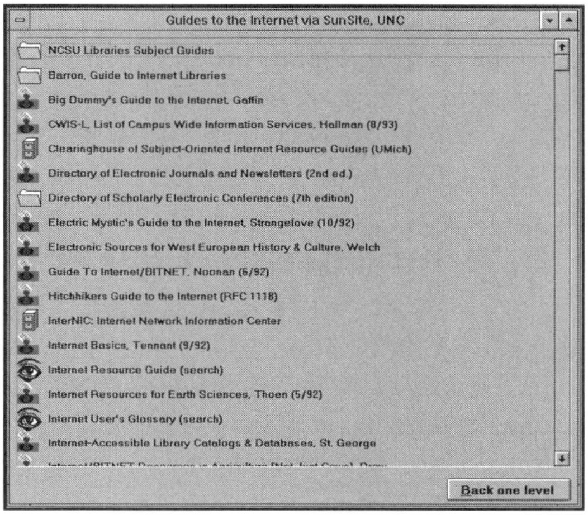

Figure 8.4. *The SunSite Gopher—guides to the Internet.*

One such guide is Big Dummy's Guide to the Internet (third item on the list), which keeps being rereleased in updated editions. Figure 8.5 shows a very, very tiny portion of this long, extensive, and extremely useful guide, one that more than repays the time it takes to download.

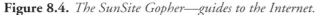

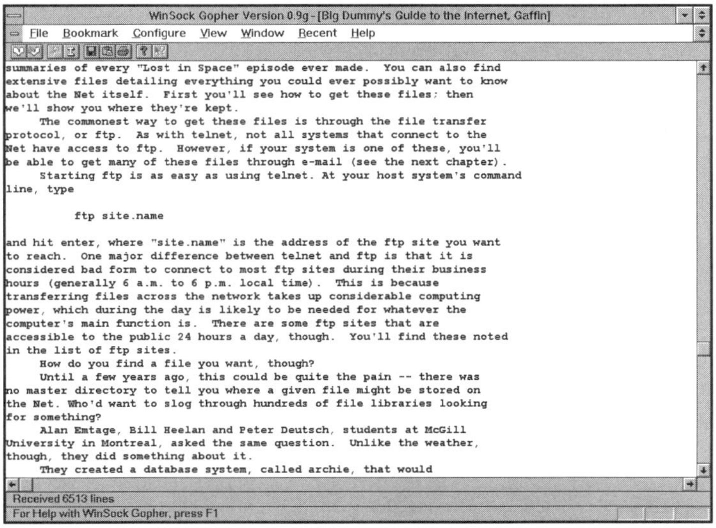

Figure 8.5. *Big Dummy's Guide to the Internet.*

From these two excursions, it's easy to see the sheer amount of information that's available through some simple Gopher browsing. In fact, with a couple of guides downloaded and text files of Internet services information, you may think there's no reason to look any further. Wrong. There's still the World Wide Web. And that's where things really start to pick up as far as teaching yourself the Internet is concerned.

Excursion 8.7. Internet Resources on European Gophers

Several strong European sites offer information about the Internet. Among the best is the BUBL Information Service, available on the UKOLN (UK Office for Library and Information Networking) Gopher at the University of Bath, UK (`ukoln.bath.ac.uk`). The BUBL (Bulletin Boards for Libraries) service contains an item entitled Internet Resources by Subject; Reference Tools, Electronic Texts, which yields the following menu:

```
1.  BUBL Beginners:Contacts, Help..Hints, News, Latest Additions, Sta/
2.  BUBL Subject Tree/
3.  Electronic Journals & Texts/
4.  Employment Resources and Opportunities/
5.  Grants Available & Competitions You Can Win/
6.  Major Networked Services/
7.  Networking Groups on the Internet/
8.  Networks and Networking/
9.  Non-Networked Groups on BUBL/
10. Reference Resources: Acronymns, Directories, E-lists, Glossaries/
11. Software for Teaching and Using to Aid Your Work/
```

From here we can move to Networking Groups on the Internet (although some others in the menu are useful), and that choice leads us to this list (truncated here):

```
2.  Association for Progressive Communications (Connection details) -.
3.  CAUSE - Assoc for managing & using IT in HE - H2B15/
4.  CEPES-UNESCO - H2B13//
5.  CHEST - H2B12/
6.  Chemical Abstract Service STN Internet Contact - H2B08/
7.  Committee to Protect Journalists.
8.  Connect - IBM PC Users - H2B04/
9.  EARN Information Service/
10. Electronic Frontier Foundation (EFF) - H2B19/
11. Greennet - Environment - H2B03/
12. INTERNIC: The Internet Network Information Centre/
```

Once again, several of the items are useful for learning the Net, but EARN Information Service (also available from `gopher.earn.net`) is of primary use. We already met EARN in Excursion 8.5, but here the material is of greater depth.

```
1.  About EARN/
2.  User Services Documentation/
3.  EARNEST, the EARN Newsletter/
4.  CNRE - Computer Networks for Research in Europe/
5.  Network Services Conferences (NSC)/
6.  Public LISTSERV archives/
7.  Related Internet Documents/
8.  Topology and Performance of the Network/
9.  Network information/
```

If you want a solid grasp of what EARN does (and, consequently, the state of the Internet in Europe) choose EARNEST, the EARN Newsletter, and read the latest issues. If you're more interested in technical and performance issues, download the PostScript files found under the Topology and Performance of the Network item.

Another important European network is EUnet. At the address `gopher.EU.net` we find the following short menu:

```
1.  EUnet Country Guide/
2.  Profile: EUnet.
3.  Traveller/
```

The EUnet profile is worth reading, but instead we'll enter the EUnet Country Guide, where we find the following:

```
1.  Austria.
2.  Germany/
3.  Greece/
4.  Ireland/
5.  Other Countries.
6.  Slovakia/
7.  Spain/
8.  Switzerland/
9.  The Netherlands/
```

Any of these items will give us more information on EUnet, and some of the Gophers are more fleshed out than the others. One of the lesser developed (but interesting nevertheless) is Spain, which leads us to the following menu:

```
1.  Yo soy ... / I am ....
2.  Info on EUnet at Spain (goya)/
3.  Info on EUnet -- Paneuropean Network Services Providers/
4.  Info on Internet/
5.  Servicios - Goya/
6.  Useful Services (worldwide)/
7.  Anuncios/
8.  pruebas/
```

Selecting the second item, Info on EUnet at Spain (goya)/, yields this short menu, which demonstrates clearly that the information will be (quite naturally) in Spanish:

```
1.  Tarifas (Prices)/
2.  Informacion tecnica/
3.  GoyaHoy: anuncio de servicios accesibles via goya (eunet.es)/
4.  contratos/
```

In fact, the Informacion tecnica/ item leads to this well-stocked Gopher, with several Spanish files dealing with Internet details:

```
4.  AUP: Condiciones de utilizacion de los servicios.
5.  Configuracion del correo con UUPC 1.10.
6.  Direcciones: secretaria, soporte, listas de distribucion, ....
7.  E-mail, News e IP: propaganda.
8.  E-mail: Correo electronico.
9.  FTP anonimo.
10. FTP mail: ftp anonimo via E-mail.
11. FTP: Bases de Datos on-line.
12. INDEX.
13. IP over IP.
14. Indice comentado de documentos.
15. Informacion administrativa sobre EUnet Espana / GOYA.
16. Instalacion de UUCP en una maquina UNIX via modem RTC.
17. ListServ: listas de distribucion.
```

The World Wide Web

As Day 7 demonstrates, the World Wide Web offers a visually appealing means of exploring the Internet. It does more than this, however; it makes possible the kinds of learning tutorials available in today's graphically oriented software, such as Lotus 1-2-3 for Windows or for OS/2, or PowerPoint 4.0 for Windows or for Macintosh. Tutorials such as these are only beginning to appear on the Web, but you can probably rest assured that their numbers will quickly increase. Among its other strengths, the Web promises graphically rich interactivity.

It's no surprise that, as a teaching and information medium, the WWW has so far perhaps been best used to teach about itself and the Internet in general. The Net, after all, is a good test subject: because one of the Web's primary functions is to allow easy links to other sites, and because there's a great deal of Internet information on a wide range of sites throughout the Net, it's only natural to use the Web to point to these sites. In other words, using the Web as an Internet tutorial and resource guide makes sense because the subject matter—the Internet itself—is already available. It's a matter of designing the interface, not the material itself.

Several good Web sites provide Internet information and the potential for self-teaching. This section explores a few of them. In addition, the extra credit section for this chapter focuses on an extremely valuable resource, Internet Web Text. I encourage you to turn to it after you've visited these preliminary sites.

Excursion 8.8. GNN: The Global Network Navigator

One of the first truly well-designed WWW sites, The Global Network Navigator (GNN) offers a wide variety of Internet information and help with tools. Figure 8.6 shows GNN's home page.

> **Tip:** The address shown in Figure 8.6 isn't the actual GNN home page address, which is `www.wimsey.com/gnn/GNNhome.html`. Instead, as the GNN welcome page at `wimsey.com` suggested, I clicked a *mirrored* site. When a site becomes popular, it also becomes over-accessed, so the site owners often make arrangements to mirror the site on another server. The idea is not just to divert traffic elsewhere, but to attempt to offer users a site closer to home. In GNN's case, one mirrored site is in North Carolina (the one I've accessed here); another is in Australia. Presumably the home site was receiving

considerable Australian traffic, which is why that decision was made. Mirrored sites are becoming increasingly popular on the Internet, and it's a good idea to access them. They're often much faster than the original site, and you lose nothing by accessing them.

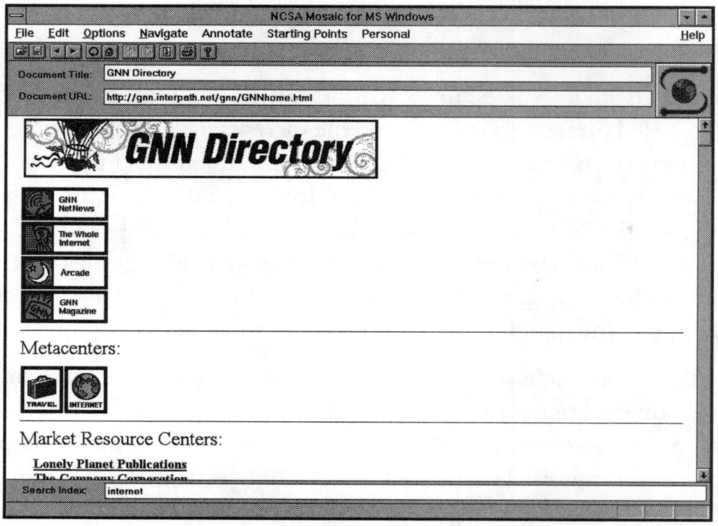

Figure 8.6. *The Global Network Navigator home page.*

On the home page are three links to useful Internet material: GNN Magazine, The Whole Internet Catalog, and at the bottom of the page the Internet Center. Figure 8.7 displays the Internet Center's main page, with links to other points of interest.

Actually, all these items offer more Internet information, but instincts suggest that the item of most immediate interest is the clickable icon called The Internet Gold Mine. As Figure 8.8 demonstrates, the instincts knew what they were doing.

One of the links from the Gold Mine page leads to a short introduction to training materials. The suggested site is Trainmat Gopher in Newcastle upon Tyne, U.K. (`trainmat.ncl.ac.uk`). Here, as Figure 8.9 shows, you can find a range of materials, including documents that are of great use to Internet trainers.

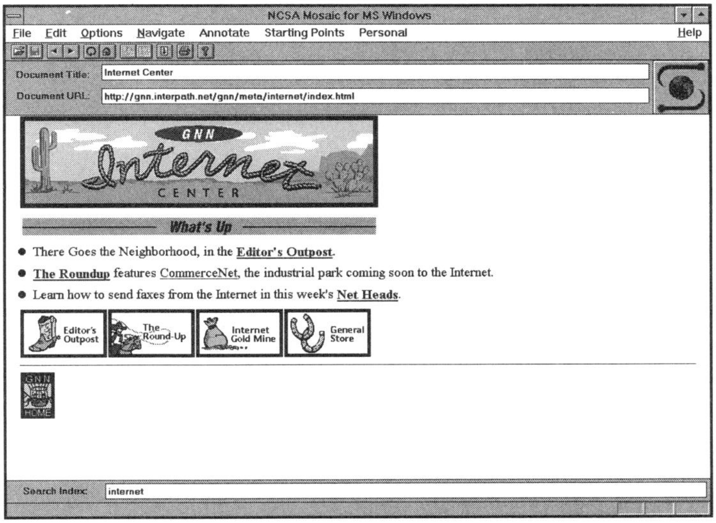

Figure 8.7. *GNN's Internet Center main page.*

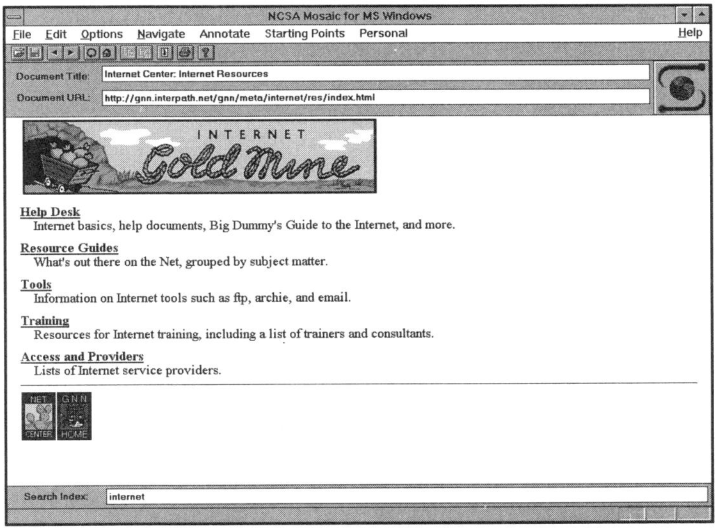

Figure 8.8. *GNN's Internet Gold Mine page.*

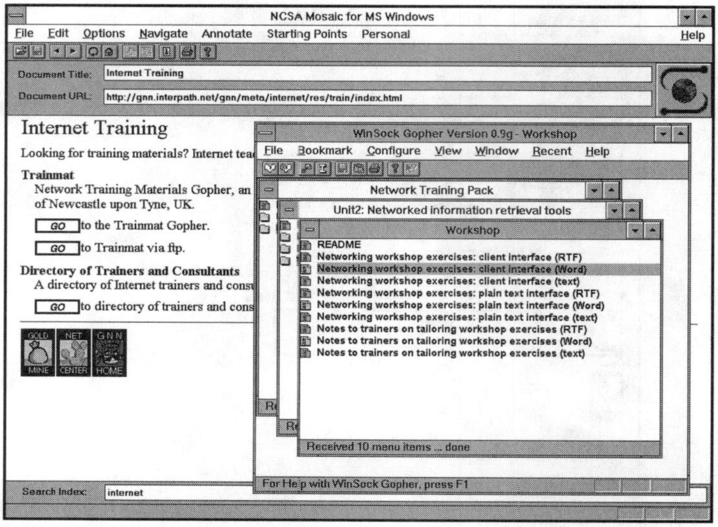

Figure 8.9. *GNN's training page with Trainmat Gopher.*

Tip: By now you're well aware that Mosaic, like its Windows competitor Cello, is more than capable of linking directly to Gopher sites. I often prefer to load a dedicated Gopher program, however, because of its greater flexibility. Using the two in conjunction with one another can help you out, especially because of the excessive time it sometimes takes for the Web browsers to reload the original page. This way, I maintain the Web page *and* download the documents I want.

Training materials are nice, but what if your real purpose is to train yourself, not others? Well, GNN helps here as well. Clicking back to the Internet Gold Mine page, you find a link to Tools. This brings you to Figure 8.10, which offers links to further Web pages dealing with the specified Internet tools.

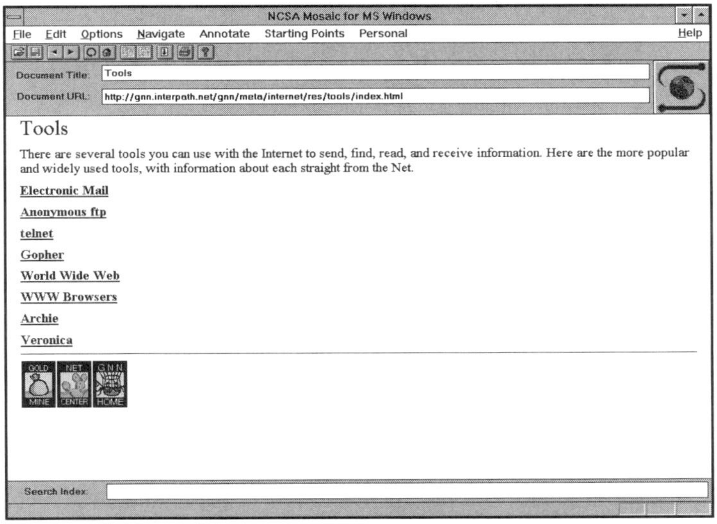

Figure 8.10. *GNN Internet Center—Tools.*

The format for each subsequent Tools page is similar. Rather than offer a tutorial or an information page at that point, GNN links you to WWW, Gopher, or FTP sites to download documents with the details you wish.

Having worked with Archie on Day 6, you might want to check out these alternate sources of information.

Excursion 8.9. GNA and CUI

An interesting Web site promises full courses offered over the Net. The Globewide Network Academy (or GNA, as it's certain to be referred to) began posting details about a course on the Internet in early spring of 1994, with plans to begin a bit later on. The idea is that you can sign on to the course, which is a series of interactive demonstrations and hands-on activities of the various Internet tools.

Figure 8.11 shows the introductory page for the course (`http://uu-gna.mit.edu:8001/uu-gna/text/Internet`). Of interest here is the concept of the *online consultant*—a real live instructor, complete with office hours, who will help you through the Internet maze.

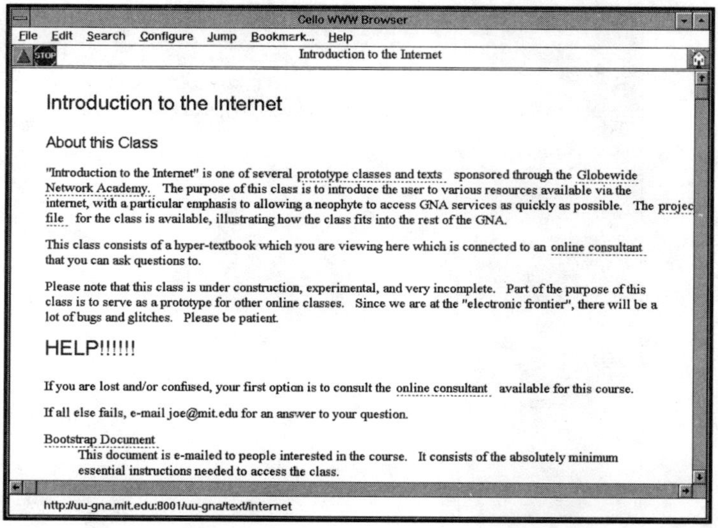

Figure 8.11. *GNA's online interactive course on the Internet.*

The possibilities for this course present themselves in Figure 8.12. From here, the trainee can move into a series of workshops and exercises, which will in turn demonstrate how to use the various Internet tools. This seems well worth following, either to learn the Net from scratch or to follow up your existing knowledge.

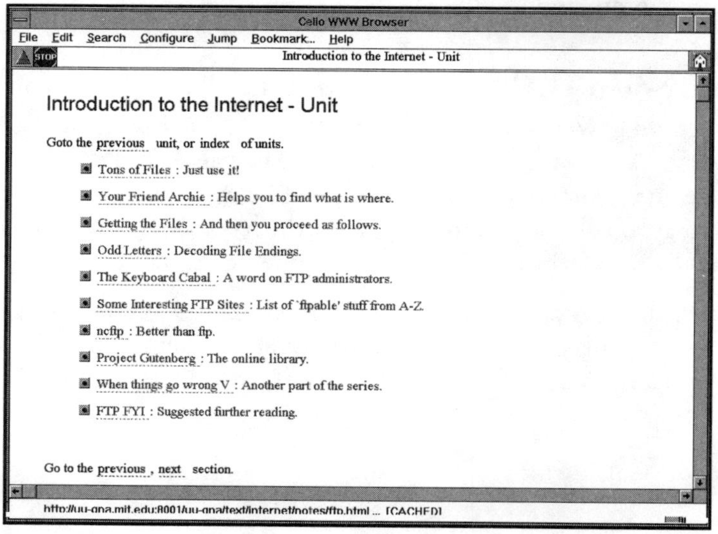

Figure 8.12. *GNA's online course—FTP section.*

Finally, there's always the Internet search pages to look through, and Figure 8.13 shows the results of a search through CUI's excellent locator (`http://cui_www.unige.ch/w3catalog`). The search here was for the string "internet tools," which was necessary because "internet" itself produced far too extensive a list. This result is relatively incomplete, however, although the links it contains can be used to link to many other sites.

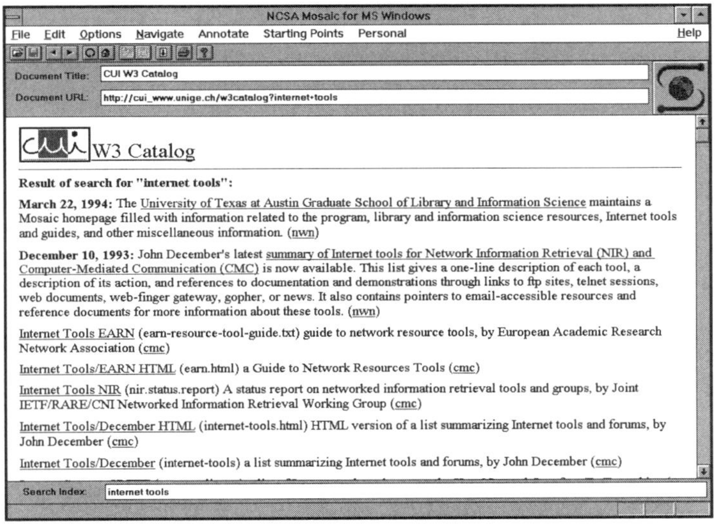

Figure 8.13. *CUI—results of searching for "internet tools."*

One of the interesting things about the CUI search (for our purposes) is that five of the links point to the Internet pages offered by Rensselaer Polytechnic Institute's John December.

Excursion 8.10. Saving the Best for Last: The Internet Tools Summary

If you want to learn the Internet tools from the Internet itself, plan to spend an extra day browsing and working with Internet Web Text, Internet Tools Summary, and Internet-CMC Page. All three are the product of John December and are featured in the extra credit section of this chapter.

Why are they placed in that section? Precisely because they'll consume a great deal of extra time. You've already used the Internet to learn the Internet, but with December's work you'll go far toward furthering that knowledge. Extra credit perhaps, but essential credit nevertheless.

I invite you, then, to spend another several hours teaching yourself the Internet...on the Internet. Turn to the extra credit section at the end of Day 8 and follow a truly thorough guide.

Warning: If you pass on today's extra credit section, you're passing on one of the Web's single most useful resources.

Summary

The Internet is filled with information and advice about the Internet itself. Through an extensive look at newsgroups and mailing lists, and by browsing and searching Gopher, FTP, and World Wide Web sites, you can increase your knowledge of the Net and your efficiency at using it. Already under way are hands-on workshops available over the Web, and full multimedia versions will undoubtedly follow before too long. Once you've worked your way through this book, it should be relatively easy to keep fully up-to-date on the Net and its associated tools.

Task Review

On Day 8, you have done the following:

- ☐ Joined newsgroups dealing with Internet tools and issues.
- ☐ Subscribed to mailing lists about the Internet and its tools.
- ☐ Used Gopher to access information about the Internet's resources and tools.
- ☐ Downloaded Internet guides and other information from FTP sites.
- ☐ Browsed and searched the World Wide Web for Internet tools materials.

Q&A

Q If all this material is available on the Internet itself, why did I buy this book?

A Apart from helping me put my kids through university, working through this book has offered—and will continue to offer as you go along—a number of advantages over taking all your information off the Internet. The first, of course, is that it points you toward the very fact that the Net offers its own learning resources, something you might not otherwise discover. Second, you can take it with you on the plane, or you can read it while lying on the couch with a cup of tea in your other hand, neither of which you can do (without a great deal of technical resourcefulness, at least) while on the Net itself. Third, the book is formatted much more pleasantly than a long file of plain ASCII. Fourth, it's designed to move you from point to point in your explorations, which Net-based tools are only beginning to do. Finally, if you actually pay for your Internet access, the book may well be cheaper than working your way through online tutorials or downloading several files. And there *is* that point about my kids and university....

Q Why doesn't someone make learning easier by designing a single, all-purpose Internet interface?

A In many ways, that's what both Gopher and the World Wide Web try to do. Combine the two, in fact, and wait while all the details are worked out, and you may well have the single all-purpose interface you're looking for. Either, in fact, will be enough for most users. But the Internet is based on flexibility, mainly because its controlling operating system, UNIX, is also based on flexibility. UNIX people have always *wanted* to create their own interfaces, their own ways of doing things, and the variety of Internet tools reflects that. So you won't see a full all-purpose interface for several reasons:

- ☐ UNIX programmers will always be developing additional tools, which can only be incorporated in a single-purpose interface at a later time.
- ☐ It's almost always faster and more flexible—even if not easier—to work with the tools individually.
- ☐ Many people don't want a standard all-purpose interface, because it could restrict what they can actually do.

Extra Credit: John December's Internet Web Text

Professionally, my interest in the Internet lies in its capabilities and ramifications as a communications medium (nonprofessionally, I just like surfing). Imagine my enthusiasm, then, when I found out, through the net-happenings list discussed in this chapter, about a World Wide Web page devoted to Computer-Mediated Communication (CMC). I fired up Cello immediately to check it out.

Excursion 8.11. Internet Web Text

What I found was nothing short of mind-boggling. Some guy named John December at Rensselaer Polytechnic Institute (RPI) had constructed this long, detailed Web page with a seemingly endless series of links to other sites. The links had much to do with CMC itself, and many of them pointed to Web, Gopher, FTP, and Telnet sites dealing with a huge array of Internet tools. I spent hours working from this page, learning about tools I'd never even heard of.

As my Web browsing continued, I began to see December's pages referenced from a great many other pages. It turned out that the CMC and Internet Tools pages weren't the only ones he'd prepared, In fact, perhaps the most interesting of the lot was Internet Web Text, as handy an introduction to the Internet as I'd seen. Together, these pages comprised a fascinating, comprehensive reference guide to the Internet, and I decided that they had to be featured in this book.

First, though, a quick introduction to John December. What better way than to use the Web itself? (See Figure 8.14.)

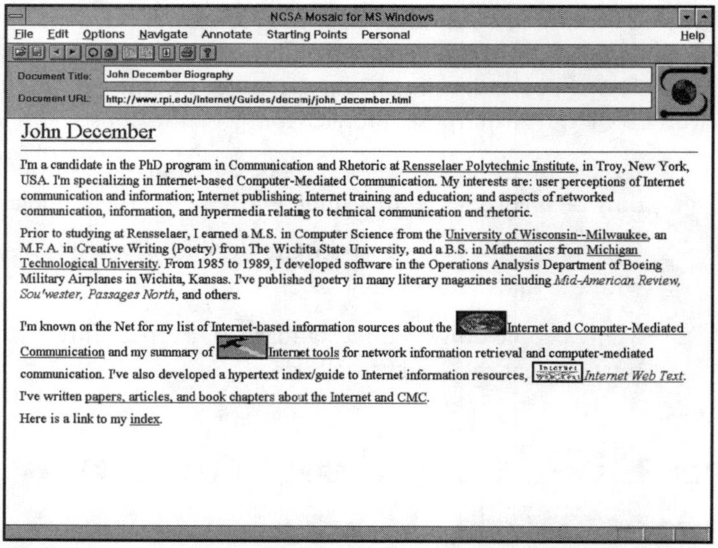

Figure 8.14. *An introduction to John December.*

Next, a look at December's extensive linking of Internet tools, called, appropriately, the Internet Tools Summary (`http:www.rpi.edu/Internet/Guides/decemj/internet-toolshtml`). This long Web page offers instructive reading all by itself, even before you begin clicking on the huge variety of links. A quick scan of the page will probably make you aware of tools you didn't even know about, and you can click any of the links to find out more about that particular item. Figures 8.15 and 8.16 show various portions of this huge page.

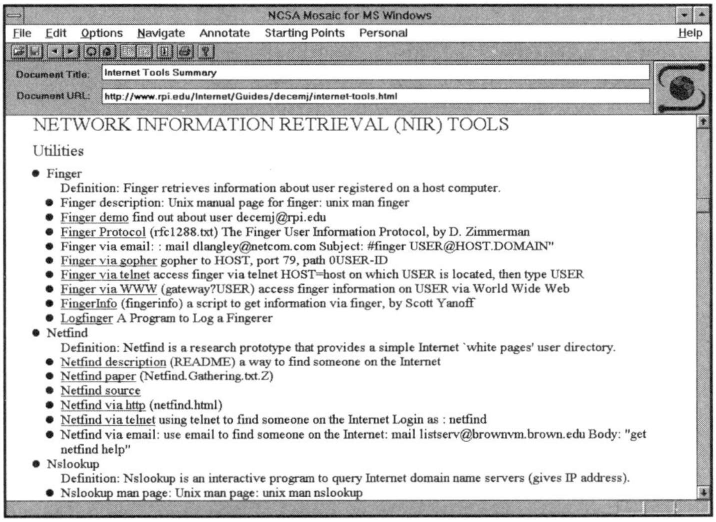

Figure 8.15. *Finger and Netfind portions of the Internet Tools Summary.*

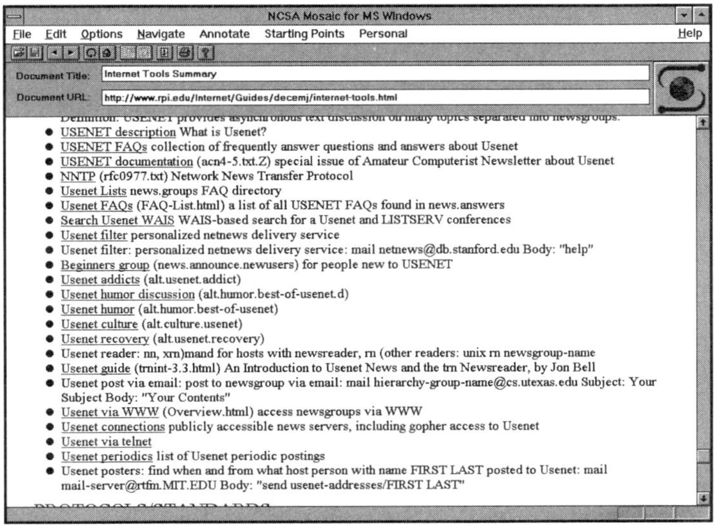

Figure 8.16. *USENET portion of the Internet Tools Summary.*

Internet Web Text

by John December

I created Internet Web Text for a graduate course in computer-mediated communication at RPI that I helped teach in the spring of 1994. My goal was to create an Internet-based interface that students could use to tap into the rich store of knowledge on the Internet and learn about it.

Having had the experience of maintaining a list of information sources about the Internet and computer-mediated communication (URL `ftp://ftp.rpi.edu/pub/communications/internet-cmc`) for more than a year and half, I knew that the Internet itself was a rich resource for Internet information. I also knew which sources on my list were particularly helpful for particular purposes.

The Design of Internet Web Text

My design goal was to create a hypertext guide with flexible ways for users to encounter information. I wanted to link together Internet resources for orientation, guides, reference, browsing and exploring, subject- and word-oriented searching, and information about connecting with people. I wanted to create a design that would allow users to encounter the information in a variety of ways (both in list form and in narrative form) in "chunks" that did not overwhelm. I also wanted to use icons to create memory aids to help users remember the resources. I wanted to weave the whole package of information together with links so that a user could easily move from one area of the text to the other.

My resulting design meets these goals. From the front Web page (URL `http://www.rpi.edu/Internet/Guides/decemj/text.html`), I provide the user with an overview of the entire guide and links to other versions of it. (See Figure 8.17.) The guide itself is divided into seven subdivisions with a maximum of seven major resources mentioned in each. (Seven is a good rule-of-thumb upper limit on the number of things people can keep in mind at once.) From the front page, the user can access more information about Internet Web Text itself, release notes, and the narrative, no-icons, icons-only, and page-oriented versions of the text.

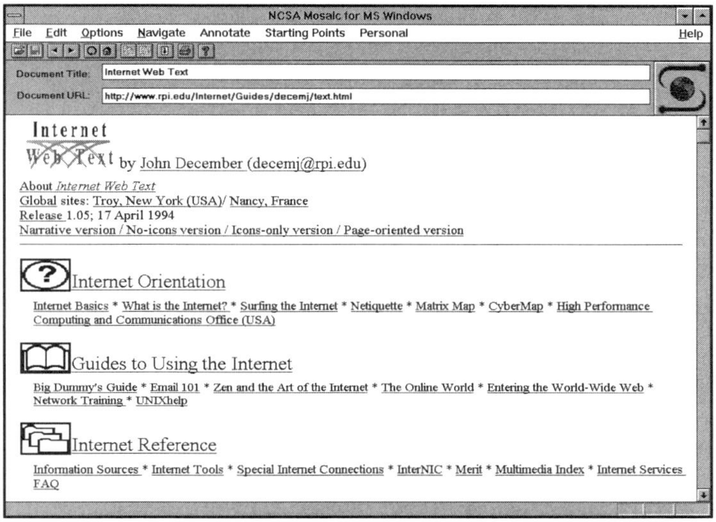

Figure 8.17. *The Internet Web Text home page.*

The narrative version (URL `http://www.rpi.edu/Internet/Guides/decemj/narrative.html`) presents the resources with an explanatory narrative (see Figure 8.18).

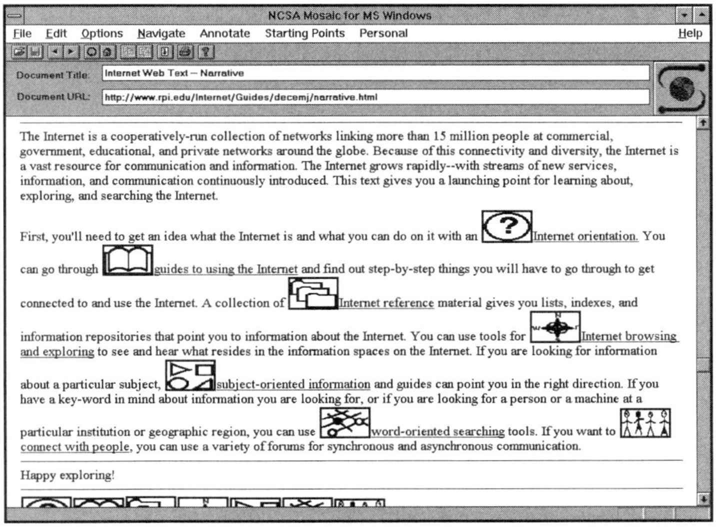

Figure 8.18. *The narrative version of Internet Web Text.*

Besides the top-level narrative version, each of the seven subdivisions of the text has a narrative version of its own. In the narrative version of each subdivision, I describe seven major resources, including icons in the narrative to identify these seven resources. (See Figure 8.19.) In addition, I provide links to supplementary or further resources that are useful, but I don't provide icons for these links in order to preserve the "major" feel of the seven major resources in each subdivision.

For each page of narrative for the seven subdivisions, I have an accompanying list version that presents only the seven major resources for that subdivision. In this way, the reader can quickly get a list of the major resources without having to read through the narrative. In this way, the list version serves as a more "expert" layer for this information.

The icons-only version of the text (URL `http://www.rpi.edu/Internet/Guides/decemj/icons.html`) presents only the icons of the major resources of the text. The icons-only version serves as a compact jumping-off point for users who are familiar enough with the resources that they can recognize them by the icons only. In contrast, the iconless version of the text presents only a list of the resources with no icons. This is particularly useful for those people who are not using a graphical browser or who do not want to bring up any icons.

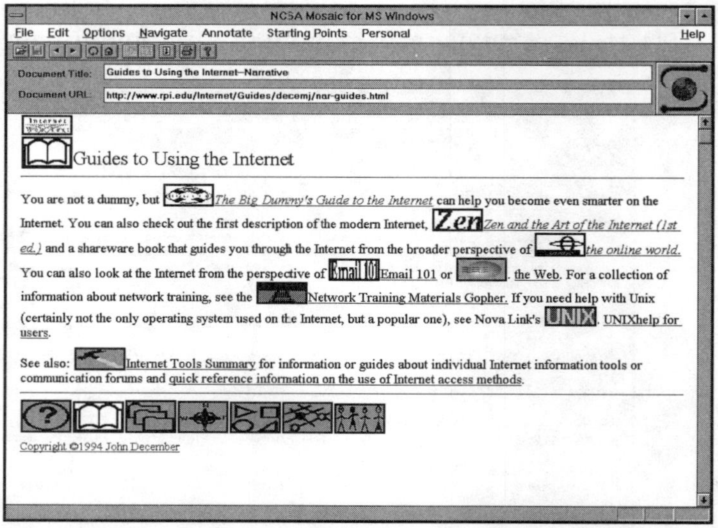

Figure 8.19. *The Internet Guide's subdivision of Internet Web Text narrative version.*

Finally, I've designed links among the pages so a reader can encounter the information using multiple paths, and jump from one version to the other. At the bottom of each list or narrative page, there is a row of icons with links to any of the seven major categories. You can go from any page-oriented list version to its corresponding page-oriented narrative version by clicking on the category title at the top of the page to the right of the category icon. (Figure 8.20 shows the full, page-oriented version.) Conversely, you can go from any page-oriented narrative version to its corresponding page-oriented list version by clicking on the category icon at the top of the page. The Internet Web Text icon at the top of the page will take a user to the front page of either the list-oriented version or the narrative-oriented version, depending on in what version the user is currently located. This flexibility makes it possible for a user to quickly select the way the information is presented.

Using Internet Web Text

You can use Internet Web Text in a variety of ways. If you are an experienced user, you can probably go right to the front page (URL `http://www.rpi.edu/Internet/Guides/decemj/text.html`) and select resources from there. This front page gives direct access to all the major resources in the text. A new user to Internet Web Text or the Internet in general should first read the front page of the narrative version (URL `http://www.rpi.edu/Internet/Guides/decemj/narrative.html`) to become familiar with what the guide has to offer as well as the meaning of the icons representing the seven subdivisions. From there, a new Internet user should consider selecting the Internet Orientation subdivision (URL `http://www.rpi.edu/Internet/Guides/decemj/nar-orient.html`) to get acquainted with what the Internet has to offer and some basic information about it. An experienced user could view the list-only version of this same information. Beyond this orientation, the user then should select the subdivision that represents the kind of resource they are seeking (guides, reference, exploring, searching, or connecting with people).

The images in the guide can help users remember and become familiar with resources. However, it does take a while to load the images when using Mosaic or other graphical interfaces. Once the images are loaded, however, you can skip from page to page fairly rapidly, and gain the benefit of having the icons. When I am going to use the text for an extended time, I usually click on the icons-only version and let all the images load while I do something else in another window. A few pages do have additional images, such as the Cultural Aspects of the Internet collection (URL `http://www.rpi.edu/Internet/Guides/decemj/culture.html`). There is currently a European mirror site for the Internet Web Text (URL `http://www.loria.fr/~charoy/InternetWeb/text.html`), which makes it faster for European users to load the images. I am currently working with people in Japan and Mexico to provide similar mirror sites.

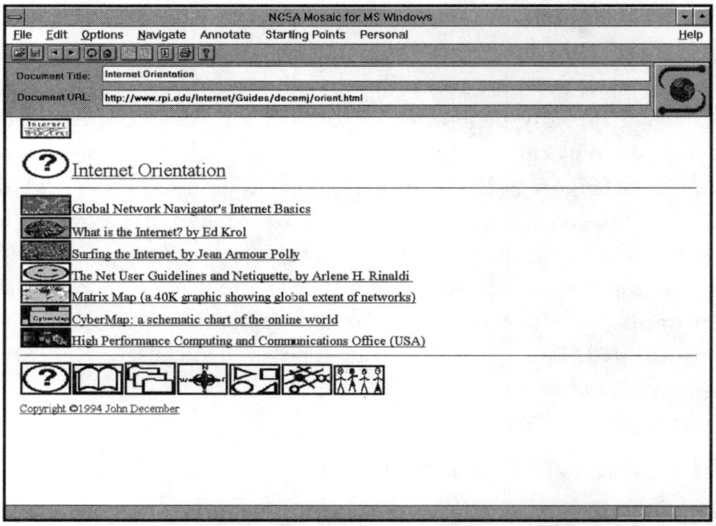

Figure 8.20. *The page-oriented version of Internet Web Text.*

9

WEEK 2

Location, Location, Location: Finding the Best Places in the World to See

Day 9 focuses on travel information available on the Net. In this chapter, we'll examine newsgroups and mailing lists devoted to travel, and we'll explore FTP, Gopher, and World Wide Web sites in search of the perfect destination. Eventually you'll want to turn off the machine and actually visit some of these places, but today virtual traveling will more than merely suffice.

Today you will:

- ☐ Subscribe to mailing lists that focus on travel issues.
- ☐ Join newsgroups that deal with travel destinations and concerns.
- ☐ Retrieve information about travel from FTP sites.
- ☐ Explore Gopher sites for details about travel destinations and issues.
- ☐ Browse the World Wide Web for multimedia presentations of travel destinations.

Traveling with the Net

This one, you'd think, should be the easiest surfing there is. The Internet is all about different destinations, after all, and even though most of those destinations are computers, you'd expect to find an almost infinite amount of information about the geographical sites in which those computers reside. Everybody's putting that material online, aren't they?

Some are, yes. But finding travel and tourism information isn't the cakewalk it might seem to be. And, on reflection, this may not be so hard to understand. The Internet was originally a collection of research sites, and putting details about local bed-and-breakfast establishments in FTP sites was quite naturally frowned upon. In all likelihood, there was a feeling that making this kind of information readily available would actually detract from the Internet's purpose, so it took a while for the resources to build up. Then there's the other major point: The Net is supposed to overcome the notion that people are actually *located* somewhere. Virtual worlds and all that.

When Marion Muirhead expressed an interest in locating travel information, I figured she'd spend 8 to 10 hours collecting archive after archive with details about places to visit, tourist traps, restaurants and theaters, prices of all kinds, customs and immigration assistance, and everything else associated with travel and tourism.

A few weeks later, she was clearly dissatisfied. There was no problem with the messages from other Internetters—one newsgroup and one mailing list had provided hundreds of travel anecdotes and words of advice—but the rest didn't seem to be falling into place. Gopher and FTP sites proved useful, but primarily for collecting travel stories from other Net users—valuable, to be sure, but still not enough for a strong collection.

A breakthrough of sorts came with access to the World Wide Web. While newsgroups, mailing lists, and Gopher/FTP sites provided travel *stories*, the Web offered travel *details* (and some stories as well), taking good advantage of the graphical capabilities. Virtual touring on the Web is addictive, informative, and more than a little entertaining. But after hours upon hours of WWW exploration, I'm about to concede that the travel stories from the other sources are every bit as—maybe even more—valuable. The Web lends itself to Fodor-like travel guide material, while the trials and tribulations of real travelers appear on the less glamorous newsgroups and mailing lists.

The Web's potential as a repository of travel and tourism information is enormous, but it hasn't even begun to be realized. When I can use the Web as my personal travel agent, making aircraft and hotel reservations and checking out local attractions, restaurants, theater, and shopping in a fully interactive way, then I'll know it's working. Until then, the Internet offers a good—but not superb—set of travel resources, and here we outline the best of them.

About the Contributor

Marion Muirhead is a doctoral candidate at the University of Waterloo, Canada. She has plans to use the Internet for a variety of different purposes, travel information being one of them. Here she recounts a journey of a different kind, through the Internet to find material about travel locations.

Searching for Travel Resources on the Internet

by Marion Muirhead

I began with no particular destination in mind; I just wanted to find out what information was available on destinations all over the world. It seemed like a good idea to get as much specific information as possible before making a decision about where to go, and then I wanted to know exactly what to expect.

Chances are your travel agent won't give you the most honest evaluation of destinations or hotels, or give you warnings that might frighten you off, but people compiling travel archives or subscribing to mailing lists usually have no reason to lie (although they may embroider the truth a bit now and then). I like to know what I'm getting into before I leave—I've had some fairly arduous adventures in the world already! One of the wonderful things about the Net is that it tends to be devoid of commercial motives; knowledge and information exchange are the prime values here.

Excursion 9.1. The TRAVEL-L Mailing List

First, I subscribed to a mailing list—TRAVEL-L—that discusses all aspects of travel: transportation, accommodations, tours, agents, food…everything. You can lurk and learn from discussions other subscribers are having.

Subscribing to and Maintaining TRAVEL-L

To subscribe to the TRAVEL-L electronic mailing list, send an e-mail message to this address:

```
listserv@trearn.bitnet
```

Your message should read

```
subscribe travel-l firstname lastname
```

Warning: As always, when subscribing to a mailing list, be sure to leave the subject line blank, and remember to erase your signature.

You will receive a message within a short while confirming your subscription. Every so often you are required to renew your subscription with the message

```
confirm travel-l
```

You will be prompted by an announcement sent to all subscribers when this is necessary; you will receive a message that can simply be forwarded back to the list without having to compose anything, if you prefer.

Note: Confirming a subscription isn't usual with mailing lists, but it's possible with an unusually high-volume list. If you join TRAVEL-L, or any other list with required confirmation, simply follow the instructions. One advantage of this procedure is that if you *don't* want to continue with the list but you forget how to unsubscribe, you'll be spared the necessity.

If you plan to be away from your computer for some time, you can sign off from the list to avoid being swamped by an accumulation of mail when you return. The message to send is

```
signoff travel-l
```

You can resubscribe whenever you want.

Tip: Again, with a high-volume list of this type, the `signoff` message can be invaluable. It's not unusual for TRAVEL-L to send 50 or more messages in a day.

If you should want, at some time, to send mail to all subscribers—if perhaps you had a request for specific information about some aspect of a destination—you can send an e-mail message to this address:

```
travel-l@trearn.bitnet
```

If you're after information about a specific travel location, TRAVEL-L maintains an archive of past discussions you can access. Send the message

```
index travel-l
```

to `listserv@trearn.bitnet`.

Warning: Be sure to send this type of message to the `listserv@trearn.bitnet` address, and not to the mailing list at `travell@trearn.bitnet`. Some people get cranky about the volume of material from this mailing list, so remember: If you send this or any other maintenance message to all subscribers, you may become instantly disliked.

When you have decided what files you want, send the message

```
get travel-l log file_number
```

to receive files, replacing *file_number* with the correct numbers for the file.

What TRAVEL-L Offers

One of the advantages of the mailing list is that you get different opinions. Sometimes people disagree (sometimes violently—or, at least, as violently as one can be with only a keyboard as a weapon) on what is good or bad about a destination, so you can make up your own mind from the information you find in a discussion.

For example, someone recently posted a message requesting suggestions as to what to see in New York. Someone else wrote back with all the usual tourist attractions and directions for the easiest way to get to them. At this point another subscriber, presumably someone from New York or at least very familiar with the city, asserted that the first respondent's suggestions were overly "touristy" and proceeded to list out-of-the-way places, including ethnic restaurants that were her favorites. The first respondent rejoined, commenting that the second respondent's suggestions were "the most Bohemian places he'd ever heard of." They flamed each other, but it really was perfectly instructive on the whole, despite the insults, for anyone interested in going to New York.

Usually the discussions are pretty amicable, but occasionally something untoward is suggested, someone reacts, and subscribers get sarcastic. If you don't find it entertaining or at least instructive, you can just tune in to a more sedate discussion. Often people just want to be helpful and share the useful things they've found. For example (with names and numbers altered for privacy's sake):

```
From: "Walcott P. Thompson" <WPTHOMPSO%CCVAX.BITNET@vm.hhh.de>
Subject:      Toll-free line, British Tourist Authority
Comments: To: travel-l@trearn.bitnet
To: Multiple recipients of list TRAVEL-L <TRAVEL-L%TREARN.BITNET@vm.gmd.de>

This was in my Sunday paper yesterday. Thought it might be of interest.

"The British Tourist Authority is introducing a new nationwide toll-free
telephone number, (800) 462-2748, for prospective travelers seeking
information. There service, scheduled to begin tomorrow, (Monday April 4) will
be available from 9:30 a.m. to 7 p.m. Monday to Friday. In Manhattan, callers
should dial 555-2200."
```

TRAVEL-L is a hugely active list, with messages coming in constantly. You really have to keep up with it, or else deal with going through the hundreds of messages that will accumulate. This can take hours. Assuming your mail reader gives you a subject line for each message, you can delete any that don't interest you without having to read them. Or you can receive all the messages from TRAVEL-L under one heading with a subdirectory, so that your other mail messages don't get swallowed up in the deluge.

Tip: If you're serious about maintaining travel information, set up a series of appropriate folders in your mailer. I saved useful messages in my Pine mail folder (organized by country, area, or topic) using the `s` (save) command. You can do so with other mailers as well.

The Internet tends to cater to a wide range of lifestyles, so quite often information that would be hard to find elsewhere will be highlighted here.

Tip: On the TRAVEL-L mailing list, postings frequently appear detailing other sources of information. These may be other Internet sites, regular snail-mail lists and newsletters, or books and travel guides recommended by subscribers. Also, people may be advertising accommodations for rent at a travel destination. And, of course, there are always a number of discussions going on about things to see and do and places to stay and eat at various travel destinations by people who have spent time there. A lot of these people have traveled extensively and have good advice to give.

If you require any specific information, you can post a message to all or one of the list subscribers. People in the list suggest that very general questions should be avoided. Decide exactly what you need to know. You might want to e-mail someone who is active in the list and seems knowledgeable in your area of interest.

If you are new to the list, it is best to read messages for a few days to get a feel for appropriate topics. People get quite upset if they read something unrelated to the topic. Also, if you are looking for other sources of Internet information, it won't likely help to make a request here. Many subscribers have e-mail capabilities only, so they have no interest in Gopher, FTP, or WWW sites, and they even seem to resent those who do. They may be so blunt as to tell you to buy a book.

Excursion 9.2. Travel-Oriented Newsgroups

Usenet newsgroups that focus on air fares, accommodations, and a variety of general advice can be accessed through trn or any other newsreader. The first such group I tried was the popular `rec.travel`. To access this newsgroup, I typed the command **rn** to start the rn and then issued the following command at the prompt:

```
get rec.travel
```

Here are a few sections from the advice of a seasoned traveler:

```
What to take when traveling abroad? There's an old saying that aptly applies:
Take half as many clothes and twice as much money.

lomotil for diarrhea
anti-histamine dalmane or halcion to sleep on the plane
combid spansules (prochlorperazine & isopropamide) for nausea & diarrhea
```

A few other newsgroups you might want to try are `travel.air` and `travel.marketplace`. The `rec.vacation` group has information on cheap fares, meals, airline 1-800 numbers, frequent-flier deals, service records for various airlines, and instructions on how to complain effectively if you've had a bad flight. Some suggest that complaining doesn't help unless you suggest some remedy or compensation the airline could make for you. Mere complaining tends to be ignored.

Following are three examples of postings from the various newsgroups to give you an idea of what to expect. The last of these is fairly rare, an announcement of a World Wide Web site devoted to travel. You don't usually see postings informing you of other Internet sites, at least not on the travel newsgroups.

```
------------------------------------------------------------------------
We arranged a 1 week package that included r/t air from Riga, Latvia to
Larnaca, Cyprus, hotel transfers, and 7 nights in a 3 star hotel in Agia
Napa (or Ayia Napa). The hotel was $28.00 /night per person in a double
(so essentially $56.00 per night). The hotel (Napa Mermaid) was right
across the street from a beautiful white sand beach. There are also hostels
in the main areas that are around $10.00per night. We had no idea what to
expect so we booked a hotel ahead of time, but would do the hostel route next
time since so little time is spent indoors.

Since Cyprus is mainly Greek, it feels and looks much like Greece. It has
all the charm, but since it is so small you don't have to go far to get a
completely different "hit".
```

```
-------------------------------------------------------------------
Could someone tell me more about the Eurail Youth Flexipass, I'd like to buy
the 5 travel days in 2 months pass. My specific questions:
        1) do you need a youth i.d. card?
        2) should we make reservations for the specific trains?
        3) what kind of trains can we take?

At this late date, what is the cheapest (and available) fare I can get for
flying from Nashville to Paris (16 Sept) and returning via Madrid (4 Oct)?
Right now, I was quoted a price of $925.95.

-------------------------------------------------------------------

**The Avid Explorer** - A World Wide Web server providing a variety of
information on travel destinations around the world is now available. In
addition to providing convenient links to the wealth of travel information
on the Internet, The Avid Explorer presents specific and up-to-date
information of interest to special groups of travelers. Current areas under
development include *scuba* and *skiing/snowboarding*; other areas will be
developed based on user feedback. In addition, we offer the *Travel Bazaar*,
a growing forum where you may find information on a variety of travel
product and service providers.

The Avid Explorer also features the latest information on cruises, tours,
FIT's, and domestic vacation alternatives. Special value packages will be
presented and updated frequently. Our goal is to provide a fun place on the
Web for exploring the incredible diversity of travel options now available.
Connect with Mosaic or other graphical or character-based browser via:

URL = http://www.explore.com
```

Like the mailing lists, travel-oriented newsgroups abound with hints, tips, and stories. For anyone trying to determine where to vacation or travel, they can be invaluable.

Excursion 9.3. Gopher Sites

As always, Gopher sites are among the easiest to access and use. They also contain a variety of information, ranging from travelogues to country and regional information. But they take some digging, and the resources tend to be a bit disappointing. Still...

CNS, an Internet provider in Colorado, has developed a strong Gopher site. Included are some very useful travel items. Type the command **gopher cscns.com** to connect. You can find lots of ski information here, on facilities, locations, rates, classes, addresses, and phone numbers, as well as other subjects. You can also access the electronic version of the *CIA World Fact Book* through CNS (through the item path Enter the CNS Gopher, then Reference - The CIA World Fact Book), and this will give you geographical information as well as cultural facts about different countries.

Cultural information can be extremely useful for planning a trip. A strong source of cultural information exists at `ukoln.bath.ac.uk`, through the following directory lists: BUBL Information Service/ BUBL Subject Tree: Links to Resources in Gopherspace and on BUBL/ 008 - Cultures and Civilizations.

From this Gopher you can access a range of cultural and ethnic information, including details on Israel, Scandinavia, Greece, and Romania. You can also find information on Edinburgh in this directory. There are also files on French, Polish, Indian, Native American, and Tibetan cultures.

While I was at the Bath Gopher, I decided it might be a good location for a Veronica search. The University of Cologne (Germany) is one option for this type of search; I used the keyword `travel`. The search took some time, resulting in a huge list with 200 items, plus a closing reference to about 6,000 additional items. However, this material was not organized hierarchically (or in any other way, for that matter). Some items were only very small blurbs on some book or a message from a discussion group. It took a great deal of browsing work to find out which items were worthwhile.

Pennsylvania State University maintains a large archive that can be accessed through Gopher at `genesis.ait.psu.edu`. This leads to a Telnet site (you can also simply Telnet to `psupen.psu.edu` if you want to access it directly) that contains travel information, including advisories. Log in as `PENPAGES` (if you're in the U.S.) or `WORLD` (if you're anywhere else) and follow the prompts to the keyword search. Search for `travel` and choose `L` to list the files. Here's a sample of those available:

```
TRAVEL
33 documents found
---------------------------------------------------------------------------
(L) List Titles     (R) Reduce Selection     (S) Search Again     (?) Help
                    (E) Expand Selection     (D) Display Options  (@) Exit
---------------------------------------------------------------------------
Enter choice: <L>
List of Titles
---------------------------------------------------------------------------
TRAVEL

From: 26-APR-1994     To: 21-DEC-1988          TOTAL DOCUMENTS: 33

   #              TITLE                                      DATE
   1    Sources on Mexican Americans/ Chicanos (NLS3a)     26-APR-1994
   2    Sources on Mexican Americans/ Chicanos (NLS3b)     26-APR-1994
   3    Traveler's Tips                                    30-JAN-1994
   4    What Does the Peace Corps Offer?                   30-JAN-1994
   5    American Express Billing Inquiries                 15-DEC-1993
   6    Club Discounts                                     15-DEC-1993
   7    Contracted Travel Agencies                         15-DEC-1993
   8    Corporate Hotel Discounts                          15-DEC-1993
```

```
   9     Insurance Coverage                                  15-DEC-1993
  10     Rental Car Discounts                                15-DEC-1993
  11     Research on Needs of Female Business Travelers      22-AUG-1993
  12     Ideas for Better Living (July 1993)                 12-JUL-1993
-----------------------------------------------------------------------
(N) Next Titles     (R) Reduce Selection     (S) Search Again     (?) Help
(P) Previous Titles (E) Expand Selection     (D) Display Options  (@) Exit
-----------------------------------------------------------------------
```

While the advisories are intended for American citizens, much of the information is useful for other travelers. Information on most countries includes the political situation, crime rate, and penalties for breaking laws, among other things. The archive has a directory on Africa that includes information on biking in Africa as well as African art.

If you are interested in museums or botanical gardens, information can be found that includes exhibits, their locations, and hours, through the Internet. The Bishop Museum in Honolulu maintains a Gopher that can be accessed by this command:

```
gopher bishop.bishop.hawaii.org
```

Other Museum Information and Services contains information on exhibits, hours, admission prices, and other pertinent data at major museums around the world. You can browse the frog and toad collection at the Museum of Natural History at UGA, but it's not quite the same as being there. If you want to preview exhibits where you are headed, this is definitely one way to check them out.

Other link possibilities from this Gopher abound. If you have audio capabilities on your computer, you can enjoy whale sounds at the Museum of Paleontology in UC Berkeley in Sun Audio (`.au`) Format (see Day 2 for details on Internet audio), a directory in Remote Nature Exhibits. If you have graphics capability, you can download images of birds, plants, and environments, also from Remote Nature Exhibits file. A new spot for museum info can be found in Greece by Gopher. The address is `ithaki.servicenet.ariadne-t.gr`.

The directory includes Hellenic Civilization, with sculpture, painting, music, literature, and theater. At the time of writing, Some files were still unavailable. In fact, the Internet has no shortage of museum exhibits to visit, the only problem being that all such visits are virtual. Still, if you're interested in planning a trip with visits to museums, Gophers such as these can be an excellent starting point.

If you wish to search for books or articles on travel, you can Telnet to the Electronic Newsstand at `gopher.internet.com` and log in as `enews`. I searched `travel travelogue` and came up with articles and books that contained the keywords. I did find a magazine of interest, but it was not an electronic journal. `Enews` has samples of contents from magazines and subscription information. I found an ad for *Today's Traveler Magazine*, a magazine that focuses on travel as a learning experience rather than the bargain-hunter perspective of some mailing lists.

Excursion 9.4. Learn Your FTPs

One good source of travel information is the `rec.travel` archive at the University of Manitoba. You can reach this archive through anonymous FTP to `ftp.cc.manitoba.ca` (see Day 6 for details on anonymous FTP), then changing to the rec-travel directory. The archive is organized according to region of the world (and a few other topics), and has information on most countries, including the travelogues from people who have been to them.

When you have chosen a file to view, type **`get`** *`filename`*. The file will be transferred to your account. At this site you will find a directory of information on most countries, as well as airline, restaurant and cultural information, rates, pen-pal clubs, and online ski information.

Here is an example of the files found at `umanitoba` in `/rec-travel/north_america/mexico/`:

```
-rw-r--r--   1 1000      104          29 Feb 13 06:43 0
-rw-r--r--   1 1000      104        1271 Apr 18 08:01 README.html
-rw-r--r--   1 1000      104        2167 Feb 13 06:57 baja-california
-rw-r--r--   1 1000      104       10384 Feb 13 06:59 cancun.misc
-rw-r--r--   1 1000      104       73216 Apr 17 07:19 cozumel.trip
-rw-r--r--   1 1000      104       10451 Feb 13 07:01 kailuum.trip.sopelak
-rw-r--r--   1 1000      104       13155 Feb 13 07:02 mazatlan.trip
-rw-r--r--   1 1000      104         892 Feb 20 20:34 mexico-faq
-rw-r--r--   1 1000      104       18624 Feb 13 07:05 oaxaca.trip.cisler
```

Another strong archive of travel and recreation information at MIT can be accessed by FTP at `rtfm.mit.edu`.

Once you are connected, type **`cd pub/usenet`**, and at the next prompt, type **`dir`**. This archive contains a file on travel "frequently asked questions," or FAQs. You also can find socio-cultural FAQs and files on vegetarian restaurants in various places in the world. This archive is organized conveniently for easy access to information.

Green Travel is an ecology-oriented agency with an FTP site located at `igc.apc.org/pub/green.travel`. These are large text files (some are over half a megabyte) containing a wide range of travel and tourism items.

The Omni-Cultural Academic Resource (OCAR) archive contains a variety of interesting files, including photographs with captions, taken in Africa. This is an abbreviated list:

```
Following this index, I'm going to post Egypt 256-color pics
taken in my trip in Cairo, Luxor and Sharm el Shaykh in April.
Enjoy

Egypt03.jpg -- Evening in Street of Cairo, 799x556
               Shopping after sunset is enjoyable in Cairo.

Egypt13.jpg -- Church of Al Muallaqa (Coptic), 521x800
               One of the oldest Christian places in Egypt.
               The Coptic Christianity came to Egypt in the
               1st century AC.

Egypt14.jpg -- Dawn in Luxor, 700x482,
               Luxor started 4000 years ago on the site of
               ancient Thebes. Its excellent preservation of
               historical sites makes it as the most
               attractive center for tourists.

Egypt16.jpg -- The west bank of the Nile in Luxor, 800x504
               It is the necropolis of the ancient Thebes
               (present Luxor), including tombs for the Kings
               and even ordinary workers. It seems a museum
               of technology for construction, decoration and
               concealment of tombs.
```

You can reach it by FTP at `ftp.stolaf.edu`. Or, you can access it by Gopher at `gopher.stolaf.edu`, through the path Internet Resources, then St. Olaf Sponsored Mailing Lists, then Omni-Cultural Academic Resource, and finally Going Places. These locations (FTP and Gopher) offer files dealing with travel advice, airline info, maps, slides, travel agent recommendations, travelogues, and information on an info-line in Japan. OCAR also contains a file with addresses of YMCAs in Asia and Australia. One file in the directory is called Share the World, a program for adult cultural exchange. You can find people who live in places you want to visit who share your interests, and then arrange to visit one another.

Excursion 9.5. Telnet

By Telnetting to France, you can access an interactive map called a *subway navigator* that will navigate you through subway systems in various cities around the globe. The command is `telnet metro.jussieu.fr 10000`.

When you access the site, you receive instructions for logging on. A sample opening session is displayed below:

```
Quelle langue desirez-vous ?            ¦ Which language do you want to use ?
Votre choix ? (Francais/Anglais)        ¦ Your choice ? (French/English)
Choix/Choice [Francais] : English

Do you want to use the X Window System [No] :

Choose a city among these ones:
canada/montreal         hong-kong/hong-kong
canada/toronto          nederland/amsterdam
france/lille            spain/madrid
france/lyon             united-kingdom/london
france/marseille        usa/boston
france/paris            usa/new-york
france/toulouse         usa/san-francisco
germany/frankfurt       usa/washington
germany/muenchen

Your choice [france/paris] : nederland/amsterdam

The network includes all Amsterdam subway and train stations.

Times are estimates for a "normal" day (outside off hours).
Note:
  GVB = "Gemeentelijk Vervoerbedrijf Amsterdam" (Municipal Transport Company)
  NS = "Nederlandse Spoorwegen" (Dutch Railways)
Source : From a september 1993 map supplied by Gerben Vos.
All electronic data supplied by Gerben Vos.

Departure station [no default answer] :
```

For information on skiing in British Columbia, Telnet to `CIAO.trail.BC.ca` and log in as guest, then follow the menus to Health and Recreation.

Excursion 9.6. The World Wide Web

With a WWW browser at your disposal, you can access a wealth of travel information by clicking the hypertext links highlighted on your screen. Some of the best travel information (some of it nearly in travel brochure form) is accessible this way.

Canadian Airlines operates a WWW site that promises departure information in the near future. At the time of writing, these features had yet to be implemented, but soon this site should enable you to type in your preferred days of departure and arrival in cities of your choice, and in return give you a response that enables you to choose flight times. The Canadian Airlines International WWW Page (see Figure 9.1) can be accessed at `http://www.cdnair.ca/`.

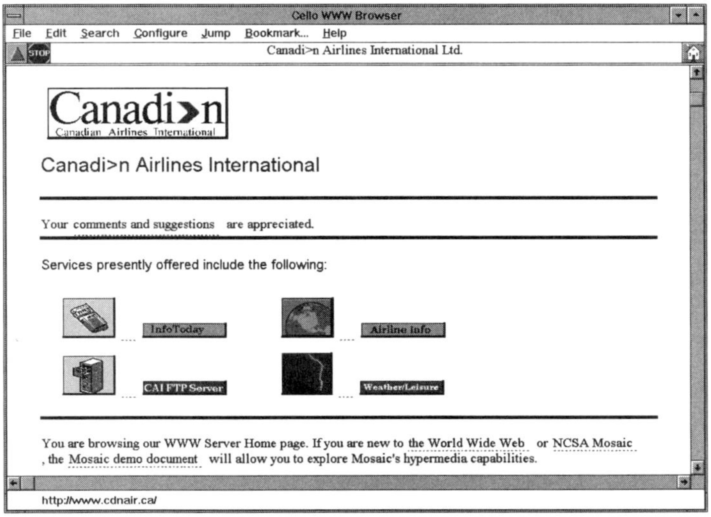

Figure 9.1. *The Canadian Airlines International home page.*

The page lists Weather/Leisure, Travel, and Accessories as options. I decided to choose the Weather/Leisure menu item.

Here, I found several weather information maps. The site also contained ski information from British Columbia and included current slope conditions. My favorite feature here was the scanned trail map files that showed mountains, trails, lifts, and chalets in relief (see Figure 9.2).

The address is `http://www.wimsey.com/bcski.html`, if you're interested in a ski trip to Whistler Mountain one day soon (and who isn't?).

Time for a site change. This time, I thought I would peruse The Singapore Online Guide (`http://www.ncb.gov.sg/sog/sog.html`) issued by Singapore's tourist board (see Figure 9.3).

These people have put together quite an extensive sampling of information, but because I didn't know what to expect, I decided to have a look at What to Expect in Singapore (see Figure 9.4).

Other selections include history, culture, etiquette, food, sight-seeing, and geographical details, to mention but a few. It's a pretty thorough guide and worth checking out if you're planning a trip to Singapore (or just want to do some traveling from your computer).

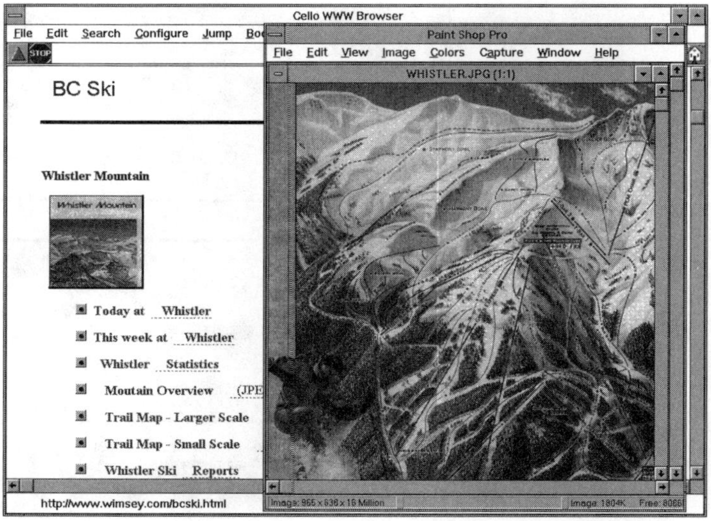

Figure 9.2. *A scanned trail map from B.C. Ski Information.*

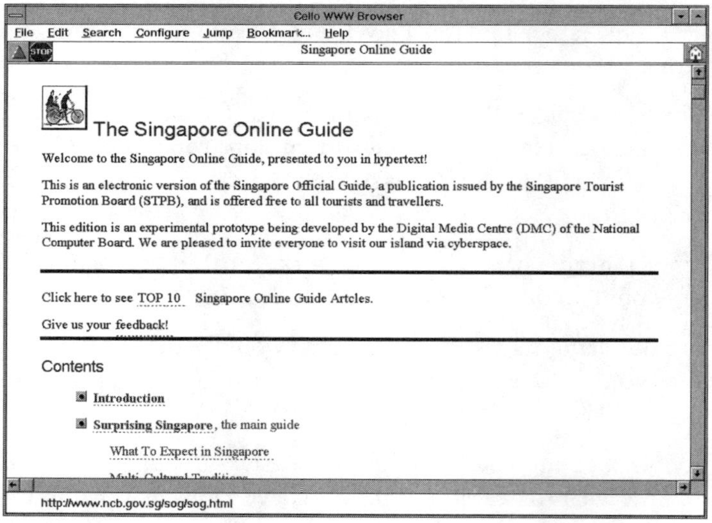

Figure 9.3. *The Singapore Online Guide.*

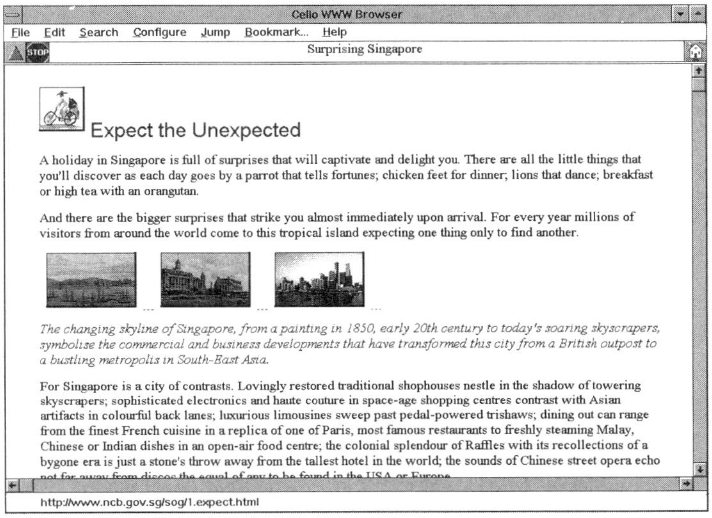

Figure 9.4. *Expect the Unexpected, from The Singapore Online Guide.*

Another nice WWW site for travel is Costa Travel (`http://mmink.cts.com/costatravel.html`). Costa Travel has information on travel discounts, flight bargains, reservations, coupons, and rebates. Through Costa's For Information and Reservations item, I accessed a tour of New Zealand (see Figure 9.5).

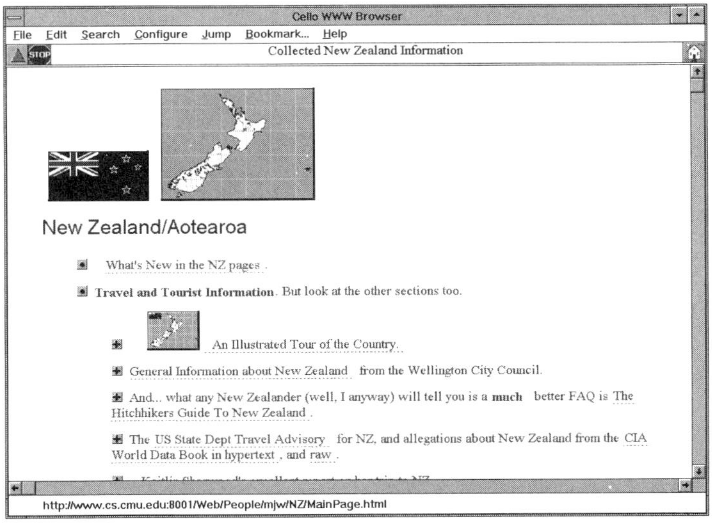

Figure 9.5. *New Zealand/Aotearoa, through Costa Travel.*

From the Travel and Tourist Information item, I chose the first option, An Illustrated Tour of the Country, which produced a map of New Zealand (see Figure 9.6).

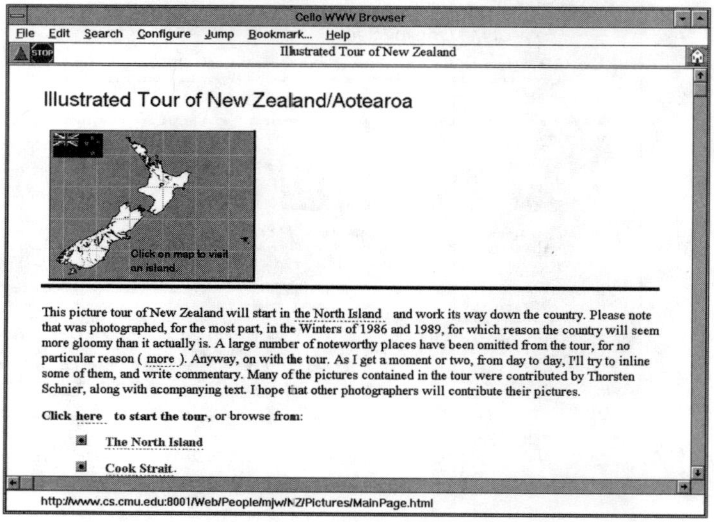

Figure 9.6. *An illustrated tour of New Zealand.*

By clicking the island of your choice, you start a guided tour complete with photographs, history, places to see, and information about the area.

Another interesting stop on my Web travel was the GNN Travelers' Center (see Figure 9.7). This site is among the best sources of travel information on the Web, and it can be accessed at `http://nearnet.gnn.com/gnn/meta/travel/index.html`.

The main menu includes direct links to featured articles and information as well as a subdirectory including Editor's Notes, Notes for the Road, Internet Resources, and the Travelers' Marketplace. The Travelers' Marketplace (which is called Travel Marketplace once you reach it) offers only a few choices, but one of them, Travelers' Tales Books, features some intriguing and informative reading (see Figure 9.8).

The Marketplace includes ads for travel books that show the cover and give a sample of the writing, including Thailand Guides and a Bangkok city guide, Lonely Planet Publications, and Travelers' Tales. In addition, an interactive forum in which you will be able to chat with travel authorities is planned for GNN.

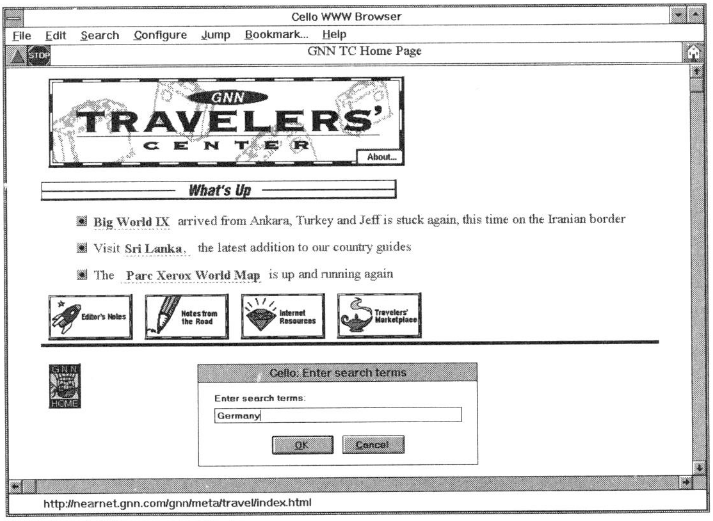

Figure 9.7. *The GNN Travelers' Center, including search box.*

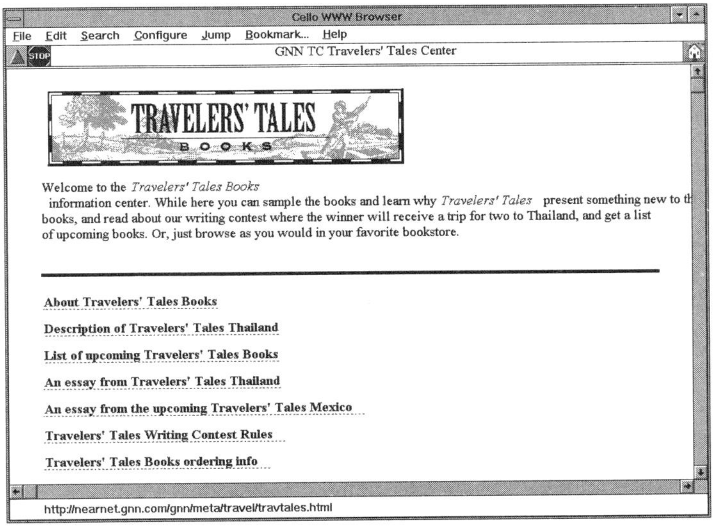

Figure 9.8. *Travelers' Tales Books, from GNN Travelers' Center.*

One of the best features in the Travelers' Center is Internet Resources (see Figure 9.9). From here you can access a range of travel-related sites, but before doing anything else be absolutely sure to click Net Travel - Using the Internet to Prepare for a Trip. It's excellent supplementary reading for this chapter.

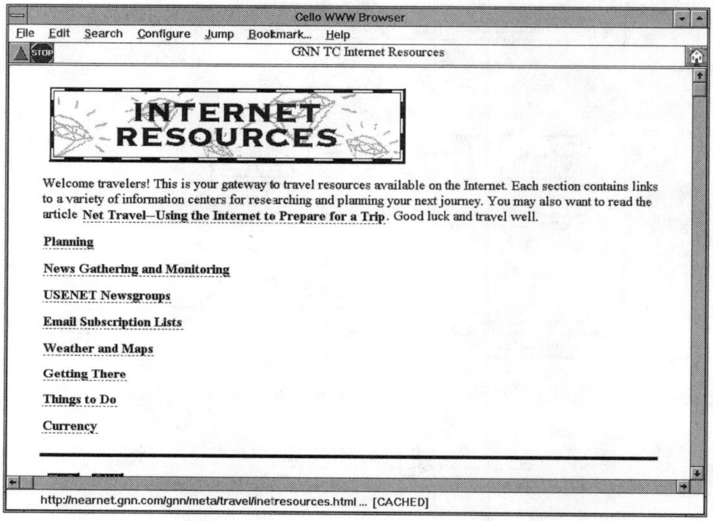

Figure 9.9. *The Internet Resources page from the Travelers' Center.*

There was more to discover, though, so I pressed on. Clicking this page's Things to do item led me to a number of links to a variety of pages. One was for skydiving, and I was tempted. But sun, sand, and surf still beckoned, so I clicked the entry for SurfNet. The result was Figure 9.10.

This resource (Figure 9.10 shows only a small portion of the page) gives you current water temperatures, wave heights, and other surf information for different locations including California and, of course, Hawaii. You can call up surf reports from different areas of the world and see if it might be worth your while to leave the computer, jump in the car, and cruise down to the beach. Also featured is a .GIF of the Wave of the Day, something worth checking if you're deciding which beach to visit. Among the more interesting demonstrations of the WWW is the SurfWindows item, which is a live video feed of the surf from Carlsbad, California.

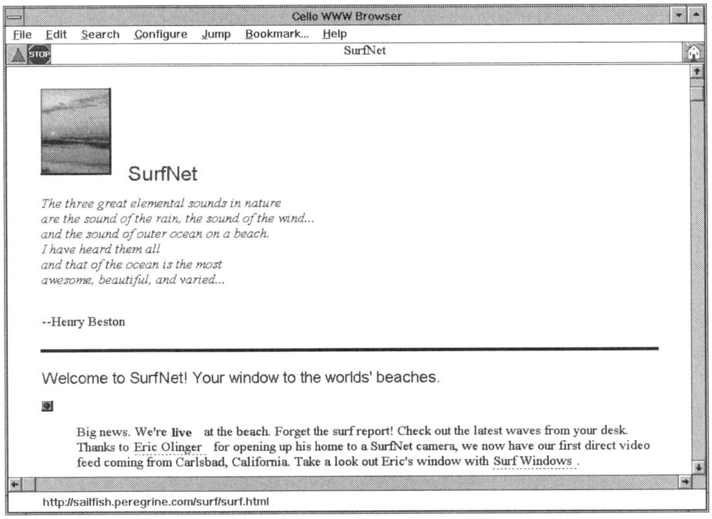

Figure 9.10. *The SurfNet home page.*

Warning: As this page shows, you must set up your WWW browser properly to view the videos. Because these files are in Microsoft Video for Windows (VFW) format, that means pointing the .AVI extension in your MOSAIC.INI or CELLO.INI file to MPLAYER.EXE, which will display VFW files. This is outlined in the link Setup Mosaic to watch surf videos, which you should follow. Note, however, that you can substitute Cello for Mosaic if you use Cello instead. See Day 2 for a more extensive discussion of WWW videos.

The same menu that provided access to SurfNet also has other interesting and useful items—for example, interactive currency conversion, airline information, and weather reports. There are options for all kinds of different tastes, including a list of restaurants in Boston, and climbing and skiing information sources. I wanted to check out restaurants in Boston and found that the file focused on moderately priced fare, brew pubs, and places to drink cider, interestingly enough.

Some of these ideas should help get you into travel on the Web. You will, no doubt, find other resources that fit your interests as you surf around with your browser. The web is expanding rapidly, so more exciting sites are on the horizon!

If you have a particular interest that leads you to travel—let's say, art and architecture, for instance—you might want to focus your search for information that way. Perform searches on art exhibits and note the locations where the most interesting art can be found. This approach should narrow down the destinations you have to read up on in the mailing lists and archives.

However you approach your search for travel information, you are sure to discover much more than you anticipated on the Internet. It's a great trip in itself!

Other Travel Information on the Web

Marion's search has yielded an extensive amount of information, including resources for searching the Net even further. I'd like to spend the rest of this chapter exploring the Web a bit further, to let you see some of the other resources available and the way in which these resources are growing.

Excursion 9.7. The Virtual Tourist and Beyond

An extremely worthwhile stop on your travel search is the Virtual Tourist (`http://wings.buffalo.edu/world`), which provides a clickable map of the world (see Figure 9.11).

By clicking one of the inset sections, you call up a more detailed map of that region. Figure 9.12, for instance, shows the detail map of Europe.

Nor is this the end of the interactive map chain. Several of the sites in the Virtual Tourist display lead to other clickable maps, such as the UK map displayed in Figure 9.13.

> **Warning:** When using a clickable (interactive) map, be sure to check the map's key before making your choice. Some of the locations point to WWW sites (including other maps), while others lead to Gophers or even text files. Furthermore, don't expect most sites to be travel-oriented. The vast majority

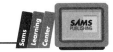

of these links are to universities or governmental institutions, not to travel destinations. Still, some of the educational sites offer links to sites dealing with the local area and to other informative sites within the same country.

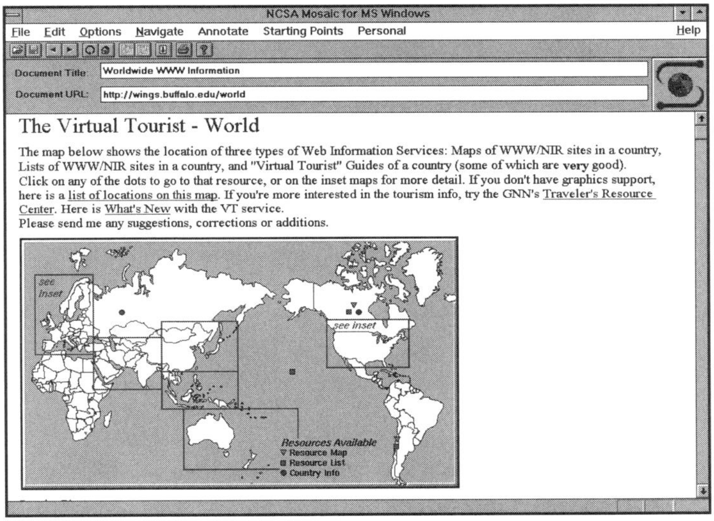

Figure 9.11. *The Virtual Tourist's clickable world map.*

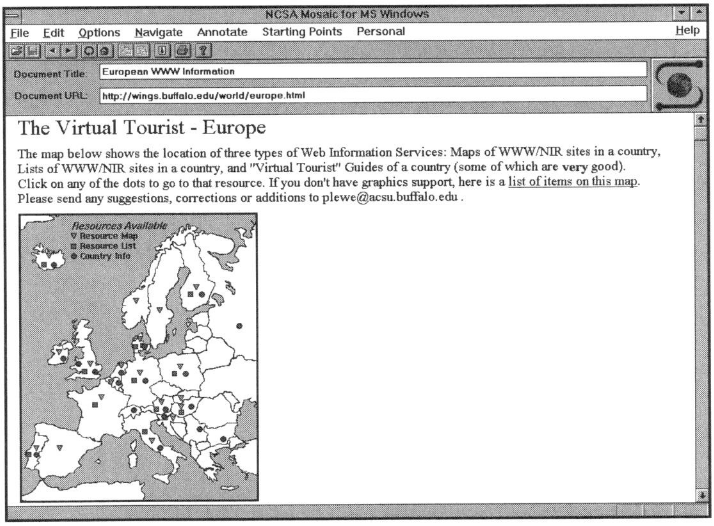

Figure 9.12. *The Virtual Tourist European map.*

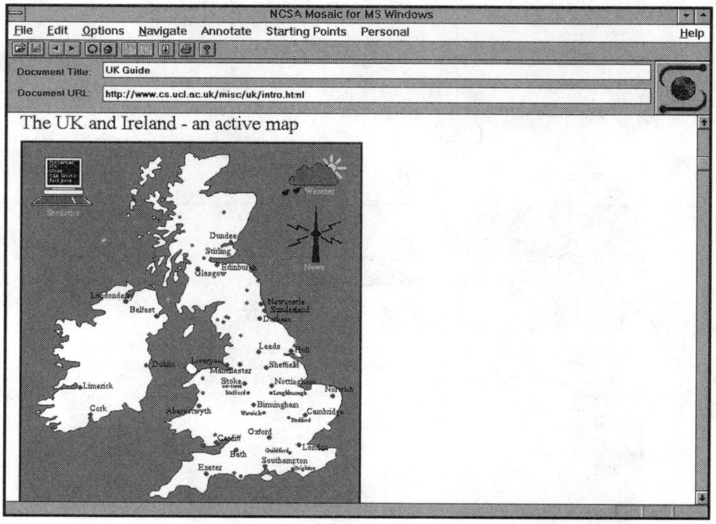

Figure 9.13. *The clickable map of the U.K. and Ireland.*

The U.K. and Ireland are nice places, to be sure, but we have more exotic fish to fry (or whatever the metaphor is). So let's head eastward from the enchanted isle and get a smattering of what else is available.

First stop, Paris. Oh, why not? There are other Web sites scattered throughout France, but it's spring as I'm writing this, and Paris and spring form an irresistible cliché.

Figure 9.14 shows a home page for Paris, including a link to some virtual tours. One such tour leads to a historical walk through the city, including an informative and colorful view of Paris's historic river, the Seine.

Skipping an unbelievably large portion of the world, we arrive in Australia. Australia has a number of worthwhile Internet sites to visit, but an excellent starting point is the home page at `http://life.anu.edu.au:80/education/australia.html` (see Figure 9.15), which offers a variety of travel, government, and education links.

A link to a wildlife and parks page leads us to another link, this time to Tasmania. Having always been fascinated by this island state (and what Bugs Bunny fan hasn't?), it's only natural that I would want to travel there, even if only virtually.

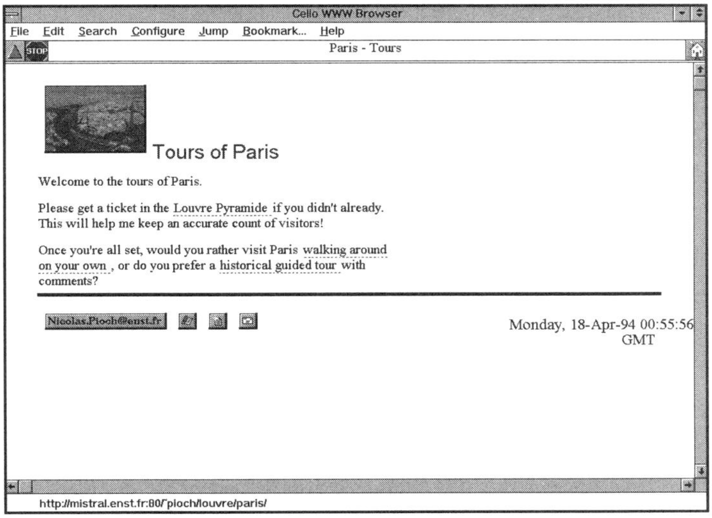

Figure 9.14. *The Paris home page.*

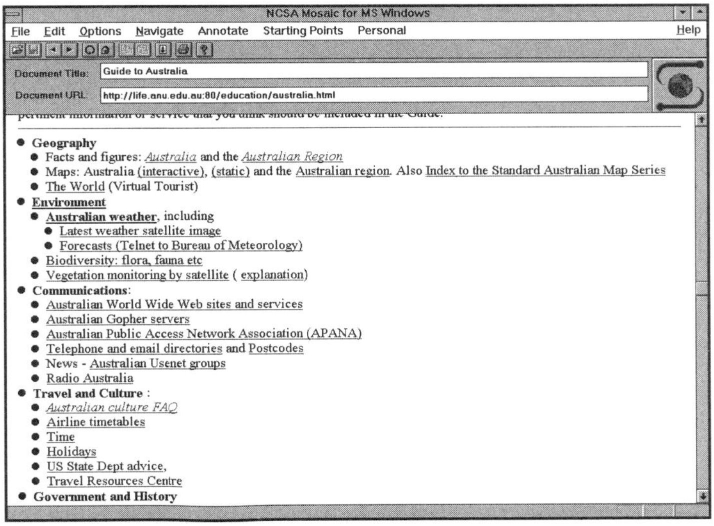

Figure 9.15. *The Australian home page, with travel and other links.*

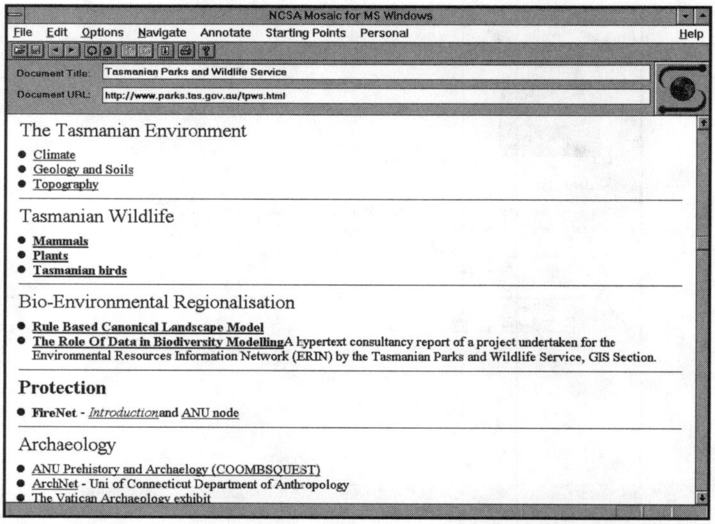

Figure 9.16. *The Tasmanian home page.*

And, yes, I have to admit I couldn't resist. There's a link here to Tasmanian mammals, which I clicked to reveal Figure 9.17.

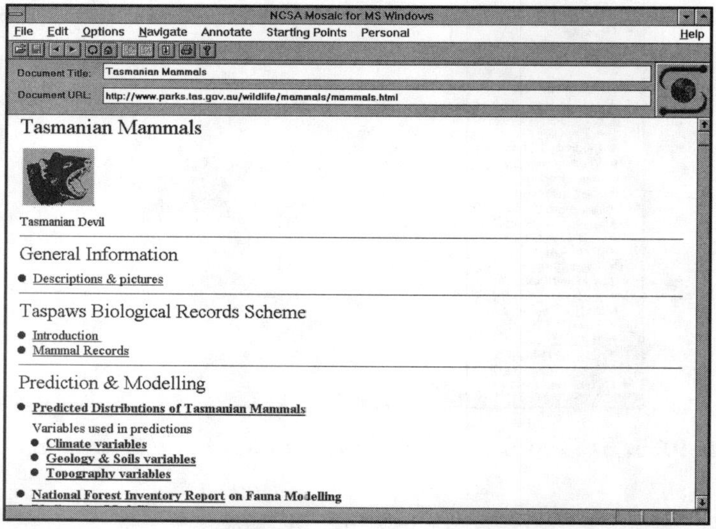

Figure 9.17. *The Tasmanian mammals page.*

Here, on the Net, is proof that the Tasmanian devil exists. He's not quite as flashy as the TV star, but still worth a trip to see. Maybe even for real some day.

Last stop, Japan. While the Japanese have only begun building their presence on the Internet, it's clear from their earliest efforts that when the construction begins in earnest it's going to be little short of spectacular. We visited Japan briefly on Day 1, and we'll do so again on Day 11, but here is a source of information particularly valuable to anyone wishing to visit the islands.

Figure 9.18 is part of the growing Japan information section of Stanford University's Japanese WWW initiative. From here are several obvious links to Japanese travel and tourism.

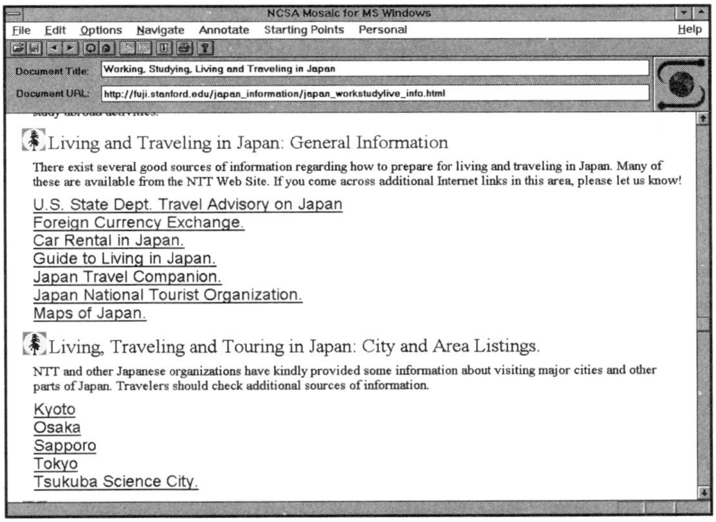

Figure 9.18. *Stanford's Living and Traveling in Japan.*

The Japan Travel Companion link takes us to Figure 9.19 (residing, as the URL address shows, on a computer in Japan itself), which not only gives us travel information, but also promises details on how to travel cheaply. Since we've all probably heard that Japan is an extremely expensive country to visit, this will surely be of interest.

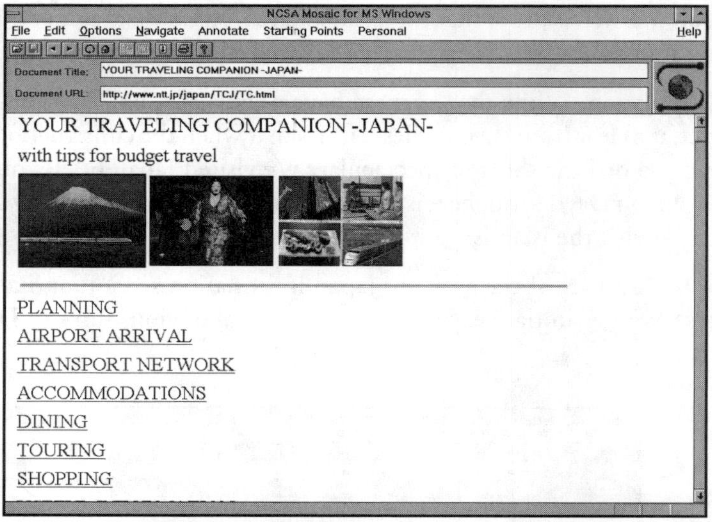

Figure 9.19. *The Japan Travel Companion.*

Is the World Wide Web the best Internet site for travel information? In one way, yes, because it points to practically all other resources. In another way, however, the Web seems to be establishing itself as a source for appealing but undetailed information, along the lines of a published travel guide or (perhaps at best) an encyclopedia entry.

After more common Web access is available, however, this will likely change, if the history of Internet usage is any indication. Before long, we should see travel journals and collections of travel stories (both the wonderful and the horrific) make their way in numbers onto the Web, counterbalancing the tame multimedia efforts so far established. In addition, we'll start to see in-depth guided tours that will enable you to learn about these places in much greater detail.

A very tiny percentage of us will visit more than 10 percent of the nations of the world, so multimedia traveling via the Web can, if it's done right, make a big difference in our appreciation of other lands—as long as it becomes a technology for virtual *travel,* not just virtual tourism.

Summary

Day 9 explored the variety of travel resources on the Internet. Mailing lists and newsgroups demonstrate the Net's capacity for letting travelers and would-be travelers correspond and share stories and details, while FTP and Gopher sites provide access to graphic and (predominantly) text files that can help us determine our next travel locations. Finally, an extensive travel tour on the World Wide Web showed both the benefits and the potential drawbacks of multimedia travel planning, with information about a variety of different locations.

9

Task Review

On Day 9, you:

- ☐ Subscribed to a mailing list that focuses on travel details and stories.
- ☐ Found and joined newsgroups that deal with travel destinations and concerns.
- ☐ Retrieved information about travel from FTP sites.
- ☐ Explored Gopher sites for details about travel destinations and issues.
- ☐ Browsed the World Wide Web for multimedia presentations of travel destinations.

Q&A

Q Will I ever be able to use the Internet exclusively for making travel arrangements?

A Probably. In the works as of this writing is a "secure" version of NCSA Mosaic, designed expressly so that organizations can accept such items as credit card information over the WWW (right now, the Net is too open for this to be completely safe). Once that's in place, you'll begin to see a range of commercial sites that will let you place orders. Combined with the Web's forms capabilities (which Mosaic now offers and which Cello will offer in its next release), there's no reason whatsoever that you won't be able to access tour and travel information, figure out via a series of multimedia presentations where you want to go, then make transportation and accommodation arrangements by filling in the appropriate forms. Of course, it will likely be a long while before the less traveled parts of the world make their debut this way, so if you're interested in unusual locations, you may not find the Net of as much use, except through newsgroups and mailing lists.

Q Will the degree of detail about individual locations improve significantly?

A Yes, I definitely think so. There's every reason in the world for individual towns and cities (and countries, for that matter) to provide extensive information over the Internet, through both Gopher and Web sites. Cities are in competition for tourism dollars, but they're also fiercely competitive about corporate relocations. As corporations and other organizations move onto the Net, they'll want to use it as a research tool for this kind of information. What could be more immediately attractive, from the standpoint of a technologically savvy corporation, than to see an equally savvy community demonstrating itself in multimedia fashion on the World Wide Web? If you're currently working for a town or city, think about starting the process.

10

WEEK 2

The Lure of the Masters: Building an Archive of the World's Great Works of Art

With all the files available through Gopher, FTP, and World Wide Web sites, it's hardly surprising that some of them are digital reproductions of works of art. Digitized art has been available ever since someone first designed a computer monitor capable of displaying it, and today's graphics-capable monitors have made downloading reproductions more appealing than ever. Your favorite Michelangelo or Picasso in .GIF or .JPG form, after all, can be displayed when your computer boots up, and if you have enough of these on your hard drive you can assign them to appear randomly as wallpaper or screen savers. Day 10 offers a glimpse at the horde of artwork the Internet holds.

In Day 10, you will learn how to:

- ☐ Use e-mail to contact other art enthusiasts.
- ☐ Subscribe to newsgroups that contain information about digitized art.
- ☐ Explore for art files using the resources of Gopher.
- ☐ Find and retrieve reproductions from the World Wide Web.
- ☐ Search for art using Veronica.
- ☐ Use the World Wide Web to learn of artist activities on the Internet.

Art and the Internet

The goal of art is human expression. To attain that goal, artists have always been eager to explore new media. A wall in a cave, a ceiling in a church, a slab of marble, a square of canvas: these have been only some of the artistic media used in the past, and it takes little knowledge of the fine arts to list a dozen more. Far from being frightened by the new media offered through high technology, artists have in fact consistently been among the first to embrace it. Artists dipped their brushes into computer pixelization almost the moment the technology existed, and computer art has been expanding into a new set of genres over the past quarter-century. Small wonder, then, that the Internet should attract artists now.

Most artwork on the Internet consists of graphics files. Find one, and you can download it or (in some cases) view it online. Increasingly, though, we're starting to see Internet-specific experimental art work its way onto, primarily, the World Wide Web. Within a year and a half, artists will undoubtedly have found a way to parlay the power of this new global interactive medium into yet another method for articulating their vision. That's the way it's always been, and thankfully it's not about to change now. The problem, of course, is that the Internet relies exclusively on flat-image, nontactile materials, but maybe that too will eventually change.

In the meantime, there's lots to explore. Whether your choice is modern or ancient, you have a significant amount of material available to you. And because traveling around the world building a collection of great art is something most of us have at least thought about, navigating the Internet in search of the images you want seems merely a natural (or is that virtual?) progression.

One such searcher is Celine Latulipe, who takes you on an artistic odyssey for the duration of this chapter.

About the Contributor

Celine Latulipe is a relative newcomer to the Internet, but she is one of the fastest learners I've ever had the pleasure to work with. An undergraduate in Economics, she is an artist in her spare time, and she almost leaped at the opportunity to explore the Net to find some of the works she admires. This is her experience in building an archive, and it's certainly one any new Netter can follow and emulate.

10

The Lure of the Masters

by Celine Latulipe

Art has always been a hobby of mine, but since high school, my time constraints have doubled and my watercolor painting has practically become a thing of the past. I've always wanted to be a collector of great art, but being a university student, it seemed completely out of the question. Buying art, even in print form, is far too expensive, and I've never liked buying books containing plates because you often end up paying for pictures you don't even like. All I really wanted was to be able to find paintings that I enjoy looking at and have them at my disposal to appreciate when I please.

I thought I was asking for the world until I realized the resources available over the Internet. Since I began my search, I've collected many masterpieces, by the masters as well as currently working artists. The great thing is that the search is never-ending, and whenever I have a few minutes, I go hunting for more specimens for my collection. It has become something of an obsession (always a danger for Netters) and a very private, self-centered obsession at that.

My first thought was that I would be doing a million keyword searches, so in anticipation, I scribbled out a bunch of subjects and names on a Post-it and stuck it to the side of my screen. Being an eclectic sort of art collector, there was no specific artist or group of artists

I was looking for; all I knew was that I liked paintings and pen and ink sketches, but I didn't really appreciate sculpture, photography, and a few other media. So my list included a few of my favorite painters—Leonardo Da Vinci, Vincent Van Gogh, Georges Seurat, and Lauren Harris—as well as some general subject titles: fine art, art, paintings, pictures, and gallery. I later realized that, in the art subject at least, keyword searches are necessary only a fraction of the time, especially when you don't know exactly what you're looking for.

Excursion 10.1. Newsgroups

Newsgroups are something I had trouble with from the beginning; user-friendly is a concept that newsgroup reader programs such as trn (which I used) have managed to evade. I could get in, and I learned fairly quickly that pressing `s` subscribes and `u` unsubscribes, but useful things like typing `h` for help isn't found on the screen. Fumbling through the reading of messages was easy, but I couldn't figure out how to respond to any particular message. It took awhile, but with the aid of the help menu, I finally was able to search for newsgroups, and at this point my list of keywords was put to use.

To demonstrate some of the confusion with using trn, here is the kind of result I came up with when I did my first search (note—boldfaced text represents what I typed):

```
****** End of newsgroups — what next? [npq] l fineart
Completely unsubscribed newsgroups:
[Type Return to continue]

Unsubscribed but mentioned in /home/clatulip/.newsrc:

****** End of newsgroups — what next? [Npq] l art
Completely unsubscribed newsgroups:
alt.artcom
alt.arts.nomad
alt.ascii-art
alt.ascii-art.animation
alt.autos.karting
alt.binaries.clip-art
alt.binaries.pictures.cartoons
alt.binaries.pictures.fine-art.graphics
alt.destroy.the.earth
alt.fan.kali.astarte.inanna
alt.party
alt.pave.the.earth
alt.save.the.earth
alt.sport.darts
alt.startrek.creative
alt.startrek.klingon
alt.support.abuse-partners
alt.support.arthritis
```

When this screen appeared, I was in the middle of trying to find art related newsgroups. At the top I typed **`l fineart`**, which tells the Usenet program to locate all newsgroups containing the word sequence `fineart`. Obviously, there were none. So, only slightly discouraged, I tried a broader category—**`art`**. What is shown in the previous screen is only the very first part of the list, but notice that many of the items listed are not at all what I am looking for.

> **Note:** When you search newsgroups, you'll almost always get more than you bargained for. trn pulls out anything with the successive letters *a*, *r*, and *t* in that order, so I ended up with newsgroups like `alt.support.abuse-partners` and `alt.party`. Cool (well, the last one anyway), but not what I wanted.

10

The first two newsgroups I came up with were `alt.binaries.pictures.fine-art.graphics` and `rec.arts.fine`. The first, which looked like the most interesting and applicable to my interests, turned out to be very inactive; I didn't see a single message posted there in a span of two weeks. Undaunted, I pursued the second group, and found some interesting (and some uninteresting) conversations going on.

A discussion of the use, supply, and pros and cons of using masonite as a base for oil paintings was probably great for anybody actually involved in the activity, but having tried oils only twice (and never having had any success), I ignored that thread. There was, however, a somewhat controversial discussion going on concerning the impact of (homo)sexuality on the works of different artists. I learned a lot about a few different artists and felt as though I got to personally know some of the group contributors. It was an experience that made me realize how small the world can quickly seem to someone who uses the Internet regularly. I read a message typed probably a minute earlier by someone on the other side of the ocean in reply to someone else on the other side of the continent.

So far, though, I wasn't much closer to finding what I'd set out to find. That began to change, though, as soon as I saw the following posting (I've only reproduced a portion of it here):

```
This is intended to be the same sort of information that would be
included in an art book.

A long-term goal would be to assemble an art book and/or a CD-ROM
```

```
based on the work submitted. (Of course, we would request the consent
of each poster prior to including their work.) This would include
the possible non-profit distribution to art departments worldwide.

People wishing to discuss the use of computer graphics in fine arts
may submit their postings to alt.pictures.fine-art.d

archives can be found in the file
/pub/fine-art
on uxa.ecn.bgu.edu
by anonymous ftp.

The file "list" will contain a list of what we have.

(Remember to set binary — most everything is binary or compressed
```

Taken from the `alt.binaries.pictures` newsgroup, this message states that the pictures that had been posted to the newsgroup were available for downloading at an FTP site. Most newsgroups have this type of thing in operation: the sites are known as *archives.* There are even search tools designed specifically for searching archive sites. The sites can hold a lot of completely unimportant stuff, especially if the unnecessary messages aren't weeded out before being archived. However, tons of information is available at these sites, and I checked out the one recommended in this posting.

Excursion 10.2. Gopher

My first Internet account was through Carleton University in Ottawa, and my Gopher search therefore began at the Carleton University Gopher. The Carleton Gopher itself didn't provide much in terms of art, but it did enable me to access Gopher Jewels (`cwis.usc.edu`), a Gopher site with, in my opinion, an extremely appropriate name. From Gopher Jewels I searched a ton of different directories, including Arts and Humanities; Museums, Exhibits and Special Collections; and a few others for good measure. These directories all had great stuff in them, but they weren't specifically what I was looking for. Then I chose a directory called Gophers With Subject Trees, which led me to a number of hot spots. Under the University of Texas, I found an arts directory, which brought me back to Canada to the Victoria Freenet and a set of numbered (but unnamed) picture files. There I found a Dali picture I wanted, so I used Gopher to save it in my home account. I bookmarked the Gophers With Subject Trees menu, for future reference.

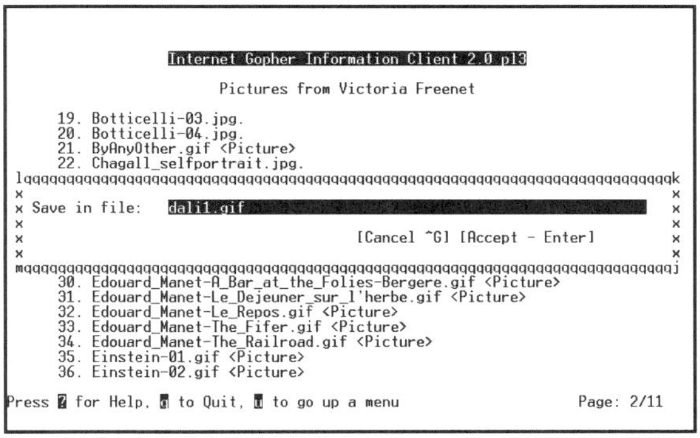

Figure 10.1. *Gopher menu showing Pictures from Victoria Freenet.*

Figure 10.1 demonstrates one of the problems with searching for files across the Net. This screen shows a portion of a list of pictures available from Victoria Freenet. The one I chose was obviously a Salvador Dali print, but the filename `dali1.gif` did nothing to help me figure out which Dali I was getting. This is one of the main problems with downloading files from directories such as this one; the filenames aren't often the most descriptive.

At this point, I went back to the Gophers With Subject Trees menu, which I had bookmarked earlier, and chose the AMI menu item (available directly by Gophering to `gopher.mountain.net`). Under the AMI Gopher I found two great directories: the Art, Images, Sound, and Humanities directory, and the Images and Pictures directory. In the Art, Music… directory I tried a number of menus, the most interesting of which was the RiceInfo (Rice University Arts) Gopher (see Figure 10.2).

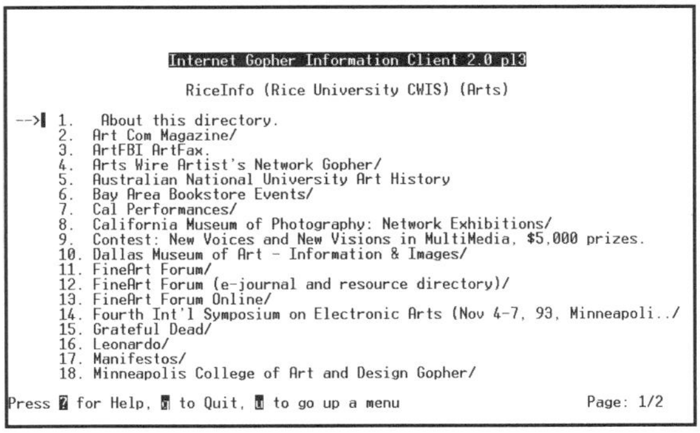

Figure 10.2. *Rice University Arts Gopher menu.*

From Rice, I Gophered into the Dallas Museum of Art and a directory called Museum Galleries (images).

The Museum Galleries (images) menu appeared familiar, and I realized that I had already been there—through a useful Gopher site called The Well (a bulletin board in San Francisco). Last time I hadn't bookmarked the site, though, so this second time I did. In the Museum Galleries directory were subdirectories dividing the available online art into Europe, Americas, Asia & Contemporary art. Some directories had no files in them, but most had a few. It looked like the whole Museum Galleries directory was fairly new; the number of available image files would probably increase over time.

After bookmarking the Museum Galleries, I examined the AMI directory Images & Pictures, finding a few items that looked interesting. I checked out several, but I was most impressed by the Art & Images directory, which contained a plethora of art sources. My two favorites were Impressionist Art from University of Vermont and Postcard Collection from University of Vermont. From these sources I downloaded a bunch of .JPG files.

Figure 10.3 shows one of the pictures I found. The shot shows the graphic file itself displayed in PaintShop Pro, and Winsock Gopher in the background. As the Gopher windows show, I started in the AMI Gopher. From AMI, I chose Images and Pictures, and then chose Art and Images. I finally ended up at Impressionist Images From the University of Vermont, where I chose the Renoir picture, "Young Women Talking." I downloaded it to my hard drive, but notice the title bar in the Paint Shop Pro screen: The computer renamed it RENOIR.GIF. It can sometimes be a problem when the computer shortens a UNIX name to fit DOS's filename format; the new names are often even more ambiguous than the UNIX ones.

At this point, I decided to turn to the World Wide Web browser Mosaic. Even though Mosaic is a World Wide Web browser, it handles Gophering extremely well. Figure 10.4 shows an art directory I located in the Netherlands after clicking on several Gopher items. Here, I have found a site offering numerous picture files in .GIF or .JPG format. I can't remember how I found the site (I could have used Mosaic's history feature, but only while engaged in the same session), or what it's called. But it really doesn't matter. Below the menus is the Document URL box showing which Gopher or FTP site is being visited; all I have to do is use Mosaic's Open URL feature to return there.

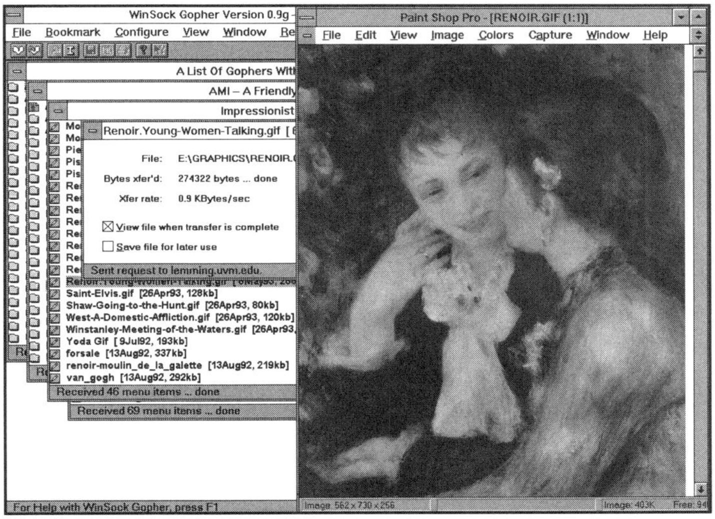

Figure 10.3. *Renoir's "Young Women Talking" from University of Vermont.*

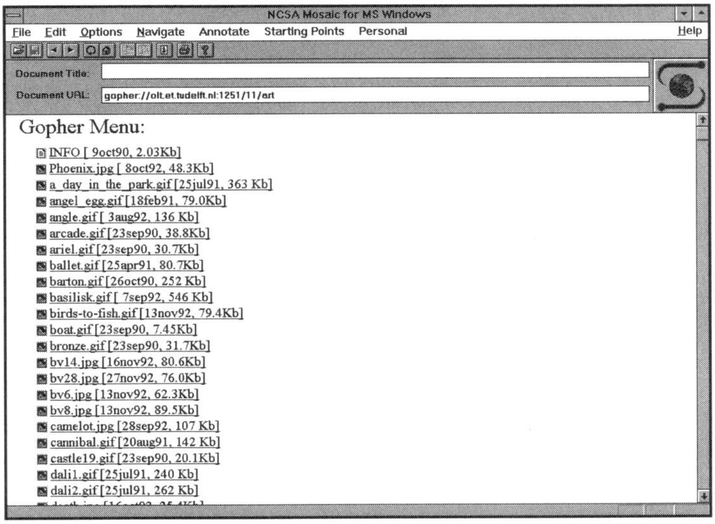

Figure 10.4. *Netherlands Gopher site with downloadable art.*

Excursion 10.3. When Searching Fails, Ask

I was pleased with my searching so far, but I felt I should be finding much more. So I turned back to the newsgroups to see what I could come up with. Having joined the `rec.arts.fine` Usenet newsgroup, I decided to get aggressive and just ask for what I wanted. So I posted a message asking for information on online galleries. Within a day I had received four responses, offering more sources. One of them pointed me to another Usenet group called `alt.binaries.pictures`, where pictures are sometimes posted. Another person sent me the names and e-mail addresses of three people involved in the area. I promptly thanked the people who had sent me information, and then wrote e-mails to the new sources. The last e-mail I received gave me a direct source: an FTP site in Sweden that apparently had a huge number of masterpieces online. With David's permission, here's the first part of the message:

```
Date: Mon, 7 Mar 1994 10:23:30 - 0600 (CST)
From: david furstenau <df@unlinfo.unl.edu>
To: clatulip@ccs.carleton.ca
Subject: ONLINE ART

   Dear Celine ...

     Though I paint and draw with traditional tools, I'm
primarily an airbrusher. Whilst surfing the Net to see if I could
find anything of value for like-minded individuals, I fell into the
most impressive art collection I've seen on the Net. Mostly .gifs and
jpegs, but they are images from most any significant artist you can
name: Dega, Van Gogh, Monet, etc. Etc. Even modern people like
Geiger, Escher, and Patrick Nagel.
     Being an airbrusher, I was especially drawn to the
impressive works of: Hajime.Sorayama, and Boris.Vallejo. Simply:
          ftp ftp.sunet.se (ANONYMOUS)
     It's at the University of Sweden, so keep in mind the time
difference.
```

This reply was among several I received, but it was by far the most helpful. In fact, it was the first reply I got after posting, and it was on my computer when I logged on the very next morning. That's one of the beauties of the Internet, especially in contrast to snail-mail: Responses can be instantaneous. The message came from an Internet user who is obviously very happy about what he's found, but who is also clearly very guarded. In it, David basically warns me that I should remember my Netiquette and keep in mind the time difference between here and Sweden, so as not to force them to restrict access and therefore ruin the source for the rest of the Internet world.

Warning: Many FTP sites are not designed exclusively for public use; in most cases, that is the last purpose. In other words, many sites are corporation or government department computers that are already heavily utilized during the day, and public users may not be completely welcome during work hours. For this reason it is always a good idea to consider the time difference and FTP only during off-hours.

So taking good care to watch my netiquette, I checked the site out using my university account (which I was in at the time). The route there is to type **`ftp ftp.sunet.se`**, then log in anonymously (see Day 6 for information on anonymous FTP), and then change the directory to the appropriate path: `cd pub/pictures/art`. Next I typed the list command (`ls`) to see what was there. Part of the result was as follows:


```
Michelangelo
George.Ouanounou
Eric.Jordan
Leonardo.da.Vinci
William.Blake
Ken.Kelly
Dennis.Lu
Thomas.Cole
Camille.Pissarro
Ken.Foote
Berthe.Morisot
Gustave.Caillebotte
Alan.Lee
Edgar.Degas
H.R.Giger
Zhou.Jun
Stephen.Whealton
Stefan.Torreiter
Boris.Vallejo
Limbourg brothers
Mihaly.Zichy
226 Transfer complete.
631 bytes received in 0.51 seconds (1.2 Kbytes/s)
ftp>quit
```

David was right; a great selection was available. Within the art directory, there were directories for a number of different artists, including Degas, Da Vinci, Monet, Blake, Van Gogh, and many others. I left my university account and fired up my commercial one, then used Cello to FTP to the site and downloaded straight to my hard drive (a bonus with this account) and checked out my findings in PaintShop Pro. At this site I found my favorite Escher print, then downloaded it to my hard drive.

Excursion 10.4. We Want More: Veronica

I decided to try out a few other Internet tools; after all, why limit myself? So I took off to Winsock Gopher once again and tried a Veronica search. The question was, which Veronica site to use. After such considerations as the time of day, I chose to search only for directory titles and chose the University of Cologne Veronica searcher.

The search keyword I chose was `pictures`, and the response I received was mind-boggling. Veronica gave me 201 Gopher items containing the word `pictures`, and when I scrolled through it to the bottom of the list, I found a terrifying message: `"There are 1574 more items matching the query 'pictures' available"`. It is this kind of message that is actually discouraging to Net users; the thought that there is that much information available is great, but knowing where to go at this point is impossible. I tried several, downloaded a few files, but I realized there was a great deal more to find. Still, the search had been extremely valuable.

Excursion 10.5. The ANIMA Project

I'm a firm believer in Murphy's Law. Maybe that's why, after spending a large number of hours browsing the Net looking for masterpieces online, I got another response to my Usenet request for online images information that seemed to be the answer to all my problems. It seemed that almost all of the time I had spent in searching could have been saved had I known about one single resource—ANIMA—right from the start. Actually, that's an exaggeration; some of the parts of the resource were accessed more easily by direct Gopher or FTP, but in many instances ANIMA was the perfect Internet resource for artists. Here is a portion of the e-mail message I received; I reproduce it here because it also demonstrates the friendliness and goodwill on the Internet, which never fails to amaze me.

```
Date: Wed, 9 Mar 94 02:18 PST
From: Derek Dowden <ddowden@wimsey.bc.ca>
To: Celine Latulipe <clatulip@ccs.carleton.ca>
Cc: ddowden@wimsey.bc.ca
Subject: Re: On-line Masterpieces

Hi Celine,

As a Carleton graduate myself I thought you might be interested in my
current on-line art project ANIMA. (I have been running art networks on-line
since 1984 with ArtNet out of Toronto). It is really useful to somehow get
Mosaic access to the net, there is a hell of a lot of art now available
only through the World Wide Web. Good luck with your book on the internet.
Please let me know if you find any art resources on the net we don't have
in ANIMA.
```

```
Here is my current release blurb:
ANIMA - Arts Network for Integrated Media Applications

    The WebWeavers presents the premiere of the public version of 'ANIMA -
Arts Network for Integrated Media Applications'. The ANIMA information
service provides a network source for information focusing on the
intersection of arts, technology and media.

    ANIMA is a newly available multimedia cultural information service now
distributed over the World Wide Web global hypertext network. ANIMA
provides on-line access to cultural theory and expression, ideas and
research.

    ANIMA explores the possibilities of networking as an information resource
and tool for research in art and technology, the development of virtual
communities for creative collaboration, and the network as a medium for
artistic exploration and expression.

    Currently available ANIMA features includes
ArtWorld: a service center for the arts on-line;
Spectrum, a selection of electronic publications,
NEXUS: an on-line gallery space for artists projects;
ATLAS a reference library on art and technology,
Sphere: a journal for communications theory;
Techne: research on media tools and techniques;
Virtuality: the impact on the interface of interactivity and immersion; and
Persona: a community forum for empowering voice and vision on the net.
Many new features will be released over the upcoming weeks on a regular
basis.

ANIMA can be now be accessed with a direct connection to the internet
using Mosaic software available for Macintosh or Windows. The URL for ANIMA
is - http://wimsey.com/anima/ANIMAhome.html.

    For further information on how to connect, contribute or participate in
ANIMA please email anima@wimsey.bc.ca.

_____________________________________________________________________________
Derek J. Dowden,
The WebWeavers, anima@wimsey.bc.ca
ANIMA - Arts Network for Integrated Media Applications
URL http://wimsey.com/anima/ANIMAhome.html
```

I checked out this ANIMA network, specifically the ArtWorld section. Figure 10.5 shows the ArtWorld home page, one page below the ANIMA home page.

The title ArtWorld was underlined, indicating that it is a hypertext link. Clicking it brought up the linked screen. On this page I found such items as Derek's Guide to On-line Galleries and Traditional and Fine Arts. Under this last item I found a lengthy list of online art, with the title Experimental Art: Web Art. The list included the OTIS project, a Random Portrait Gallery, Off the Wall Gallery, the Marius Wate Home Page, Underworld Industries, Playground Gallery, and a whole host of other directories. The great thing about ANIMA is that in many instances, the creators have given a description and critique of the sites, galleries, and so on, which make up the user's options. This is a nice feature; most other art browsing sites don't offer it.

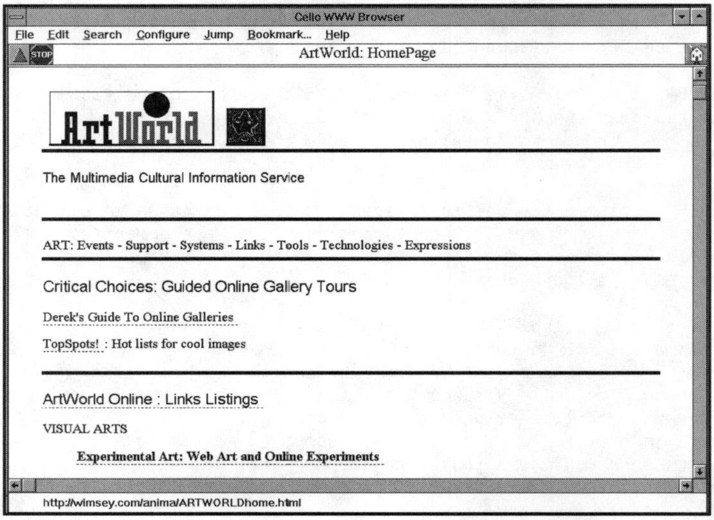

Figure 10.5. *ArtWorld home page, from ANIMA.*

Anything with a title Off the Wall Gallery simply has to be checked out, so I did. Figure 10.6 shows two pages deeper in the ANIMA directory, and demonstrates one of the nicer aspects of ANIMA—relatively thorough descriptions.

Artists' names are in hypertext, and when I clicked them and I got directories that let me see their work. I downloaded some files and discovered (although I wasn't really surprised) that some really interesting stuff was in there. The fact that this collection changes monthly is also nice; it's like having a neighborhood gallery featuring different exhibits and free admission.

The part of ANIMA I checked out was minimal—the service is obviously very extensive, and not limited to my specific topic of painting. Like many other of the sites mentioned in this chapter, the arts in general are represented extensively on the Internet. I came across directories for dance, theater, literature, sculpture, television, graphic design, architecture, and numerous other subjects. Any of the main directories that have been mentioned are good starting places for searches on any of these or related topics.

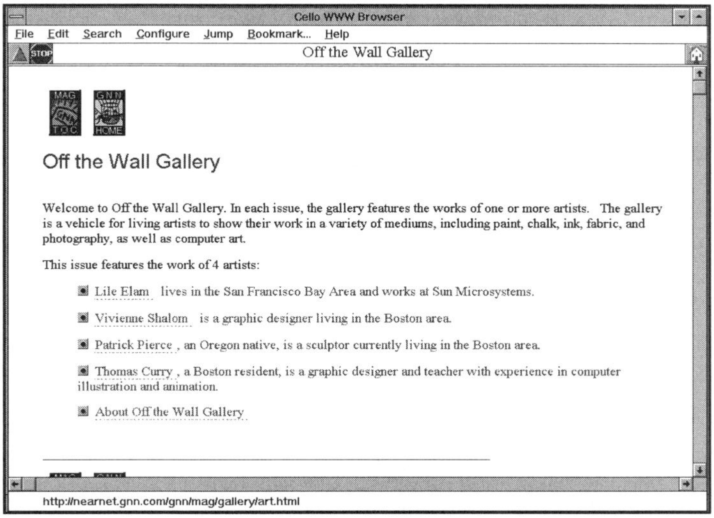

Figure 10.6. *Off the Wall Gallery page.*

Of course, there also is a ton of directories, newsgroups, FTP sites, and so on, for computer art of all sorts. Simply start searching, and I guarantee you'll find more than you thought you were asking for.

Note: The image (.GIF, .JPG, and so forth) files that I have mentioned also are not exclusively for paintings, and there are .GIFs of photographs all over the Net, as well as .GIFs of photographs of other arts (architecture, sculpture, design).

For me, the search for art is never-ending, and even if my monitor gives me only 16 colors and mediocre resolution, I'm not about to stop. Half of the fun, after all, has been the challenge of finding the masterpieces to which I want ready access. If I really want to have a good copy of them, I can take the file to a store that does laser printing, and get my "print" there, or have them turn my files into slides. And the great masterpieces aren't the only material I ended up with. I even went out, for example, and found a .GIF file of a photograph of my roommate's favorite: penguins. Of course, I have no idea where I downloaded it to or what it got named when it was downloaded, so I haven't looked at it yet, but I know it's on my hard drive somewhere.

I now know how to navigate the Internet. Now, if only I could figure out how to use my own computer....

Summary

As Celine has demonstrated, the Internet is a rich and intriguing resource for starting your own art collection. In fact, it's equally rich for establishing an archive of photographs or related documents. Despite the wide range of searching and downloading Celine went through, she readily admits that she hasn't even begun to explore the Net's wealth of information about art, art history, and other art-related issues. What she has done, however, is make an excellent start.

The combination of tools demonstrates the multimedia nature of art. Not only are newsgroups and e-mail extremely useful, but Gophers and FTPs also are essential to make the collection happen at all. Then, too, there's the issue of actually viewing what you've downloaded, and here a knowledge of your own computer's software is needed. I have a feeling that the World Wide Web will soon receive the majority of attention from Internet artists, but so far that hasn't happened. Still, if resources like ANIMA are any indication, that day can't be far off.

Task Review

On Day 10, you learned how to:

- ☐ Use e-mail to contact other art enthusiasts.
- ☐ Subscribe to newsgroups that contain information about digitized art.
- ☐ Explore for art files using the resources of Gopher.
- ☐ Find and retrieve reproductions from the World Wide Web.
- ☐ Search for art using Veronica.

Q&A

Q I've downloaded several pictures using Mosaic, but I can't find them anywhere on my hard drive. What gives?

A When you click a graphics file in Mosaic, it's not automatically downloaded to your hard drive. Instead, Mosaic interprets the click as an indication that you want to view the picture rather than download it. So it brings it into your system, after which it fires up the appropriate viewer (see Question 3) and lets you look at it.

Next time, go to Mosaic's options menu and select Load to Disk. Now when you click a file, you'll get a standard dialog box asking where you want to put it. Name the file whatever you want and put in on whatever drive and in whatever directory you want.

Why is all this necessary? It has to do with the simple fact that Mosaic was designed originally as a program for UNIX workstations with high-speed (that is, direct) Internet connections. The idea was that you'd bring in a graphics file at ultra-high speed—your 14,400 bps modem doesn't even qualify as a kiddie-car by real access standards—and then view it and decide if you wanted to keep it. Only then would you save it on your drive. Modem hook-ups to the Internet, however, don't work this way, but Mosaic hasn't been rethought with the home Netter in mind.

Q When I download pictures using Cello, they keep showing up in a directory I don't want them in. How can I change this?

A Unlike Mosaic (see the preceding answer), Cello defaults to downloading clicked items to your hard drive. The problem is that it doesn't present a dialog box, asking where you want to put it. Instead, it downloads automatically to a default directory, which you can specify in the program's Configure menu. From the Configure menu, choose Files and Directories, then choose Download Directory from the cascaded menu. Then type in the directory in which you want your downloads. Note that you can change this whenever you want—if you're downloading a number of things for a specific purpose, for example—but Cello saves the most recent configuration when you exit.

Q Now that I've downloaded some pictures, how do I go about looking at them?

A As mentioned throughout the chapter, you need viewers. This isn't a special Internet problem; it's endemic to all computing activity. If you have a certain kind of file on your hard drive, you need a program that will let you work with it. In the case of graphics files, you'll find, for the most part, two major types. The first has the extension .GIF, the second the extension .JPG. Many graphics or paint programs let you view .GIFs—in fact, it's likely your system shipped with some kind of .GIF-capable program or another. To view .JPG files, however, you may well need a separate program. Fortunately, shareware and freeware packages abound, and they're available on the Net, on commercial services such as CompuServe or America Online, or on shareware floppies or CD-ROMs.

A more difficult issue is setting up your Gopher or Web program to let you view pictures automatically. In all cases, the installation instructions will guide you through the procedure of associating various types of files with specific programs, but don't expect it to be easy. Windows Mosaic is hopelessly convoluted in this regard, for example, and even the friendlier Cello could use some help here. Gopher programs range in ease this way, and you can expect most programs to assume that you have more knowledge about this kind of thing than you may well have. Fortunately, it's not easy to botch things up completely, so do some experimenting.

The general principle is this: If you want to automatically view a file as soon as it downloads, you have to associate that type of file with a specific viewer program. In other words, if you plan to use PaintShop Pro for Windows (as Celine has done throughout her exploration) to view .JPG files in Mosaic, you have to specify somewhere in the program's configuration file that .JPG extensions will be associated with `c:\pshop\psp.exe` or whatever your path and filename may be for the program. Next time you download a .GIF file in Mosaic, PaintShop Pro will automatically load and display your picture.

Q I've just found an archive of experimental computer art, and I've downloaded some of the best. Am I allowed to use them in my business presentations?

A In a word, no. Several online galleries contain a readme file of some sort that states quite clearly the conditions surrounding the use of downloaded files. Usually it goes something like this: You may use the files for personal or noncommercial use, but any commercial use is strictly off-limits. A business presentation is a commercial use, even if you're a member of the firm's nonprofit R&D facility.

There's an easy way around this problem, although it takes a bit of planning. There's almost always an information area for galleries, containing the names of the people involved in setting it up. E-mail them and ask permission. If the permission isn't theirs to give, they'll let you know who can do so. This is a good idea for noncommercial use of the material as well, even though it might not strictly be necessary.

Q Is there anything I can do to speed up the downloading of these pictures?

A Yes. Either buy a new modem or establish a high-speed direct line. Buying a new modem requires a knowledge of your service provider's options: If you nip out and get a spanking new 28.8 kbps model, for example, it won't do you any good if your service provider is using only 14.4 kbps modems. As for the direct line approach, it's a great idea, but it's extremely expensive (possibly a few hundred dollars a month).

Two ways around the cost. First, your company might already provide a high-speed Internet connection; check with your systems people. For the home user, keep tabs on the developments at your local cable-TV company. As I write this, for example, I've just learned that a cable-TV provider in Massachusetts is beginning a high-speed Internet service through the cable system. It's quite expensive, but it's very fast.

11

WEEK 2

A Matter of Degrees: Choosing a University…or Universität

A Matter of Degrees: Choosing a University...or Universität

Day 11 examines the growing amount of available information on the Internet about universities and colleges. Specific departments or centers have been offering information about their activities since the Internet's early history—and recently, entire schools have made an effort to include the kind of information students need to make a choice. Primarily through Gopher and the World Wide Web, it's now possible to browse—sometimes even visit—before you sign that first tuition check.

During Day 11, you will perform the following tasks:

- ☐ Use Gopher to locate information about a range of universities.
- ☐ Use e-mail to obtain information from others regarding universities.
- ☐ Examine newsgroups for university information.
- ☐ Examine one university in detail.
- ☐ Explore other university offerings on the World Wide Web.

Selecting the right university may be the first truly important decision of an adult's life. Many people, however, make the decision almost by default. The assumption is that just about any university or college will fulfill your educational needs, and that the only real difference is in how much it costs to attend. Money, of course, is always a concern, but the type and quality of education should matter even more.

So far, there isn't an Internet-based ratings system for post-secondary institutions. I suspect it won't be long until there is one. Much of the truly creative Gopher and World Wide Web activity is springing from the work of students, and surely someone somewhere is working on a means of surveying all Internet users with very specific questions about education at their schools. If not, maybe this chapter will spur such an activity.

It's needed, and it's timely. With the global reach of the Internet, there's never been a better time to inform all would-be students (and all existing students looking to transfer) of the huge range of educational possibilities at the university level. Nor has there been a better time for post-secondary institutions to design Gophers and Web pages that show people exactly what they have to offer. A good server can be extremely specific, going so far as to include course descriptions, assignment profiles, faculty information, program options, book lists, and fee options—and that's only a start.

With more and more high schools taking advantage of the Internet, it only makes sense for universities to make this kind of material available. Call it informing, call it advertising, call it school spirit if you will, the fact is that prospective students want to know it. The amount available thus far is still quite limited, but a few shining lights are changing that for good.

There's more to choosing a university than just determining which institution has the best program for your needs. You also need solid information on the school's location, surroundings, academic disciplines, student resources, library holdings, laboratories, housing, and much more.

While you can't judge an institution by its Gopher or World Wide Web information, you might be able to come close. In this sense, the Internet can serve as a kind of education counsellor, in much the same manner as the traditional guidance counsellor.

As an example, look at the excellent main Gopher menu from Rice University in Texas (`riceinfo.rice.edu`):

```
1.  About RiceInfo
2.  More About RiceInfo and Gopher/
3.  Calendars and Campus Events/
4.  Campus Life at Rice/
5.  Computer Information/
6.  Health and Safety at Rice/
7.  Houston Information/
8.  Information by Subject Area/
9.  Library Services/
10. Other Gopher and Information Servers/
11. Research Interests and Opportunities/
12. Rice Campus Directory/
13. Rice Course Schedules and Admissions Information/
14. Rice University and Departmental Policies/
15. Search all of RiceInfo by title/
16. Weather/
```

Items 2-16 are directories, each containing more information. With topics such as health and safety, campus life, library services, and course schedules and admissions information, you have everything you need to get started thinking about Rice as a possible school for you or your children. Not all university gophers are this instantly informative, and that, too, might tell you something about the school. Clearly, Rice is determined to get the information out.

An example of a less developed Gopher site, but an informative one nonetheless, is at Rhodes University in Grahamstown, South Africa (`gopher.ru.ac.za`):

```
1.  About the Rhodes University Computing Services gopher  [ 7Apr94, 3k..
2.  Rhodes University/
3.  South African Politics/
4.  African Networking/
5.  Gopher-Jewels/
```

```
6.  Information About Gopher/
7.  Interesting services - after hours/
8.  Interesting services - working hours/
9.  Other Internet Gopher Servers/
10. Rhodes University WWW Server <HTML>
11. Rugby Information/
12. Search Gopherspace with Veronica/
13. The CricInfo Cricket Database/
14. The Internet Hunt/
15. xperimental/
```

Again, there's not as much information here about Rhodes University as there was about Rice, but any Gopher pointing to a cricket database can't be bad.

Much more complete is the main Gopher menu for the University of Bath in England (`gopher.bath.ac.uk`):

```
1.  About the University/
2.  Courses, Seminars and Events/
3.  University Services/
4.  - Administration/
5.  - Computing Services/
6.  - Library/
7.  Academic Departments/
8.  Staff Societies/
9.  Student Services and Societies/
10. Publications, Documentation and Minutes/
11. Equipment, Price Lists, Shops and Supplies/
12. Weather, Travel, Entertainment etc./
13. Directory Services/
14. Fact Files/
15. Keyword Searches of Bath Information/
16. Other Information Services/
17. Information about this Service/
```

Choosing item 9, Student Services and Societies, brings us to the following menu, which despite its brevity offers useful information to anyone checking this university out:

```
1.  Bath University Christian Union/
2.  International Students News/
3.  University Radio Bath/
4.  Wine Society/
```

Judging from item 4, this sounds like a perfect place to be. Wine, a Roman bath, what more could you ask of a university?

There's much more to discovering information about universities than simply checking Gophers, but why not use them for a start? At the very least, they should help you eliminate places you simply don't want, and that, too, is an important part of the selection process.

About the Contributor

Angela Pollak is a graduate student at the University of Waterloo (Canada). Like any number of advanced students, she's making decisions about what to do next, and also like many of them, she's wondering what she might have done instead (and, for that matter, might still attempt). Here is her experience at searching the Net for university information.

Using the Internet to Help Choose a University

by Angela Pollak

My mission was to find information about universities in many parts of the world: the United States, Europe, Asia, *anywhere*. Early in the project I decided to focus sharply. I wanted to find universities that offer courses in marine biology and oceanography. Then came the questions. How do I tackle this? Where do I look? The world is a big place, you know.

I'm an English major, but I think in another life I would have chosen to be a scientist. In fact, in my upcoming life, I still might. So, I've narrowed the courses I'm interested in to those dealing with marine biology. (Actually, I suspect I am more in search of a warm environment in which to study, close to a large body of water.) Given that English is my mother tongue, I expect eventually to limit my search to English-speaking universities. Dreams of mastering every language on the planet—or even on this one continent—have long since faded away.

Note: I will be looking for information about the courses each university offers, along with the school's facilities and faculty. Information about the community surrounding the university also gives insightful information to prospective students. After all, relocating to a new university affects your personal life too, not just your academic life. Even knowing what the weather will be like is a relevant factor to consider.

Excursion 11.1. Checking Your Local University Gopher

Most universities on the Internet offer a main Gopher. Mine is no exception. Through UWINFO (the University of Waterloo Gopher at address `uwinfo.uwaterloo.ca`), I can connect to any number of other Gopher sites, including the huge main Gopher home at the University of Minnesota (`gopher.micro.umn.edu`). I could start, of course, by exploring my own university, but since I'm here I think I'll go further afield.

Tip: If you're already at a university, use your local Gopher to find out all sorts of information you might have forgotten to read in the university calendar (you know, the paper thing). Most will offer solid, concise information about the university itself, along with its projects, official documents, facilities, departments, courses, faculty, and even news bulletins and weather. These selections lead to online periodical reviews, lists of other schools, and newspaper reports from other universities.

Knowing what my university makes available over the Internet is important for several reasons. First, I'm familiar with my own university. I know where the campus is. I know what the city is like. I know what programs and degrees and courses my own offers. Because of my familiarity with the school, the only new thing to learn will be how to access this information over the Net. In short, I will learn how to find that information, but I won't be concerned about its accuracy (I'll already know that). After I become familiar with the Internet, I fully expect this process to reverse itself until I find the school I'm looking for. When I access other universities, I want the information to become primary, and Internet techniques to be secondary.

Like all good university Gophers, mine offered information on the institution's history: its founding, its date of incorporation as a university, how specific programs have originated and enhanced its reputation. It told who the professors were, and it detailed their strengths and interests. It described student associations and recreational facilities, and it listed courses and exam timetables. In other words, it told me just about everything I need to know about life on campus.

On the basis of what I encountered here at home, I decided there are two ways to find the information I'm looking for. First of all, my university isn't likely to be singularly vain in posting this specific campus information for public use. If I could get into systems at other universities, it was just a matter of finding this bragging section.

Secondly, I could interact directly with other people through e-mail. This would be good interactive information that would apply specifically to my questions—and it would be a good source for the information I can't find on Gophers or Web pages, or information that universities are less willing to share. Questions regarding school reputations, school connections to resources and employment, and campus night life or information about the city atmosphere are all questions many students likely have down-to-earth answers for. The answers forthcoming from university public offices won't always tell all sides of the story. I wasn't expecting objective answers, and I honestly didn't want any from my e-mail interaction. I wanted the anecdotes.

Excursion 11.2. Using E-mail to Get Information from Real People

Although most of my searches start with Gophers and proceed from there, I decided to take a somewhat different route. I was in trn, my newsgroup reader, and I did a search for marine biology groups. I didn't find a lot that immediately interested me, but through some messages I pulled some e-mail addresses for information.

Loading Pine, my preferred e-mail program, I sent e-mail requests for information on marine biology to `trop-bio@net.bio.net`, and to `Womenbio@net.bio.net`. Very quickly, I received six replies. One correspondent, Sara, suggested I look into Stanford University, Boston University, and the University of California at San Diego. Another, Shannon, recommended the University of Texas, while Cathy suggested the University of California at Santa Cruz and Kris suggested Oregon State University. The next relevant message was from Donna, who said to check out the University of Hawaii and the University of Guam. Finally, Karen suggested Long Island University.

Kris's message looked like this:

```
Having worked at Botany and Plant Pathology for a while I know Oregon State
University had a pretty solid faculty in Oceanography and Marine Biology.
They run the Marine Science center on the coast at Newport, OR. You might
want to check them out if the Pacific Northwest interests you. A warning
though, state funding due to a thing called Proposition 5 is causing severe
problems. Question them closely and if you do decide they are worth a look,
question current students even more closely.
```

Note: I liked Kris's message because she was kind enough to let me in on the potential funding problems at this university. Comments like these comprise the necessary information students should have to make informed decisions.

From Cathy, the following:

```
Well, there's the University of California at Santa Cruz: the weather is
gorgeous, the ocean is a couple of miles from campus, and you have all of
Monterey Bay to play in!

Now, seriously, UCSC does have marine biology programs at all levels and
there are faculty members with a wide variety of interests, both plant and
animal...

Good luck in your search!
```

Note: As apparent in this and other messages, Cathy has an excellent sense of what students are looking for in a school. The geographic location and weather patterns are as much a part of choosing a place to live as are expenses and transportation. In the case of studying marine biology, proximity to the ocean really seems an important factor. Why not study biology in its natural habitat?

Pleasantly surprised, I read the encouraging messages from total strangers across the continent. The notes were so friendly, it was as though we had been corresponding for years rather than passing a few computer connections at the same time. As a bonus, these mail messages also described to me in more detail what the field of marine biology involves. For instance, oceanography is, if not a synonym for marine biology, at least closely related. And the field itself consists of plant *and* animal life studies. I didn't know that before (I'm an arts major, remember?).

Excursion 11.3. Gopher Searching for Other Universities

I began my adventure at the aforementioned UWINFO (`uwinfo.uwaterloo.ca`) Gopher, choosing About the University of Waterloo. The idea was to move from here to information about other Canadian universities, and this was possible through item 12, List of Universities Across Canada:

```
7.   Highlights
8.   History
9.   Names and Departments
10.  New President
11.  Statistics and Data Files
12.  List of Universities Across Canada
```

This item gave me the option of performing a search, which I did. When prompted for key words, I responded with **`universities`**. The computer spat back a list of 23 articles and article reviews on Canadian universities. There were entries on the social contract issue, Alberta Universities Grants, and a review of Maclean's Magazine's ranking of Canadian Universities. A good beginning, but not quite what I was looking for, because nothing pertained to the discipline I'd decided to pursue. Still, for anyone thinking of attending a Canadian university this would be an extremely good option.

Through News from Other Universities, the last item on this menu, I got into a number of newspapers and even found a number of Canadian University newspapers (like Queen's, University of Victoria, York, Calgary, Waterloo, and Simon Fraser), and these gave me an excellent idea of what was happening at those schools. But I still wanted marine biology information, and not especially in Canada.

Backtracking brought me to the main UWINFO menu again, and I selected item 9, Electronic Resources Around the World (an entry like this exists on virtually all university Gophers). I saw a listing of information on library catalogues, electronic texts, journals and dictionaries, Gophers from around the world, FTP sites, and Wide Area Information Server (WAIS) Databases. I chose item 4 to see where Campus and other Information Systems might take me:

```
ELECTRONIC RESOURCES AROUND THE WORLD

1.  About Electronic Resources Around the World
2.  UW Library's Finding Information Area
3.  Guides to Internet Services
4.  Campus and other Information Systems
5.  Library Catalogue
6.  Electronic Texts, Books and Journals
7.  Electronic Dictionaries, Gazetteers etc.
8.  FTP Services (File Transfer Protocol)
9.  WWW(World Wide Web Servers via telnet)
10. Finding Someone on the Internet
11. University of Waterloo Gophers
12. WAIS (Wide Area Information Servers) databases
```

Item 4 gave me this next menu:

```
CAMPUS AND OTHER INFORMATION SYSTEMS

1.  Veronica
2.  Gophers added lately
3.  U of W Gophers
4.  Ontario
5.  Canada
6.  USA
7.  Mexico
8.  Costa Rica
9.  South America
10. Europe
11. Pacific
12. Asia
13. Africa
14. Middle East
15. Gophers of Scholarly Societies
16. International Organizations
17. Subject Specific Info Servers
18. Free Nets and Community Information systems
19. Terminal Based Information
20. All the Gopher Servers in the World
```

One of the most enticing items in Campus and Other Information Systems was All the Gopher Servers in the World. It sounded like a place to begin a really broad search, so why not? Unfortunately, the next menu took a long time to appear, and because of its size it wasn't especially useful. It did, however, contain an item for starting a Veronica search. I started by reading the section on composing Veronica queries to search the Gophers (it's always good to refresh your memory about specific features and techniques), and recalled that searching through Veronica is a lot like conducting a fairly simple Boolean search in many online libraries. You select keywords for your subject and the search gives you results showing documents containing those keywords. In addition to the regular library commands, Veronica recognizes the `<not>` command, which is essential for limiting the search. Veronica automatically lists 200 entries unless I choose to alter the default setting, in which case it lists the number of entries I specify.

```
All the gophers in the world
   1.       Search gopher space using Veronica
   2.       Script to automate your local Veronica Menu
   3.       Frequently Asked Questions about Veronica
   4.       How to compose Veronica Queries
```

Okay, it was time to give Veronica a try.

I selected item 1, Search gopher space using Veronica. At the search dialog, I typed **`universities marine biology`**, thinking those were safe and reliable keywords. The computer responded, `"too many servers. Try later."`

I then typed in **`universities marine biology women`** but got the same response: `"too many servers. Try later."`

Thinking that maybe the instructions on how to use Veronica lied to me, I tried the example they gave to see if Veronica really works. I typed **`Internet`**. The computer responded: `"Revealed 200 entries and suggested 30024 more."` Good. That was exactly what the example said should happen. What was I doing wrong, I wondered.

I tried different keywords, and typed in **`dolphins`**. The computer responded: `"200 entries and 233 more."` Terrific. Finally, I was making progress! I selected `view` to read these entries. To my dismay, the computer confronted me with a screen of references to the Miami Dolphins.

I decided to try again, but this time to limit my search to exclude the football team. I typed in **`dolphins marine, not Miami`**. The computer responded: `"Too many connections. Try again soon."`

Time to make it simpler. This time I searched for marine biology. This time, I received five screens of items, a portion of which looked like this:

```
11. Biology (Ecology, Evolution, and Marine Biology)/
12. Biology Department Information, UCSB Marine Lab, Classes/
13. 155. Biology of Marine Mammals. S.
14. 0. Marine Biology Introduction.
```

```
15. Oregon Institute of Marine Biology.
16. Marine Biology/
17. Marine Biology and Biological Oceanography.
18. 93-03-15-04: *Information on Marine Biology Requested*.
19. 94-04-21-20: Best university for marine biology??.
20. 94-03-29-10: Resource Guides for Marine Biology Labs?.
21. 94-03-31-14: Resource Guides for Marine Biology Labs.
22. Joint Program on Molecular Biology of Marine Organisms.
23. Glen Geen Graduate Scholarship in Marine Biology                    ...
24. Marine Biology/
```

Now this was exciting. Especially fascinating was the title of item 19, Best university for marine biology?? There it was. I had it. Someone would tell me exactly what I wanted to know.

Nothing there. Nothing at all. And very little else gave me a strong idea. Oh, well. Back to the drawing board.

Moving back up to the Campus screen, I selected item 2, Gopher Servers Added Lately, just to get a flavor of what's new and up-to-date on the Net. Any time you want to feel completely out of date, find a screen of new additions. In this case, I got 22 screens with 381 new Gopher additions.

There were many more universities and organizations added recently than I anticipated, organizations from the Los Alamos National Lab to the National Science Foundation. A Software Tool and Die entry caught my attention because my husband works in this field. This server was sponsoring an essay contest about using computer software in the tool and die trade. More closely related to my search, the Honolulu Community College was having a science fair. One category of entries is forensics. According to the Gopher, the college hopes to stimulate an interest in police work.

From the Campus screen I selected `USA` this time, and it led me to a new menu listing all the servers in the USA, general information, and an alphabetical listing of the states. I selected `All` and found myself staring at 52 pages of school Gophers. If I ever doubted that I'd find information about universities, this ended that doubt forever. I paged through the list using the spacebar (the usual paging option), hoping for a title that might be helpful. I found Biosci—a bionet biology newsgroup server. I took note of this, hoping I could find more e-mail addresses in this section later.

Just for fun I ventured off to Europe to browse for a while. I hadn't actually been thinking of Europe (and I probably can't afford it), but it's always a nice dream. Norway is exotic (not warm, maybe, but interesting), so I took a peek to see what universities they have, and to see also if any might be accessible in English. Unfortunately, language appears to be a barrier for me at this point. But that's okay; it's much better to discover this *before* I make a commitment to finding extensive information.

Quite finished with my exploring for the moment, I searched the United States section of the Gopher for suitable programs in marine biology and oceanography. American education is primarily in English, releasing me from the language barrier (that is, the fact that I only know one). As well, the country is surrounded by three major bodies of water—the Pacific and Atlantic oceans to the west and east, and the Gulf of Mexico to the south—all of which probably support a multitude of oceanographic studies.

The e-mail messages from Excursion 11.2 suggested mostly American schools. The universities I decided to pay attention to, therefore, included those from the states of California, Hawaii, Massachusetts, New York, Oregon, and Texas.

Boston University in Massachusetts was a quick find (`gopher.bu.edu`), and the initial menu was inviting:

```
Boston University
   1.      About this service
   2.      Campus Facilities
   3.      Who, What, Where, When
   4.      Opportunity Knocks
   5.      Things you should know
   6.      Resources at your fingertips
   7.      Metro guide
   8.      Title Search
   9.      Text search on all catalog entries
```

I selected item 8, the title search, and tried to search for a Marine Biological Laboratory. Nothing came up, so I decided a simpler search, this time for marine. The following menu appeared:

```
1.  BI 260  Marine Biology
2.  Marine Program
3.  Conc in Biology with Marine Sci/
4.  Mass Bay Marine Studies Consort
5.  Marine Science Association
6.  BI 260 Marine Biology (EBE)
7.  BI 261X Curr Topics Marine SCi
8.  BI 465X Marine Physiology (PA)
9.  BI 466X Marine Ecology (EBE)
10. BI 478X Experimental Marine Bio
11. GG 341 Ocean Res & Marine Mng
12. Boston Univ Marine Program/
13. GL 440 Marine Geology
14. GL 455 Princpl Marine Pollution
```

Lots here, and well worth exploring. After doing so, I had a much better idea of what the university had to offer. Still, because the idea was to learn about the university as a whole and not just the marine biology offerings, I decided to browse through the Gopher menus to get a feel for the university.

Item 2, Campus Facilities, discusses only computing and library services. I hoped to see course selections or something similar. There were 10 selections including information on UNIX, VMS, software distribution, and computing ethics. Computing ethics? As it turned out, this section contains a disclaimer explaining how Boston University retains the right to inspect all files, and a list of rules and regulations for using the system. A rather stuffy introduction to the school, although probably not atypical.

Under Resources at Your Fingertips, I found references to recreation and learned that Boston University offered recreational facilities including dancing, health and fitness, intramural programs, phys-ed courses, and a sailing program. Participants must pass a swimming test to ensure safety, but the school provides classes to faculty, staff, students, and the public upon meeting this condition. There was an invitation to join the boating team, and students can even take classes in boating as part of their regular curriculum at no extra cost. Recreational sailing is available to students at $25 and to the public at $75. As well, I found a section describing the shopping available on campus and the shuttle bus, and a small section on admissions, financial aid, employment, and international programs. This material would clearly help me in considering whether or not to apply.

Excursion 11.4. Exploring One University in Detail

Everything I saw at Boston University was good, and browsing through other Gophers proved equally or even more interesting. But, to be quite honest, I was getting a bit impatient. Not even an extensive search of Gopher Jewels (see Day 6 for details on this excellent resource) gave me a huge amount of information. A few more Gopher menus later, I had almost decided to give up and come back another day, no closer at all to finding my dream university. One last try, I thought, and then I'd log off and go home.

And that's when I encountered the University of Hawaii Gopher, UHINFO. Its address is `gopher.Hawaii.edu`, and it's a superbly constructed resource.

From the moment I entered the University of Hawaii information system, I knew where I was, where I wanted to go, how to get there, and even what kind of information I would find. Only rarely were my expectations not satisfied; usually, I received more than I even thought to ask for.

For instance, the University of Hawaii system has 15 sections. Section one contains notices and updates. Section two explains the UHINFO system, welcomes users, and shows how the organization of UHINFO works. This is invaluable advice. Additionally, it offers assistance on how to use the Gopher system to get what you want.

```
UHINFO
1.  Important Notices
2.  About UHINFO
3.  Around Town
4.  Computing and Technology
5.  Employment Opportunities
6.  Library and Research Tools
7.  News and Events
8.  Other Gopher and Information Servers
9.  Phone Directories
10. Search All UHINFO menus
11. Student Information
12. UH College Information Services
13. UH General Information
14. University Services
15. What's Happening Today
```

For a little taste of the information available through UHINFO, Around Town describes movie theater schedules and listings, radio stations, television channel guides, and public transit information (prices and routes). The technology section explains the computing technology used with the Internet, details how to purchase computers (including price lists), and offers services through the UH Computing Center.

I found a listing of employment opportunities and career resources, library catalogs, Internet libraries, and federal libraries. The news and events section offers weather, news highlights, journals, newsletters, and the campus paper. There are phone directories for students, faculty and staff of UH, and emergency numbers.

Another section identifies statistics about the student population, extracurricular activities, exam schedules and other student services, as well as the school's policies, codes, and procedures.

Finally, there is a complete list of other university services including the bookstore, campus center, food services, banking, and transportation. I was *very* impressed. The University of Hawaii definitely knows how to portray a thorough image of itself.

> **Note:** As an example of how carefully designed the UHINFO system is, item 2, About UHINFO, has an entire overview of the UHINFO system. I printed out the information and discovered that the printout functioned as a table of contents. I only had to look at this printout then to figure out where I was and how to get where I wanted to go.

The University of Hawaii Catalog is online, and I leisurely browsed through it. This large document is, as I expected, an electronic version of the 1993-1995 academic calendar. The authors have cross-referenced the Internet screens by page number with the actual printed catalog and have provided options for photos and graphics, when technology permits. The catalog contains information about the university campus, student services, tuition, admission requirements, course descriptions, a list of the faculty and their academic backgrounds.

Clearly, this is a model for all post-secondary institutions to examine as they compile their online information resource center. From the information available in UHINFO, I was able to determine, quickly and easily, whether or not that university might be for me. Because I liked everything I read, including the details in other menus about the marine biology programs, I decided that the University of Hawaii was unquestionably worth exploring even further.

Now it's time to read the information in Day 8, so I can find a job to get enough money to actually go there.

Excursion 11.5. Researching Other U.S. Universities Through the World Wide Web

Like most students at the high school or post-secondary level, Angela's information searches were restricted primarily to Gopher access. Gopher is far and away the most common method of browsing the Net—first because it's available practically everywhere, and second because it requires no special graphical hardware. For many purposes, it's really all you need.

But choosing a university, as Angela suggested throughout her search, depends on efficient, attractive access to well-designed screens. Here as elsewhere, the World Wide Web is beginning to show the way. Graphical Web browsers like Mosaic or Cello can include Gophers, which means they lose nothing in the translation, and in addition they can easily display graphics and even incorporate video and sound. For universities, this means the capability of showing their campuses rather than just describing them with text. The difference, as the following examples demonstrate, can be quite striking.

> **Tip:** To get to these pages, load Mosaic or Cello (see Day 7 for details). In Mosaic, choose Open URL from the File menu; from Cello, select Launch URL from the Jump menu. Then type the `http://` address shown in the Document URL box of these Mosaic screens.

First, let's look at a primarily text-based WWW page. Figure 11.1 offers an introduction to the Undergraduate Computational Engineering and Science at Clemson University.

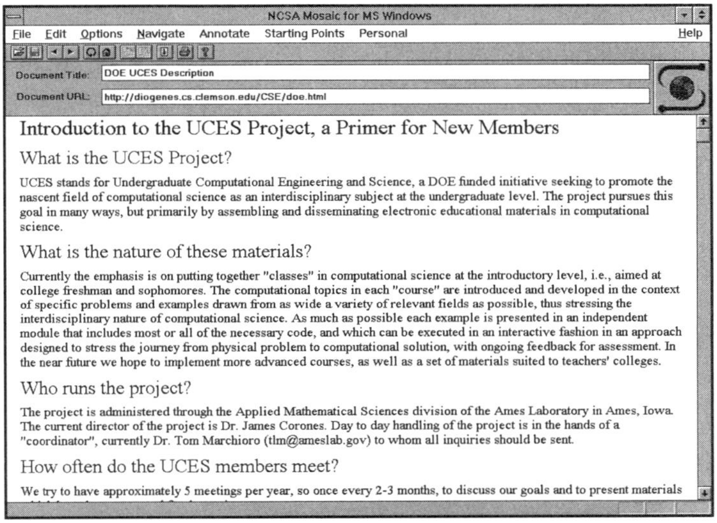

Figure 11.1. *WWW page for Clemson University.*

This is only one page in Clemson's fairly extensive Web collection, but it clearly points out the features of the program.

Equally informative is Figure 11.2, which is the home page for the Undergraduate Research and Curriculum WWW Guide in the Department of Biology at Carnegie Mellon University.

Here you can see hypertext links to a variety of other information about the program in biology. Although learning about advisors and mentors will certainly be useful soon, let's examine the requirements for the Bachelor of Science degree first. Figure 11.3 makes it all very clear, and from this page you should get some idea of whether or not this is the program for you.

Another approach can be seen in the presentation by the University of California, Irvine. Figure 11.4 shows the home page for the Office of Academic Computing, which points clearly to a campus Gopher and FTP server.

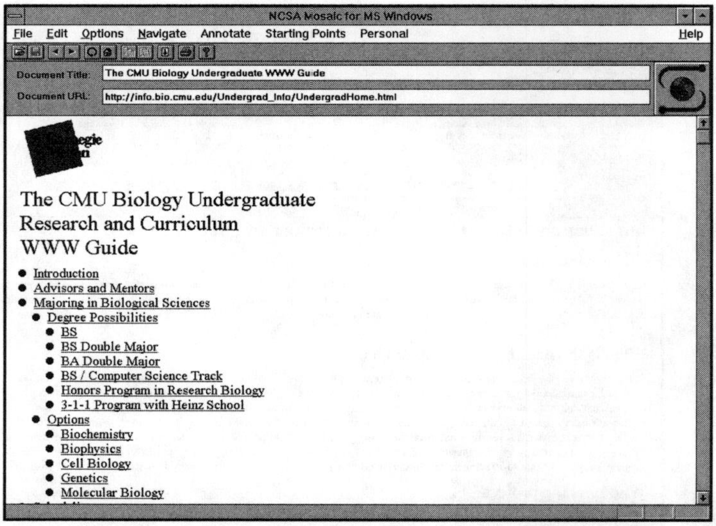

Figure 11.2. *CMU's Department of Biology WWW page.*

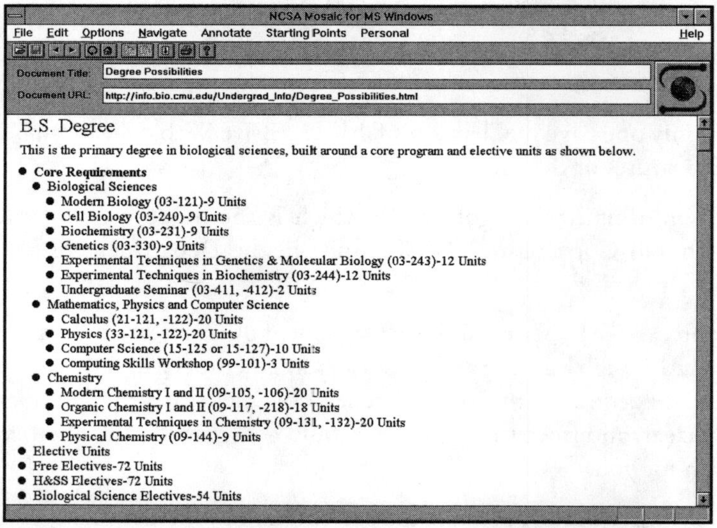

Figure 11.3. *CMU requirements for Bachelor of Science degree.*

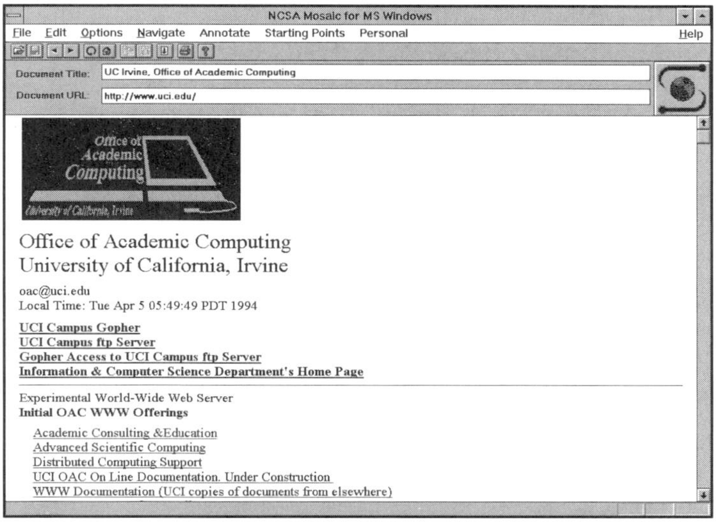

Figure 11.4. *Office of Academic Computing, UCI.*

Further down this page you can find a link to the Web server for the UCI Bookstore; as any student can tell you, the campus bookstore is always a good place to learn something of the institution's culture. Figure 11.5 shows this attractive page, from which you can even order essential student items like sweatshirts.

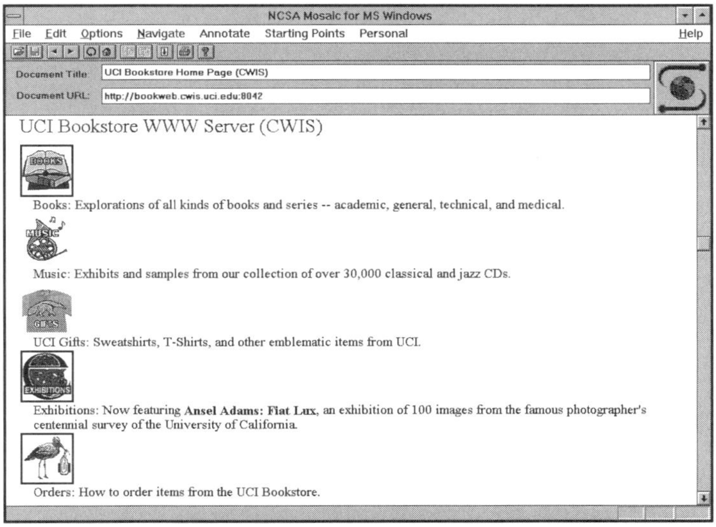

Figure 11.5. *UCI Bookstore home page.*

For now, though, let's select the books section (everyone has to be scholarly for at least a small part of their school research time) and see what's offered. Figure 11.6 gives a good sense of what's making the WWW headlines here. This is a presentation with short reviews of books that talk about cyber-culture, an obviously appropriate discussion for a Web page.

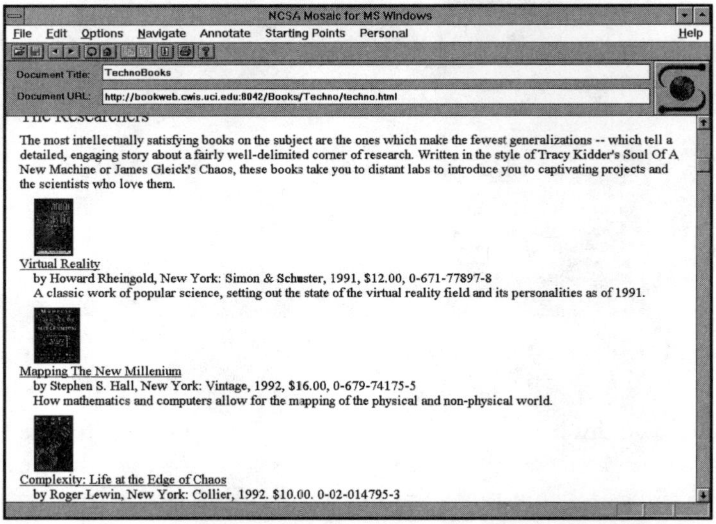

Figure 11.6. *Cyber-culture list at UCI bookstore.*

But let's go a bit further afield—or, in this case, awater. Angela already pointed out the effort made by the University of Hawaii in presenting their campus and programs to the fullest through a detailed Gopher server, and Figure 11.7 shows another Hawaiian institution strutting its stuff across the Net. This time it's Honolulu Community College, with an extremely strong pictorial home page shown.

More and more, Web page designers are using interactive maps to offer visual links to other pages. Figure 11.8 shows HCC's attractive and usable campus map. From here it's just a matter of clicking the building you're interested in, or the list beneath the map.

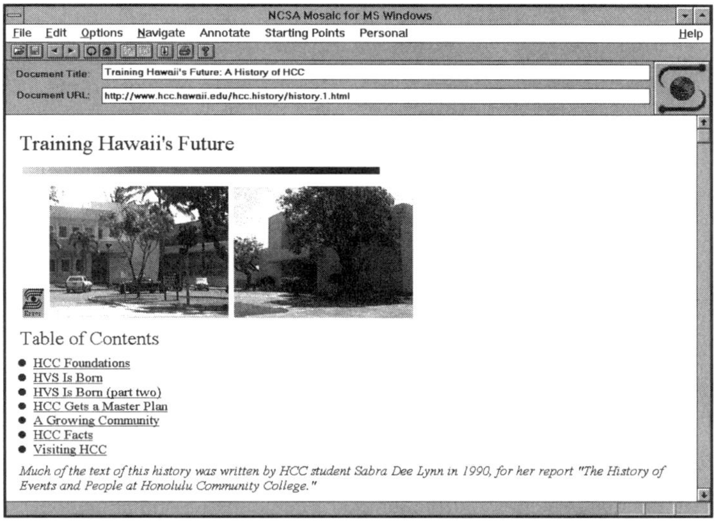

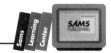

Figure 11.7. *Honolulu Community College home page.*

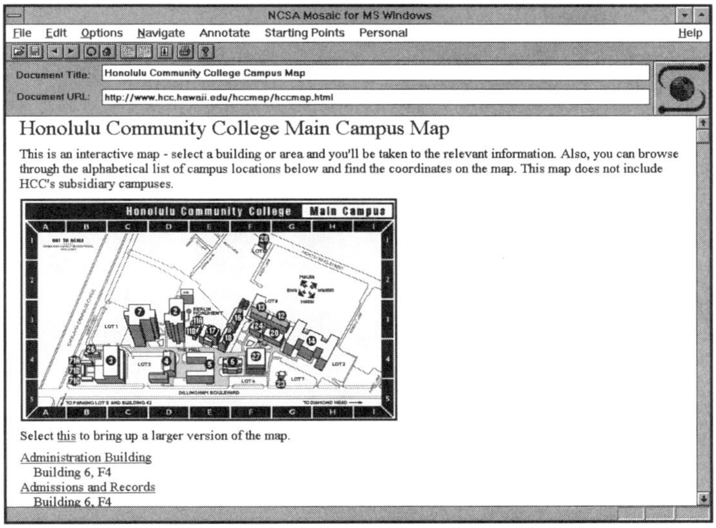

Figure 11.8. *Clickable campus map at HCC.*

One of these links leads to a picture and description of the Educational Media Center (see Figure 11.9). Again, the point for a would-be HCC student is that the page offers both a glimpse of the college as well as textual information.

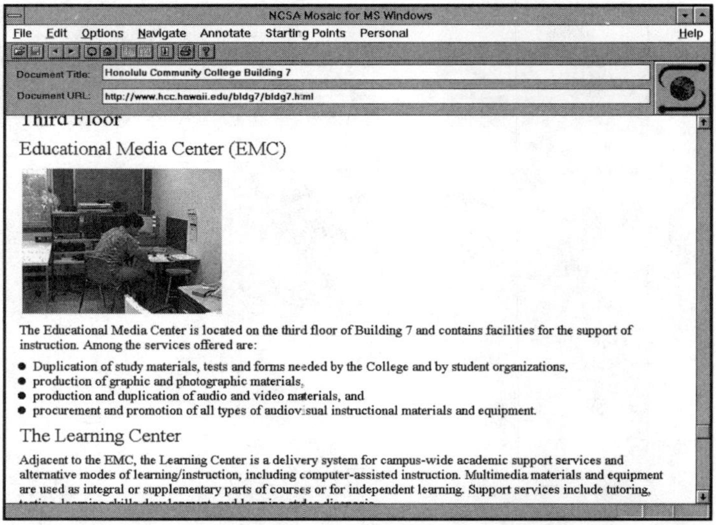

Figure 11.9. *Educational Media Center at HCC.*

Finally, take a look at a publication produced at HCC. This one, The Technological Times (see Figure 11.10), offers a wide range of interesting articles; if you're looking for this sort of involvement as a student, the Web page gives you a good indication of what to expect.

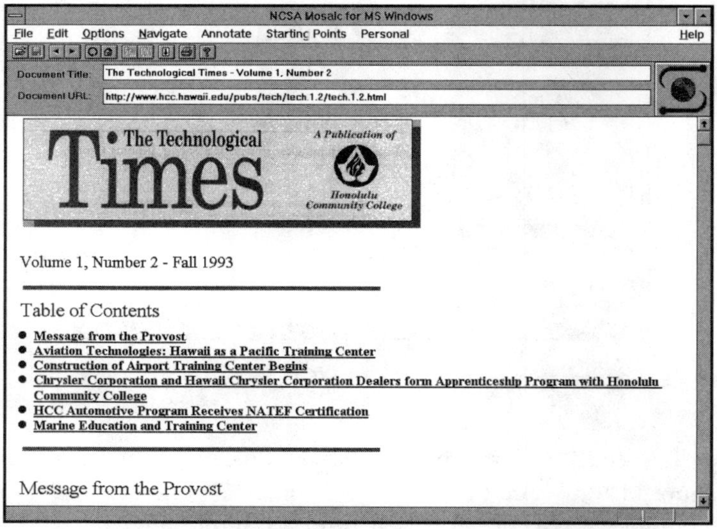

Figure 11.10. *Web page for an HCC publication.*

As you can see, World Wide Web pages may offer the same amount of raw information as an equivalent Gopher server, but the information is structured and presented far differently. In many ways, a Web page is like a colorful book about the campus you're exploring. But in some aspects it's very different: First, you don't have to buy it, and second, you can do all your browsing without leaving your study.

Soon, with luck, you'll be able to register over the Web. When that happens, the process of selecting a university will have changed for good.

Summary

Most universities offer Gopher servers with information about their campuses and programs. Many areas also are beginning to offer well-developed World Wide Web pages, complete with maps, graphics, and in some cases even short videos. Expect more of these graphical information sources as more and more people gain access to the Web in the near future.

Gopher and Web pages can help you learn a significant amount about universities, whether you're examining possibilities for yourself, for a friend, or for your children. You can retrieve course descriptions, location information, details about services, and documents about the university's policies and procedures. You can also learn who's on faculty, an extremely important decision for graduate students. By no means should you restrict your search to the Internet, but it's an excellent starting point.

Task Review

On Day 11, you performed the following tasks:

- Used Gopher to locate information about a range of universities.
- Used e-mail to obtain information from others regarding universities.
- Examined newsgroups for university information.
- Examined one university in detail.
- Explored other university offerings on the World Wide Web.

Q&A

Q After I find the university I want, why can't I use the Internet to register? And after I'm enrolled, why can't I use it to select courses and put library books on hold?

A Patience, patience. In some cases, holding library books is already possible, and I don't expect it to be too very long before registration and course selection become possible over the Net as well. The problem is this: While Web pages can be fairly independent of the main university academic computing systems, registration and course selection must be linked directly (and thoroughly) to these systems. That will take a while.

Q If I'm looking for a university overseas, will the Internet help me?

A Yep. See the following Extra Credit section.

Q Should I rely on the Internet for all the information I need about a particular school?

A No, any more than you should rely on that school's academic calendar. If you're seriously thinking about attending an institution, be sure to check not only the official documents but also articles in the press, any books that might deal with the school, and just plain hearsay to find out more. At some point, most of this material will find its way onto the Net, but for now it's simply not there. But you'll be spending several years, a great deal of money, and huge reserves of energy at the location you choose, so you owe it to yourself to gather as much information as you can. The Internet can help, but it can't do it all.

Extra Credit: Universities Around the World

As if the wealth of information on North American universities wasn't enough to make your search seem never-ending, post-secondary institutions in other parts of the world have already been making their Internet presence felt. This Extra Credit section examines a range of institutions, seeing what kinds of Web pages each has to offer.

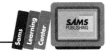

Tip: One exceptional place to start on the World Wide Web is the sensational interactive world map offered by the State University of New York (SUNY), Buffalo, as part of their Virtual Tourist display. You can see the map among the Web treasures shown in Day 7, but once again the address is `http://wings.buffalo.edu/world`.

Excursion 11.6. Universities Around the World via WWW

First, and to continue our westward journey from Excursion 11.5, let's stop in on Australia. Figure 11.11 shows the main page for the Australian National University Library, with a wide range of information and a number of useful links to other servers. One such server is shown in Figure 11.12. Here we have an extremely useful collection of links to servers across the Asian continent.

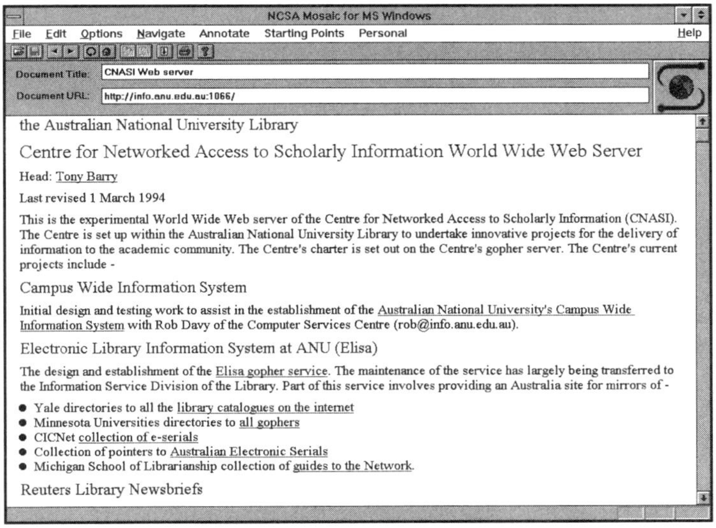

Figure 11.11. *ANU Library Web page.*

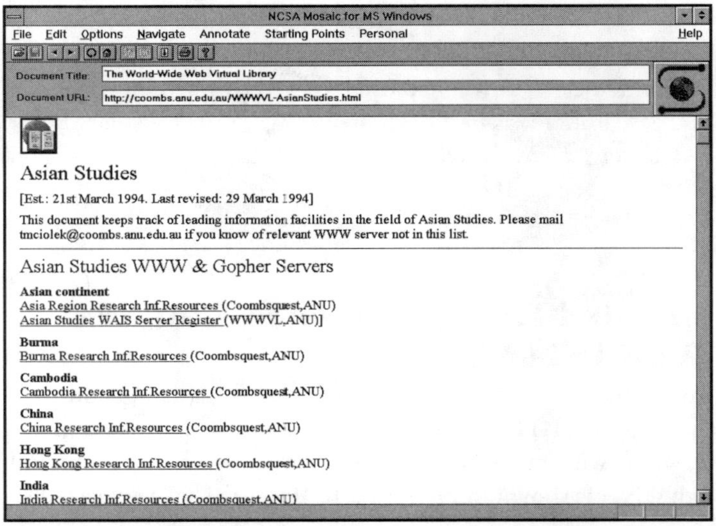

Figure 11.12. *Asian information via ANU.*

Now to Japan (okay, so we're going north now). First stop is the excellent Japan-U.S. program home page at Stanford University in the U.S. (see Figure 11.13), which contains links to several international sites.

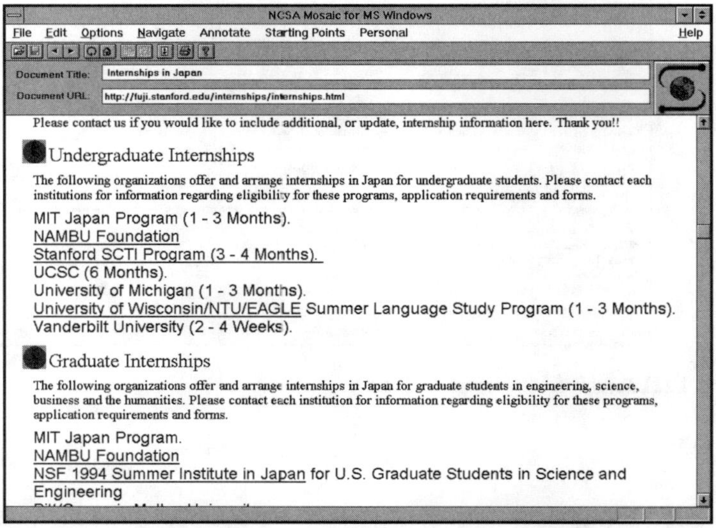

Figure 11.13. *Stanford University Japan page.*

Next we arrive at Japan proper—specifically the Campuses of the University WWW page for the University of Tokyo (see Figure 11.14). The most enticing link on this menu is to the map, which you can see in Figure 11.15.

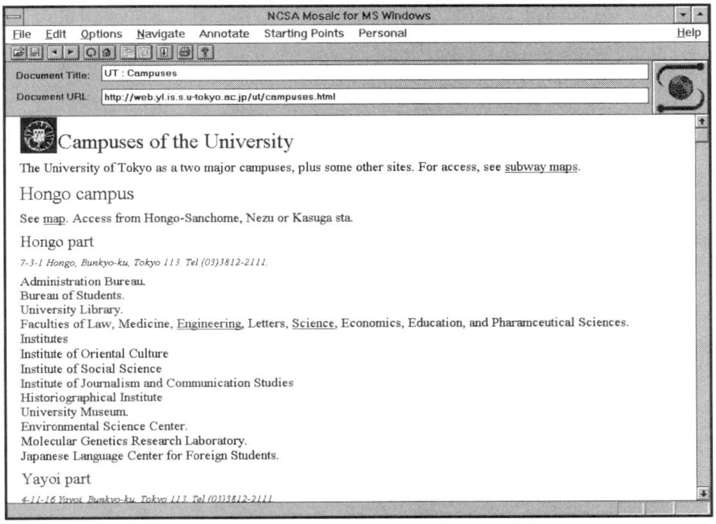

Figure 11.14. *Home page for the University of Tokyo.*

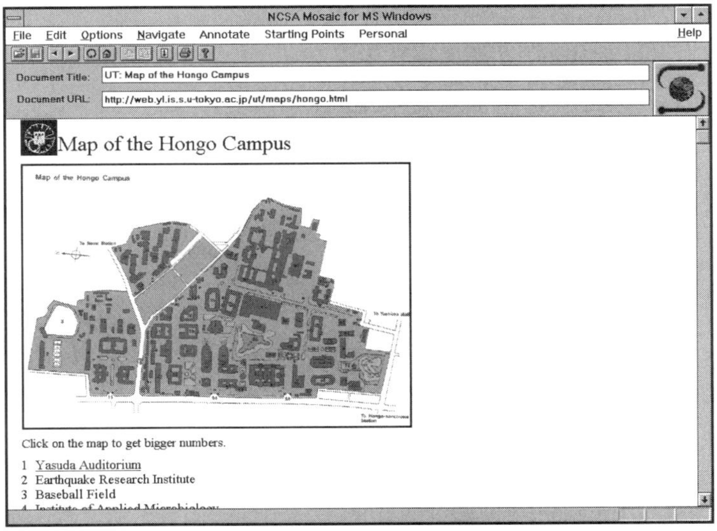

Figure 11.15. *University of Tokyo campus map.*

Unfortunately, this map isn't quite as interactive as the Virtual Tourist map or the one provided by the Honolulu Community College, but the links beneath it let you roam where you will. So let's roam. Figure 11.16 offers an enthralling image of the campus's Sanshiro Pond, and a hypertext link below the picture takes us to an equally lovely shot of the Clock Tower (see Figure 11.17). Any wonder why someone might decide to think about heading for a degree in Tokyo?

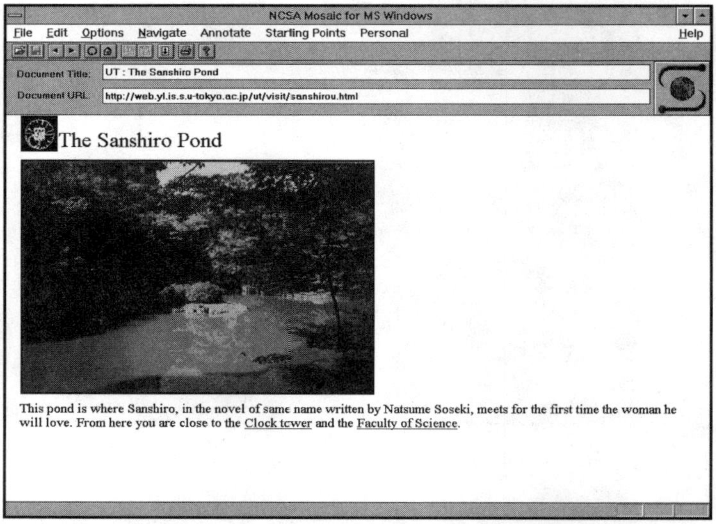

Figure 11.16. *Sanshiro Pond, University of Tokyo.*

South again. Southwest, actually, and into Singapore. On Day 9 you got a taste of Singapore through its nicely presented tourist pages, and now we're back, this time with education pages. The home page for the Institute of Systems Science, National University of Singapore (see Figure 11.18) gives several worthwhile links to university information, one of which is to a highly useful page explaining the Diploma in Knowledge Engineering (see Figure 11.19).

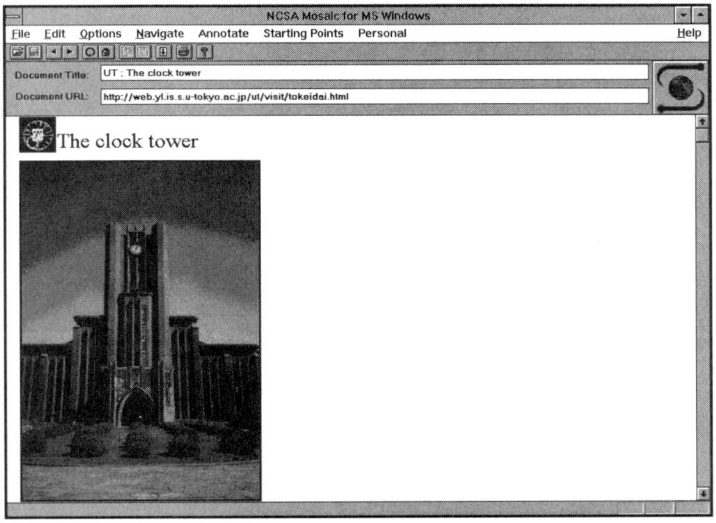

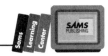

Figure 11.17. *Clock Tower, University of Tokyo.*

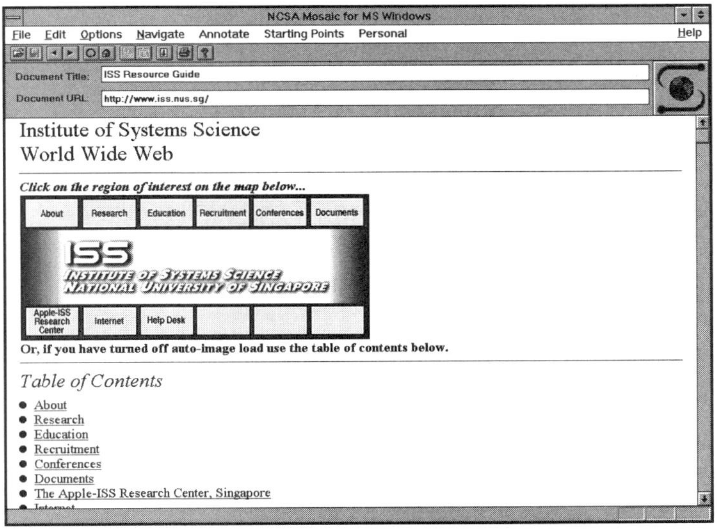

Figure 11.18. *National University of Singapore Web page.*

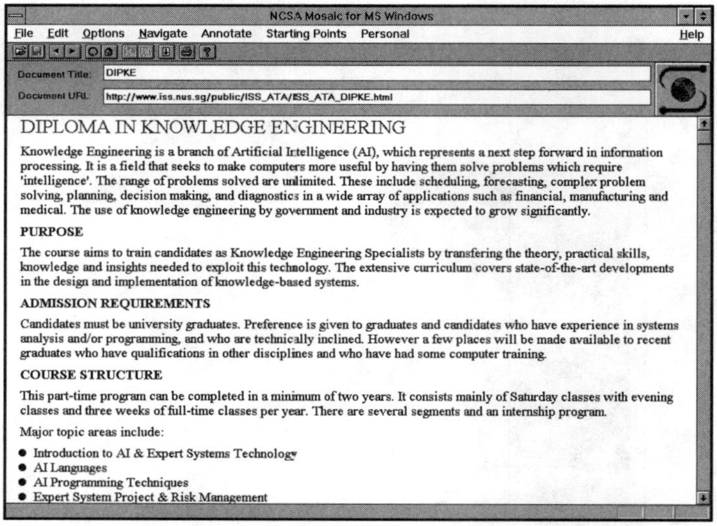
NCSA Mosaic for MS Windows

File Edit Options Navigate Annotate Starting Points Personal Help

Document Title: DIPKE

Document URL: http://www.iss.nus.sg/public/ISS_ATA/ISS_ATA_DIPKE.html

DIPLOMA IN KNOWLEDGE ENGINEERING

Knowledge Engineering is a branch of Artificial Intelligence (AI), which represents a next step forward in information processing. It is a field that seeks to make computers more useful by having them solve problems which require 'intelligence'. The range of problems solved are unlimited. These include scheduling, forecasting, complex problem solving, planning, decision making, and diagnostics in a wide array of applications such as financial, manufacturing and medical. The use of knowledge engineering by government and industry is expected to grow significantly.

PURPOSE

The course aims to train candidates as Knowledge Engineering Specialists by transfering the theory, practical skills, knowledge and insights needed to exploit this technology. The extensive curriculum covers state-of-the-art developments in the design and implementation of knowledge-based systems.

ADMISSION REQUIREMENTS

Candidates must be university graduates. Preference is given to graduates and candidates who have experience in systems analysis and/or programming, and who are technically inclined. However a few places will be made available to recent graduates who have qualifications in other disciplines and who have had some computer training.

COURSE STRUCTURE

This part-time program can be completed in a minimum of two years. It consists mainly of Saturday classes with evening classes and three weeks of full-time classes per year. There are several segments and an internship program.

Major topic areas include:

- Introduction to AI & Expert Systems Technology
- AI Languages
- AI Programming Techniques
- Expert System Project & Risk Management

Figure 11.19. *Web page showing information on diploma at Singapore.*

Of course, there's always the possibility that Europe holds an even greater lure, given its ancient universities and the reputation of both its educational systems and cities. If so, check out the growing host of post-secondary WWW sites on that continent, including the English-language page in Austria at Innsbruck's Physics Department (see Figure 11.20).

Or, if you'd like to be France-bound, why not think about the lovely city of Lyon? Figure 11.21 shows their French-language home page, while Figure 11.22 demonstrates that English-language pages are appearing as well.

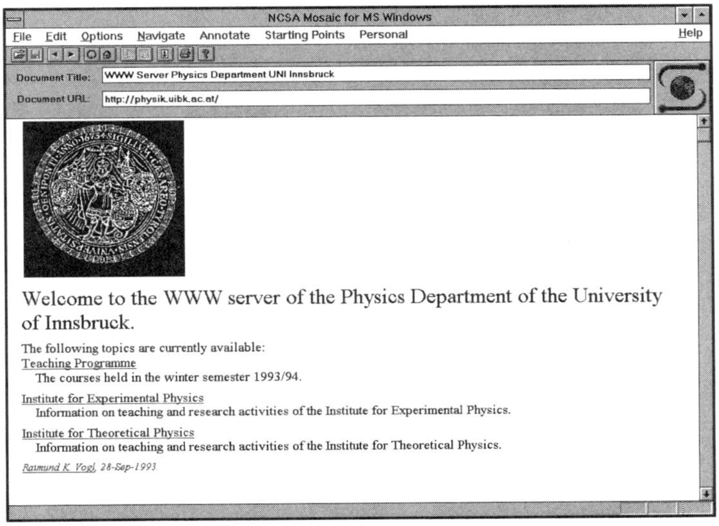

Figure 11.20. *Physics Department, Innsbruck, Austria.*

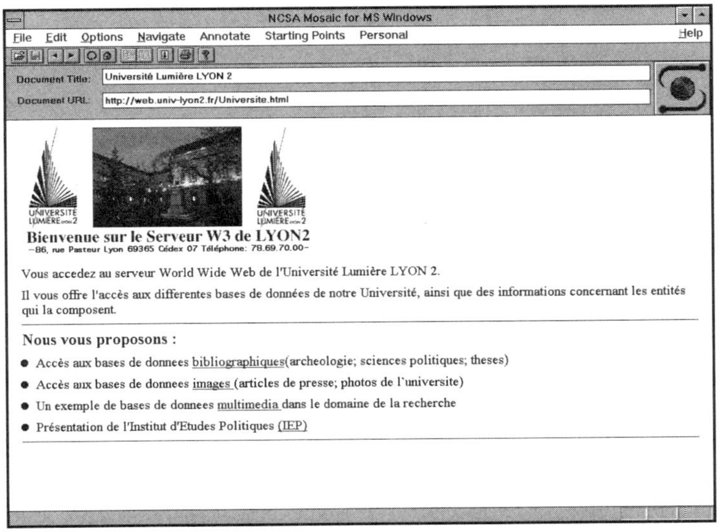

Figure 11.21. *French language home page for Lyon.*

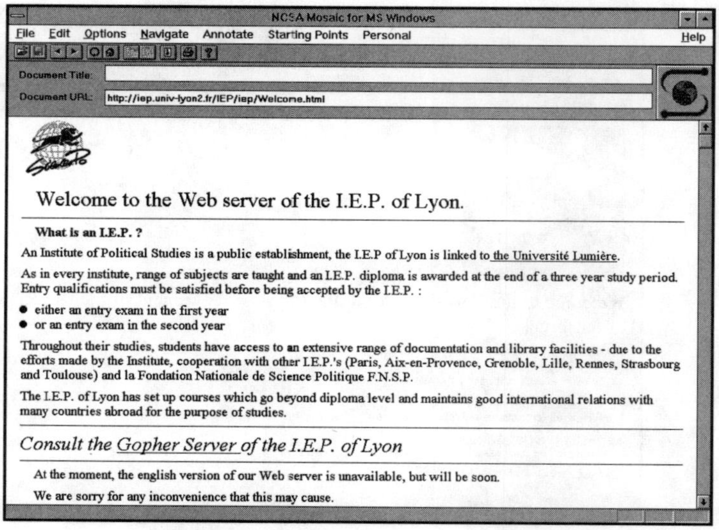

Figure 11.22. *English language home page for Lyon.*

There's more, lots more. Explore to your heart's content, then make your university the one you really want.

WEEK 2

12

One Hand on the Wallet: Searching the Globe for That Elusive Job

The Internet is no substitute for the Help Wanted or Careers section of a good newspaper. However, it has started to become a worthwhile addition to a job-finding strategy, and there are definite signs that it will become more important still. As corporations and other organizations who employ people develop their own presence on the Net, they will almost inevitably turn to it as a means of finding the best possible employees. The Internet is in many ways cheaper than conventional job advertising, and it has a wider reach than all but the largest publications. Furthermore, employers can rest assured that anyone who has discovered and responded to the advertised position on the Net has more than a marginal degree of computer competence.

So far, the choices for job searchers are limited. But they're growing, and they're well worth checking out. This chapter shows one user's search for a job and for information about a particular company.

On Day 12, you will learn how to do the following:

- ☐ Use Internet resources to find job postings.
- ☐ Search through job-related Gophers and World Wide Web sites.
- ☐ Make use of Internet resources to help with career planning and the job search.
- ☐ Find information on the Internet about prospective employers.

Using the Internet to Find a Job

by Jim Hartling

To begin my job search, I set a few goals for myself to provide a loose framework for my search. I wanted to see what job opportunities were available in the field of technical communications, in both academic and nonacademic capacities, and I also wanted to see what background information I could find about a specific company. So, with nothing to lose, I fired up my computer and started looking.

My search of the Internet for employment resources started off as a fairly unorganized endeavor. I wasn't entirely sure what I was really looking for, and I wasn't even sure where I was going to look. I didn't carry out any thorough, all-encompassing keyword searches or really plan any definite strategies. I simply did what seemed best-suited to the Internet—I jumped right in and tried to make sense of where I was and what resources were around me. As I soon learned, my approach might not have been that bad.

Finding a Job Through Gopher Searches

The first Internet tool I decided to use was Gopher. Even when I had my basic UNIX account at school, I always found Gopher to be one of the easiest search tools for finding information on the Internet. When I finally got a direct-access account through a local Internet access provider, Gopher became all that much easier, because the package included with the account, Winsock Gopher, offers a point-and-click interface and a number of preset bookmarks. Even with this program, however, I still returned frequently to my UNIX shell account as well, examining the more common numbered Gopher menus.

Excursion 12.1. Employment Information through Gopher Jewels

From my home Gopher server, I selected Internet Resources (`owl.nstn.ns.ca`). One of the menu items was Gopher Jewels (`cwis.usc.edu`, in the path Other Gopher and Information Resources, then Gopher-Jewels), and I was fairly certain that I'd seen some reference to employment information there before. As it turns out, I'd remembered correctly, and there was an entry for Employment Opportunities and Resume Postings, shown in part below:

```
10. Books, Journals, Magazines, Newsletters, and Publications/
11. Botany/
12. Chemistry/
13. Computer Related/
14. Disability Information/
15. Economics and Business/
16. Education and Research (Includes K-12)/
17. Employment Opportunities and Resume Postings/
18. Engineering/
```

I selected Employment Opportunities and Resume Postings, which opened up another menu containing 54 items. The first half of the menu looked like this:

```
1. ACADEME THIS WEEK (Chronicle of Higher Education)/
2. Academic Position Network/
3. American Physiological Society/
4. BIONET/
5. CNIDR (American Astronomical Society Jobs Listings) <?>
6. California State Univ, Chancellor's Office/
7. Columbia University Experimental Gopher/
```

```
 8. Dana-Farber Cancer Institute, Boston, MA (Institute Positions
 9. Dartmouth College (Job Openings in the Federal Government)/
10. Dept. of Labor Occupational Outlook Handbook 1992-93 - U. Min
11. Go M-Link (Federal Jobs List)/
12. Go M-Link (Michigan Jobs available from Online Career Center)
13. HoodInfo CWIS (Hood College, Frederick, MD)/
14. IUPUI Integrated Technologies (Staff Job Openings)/
15. Indiana Univ. (Int'l Career Employment Network)/
16. Job Listings From Around the Globe - University of Texas/
17. Jobs and Employment - RiceInfo (Rice University CWIS)/
18. Library of Congress (LC MARVEL)/
19. MIT Personnel Office Job Listing/
20. Metropolitan Tucson Electronic Communications Network (METCOM
21. Mississippi State University/
22. Msen Vendor Emporium (gopher.msen.com.)/
23. Online Career Center (at Msen)/
24. Purdue Univ, BMEnet Whitaker Biomedical Engineering Informati
25. Saint Louis University.
26. Syracuse University CWIS (Employment Opportunities)/
```

Many of the other menu items were links to specific university Gopher servers, each with their own employment resources. I decided to start from the top and work my way down through the listing to see what I could find. The first item on the list was ACADEME THIS WEEK (Chronicle of Higher Education), and it sounded like as good a place to start as any. Besides, I was interested in seeing if I could find an academic teaching position in technical communications, something this item would surely contain.

Excursion 12.2. Searching the Employment List in *ACADEME THIS WEEK*

I selected ACADEME THIS WEEK (Chronicle of Higher Education)—retrievable directly by Gophering to `chronicle.merit.edu`)—which opened up another menu containing the following two entries:

```
1. SEARCH using The Chronicle's list of job titles/
2. SEARCH using any word or words of your choosing/
```

Since I wasn't sure what the Chronicle's list of job titles included, I decided to set the parameters of the search myself and take my chances with the second entry. I selected SEARCH using any word or words of your choosing, which gave me the following choices:

```
1. Search the entire jobs list for a word or phrase <?>
2. Limit search to jobs in the Northeast <?>
3. Limit search to jobs in the South <?>
4. Limit search to jobs in the Midwest <?>
5. Limit search to jobs in the West <?>
6. Limit search to jobs outside the United States <?>
```

I was pleased to see that I could limit my search to a specific area. Since I wasn't sure how long it would take to search the entire job list, I decided to concentrate on the Northeast USA. I selected Limit search to jobs in the Northeast and was given the following search box:

```
1. Search the entire jobs list for a word or phrase <?>
2. Limit search to jobs in the Northeast <?>
3. Limit search to jobs in the South <?>
4. Limit search to jobs in the Midwest <?>
 +-----------------Limit search to jobs in the Northeast-----------+
 |                                                                  |
 | Words to search for  technical communications                    |
 |                                                                  |
 |                                  [Cancel ^G] [Accept - Enter]    |
 |                                                                  |
 +------------------------------------------------------------------+
```

As shown above, I entered **technical communications** in the search box and pressed Enter. Now all I had to do was sit back and see what the search would come up with. After a few seconds, 22 menu items were returned, including the following:

```
 1. Dir of Dev & Communications — Social service organization —
 2. Director, Administrative Data Processing — Brandeis Universi
 3. Full-time Faculty Positions — Holyoke Community College — M
 4. Library — U of Delaware — DE.
 5. Benefits Administration Marketing Mgr. — Fidelity Investment
 6. Technical Communications — Clarkson University — NY.
 7. Director of Library Systems — Dartmouth College Library — N
 8. Director of Writing Laboratory — Jersey City State College -
 9. Editor, Bucknell World — Bucknell University — PA.
10. Director, Administrative Computing — SUNY at Binghamton — N
11. Editing - Science — Publication — VT.
12. Advertising — University of Hartford — CT.
```

While some of the menu items didn't look overly promising, the entry for Technical Communications — Clarkson University — NY was a direct match, so I selected it and received a text screen showing the job posting. Naturally, I applied, but I suspect 200 or so others did as well.

Excursion 12.3. Searching the Online Career Center

Well, so far the search had been incredibly easy and extremely painless. I spent another half hour or so using different keywords for my searches and browsed through a number of other job listings. After a while, I bookmarked the site so I could easily get back to it later, and returned to the Employment Opportunities and Resume Postings menu to see what other job openings I could find outside of the academy. Figure 12.1 shows some of the possibilities, this time through the program Winsock Gopher.

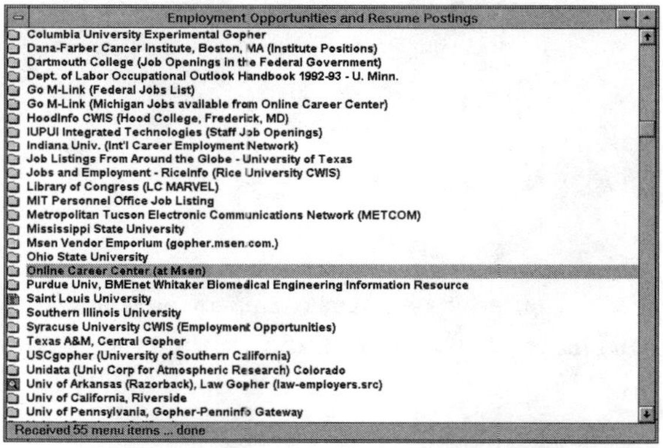

Figure 12.1. *Gopher menu showing link to Online Career Center (at Msen).*

I scanned through the menu items and decided to give the Online Career Center (at Msen) a try. I selected Online Career Center (`garnet.msen.com`) and, once again, waited to see where I'd end up. The main menu items are shown in Figure 12.2.

I selected *Search Jobs from the listing, which opened up another menu allowing me to search for jobs in a number of different ways. This menu is shown in Figure 12.3.

Instead of searching by area this time, I decided to try a search by **`Skill/Classification`**, which opened up another menu containing several items covering specific jobs from many different disciplines. Figure 12.4 displays some of this list, including my highlighted choice.

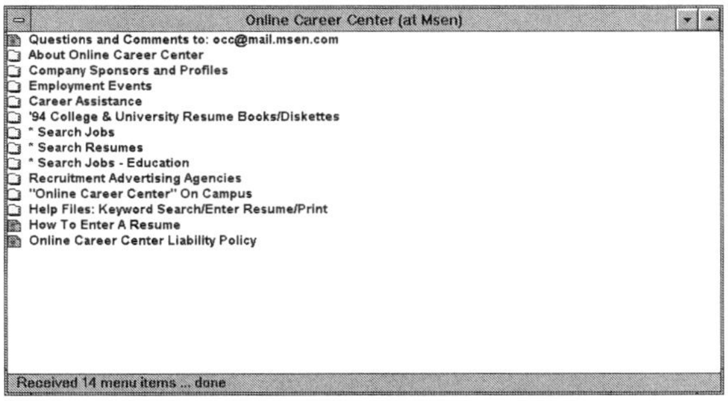

Figure 12.2. *The Online Career Center Gopher menu.*

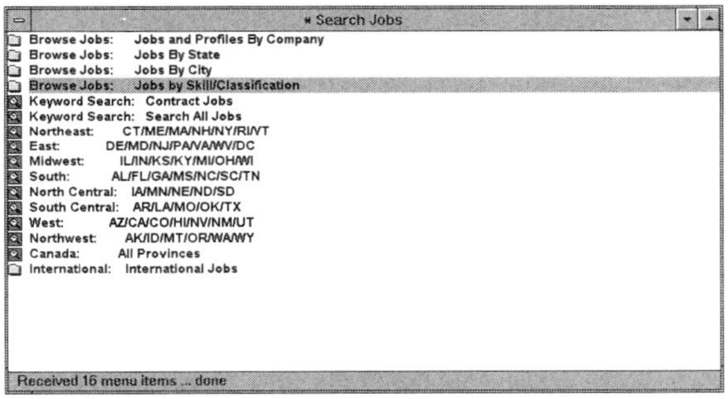

Figure 12.3. *Job search menu through Online Career Center.*

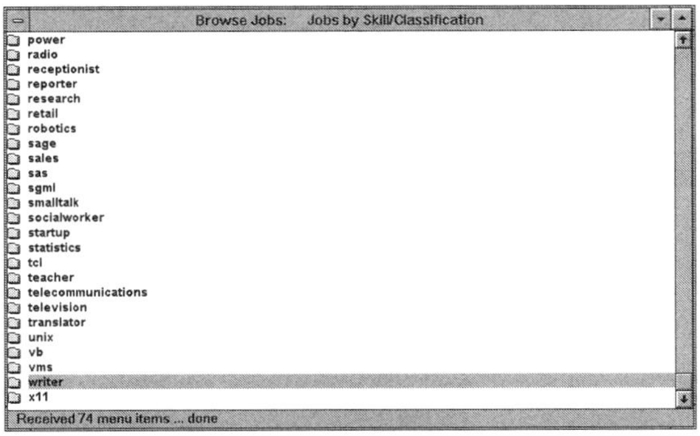

Figure 12.4. *Online Career Center menu showing several disciplines.*

I was looking for technical communications positions, so I chose writer from the list of menu items since there were no specific references to technical writing. The menu listing that opened up included 258 items advertising jobs worldwide. Most of the subject lines were clear, and included job title and location, making the listing very easy to scan. I didn't have any difficulty finding jobs that interested me, so I decided to look for jobs at companies I'd heard of. Figure 12.5 shows one of my highlighted choices.

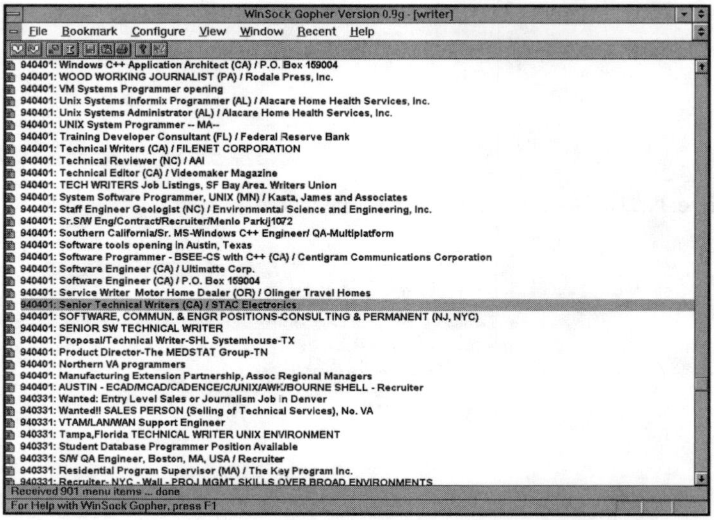

Figure 12.5. *Partial listing of writing jobs from Online Career Center.*

True, the company wasn't in the Northeast, which I'd already set for my location criteria. But I knew of this company's products and thought I'd check it out. This is what the first part of the job listing looked like:

```
From: hwusa@mail.msen.com
Subject: Senior Technical Writers (CA) / STAC
Electronics
Date: 1 Apr 1994 00:40:50 -0500
Location: inFlorida inSouthern

Senior Technical Writers (CA)

STAC Electronics
5993 Avenida Encinitas
Carlsbad, California 92008

Contact: Mail or Fax resume to Human Resources Department TD-3 13
Fax: 619 431-0271
Business Line: Technical Writer
Computer Data Compression
```

```
Description:
Senior Technical Writer

Qualifications:
Ideal candidate will be a top-notch technical writer with at
least 5 years' experience writing PC software user manuals.
```

Note: Excursion 12.3 demonstrates one of the chief benefits of searching for a job on the Internet. Although my original search locations were restricted to the Northeast, by searching skill sets instead of location I found several jobs in locations I'd never even considered. Unlike newspapers, which are almost always local or at least primarily local, the Internet's job ads open your eyes to all sorts of other possibilities. Keep in mind, though, that when you do your job searches after reading this chapter, some of these jobs will no longer be listed.

Once again, it was easy to find a job that interested me. I spent the next hour or so in the Online Career Center (at Msen) searching for jobs by area, title, and city. In most cases, I usually found something interesting in the search results. I also found worthwhile information in the Career Assistance menu, including listings of various books and publications dealing with job searches that were available.

Excursion 12.4. Other Gopher Sites for Job Searching

I spent even more time playing around with some of the other Gopher sites listed in the Employment Opportunities and Resume Postings menu and was again overwhelmed by the amount of job information available. While I won't list all the other sites I found, I will note a few of them that really are worth looking into:

- The Department of Labor Occupational Outlook Handbook Gopher (`marvel.loc.gov`) provides Bureau of Labor statistics and employment projections, job interview tips, job listings, information on what to put in a resume, and specific information and forecasts for a wide variety of disciplines.
- The Job Listings From Around the Globe Gopher (`bongo.cc.utexas.edu`) provides separate worldwide job listings for university, government, and miscellaneous positions, and a separate item for student jobs. In addition to job postings, the Gopher provides an abundance of resources on disability-related information and job searches.

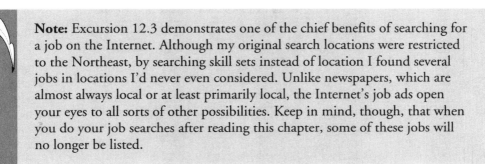

- The Academic Position Network (`wcni.cis.umn.edu`) permits job searches for academic positions both by state and worldwide. It posts a large number of job opportunities.

Having briefly explored a number of Gopher sites, I decided to investigate other ways I could gather information on the Internet.

Finding a Job on the World Wide Web

After having frantically double-clicked my way through countless Gopher trees, I decided it was time to take a different approach. I decided to see what the World Wide Web had to offer. I wasn't entirely certain that I'd be able to find anything new, but it couldn't hurt to try. At the very least, I'd be able to see if my Gopher searches had been as exhaustive as I had hoped. So, once again, with no particular search strategy or definite leads to valuable job resources, I turned to NCSA's World Wide Web browser, Mosaic, to see what I could find.

Note: As explained in Day 7, Microsoft Windows users could use LII Cello instead; UNIX users without a graphical environment could use Lynx.

Excursion 12.5. Searching through the WWW Virtual Library

Like so many of my other searches, this one began with the all too familiar question "where should I begin?" Fortunately, the Web makes things quite easy, providing resources such as the WWW Virtual Library, with its reference to many topics and other virtual libraries. Its home page is shown in Figure 12.6.

Like the Gopher Jewels listing of subjects, the WWW Virtual Library: Subject Catalogue provides some excellent starting points for all kinds of general interest subjects ranging from Aeronautics to Sports. Unfortunately, there weren't any specific hypertext links to job search subjects. But like any good library, there was a reference to where I might be able to find the information I was looking for. I clicked Other virtual libraries, which displayed Figure 12.7.

As the first sentence on the screen reads, this page provides hypertext links to other useful information resources. I'd already looked through some of the searchable libraries for information on other topics, and didn't remember seeing any references to job resource sites I hadn't already visited. One library I hadn't used was the W3 searchable catalog, so I decided to give that a try. I clicked W3 searchable catalog from the list and received Figure 12.8.

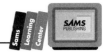

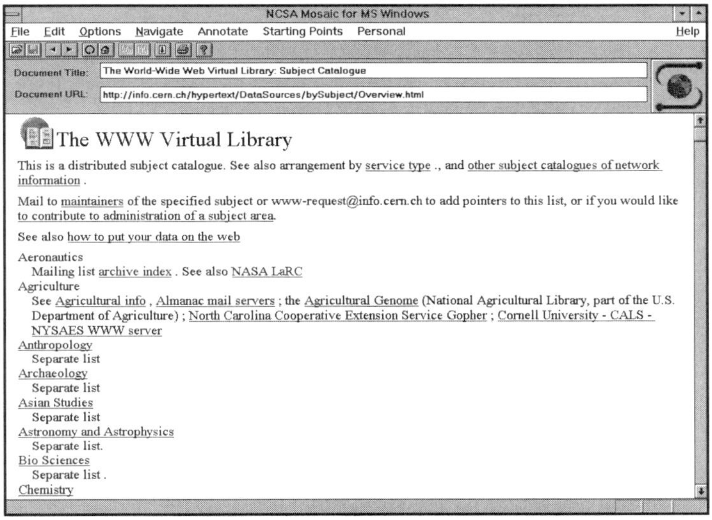

Figure 12.6. *The WWW Virtual Library home page.*

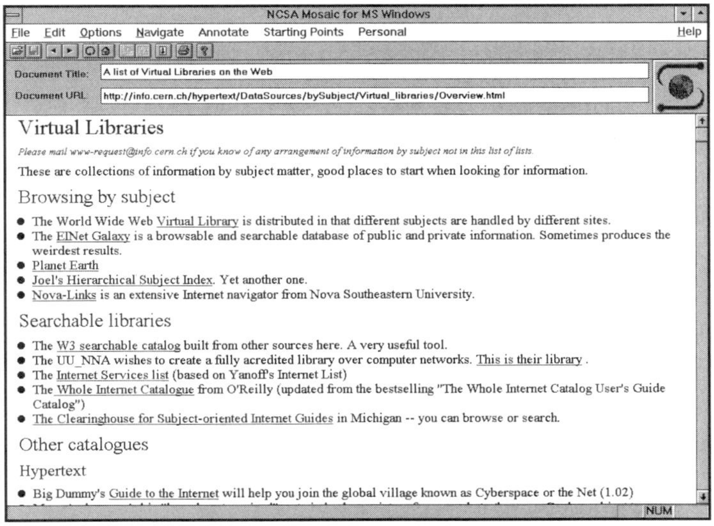

Figure 12.7. *The Virtual Libraries page in Mosaic.*

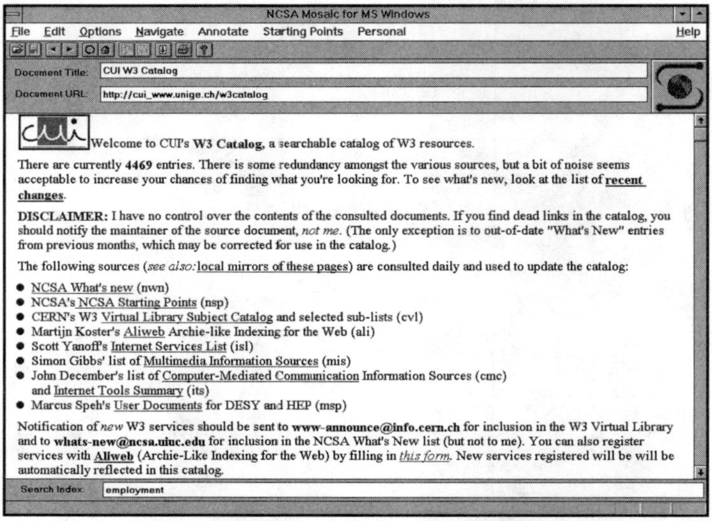

Figure 12.8. *The main page from CUI's W3 Catalog.*

I carried out a number of searches using `jobs`, `career`, `resume`, and `employment` as keywords. The results were fairly similar, so I proceeded from my last search for `employment` (as shown in the Search Index box at the bottom of Figure 12.8). Figure 12.9 displays the search results.

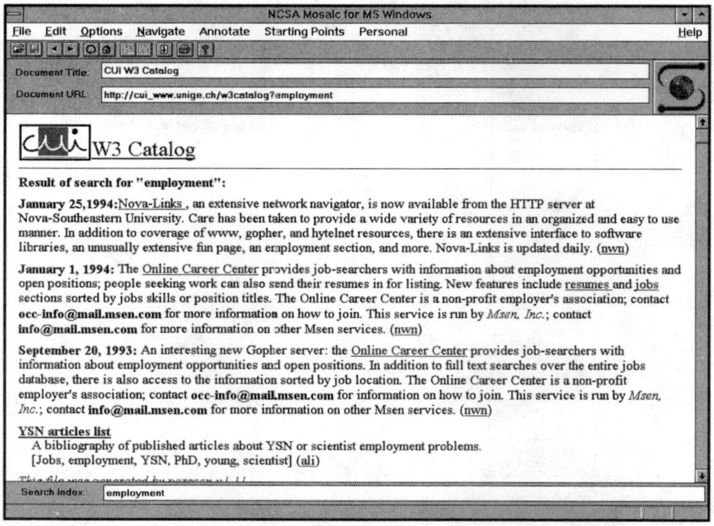

Figure 12.9. *The results of a search using the keyword* `employment`.

Since I had already spent a lot of time looking through the Online Career Center, I decided to take a look at Nova-Links. Nova-Links (`http://alpha.acast.nova.edu/start.html`) had the same keyword search, so I used `employment` again and didn't come up with anything new. The search found resources such as the following:

- The Chronicle for Higher Education
- Help Wanted USA
- Online Career Center
- US Academic Position Network
- Summer Job Network (Cornell)
- Jobs in Federal Government

Clearly, there were a number of paths leading to the same information sources. Even though there was nothing new here, I figured I'd be visiting these sites again, so I used Mosaic's Menu Editor feature to save the address for later.

Excursion 12.6. Searching through the EINet Galaxy

I returned to Virtual libraries and clicked the hypertext link to EINet Galaxy from the Browsing by subject section. Much like the other libraries, EINet Galaxy includes a search index. The index is a little different, however, in that it allows you to specify what specific areas of the Internet you want your search to include. Since I was only interested in finding sources on the Web, I clicked the middle box, entered `employment` as my keyword, and waited to see what would come up. This action is shown in Figure 12.10. The search results came up with one promising entry, Employment Resources, shown in Figure 12.11. This link led me to a page entitled Employment Opportunities. I clicked here and was presented with Figure 12.12.

The listing returned several entries, but all of them were references to Gopher servers listed in Gopher Jewels. Having looked through most of them previously, I realized that I probably wasn't going to have much more luck finding any employment sites specific to the Web. While being just a little disappointing, the results of my search on the Web did show me that I'd covered most of the important resources already with Gopher.

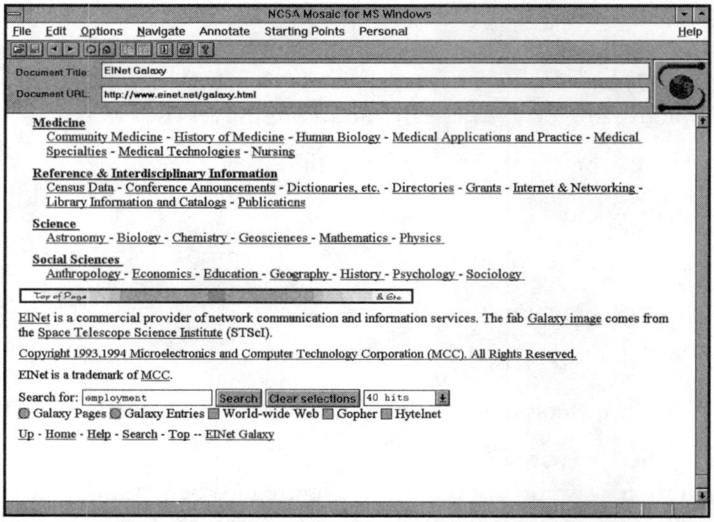

Figure 12.10. *Conducting a search in EINet Galaxy.*

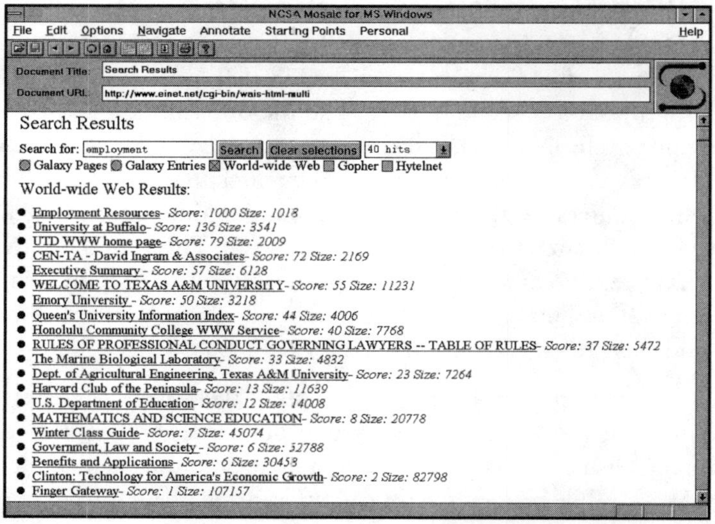

Figure 12.11. *Employment Resources search result from EINet Galaxy.*

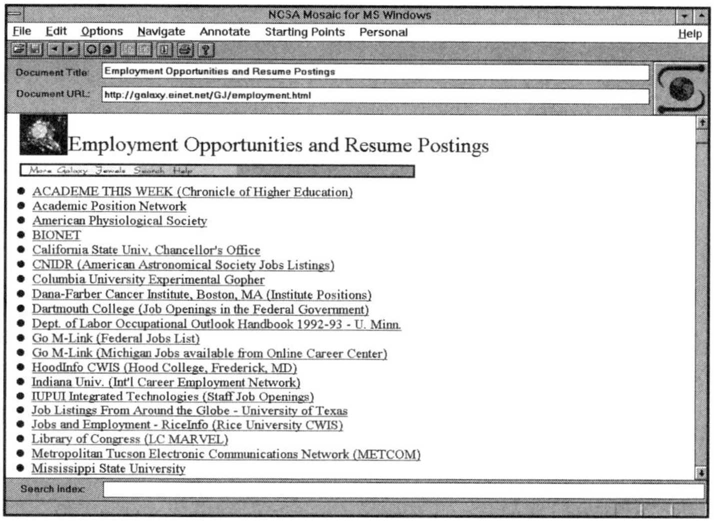

Figure 12.12. *Employment Opportunities from EINet Galaxy.*

Finding a Job by Reading the News

In the past, I've relied extensively on the employment, business, and career sections of different newspapers for job listings. While newspapers still provide invaluable assistance to someone looking for a job, many of the Usenet resources available on the Internet are even better.

Excursion 12.7. Searching for Applicable Newsgroups

The first thing I wanted to do was find out what employment resource newsgroups were available to me. I use the TRN news reader, so after typing **`trn`** at the command prompt to start up the reader, I typed **`l jobs`** to find out what groups existed that contained the string **`jobs`**. The following listing shows the results:

```
* * * * * * End of newsgroups - - what next? [npq] l jobs
Completely unsubscribed newsgroups:
ab.jobs
aus.ads.jobs
ba.jobs.contract
```

```
ba.jobs.misc
ba.jobs.offered
bionet.jobs
bit.listserv.biojobs
biz.jobs.offered
can.jobs
chi.jobs
dc.jobs
de.markt.jobs
kw.jobs
misc.jobs.contract
misc.jobs.misc
misc.jobs.offered
misc.jobs.offered.entry
misc.jobs.resumes
ont.jobs
tor.jobs
ucd.cs.jobs
uk.jobs
uk.jobs.offered
uk.jobs.wanted
```

Excursion 12.8. Joining One Particular Jobs Newsgroup

While I didn't think the list was exhaustive, it was, nevertheless a good starting place. I decided to join just one group, `can.jobs` (a listing of job opportunities in Canada, which is where I'm based) for the time being to give me an overview of what was available. To subscribe to the newsgroup I typed `g can.jobs`, and then typed **y** for yes when prompted whether I wanted to subscribe.

I was surprised that the first time I browsed through the `can.jobs` newsgroup, I immediately found a job that interested me. The posting was for a technical writing position that had been posted to the newsgroup the previous day. Parts of the posting follow:

```
Subject: Technical Writer/Montreal
Date: Tue, 15 Mar 1994 15:02:00 GMT

Visual Edge Software Ltd. is the leading supplier of GUI development tools for
UNIX. Our product, UIM/X, is an award winner.

Technical Writer
================
```

```
You possess strong planning, writing, and editing skills, a solid grasp of
printed and on-line documentation techniques, and a strong technical
background or aptitude. You have experience developing software documentation,
have worked with GUI applications on UNIX or MS Windows, and are familiar with
desktop publishing software such as FrameMaker.
```

Now maybe this was simply a lucky find, but it was still fairly impressive considering the small amount of effort I had actually put into the search at that point. On the whole, the `can.jobs` newsgroup contained a few jobs that interested me, and an even larger number of jobs that didn't. All I had to do was scan the subject line of each post until I found something that interested me.

Excursion 12.9. Scanning Other Newsgroups for Job Postings

Chances are, if you're interested in something specific, there's a relevant newsgroup. Instead of simply subscribing to general newsgroups that post job opportunities, try subscribing to newsgroups specific to your field.

For example, I subscribe to a number of different Listservs and newsgroups dealing with technical and professional writing issues. Every so often, someone posts a job opportunity they stumbled across or heard about. The other day I was reading through `bit.listserve.techwr-l`, a group devoted to the discussion of technical writing issues, and I came across the following post (which I've included parts of):

```
. . . I seem to remember that a couple of our posters from the San Diego area
recently lost positions so I thought I would forward this to the list . . .

---- Begin Included Message ----
Subject: Sr Tech Writer@Cadence, San Diego, CA
Date: Thu, 24 Mar 1994 19:32:26


Senior Technical Writer

Write user and reference manuals, training and online help for Windows and
UNIX-based software for designing printed circuit boards. Software is
developed in multiple cross-country sites through project teams, and documented
using FrameMaker publishing software.
```

Tip: While it doesn't happen all that often, jobs posted to specialty discussion groups provide a great supplement to some of the other groups devoted entirely to general job listings. Even if you don't find postings to these groups that often, they are still an excellent resource for finding a job. By subscribing to discipline-specific groups, you can keep up with current trends and activities in your field. By following the different discussion threads, you can find an abundance of information on developments and changes within your field. For example, I read several times last year about some of the new software packages companies were considering for producing documentation. One product that kept coming up in the discussions was FrameMaker. Over the course of a few months different posters discussed the merits and drawbacks of the package. The trend continued, and it became clear that more and more companies were indeed considering switching to this package for writing their documentation. I decided I'd better learn it, and the preceding job posting proved me right.

Overall, reading a combination of general and specific newsgroups provides an excellent supplement to any good Internet job search.

Researching a Prospective Employer

Having already found a number of promising employment resources, I decided to see if I could fulfill the other goal I had set for myself at the beginning of my search—to see what information I could find about a specific company that would be useful for an interview.

Tip: Researching a prospective employer is an extremely important, yet often overlooked, aspect of the job search. In today's tough job market, a successful job search depends on knowing as much as possible about a prospective employer. Whether you already have an interview scheduled, or are just interested in what a specific company does, research provides valuable information that could give you an added edge over other job applicants. At the very least, research allows you the opportunity to see if your interests are compatible with a specific company.

One Friday afternoon, I received a message from a company asking if I'd be able to come in for an interview on the following Monday morning. I called Human Resources and said that I'd love to come in. I was told that they were looking for a technical writer and that they'd like to talk to me. Great!

Wait, a second…not so great! It was late Friday afternoon and the career center I used was closed for the weekend. There was practically no way that I was going to be able to find any information about the company or what they did. I had some idea, but not enough to demonstrate any semblance of intelligence during the interview. Fortunately I knew a handful of people who had worked for the company, and they were able to answer most of the questions I had. Of course, if I'd known that answers were available through my own computer, I probably could have spent a little longer relaxing that weekend.

Excursion 12.10. Finding Information about a Specific Company

If you're up for a job, or even if you're in one, the Internet can provide you with a considerable amount of information about the company. For the sake of example, I decided to see what information was available on the Internet about the company I currently work for—AT&T, Global Information Solutions. While I didn't expect to find any information on the specific business unit I work for, I wanted to see if I could find any general information that might have made my first job interview a little easier.

I remembered seeing a directory in the Online Career Center that provided company profiles. This sounded like a good starting point. I started up Winsock Gopher again, and returned to the Online Career Center using a bookmark feature.

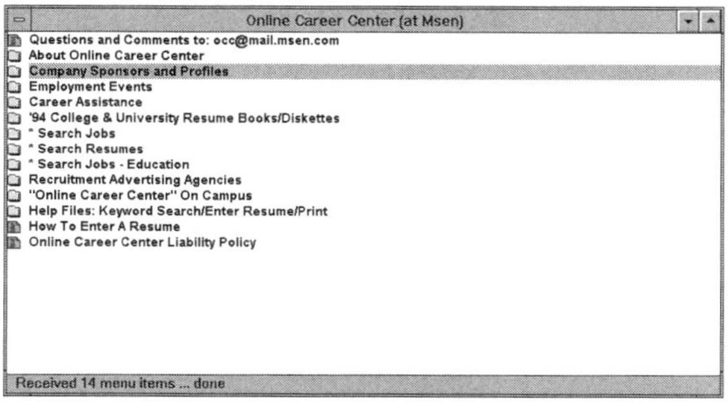

Figure 12.13. *The Online Career Center showing Company Sponsor and Profiles.*

Figure 12.13 shows the Online Career Center Gopher. The item I remembered seeing was Company Sponsor and Profiles. If there was anything available on my firm, it would likely be here.

I clicked Company Sponsors and Profiles, which opened up a listing of numerous items. Part of that list is shown in Figure 12.14 below:

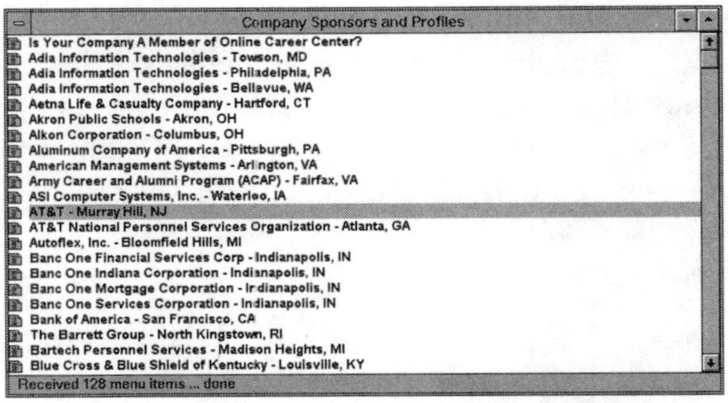

Figure 12.14. *A partial listing of company profiles.*

The list included a number of large and small companies across the United States. I'd imagine that this list will only continue to grow as other companies start including their profiles in this directory, making this a valuable resource for researching an employer. For now, however, it seems like the majority of entries were for larger companies. But, already I'd found what I was looking for. Near the top of the listing were AT&T - Murray Hill, NJ and AT&T National Personnel Service Organization - Atlanta, GA.

Thinking that the first AT&T reference would provide a good overview of the company, I clicked AT&T - Murray Hill, NJ. The first part of the document was as follows:

```
AT&T - Murray Hill, NJ
                             AT&T
AT&T'S BUSINESS

AT&T is a global company that provides communications services
and products, as well as network equipment and computer
systems, to businesses, consumers, telecommunications service
providers and government agencies. Our worldwide intelligent
network carries more than 140 million voice, data, video and
facsimile messages every business day. AT&T Bell Laboratories
engages in basic research as well as product and service
development. AT&T also offers a general-purpose credit card
and financial and leasing services. AT&T does business in
more than 120 countries.
```

The document goes on to describe the company's business, corporate history, and structure. Overall, it's a fairly good overview of the company. More importantly, it would be something you could use in an interview to demonstrate a working knowledge of the company and formulate some questions to ask the interviewer. Many companies provide similar or even more extensive information over the Net.

Excursion 12.11. Back to the Web for More Information

For my interview, it would have been nice if I'd known more about AT&T Bell Laboratories, which was mentioned in the company profile. Now that I had the job, I still wanted the information, so I went back to the World Wide Web to see what I could find, by using the search capabilities of the CUI W3 Catalog, shown in Figure 12.8.

Once again, just a matter of seconds, and the CUI W3 Catalog page appeared on the screen. I entered `AT&T` in the search box and waited to see what would come up. Figure 12.15 shows the results of the search.

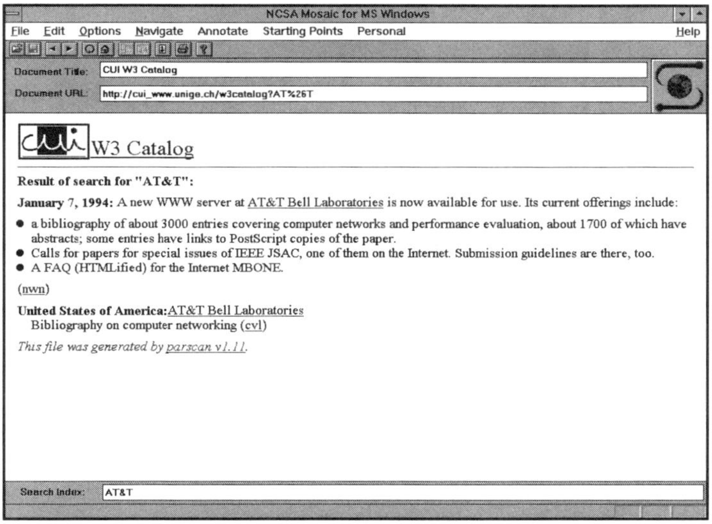

Figure 12.15. *The results of a W3 Catalog search for AT&T.*

Note: In many searches on the World Wide Web, search results are often followed by brackets containing letters—(`nwn`) and (`cvl`), as shown in Figure 12.15. These brackets provide a hypertext link to the original list or source the entry was taken from. For example, clicking (`nwn`) provides a hypertext link to the NCSA What's New page (`http://www.ncsa.uiuc.edu/SDG/Software/Mosaic/Docs/Whats-new.html`). Clicking (`cvl`) would open up CERN'S W3 Virtual Library Subject Catalog (`http://infocern.ch/hypertext/DataSources/bySubject/Overview.html`).

Just what I was looking for: AT&T Bell Labs. I clicked AT&T Bell Laboratories and waited to see what information it would provide me with. The result is shown in Figure 12.16.

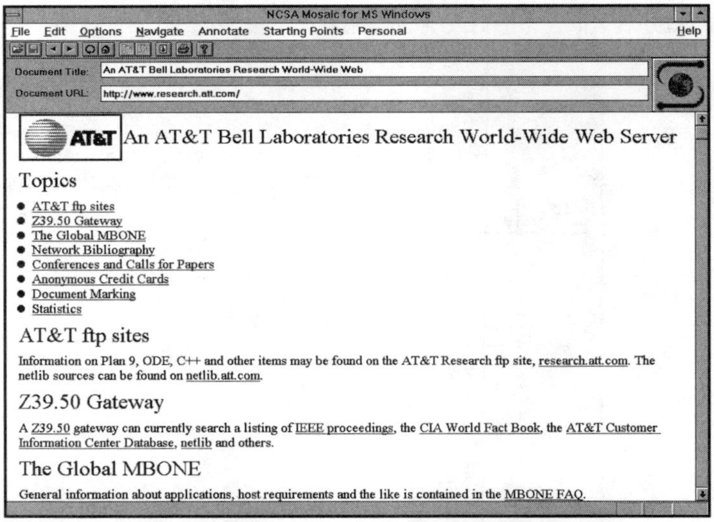

Figure 12.16. *World Wide Web page for AT&T Bell Laboratories.*

Not bad—a server devoted entirely to AT&T activities, information, and files. I spent a little while searching through each of the entries, trying keyword searches, and collecting usable information. Overall, the information I found would be extremely useful in an interview. If I was asked if I had any idea about what the company did, I would be able to talk generally about some of the information I had found.

> **Tip:** Don't forget to check new Internet resources on a regular basis. Information in the Online Career Center and other employment search areas can change daily, even hourly. Company information might appear any time. You'll probably want to check once every couple of days, or even daily as you read the help wanted ads in your newspaper.

Excursion 12.12. A Reason to Check the Resources Regularly

In Excursion 12.10, I said that I didn't expect to find any information about the particular business unit I worked for when I was looking for references to AT&T. There wasn't anything available then, but… .

A week after the first search, I found what I was looking for. I wasn't intending to, though. Instead, I was on my account, checking out new items on the Internet. This time I was using a commercially available Gopher program called WinGopher (see Day 2 for more on WinGopher). As I usually do, I chose an extremely useful menu item called Gopher servers added lately to the net at Gopher address `liberty.uc.wlu.edu`, in the path Explore Internet Resources, then New Internet Sites, and finally New Gopher Sites. Scrolling down, I saw the screen pictured in Figure 12.17.

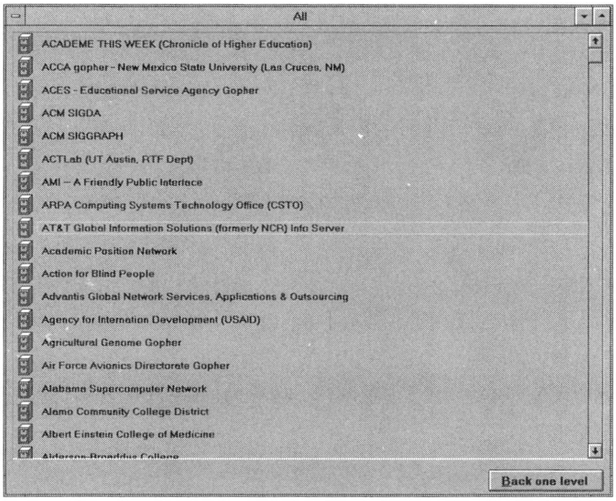

Figure 12.17. *A partial listing of new Gopher sites.*

There it was, the second entry, AT&T Global Information Solutions (formerly NCR) Info Server. It never fails, when you're not looking for something, it always turns up in unexpected places. The server had been added the day before! So, I decided to check it out. I double-clicked and found Figure 12.18.

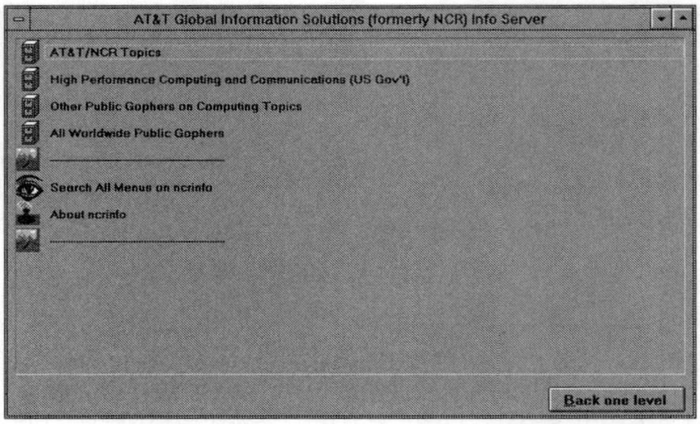

Figure 12.18. *The Gopher menu for AT&T Global Information Systems.*

I browsed through each of the entries and found that the server had been established to provide information about products, and computing-related topics in which AT&T Global Information Solutions has interest and expertise. Again, this is information that I would have found extremely useful for my interview, and it clearly demonstrates why you should keep checking the Net for new information.

Excursion 12.13. International Job Sources

Looking for a job outside the U.S. or Canada isn't nearly as easy as all of this. There's no European or Asian equivalent to the Online Career Center as yet, and there simply aren't as many companies on the Internet in other parts of the world.

Still, there are two strategies worth trying. First is the ACADEME THIS WEEK (Chronicle of Higher Education) searchable Gopher shown in Excursion 12.2. By selecting the items SEARCH using any word or words of your choosing, then Limit search to jobs outside the United States, you can narrow down the possibilities. Below is the result of a search for jobs using the keyword `marketing`, showing three jobs available in New Zealand.

```
1.  Management — University of Canterbury — New Zealand.
2.  Lect: Dept of Consumer Tech; Educ & Marketing — Massey University...
3.  Multiple Faculty (Soc, Biochem, Ed, etc) — University of Auckland...
```

Another listing of jobs, this time using the keyword `management`, is shown here:

```
1.  Management — University of Canterbury — New Zealand.
2.  Coordinator of Business Studies — U of the South Pacific — Fiji.
3.  Faculty Positions — Lincoln University — New Zealand.
4.  Multiple Faculty (Soc, Biochem, Ed, etc) — University of Auckland...
5.  Vice Chancellor — U Western Sydney — Australia.
6.  Reader, Professor in Business — U of the South Pacific — Fiji.
7.  Lect: Dept of Consumer Tech; Educ & Marketing — Massey University...
8.  School of Banking and Finance — U of New South Wales — Australia.
```

Notice that all are based in educational institutions. This is often the case with international Internet information at this stage in the Net's existence.

The other strategy is to use Gopher or the World Wide Web to surf from country to country, finding organizations you might want to work for, then getting contact information from the files you discover. An example of this is the following information, discovered by surfing through new Gophers on the Internet. The company is The Internetworking Company of South Africa (TICSA), whose Gopher can be found at `gopher.ticsa.com`:

```
1.  About This Gopher.
2.  African Networking (Rhodes University)/
3.  Information by Subject Area (rice.edu)/
4.  Other Gopher and Information Servers/
5.  Request For Comments (RFCs) <ncren.net>/
6.  TICSA Information/
```

Selecting the last item, TICSA Information, yields a file with information about the company. While they're not advertising for employment, they provide contacts you might want to use if you're thinking of working in South Africa and you're Internet-savvy. It's certainly worth a try.

Conclusion

While my employment search of the Internet was by no means exhaustive, I did manage to accomplish the goals I had set for myself in the beginning. By spending just a few hours, I managed to find numerous job postings that interested me and an abundance of information on career planning and job searches. Looking back, I know that the resources available on the Internet would certainly have made my job search a whole lot easier.

Summary

Using the Internet as one means of finding a job is a worthwhile idea. An increasing number of companies are posting to the Net, recognizing its potential at reaching a wide range of people with varied and advanced skills. Currently, the information is far from extensive, but the Internet offers search tools that help you narrow your focus. You can search in Gophers and in the World Wide Web, and you can keep tabs on possible employment through newsgroups.

It's also an extremely good idea to conduct background research on a prospective employer, especially if you've been called for an interview. Here, too, the Internet can easily help. While a number of services are appearing that charge for the extensive financial information they contain, there may well be enough in locations like the Online Career Center to get you started.

By no means should the Internet be your only job-finding strategy. But nor should any other single venue. Instead, the Net should become one of many search tools, which, when combined, give you the best possible chance of landing a position, even in today's very tough employment climate.

Task Review

On Day 12, you:

- ☐ Accessed the Chronicle of Higher Education job listings through Gopher.
- ☐ Accessed the Online Career Center through Gopher.
- ☐ Used the CUI W3 Catalog and the EINet Galaxy on the World Wide Web to search for job postings.
- ☐ Followed newsgroups to help you find available positions.
- ☐ Used the Internet to research prospective employers.

Q&A

Q The Internet isn't the only online service that posts career opportunities, is it?

A By no means. All of the commercial services—including CompuServe, Prodigy, and America Online—have career areas, and many of these are better developed than anything on the Internet. The only drawback is that those services can sometimes cost more money than the Net, especially if you're not paying for your own Internet access. Still, if you're serious about searching for a job and you're not concerned about specific location, you owe it to yourself to check out all of these services.

Q Isn't posting a resume on the OCC or a newsgroup a hit-and-miss proposition?

A Yes, it is. But maybe no more than sending it in the mail to the great resume dump in the sky (or wherever these things seem to go). As more companies become aware of the Net's career areas, this will likely change, though, because many will look there before advertising locally (it's cheaper, among other things). So give it a shot anyway. Following newsgroups may be especially important, though, especially newsgroups related to that field, because then you're asking people from around the world to keep their eyes open for a position.

Q Does anyone conduct interviews on the Internet?

A Not yet. But why not?

13

WEEK 2

Getting the Word Out: Publishing a Special-Interest Magazine on the Net

Day 13 takes you through the first steps in the process of publishing your own special-interest magazine on the Internet. Creating a magazine is relatively easy, but publishing it requires several considerations. Among the possible publishing techniques are Usenet newsgroups, FTP sites, electronic journals, Gophers, and the World Wide Web. Day 13 briefly examines all these possibilities.

On Day 13, you will:

- ☐ Decide which Internet tool to use to publish your magazine.
- ☐ Learn the benefits and drawbacks of publishing your magazine as a newsgroup, a mailing list, a Gopher, and a Web page.
- ☐ Learn to create a World Wide Web page via HTML (Hypertext Markup Language).

Magazines and the Internet

Roughly an hour and a half after visiting your first Gopher-based or Web-published magazine, you'll probably start thinking about how to produce one of your own. It seems so easy, after all: Start a Gopher site, or a World Wide Web site, and you're free to publish whatever you want. Especially if your area of special interest isn't already covered by a number of similar online magazines, or if the magazines on the Web don't do your interest proud, there appears every reason to strike out on your own.

The usual follow-up to a paragraph such as the one you've just read is, "But it's not that easy." I can't tell you that, however, because in fact it *is* that easy. As long as you have a machine to store it on, you can make your magazine available in a great number of formats. The only questions are "Which format?" and "Do I have the equipment and the connection?" Answer these questions appropriately, and you're on your way.

When you have the equipment in place (which is a big when, I realize), publishing a magazine on the Internet is cheaper than publishing it in any other medium. There are no paper costs, no ink costs, no four-color production costs, nothing like that. There isn't even a distribution cost, beyond of course the equipment and the Internet connection, which presumably you have anyway. As long as you don't have to pay contributors—and this, too, has its precedent in special-interest magazine publication—you can do your magazine for no cost other than your time (which, because it's a hobby anyway, isn't a concern at all).

Of course, there's always the problem of readership, but the same holds true of any publication. On the Internet, in fact, readership is probably less of a problem than with a paper publication. Through newsgroups and mailing lists (and personal e-mail that others can forward), you can get the word out that your magazine exists, and you can get links placed on Gopher sites and on any number of World Wide Web pages.

If you're already directly connected to the Net, you can do everything yourself. You'll need to establish your computer as an FTP, Gopher, or WWW site—the last two of which require special server software—and you have to make sure your computer maintains a constant connection to the Net. If you're operating through a phone line and modem, this is obviously a problem, but it can be done.

If you're directly connected through an existing 24-hour high-speed site (through your organization, for example), there are more possibilities, but of course you'll have to work with your system's administrators to get things going. Essentially, you'll want to place your site on a fast server, one that already contains the necessary software, and the systems people can help you with this.

If you're not connected in this way, you can establish a connection with a commercial Internet provider, and then make storage arrangements with them. It might cost you some money this way, but it's worth checking out. There are also some commercial providers who specialize in providing access and assisting you with preparing your sites. While these are extremely useful, they cost additional money.

With everything in place, anything goes. So publish away, and let us all know where we should go to read it.

Magazines Already on the Internet

Before hearing from Neil Humphrey and David Randall, who will look at some of the particulars of Internet magazine publishing, examine some of the magazines with existing Net presence. Scores of these are available through Gopher, and the most recent (and probably the most interesting) are appearing on the World Wide Web.

Excursion 13.1. Gopher-Based Magazines

Figure 13.1 shows the results of a multilevel Gopher browse. Beginning with the Journals and Newspapers item in Carnegie Mellon University's excellent English Server (`english-server.hss.cmu.edu`), you see some of the huge variety of online magazines. *Future Culture* (bottom-left corner) presents text files with its full contents, whereas *The New Republic* (top-right) is available in sample form through The Electronic Newsstand. E-News, as it's called, presents sample issues and special rates for "Internauts," as it calls us. Essentially, it's a subscription service.

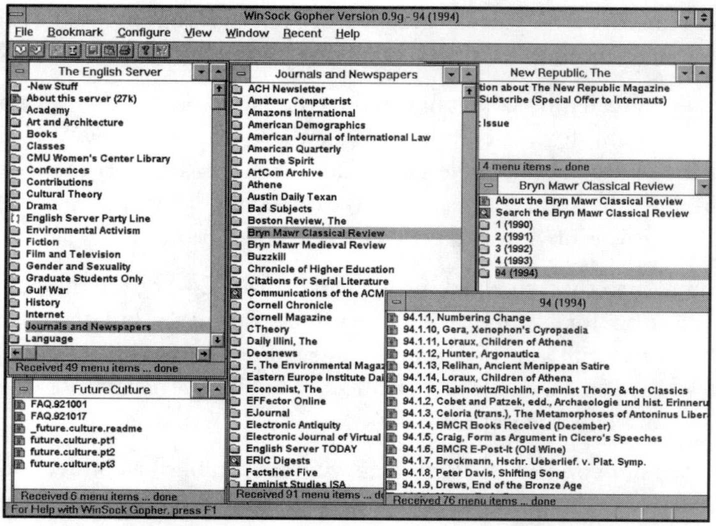

Figure 13.1. *A Gopher collection showing the* Bryn Mawr Classical Review.

The magazines available on E-News are varied and interesting, although most are quite well known and established. One such publication is the *Times Literary Supplement*, the famous book and culture review publication out of London. The following menu shows the details available from E-News, and again you'll note that this is the typical structure for this Gopher service:

```
1.  Information about The Times Literary Supplement
2.  How to Subscribe (Special Offer to Internauts)
3.  Archive
4.  Current Issue
5.  To the Rest of The Electronic Newsstand(tm)
```

Also available from the English Server Gopher, through Journals and Newspapers, then Other Journals, is a huge range of electronic publications available primarily or even exclusively on the Net. One such journal is *EuroNews* out of Finland; part of its menu looks as follows:

```
1.  05Apr93
2.  05Apr93.ps
3.  07Sep93
4.  08Jun93
5.  08Jun93.ps
6.  09Aug93
7.  09Aug93.ps
8.  09Mar93
9.  09Mar93.ps
```

Choosing the 09Aug93 edition, we receive the following (partial) publication:

```
::::::::::::::::::::::::::::::::::::::::::::::::::::::::::::::::::::::::
::                          EURONEWS 9.8.1993                         ::
::               Edited by Risto Kotalampi, rko@cs.tut.fi             ::
::::::::::::::::::::::::::::::::::::::::::::::::::::::::::::::::::::::::

FRANCE: Riviera Radio (ex-RMC Italian Service) is now operating on 702
kHz with 20 kW in English. They have plans to increase to 1200 kW.
RVI Radio World via Contact

INTERNATIONAL WATERS: The Radio Ship, Radio Brod, went off the air on
June 28th, on orders of the company owning the ship. This followed a
complaint by the Yugoslavian government to the ITU. The government of
Caribbean state of St.  Vincent, where the ship is registered, had
made the demand, on behalf of the ITU. The programming, promoting peace
in the former Yugoslavia, was financed by the European Community. The
ship is now in an Italian port undergoing overhaul, and taking on
fuel, food, and water for another three months. The editor is hopeful
they will return to operation. Radio Brod operated on 720 kHz and 97.8
MHz. Vreme, Belgrade via BBCMS via SCDX

Radio Brod v/s is Enisa Alicehic (from Paris). The correct address in
Italy is Via Bozzi 45C, c/o Gruppo Regionale Verdi, I-70123 Bari. JM

LITHUANIA: From February 1st the new commercial station, R Station
Tau, went on air 0700-1900. The station uses the former Radiocentras
transmitter in Kaunas. Address is P.O.Box 2040, 3000 Kaunas.  RP in
SWN via ARC

RUSSIA: 1089 R Teos is the first Russian Christian Radio Station. It
works since January 20th, 1993 daily from 8 am to 12 pm (local time)
and is using 20 kW transmitter. The official founder is the
Evangelical Russian Church, but it wouldn't have existed without the
support of a Canadian, Mr.Robert Lowe. Their address is P.O.Box 171,
St.Petersburg 194356. V/s was Chief Manager Evgeniy N.Nedzelskiy.
BEFF via ARC
```

13

On the right side of the screen you see, highlighted, the prestigious *Bryn Mawr Classical Review*, and in the adjoining window several of the files are available. Also available through the English Server links are publications such as *The Journal of Educational Technology*, shown in Figure 13.2.

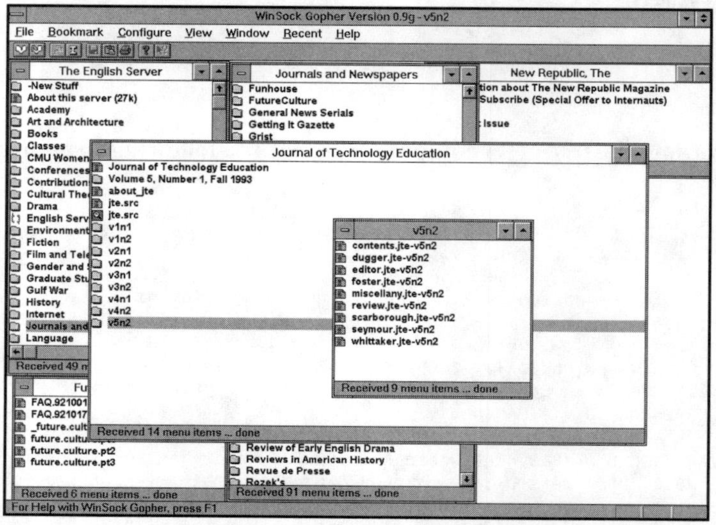

Figure 13.2. *A Gopher collection featuring* The Journal of Educational Technology.

Both these magazines, like most of those on Gopher servers, present themselves as readable or downloadable files. Usually the files are text files, but sometimes they're available in PostScript form as well, which means they're professionally formatted.

Excursion 13.2. Web-Based Magazines

When you think of magazines, you probably think of colorful, easily browsable publications. Increasingly, these are appearing on the World Wide Web, and if the early results are any indication, the Web should quickly become the medium of choice. The examples in this section demonstrate why.

It's probably no surprise that *Wired* magazine has an Internet presence. After all, its focus is squarely on cyberspace in its many forms. Figure 13.3 shows a portion of the contents page for one issue, listing some of the available features and two of its most popular columns.

More surprising, perhaps, but fully established on the Net, is the well-known alternative magazine *Mother Jones*. Figure 13.4 shows part of the table of contents for the May/June 1994 issue, with graphics identical to the cover of the print version.

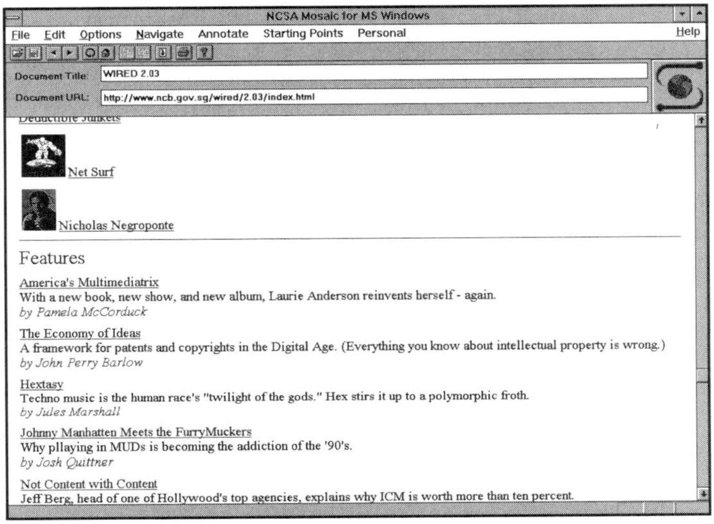

Figure 13.3. Wired *magazine contents page.*

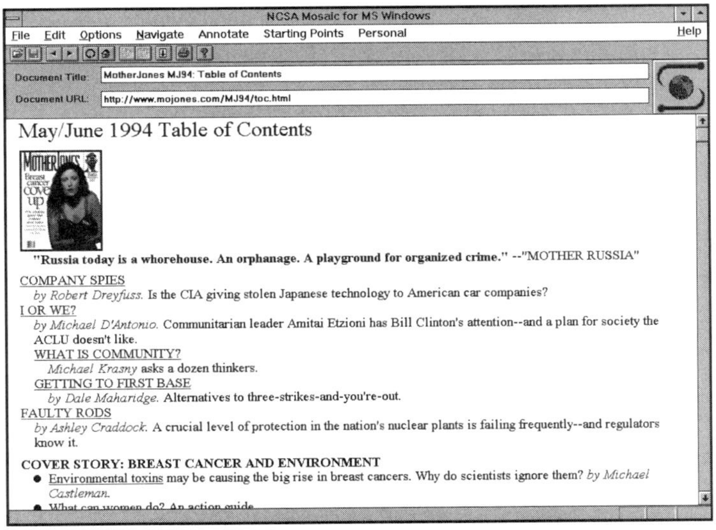

Figure 13.4. *A* Mother Jones *contents page.*

Both *Wired* and *Mother Jones*, of course, are print magazines as well as online magazines. They began as the former, and have recently supplemented their distribution through the Net (and through other online services, such as America Online, as well). The next group of magazines resides primarily (if not solely) on the Internet, and the examples show the ways they are tailoring themselves for this medium.

Figure 13.5 is a contents page for *X-Section* magazine. Its home page (not shown) says *X-Section* is staffed by students in the Nuclear Engineering Department at the University of Wisconsin-Madison. It is designed to offer information about nuclear engineering to the general public rather than to the discipline itself. It contains a number of fascinating articles.

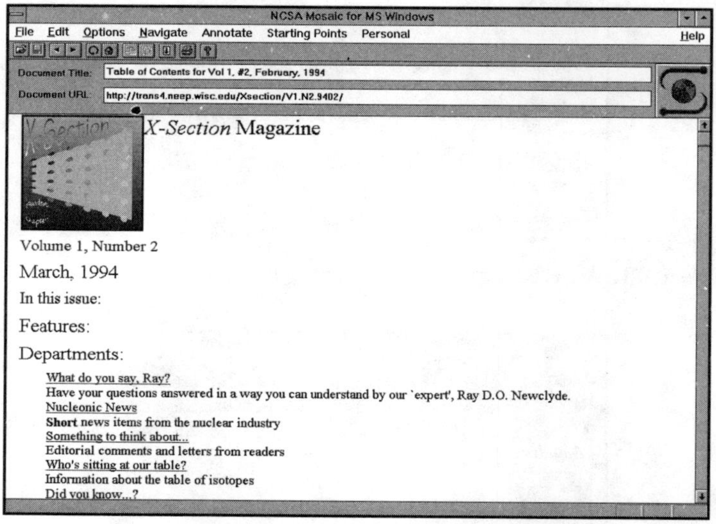

Figure 13.5. *An* X-Section *magazine contents page.*

Next up is *InterText* magazine, whose home page (See Figure 13.6.) practically jumps off the screen. On the home page is a link to a list of other electronic publications, as well as a link to an FTP site containing PostScript files of the magazine.

Figure 13.7 displays a typical *InterText* contents page and shows its division into columns and features. The page orientation of the World Wide Web seems to lend itself very well to this traditional kind of structure.

Figures 13.8 and 13.9 show two screens from *ANSWERS* magazine, which, as its home page explains, is a special-interest magazine for adults with aging parents. The Web version of the magazine acts as a kind of sophisticated ad for the magazine, and it includes a link to a subscription form. As shown in Figure 13.9, the form does not include a field for credit card information, suggesting that you will be billed the appropriate amount. (Canadians will note that this seems completely legitimate, since the additional exorbitant postage fee is in keeping with that of every other U.S. publication.)

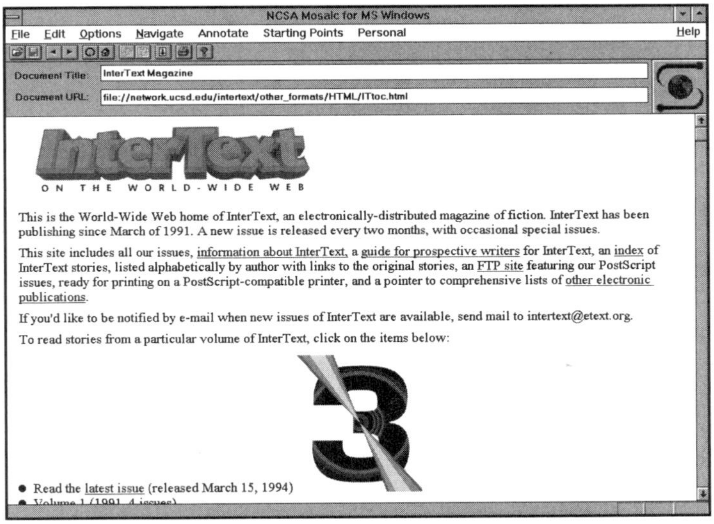

Figure 13.6. *An* InterText *magazine home page.*

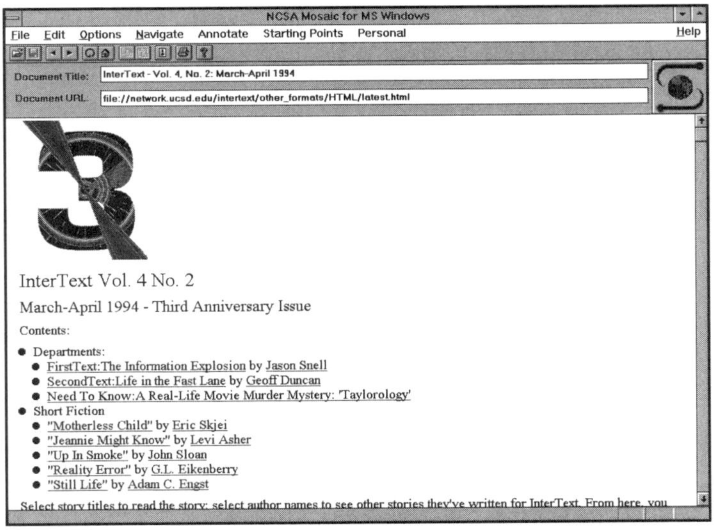

Figure 13.7. *An* InterText *magazine contents page.*

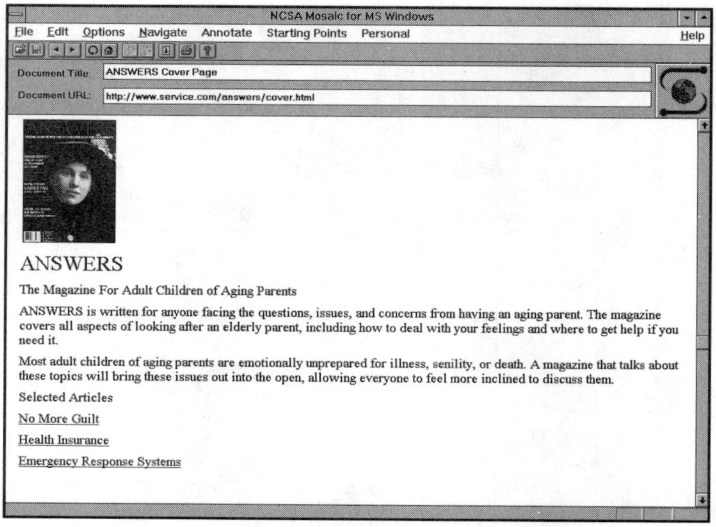

Figure 13.8. *An* ANSWERS *magazine home page.*

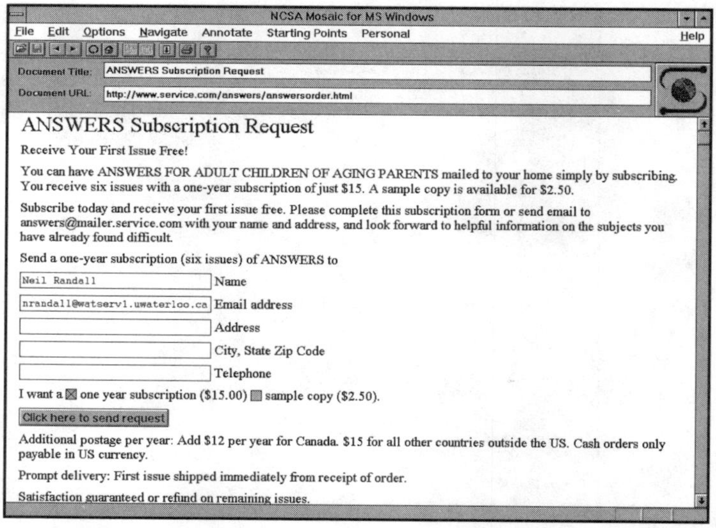

Figure 13.9. *An* ANSWERS *magazine subscription form.*

Figures 13.10 and 13.11 show another student-run publication, the *Trincoll Journal*, out of Trinity College in Hartford, Connecticut. An excellent magazine, *Trincoll* solicits submissions from writers and designers around the world (as do most Internet-based magazines, such as *InterText*), and its high graphics quality ensures the writer a strong presentation. It's worth reading, and worth writing for. In fact, writing for the online journals, although it doesn't usually pay, is a superb way for would-be magazine journalists to get started.

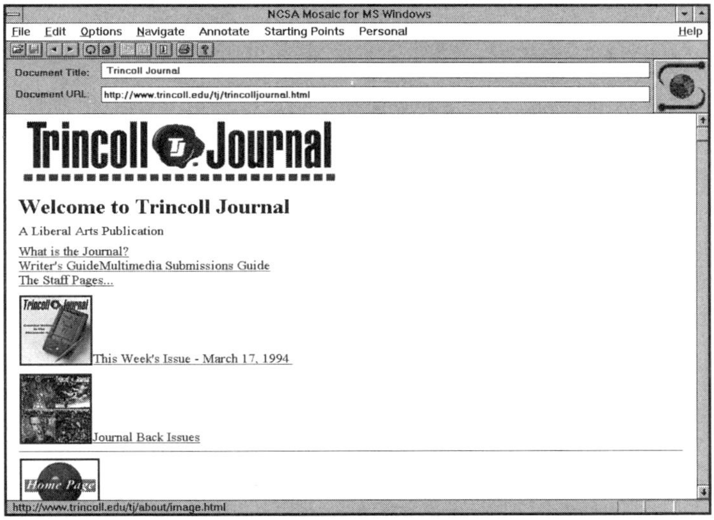

Figure 13.10. *A* Trincoll Journal *magazine home page.*

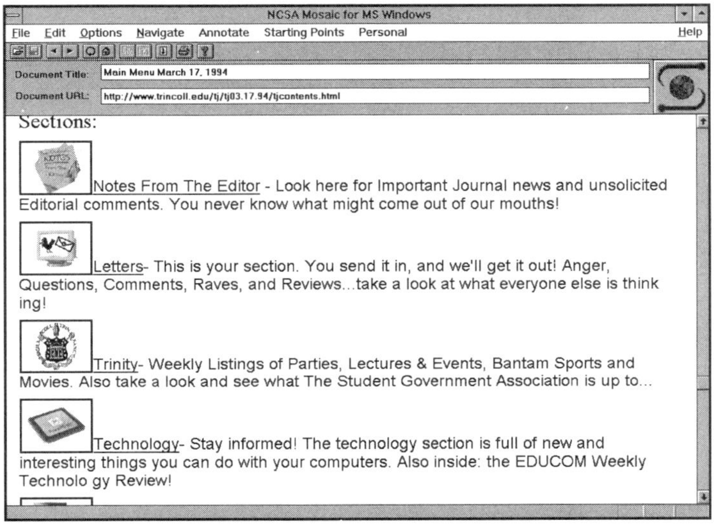

Figure 13.11. *A* Trincoll Journal *magazine contents page.*

Finally, *International Teletimes* is an online magazine out of Vancouver, British Columbia. The magazine is nicely designed and always interesting. Its home page (See Figure 13.12.) tells that it is distributed to the Net and other online points as well. A typical issue is shown in Figure 13.13.

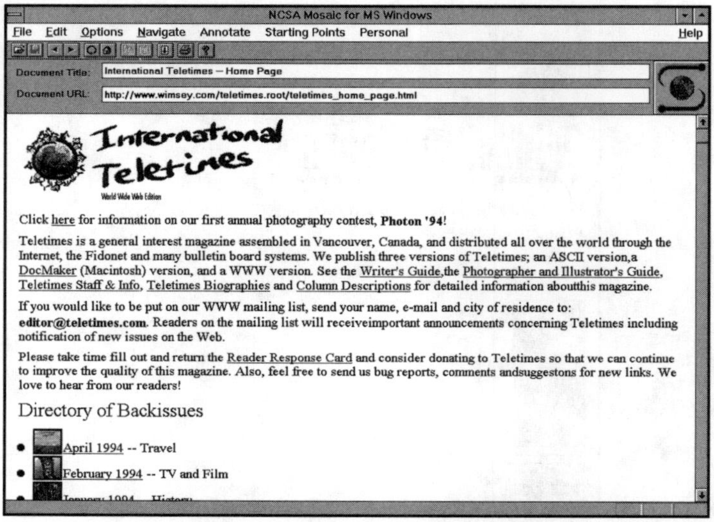

Figure 13.12. *An* International Teletimes *home page.*

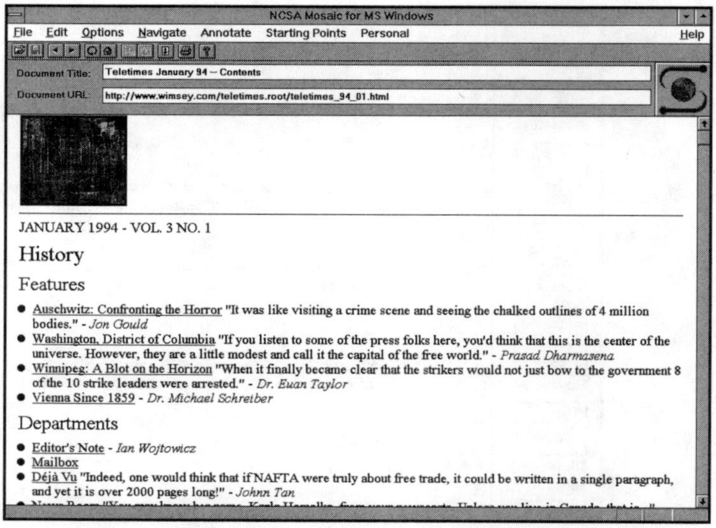

Figure 13.13. *An* International Teletimes *contents page.*

International Teletimes features another good use of the Web's forms feature (for further uses, see *ANSWERS* magazine preceding),this time as a replacement for a feedback card. (See Figure 13.14.) I rarely filled out and mailed the feedback cards from special-interest magazines, but this makes it so easy that there's no point in *not* doing so.

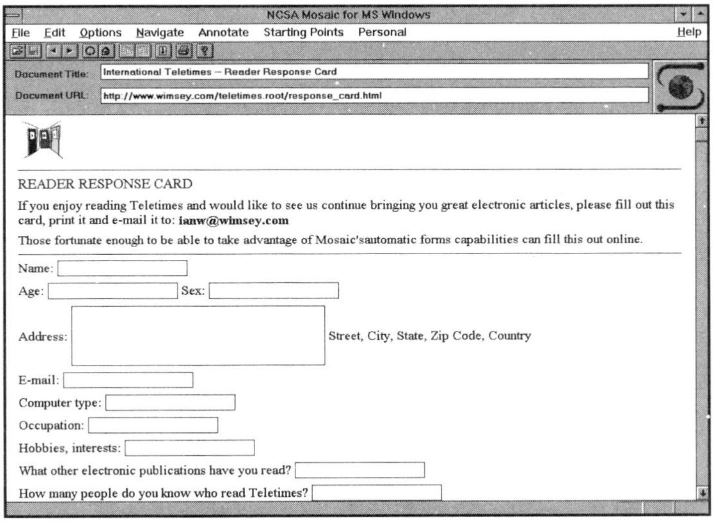

Figure 13.14. *An* International Teletimes *feedback page.*

Warning: As of this writing, NCSA Mosaic was the only Web browser to offer forms support. It will appear in the next upgrade of LII Cello, which should be shortly after you read this.

The benefits of presenting a magazine on the World Wide Web are obvious. Essentially, you're giving readers a familiar-looking product (it can resemble the paper version substantially), but you're also able to offer sound and video if you wish.

There are several ways of putting your publication on the Internet, as the previous examples clearly show. Two contributing authors will now guide you through some of the details of publishing, with the hope that soon your ideas will be available for perusal.

About the Contributors

Neil Humphrey and David Randall share an enormous enthusiasm for bicycling (they also share youth, which may well account for this enthusiasm—I'm more into motoring and mouse-clicking). They expressed an interest in working toward publishing an Internet-based cycling magazine, suggesting that the cycling community would also be interested. I asked them to write down their considerations, and they appear in the following sections.

Note: Even though the special interest for the proposed magazine is limited to cycling, the methods and suggestions for Internet publishing are not limited at all. If your interest lies with recycling, or acne prevention, or Gestalt theory, or canary breeding, these suggestions are still completely valid.

Publishing a Special-Interest Magazine on the Net

by Neil Humphrey

By now I would guess that your Internet adventures have given you at least a hint of these sentiments:

- The amount of information out there boggles and sort of scares me, and I'm beginning to feel stressed by information anxiety.
- There isn't enough information about the things I'm really interested in, such as house buying, bicycling, and the secret mating dance of the Lake Erie zebra mussel.

The first sentiment means that you can't find the forest for the trees. The second means that you want more trees, which will make the forest even more difficult to navigate.

So how do you deal with the information anxiety problem? Very simply, forget the problem of too much information and simply add to the information universe. Distract yourself from your inability to cope with the stupefying volume of the Net's information by starting your own newsgroup, discussion list, Gopher, or World Wide Web page! Each of these vehicles offers you a way to deliver your two cents to the e-doors of the world.

By starting your own source of information, not only can you impress your friends and mystify your enemies, you can also rant on and on about exactly what interests you, and you can actually feel like you have some control over the Net.

For instance, say you're a rabid but entirely mediocre bicycle fiend, as David and I are. There are heaps of ways to use the Internet to fuel your obsession:

- Start a Gopher site, WWW page, or FTP area that stocks descriptions or even .GIF maps of local rides, which you've scanned in or drawn on computer.
- Label the maps to show all the roads with lousy pavement or where the thorn bushes are on a given trail.
- Brag about your terminal velocity down (or up) a little-known hill.
- Recommend your favorite physiotherapist.
- Start a discussion list for Scottish-American cyclists who prefer to ride in kilts.
- Publish a regular e-column of wisdom from that wizened old Italian coach you found in an obscure, parts-cluttered shop in a remote, dingy hamlet.

Use your imagination. Starting your own magazine is uniquely exhilarating and empowering—few things approach the immense (and cheap) satisfaction of authorship. Following are a few ideas for getting started, and by the time you're done looking at them you should be ready to head out and do it. So good luck.

Choosing a Distribution Method

A number of distribution methods present themselves. You've experienced all of them in previous chapters, although maybe not in magazine form. Here they are:

- **Newsgroups**—A newsgroup, a kind of electronic bathroom wall, is completely public. Everybody writes on it, and everybody else gets to see and respond to what's written, adding their own comments. Newsgroups are completely text-based, and they can be wild, exciting, cutting-edge, or irrelevant, depending on who's posting replies. To read or post to newsgroups, you need access to a news-providing host and newsreading software such as the well-known rn or trn. The benefits of publishing via newsgroup are easy accessibility and constant feedback; the disadvantages are lack of formatting, over-accessibility, and no real control.

- **Mailing Lists**—A mailing list is a more private list for people more heavily obsessed with a narrower topic. Postings appear as e-mail messages, and every time someone writes mail to the discussion group, the message gets carbon copied to every member on the list. Benefits include instant awareness for subscribers (that is, as soon as they read their e-mail) and a committed readership. The disadvantages are lack of sophisticated formatting and getting people to subscribe in the first place.
- **FTP**—An FTP site is simply a storage area for files others can retrieve. Its benefits are that you can format your magazine as fully as you want (full PostScript, for instance, or Word or WordPerfect for Mac or Windows). The drawbacks? First, they rely on the reader being interested enough and technologically adept enough to get them, and that they have the software to read them. Probably the easiest way to start your publication, but also the least attractive.
- **Gophers**—A Gopher is a structured hierarchy of menus that enables you to easily point and shoot your way through a body of information. Gophers require special (but readily available) software for servers and clients. Gophers also let you search indexes, view pictures, and download files. The benefits of publishing via Gopher are easy and instant accessibility and fairly easy new-subscriber awareness. The major disadvantage is lack of sophisticated formatting, except by connecting the Gopher to an FTP site and letting readers download fully formatted files.
- **World Wide Web**—A WWW page is an HTML document whose creation is explained in some detail later in the chapter. The benefits of WWW distribution are shown in Excursion 13.2. The drawbacks are the hardware requirements for your potential readers (they need a graphics-capable machine and a direct connection to the Internet) and the need for designers to learn HTML programming.

Which one is the right one to carry your message to the world? That depends on what you want to do and what you've got to do it with. Let's look at these vehicles in more detail so you can decide which one meets your needs and resources.

Distributing via Newsgroups

This section covers the following issues:

- Newsgroups help get the word out fast.
- It's fairly easy to get a new group created, especially if it's an `alt.*` group.

- You don't install anything on your home computer, and you can't run one from home.
- Not all sites carry all newsgroups, especially if they're `alt.*` groups.
- If you start a newsgroup, you won't have much control over it.

As I said before, a Usenet newsgroup is like an electronic bathroom wall: It provides an Internet place for people to scribble about things that relate to one topic. For example, in `rec.bicycles.tech` people ask and answer each others' questions about how to fix bicycles. The newsgroup consists of electronic conversations, so it is truly group-authored, making it spontaneous, mercurial, unpredictable, and often irrelevant. You can post many, many articles to a newsgroup, but there is no one author for a newsgroup. If what you want to do is start a conversation/debate/raging argument on a new topic, the newsgroup is for you. If you want to provide and control all the information yourself, a newsgroup is not your vehicle.

Because Usenet newsgroups are popular, well-established sources of information and fun, sites all over the world provide access to them, and people all over the world read (and write to) them. Some newsgroups are limited to specific smaller areas (such as continents or countries), but many are global. So if the information you want to write or read about is strictly local in geography, a newsgroup probably isn't your vehicle either. Consider a discussion list or something else (maybe even a local electronic bulletin board service (BBS) off the Internet—but that's not why you're reading this).

The Big Seven Hierarchies: Where Do I Fit In?

These are the seven standard Usenet hierarchies:

```
Group    Discusses
comp.*   computers, hardware, software, programming
news.*   news, about the Internet itself, about the world, etc.
sci.*    science, hard and soft, physical and social
soc.*    society, for social issues
rec.*    recreation, for sports and leisure interests
talk.*   gossip, discussion, opinions on anything
misc.*   miscellaneous, for anything else
```

That's how the original Usenet people carved up all the information in the world. The big seven are carried by almost every Usenet site, but in order to create a new group in the big seven hierarchy, you have to propose the group, create a charter, go through a review and voting procedure, and wait for results. The process isn't that difficult or unreasonable (depending on what you're proposing), but it still isn't fast enough for those people who abhor any kind of administration or restriction. So some hacker-types created `alt.*` groups such as the following:

```
Group     Discusses
alt.*     whatever you want it to
```

`alt.*` groups cover virtually everything (for example, there's `alt.1d` to `alt.znet.fnet`, and everything in between) and don't have to be approved by anybody in particular. But since they can be really wild, offensive, or just irrelevant, not all Usenet sites carry `alt.*` groups, and most that do still don't carry all of them. Here are a few my site carries, as revealed by a search through my newsreader:

```
alt.angst
alt.appalachian
alt.aquaria
alt.archery
alt.architecture
alt.ascii-art
alt.astrology
alt.atheism
alt.atheism.moderated
alt.autos.antique
alt.backrubs
alt.barney.dinosaur.die.die.die
```

Obviously, the discussions can be about anything.

Starting Your Own Newsgroup

Before you try to create your own newsgroup, make sure one doesn't exist already. The easiest test is to start up your newsreader and list all the newsgroups carried on your host that share a word with the group you have in mind. If you want to start a group called `comp.cyclocomputers` or `alt.bikes.namerica`, try listing all the groups with "cyclo" or "bikes," or "namerica" in their names. If there's already a newsgroup, read it and see if it covers your intended material.

If you don't find one immediately, subscribe to and browse the newsgroups `news.announce.newusers` or `alt.internet.services` for the lists of all the publicly accessible newsgroups in the world, but remember that although these lists are useful, they're never absolutely current.

Once you know you're really creating a unique newsgroup that you think somebody else will actually read and like, then familiarize yourself with newsgroups in general and the creation process in particular. Get a feel for the culture of the Internet and its netiquette. Then look in news.announce.newusers or news.answers for articles with titles such as "How to Become a Usenet Site," "So You Want To Create Your Own Newsgroup," and "Usenet Newsgroup Creation Companion." Read these postings. They are reposted every two weeks or so. They'll tell you important details, procedures, and ways to avoid getting your head flamed off. You can get the FAQ (frequently asked questions) file for Usenet group creation via anonymous FTP to rtfm.mit.edu in the directory /pub/usenet/news.answers/ The files have long names that are fairly descriptive.

These are some files available via anonymous ftp in rftm.mit.edu in the /pub/usenet/news.answers/ directory that give newsgroup creation info:

```
news-announce-intro/part1
news-announce-intro/diff
news-answers/introduction
news-answers/guidelines
news-newusers-intro
```

Briefly, if you're creating a group to be part of the big seven hierarchies, then you have to post a Request for Discussion (RFD) to news.announce.newgroups and also to any other groups or mailing lists related to your proposed group. After discussions, a vote takes place, and if it passes, then your newsgroup will be created. That's why a brand-new, general-interest newsgroup is always easier to start as an alt.* group, which requires no vote.

13

How Will Anyone Know About My New Newsgroup?

Most newsreading programs ask their users if they want to subscribe to any groups that are new to a site. So if your group gets created, it will be passed to other sites around the world. Systems administrators will decide whether to carry your group. If they carry it, each user will hear about it. There are also lists of new groups in places all over the Net.

Distributing via Mailing List

This section covers the following issues:

- Mailing lists appear as e-mail, making them accessible to practically everyone.
- You don't have to install anything on your home computer.

- ☐ You have some control, but not full control, over a moderated mailing list.
- ☐ People have to know how to subscribe to mailing lists (see Day 4).

Mailing lists consist of e-mail messages that automatically get copied to every person on the list. Like newsgroups, they are electronic conversations, so they're not your vehicle if you want to provide or control all the information.

Discussion list topics are generally narrower than newsgroup topics—for example, there are close to a dozen `rec.bicycle.*` newsgroups (`.misc`, `.rides`, `.racing`, `.tech`, `.soc`, `.marketplace`, and so on) that voluminously cover many aspects of cycling, but tandem enthusiasts still maintain their own separate discussion list. As with newsgroups, there are more Listservs than you can shake a stick at...more than you could shake sticks at even if you taught your computer to do the shaking.

Starting Your Own Discussion List

As with newsgroups, check to avoid duplication. It's very difficult to track down all the lists that exist. There are periodic postings of lists of lists, or pointers to lists of lists in the newsgroup `alt.internet.services`; if you're Gophering, another good place to look is `gopher.colorado.edu` in the path Other Gophers By Subject, then List of Lists Resources in the Interest Group Lists item.

To set up a discussion list, all you really need is a list of the e-mail addresses and a way to distribute the mail. If you can write your own mail-processing mechanism, great. But for efficiency and ease, you should get in touch with a site that already does mail processing. Ordinarily, there's no problem getting a site that does Listserv stuff to also distribute things to your list. In some cases, all you have to do is send the message and the list to a Listserv. But you'll need the permission of your provider, and you should use a Listserver that makes sense for your distribution area—don't get some computer in Austria to do the distribution for a list of primarily North American e-mail addresses.

How Will Anyone Know About My New List?

Probably the best thing to do would be to post announcements in newsgroups related to the topic of your list, as well as in `alt.internet.services`, `news.announce`, the net-happenings list (see Day 12 for details on this list), and so on. Besides that, word of mouth still works wonders; ask people to forward their e-mail to others they know.

Distributing via Gopher

This section covers the following issues:

- Creating your own Gopher isn't an option unless you've got disk space on computers that are part of the Internet, stay on all the time, and allow public access.
- Setting up a Gopher requires a fair bit of nearly hacker-level configuration and installation. But if you're a nearly hacker-level Internet entity or have a really good friend who does this sort of thing regularly, you're set. You can also usually latch on to the existing Gopher at your local site.
- You need Gopher server software, easily available by anonymous FTP from the University of Minnesota. If you're providing a free service, the software is free. Otherwise, you pay a licensing fee. Again, check your local site, which probably already has the software you need (but licensing may still be an issue).
- You design a strictly hierarchical tree (such as a directory and files), also throwing in things such as indexes and links to other Gophers (menu trees) in other parts of Gopherspace.
- Gophers are incredibly easy to use, and they're the most popular Internet software out there.

Gopher Examples

If you remember, our publication is going to be about bicycling. It was with great satisfaction, therefore, that I found the following Gopher menu at `draco.acs.uci.edu:1071`. While we don't want extensive competition, we want to know that someone out there is also interested in biking. But try not to use this Gopher during Pacific Time working hours—it's somebody's desktop machine.

```
                Internet Gopher Information Client v1.03

                    Root gopher server: draco.acs.uci.edu

      1.  About the Rec.Bicycles FTP archives.
      2.  Bicycle term glossary (Alan Bloom).
      3.  Bulding a box to ship a tandem (Arnie Berger).
      4.  Buying an entry-level MTB (Joakim Karlsson).
      5.  Cameras to take on a tour (Vivian Aldridge).
      6.  Collection of articles on bicycle lights (Tom Reingold).
      7.  Collection of articles on bicycle trailers.
      8.  Collection of articles on bike painting (Sam Henry).
```

```
9.  Collection of more articles on bicycle lights.
10. Copy of the California Vehicle Code sections pertaining to bicycl/
11. Current FAQ (one complete file).
12. Cycle Sense for Motorists  (Larry Watanabe).
13. FAQ split apart into individual articles/
14. GIFs and other pictures/
15. ..Bill Bushnell).
16. Hypercard stack riding diary (Phil Etheridge).
17. Hypercard stack riding diary documentation (Phil Etheridge).
18. Hypercard stack riding diary readme (Phil Etheridge).
```

As with all Gophers, if the menu item ends in a slash (for example, item 13 in this example), it links to another directory, like this:

```
                Internet Gopher Information Client v1.03

                   FAQ split apart into individual articles

   1.  About the Rec.Bicycles FAQ.
   2.  Index.
   3.  Administrivia/
   4.  Marketplace/
   5.  Misc/
   6.  Racing/
   7.  Rides/
   8.  Social/
   9.  Tech/
```

If it ends in a period (for example, #2 in the main Gopher preceding, Bicycle term glossary (Alan Bloom)), it's probably a file, like this:

```
                           BICYCLE TERMS:
To keep this list to a manageable size, terms that are in everyday use, such as
tire, such as Allen wrenches and wire cutters are commonly found at your local
hardware store so are left off the list, but bicycle-specific tools like spoke
wrenches and truing stands are included. Similarly, self-explanatory terms like
"water bottle" and "brake cable" are left out, Record are not included.

Thanks to the following helpful souls who responded to my request for
corrections, comments and additions: John Forester, Harry Phinney, Brian Tomlin,
Carlos Martin, Andy (ajh), Mark Dionne, Pamela Blalock, Michael Weaver, David
Wittenberg, and Mark ? (who taught me how to spell "triathlon".) However don't
blame those folks if something isn't right — I am responsible for any remaining
errors! - Alan Bloom
```

```
ADJUSTABLE CUP: The left bearing in the bottom bracket. It screws in and out to
adjust bearing free play. See FIXED CUP.
—More—(3%)[Press space to continue, Q to quit]
```

Gopher Licensing

The Gopher programs are free to people who want them for educational and nonprofit purposes. But if you want to set up a service people have to pay for, you'll have to pay a licensing fee to the University of Minnesota. You can (and should) read more about the (quite fair and reasonable) Gopher licensing policy—you'll find it in the same place as the Gopher program files, as well as in newsgroups such as `comp.infosystems.gopher`, and `alt.gopher`.

Getting What You Need

It's up to you to get the software appropriate to your computer. Remember that you must also figure out how to let other people actually get access to your Gopher. If you set up a Gopher server on you machine at home, no one will be able to use it unless your modem is on and taking up telephone line time. That could be expensive, it will certainly be slow, and it will usually mean only one customer at a time.

But there are other options. If you're at a university, you can probably find some computer with disk space that is on all the time and connected to the Internet. If you don't have access to a university or institutional computers, see if there's a freenet in your area that will allow you to set up a Gopher server. Look and post in the `alt.internet.services` newsgroup to find out more about local freenets. If all else fails, you can cough up the cash and rent disk space and processing time from a commercial provider.

Creating Your Own Gopher

The structure and content of information is completely left to the creator of the particular Gopher (that would be you). The Gopher itself is just the list of directories and files in a particular directory on the hard disk; what the Gopher software does is sort these items either alphabetically or according to specific instructions you provide. Once the Gopher software points to your directory, it's up to you to construct and maintain the Gopher. Essentially, you just put the files in the appropriate directory, or you give Gopher instructions on where to find them. Talk to your systems administrator about how to write and store the files, or download Gopher FAQ files from any one of dozens of machines on the Net.

Gophers are darn nifty and useful. Their strengths are interface consistency, ease of use, and ability to organize information into a tight structure. Of course, if you don't follow any logical plan for your menus, users won't find your stuff.

The Drawback of Gophers: Browsing Versus Reading

Gophers are for browsing and finding, not for reading, and as a magazine producer you want people to read your stuff. If your users know what you want and what they want is big, they can save a lot of online time and money by downloading it. That is, transferring the information as a large package from its remote location to a local one. In effect, by downloading you get the information sent to you at bulk rates. Reading something big via Gopher is a bit like standing with the refrigerator door open, only worse. If you're paying for time on the computer (and who isn't?) it costs you money. It also adds to the network traffic.

To address this problem, Gophers let you mail files to yourself or download them to your computer. This means you can browse, find information in a particular file, and have it sent to your mail reader. That's handy, but it doesn't work well for a magazine, because a magazine may have 10 or 20 or 794 articles in it; if they're all separate files (separate Gopher menu items), you'll have to go into each one individually and mail or download each in turn. That's tedious.

So while providing Gopher access to your info is a good thing, you should also allow other kinds of access (for example, FTP, newsgroup, Listserv, WWW), depending on the size, form, and nature of it. A magazine, especially one with graphics files in it, would probably work best if you put it somewhere other people could FTP it, or read it over the Web. You can, of course, set up a Gopher to allow FTP access.

Distributing via the World Wide Web

by David Randall

The World Wide Web offers the most visually appealing method of distributing a magazine, primarily because you can make a Web page look like a paper-based publication. You can also add sound and video to produce a series of multimedia links, and through well-designed hypertext links you can enable your readers to browse effectively and in whatever direction they wish. The Web also makes advertising a very real possibility, although it remains to be seen if people will actually read advertising on a Web page (of course, people watch infomercials on TV when they could easily turn to another channel; as long as the ad is well designed, there's no reason it won't work here).

The problems with publishing on the Web are that not everyone has access to Mosaic or Cello, and writing Web pages takes time and skill. There's nothing I can do about the first problem, but below are some first steps towards solving the second. Good luck on creating your first HTML pages.

WWW Magazine Examples

See Excursion 13.2 for examples of magazines published on the World Wide Web.

What You Need

To create and distribute a Web page, you need the following:

- A computer with 24-hour dedicated connection to the Internet, on which your files can reside
- WWW server software on the computer
- A knowledge of Hypertext Markup Language (HTML)—see the following section
- An HTML editor, macro, or file converter (not strictly necessary, but extremely useful)

Writing a Basic World Wide Web Page

You've seen the World Wide Web in action throughout this book. It's appealing for a number of reasons, and despite its equipment requirements, it'll almost certainly be the leading Internet interface of the next few years.

Whereas the Web is in essence just another way to access files, HyperText Markup Language (HTML) allows creation of personalized "pages," into which graphics can be inserted, links to other HTML, FTP and Gopher sites can be embedded, and much more. See Day 7 for other information about HTML and creating Web pages.

Note: The purpose of this part of the chapter is not to give a history of the Web or HTML, but show the easiest way to create your own magazine or business and/or personal home page. This is not in any way an exhaustive tutorial, but when finished reading, you'll know some basics of the hypertext markup language and how to find all the documentation pertaining to it one could ever want.

Sources of HTML Information

There are many sources of information about HTML, one of them being within the NCSA Mosaic home page site (`http://www.ncsa.uiuc.edu`). A Beginner's Guide to

HTML (`http://www.ncsa.uiuc.edu/demoweb/html-primer.html`) goes through most of the information pertaining to HTML creation, right from the title to a list of special characters (mostly non-English letters and symbols). Downloading this document as a text file to an editor is a good idea, so you don't have to log in every time another mental refresher is needed. Another excellent HTML information source is the What is Hypertext page at `http://info.cern.ch/hypertext/WWW/WhatIs.html`. Still another recent addition to the HTML tutorial line is *PC Week*'s Crash course on writing documents for the Web, found at `http://www.pcweek.ziff.com/~eamonn/crash_course.html`.

Still another excellent basic guide to HTML is within the help system of Cornell's Windows-based Cello WWW browser. Fire up Cello (you don't have to be connected to the Net at the time) and click the Help menu, then the Help option within it.

After scrolling through this Help document a bit, you'll come across the heading "HTML, miscellaneous features, and other useful information." Clicking Hypertext Markup Language (HTML) pulls up a document explaining the basis of HTML usage, as shown in Figure 13.15.

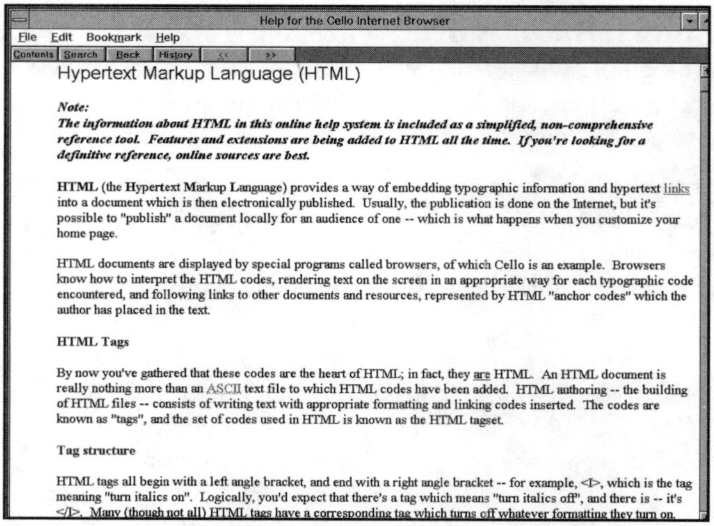

Figure 13.15. *The Cello HTML help screen.*

A good plan is to go through the entire document, clicking and reading every linked heading; although most of the information will not be remembered, this exercise will produce the handy "I think I know where I've seen that" ability. The people at Cornell are clear that there's much more and probably better information on the Net itself, which is an excellent point, considering its rapid change and growth.

Starting Your Own Home Page

To start your own home page, go into Cello or Mosaic and download a relatively simple World Wide Web page—one without a lot of live links—to your hard drive. Then load it into any word processor or editor as a text file.

> **Tip:** HTML files are simply ASCII files with formatting codes enclosed in arrow brackets (<>). You don't need special software to read or edit them, although you need a WWW browser (Mosaic, Cello, or Lynx, for example) to process them as hypertext pages.

Now all the commands and special keystroke sequences are revealed. Having read a bit about HTML creation already, either on the Net or in Cello's help system, you'll recognize much of what looked really confusing before. Now you can just go and change stuff, within the parameters of the commands.

As an example, Figure 13.16 shows the Trinity College home page as it appears on the Web through the Cello browser.

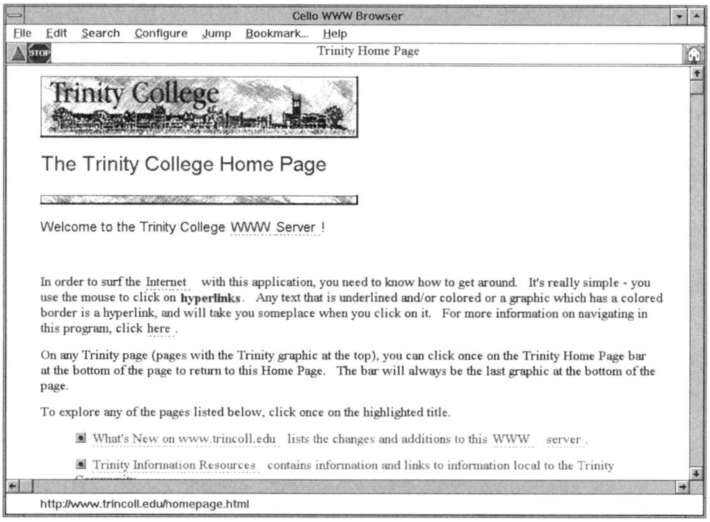

Figure 13.16. *Trinity College home page.*

Downloading the page, and omitting the graphic, we find what the first line of this page actually looks like in the HTML file:

```
<H1> The Trinity College Home Page </H1>
```

As you read in the guides, this is a level one heading, meaning basically that it's in the biggest typeface. Now, by simply overwriting the original text with your own text, change this to the following:

```
<TITLE>MY HOME PAGE</TITLE>
<H1>MY HOME PAGE!</H1>
<H2>Welcome to My First Way Cool HomePage</H2>
```

The <title> line will not show in the HTML document, but will show instead as the HTML's title in the WWW browser's title line. The entire new page, when loaded into Cello, looks like Figure 13.17.

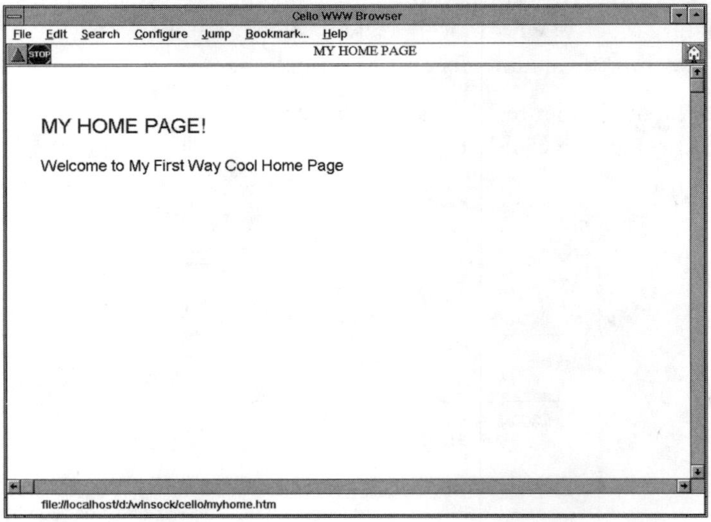

Figure 13.17. *Newly created home page.*

This, frighteningly enough, is the basis of HTML; there is much greater complexity in the commands, but here is the whole concept. Unfortunately, much greater knowledge and experience is needed to make everything actually work.

Clearly, perfecting HTML will take some time, but notice that the page is simply ASCII text with appropriate codes; simple pages take very little time to create.

Adding a Graphic

The `<src img>` lines load graphics files into the document. You can retrieve them from anywhere on the Net with an appropriate link (and as long as you have access to that directory), but usually you'll want them on your local machine. This can be a little confusing, though (at least it was for me), but reading the HTML document in Cello clears everything up.

```
..............................................................
File/FTP resource addresses

The file:// scheme is used for two purposes: to specify files which are
accessible via a local system such as your own workstation or a DOS LAN, and to
specify files which are remotely available via FTP.

For files on your machine, or otherwise accessible via DOS (say, on a Novell
LAN):

       file://localhost/c:/afull/pathto/thefile.htm

where file://localhost is mandatory and indicates that the file is on a local
system for which Net access is not necessary, and c: is the (optional) drive
designator of the DOS drive, and afull/pathto/thefile.htm is a full path to the
DOS file, with slashes reversed a la UNIX. Note that you can also use relative
pathnames:

cerntest.htm would be the file CERNTEST.HTM in the same directory as the current
document.

../oneabove.htm would be a file in the parent directory of the one containing
the current document.

For files on a remote computer:

       file://remote.host.dom/apath/toa/fileor/directory

In this case the file:// scheme is interpreted as meaning "to be fetched by
FTP". The remote computer is remote.host.dom; the remainder of the string is a
path to either a directory or a
file. Note that it is not necessary to end with a slash for directories, as
Cello checks this, shall we say, empirically.
..............................................................
```

13

I've highlighted `where file://localhost is mandatory`, because the `localhost` designation stumped me for a good number of hours one day. Here's an example of a local `<src img>` file that pulls an image from my hard drive:

```
<IMG SRC=file://localhost/e:/cim/wincim/wsmart04..gif>
```

Now add the file to the page we began creating previously. The HTML source code now looks like this:

```
<title> MY HOME PAGE</title>
<H1> MY HOME PAGE! </H1>
<H2>Welcome to My First Way Cool Home Page </H2>
<IMG SRC=file://localhost/e:/cim/wincim/wsmart04.gif>
```

To see what this looks like, fire up a WWW browser (I'm using Mosaic for this example) without going online. In the File menu choose Open Local File, and find your HTML page. Figure 13.18 displays the result.

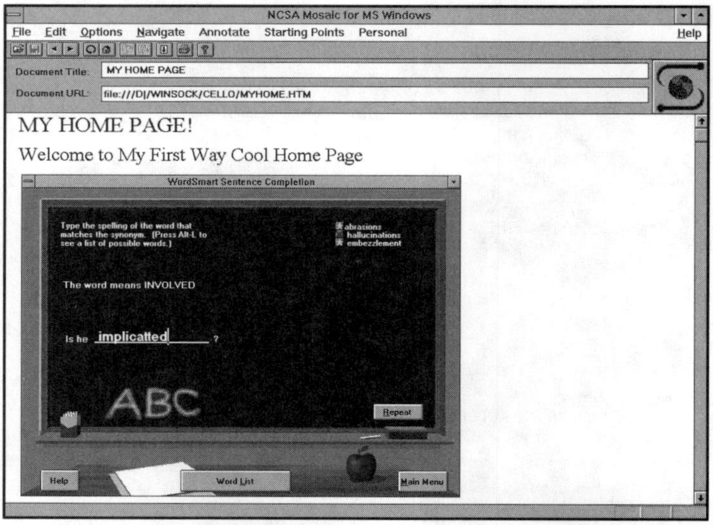

Figure 13.18. *A home page with graphic added.*

There's lots more, obviously, but this gives you an idea. As far as links to remote computers are concerned, copy one from your downloaded source code and watch it work. Then go out and find the ones you want.

When you are experienced enough at page creation, a WWW newsletter or magazine can be put online. This part is mostly time-consuming, and there are two ways of doing it. The magazine must be put in an accessible site so that people can get at it. If you wish to use your own computer as a host, be prepared to dedicate your machine to the site, as it'll have to be on 100 percent of the time.

The way to do it most conveniently is to ask your access provider, university, or other server site to set up a directory where you can keep your HTML page(s). Most sites with full high-speed access shut down only for repairs and uploading, so people will always be able to access your page's address.

Summary

Day 13 has examined several possibilities for publishing your own Internet-based magazine. Included are considerations for publishing the magazine via newsgroup, mailing list, Gopher, or the World Wide Web. This chapter has looked at the benefits and drawbacks of each, from the standpoint of reader access and control over the material. It has also looked at the basics of writing HTML pages for World Wide Web publication, because this is becoming the preferred method for magazine publication.

Task Review

On Day 13, you have:

- Examined a wide range of magazines currently on the Internet.
- Learned the benefits and drawbacks of publishing your magazine as a newsgroup, a mailing list, a Gopher, and a Web page.
- Learned to create a World Wide Web page via HTML.

Q&A

Q Do people really read magazines on-screen?

A Increasingly, yes. Although some people swear up and down that they hate reading on-screen, Internet users are becoming much more used to it. Reading a magazine on-screen is thoroughly uncomfortable, perhaps even impossible, if you don't have a good monitor with strong resolution. That's why the World Wide Web, used with a good Mac, Windows, or X Window monitor, is far and away the reading medium of choice. I hear arguments all the time, even from these users, however, that they hate actually reading (rather than just browsing) on-screen, but as hypermedia publications increase in importance, there won't be much real choice. I've reached the stage where I prefer doing some kinds of reading on-screen and other kinds on paper, and I'm pretty sure I'm not unusual in that regard.

Reading from the screen is usually more like skimming than reading (we expect a greater speed, I think), so be sure to design your publications either to make that possible, or to offer a very good reason for people to read more slowly.

Q Print magazines usually rely on advertising to make ends meet. Will Internet magazines have to do the same?

A Probably, and we'll see advertising happening soon. But it'll be different from that in print media, because there's no way people will click a Pepsi or GM ad just to read it (nobody looks for ads in magazines, they just get seen in the process of turning pages). So advertisers and magazine designers will have to be inventive about how to make their ads work. There really isn't a model for it in any medium.

Here's another point: It may well be that subscriptions—as soon as they're put into place—will be more capable of carrying the entire cost of an Internet magazine, which couldn't possibly happen with a print version. Remember that paper and printing costs, as well as distribution costs, are minimized on the Net. As long as magazines can actually get people to subscribe (there's a strong lingering notion that everything on the Net should be free), covering costs through subscriptions shouldn't be that much of a problem, especially for a special-interest publication.

WEEK 2

14

Beam Us All Up, Scotty: Building an Entertainment Archive

It's Day 14, and that means it's time for a break. Not a break from the Internet, of course. Instead, Day 14 will take a look at some of the entertainment resources on the Net, an area that is still quite small but certainly growing. The Internet can be entertaining on its own, but when combined with more conventional forms of entertainment, it promises a considerable amount of excitement. Day 14 offers an introduction.

On Day 14, you will:

- ☐ Find newsgroups and mailing lists about entertainment issues.
- ☐ Find newsgroups dealing with *Star Trek* issues.
- ☐ Explore Gophers and FTP sites for *Star Trek* files.
- ☐ Examine entertainment issues on the World Wide Web.

The Global Entertainer

The Internet has only recently become a medium open to any kind of formalized entertainment—that is, entertainment as produced by entertainment companies. As a result, very little of this type of material is currently available, although it should begin to grow spectacularly. In many ways, of course, the Internet is the basis of the information superhighway, which, according to the cable companies and the Hollywood moguls, will become the central entertainment focus for the future.

For now, though, entertainment on the Internet consists primarily of specialized archives. You can find them scattered at various locations, and by far the best way of locating them is to join and keep a watch on newsgroups. Newsgroups exist for such entertainment items as Madonna, R.E.M., *Beverly Hills 90210, Melrose Place*, and just about any other popular (or cult) show. There's a Gopher for bands such as the Beatles, the Grateful Dead, and Rush, and surely it won't be long before a Nirvana site emerges to preserve the memory of Kurt Cobain and the Seattle scene.

As far as interactive entertainment goes, there isn't much beyond the MUDs and MUD-like games featured in Day 5. You can get the latest list of top-rated TV shows, but you still can't vote for your favorite show this way. But all this is coming, and probably sooner than we might think. If there's one thing we can be sure of, it's this: Every strong new medium ever introduced has, especially in the United States, become an entertainment medium sometimes first and foremost. There's no reason to suspect that the Internet will be any different.

For now, though, the archives are what we have, and by combining them you can create a substantial archive of your own material. On Day 14, the material of choice will deal with that perennial entertainment product, the science-fiction series *Star Trek*.

About the Contributor

Christa Ptatschek is a Master's student at the University of Waterloo, Canada. Like many university students—and lots of other people, for that matter—she's followed *Star Trek* in its several incarnations more or less ever since her eyes first opened. She figured that the Internet must be jammed with Trekkies—oops, Trekkers—so she decided an interesting project would be to collect *Star Trek*-related material. The following are the results of her search.

Building a *Star Trek* Archive

by Christa Ptatschek

It was Sunday morning (okay, afternoon), and time for a break. I'd just finished watching a tape of *Star Trek: The Next Generation* episodes I'd borrowed from a friend. The Internet, as you already know, is a place of vast resources, not only for the purposes of education and scientific advancement, but also for, dare we say it, entertainment. Knowing that many computer users are also science-fiction fans, today seemed a good day to see if I could use Internet resources to build a sci-fi archive, concentrating on *Star Trek* items.

Before I actually began looking for items on the Internet, I set up a directory structure on my PC to organize the archive. Originally, it looked like this:

```
STARTREK
TOS       TNG          DS9         PICTURE      STORIES     INFO       MISC
(the old  (the next   (deep space  (pictures of (stories by (news about (interesting
series)   generation) nine)         cast, etc.)  fans)        the show)  items)
```

I created these seven directories under DOS, because most of the information coming from the Internet, I assumed, would be IBM PC-compatible. As well, the text files would be in ASCII format, and I could combine or format them more easily if they were separated by subject matter.

Tip: If you're collecting archives directly onto your PC or Mac, it's a good idea to set up the directories or folders as quickly as you can. By default, each different program (your World Wide Web client, your newsgroup reader, your FTP program, and so on) will download into its own location; if you retrieve any number of files, you'll quickly lose track of where they are. Get a sense of what's out there, then prepare locations on your hard drive for them to reside.

Excursion 14.1. Searching for *Star Trek* Newsgroups

I began with the newsgroups (always a popular choice). I typed **`rn`** at my prompt, and then, after getting into the news reader program, I typed **`l trek`**. This command means "list all of the newsgroups that have the string `trek` in their names." Your particular news program may be capable of searching for only one term at a time. The news reader gave me a list that looked like this:

```
Completely unsubscribed newsgroups:
alt.games.xtrek
alt.startrek.creative
aus.sf.star-trek
de.rec.sf.startrek
rec.arts.startrek
rec.arts.startrek.current
rec.arts.startrek.fandom
rec.arts.startrek.info
rec.arts.startrek.misc
rec.arts.startrek.reviews
rec.arts.startrek.tech
rec.games.netrek
```

In general, these newsgroups are a forum for people to talk about the shows generally, focus on various aspects of the Trek universe, or argue over specific points from episodes, movies, books, or comics. Sometimes the discussions are serious, sometimes they're detailed or esoteric, but they're always current.

Note: What is really incredible about the newsgroups is just how seriously people take things. `Rec.arts.startrek.tech`, for instance, is filled with highly-educated people trying to apply real-world science to fictional concepts. It's really fascinating to look in on these discussions, because they're often dealing with very new scientific concepts and trying to explain them to other people who have no science background. Lurking on a group like this can result in a varied (and hopelessly incomplete) scientific education.

The following is what I found in a couple afternoons of newsgroup skimming.

Excursion 14.2. Newsgroup *alt.games.xtrek*

Absolutely nothing. Really. Nothing had been posted to this group for a while. It could just be that it's hit a lull, but I have no idea what's in this group.

Excursion 14.3. Newsgroup *alt.startrek.creative*

This group contains stories of all sorts, both newly-written and archived pieces. It's also a good place to get FTP sites, because a number of the headers mention which site the story came from. There are some interesting questions being asked in this group, mainly concerning character motivation or specific details about some issue, like Vulcan or Ferengi rituals or ship construction. I also found some interesting parodies in this group, and if you like parodies of your favorite show (some people adamantly do not), I highly recommend subscribing to this group to read them.

Excursion 14.4. Newsgroup *aus.sf.star-trek*

This group is pretty eclectic. It's based in Australia, and from the articles, they have an awful time watching the episodes because they aren't shown regularly there. I guess the Australian TV stations don't take *Star Trek* seriously. I can't imagine why. The posts on this group tended to center around the episodes, and occasionally they mentioned some pretty funny bloopers. (No, I'm not going to spoil your fun!)

Excursion 14.5. Newsgroup *de.rec.sf.startrek*

This group, based in Germany, is truly eclectic. It's also written entirely in German. Actually, for a crash course on conversational written German, it's excellent! I'm adequately fluent in German, so I found this group pretty interesting, but if you aren't, you can probably skip it.

Excursion 14.6. Newsgroup *rec.arts.startrek*

This group is filled with a wide variety of questions. Often they're cross-posted to other groups. There were articles there about the Ferengi Rules of Acquisition as well as questions about what stations carry *Star Trek* in Finland. This group is a good general-information source.

Excursion 14.7. Newsgroup *rec.arts.startrek.current*

This group is different. The first article I read discussed proper responses to the "Get a life" insult. There were discussions about gender issues regarding casting, whether or not new movies were being planned, the flamewar between *Star Trek* and *Star Wars* fans, the Troi/Worf relationship, and, perhaps most importantly, information on other newsgroups, organizations, conferences, and so on. This group is probably most concerned about what's happening now. There is very little discussion about The Old Series.

Excursion 14.8. Newsgroup *rec.arts.startrek.fandom*

This group is for the true-blue die-hard fans out there. Posts centered on the actors' birthdays, the actors' heights, and generally every personal detail of every actors' lives. Movie showings, conventions with guest actors, and other activities that some of the actors are involved in were fiercely debated. There was also a raging argument over the quality of Shatner's Tekwar books.

Excursion 14.9. Newsgroup *rec.arts.startrek.info*

This is a pretty formal group. It contains the Paramount Press Releases and Air Schedules, mentions fairly academic books and articles that might interest *Star Trek* fans, and also provided this list of *Star Trek* sources. Only the first part of the list is included here.

> **Note:** This list is subtitled "The final release" because its compiler, as stated in an introductory note, needed to move on to less time-consuming pursuits. This is something to expect from mailing lists. All the work is voluntary, so we shouldn't expect it to be there for all time. Life happens.

```
                    List of Lists Archive Site Info
                        (Updated April 4, 1993)

The final release of the List of Lists is April, 1994.
-=-=-=-=-=-=-=-=-=-=-=-=-=-=-=-=-=-=-=-=-=-=-=-=-=-=-=-=-=-=-=-=-=-=-=-=-=-=-=-
                          Anonymous FTP Info. . .

ftp
~~~
netcom.com [Primary LoL Distribution Site]
-=========-
1. ftp netcom.com
2. Type "anonymous" as your name.
3. Type in your login as password.
4. Type "binary" for correct transfers. (VERY IMPORTANT)
5. cd pub/mholtz
6. get README for more info!

Note: All .Z files were compressed using UNIX's compress program.

cisco.com
-========-
A Quantum Leap List of Lists is kept in /ql-archive, along with lots of other
Quantum Leap material. The filename is ql_list_mmyy.Z.

cs.columbia.edu [Mirror of netcom.com directory
-==============-
1. ftp cs.columbia.edu
2. Type "anonymous" as your name.
3. Type in your login as password.
4. Type "binary" for correct transfers.
5. cd archives/STARTREK/List_Of_Lists
6. get README for more info.

Note: All .gz file were compressed using GNU ZIP.
```

Excursion 14.10. Newsgroup *rec.arts.startrek.misc*

This group is truly miscellaneous. A discussion of Data's use of contractions came right after an ad for a *Star Trek* auction, which was sandwiched between posts about the actors' other roles. There were also requests for GIFs (this appears to be the best way to get them—ask!) and sound files, questions about Vulcan attire and McCoy's middle name (so far he just has the initial H, although someone did suggest Horatio…). There are also posts about new (and old) FTP sites. All in all, this group is definitely varied.

Excursion 14.11. Newsgroup *rec.arts.startrek.tech*

This group is highly scientific. The discussions dealt with descriptions of ships, their purposes, their structural designs, why the hull of the *Enterprise* was round, that kind of stuff. They also talked about the various types of weapons, the lack of toilets on the *Enterprise* and other ships (apparently that lack is corrected in the starship plans), what the different classes of ships are and why they exist, and then, just for fun I guess, they threw in some calculus questions.

Here's a sample discussion from this newsgroup. Notice how the thread builds with each response in each message.

> **Note:** The following example demonstrates how mailers show the order of responses in a discussion "thread." The arrows (and colon in the first case) to the left of the text lines indicate this order: the number of prefix characters increases as the response gets older. The most recent response is always the one with no prefix characters at all. In the example following, the order is strictly oldest to newest.

> **Note:** The content of the messages following is exactly as taken from the newsgroup, except for names, which have been changed, and e-mail and real addresses, which we've edited or marked out. The same holds for all examples in this chapter. If you want to reach these people, join the group.

Message 1:

```
|> >> : This is a misunderstanding of the way special relativity works. Get
|> >> : any elementary text on special relativity, and this point will be made
|> >> : clear.
|> >>
|> >> ** I was quoting Professor xxxxxxxxx, Professor of xxxxxxxxxxx xxx
|> >> xxxxxxxxxxx Astrophysics at the xxxx Institute xxxxxxxxxxxxxx
|> >> xxxxxxxxxxxxxxxxxxxxxxxx. I think his credentials qualify him to
|> >> talk about special relativity.
|> >
|> > Regardless, I still say that he is mistaken. Special relativity very
|> > _explicitly_ forbids faster-than-light travel of particles which could
|> > conceivably carry information (that means they could interact with
|> > tardons) because of causality violation.
|> >
|> > Also, if the Universe is closed, then his answer is clearly
|> > nonsensical even if faster-than-light travel is okay. Tachyons can
|> > travel arbitrarily close to infinite speed as you like, and in fact in
```

```
|> > some frames of reference, they will be transcendant -- that is,
|> > everywhere along a great circle of the Universe at once. With
|> > tachyons, they can easily loop around the Universe before the Big
|> > Crunch and interact with matter.
|> >
|> I think you're missing something -- you assume that special relativity is
|> CORRECT, which is not necessarily the case. Everyone thought non-relativistic
|> mechanics was correct until it was found not to work at extremes, so how can
|> you exclude the possibility that, in a few hundred years' time, relativity will
|> not be found to fail at extremes as well? If this happens, what you say about
|> information not travelling at >c may be wrong. We just don't know.
|>

Not only this, but relativity itself (General) is based on an assumtion. It is
assumed that the laws of physics, including the speed of electromagnetic waves,
are constant. This means that if you were at .9 c and shone a light ahead of
you, it would travel c, not 1.9c. If these two assumtions are true (c and laws
of physics constant) Relativity would be true. But in order to explain some of
the tricks light does, they had to use time dilation and length contraction.
This means of explaining light's antics is no more valid than the laws of
physics changing (Not that either are not valid, just that they could have the
same validity)
```

A little later, and on a slightly different topic:

```
Relativity tells us that FTL travel will give violations of causality.
This is an unarguable statement. If one then assumes that causality
cannot be violated, then FTL travel is impossible (and I for one am
inclined to believe just that). However, there are physicists who
theorize possibilities where causality does not strictly hold.
Wormholes, for example, have problems with causality; and yet, the
possibility that they exist is considered by some theoretical
physicists.

So, you see, saying that "Relativity strictly implies that FTL travel
is impossible" is not quite correct. What one should say is that
Relativity along with the principle of causality together imply that
FTL travel is impossible. It is a simple difference, but it makes the
statement precise.
BTW. StarTrek communities is definitely NOT the place for
meritable scientific discussions.
```

Well, this last sentence seemed to say it all. Still, I was impressed by the level of this discussion. Of course, because I have no background in faster-than-light travel or supernovas….

Excursion 14.12. Newsgroup *rec.games.netrek*

Netrek is an interactive *Star Trek* game that can be played on networked systems, including the Internet itself. That's what this group is about: playing the game. There are challenges, questions, comments, and other stuff (Hey, I don't play—I'm already addicted to enough time-consuming activities!) concerning the game. If you want to find out about it, this group looks like the place.

> **Warning:** We've excluded the address for Netrek, for two reasons. First, it is truly addictive. Second, it's being removed from servers in a number of places because of the impact on resources. The addicted don't have much regard for things like logging on in off-hours.

Excursion 14.13. Searching for *Star Trek* Material Through Gopher

The next part of my archive search took me through Gopher. I began with the Gopher server at my local university, expanding into other Gophers as I located them. That's the nature of Gopher browsing.

Having explored the Internet before, I decided to begin with search types that I thought would probably not get me too far, and work up to the more successful searches later.

> **Tip:** By searching from least likely to most likely, you are less likely to ignore possibilities. If you're successful to begin with, there's a good chance you won't bother with the other search tools. As a result, you might easily miss something important.

My first search involved the Wide Area Information Servers, or WAIS. I moved through the Gopher and entered the Subject Sorted WAIS Databases from Sweden area (available from many Gophers, but try `gopher.physics.utoronto.ca` in the path Other Gopher and Information Servers, then WAIS Based Information), then scanned through their alphabetical subject listings, looking for anything science-fiction related. I found a lot of science-related information, but nothing at all fictional.

I also tried some keyword searching using `star`, `trek`, and `sf`. I found a grand total of nothing. WAIS seems (to me at least) to be eclectic and academic-oriented. Sometimes there's a lot of information on a subject, sometimes there's nothing, and you're never sure which it will be. After poking around the WAIS for a while, I gave it up. There were other Internet options to explore.

Next I turned to Veronica, and here I was wildly successful. I selected the Veronica option in my Gopher (again, Veronica searches are available on many Gophers). In the search box, I typed the specification **`star AND trek`** (that is, I told Veronica to find the two words together). I also selected a directory search only, to keep the list limited.

Tip: Searching for directory names in Veronica helps you avoid receiving things like saved news postings and other files that are duplicates of articles in the directories. It's usually best to begin this way.

I ended up with 12 screens of information, giving me a total of about 200 directories to look at immediately. When I scanned to the end of the 12th page, I found that the last entry read:

```
** There are 1810 more items matching the query available.
```

That's a lot of directories to look through. But somebody had to do it....

Most of the resulting directory names were simply some version of *Star Trek.* As a matter of fact, I'd often find 10 or 20 directories in a row, all called `star trek` or `Star_trek`. My best advice is to run the same Veronica search (remember the `AND` between `star` and `trek`), and go from there.

Excursion 14.14. Results of the Veronica Search

One of the first directories I looked at was an excellent collection of reviews that I immediately captured, at `chop.isca.uiowa.edu`. The directory was divided into The Old Series (TOS) and The Next Generation (TNG), which included Deep Space Nine (DS9). Then each of these directories was divided into seasons and each season was divided into episodes. A file for each episode gave a plot and critical review, identified quotes, examined the music and special effects, and speculated about how the episode was influenced by and would influence other episodes. Each episode also received a numerical ranking. (Whew! I'd hate to have to do all that work! You've got to admire some people's dedication.)

The reviews were pretty amazing. They were often insightful, examined both the personalities and motivations of the characters, and also stepped back to examine how major events or revelations would affect future episodes (in terms of opening up or limiting plots) and the Paramount marketing strategies. The reviewers cared about their subject matter but weren't blind to its commercialism. The reviews were all very different, but often contained some fascinating insights.

I then started looking at some of the story directories (see the Gopher at `world.std.com`, through the path FTP, then The World's Anonymous FTP Archive, then OBI, and finally into Star Trek Stories), and it's pretty obvious that *Star Trek* fans are an incredibly prolific bunch. I spent a lot of time reading stories, both good and bad, and many of them were highly insightful. Often the writers had opinions about the characters that didn't match my own. For instance, I still see Troi as a useless floozy most of the time (I'm sorry, I just don't see the use of a character who says things like "I sense that they are confused" when, lo and behold, the aliens (latex-headed beings) are running around in circles, or "I can't sense anything" when it would be really useful if she could), but numerous authors focused on that character as the basis of their stories. Tastes differ.

Generally, the stories focused on one or two characters, and, if the author was half-way serious, tended to get highly involved with the personalities of those characters. Often the situations within the stories led to lots of character growth and development, none of which, unfortunately, actually shows up in the episodes or movies.

Excursion 14.15. Exploring the Parodies

Also in the world.std.com FTP archives was a listing of the many *Star Trek* parodies available. As the retrieved item below demonstrates, there are several such sources, and a huge number of parodies waiting to be accessed. This is only a tiny portion of the full listing.

```
There is a collection of Star Trek parodies is available via
anonymous ftp from math.princeton.edu in the directory pub/rjc/st.
Consult the file "p.files" for an index of the contents. Note
that all files in that directory have been compressed so you have
to type the command "image" in "ftp" before doing a "get".

People who can't ftp can obtain the files via email. Type this to your
unix-like machine

     echo send filename ¦ mail -s Command rjc@math.princeton.edu

replacing "filename" with the actual name of the file you want.
Since mail servers are frowned upon by most system administrators,
I ask that you use ftp if at all possible, and that if you have
to use the mail server, to limit yourself to three requests total.
```

```
The following is the file "p.files":
----------------------------------------------------------------------
File      Last Changed   Title(s)  Author(s)

p.files   (see above)    (this file)
p.addrs   1990 09 18     (email addresses)

p.001     1989 09 24     Internet Star Trek
               - Jeff Okamoto
p.002     1989 09 24     Star Trek: The Next Generation
               Episode XIX: Peace Restored
               - Seth Meyer
p.003     1989 09 24     Star Trek: The Next Generation
               Episode XX: Share Minds but Kill the Kid
               - Seth Meyer
p.004     1989 09 24     Star Trek: The Next Generation
               Episode XXI: Who's The Better Crew?
               - Seth Meyer
p.005     1989 09 24     Star Trek: The Next Generation
               Episode XIII: Willi
               - Leonard Bottleman
```

Often the parodies require an almost-perfect recall of the original scene, whether it is from a movie or TV episode. I like *Star Trek*, but I do need brain cells to do other things (like get through school), so I understood some of the parodies, completely missed others (don't feel bad if you don't get all the jokes—50 percent is an excellent score!), and only vaguely understood the rest.

Excursion 14.16. More *Star Trek* Information Files

At other Gophers, such as the Gopher at `cscns.com`, in the path Enter the CNS Gopher, then Entertainment, then Star Trek, there is a huge amount of additional information drawn from Gophers around the Net. Some are whole directories consisting of poems and songs, usually parodic. Also available is a huge amount of information about all, and I do mean all, of the actors who had ever been involved with *Star Trek* (main characters, guest stars, walk-ons, expendables—also known as phaser bait—you name it). You can find details on all characters, all *Star Trek* novels, all starships and other space ships, everything you could possibly think of.

Obviously, these files are all an incredible amount of work, and it amazes me that so many people can find the time, energy, and creativity to maintain these sources. They're accurate and interesting to look through, but I can't even imagine compiling them.

Excursion 14.17. Sound Files

It was around this point that I discovered something really neat. All over the Internet are sound files that, once you've downloaded and got onto your own computer, you can pipe into a utility and play. You can, for instance, have Kirk saying "Two to beam up" or McCoy saying "I'm a doctor, not a bricklayer." Helpfully, the first directory I found sounds in was labelled Star Trek (TOS) Sounds (at `gopher.med.umich.edu`, through the path Entertainment, then Sounds, and finally Star Trek (TOS)—there's also a *2001* and a *Three Stooges* archive here), and all of the files it contained had the extension `.au` (Sun Audio files). Having figured out what sound files were was only half the battle, however. When I found the sound files, I had nothing to play them on and no idea where to get such a utility.

> **Warning:** Sound files are often very large. You can recognize them because they have the extensions `.au`, `.voc`, `.snd`, `.wav` (and others). Be prepared for long downloads in some cases. In addition, you need the proper hardware and software to play them. The software can usually be found on the Internet; the hardware you must go out and buy.

Then I did what everyone exploring the Internet should learn to do: I asked someone. Actually, I asked a number of someones, and was finally pointed toward a source that had the right software: the CNS Gopher (`cscns.com`), which I've already mentioned.

After choosing Enter the CNS Gopher, I saw an entry File Area via gopher, which I entered, and then went into File Areas for Special Topics. From there it was on to Audio, which gave me links to several other Gophers with sound information and software. I chose DOS and Mac listening software, which gave me Sound Exchange, a sound program for DOS. The file was in compressed format, and the decompression utility was also available in the sound directory. After I moved the file onto my IBM, I could play all of the sound files.

Temptation struck again, and I decided to head back to the Entertainment directory, and then into Star Trek. While nothing had been added since my last visit, I downloaded a number of the sound files (now that I could play them), and I became interested in files containing information on stardates and correct spellings. These files, from the Star Trek Library at `wiretap.spies.com`, are listed in Figure 14.1.

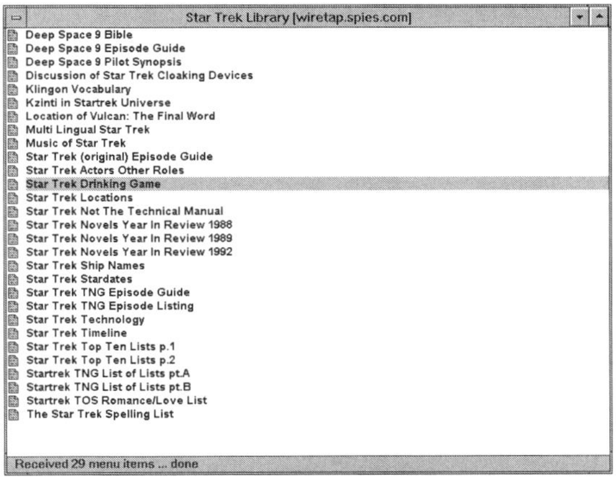

Figure 14.1. *Gopher menu for Star Trek Library.*

Excursion 14.18. The *Star Trek* Drinking Game (Explore with Caution)

One of the most fascinating items in the Star Trek Library (again, at `wiretap.spies.com`) was the "Star Trek Next Generation Drinking Game." For those of you who are wondering, yes, you can indeed get incredibly drunk on just one episode (dutifully, I conducted a usability test on the game), especially if it has Troi or Wesley in it. The game is also a lot of fun just to read through. Here is a tiny portion of this file, but I highly recommend downloading it if you are a *Star Trek* fan and have appropriate refreshments available.

```
=========================================================================
Requirements: Episode(s) of ST:TNG
              This list
              People (the more the merrier)
              Beverages of your choice

Instructions: Simple. Watch the show, and whenever a condition is met,
              take the appropriate number of drinks. The definition of
              "drink" should be decided before game play starts. Usually,
              a good mouthful will suffice. Optional rules are included
              at the end of the list for fun variations on the "standard"
              game.

Compiler's Note: I would advise taking some time before game play starts
                 to decide which conditions to use and which to ignore.
```

```
                 Remember that this list is canonical, so you probably will
                 _not_ want to use them all (especially with a new episode,
                 since you'll spend all your time reading the list, rather
                 than watching). Please send any corrections, suggestions,
                 requests, submissions, flames, etc. to the address listed
                 above.

============================================================================
Category: Condition                                      : Number of Drinks
============================================================================
General :  "Open hailing frequencies"                    :          1
Quotes  :  "Medical emergency"                           :          1
        :  "Belay that order"                            :          1
        :  "Energize"                                    :          1
        :  "Hell", "Damn" and other swearing.            :          1
---------------------------------------------------------------------------
General :  A female crewmember has flawless makeup after :
Actions :      she's been put through the ringer         :          1
        :  A crewmember straightens his/her uniform      :          1 ea.
        :      SEE ALSO: Picard's special uniform rules. :
        :  A crewmember drinks (outside of 10 Forward)   :          1 ea.
        :      SEE ALSO: Picard's special drinking rules.:
        :  A bridge officer is seen in casual clothes    :          1 ea.
============================================================================
Picard  :  "Make it so"                                  :          1
Quotes  :  "Engage"                                      :          1
        :  "Come"                                        :          1
        :  "Come" (in personal quarters)                 :          2
        :  "Captain's Log"                               :          1

Whenever Data embarasses himself, drink until somebody stops him.
```

Excursion 14.19. ASCII Pictures

You may have noticed that by now I've found information to fill up almost all of the directories I originally created, and create a new directory for sounds. That leaves one directory, pictures, empty. I started looking for pictures in my Veronica items, and came across a collection of ASCII art files at `gopher.cs.ttu.edu`, in the path Art and Images, ASCII Clipart Collection, then Star Trek. Here I found several files containing ASCII art, including this one under the heading Federation Star Ships:

Ambassador Class (Enterprise-C)

```
                                  _________
    ____________________     ___..'---------'--..____
   (___________________LL_) ==============================
         ___|   |_________/_      '--..________..--'
       /_________              ' -,/
                 '.               |
                   '._          _/
                      '-------'
```

```
              ___
        ____..--'--'--..____
==============================
   '--'--..________..--'--'
     "----' \_|_/ `----"
           |  .-.  |
           \  '-' /
            '--'
```

Constellation Class (Stargazer)

```
          _       _
         |_|==I==|_|
              |
             _-_
     ____.--'--'--.____
     \__________________/
         ~~'-_-'~~
              T
          _   |   _
         |_|==I==|_|
```

```
                      _________________
                     (_=_=============/
                            ,'  /
          _-_
    ____.--'___'--.___,'__/
    \__________________]_O_]
       ''~~'--_--'~~  --',  \
                        ____',_\________
                     (_=_=============\
```

Constitution Class (Enterprise)

```
   __________________            _-_
   \_________________|)____.--'--'--.____
                 ||       \----.__________.----/
                 ||         / ,'     '--'
                 ||_,--'       -._
            ____||              ||(
           /____
                 '--.______-'
```

```
    _       _-_       _
  _(_).--'--'--.(_)_
  \----.__________.----/
     '\    ']-['    /'
       '\.'  _  './'
         (  (_)  )
           '._.'
```

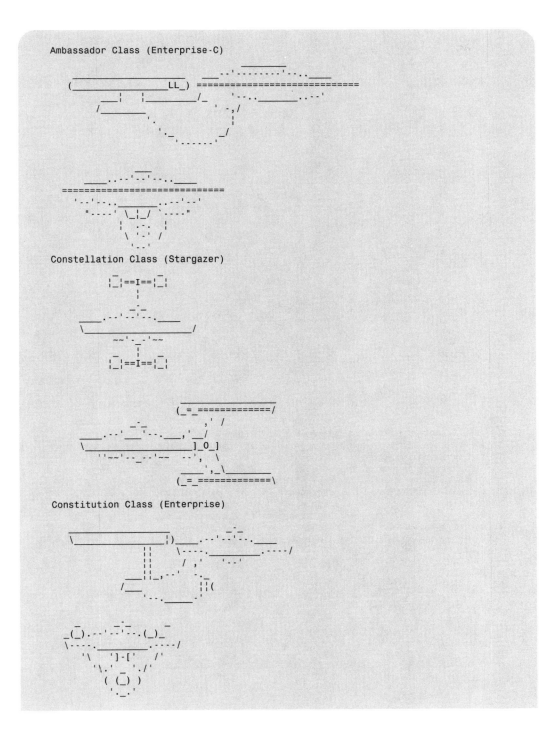

```
Constitution Class - Refit (Enterprise-A)
```

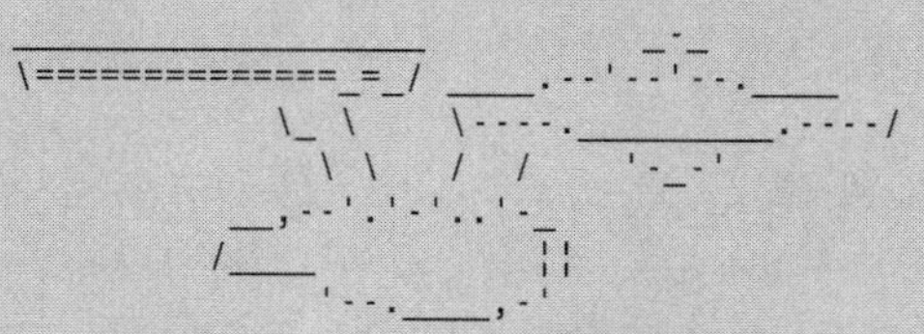

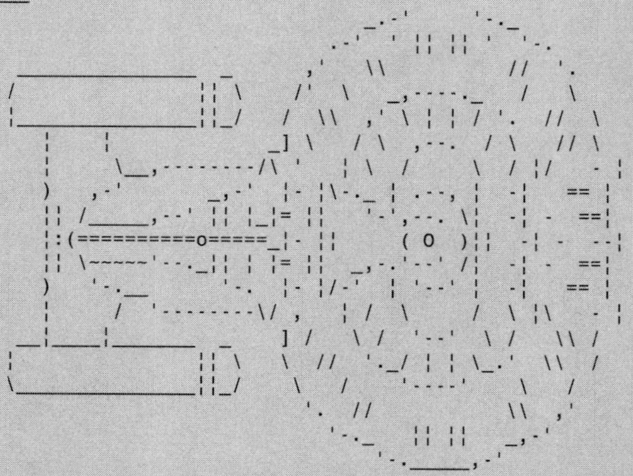

```
    Still another advanced starship concept would call for
variable-geometry warp nacelle pylons, permitting optimization of
field stress during extended Warp 8+ flight, resulting in
significantly improved engine efficiencies. This design study
features a saucer section composed of wedge-shaped modular
segments that could easily be replaced as mission demands change
and new technology becomes available. This concept calls for an
internal volume approximately 40% less than the present Galaxy
class starship, but is expected to perform similar mission
profiles within normal cruise ranges because of the relative ease
of spacecraft segment swapout.
```

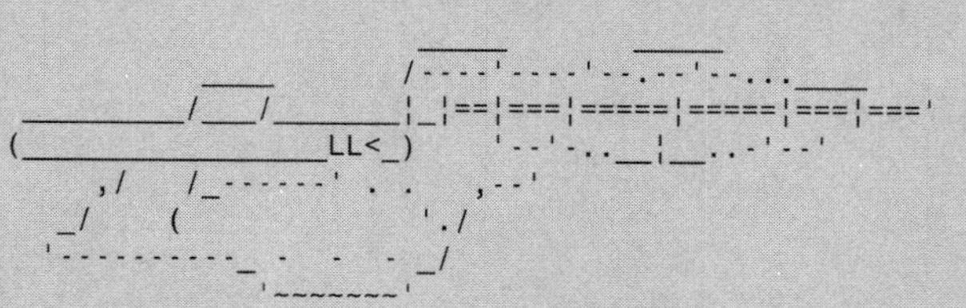

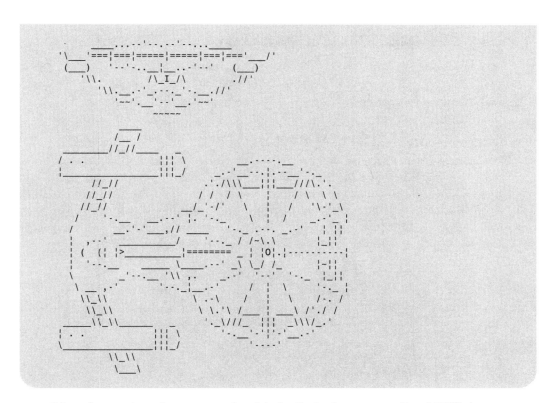

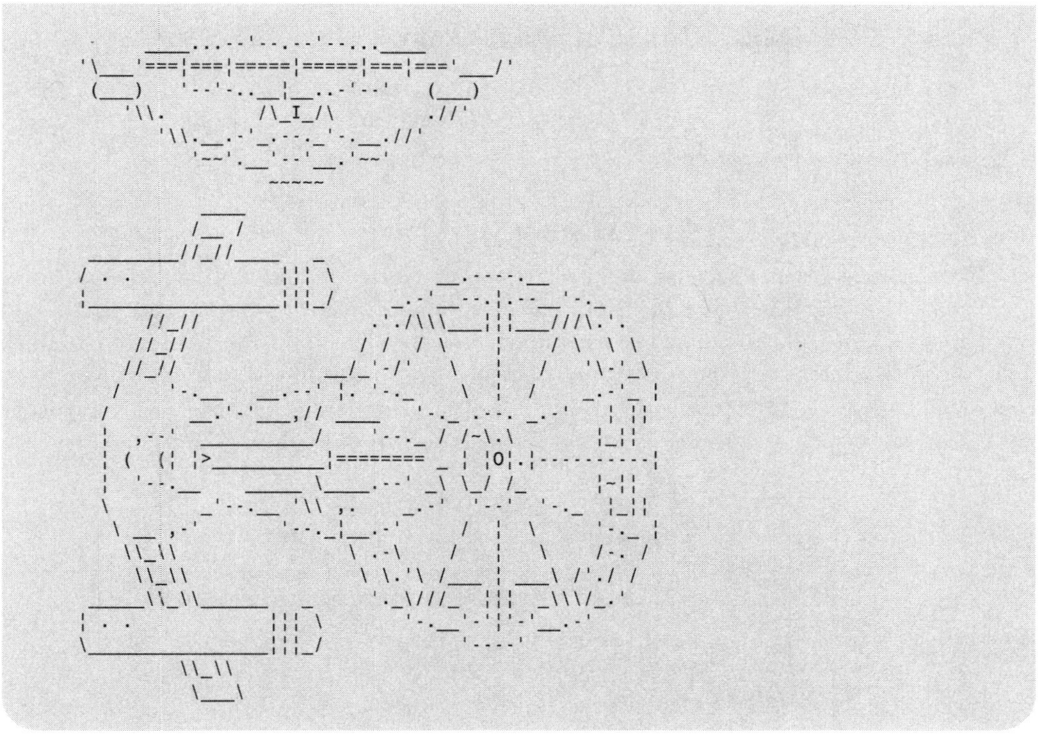

It's truly amazing what you can do with the limited resources of an ASCII character set. All of these images are simply typed on a normal keyboard. Often, you'll see images like this in the `.sigs` from the news postings. I wouldn't have the patience (or the artistic skill) to create images like this, but I'm intrigued by what some people can come up with.

Star Trek isn't the only fictional creation that's developed a following. There's a whole Anne McCaffrey subculture out there, focusing on her Pern books. *Star Wars* is also represented, as is *Quantum Leap*. When you go looking, I'm sure you'll find more. By the way, did you know that Harlan Ellison, who wrote "City on the Edge of Forever," is now a consultant for *Babylon 5*? It's amazing how incestuous science-fiction series are. (Walter Koenig, Chekov on *Star Trek*, recently guest starred on *Babylon 5* as an amazing villain!) Anyway, enjoy yourself! The Internet has some amazing stuff just waiting for you.

Other Entertainment Archives

As Christa pointed out, *Star Trek* isn't alone in getting its share of Internet treatment. It's probably the most extensive example, however. Still, it's worth looking for others, and here are a few examples.

Excursion 14.20. *Babylon 5*

A character-oriented science-fiction series has attracted its share of fans as well. Some would say the series has eclipsed *Star Trek*, simply by making some assumptions about human nature that seem much closer to what we'll be like in the future (heaven help us). If this is true, then *Babylon 5* has eclipsed *Star Trek* in another way as well: B5 archives are appearing, complete with loving graphic detail, on the World Wide Web. Called The Lurker's Guide to *Babylon 5*, its home page is shown in Figure 14.2.

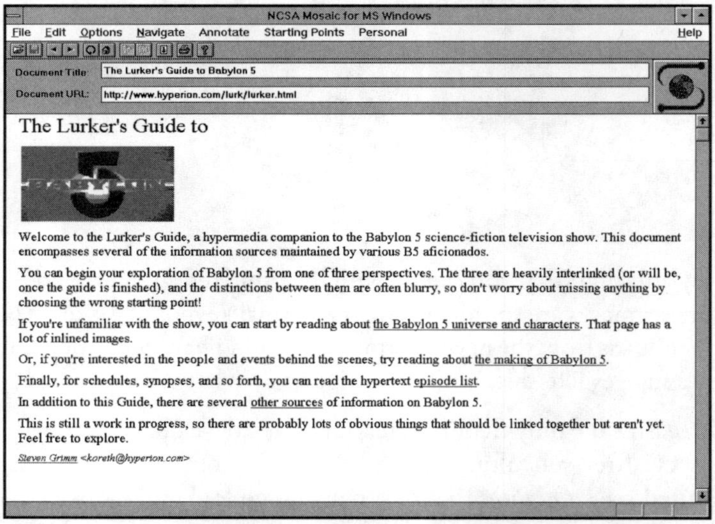

Figure 14.2. *Lurker's Guide to* Babylon 5 *home page.*

The show's cast is presented on a linked page, as shown in Figure 14.3. Each of the links here leads to information about that cast member, and this information will continue to expand. This is very nicely done, and *Star Trek* is clearly in need of such a presentation, if only to keep up with the competition.

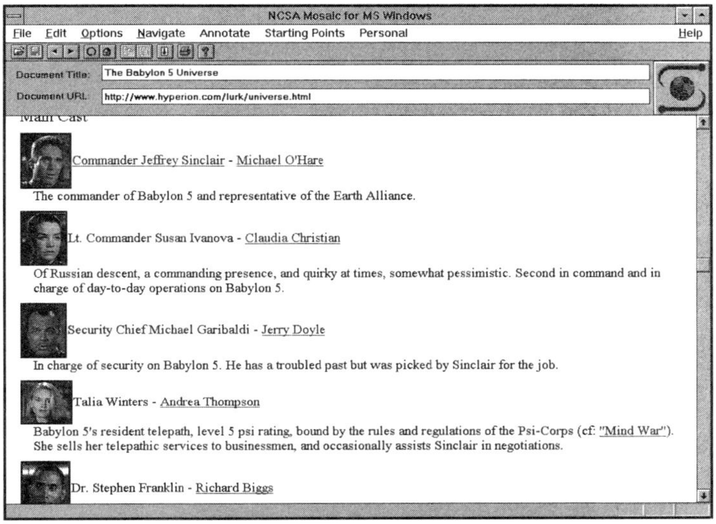

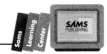

Figure 14.3. *WWW page showing* Babylon 5 *cast members.*

Excursion 14.21. Music Archives

Although MTV fans have only a limited amount of Internet information available—you can Gopher to `mtv.com`, but this site is *not* an official MTV archive—lovers of contemporary (and not-so-contemporary) music are beginning to have a fairly wide range of choices.

Figure 14.4 displays the home page for the Internet Underground Music Archive, a small but developing center for music with links to some (but as yet not many) other areas.

In Figure 14.5, we see a U.K.-based home page dealing with bands from that part of the world. While the Wonder Stuff may be old news, others here aren't. Unfortunately, the information about the bands is extremely limited, so we can only hope that the page is maintained and expanded.

And then there's Frank Zappa. It's hard to know if he of yellow-snow fame actually got to see what was available about him on the Internet, but I can't help but think he would have approved of the idea, if not necessarily the content. Figure 14.6 shows one such site.

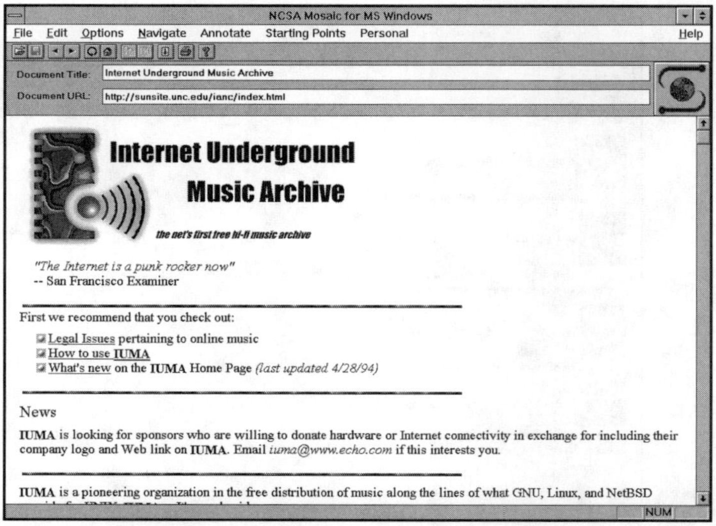

Figure 14.4. *Internet Underground Music archive.*

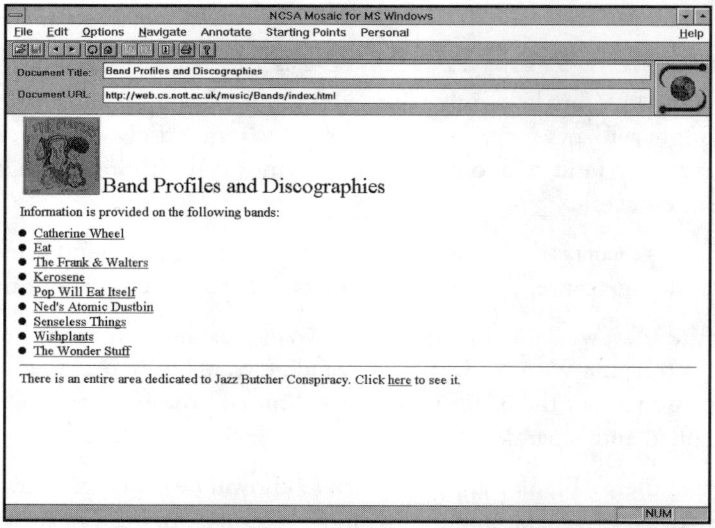

Figure 14.5. *WWW page showing information on U.K. bands.*

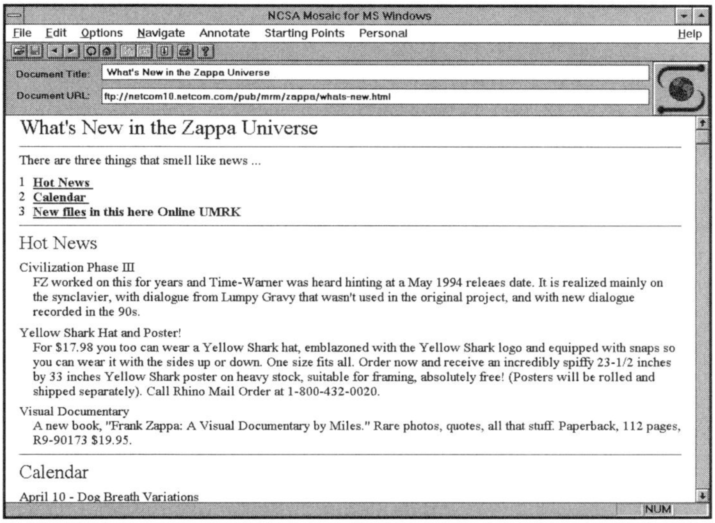

Figure 14.6. *Internet site for Frank Zappa material.*

Excursion 14.22. The Grateful Dead

And why not? Because Deadheads have appropriated just about every technology introduced since the glory days of Haight-Ashbury to spread the word of their favorite band (their *only* band, in many cases), it's hardly surprising to find Dead information on the Net. Without further commentary, I present Figures 14.7, 14.8, and 14.9 for your perusal.

Summary

Building an entertainment archive takes diligence and patience, but it can be done. Still, perhaps the Internet's most important advantage here is that it lets you find other people, all over the world, who are fans of the same things you are. To date, newsgroups and Gopher/FTP sites are the most common repositories for entertainment information, but before long, as the *Babylon 5* example demonstrates, the World Wide Web will almost certainly come to the fore. It is, after all, the most entertaining interface the Internet has to offer.

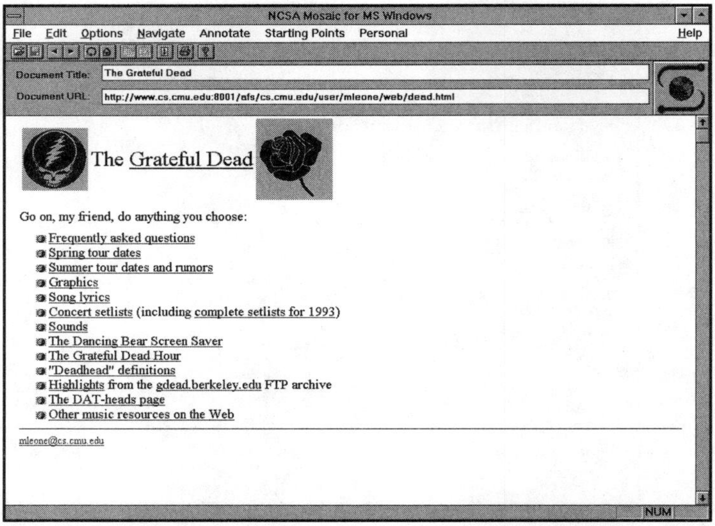

Figure 14.7. *Grateful Dead WWW home page.*

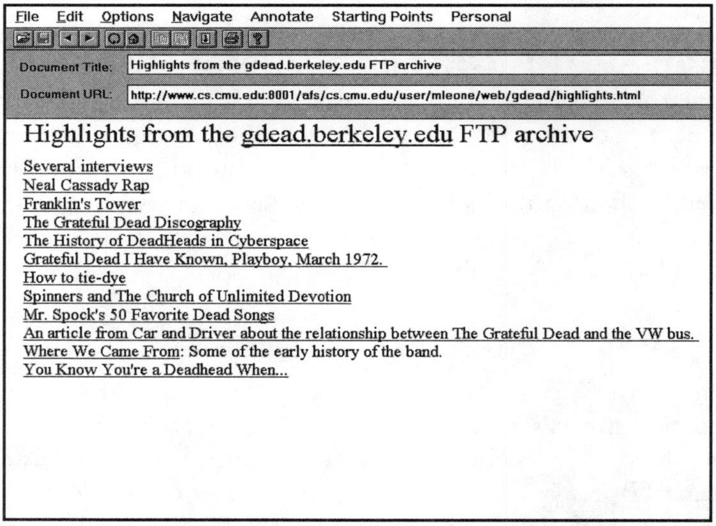

Figure 14.8. *Grateful Dead FTP archive.*

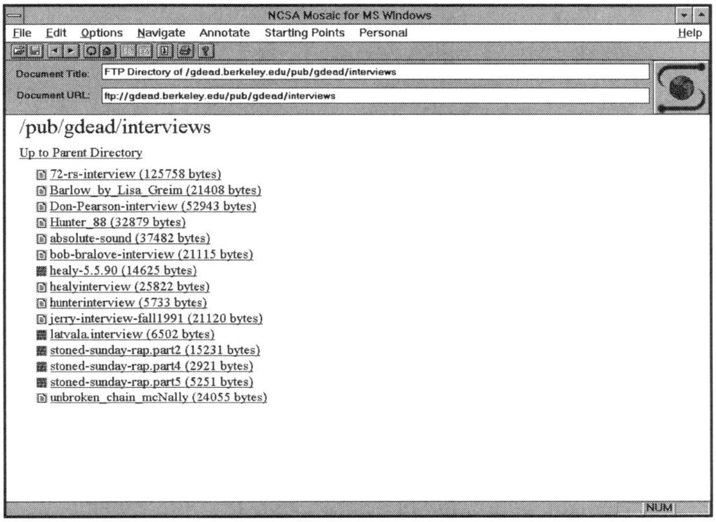

Figure 14.9. *Collection of Grateful Dead interviews.*

Task Review

On Day 14, you:

- ☐ Followed newsgroups dealing with *Star Trek* issues.
- ☐ Explored Gophers and FTP sites for *Star Trek* files.
- ☐ Downloaded and examined (or listened to) these files.
- ☐ Explored other entertainment issues on the World Wide Web.

Q&A

Q Will we ever see sophisticated interactive entertainment on the Internet?

A Yes, but it will develop fairly slowly. There are several main reasons for this. First, interactive entertainment beyond very simple interactive games demands high-speed access, and until more cable and phone companies offer this access, only the universities, research organizations, and government institutions have it. None of these organizations is likely to promote interactive entertainment. Second, true interactive entertainment, complete with graphics and sound, chews up huge amounts of bandwith, and requires constant, reliable access to host computers. Until hosts are established that exist solely for this purpose, it won't happen, and the only way such a host will be established is if its owners can charge its users. So don't expect sophisticated entertainment that's free. Finally, it's likely that other systems—dedicated systems connected in customized ways—will beat the Internet itself to the punch…which is probably what the Internet maintainers actually want.

Q Why don't all entertainment producers set up Internet archives of their products?

A There's no money in it yet. Why should they, when most people would rather rent videos or buy glossy books about the topic? It will happen only when they perceive, say, a Web page's usefulness as a promotional device.

Q Why does entertainment material appear so sporadically, and occasionally disappear?

A Putting together an archive is voluntary, and it requires a huge amount of time and energy (and see the first sentence in the preceding answer in this section). Still, if an archive about your favorite entertainment item stops being maintained, volunteer to take it over yourself.

WEEK 3 AT A GLANCE

Using the Internet Professionally

15

16

17

18

19

20

21

15

WEEK 3

Business 101: Making the Case for Full Internet Access

Business 101: Making the Case for Full Internet Access

With the knowledge of the Internet you now have, you might well be convinced that you need full Internet access where you work. But explaining the Net can be a very difficult task, and persuading your firm to spend money on it could prove to be more difficult still. Day 15 offers fuel for your argument.

Today's goals are to use:

- ☐ Gopher to find electronic journals that relate to economics.
- ☐ Veronica to search for an economics term such as *finance.*
- ☐ The NCSA Mosaic "What's New" Page to find recently added economic resources.
- ☐ FTP to transfer a file containing a table of data.
- ☐ The World Wide Web to find out what today's foreign exchange rates are.

If you don't have full Internet access at your office, you're likely to want it before too long. As an Internet devotee, you're already aware of the range of research possibilities the Net opens up, and you have no problem seeing how those possibilities would enhance the research efforts of your coworkers. You're also probably becoming increasingly convinced about the full communication potential of the Internet—enhancing both internal and (especially) external communication—and you want your organization to be state-of-the-art in this regard as well.

How do you go about convincing the powers that be? How do you demonstrate to them that the Internet is far more than the main media buzzword of the mid-1990s, more than just the underpinning of Vice President Gore's much-hyped information superhighway? You can start with the Net's history, of course (see Day 2), but if you're working for a business that might not help because until recently, businesses and the Internet were a bit like oil and water. In fact, they were mandated not to mix.

The only real way to make your point is to spend hours scouring the Net, retrieving information, making contacts, developing a network of your own. Of course, you want to make sure that you don't step on anyone's toes in your organization while doing all this, but putting forth this effort is the only way to be truly convincing. Then, when you're ready, put together a presentation. With office politics firmly in mind, try the presentation on a few key people, then see where your efforts take you. In other words, it's like proposing anything else that will cost both money and resources.

Tip: Use the Internet to help you. Scattered around numerous FTP, Gopher, and World Wide Web sites are presentations, text files, maps, charts, and tables, all explaining the growth of the Net and its capabilities, its future potential, and its benefits. Weed out the hype, then develop a proposal using these materials. Contact the official Internet organizations as well; the Internet Society and the various Internet task forces have information that you will almost certainly be welcome to use. To find these organizations, find the Internet Resources section of your local Gopher (it may have a slightly different title), and start exploring.

In this chapter, Celine Latulipe takes you through her own experience of attempting to persuade her superiors that the Internet could be of significant help to them. As will be the case for most people, she did this entirely on her own, in her spare hours off work, and you should probably expect to do the same. It would be nice to be given work time to put a solid presentation together, but that will only happen, of course, if your organization already sees some potential to Internet access and wants further information. The scenario being played out here is more likely, especially with smaller organizations. You may well know the Internet's value, but nobody else has even begun to understand it. Like Celine, you'll be essentially on your own.

About the Contributor

See Day 10 for Celine's biography.

Note: There is, of course, far more to the full persuasive effort than Celine's write-up includes. Primarily, you'll need to determine the full range of costs: equipment, communications lines, software, training, maintenance, and so forth. But that may be more than you're capable of doing, maybe more than you'd be permitted to do. In this chapter, Celine's goal is very simple. Rather than try to get her superiors to adopt the Internet, she merely wants them to understand it to the point where they will push for full access themselves.

Tip: The following scenario examines the value of the Internet from the standpoint of a research organization. If you'd like more information about commercial activities on the Net, see Day 16 as well.

Convincing Your Office of the Benefits of Full Internet Access

by Celine Latulipe

When I wrote this chapter, I was on a four-month work term as a co-op student through the Co-operative Education Program in the Department of Economics at the University of Waterloo (Canada). The group of people for whom I worked were consultants. They were involved in studying the competitiveness of Canadian industry mostly through hypothetical cost/benefit analysis. Much of the work that I and my co-workers did involved research in the field of financial economics and general background searches into different sectors of the economy. I had to make frequent trips to the library to find a wide variety of information. Quite often our workplace library was unable to supply the information that we needed, or we had to wait days or weeks for the librarian to locate and retrieve the information from other libraries.

Our workplace operated through a wide-area network, which had recently been connected to Internet. We only had Internet e-mail access, however, and the use of this resource had not been widespread in the office. I'd spent a lot of time browsing the Internet because I have full Internet access at home, and it came to my attention that there could be potential benefits to my coworkers if our Internet access could be expanded. Therefore, I took it upon myself to fully explore these benefits in the hope of convincing our manager to arrange full Internet access.

Excursion 15.1. Financial Information via Gopher

To begin my project, I asked some of my coworkers to give me examples of information searches that they have recently performed or are in the midst of performing. Following, I have listed some of their examples:

- Background information on Canada/United States anti-dumping procedures, especially with respect to steel.
- Background information on the use of chlorine, especially with respect to the auto and forest industry.

- A listing of all companies that traded on the Toronto Stock Exchange in 1992.
- Statistics for the Canadian and American food and automobile industries.
- Gross domestic product (GDP) and consumer price index (CPI) statistics for North America.
- Company data and financial statements for North American companies.
- Information on the weighted average cost of capital for Canada, the United States, and Finland.
- Financial information on North American pulp and paper companies.
- Exchange rates and trade data.
- Population statistics.

As you can see, the searches vary in terms of how specific the need is, and with respect to its subject matter.

Before setting out to look for specific information, I did a general economics search to see what was out there on the Internet. I began by using Winsock Gopher, probably the easiest (and most unlikely to crash) Internet tool available for the Microsoft Windows environment. I'm connected to the Internet through a commercial service, and so I've configured my `wsgoph.ini` file to automatically load that service's home Gopher. From there I moved to the University of Waterloo Gopher to start my search. Located at the Gopher address `uwinfo.uwaterloo.ca`, this Gopher is well organized and well maintained. From here, I chose the Electronic Resources Around the World item and then selected Electronic Texts, Books, Journals and News Services. At this juncture, I found a long list of different resources not specific to any subject area. I think it's an interesting spot; I have listed some of the menu items following, just to give you an idea of what's there.

```
1.   Electronic Journals;
2.   CIA World Fact Book;
3.   Electronic Serials at CICNet;
4.   Gutenburg Ebooks;
5.   North American Free Trade Agreement; and
6.   The Maastricht Treaty on European Union.
```

I checked out The Maastricht Treaty Gopher, because one of the consultants followed trade issues quite closely and I thought he might be interested. The files that are available under this Gopher can be seen in Figure 15.1.

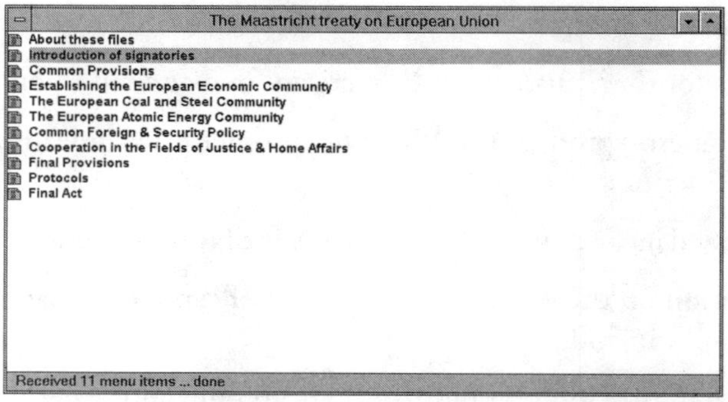

Figure 15.1. *Gopher screen showing documents from Maastricht Treaty.*

Under Electronic Journals, I found the *Journal of Statistics Education*, which I looked at briefly and then bookmarked. It's not something that could have been of a lot of use to the people at work, but I didn't want to ignore any possibilities. Under Electronic Serials at CICNet, I chose General Subject Headings, and then Business. Here I found a very interesting list of items that actually looked relevant to my search. Once again I've included a list of some of these items.

```
1.   Center for Economic Policy Research Bulletins;
2.   The Financial Times;
3.   International Business Association of Atlanta;
4.   Internet Business Journal
5.   Trade News
```

I won't go into the details of what I found under each menu item, but I will say that some items were not what I expected.

Warning: Don't get your hopes up when you see the name of your favorite magazine or newspaper on a Gopher menu. It doesn't mean you get the whole thing free. Quite often magazines publish a few selected articles or an occasional full issue for free on the Internet; there are very few magazines that are offered consistently for free online.

Most publications do offer subscription information online, however, and there is even a new service available—Magnet Online Magazine Subscriptions—that enables you to order magazines over the Internet. The address for this service follows:

```
http://branch.com:1080/
```

Returning to the previous menu, I clicked the Electronic news sources item and found the Electronic Newsstand (available directly through `gopher.internet.com`). Here I chose Titles Listed By Category, and then opened the Current Affairs—Business, News, Politics menu. I went into the Business Gopher and found a bunch of great archives. Figure 15.2 shows how I got to this point and lists what is available.

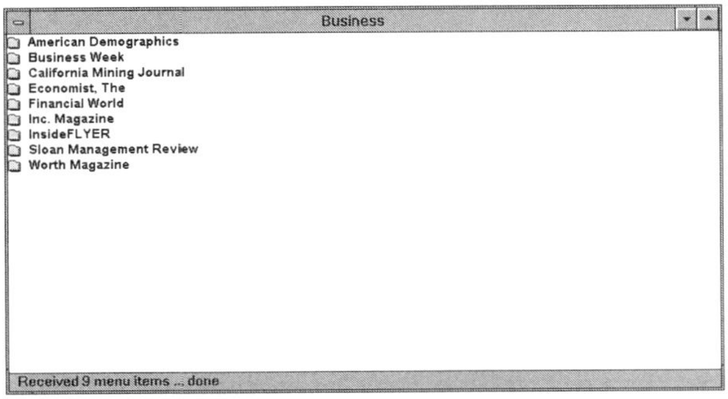

Figure 15.2. *Electronic Newsstand Gopher.*

Once again, my warning about online magazines is applicable, but the information available here is useful.

Excursion 15.2. Financial Information via the World Wide Web

At this point, I ended my Gopher search and began my vague World Wide Web search using the Cello browser. From the Cornell Home Page of Cello (`http://www.law.cornell.edu`), I found a direct economic resource: the Nasdaq Financial Executive Journal (`http://www.law.cornell.edu/nasdaq/nasdtoc.html`). (I later saw several other pointers to this journal, and realized that it was a well-documented site.) The Cornell Home Page also led me to the NCSA Mosaic Demo Document, which I could just as easily have opened in Mosaic. Once there, I chose the Global Network Navigator (`http://www.wimsey.com/gnn/gnn.html`), and found The Whole Internet Catalog (`http://www.wimsey.com/gnn/wic/newsrescat.toc.html`). In Figure 15.3, you can see part of the catalog's WWW page.

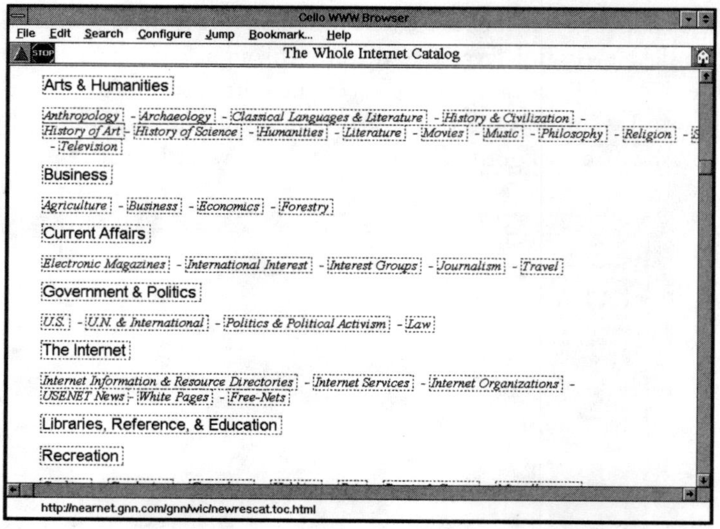

Figure 15.3. *Whole Internet Catalog home page.*

I chose the Business item from the Catalog and found three interesting menu items. The first was the Stock Market Summary, but unfortunately the site was not available at the time, so I bookmarked it. There was also the EconData Gopher server listed, which I will talk about a little later. Finally, I clicked on the Rice Economics Gopher (`chico.rice.edu`), where I found one of the items that was on my coworker's list—Foreign Exchange Rates. After all this searching with only mediocre results, I got so excited at seeing this Gopher that I almost forgot to bookmark the site! The data that I retrieved gave me that day's spot rates at 10 a.m. for all the industrial currencies, as shown in Figure 15.4.

I decided to try browsing in Mosaic as well, because there are few features in Mosaic that I like better than Cello's. My home page in Mosaic defaults to the page constructed by my commercial service provider; I've adjusted my `mosaic.ini` file exactly the same way I adjusted my `wsgoph.ini` file. The service provider's home page consists of The Internet Mall, which is built around the shopping mall metaphor and contains shops for just about everything. The two shops that interested me the most were The Bank and The Research Library.

I tried the research library first, at the URL address `http://hookup.net/library.html`. In the library I found a menu item entitled Spirit of the University of Connecticut (`http://spirit.lib.uconn.edu`), which I decided to check out. Once inside their

Gopher, I chose the Academic Subjects and Services menu and then the Business & Economics item. Through the last menu (Economics & Business at Rice University), I chose the Rice University Economics Gopher (available at `riceinfo.rice.edu`) and found the important financial database called Edgar.

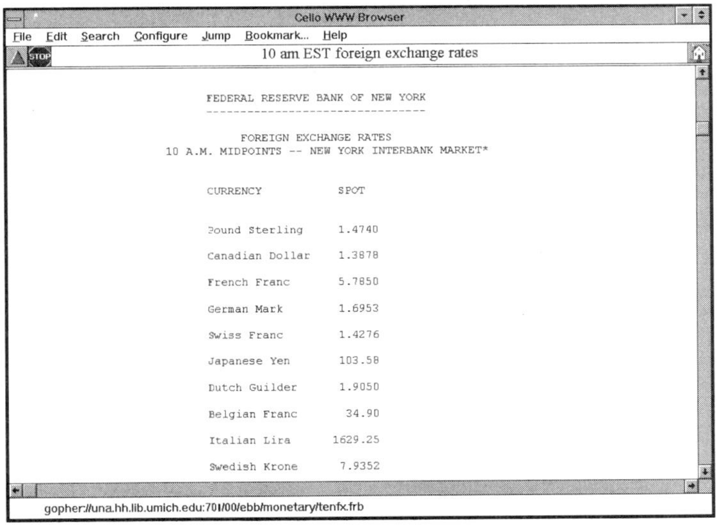

Cello WWW Browser
File Edit Search Configure Jump Bookmark... Help
10 am EST foreign exchange rates
FEDERAL RESERVE BANK OF NEW YORK
FOREIGN EXCHANGE RATES
10 A.M. MIDPOINTS -- NEW YORK INTERBANK MARKET*
CURRENCY SPOT
Pound Sterling 1.4740
Canadian Dollar 1.3878
French Franc 5.7850
German Mark 1.6953
Swiss Franc 1.4276
Japanese Yen 103.58
Dutch Guilder 1.9050
Belgian Franc 34.90
Italian Lira 1629.25
Swedish Krone 7.9352
gopher://una.hh.lib.umich.edu:70I/00/ebb/monetary/tenfx.frb

Figure 15.4. *Information on Currencies from Foreign Exchange Rates.*

Edgar consists of company data that would normally be filed with the Securities and Exchange Commission (SEC) and available for public use. The difference between Edgar and the information that is physically held at the SEC is, of course, that the data in Edgar is available online through FTP or electronic mail. According to the description, there will be 15,000 companies with data available online by the end of 1994. The information available is only on American companies and is not retrospective; that is, only information pertaining to 1994 or later is available. Figure 15.5 shows the Edgar information screen.

Excursion 15.3. Retrieving Company Information from the Edgar FTP Site

I decided to FTP to the site via anonymous FTP to `town.hall.org/edgar`. When the connection was complete, I downloaded the `readme` file and opened it in my word processor. It directed me to a file called `general.txt`, which I next FTPed and read. That file explained how the site was organized. By retrieving the `company.idx` file from the full directory, I was able to find out what files contained information about pulp and paper companies. A warning, though: the `company.idx` file is over 2MB in size, and even with a 14.4 kbps modem it will take about half an hour to download it.

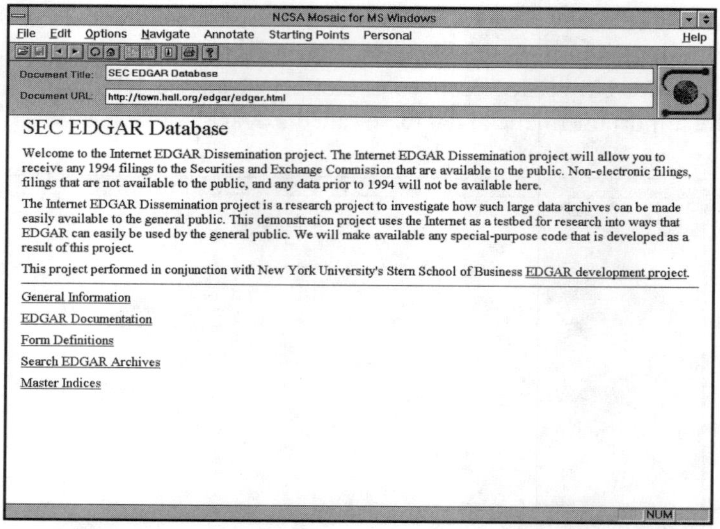

Figure 15.5. *Edgar database information screen.*

I then went back to the FTP site and retrieved a file on Georgia Pacific, an American pulp and paper company. The file contains information on the company's annual meeting, its board of directors, its shareholders, and a number of other items. This was only one of about 10 different files on the company, so I imagine that some of the other files contained balance sheets and other financial data. I'm really quite impressed with what seems to be available. Of course, working in Canada, I quite often need information such as this on Canadian companies (which often is simply not available online), but being able to get information on U.S. companies is definitely handy, partly because of the importance of trade between the two nations. I have no doubt that this kind of information will be made available for Canadian companies, as well as those of other countries, as the Internet continues to grow.

Excursion 15.4. Two More Sources of Financial Information

I still hadn't checked out the The Bank, so I went back into Mosaic and browsed there for awhile. The most interesting feature available at The Bank was The World Bank (`http://www.worldbank.org`). When I clicked this hypertext, I was given a choice of The Public Information Center or the World Bank Publications; I chose the first (`http://www.worldbank.org/html/PIC.html`). Here I found Economic Reports, but unfortunately there was nothing available under this section. So instead I chose Environmental

Data Sheets. There was a ton of files under this category, but when I chose to view them alphabetically by country, I realized that all of them contained information about developing countries rather than Canada or the United States. Figure 15.6 shows all of the resources available at The World Bank Public Information Center; take note that Mosaic displays the URL address below the menu bar.

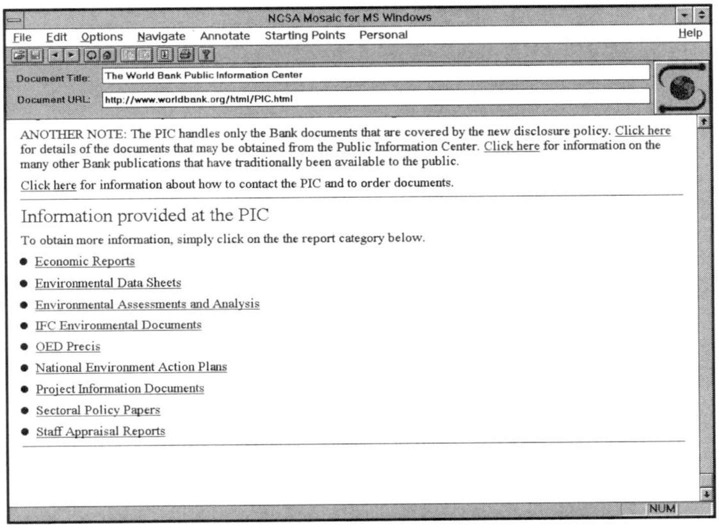

Figure 15.6. *Resources available at World Bank Public Information Center.*

Next, I decided to try the NCSA "What's New" page. This is a page to look at when you have a spare half-hour. There is so much great information here that the page merits revisiting often, but the links are not really in any particular order, other than (it seems) the chronological order in which the authors learned about them. Nevertheless, here I found the University of Texas Economics Server. This led me to a reference that I'd seen in a few other spots—The Kiwi Club. I assumed this was a Gopher for New Zealanders or something like that (well, with a name like The Kiwi Club that seems only natural), but it's actually an economics-related World Wide Web page (there's also a Gopher). Figure 15.7 is the opening page of the Kiwi Club server (`http://kiwiclub.bus.utexas.edu/finance/kiwiserver/kiwiserver.html`).

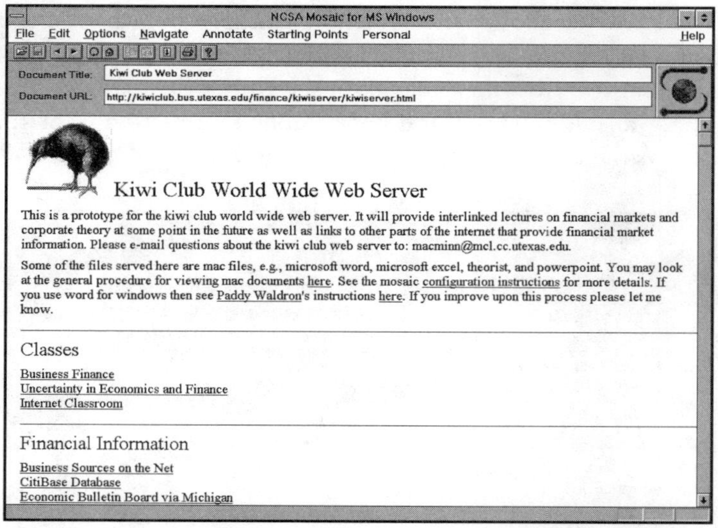

Figure 15.7. *Kiwi Club home page.*

Under the Kiwi Club, I found a number of interesting menu items, including one called Holt's Stock Market Reports. I tried to open a few of the documents contained under this menu item, but none of the documents could be read without BinHex conversion software, which I don't have. I've made a note to myself to download such software if I ever see it, and I've bookmarked the site so that I can go back when I'm better equipped.

Excursion 15.5. Financial Information Through Newsgroups and Mailing Lists

Another method of browsing for economics data, which takes less effort but more time, is to wait for someone else to tell you about available sites. This can be done by subscribing to newsgroups that inform you about different resources that come online.

The newsgroup that I joined for economics information is called `sci.econ.research`, and I have found it an interesting newsgroup to follow. One of the sources that I discovered through this newsgroup was the Census Bureau Internet Site, and because one of my coworkers had asked about the availability of population statistics on the Internet, I took note of this posting. Following is the article that tipped me off and may be of interest to users of census data.

```
---------------- BEGIN FORWARDED MESSAGE -------------
Newsgroups: comp.infosystems.announce
From: calliope@netcom.com (Gary Goldberg)
Subject: ANNOUNCE: U.S. Census Bureau Internet Site (Web, Gopher, FTP)
Date: Mon, 21 Mar 1994 21:16:23 GMT
Lines: 24
Approved: announce@ibm.cl.msu.edu
Message-ID: <calliopeCMq5rB.2yt@netcom.com>
NNTP-Posting-Host: ibm.cl.msu.edu
The United States Bureau of the Census has opened an information
server on the Internet. Please explore our service and tell us
what you think. Connect to our beta site by pointing your client
software to our universal resource locators (URL's):

     http://www.census.gov/          # use with mosaic, lynx, etc
     gopher://gopher.census.gov      # use with gopher

     ftp://ftp.census.gov/pub        # use with ftp

Also, we plan to offer a majordomo mail server in the near future.

If you have problems, questions, suggestions, etc, send email to:

     gatekeeper@census.gov

Please broadcast, netcast, and publish this information widely.
```

Clearly, the information from this one message alone will be of immense help to my colleague, and I passed the information along to him. It demonstrated another reason for my department to consider acquiring full access to the Internet.

Like newsgroups, mailing lists are valuable sources of information, and all you need to join one is Internet e-mail access. For instance, I belong to Gleason Sackman's indispensable net-happenings list, and I've included a few messages following that come from the list and are economics-related.

```
Date: Thu, 17 Mar 1994 18:43:37 -0800
From: Gleason Sackman <sackman@plains.nodak.edu>
Reply to: net-happenings@is.internic.net
To: Multiple recipients of list <net-happenings@is.internic.net>
Subject: Mother Jones Magazine March/April on WWW (fwd)
Forwarded by Gleason Sackman - InterNIC net-happenings moderator

Mother Jones Magazine has just released the March/April issue
on the World Wide Web. See our home page at URL
http://www.mojones.com/motherjones.html
The major package is on jobs and the economy: Where is our economy headed?
What is the jobs outlook? John Kenneth Galbraith, Lester Thurow, and other
experts try to answer these questions, and ordinary people tell their
stories in several articles of varying length.
```

```
We've also got pieces on Bob Maxwell, a banker who got sucked into a CIA
nightmare, Chelsea, one of the poorest communities in the US, the right
wing takeover of public schools, and all our usual columns and short bits
including Paula Poundstone and a nasty letter from the EPA.
Check it out on us!
```

```
Date: Thu, 3 Mar 1994 06:17:46 -0800
From: Gleason Sackman <sackman@plains.nodak.edu>
To: Multiple recipients of list <net-happenings@is.internic.net>
Subject: Internet Guide to Govt. Business & Econ. Sources (fwd)
Forwarded by Gleason Sackman - InterNIC net-happenings moderator
After several months of searching/evaluation plus an additional two
months of ironing out format problems, we would like to announce the
official appearance of a guide to government business and economic
sources on the internet.
The guide is available through the Clearinghouse of Subject-Oriented
Internet Resource Guides currently residing on the University of Michigan
Libraries gopher and is roughly 122K (50 pages). Access information follows:
Anonymous FTP:

host:  una.hh.lib.umich.edu
path:  /inetdirsstacks/govdocs:tsangaustin
Gopher:
   via U of Minn. list of gophers
   menu:  North America/USA/Michigan/Clearinghouse of Subject-Oriented
          Internet Resource Guides
URL for WWW/Mosaic:
gopher://una.hh.lib.umich.edu/00/inetdirsstacks/govdocs%3atsangaustin
We had a lot of fun compiling this (most of the time) and hope you find
it useful.
```

This is actually something that the consultants with whom I work could already have been reading, because they have Internet e-mail access. However, because they don't have full Internet access and therefore can't visit Gopher or WWW sites, learning about Internet resources for economists seemed somewhat pointless.

However, there are other things that the consultants could have been accomplishing with their e-mail, and I'll use a little bit of space here to explain how I planned to convince them that they are not using e-mail to its full potential. The most important e-mail possibility for them had to do with the Financial Economics Network (FEN). FEN operates as an automatic Listserv, and following I've included part of one of the Listserv messages that demonstrates the extensive and highly specialized fields to which FEN will appeal:

```
The Network consists of a master subscription, called AFA-FIN,
with 40 channels or sublists. Currently 39 channels are available
to AFA- FIN subscribers. The total list is:

AFA-ACCT (Accounting and Finance)  AFA-INV  (Investments)
AFA-ACTU (Actuarial Finance)       AFA-JOB  (Job Openings)
AFA-AGE  (Gerontology Finance)     AFA-LDC  (Bank/Fin in LDCs)
AFA-AGRI (Agricultural Finance)    AFA-LE   (Law & Economics)
AFA-AUDT (Auditing)                AFA-MATH (Mathematical Fin.)
AFA-BANK (Banking)                 AFA-MKTM (Mkt Microstruc.)
AFA-CORP (Corporate Finance)       AFA-PERS (Personal Finance)
AFA-CFA  (Financial Analysts)      AFA-PUB  (Public Finance)
AFA-DER  (Derivative Securities)   AFA-REAL (Real Estate)
AFA-DEF  (Defense/Mil. Reconfig.)  AFA-REG  (Regulation)
AFA-ECOM (Electronic Commerce)     AFA-RES  (Job-Seeker Resumes)
AFA-ECMT (Econometrics and Fin.)   AFA-RMI  (Risk Mgt & Ins.)
AFA-EDU  (Education Finance)       AFA-S-IV (Small Investor)
AFA-EMKT (Emerging Markets)        AFA-SBUS (Small Business Fin.)
AFA-ENGR (Financial Engineering)   AFA-SINV (Social Investing)
AFA-ENVI (Environmental Finance)   AFA-SOFT (Financial Software)
AFA-GORE (FinanceNet) -- NOT READY AFA-TECH (Tech. Invest. An.)
AFA-HEAL (Health Finance)          AFA-THRY (Financial Theory)
AFA-INST (Teaching/Instruction)    AFA-VCAP (Venture Capital)
AFA-INT  (Internat'l Finance)      AFA-WA-R (Real Est.in WA st.)
************************************************************
To request a free subscription, contact John Trimble at Internet
address: trimble@vancouver.wsu.edu; telephone: (206) 737-2039;
facsimile (206) 750-9701. Or contact Wayne Marr at Internet
address: marrm@clemson.clemson.edu; telephone (803) 656-0796
(voice) or send a facsimile to (803) 653-5516 (fax).
*****************************************************************
```

This network provides excellent opportunities for networking with other professionals who are in the same field, and the cooperation is always outstanding. For instance, someone put a message on the network asking for information on accounting principles in Argentina, and I remembered that a friend of mine had an Argentinian accounting professor last term. I sent an e-mail to the requester containing the name and school of the professor. Later, I posted a message asking for information on the differences among the weighted average cost of capital in Canada, the United States, and Finland. The same person sent a message back thanking me for the professor's name and in return gave me a huge list of resources to answer my question:

```
Date: Tue, 15 Feb 94 22:37:48 EST
From:xxxxxxxxxxxxxx
To: Celine <clatulip@ccs.carleton.ca>
Subject: country risk

Hello again, Celine.
```

```
Thanks for putting me in touch with Prof. Diego — he was a tremendous help
on my project. I'm glad to be able to return the favor.

The place you want to start looking regarding country risk is Canada's own
Export Development Corp. (EDC) in Ottawa. The corporation is divided
functionally into a finance division and an insurance/guaranty division; you
want the latter. I have their annual report at my office, and am sure I could dig up a
couple names and phone numbers. Send me a message, s.v.p., to remind me to do that if
you need the information.
```

Some of the messages also contain great references to related resources on the Net.

Another way that Internet e-mail could be of use to the consultants is in exchanging information with clients and industrial or commercial contacts. For instance, my coworkers often had to spend inordinate amounts of time calling industrial managers and reminding them to fill in and mail surveys that had already been sent.

Time could be saved here in a number of ways. First, the surveys could have been created using forms software. Second, they could have been sent in seconds if e-mail rather than snail-mail had been used. Third, they could have been returned the same way. Granted, some of the companies being dealt with may not have Internet e-mail, but that problem will more than likely disappear over the next year or so. There is also the problem of confidentiality. If the information being exchanged was in any way confidential, it may not be considered safe to send it by e-mail. This, however, will also likely change. The point is that many organizations already have Internet e-mail, and while e-mail is only a small part of Internet access, it can still be an extremely valuable part.

Excursion 15.6. An Example of a Wide-Ranging Financial Information Search

One of the projects that I am directly involved in at work deals with the pulp and paper industry (particularly the Canadian industry), and I can't count the number of general background information searches I have had to do in that area. Thus, this was the first specific information search I performed on the Internet. Using Gopher, and beginning with my standard home site, I routed myself to a list of Canadian Gophers. On this list I found a Gopher called Ministry of Environment, Lands and Parks, BC, Canada (`gopher.env.gov.bc.ca`). This looked promising, so I investigated, and sure enough under Other Gophers I found documents related to the forest industry. I opened this and found a number of interesting items that I downloaded for my coworkers. Figure 15.8 shows some of the available files.

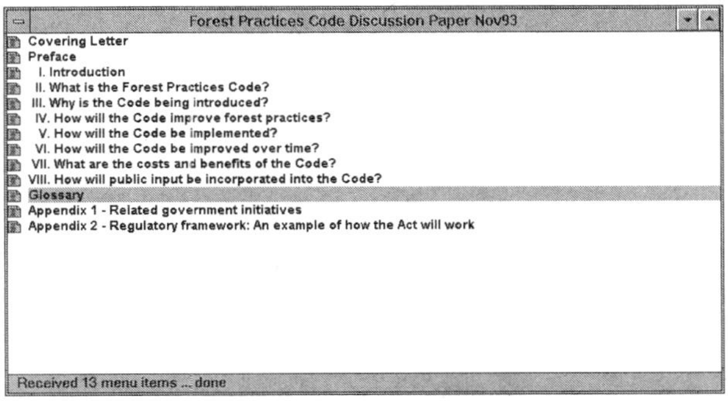

Figure 15.8. *Documents related to the forest industry.*

Another forest industry source that I found almost by accident was a document on the softwood timber supply and the future of the southern forest economy. It turned out to be only a bibliographic reference, but I took note of it anyhow—it could be just the kind of resource my coworkers needed. When I say I found it by accident, I mean that I was doing a Veronica search using the search term *econ*, and this was just one of many economics resources that I came across. Figure 15.9 shows exactly what route to take to do the Veronica search without the accidental part.

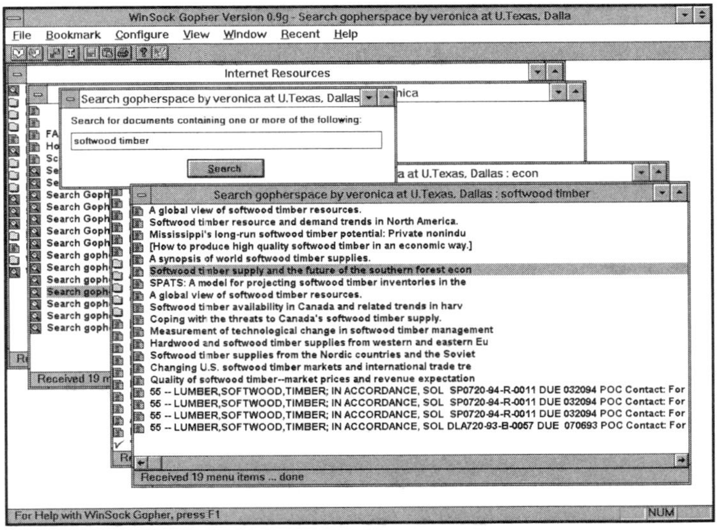

Figure 15.9. *Veronica search for information on softwood timber.*

Continuing my search for information in all of the subject areas that my coworkers described (see the list in Excursion 15.1), I decided to investigate the Statistics Canada Talon Service (`talon.statcan.ca`).

Once here, I chose the English language Gopher (my French isn't as strong as it should be), and then I read the About Statistics Canada file. I checked out a few files that described the classification system, but they weren't very interesting. Then I tried the Statistics Canada FTP Site, and became quickly frustrated by the ambiguous or useless filenames that I found. I opened the Daily Listings directory, and all of the 73 filenames were simply dates. I retrieved one, just to check it out. The file contained a lot of interesting statistics and articles, as well as pointers to Statistics Canada publications. I've included a few bits from the file, including the "Table of Contents," following. Many of the items in the first list would definitely be of interest to my coworkers, and I've included a couple of the particularly relevant clippings.

```
**  What's in today's DAILY ****************************************
Canada's International Transactions in Securities, Labour Markets and Layoffs
During the Last Two Recessions, Private Security and Public Policing, Steel
Primary Forms, Railway Carloadings, Local Government Long-term Debt, Traveller
Accommodation Statistics, Women's Sportswear Industry, Other Furniture and
Fixture Industries, Metal Tanks (heavy gauge) Industry, Metal Closure and
Container Industry, Metal Dies, Moulds and Patterns Industry, Hand Tool and
Implement Industry, Machine Shop Industry, Motor Vehicle Wheel and Brake
Industry, Railroad Rolling-stock Industry, Sign and Display Industry, Canadian
Economic Observer.

PUBLICATIONS RELEASEDTable 1 - Canada's international transactions in securities
************************************


 94 03 24 08 30Thursday, March 24, 1994 For release at 8:30 a.m.
--------------------------------------------------------------------------------


Steel Primary Forms
Week Ending March 19, 1994 (Preliminary)

Steel primary forms production for the week ending March 19, 1994 totalled 274
364 tonnes, down 4.0% from the week-earlier 285 697 tonnes and down 2.0% from
the year-earlier 279 842 tonnes.
 The cumulative total at the end of the week was 2 865 784 tonnes, a 5.9%
decrease from 3 046 329 tonnes for the same period in 1993.
 For further information on this release, contact Greg Milsom (613-951-9827),
Industry Division.

--------------------------------------------------------------------------------
Traveller Accommodation Statistics
1989-1991

Data for 1989-1991 on the accommodation service industries are now available.
```

```
 Traveller Accommodation Statistics, 1989-1991 (63-204, $22) will be released
shortly. See "How to Order Publications".
 For further information on this release, contact Sam Lee (613-951-0663),
Accommodation and Food Services Section, Services, Scence and Technology
Division.
-----------------------------------------------------------------------------
```

The important thing about the information available here is how current it was. The two clips I've included were the two that were most applicable to our work, dealing with the steel and tourism industries. The major drawback to the information at the Talon service is that it doesn't seem to be indexed very usefully. Of course, the service is new, and it may very well be that the indexing just hasn't come online yet.

I got out of the FTP site and, still in the Statistics Canada Talon Gopher, proceeded to the Internet Tools Gopher. Here I found a listing for the U.S. Department of Agriculture, Economics and Statistics, under which I saw a Trade menu. This seemed promising, as one of my coworkers had said that he often needed to get trade statistics. I opened up this Gopher and found more promising Gophers, some that seemed quite specific. For instance, there was a Gopher on Global Competitive Advantages, which I was sure my "cost of capital" coworker would be interested in, and one called Processed Food Trade Tables, which was another important project for some of the consultants.

Both of these Gophers contained data files in table forms, so I downloaded a few of them and then took them into work to check out using Excel. The data was interesting, although not quite as up-to-date as the data at the Statistics Canada FTP site. Once again the problem was with the ambiguity of the filenames, and I couldn't find an index file like the one that the Edgar FTP site provided. Figure 15.10 demonstrates the route to and through the Statistics Canada Gopher.

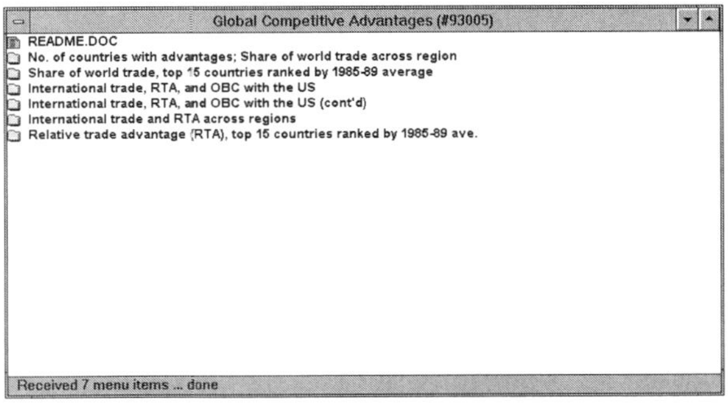

Figure 15.10. *Information on trade from U.S. statistical source.*

At this point, I decided to try another Veronica search. The results are shown in Figure 15.11.

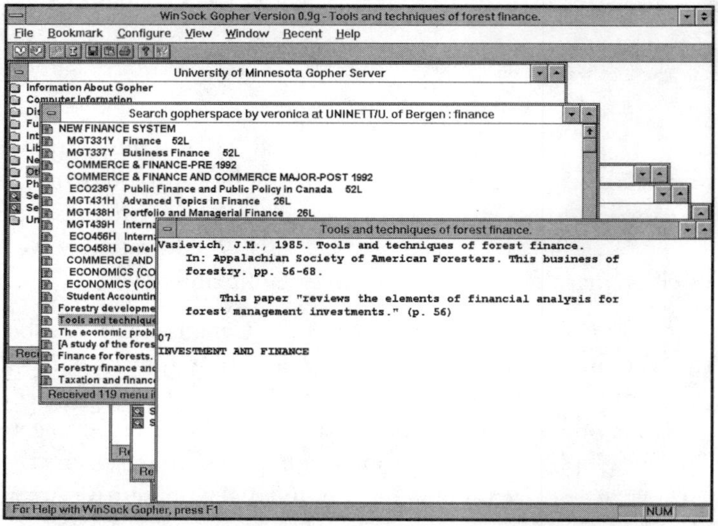

Figure 15.11. *Results of Veronica search for finance.*

In this case, the information I found was again related to the forest industry, but I found it by searching with the term "finance." This actually pleased me immensely, because all of the analyses that we do are financially based. Therefore, finding financially based background information is perfect. The information here is merely a bibliography of a book that is available, and the book isn't exactly recent, but the information we need when doing background research often doesn't need to be right up to date.

One of the most interesting projects that the consultants were doing involved research on chlorine. It's a study that had just been started, and the premise behind the study, in a few words, was that environmental extremists have convinced North American governments to ban chlorine from all manufacturing processes and the impacts of such a ban on employment, industry, and everyday life are immense and terrifying.

The consultants, in cooperation with other organizations, wished to publish a paper outlining the hazards of such a ban. However, the chlorine industry is not one that the consultants were familiar with, and therefore, much background information was needed. They needed to know every product that uses chlorine in its manufacturing processes, what substitutes were available, the environmental dangers of chlorine, the number of people employed directly and indirectly by the chlorine industry, and so on.

I set out to see what kind of information I could find on the Net.

I initiated my search in Winsock Gopher once, maneuvering into the Veronica search area. Here I chose Search Gopher Directory Titles at The University of Manitoba. My search term was, of course, `chlorine`, and when the results were in, there were over 150 items. The following is a condensed version of the list—just a few items that I thought might be applicable to our project.

```
Ozone Depletion FAQ Part II: Stratospheric Chlorine and Bromine
Chlorine
Study Zaps Chlorine In Mills
CALCIUM HYPOCHLORITE (65% CHLORINE)
chlorine.data
Ontario's Chlorine Ban
Chlorine.html
Chlorine's Industrial Ecology
Manufacturing and Use Information (chlorine)
Chemical and Physical Properties (chlorine)
Safety and Handling (chlorine)
Substance ID (chlorine)
Toxicity and Biomedical Effects (chlorine)
10980 Ban Chlorine? 980byte
Section 266.107 - Standards to control hydrogen chloride (HCl) and chlorine gas (Cl2)
emissions
CFC's & chlorine
chlorine.density
02-25  5:06a  Industry Spokesman Defends Use of Chlorine
02-27 11:48a  Talk Of Banning Chlorine Has Industry Poised For Battle
Canada Strategy Needed for Chlorine Phaseout 2/17
(Sconce) Chlorine
Chlorine free paper
```

Tip: The references that begin with either numbers or dates/times are usually either postings to newsgroups (sourced from newsgroup archives) or e-mail postings from Listservs (also sourced from archives). These files may or may not contain valuable information, but it is easy to find out either way. You probably only need to open and read one of the files to determine whether all of them will be of any use to you.

Conclusions

I started out looking for information on a number of different subjects, although all related to economics: forestry, steel, chlorine, food industry, cost of capital, population, exchange rates, trade data, company data, and others.

I cannot say that I was successful in finding information on all of those topics. I found the exchange rates, the population statistics (although only for the United States), some trade data, and the chlorine background information. I found lots of forestry information, and I found company data for American companies.

I didn't find a listing of the companies trading on the Toronto Stock Exchange, nor did I find GDP or CPI statistics. However, the fact that I didn't find them doesn't mean that they are not available online. I didn't spend a huge amount of time looking for any of the previously mentioned items (after all, this was an extracurricular project, and I still had my real work to do), so it's not surprising that I was not fully successful.

That brings up a major point to consider. If you're going to come up with a full-scale rationale for acquiring full Internet access, plan to spend a considerable amount of time doing it. Don't just find a few items and then stop. Be sure to gather appropriate information from a variety of locations, preferably the kind of material not easily obtained elsewhere. If you're doing it on your own, expect to take a great deal of your own time to put the rationale together.

Looking back on what I've done, I would say that there is a great deal of substance to my original argument. If the consultants with whom I work could have full access to Internet, there could be definite time-saving benefits, and possible quality improvements due to the expanded amount of information available with Internet access. Of course, with Internet access comes the possibility of Internet addiction—surfing for its own sake—and this can easily cancel out the time savings. Nevertheless, I would definitely recommend full Internet access at my workplace. Wouldn't you?

Summary

The Internet is immensely useful as a research and communications tool for a growing range of organizations. Determining precisely how valuable, however, depends entirely on the organization you wish to convince. By finding out the kinds of information your colleagues need, and then using the Internet to retrieve this information and establish contact with other professionals in your coworkers' fields, you can present a convincing argument for the acquisition of full Internet access.

Task Review

In this chapter, you learned to perform the following tasks:

- ☐ Use Gopher to find electronic journals relating to economics.
- ☐ Do a Veronica search for an economics term such as *finance.*
- ☐ Use the NCSA Mosaic "What's New" Page to find recently added economic resources.
- ☐ Use FTP to transfer a file containing a table of data.
- ☐ Use the World Wide Web to research today's foreign exchange rates.
- ☐ Use the Internet to establish an argument for full Internet access.

Q&A

Q I'm convinced that the Internet is exceptionally useful for research. What about communications in general?

A If your organization already operates in a wide-area network, chances are the Internet's e-mail capabilities by themselves won't be a selling point. After all, you can already e-mail everyone else. But Internet e-mail offers some advantages. First, you can communicate easily with anyone else on the Net, including clients who are also on the Internet. Second, you can use e-mail to subscribe to mailing lists related to your organization's (or your clients') activities. Third, an Internet e-mail address is as close to a universal e-mail address as exists these days, and—believe it or not—it looks good on a business card.

You can also use the Internet for a variety of customer service activities. Through e-mail, you can send press releases, product updates, technical updates, and so on. Many companies now have anonymous FTP sites through which customers can access important documents. Many have also established Gophers containing product information, technical descriptions, answers to commonly asked support questions, and a wide range of other information they want their customers to see. More ambitiously, several are now establishing World Wide Web sites as well, sometimes with forms for customer use.

Q If I'm scheduled to make a presentation about the Internet, should I use a live demonstration or simply capture some screens and present them as slides?

A A live demonstration is always more impressive, but only if it works. If not, it will do more to dissuade than convince. If you're running your demonstration through a modem (which is likely since you don't already have Internet access), remember that downloading World Wide Web graphics takes a long time—be prepared either to turn them off or to speak usefully as they are downloading. Also remember the item of netiquette repeated throughout this book: Pay attention to the local time at the destination Gopher, Web, or FTP site. If you're doing your presentation at 9 a.m. Eastern time, and the bulk of your material is available in Mountain or Pacific time locations, by all means give it a try. The same presentation late in the afternoon stands a much better chance of coming up against inaccessible sites.

Ideally, your presentation will include both a live demonstration and carefully prepared slides and handouts. Don't count on just one, any more than you would in any business presentation.

16

WEEK 3

Business 201: Doing Business on the Internet, at Home and Abroad

Soon the number of Internet addresses in the commercial domain (`.com`) will exceed those in the historically more populous educational domain (`.edu`). Businesses are moving onto the Internet quickly, developing ways of using the Net for a variety of corporate functions. But the corporate world has a great many questions about what it means to do business on the Internet, and on Day 16 we'll explore some of the possible answers.

On Day 16, you will do the following:

- Examine newsgroups dealing with business issues.
- Determine which mailing lists might be helpful for your business.
- Work through Gophers dealing with business concerns.
- Examine how businesses have developed the World Wide Web for corporate purposes.

Business and the Internet

With the changes surrounding the NSF's Acceptable Use Policy discussed in Day 2, the Internet took on new potential as a place to do business. But what exactly does this mean? Below are some of the questions that are now being asked and others that will be asked in the near future:

- Will the Net become just a different version of television's home shopping phenomenon?
- Will it offer a more interactive form of infomercial?
- Will you be able to publish a product catalog with interactive feedback and ordering systems?
- Can buyers custom-order a computer or a car by filling in World Wide Web forms?
- Does the Web have potential as a videoconferencing medium for business meetings?
- Can it assist product groups with market research and analysis?
- Will deals be struck without two parties ever physically meeting?
- Will the Net allow consortiums and alliances to collaborate on research and development, public relations, and even financial details?

- Can transportation complexities be resolved by tapping Net resources?
- Is it possible to use the Net to establish and implement distribution systems throughout the world?
- Will the Net enhance customer- and technical-service capabilities?
- Can it be set up as a legal and financial consulting medium?

You can undoubtedly add to this list. Just think of the potential of a truly global network with increasingly easy access to businesses and potential customers alike. Questions about your particular business or business interest should immediately spring to mind.

The Internet as Marketplace

The Internet represents a potentially large market, accessed by users who are open to any number of possibilities. It's even open to advertising, albeit a far different kind of advertising than that found in radio, television, or the print media. If you send promotional material via e-mail to an entire list or newsgroup, you'll be inundated with responses indicating contempt, disgust, and even hatred. Unlike junk mail, blanket postings can be responded to, and usually they will be. It's not inconceivable that some particularly irate users will program their computers to respond to such postings by returning them to their senders ten, twenty, even a thousand times over, thus clogging up the offenders' accounts.

For now at least, the Internet population is still committed to an open and essentially noncommercial network. That doesn't mean businesses aren't welcome (although many users still abhor the possibilities); what it means is that advertising over the Net is acceptable as long as participation is voluntary. If you put your product catalog on the Net as a Gopher and WWW site, for example, you should let people know it's there, but don't force it on anybody. The same goes for any other kind of service.

One important point about the Internet, even at this stage in its development, is that its users are already segregated by area of interest. From a marketing standpoint, this means there is a need to develop specialized promotional materials rather than the one-size-fits-all model of broadcast advertising. In fact, the Internet may be the first real example of a technology that not only allows but *requires* narrowcast marketing, with all the attendant pluses and minuses. It's doubtful that the Net will ever be the right place for marketing bathroom tissue, but it may already be precisely the right place to develop awareness of niche market items.

The goal, of course, is transforming product awareness (and I use the term "product" in its broadest sense here) into actual sales or contracts. Right now, the only direct possibility lies with the World Wide Web and its interactive forms (which are discussed later in this chapter). But you can place phone numbers and e-mail addresses on Gopher servers, in newsgroups or mailing list messages, and in files in FTP sites, specifying full contact information. And keep in mind that any magazine ad carrying an e-mail, Gopher, or WWW address is certain to catch the attention of Internet users, who may well check it out the next time they log on. It's probably a temporary advantage (the way fax numbers were at first), but it's well worth paying attention to.

The Internet as Communications Technology

Businesses have been using the Internet as a communications tool for years. In this context, think of the Net not as a LAN (local-area network), not even as a WAN (wide-area network), but rather as a SWAN (super-wide-area network). (I just made this one up.) It doesn't get any wider than this. Anyone with an Internet account can be contacted through e-mail, and you can establish newsgroups and mailing lists as well. Like any e-mail system, you can use the Net to have your personnel keep in touch with you—and they can do so easily (and cheaply) from anywhere in the world. Clients and associates can also communicate easily with you, to the extent that face-to-face meetings may well be minimized.

E-mail is fast, relatively inexpensive, and often more effective than telephone contact (especially since voice mail has made actual contact nearly impossible). But there's no reason to restrict your communications to e-mail. Mailing lists and newsgroups can work, but you probably don't want to commit sensitive information to them. Telnet and FTP sites, on the other hand, can be password-protected, as can Gopher sites. Security is always a concern, but a well-considered security scheme can make it possible to do *most* global-wide communication on the Net. (The truly sensitive data and communications you will want to restrict to other technologies.)

The Internet as Collaboration Tool

Research groups have been using the Internet as a collaboration medium since its inception. Through e-mail, FTP, and other tools, scientists working on collaborative projects have exchanged data and communicated findings, and more recently they have utilized Gopher and the World Wide Web to make their results public.

It takes only a short stretch of the imagination to see corporate collaboration occurring in much the same fashion. In an era of alliances, industry task forces, and the sharing of resources, collaboration over the Net makes sense. Design work could be handled over the World Wide Web (see Day 10 for examples of collaborative art being developed this way), as could frequent presentations of project milestones. In fact, project planning and (to a degree) project management could be covered on the Web as well, through a series of interactive flowcharts, diagrams, and graphs. And as full-motion video becomes more fully implemented on the Web (requiring top-speed access), other possibilities will be created for collaborative meetings and ventures.

The Internet as Service Bureau

Customer service and product support are always important considerations, and they're not about to go away, especially in a competitive business climate. It makes sense, therefore, to utilize all available means of serving clients and customers and to demonstrate a commitment to satisfying their needs. The Internet is one of those means.

While you may not like the idea of conducting private communications on a massively public network (even with full internal security in place), service is, by its very nature, a public activity. Why not establish an Internet presence in addition to the usual service features such as toll-free numbers, fax feedback, and whatever else your firm offers? E-mail alone is a possibility, although it absolutely must be staffed. People who send e-mail expect faster responses than those who send faxes.

As the World Wide Web examples in the last part of this chapter demonstrate, several companies have already begun turning to the Net as a service feature. Clients can read and/or download frequently-asked questions or technical documents from FTP, Gopher, or Web sites, and through mailing lists and newsgroups they can communicate with other customers as well. (This can be dangerous, of course, if complaint becomes the chief mode of expression.) Fax services are already in place for this type of material, and adding Net service is, from a client's standpoint, another positive step.

You can also develop interactive feedback or upgrade forms to be handled on the WWW, and there's no reason not to design Web-based tutorials for specific problem areas or improved performance or installation techniques. Start thinking of the Net as a 24-hour support representative, and you'll start getting a sense of the possibilities.

Business Resources on the Internet

In the following section, we'll look at newsgroups, mailing lists, and Gophers of interest to business people. In most cases, the material here represents either information about businesses, or communication between people interested in specific business issues. In the subsequent section of this chapter we'll turn to businesses with an existing presence on the Net.

Excursion 16.1. Newsgroups

The Usenet offers two major kinds of business-oriented newsgroups. The first, under the `biz` hierarchy, represents newsgroups dealing with specific businesses, some of which were started by those businesses. The second are more wide-ranging discussions about business issues in general and often attract owners or would-be owners of small businesses.

The *Biz* Hierarchy

One of the Usenet hierarchies (`biz`) is devoted to discussions about business and businesses. Here is an abbreviated list of these groups:

```
biz.americast
biz.americast.samples
biz.books.technical
biz.clarinet
biz.clarinet.sample
biz.comp.hardware
biz.comp.mcs
biz.comp.services
biz.comp.software
biz.comp.software.demos
biz.comp.telebit
biz.config
biz.control
biz.dec.decathena
biz.dec.decnews
biz.dec.ip
biz.digital.announce
biz.digital.articles
biz.jobs.offered
biz.misc
biz.newgroup
biz.next.newprod
biz.oreilly.announce
biz.pagesat
biz.pagesat.weather
biz.sco.announce
biz.sco.general
biz.sco.magazine
biz.sco.opendesktop
biz.sco.sources
biz.sco.wserver
biz.test
biz.univel.misc
biz.zeos.announce
```

Some of the groups here have been started by the companies themselves, while others are concerned with the products of those companies. The SCO and DEC groups, for instance, deal with issues regarding the Santa Cruz Operation and Digital Equipment Corporation, respectively, and are read and responded to by personnel from within those organizations. The following message shows a question from a subscriber (preceded by the > markers), and part of the response from an SCO support representative:

16

```
>Is there a way to get the screenblanker, one might activate by setting
>TBLNK to an other value than 0, to blank *both* displays - the VGA *and*
>the HERCULES? If not, does anybody know of a pd piece of code that could
>be used for this?

Currently, the screen blanker will only blank a VGA screen, and will not work
on CGA, EGA, or Mono video cards.

Since the individual screen driver is what handles the screen blanking,
some work would have to be done in the drivers to support the
correct adapter calls, AC_ONSCREEN and AC_OFFSCREEN as defined in
/usr/include/sys/vid.h.
```

Other questions may be answered by individual subscribers to the group. From the same SCO group comes the following, this time with a very direct and perhaps cryptic answer, from a subscriber rather than a company representative (who presumably would have elaborated a bit):

```
>Can Anyone explain to me how I would go about doing either a full screen
>capture under opendesktop 3.0? I need the information then placed into a
>word processor file so I can put together a manual describing how my
>system works and actual usages helps to expain to new users.

man xwd
man xpr
```

One of the major points here is that setting up a `biz` hierarchy newsgroup enables you to respond quickly to specific questions from users, and through those answers to compile lists of questions to be used for product redesign or distribution to other support people. As with any such venture, however, be sure that if you set the newsgroup up, you staff it accordingly. Once it's in place, Internetters will use it, and they expect responses.

General Business Newsgroups

You can find several newsgroups dealing with business issues in general. Among the more interesting are `alt.business.misc` and `misc.entrepreneurs`. The discussion is far-reaching in both of these groups, and subscribers tend to be owners of small or one-person businesses.

The following are some discussions from `alt.business.misc`:

Note: Here as elsewhere in the book, I've changed names and addresses in the messages, as a matter of courtesy. (I don't give out phone numbers, either.) If you want to contact these people, join the newsgroup.

```
-------------------------------------------
I am working in economic development in Claremont CA and work with small
businesses. I am working right now with a company that has a coffee and
gift shop. He buys chocolate from a local chocolate shop and packages it
to sell. One product that he buys costs him $.45 and the packaging costs
$.65. He wants to find a way to buy cheaper packaging.

He needs a box that is 2 1/4" wide, 4 1/2" long and 3/4" high. It must be
a see through box. Right now he is using a molded plastic but he could
also use a cardboard box with a window covered with a clear plastic. The
important thing is that it is the right size. There are jewelry boxes
like that but it has to be designed for candy. Does anyone know of a
company that produces that type of packaging?
```

At last count, the poster had received about eight responses, including one that apparently worked things out.

```
-----------------------------------------------------
                       NAFTA for Windows!


 Ideal for the business person exploring new North American import/export
 opportunities for the first time, or for the experienced professional
 who needs easy access to all the detailed NAFTA terms....quickly! The
 complete text of the North American Free Trade Agreement is now available
 as a user-friendly Windows 3.1 HELP File! Powered by the standard Windows
 WINHELP.EXE program, this is one megabyte of invaluable information for
 companies who want to improve their bottom line!
```

```
+  Hypertext format, infinitely more readable than the
   1000 page printed document!

+  Access topics through Menus, by Key Word Search, or
   sequential browsing forward and back.

+  Comprehensive, but concise Synopsis of all key points
   instantly available in a second Window!

+  Direct cross-referencing to all related Chapters, Articles,
   Schedules and Annexes.

+  Includes Specific Rules of Origin!

+  All "specially-defined" NAFTA phrases and words keyed
   as pop-up definitions!
```

This, clearly, is an ad, and they appear fairly regularly in business newsgroups. Even though they're generally welcome, however, there is still a fairly rigid protocol about them. Some ads have become the center of sub-discussions, especially those that prove to be suspect or even fraudulent.

```
------------------------------------------------------------------

Business Opportunity:   (Non-MLM)

South Carolina based manufacturer's rep firm looking for an additional
associate.

Our specialty is providing solutions to indoor air quality problems for
industrial customers. These solutions often include a combination air
handling systems, scrubbers, and close-capture exhaust systems.

We work primarily with industrial end-users, mechanical contractors, and
design/build general contractors who specialize in value engineering.

The person we're looking for has a good grasp of mechanical concepts, has
a broad-base understanding of various manufacturing processes, and is people
oriented. We will provide all necessary training to the right person.

We are not as concerned about what's on your resume as we are about who you
are and what you're looking for in a business opportunity. There is no
limit to what you can earn as this is a commission-on-sales situation.

If you're looking for a salary, expense account, and company car, this is
not for you. If you're looking for an opportunity to function as an
independent contractor, be your own boss, and control your own income, leave
me an e-mail message.
```

This is yet another kind of ad, this time for help wanted. The last paragraph alone should attract a few people, although no response was noted on the newsgroup itself. At the bottom of this ad was a personal e-mail address, along with instructions to respond there instead.

```
-----------------------------

ALO Energy, Eastern Europe's largest space organization, is seeking professional
distributors for its space souvenir items. T-shirts, hats, posters, mugs,
photographs and pins commemorating Russian space programs. Upcoming joint
Russian-US space flights are already heightening interest. Licensing
arrangements also possible.

-----------------------------

Entrepreneurial Solutions, a West Virginia company seeks working partner with
capital. Just completed one and a half years of research and develop-
ment. Complete business plan available after signing a non disclosure.
Our companies main activities are customized PC based online systems.
For serious inquires, you may call 1-800-Online-5. From the main voice
menu, select online system sales. For E-Mail; carlucci@ins.infonet.net
```

These, too, are fairly common: ads searching for licensing or business partners. Again, personal e-mail addresses are included, so responses weren't posted to the group.

```
-------------------------------

Hi everyone!

I have compiled a book containing 5 reports that will show you how to do
the following:

Report #1
HOW TO GET FREE ADVERTISING

I will show you who to contact, where to go to, and exactly what to do.
Use these secrets to help advertise your business or event. This
information can translate into HUGE SAVINGS to you as a business or an
individual.

Report #2
GETTING FREE PUBLICITY

I will show you this little known method in getting FREE PUBLICITY. How
to approach these people giving away the publicity. And give you actual
examples of successful methods of gaining free publicity.

Report #3
THE SECRETS TO MAKING MONEY IN MAIL ORDER
```

As always, the get-something-free message is intriguing. Presumably this idea will eventually mean spending some money, but the advertiser certainly makes it easy.

What becomes clear after reading only a few messages on these newsgroups is that if you ask a sensible question you will more often than not get at least one response, and usually several. Keep your questions short, don't flaunt advertising, and you'll be helped by people who've been there and who know the ins and outs. All for the measly price of a Usenet connection.

Excursion 16.2. Mailing Lists

The differences between mailing lists and newsgroups on business topics are much the same as for any other topic. Newsgroups are less formal, a bit more difficult to work with, and more open to a wide-ranging discussion. They're also at least somewhat open to advertising, which few mailing lists are. Some companies have established newsgroups and mailing lists to serve essentially the same function, but the lists shown below are more serious research-based lists.

Here are several worthwhile lists, each with a different topic, and complete with a portion of their "official" descriptions. The author followed six of them for a month. It became clear that they do what they were designed to do, and the messages, while ranging freely within the topic, stick precisely to that topic in almost all cases. That, too, distinguishes mailing lists from newsgroups on the whole.

This is just a selection, but from them you'll learn of other lists as well. See Day 4, "Birds of a Feather: Newsgroups and Mailing Lists," for information on joining a mailing list.

- `AJBS-L@NCSUVM.BITNET`—The Association of Japanese Business Studies, devoted to research and discussion of Japanese business and economics.
- `HHI-RES@UTARLVM1.BITNET`—HHI Research Findings, dealing with issues of general interest to real-estate researchers.
- `E-EUROPE@NCSUVM.BITNET`—Eastern European Business Network, on doing business in Eastern Europe countries, with a goal toward helping these countries in their transition to market economies.
- `IBJ-L@PONIECKI.BERKELEY.EDU`—Internet Business Journal, distribution list for this FTP-retrievable journal dealing with business on the Internet.
- `ICEN-L@IUBVM.BITNET`—International Career and Employment Network, self-explanatory.
- `JMBA-L@ISRAEL.NYSERNET.ORG`—Jewish MBA List, dealing with issues of being Jewish and in business or in an MBA program.

- LATCO@PSG.COM—Latin American Trade Council of Oregon list, devoted to information and ideas regarding business and trade with Latin America.
- MARKET-L@UCF1VM.BITNET—Marketing List, for academic and day-to-day discussions of issues related to marketing.
- MBA-L@MARIST.BITNET—MBA List, with information and discussion about MBA programs.
- ORCS-L@OSUVM1.BITNET—Operations Research and Computer Science, for researchers and practitioners alike.
- PA_NET@SUVM.BITNET—Public Administration Network, on public admin issues.
- FLEXWORK@PSUHMC.BITNET—Flexible Work Environment, discussions on how people handle flexible work situations.
- TRDEV-L@PSUVM.BITNET—Training and Development Discussions List, about the development of human resources.
- SPACE-INVESTORS@CS.CMU.EDU—Investing in space-related companies, including new products, contracts, venture capital, etc.

Excursion 16.3. Gophers

As ever, Gophers are easy to browse, and hidden beneath their menus is a wealth of information. Several businesses have established Gophers on the Net, complete with FAQs and downloadable technical and marketing information (including such items as press releases and product announcements). These are on the increase. For now, let's look at Gophers featuring information about business in general, rather than specific companies or industry details.

A good starting point is Gopher Jewels, at cwis.usc.edu (and mirrored on several other sites). The Economics and Business item yields the following menu:

```
                        Economics and Business

1.  Bureau of Labor Statistics, US Dept of Labor - Sam Houston State U../
2.  Business - Go M-Link/
3.  Business - Texas A&M/
4.  Business - The Management Archive/
5.  Business - Univ of California, Berkeley, Library (InfoLib)/
6.  Business, Economics, Marketing - University of Missouri-St. Louis/
7.  Commerce Business Daily - Vai CNS, Inc Gopher/
8.  Economics - Resources for Economists - Washington Univ., St. Loui../
```

```
9.  Economics - Berkeley Roundtable on the International Economy (BRIE../
10. Economics - Budget of the United States Government, Fiscal Year 19../
11. Economics - Computing Centre for Economics & Social Sciences (WSR)/
12. Economics - Economic Democracy Information Network (EDIN)/
```

The M-Link Gopher (directly accessible through `vienna.hh.lib.umich.edu`) offers another very healthy source of material.

16

```
1.  Business Gophers/
2.  Business Journals from CICNet/
3.  Business Sources on the Net /
4.  Business Statistics/
5.  Catalog of Federal Domestic Assistance/
6.  Commerce Business Daily/
7.  Current Stock Market Reports <TEL>
8.  Defense Conversion and Reinvestment (SPARC)/
9.  Employment/
10. Industry/
11. International Business & Exports/
12. Michigan Business/
13. NASA Shuutle Small Payloads Info/
14. Occupational Safety and Health (OSHA) Regulations/
15. Querri Database (Community Resource Development) <TEL>
16. Safety Information Resources on the InterNet/
17. Small Business/
18. TQM/
```

Lots to work with here, but let's start somewhere. Near the bottom is a directory for Small Business, which will obviously be of interest to anyone in that category. Selecting it, we find the following short menu.

```
1.  Basic Guide to Exporting (NTDB) /
2.  Catalog of Federal Domestic Assistance/
3.  Newbiz <TEL>
4.  Overseas Business Reports  (NTDB) /
5.  Small Business Administration Industry Profiles /
6.  Small Business Administration State Profiles /
```

Let's assume an interest in overseas markets. Selecting item 4 takes us to the following (partial) menu, which presents reports on a variety of nations outside the U.S. (whether technically "overseas" or not).

```
                    Overseas Business Reports  (NTDB)

1.  ***** Via the University of Missouri-St. Louis *****   .
2.  ARGENTINA       - OVERSEAS BUSINESS REPORT - OBR9211    .
3.  AUSTRIA         - OVERSEAS BUSINESS REPORT - OBR910903  .
4.  BAHAMAS         - OVERSEAS BUSINESS REPORT - OBR9208    .
5.  BOLIVIA         - OVERSEAS BUSINESS REPORT - OBR9212    .
6.  BRAZIL          - OVERSEAS BUSINESS REPORT - OBR9205    .
7.  CANADA          - BUSINESS GUIDE           - OBR9304    .
8.  CHILE           - OVERSEAS BUSINESS REPORT - OBR9210    .
9.  GABON           - OVERSEAS BUSINESS REPORT - OBR9109    .
10. GERMANY,-W.     - OVERSEAS-BUSINESS REPORT - OBR9102    .
```

The following is a tiny portion of the Brazil business report. Included in the full report are statistics for each Brazilian industry, methods for exporting, trade policy and role of government, and so on. Useful for every company, not just a small business, with designs on the Brazilian marketplace.

```
Introduction

This report is designed to acquaint the U.S. business community with
Brazil's economic and commercial environment and provide guidance on
exporting to Brazil. Brazil's rules and regulations affecting trade and
investment are in a state of rapid change as the Brazilian government
implements various programs intended to stimulate economic competitiveness
through opening its traditionally restricted and protected markets to
greater foreign and domestic competition.

Considerable attention has been given to the details of Brazil's import
system because it is important to understand how the system operates.
Exporters must be familiar with Brazil's import procedures and documentation
requirements, which are stringently applied. Non-compliance inevitably
results in delays and financial penalties. Information is also provided on
Brazilian regulations affecting foreign investment.
```

Also from this Small Business item comes the Catalog of Federal Domestic Assistance Gopher, which features only two items, as follows.

```
1.  Introduction to the Catalog of Federal Domestic Assistance .
2.  Search the CFDA.src <?>
```

A quick search using the keyword "loans", however, reveals how extensive the information is. Below is the first portion of a five-page menu containing files dealing with loans.

```
                    Search the CFDA.src: loans

1.  84.032 Federal Family Education Loans.
2.  10.410 Very Low to Moderate Income Housing Loans.
3.  10.406 Farm Operating Loans.
4.  64.114 Veterans Housing_Guaranteed and Insured Loans.
5.  10.051 Commodity Loans and Purchases.
6.  10.404 Emergency Loans.
7.  59.008 Physical Disaster Loans.
8.  59.041 Certified Development Company Loans (504 Loans).
9.  10.416 Soil and Water Loans.
10. 10.407 Farm Ownership Loans.
11. 10.768 Business and Industrial Loans.
12. 59.012 Small Business Loans.
13. 10.766 Community Facilities Loans.
```

Since we're in the Small Business Gopher, why not check out the information on Small Business loans, item 12. Here's part of the Applications and Award section of the resulting (fairly short) document.

```
APPLICATION AND AWARD PROCESS:

Preapplication Coordination: None. This program is excluded
from coverage under E.O. 12372.

Application Procedure: Applications are filed by the
participating lender in the field office serving the territory in
which the applicant's business is located. Where the participating
lender is in another territory, applications may be accepted and
processed by the field office serving that territory, provided
there is mutual agreement between the two field offices involved.
(See listing of field offices in Appendix IV of the Catalog.)

Award Procedure: Applicant is notified by authorization
letter from district SBA office, or participating bank.

Range of Approval/Disapproval Time: From 1 to 20 days from
date of application acceptance, depending on type of loan and type
of lender program.
```

Similarly, the Gopher menu at Texas A&M (`gopher.tamu.edu`) contains a wealth of business-related material, much of which points to international sites.

```
1.  Internet Business Pages/
2.  Singapore's IT2000 Nation-wide Plan for Info Technology/
3.  Trade News/
4.  Arizona State Economic Development Database (3270) <TEL>
5.  Asia Pacific Business & Marketing Resources/
6.  Automated Trade Library Service at Cal State Fresno (vt100) <TEL>
7.  Business Information Directory from Tucson, Arizona/
8.  College of Business at Florida State University/
9.  Current Business Statistics/
10. Descriptions of Information Products, Office of Business Analysis/
11. East and Southeast Asian Business and Management/
12. Economic Bulletin Board via U Michigan/
13. Finance software (DOS)/
14. Israel_Business_Today/
15. Izviestia/Financial Times Newspaper (Sample Issues - Russian) /
16. Japan Economic Newswire/
17. Pacific Region Forum on Business and Management /
18. Pennsylvania State Economic Development Information Network (.. <TEL>
19. Pragati/
20. Small Business Development (from WiscInfo)/
21. The Internet Business Journal/
22. Travel Information/
```

One example of the kind of material available here is shown in the next menu, yielded by selecting item 11, East and Southeast Asian Business and Management.

```
1.  Communicating to Asia-Pacific Consumers.
2.  Cross-Cultural Face-Negotiation.
3.  Globalization & Human Resource Management.
4.  Government & Business Relations in Indonesia.
5.  Negotiations with the Pacific Rim.
6.  Networking & Business in Southeast Asia.
7.  Political Change & Business Dynamics in Vietnam.
```

All of these could be of use to anyone about to conduct business in Southeast Asia. Selecting item 2, Cross-Cultural Face-Negotiation, brings up the following essay/report, which elaborates considerably on these four areas. This, once again, is but a small portion of a highly recommended paper.

```
3. Uncertainty avoidance. Hofstede found that Canada and the US are low
in uncertainty avoidance, i.e., we like to take risks, take individual
initiative, and enjoy conflict. Whereas cultures like Japan, Hong Kong,
and South Korea are high in uncertainty avoidance, i.e., do not like
conflict, but pursue group harmony; people within these organizations
need clear rules, procedures, and clearly defined job responsibilities.
```

```
4. Masculinity versus femininity. This dimension has been controversial
because many people feel it is sexist. Hofstede discovered that Japan
rated high on masculine dimensions (males expect an "in-charge" role).
In contrast, countries like Norway and Sweden have a stronger feminine
dimension, which means that roles are more fluid between males and
females.  Canada rated high on the masculine dimension compared with
many Northern European organizational practices.
```

Finally, let's examine a Gopher established by a company. In this case, we'll choose Bell Atlantic, for no other reason than it has perhaps the most easily remembered Gopher address of all (`ba.com`). Entering this Gopher gives us the following menu.

```
1.  +Welcome.
2.  Company_History/
3.  Congressional_Hearings/
4.  Education/
5.  Financial/
6.  Information_Law_Alert/
7.  Media_Contacts.
8.  News_Releases/
9.  Other_Gophers/
10. Speeches/
11. Video/
```

None of these items is, as of this writing, fully fleshed out. The idea, though, is that providing a well-designed shell will offer expansion capacity later. For now, though, Bell Atlantic has posted recent speeches and other media information, as well as public legal and financial details. From the `Financial` item we can get the 1994 reports, including this portion from 1st Quarter 1994.

```
Reported net income for the first quarter of 1994 was $389.2
million compared with $329.2 million for the first quarter of
1993, an increase of 18.2 percent. Total operating revenues
for the first quarter of 1994 were $3.37 billion, an increase
of 6.6 percent compared with $3.16 billion for the same period
last year. Revenues, excluding financial services,
increased by 7.3 percent over the first quarter of 1993.
Wireless revenues, including cellular and paging, were 42.3
percent higher than the first quarter of 1993.
```

Bell Atlantic's Gopher provides a good model from which to work. Don't worry about getting overly elaborate all at once. Post information that you know people will want, and let their reaction determine much of the rest.

Excursion 16.4. Businesses Already on the Net

This excursion looks at some businesses that have already committed to an Internet presence. All of the examples shown here are from the World Wide Web. The reason, quite simply, is that the Web enables businesses to appear in the most attractive possible light. However, most businesses with a WWW site also offer Gopher and/or FTP sites. Few have committed exclusively to the Web, because far more users have access to Gopher than Mosaic or Cello. Soon, that is almost certain to change.

The Web offers the following advantages:

- *Graphics:* Imagine relying on letters alone to make potential customers aware of your products and services and you will quickly understand why e-mail and downloaded text files have severe limitations. Through Mosaic or Cello, customers can be shown visually striking designs, which is crucial to any marketing or communications strategy.
- *Sound:* Commercials, showrooms, videoconferences, strategy sessions—they all have a sound element. Try to conduct business for one single day without it, and you'll get an idea of why it's so important. Without the Web's sound capabilities, the Internet is nothing more than a sophisticated print medium; with it, it merges and amplifies several media.
- *Video:* Television is the most popular medium for a very good reason. There is movement, dialog, and music, all at the same time. Except for the music (and the impossible story lines), it's just like real life. The still-life media—print and even radio—rely heavily on the user's imagination. The premise of television is that most people want things imagined *for* them. As the Web develops, it is likely to become more like television.
- *Interactive Forms:* The Web is interactive. That's why its potential as a business tool is even stronger than TV's. Interactive TV, at this point, means that a user sees a phone number on the screen and places a call. But most people don't want to get up from the couch and do that—they might miss part of the show, they can't remember the phone number, they don't want to go get their credit card, they'll do it later. People on the Web, by comparison, are in interactive mode from the minute they log on. Show them a form they can fill out and then send with the click of a mouse, and you have a potentially ideal tool. These forms—currently available only in the UNIX and Microsoft Windows versions of Mosaic but soon to appear in MacMosaic and in Cello—make it possible for customers to order products, to offer feedback, to complete surveys,

and even to participate in online meetings. Currently, one major concern is with security, but that may well be addressed by the preparation of a "secure" version of Mosaic, which has recently been announced.

- *Ease of Use:* Let's face it—if the future of business on the Internet depends on your customers, clients, and personnel knowing the intricacies of Telnet and FTP, you can close up shop right now. Gopher is an exceptionally strong interface, but even a graphical Gopher program doesn't provide the Web's ease of use. At this stage in its development, the biggest problem with Mosaic and Cello is setting it up, not using it, and that situation will only improve. Eventually, even complex operations like configuring download directories will be taken care of automatically. These programs let people see something and then click on what they want next. Using the Web will eventually be as easy for your customers and associates as using the most basic features of their TV's remote control. Maybe easier.

An excellent place to start exploring businesses already on the Web is the List of Commercial Services page at `http://tns-www.lcs.mit.edu/commerce.html`. As you can see from Figure 16.1, which displays only the top portion of this page, the list is extensive. Also, as you might expect, a number of high-tech firms appear prominently, but there are others as well.

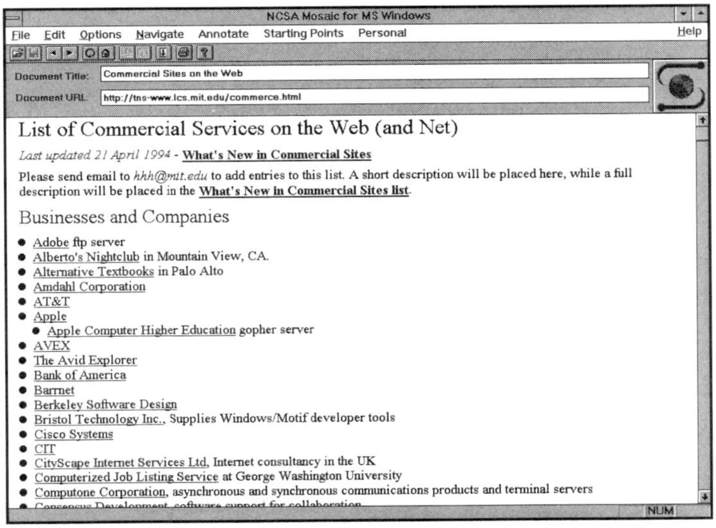

Figure 16.1. *List of Commercial Services on the WWW and the Internet.*

Further down this page, the links are divided according to server. CommerceNet, for example, is being coordinated by Enterprise Integration Technologies and represents a consortium of different firms. The links of most of those firms are gathered under one major link, as shown in Figure 16.2.

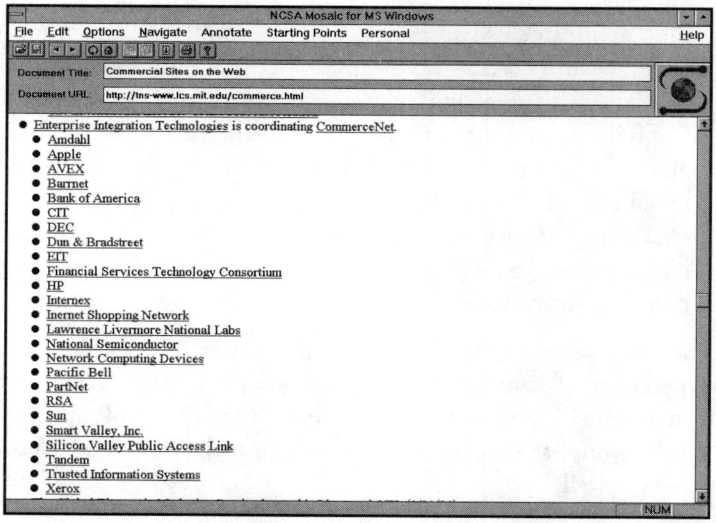

Figure 16.2. *List of Commercial Services—CommerceNet.*

The CommerceNet idea looked intriguing, so let's click on the appropriate link. This takes us to the CommerceNet home page, which offers a selection called Directories. Choosing this brings us to `http://www.commerce.net/directories/directories.html`, the CommerceNet directories page, as displayed in Figure 16.3.

As of this writing, this site was very much under construction, but already we can see the focus it will take. We also see how corporate interests view the potential of the World Wide Web; the color and easy accessibility of this page are exemplary, even if, with a slow connection, it takes a long time to load. The point is that Internet access will soon be faster, and pages like this will no longer be a problem.

Another intriguing offering from the List of Commercial Services is The Internet Mall (`http://www.kei.com/internet-mall.html`). This is another page listing commercial ventures on the Net, and it includes a number of Telnet and FTP sites in addition to the more obvious Gopher and Web sites. Figure 16.4 shows the Mall's home page.

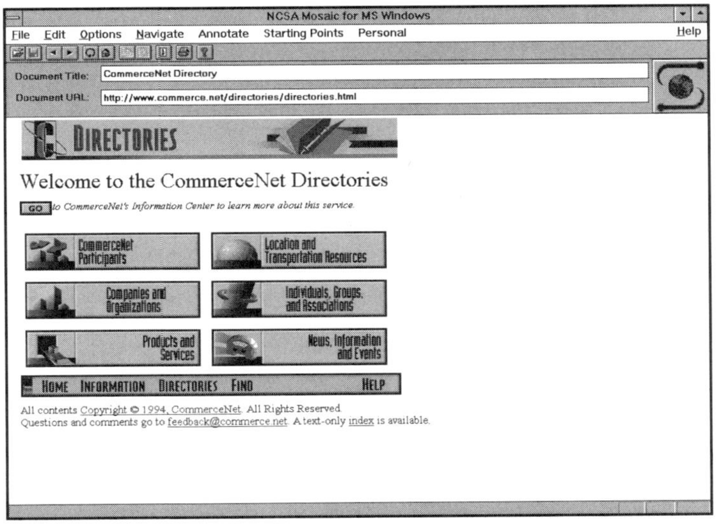

Figure 16.3. *CommerceNet directories.*

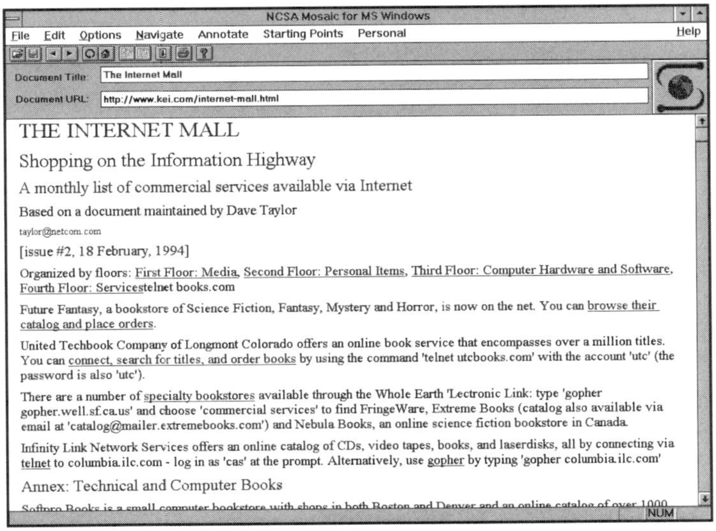

Figure 16.4. *The Internet Mall—a list of commercial Net sites, updated monthly.*

From here it's a click onto the Document Center, whose main page is shown in Figure 16.5.

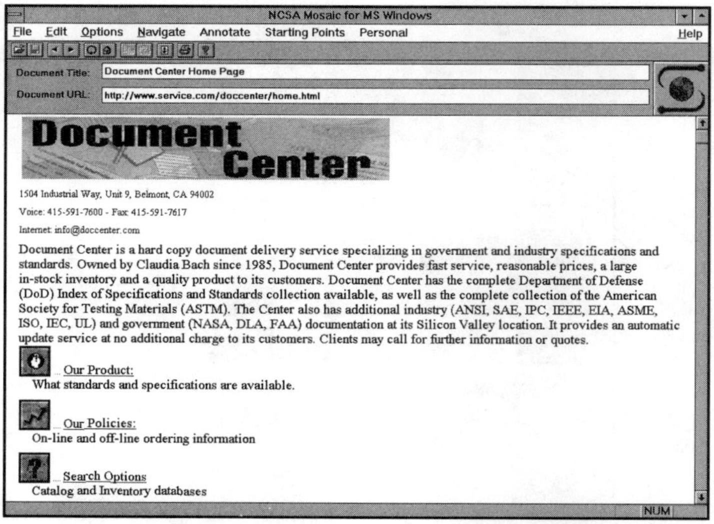

Figure 16.5. *Document Center home page.*

This colorful page explains what this company does, and it offers quick, easy links to its product information, policies, and search area. Figure 16.6 is the result of a click on Our Product, which includes a form for ordering documents.

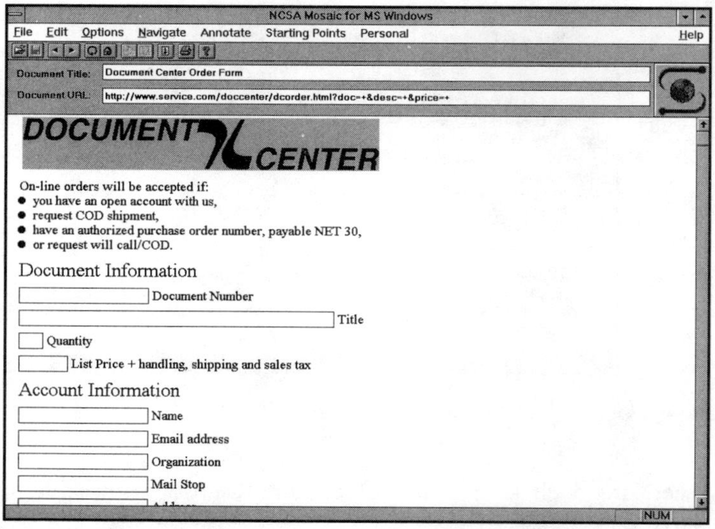

Figure 16.6. *Document Center order form.*

Here, the ordering is predicated on the customer's already having an account, or on a purchase order or a C.O.D. shipment. Pricing information is linked, and once you select your documents and specify the details, you can send the form online. This is our first example of online ordering.

Note: Once again, this kind of form is available, as of this writing, only with Mosaic for UNIX and Microsoft Windows. MacMosaic forms are being developed, as is forms capability in Cello.

Back to the List of Commercial Services, and this time let's click on the What's New link near the top of Figure 16.1. This leads us to the screen in Figure 16.7, which is directly accessible at `http://tns-www.lcs.mit.edu/commerce/whatsnew.html`.

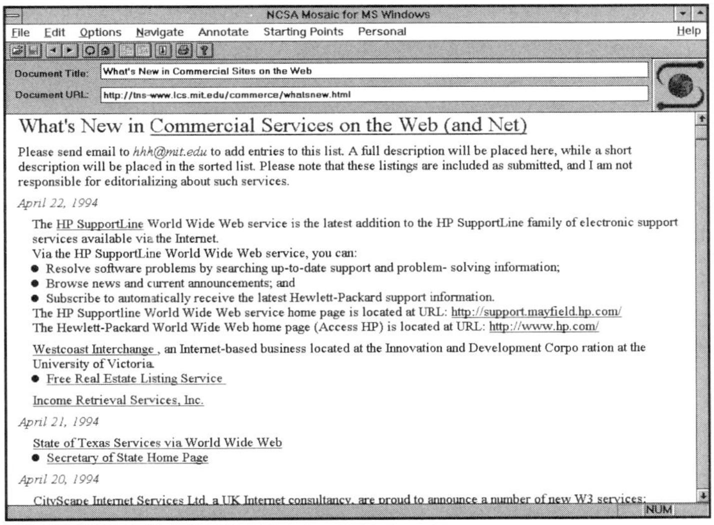

Figure 16.7. *List of Commercial Services—What's New page.*

We see a link to the HP SupportLine, Hewlett-Packard's new customer- and technical-support page. Other HP links are shown here as well, so let's start with the company's home page. Choosing this, we receive Figure 16.8.

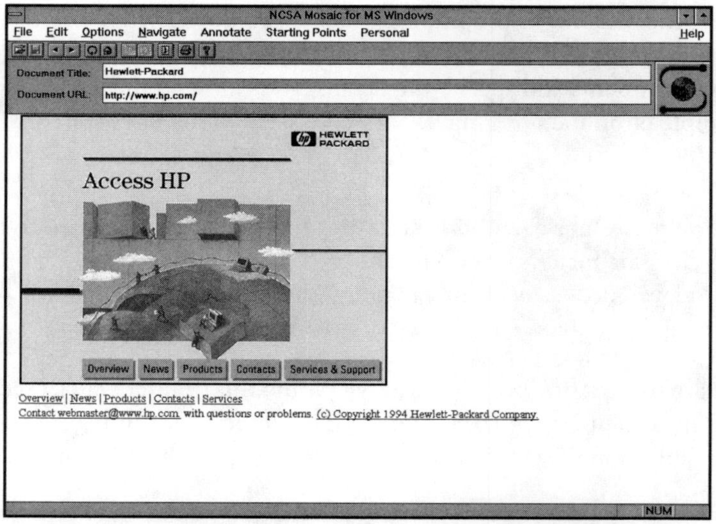

Figure 16.8. *Hewlett-Packard home page.*

This is a well-developed page for a number of reasons. First, all the information is accessible by clicking on named boxes, *or* (and this is important for many users) through text links below the graphic as well. Second, the page is graphically consistent with the company's well-known packaging designs, and therefore acts as part of the overall marketing effort.

But let's see what the new SupportLine offers. Clicking on Services, we come to Figure 16.9.

This page demonstrates several possible functions of a support feature on the Internet. Available here are news and announcements, documents, and searchable databases for solving technical difficulties.

From the U.K. comes CityScape Internet Services (`http://www.cityscape.co.uk`), which is establishing an online directory and which allows limited free advertising on the Web. Figure 16.10 shows the company's home page.

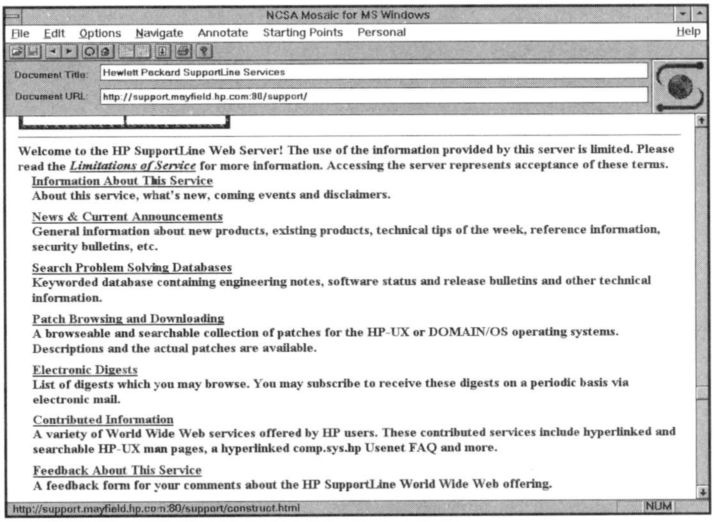

Figure 16.9. *Hewlett-Packard SupportLine page.*

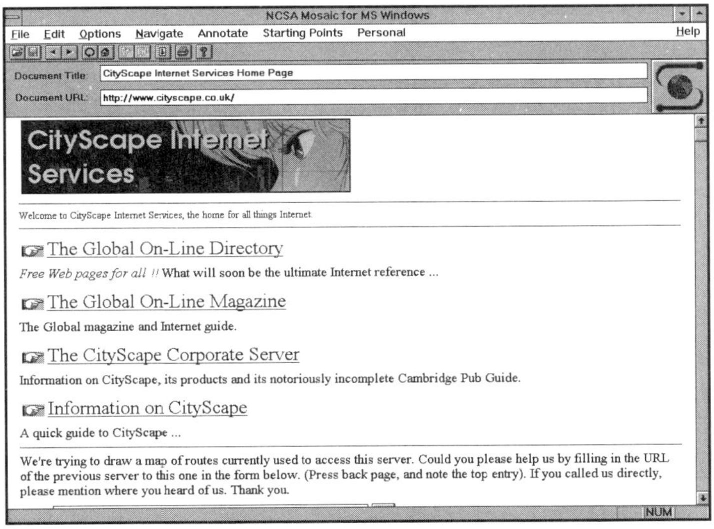

Figure 16.10. *CityScape Internet Services home page.*

Back across the Atlantic (or the Pacific if you prefer), we come to British Columbia. Figure 16.11 shows the home page for the Westcoast Interchange, which offers a link to its Free Real Estate Listing Service, although at the time of this writing the service was new and very few listings were available.

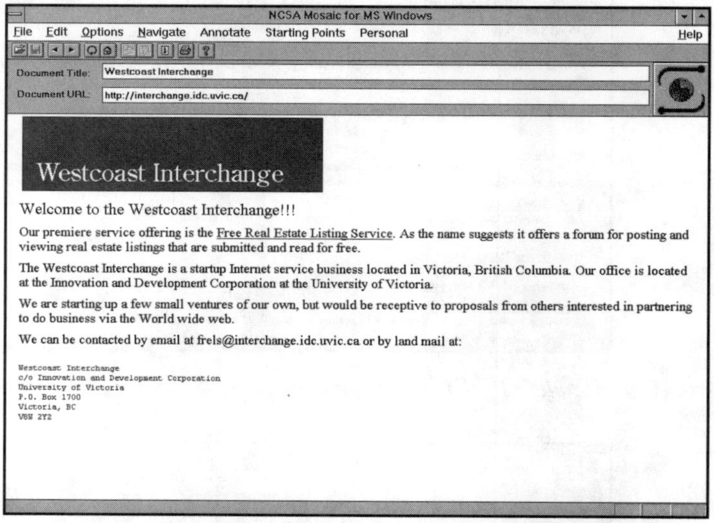

Figure 16.11. *Westcoast Interchange home page, including proposal invitation.*

An example of what such a service will eventually offer is shown in Figure 16.12. The National Real Estate Service offers information about a number of locations, including this rather attractive site in the Turks & Caicos. The Paint Shop Pro window shows the JPEG photo displayed in the link at the top of the page.

Clearly, the Internet—and especially the Web—has excellent applicability for real-estate firms, especially as access to the Net becomes more common. Entire walk-throughs of houses and neighborhoods could easily be part of a company's presentation.

Next we come to Novell, Incorporated, whose home page (`http://www.novell.com`) uses an entirely different metaphor (see Figure 16.13). The click-on-the-picture idea is the same as many, but this time the pictures are of books or manuals. Because the idea of the page is for technical support, and because Novell's product line tends to be technically oriented, this is probably a sound idea.

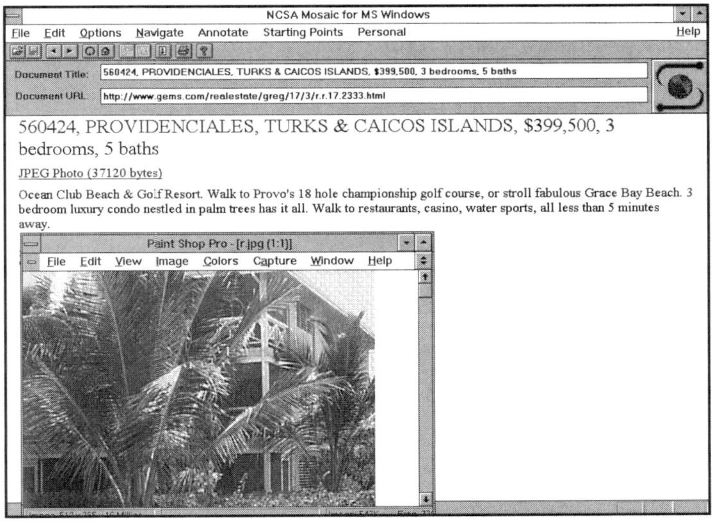

Figure 16.12. *National Real Estate Service—listing in Turks & Caicos.*

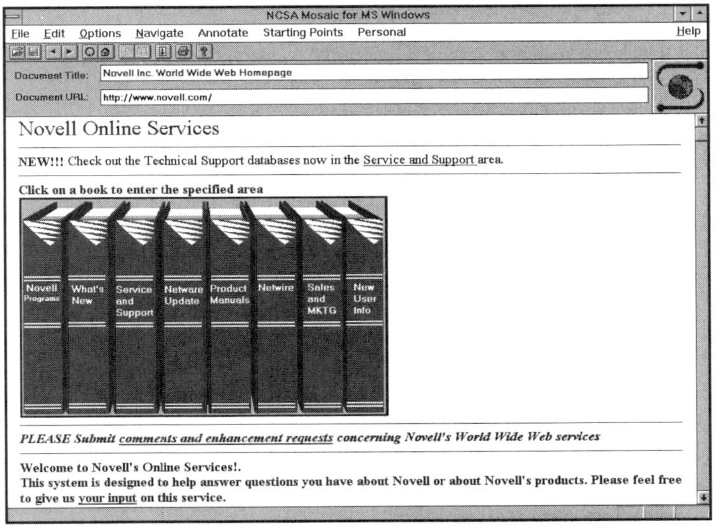

Figure 16.13. *Novell Online Services home page.*

A reduced-size continuation of the books metaphor reappears on Novell's searchable support database (see Figure 16.14), which enables such features as Boolean searching.

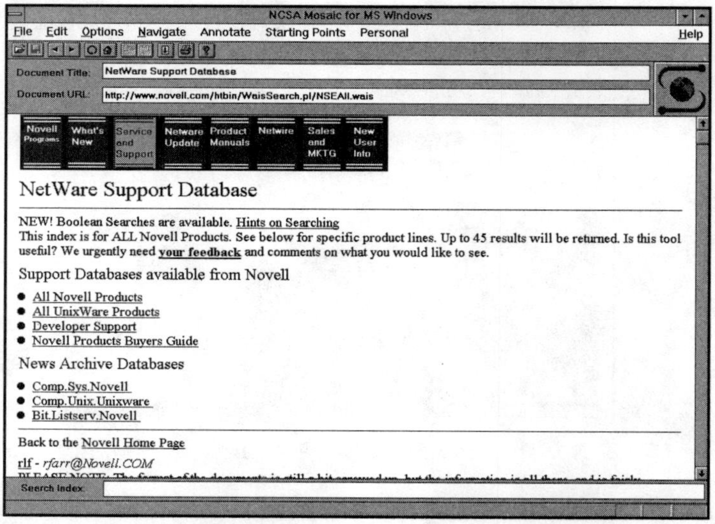

Figure 16.14. *Novell searchable support database.*

After a link to Hints on Searching, it's simply a matter of entering your search string. Let's make things easy by typing **`NetWare`**, one of Novell's chief lines. The result of the search is displayed in Figure 16.15. Each link is to a separate downloadable document.

Moving out of high tech and into finance, we arrive at the Bank of America home page (see Figure 16.16). Here we see very clearly how a major bank plans to offer Internet services. Most of this page is still under construction, but the goal is quick, easy, and reasonably detailed access.

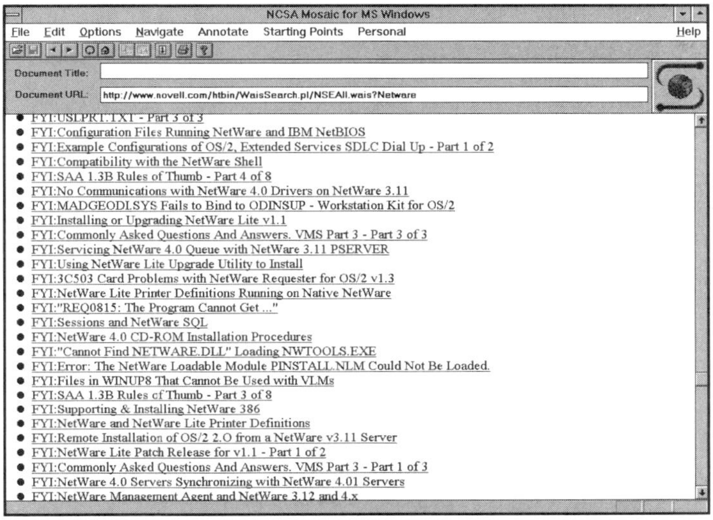

Figure 16.15. *Novell support database—search results for* `NetWare`.

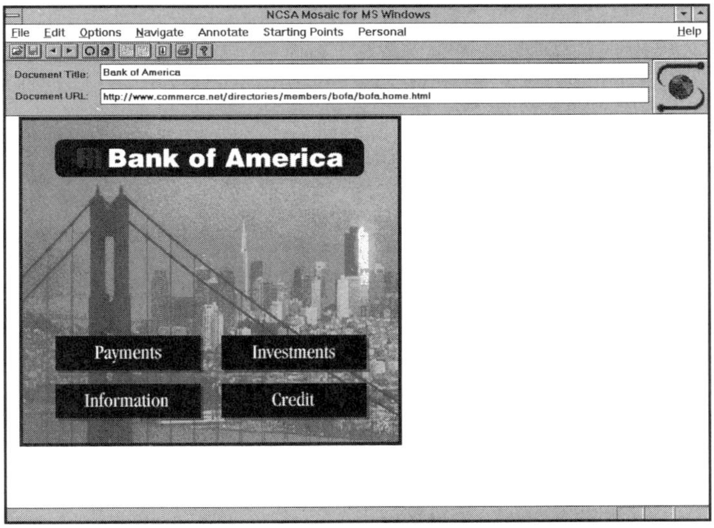

Figure 16.16. *Bank of America home page.*

Selecting Payments, for example, leads to Figure 16.17. This is another example of the use of the Web's interactive forms, this time to establish payments. Similar forms in these pages will enable investment and credit information as well.

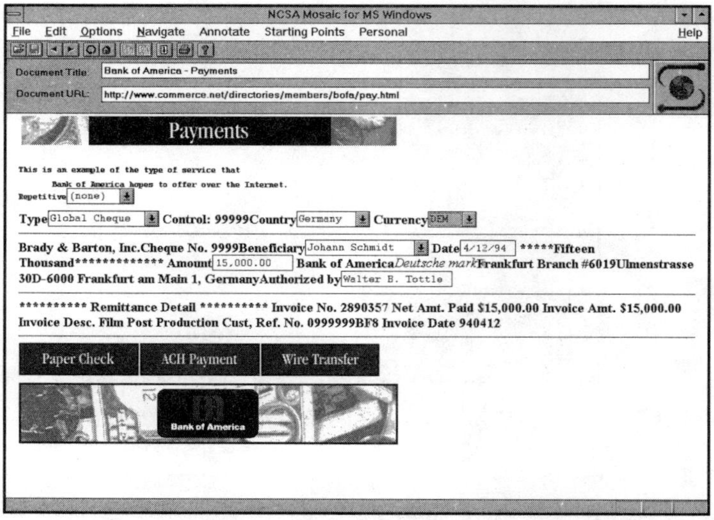

Figure 16.17. *Bank of America—payments service (under construction).*

The next two screens show the Web offerings in the Future Fantasy Bookstore. From the home page (see Figure 16.18), you can obtain information about upcoming signings or you can use the store's online catalog. A nicely designed search form appears when you select the catalog, and after a search we get Figure 16.19, this Web site's coup de grace: a chance to order the book online, an extremely important service for this kind of potential impulse buying. This is an excellent example of making Web forms work for your business.

Figure 16.18. *Future Fantasy Bookstore home page.*

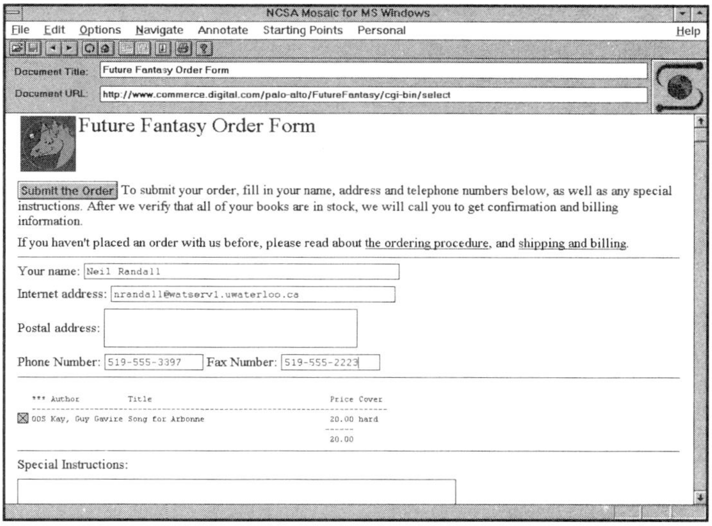

Figure 16.19. *Future Fantasy order form.*

Now, let's look at the efforts of two particular cities to make its businesses accessible through the Web. First up is Austin, Texas, from whose home page we can get detailed information about the famous Austin music scene and other Austin businesses (see Figure 16.20).

To demonstrate how prominent this idea might well become, we head across the Atlantic to Norway, where the Oslonett Marketplace's home page is clearly beginning to take shape (see Figure 16.21).

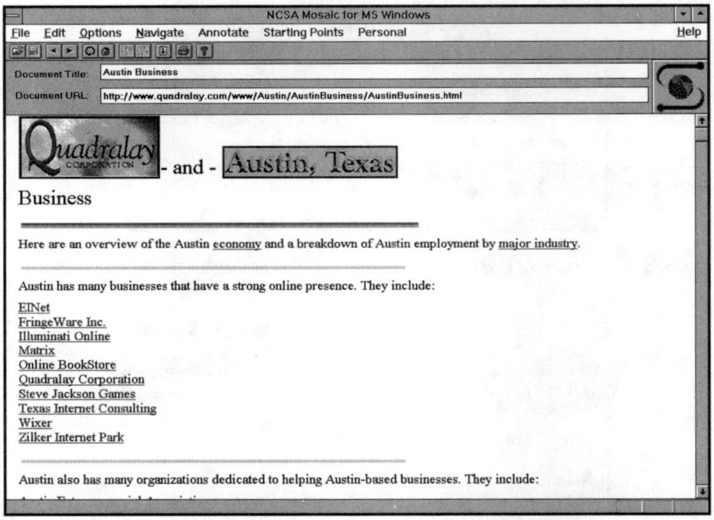

Figure 16.20. *Austin Business WWW page.*

These are only a few of the companies beginning to appear on the Web, offering a range of services and a number of different ideas about how to use the Internet in business.

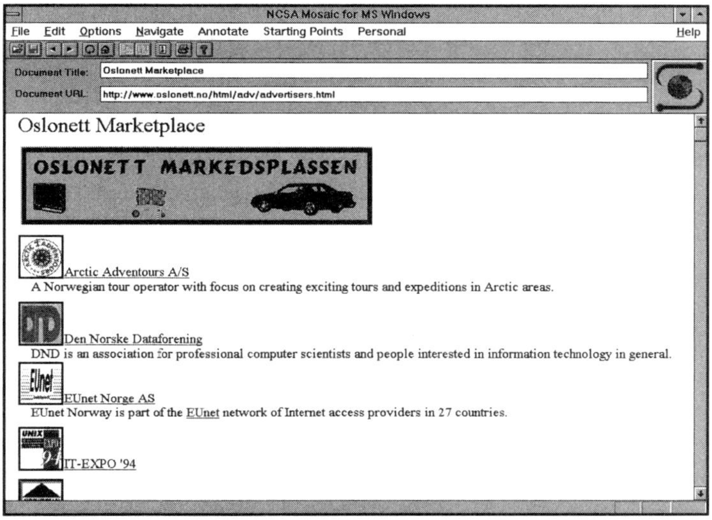

Figure 16.21. *Oslonett Marketplace home page.*

Summary

Day 16 has provided an introduction to using the Internet to conduct business. There are options for discussing business concerns, for engaging in advertising and product awareness, and for researching business issues through Gopher sites and elsewhere. In addition, we looked extensively at some of the businesses that have established a strong presence on the World Wide Web, looking at what they offer and what they plan for the future.

Task Review

On Day 16, you did the following:

- Examined various newsgroups dealing with business issues.
- Got an idea of which mailing lists your business might want to participate in.
- Worked through business-oriented Gophers and examined available documents.
- Explored how businesses have developed the World Wide Web for corporate purposes.

Q&A

Q How should my company start establishing an Internet presence?

A The first step, of course, is getting an Internet account. This can be done through a service provider, which is recommended until and unless you're planning to go whole-hog. You'll need an Internet account to allow your customers/clients/associates to reach you via e-mail. Next, it's probably a good idea to develop a Gopher, and you'll have to decide whether to maintain it yourself or have it stored on a provider's system. For a while, unless you have someone in your firm technologically capable (and with enough time) to develop and maintain it, the latter is probably a better option. Talk to your provider about this, or look to the Net for companies willing to do this. Third, get the Gopher up and running, make completely sure that it works properly, and then send a message to your clients and associates telling them it exists. If you want greater publicity, send a notice to the Gopher Jewels or Net-Happenings mailing lists (see Day 4 for information about the latter), and post to an appropriate newsgroup or two. Then, determine if you want to start a newsgroup or mailing list of your own.

Once all this is in place, decide whether or not a WWW site would suit your purposes, and how extensive you want that site to be. By this point, you'll want to hook up with an established provider or consultant to give you expertise on developing the site, and to put it on equipment you know will be dependable. Through all of this, start training your own people to use the Internet in a number of ways, and establish a team to maintain your Internet site. At some point you'll have your own people and equipment devoted to Internet functions, but that can be a year or two down the line.

Q If my Internet pages contain links to other sites, won't I simply lose browsers before they have a chance to explore my information thoroughly?

A This is an excellent question, and it brings up another point. One of the strengths of a Web page or a Gopher list is that it provides instant links to other sites. That means that someone who visits your site can just as easily leave it, never to return. As a hypothetical example, let's assume you've developed a cracker-jack home page that included colorful, appealing links to the home pages of some of your own clients (by cooperative arrangement, and all that). Someone lands on your page, thinks it looks fascinating, but before getting to the order form, they decide to head for your client's page instead. Even if your client has included your firm as a link (you'll make sure of this, of course), there's no guarantee that the browser will *ever* return to you.

A couple of possible solutions present themselves. First, make sure your page is referenced on a wide number of other pages. This can be done through a series of mutually cooperative ventures. Second, and more importantly, design your page so that browsers will stay and visit. How? Nobody knows yet. This is one of the most interesting and potentially rewarding challenges for a design artist in this decade (a similar problem to those faced by TV advertisers who have to deal with channel-surfers). How do you get people to stick around? Hmmm. It sounds like another business opportunity to me.

17

WEEK 3

Education 101: Exploring Internet Resources for K-12 Teachers

Day 17 focuses on the growing use of the Internet by K-12 educators. Particularly in the U.S. (and increasingly in Canada and elsewhere—see Excursion 17.3 later in this chapter for examples from Russia, Bosnia/Croatia, and Central America), teachers and curriculum designers are using the Internet to communicate with one another, to make resources available, and to involve their students in a variety of online projects. This chapter illustrates a portion of this explosion of activity.

Today, you will do the following:

- Use Gopher to access the growing number of information servers in the K-12 arena.
- Consult WAIS to conduct a search for K-12 documents and information.
- Find mailing lists to keep abreast of new developments in education and educational technology.
- Locate educational information on the World Wide Web.

Education and the Internet

The Internet may have started as a communications tool, quickly becoming an essential component of research as well, but there's never been any doubt of its potential as a teaching tool. Combine up-to-the-minute research and data with fast, global communications, and you have all the components necessary for an efficient, state-of-the-art education resource with previously unheard-of power and flexibility.

What *has* been in doubt is the degree to which teachers at all levels would have access to the Internet. University professors have been on the Net since its early days, and slowly but surely most universities and colleges in the United States, Canada, the U.K., and a host of other countries have gained access as well. But most of this access has been funded by research organizations to which elementary and secondary institutions have rarely had access. The types of infrastructure grants that have enabled universities to build the systems necessary for high-speed Internet connections simply haven't been available to educators at the lower levels.

Recently, things have changed. Through a variety of means (often very creative), K-12 institutions have established Internet access, and in an explosion of activity they are establishing mailing lists, Gopher servers, and even, in a few cases, World Wide Web sites. Gopher is, far and away, the most common K-12 tool currently in action, and the sheer number of these things springing into existence is almost overwhelming. Everything from working papers through course outlines is showing up on the menus, and teachers from everywhere in the world are invited to see what's going on.

And, in all likelihood, this type of activity has merely begun. With the Clinton administration's push for wider access to telecommunications resources (whether or not the much-touted "universal access" ever comes to pass), schools, school boards, education departments, and every other related institution will almost certainly strive for complete Internet access. Once in place, and with equipment in the schools themselves (yes, I'm aware of the enormous problems with supplying all of this), it's only a matter of time until the Internet becomes a resource at the classroom level as well. It already is, in a limited number of locations, but this kind of pedagogical activity will expand quickly. In fact, it may be no exaggeration to suggest that K-12 activity will do more than even commercial activity to push the Internet's technologies to their limits.

About the Contributor

Carol DeVrieze is a high school teacher in Kitchener, Canada. Although she'd heard of some of the K-12 Internet activity in the United States and Canada, it wasn't until she began exploring the resources fully that she realized what was happening out there. More than any other contributing author in this book, because of the staggering amount of information available, Carol first became awestruck and then quickly overwhelmed by the possibilities. As soon as her eyes stop burning from staring at the screen for hour after late evening hour, she'll move quickly to bring these possibilities into her classrooms.

Internet Resources for K-12 Teachers

by Carol DeVrieze

In the United States and Canada, as well in many other countries, educational reform is occurring on many levels.

Public education faces government cutbacks that naturally force reform of the school system. Educators are faced with the dilemma of providing a high-quality education with less funding, with more students in our classes, with cuts to social programs forcing the schools to provide these services, and so on.

Along with these changes comes the challenge from the business world demanding that its future employees, our students, be educated to keep up with the rapidly changing technological advancements to be competitive in a global economy. Educators also are dealing with the public outcry for accountability. Parents and taxpayers demand quality education; and, in some cases, standardized testing is seen as a way to ensure that learning has occurred.

But educational reform also is coming from educators themselves, who realize that changing the system is necessary to cope with the students we face in our schools every day. Educators are working hard to create new programs to get kids to school at an earlier age—with such programs as junior kindergarten—and to keep them in school instead of dropping out before high school graduation. Programs constantly are being developed to reduce violence in our schools, to help reduce teenage pregnancies, to make students aware of life-threatening diseases such as AIDS, and on and on.

Along with all these programs, teachers are still looking for ideas: new and creative ways to teach literature or science or math to their students; ways to teach and integrate students with learning disabilities within the regular classroom; methods for conflict mediation and resolution strategies with and among students; and techniques to expand the curriculum to be more inclusive of gender, race, and sexuality issues, just to name a few of the current initiatives in education today.

Like many teachers, I'm left questioning whether all of these demands can be satisfied.

With the help of the Internet, I thought I would be able to get a handle on all of the latest information and current ideology. However, I did not find this to be the case. Rather than using the computer to keep me apprised of the prevailing educational trends, I found that there was such a barrage of information related to education that I became even more overwhelmed.

What I discovered is that there is a tremendous quantity of information on the Internet on almost any topic related to education, more information than one person can even hope to assimilate.

I've also learned, however, that the Internet is a potentially valuable tool for educational use. Some of its most worthwhile uses include:

- Getting educators in touch with other educators through mailing lists and newsgroups.
- Finding educational software.
- Keeping informed of daily government decisions and comments on educational issues.
- Finding lesson plans on a wide array of curriculum areas.
- Locating current articles and educational research for the professional development of teachers.
- Determining useful ways students in a classroom can use computers, specifically the Internet, to foster learning.
- Linking students with other students from other parts of the country or the world to discuss issues of concern on a personal level as well as a global level.

Because education is becoming one of the most rapidly developed subjects on the Internet, and since I have only a limited amount of space, I will describe only a few of the great places that I have found.

Excursion 17.1. The New York State Education Gopher

One Gopher system with a highly useful educational component is the New York State-developed Gopher. It is located at `unix5.nysed.gov`. When you connect with this Gopher system, a list of directories is available to you. Remember, these directories frequently are changed and developed, but when I last explored I found the following items:

```
1.   New York State Documents Ftp Archive/
2.   Search the New York State Library Catalogue (OPAC) <TEL>
3.   Search the Internet/
4.   Network Learning Success Stories/
5.   State Library's Ftp site (test only)/
6.   NYSERNet's Ftp site (test only)/
7.   About This Gopher/
8.   Conferences, Calls for Papers/
9.   Government Information/
10.  Higher Education/
11.  Internet Resources/
12.  K-12 News/
13.  K-12 Resources/
14.  Requests for Comment/
15.  Telecomm Information/
```

Tip: As always, to reach this Gopher site type **`gopher`** and then the address. For this example, type **`gopher unix5.nysed.gov`** to reach the New York State Education Gopher.

Selecting number 12, K-12 News, presents a wide range of new items to choose from. As expected in a Gopher browse, some of these items are additional directory names, each with even more items to explore. Remember what I said about being overwhelmed? Some of the titles in the K-12 directory that I found intriguing included the following:

```
1. News from the North (Arctic Trip)/
2. Wildlife News
------------------------------------------------
6. Reviews of Book on History of Punctuation
------------------------------------------------
11. Online Commercial Curriculum Service
------------------------------------------------
15. Text Analysis Resources at University of Virginia
------------------------------------------------
17. 'Net Training for Rural Teachers
------------------------------------------------
20. Email Educational Projects List
21. Johns Hopkins Journals Online
------------------------------------------------
28. How to Get NASA Internet Video
------------------------------------------------
34. Classroom Mailing List
------------------------------------------------
36. NII Mailing List
37. Sixth Grade Web Server
```

Warning: When you access this Gopher, remember that some of the menu items might no longer be available. A greater likelihood, however, is that there will be even more to choose from. This Gopher is constantly growing.

One of the directories that is particularly useful for my purposes is item number one, News from the North (Arctic Trip). When you select this directory, you will get a listing of two other directories called Arctic Bites and News from the North. Choosing the first option, Arctic Bites, gives a list of file titles such as March 04, March 08, and March 16, just to name a few. Choosing any one of these files reveals short stories or excerpts of longer stories written about Arctic life or written by natives from this geographical area.

One of the courses that I teach as a high school English teacher deals with regional literature. These stories from the Arctic fit in perfectly with the curriculum and are an excellent way to introduce the North. As a result, I decided that I would like a copy of these stories. At the end of each file, the prompt `: Press <return> to continue, <m> to mail, <s> to save, or <p> to print` appeared. I typed `m` and then my e-mail address. Simple enough to do, and now I have a great resource to use when I teach that unit of the course. Under the other directory in News from the North (Arctic Trip), entitled News from the North/, you will find four more titles:

```
1.    Introduction
2.    International Arctic Project Team Profiles/
3.    Reports from the IAP/
4.    Wildlife News/
```

Introduction explains what this directory is all about. It seems that teachers from various parts of the world are working together on a project to explore the Arctic. The second item, International Arctic Project Team Profiles, gives a short biography and country of origin of each person on the trip; and the third heading, Reports from the IAP/, actually gives updates by the team as they are traveling through the North.

I can see many uses for this information not only by the classroom teacher but by students connected to the Internet in the classroom too. Students in geography classes could actually follow the team day by day on their journey, mapping out the route and learning from a firsthand description of the land, climate, culture, and so on.

Bear in mind that we have only examined one directory out of 37 options in the directory K-12 News of the New York State Gopher. By choosing other options, helpful information is available regarding other places you can find information such as the NII Teacher Mailing List, the Email Educational Projects List, the Online Commercial Curriculum Service List, and the Johns Hopkins Journals Online.

It's already easy to feel overwhelmed, and we've barely even started.

The second directory of interest to elementary and secondary school educators is K-12 Resources. This directory has perhaps more practical uses for teachers. When it's selected, the following options appear on the screen:

```
1. Arts and Humanities/
2. Disability Resources and Information/
3. English - Language Arts/
4. General/
5. Health, PhysEd and Home Ec/
6. Languages Other Than English/
7. Math, Science and Technology/
8. Other Educational Gophers/
9. Social Studies/
```

Determine your selections by the subjects you teach. Not all of the directories are developed equally, but they all present numerous entry points into your subject area.

I first chose Arts and Humanities, which listed some interesting options such as All Music Guide, Animal Sounds, Art Resources from UT Dallas, Dallas Museum of Art, Art

Lessons from Ask ERIC, Student Journalism Gopher, plus many more. I surfed through some of these directories and found interesting files on music and art lessons.

The most interesting directory from these options for me was the Student Journalism Gopher. Even though the students at which these files are aimed are college students, having senior high school students access this type of directory would help them become aware of the kinds of writing and projects they can become involved in when they go on to a college or university.

The directory that I was most pleased to discover as an English teacher was English-Language Arts. This selection provided me with the following list:

```
1.    Acronym Dictionary <?>
2.    American English Dictionary <?>
3.    Book Discussions and Reviews
4.    Collection of Mini-Lesson Plans from Ask ERIC all grade levels
5.    English Instructors Source Book for Running a Discussion
6.    Essay Starters
7.    Index of Poetry Magazine <?>
8.    Palindrome Collection
9.    Roget's Thesaurus <?>
10.   Spoonerisms and Mannerisms
11.   Student Journalism Gopher/
12.   Works of Literature in Electronic Form
13.   BooKBraG v1n1 (Americ's Past)
14.   Dogwood Blossoms - Q Haiku List
15.   Poetry Readings - Under Construction
```

Selecting item 15, Poetry Readings, yields a list of several famous celebrities reading some of the great poetry classics, and even in some cases, the authors reading their own works, but the files in this directory are not yet complete. These files would be great to access within a classroom. Students could actually listen to T. S. Eliot reading "The Waste-land," Julie Harris reading some of Emily Dickinson's poetry, or Robert Frost reading "Mending Wall."

Another practical option that I found useful for my classes is in the section entitled Essay Starters. There are many great ideas that could be used in the pre-writing process and for discovering writing topics. Once again, I mailed these files to myself for later use. Here is a partial example of one of them:

```
Problem: Areas of Philadelphia were badly affected with graffiti.
Businesses were distrubed by the resulting atmosphere and by the cost
of continual cleanup.
```

```
Proposed Solution: The City developed the Philedelphia Anti-Graffiti
Network (PAGN). This program attacked the problem on several
fronts. On the enforcement front, they worked with police to develop
a program to find offenders, promoted more severe penalties for
violators, and encouraged the passage of a law restricting the sale of spray
paint. As alternative approaches, they helped to develop the amnesty
program to get offenders to pledge not to continue, and they promoted
cleanup as an alternative punishment to incarceration. More importantly,
artists were involved in working with graffiti artists in putting murals.
The murals, located throughout the city, have provided an outlet for the artistic
abilities of the former graffiti painters....

Evaluation: The program has been a success at eliminating much of the
graffiti in the city. The murals have improved the appearance of much of
the city.
```

Another excellent resource can be found by choosing item number 13. This choice gives access to a copy of a new electronic journal called BooKBraG. This journal features reviews of children's books that could be used in a classroom setting. It also has articles about many other current issues related to the student reading program along with interviews with authors of children's books.

Going back to the first screen of listings under K-12 Resources, we find the General directory, which is very good for professional development. Here are the headings:

```
1.   Compendium of Suggestions for Teaching Excellence, UC Berkely/
2.   The Interpedia Project/
3.   Library Science Collection/
4.   Researchers Guide to the U.S. Department of Education/
5.   Teacher's Guide to the U.S. Department of Education/
6.   Things to do on the Internet/
7.   Using the Internet in the Classroom/
8.   Open Texts - A Rallying Cry for School Libraries
```

By selecting item 6, Things to do on the Internet, other directories become available:

```
1.   Why Connect/
2.   How to Connect/
3.   Instructional Applications/
4.   Ethics and Etiquette/
5.   Bibliography/
6.   AskERIC Gopher/
7.   KIDSgopher/
```

The Instructional Applications directory has some fascinating files called Space Safari and Space Trek. Within these files are some very innovative lesson plans for using the Internet in a science classroom. Here is an example of one such lesson:

```
Space Trek - Students as Guides
Lesson Two
Lesson Summary: The purpose of this lesson is for students to practice
independent information seeking. Students will access NASA Spacelink,
a database of historical documents, scientific information, current events,
downloadable graphics and interactive communication opportunities.
Student teams or "crews" will be directed to develop and research a series
of questions using information found within the spacelink database...

Grade Levels...
Procedures...
Activities...
Closure and / or Evaluation...
Key Terms...
Real World Applications...
Home Learning Suggestions...
Extensions and Follow-Up Activities...
```

As you can see, I have extracted only a small portion from this file. The headings listed above indicate areas that are developed in the lesson plan itself.

The directory entitled Using the Internet in the Classroom is another superb resource for both practical ideas and theoretical implications of using the Internet with your students. Again this list is very long. Some of the options include:

```
1. About Classroom Ideas
2. Academe One Project
3. Archaeology Units
4. Ask Dr. Science
5. Ask Prof. Math
----------------------------------
7. At-Risk Students
----------------------------------
17. The History of Math
----------------------------------
19. Introduction to Computer Science for the 21st Century
----------------------------------
26. Young Kids and Language
```

I accessed the At-Risk Students file and mailed myself a copy of this fascinating article on using telecommunications to help teach at-risk students. The following is an excerpt from that article.

```
The number of students that are not graduating from traditional
schools is increasing. We as educators, need to find a way to make
these students become contributing members of society. As the computer
becomes a vital part of the future job market, we need to make sure that at-
risk students are empowered with the knowledge of computers so that they
may join the next generation of productive thinkers.
```

There seems to be an almost endless source of information that teachers can access in this one Gopher system. I'm not sure I have solved my information-overload problem, but I certainly know what type of information is available and readily accessible using the Internet.

Excursion 17.2. The California Department of Education

Another Gopher system with a wealth of educational material is located at `goldmine.cde.ca.gov`. This Gopher takes you into the California Department of Education system. You can get some excellent information about education in California, but this system enables you to explore many other educational Gopher systems as well. When you connect, the first screen lists the options:

```
1.   About this Gopher.
2.   California Department of Education - General Information/
3.   California School Districts/
4.   Daily Report Card News Service/
5.   BBN's National School Network Testbed/
6.   Other Information Services/
```

Selecting item 2 gives a lengthy list of options that are mostly related to information about schools in California, finances, charter schools, advisories, calendar of events, and so on. One of the headings I chose to explore was a Curriculum directory, which gave the following choices:

```
1.   Bilingual Education Network (BiEN)/
2.   Elementary Ed/
3.   Healthy Kids/
4.   High School Ed/
5.   Instructional Resources/
6.   Mathematics Ed/
```

```
7.   Middle Grades/
8.   Performance Levels/
9.   Science and Environmental Ed/
```

The High School Ed directory has several entries under the title News followed by a specific month. These files are basically newsletters coming from the California Department of Education. One of the newsletters that I decided to read had articles about various classroom strategies, performance assessment in the arts, promising approaches to interdisciplinary teaching in the classroom, upcoming conferences, and the like. The following passage provides you with a sample of the type of article you can find here.

```
Promising approaches to Interdisciplinary Teaching in the Classroom
by Twyla Wills Stewart, PhD.

There is no single model of interdisciplinary instruction suitable for
all situations. Approaches to interdiscplinary instruction vary significantly
by discipline in the range of practical applications use, the context for
teaching and learning, grade level demands and the focus of inquiry.
Consequently, ...
```

Backtracking to the first listing of six directories in the Goldmine Gopher system, I decided to explore a few other areas. The directory Daily Report Card News Service gives a listing of daily publications numbering more than 40 and growing every school day. Again, I decided to read only one of these publications and found several articles about various programs occurring in California schools. One engaging piece described a pilot project aimed at reducing violence in the schools by removing students guilty of violent behavior from their regular school classes and having them attend school on the weekends. The results of this program will be interesting to follow and update in future editions of the Daily Report Card.

The next item to explore from the original screen in the Goldmine Gopher is the California School Districts directory. Choosing this directory gives only one option, the San Diego City Schools Gopher Server. One of the options available here is a directory entitled Lesson Plans. I decided to explore, and I received the following list:

```
1.   About this Collection.
2.   Biology/
3.   Earth Science/
4.   English/
5.   Lessons in Spanish/
```

```
6.   Mathematics/
7.   Physical Science and Chemistry/
8.   Physics/
```

Unfortunately, not all of the directories are complete. There was nothing available in the English directory at that time, so I surfed through some of the other subject areas. In the Biology directory, four directories are developed: Cells, Miscellaneous Biology Ideas, Physiology, and Plants. Choosing the Cells directory gives you two more alternatives: Osmosis with Peas and The Secret Path of Osmosis. Here is an example of a lesson plan teaching the scientific concept of osmosis:

```
Fill a wine glass to overflowing with dried peas, pour in water
up to the brim, and place the glass on a metal lid. The pea heap
becomes slowly higher and then a clatter of falling peas begins,
which goes on for hours.

This is again an osmotic process. Water penetrates into the pea cells through
the skin and dissolves the nutrients in them. The pressure thus
formed makes the peas swell. In the same way the water necessary for life
pentrates the walls of all plant cells, stretching them. If the plant obtains
no more water, its cells become flabby and it wilts.
```

Another area to explore is BBN's National School Network Testbed (directly accessible at `copernicus.bbn.com`). This directory also is more directly available, you may recall, on the first screen of this Gopher system, and it can be accessed from either route. Choosing this directory again provides numerable options for exploring various educational topics:

```
1.   Welcome to BBN's National School Network Testbed.
2.   Copernicus Internet Server.
3.   National School Network Testbed/
4.   K-12 on the Internet/
5.   Curriculum Resources/
6.   General Information Resources/
7.   Software Libraries/
8.   AskERIC/
9.   Internet Information.
10.  State Resources/
11.  Federal Resources/
12.  Other Gopher and Information Services/
13.  Search titles in Gopherspace using veronica/
```

Items 1 and 2 discuss aims of the BBN project and the Copernicus network to enable people to construct school- or district-based Internet resources. Choosing item 3, the `National School Network Testbed` directory, links you to the national network.

> **Note:** BBN stands for Bolt, Beranek, and Newman. One of the original firms involved in Internet research and development, BBN has been contracted by the National Science Foundation to develop a test site for U.S. K-12 schools. The BBN Gopher demonstrates some of the initial results.

Two other directories I searched through were Ralph Bunche School, New York City and Shadows Science Project (both at `ralphbunche.rbs.edu`). The first directory links you to an elementary school in New York City. Once connected to this school's Gopher, you can read files about the school and their Internet project.

I accessed one of the directories called Ralph Bunche School Newspaper Stories and read some interesting articles written by students about current issues in their school (such as the recent science fair, in which many of the school's students were involved). Another directory named `Student Work` contained several files written by the students themselves, their poetry and their points of view on topics.

Going back to the main screen of BBN's National School Network Testbed with its 13 alternatives, the next area I thought might be important was item 4, the directory K-12 on the Internet. This choice yields another 12 directories:

```
1.   Best of K-12 on the Internet (from TIES, Minn.)/
2.   Acceptable and Unacceptable Uses of Internet Resources (K-12)/
3.   Consortium for School Networking (CoCN)/
4.   Empire Internet School House/
5.   Global School House/
6.   Geometry Forum/
7.   Education BBSs/
8.   Schools/districts on the Internet/
9.   Colleges of Education/
10.  Daily Report Card/
11.  CICNet k-12 Gopher/
12.  The Hub (TERC)/
```

Yet another overwhelming list of alternatives! Starting from the first option, Best of K-12 on the Internet, I began surfing once again. Choosing this directory had amazing results. Thirty-eight new directories and Gopher links appeared on the screen. I'll list only some of the selections available:

```
1.  Current k-12 Information (postings from select Ed. Listservs)/
2.  Russian Far East Exchange/
3.  The Space Science and Engineering Center (Global Satellite Images)/
4.  WOLF STUDY PROJECT/
5.  Bosnian / Croatian Exchange Project/
-------------------------------------------------------
7.  Selected PICTURES, QUICKTIME MOVIES AND SOUNDS
8.  CNN Newsroom Classroom Guide/
9.  Project Central America/
-------------------------------------------------------
11. Africatrek!/
-------------------------------------------------------
15. Geographic Server <TEL>
-------------------------------------------------------
18. Center for Great Lakes Information Service/
19. NASA/
-------------------------------------------------------
27. TogetherNet, Foundation for Global Unity/
28. K12Net/
29. News From Around the World/
30. Teacher Contacts/
---------------------------------------------------------
32. Canada's SchoolNet/
---------------------------------------------------------
34. Education Gopher at Florida Tech/
35. KIDLINK Gopher/
---------------------------------------------------------
37. StarkNet (Stark County School Disctrict, Canton, Ohio, USA)/
38. TEACHER * PAGES (Pennsylvania Dept. of Ed.) Login: TX <TEL>
```

As you can see, there are so many places to explore, too numerous for me to describe them all. Some will be of more interest to you than others. Some that I checked out include CNN, Selected PICTURES…, NASA, Teacher Contacts, and Canada's SchoolNet. All of these have excellent resources for use in classroom assignments and projects.

The Teacher Contacts directory lists teachers involved in various projects on the Internet and e-mail addresses where they can be contacted. One of the entries is written by a professor from MIT who is interested in working on computer science projects with high schools. The NASA Gopher is especially excellent for use in a science program.

Canada's SchoolNet Gopher links you to various projects currently in production such as the Whale Watching Project, the Acid Rain Project, and the Telecommunications Project, as well as a directory of projects soliciting participants.

Two of these 11other directories include CICNet K-12 Gopher and The Hub (TERC). The first connects you to several other directories or searches. One of these, Education-Related Publications, is extremely valuable for finding articles useful for teacher professional development or in the classroom with your students. Nine publications are available: Academe This Week, Academy one, Equitnews, K12ADMIN, KIDS, KIDS-94, KIDSPHERE, and Report Card.

Selecting The Hub (TERC) Gopher enables you to find specific topics in education for use in the classroom by grade level, region, and topic. The By Topic directory gives you categories such as Assessment, Gender, Math, Science, and Technology. The By Grade Level directory enables you to find classroom information for College (Undergraduate Level), High School Level, and Upper Elementary Grades.

Here are some other educational Gopher addresses to explore:

```
garnet.geo.brown.edu
gopher.mde.state.mi.us port 70
gwis.circ.gwu.edu
csd4.csd.uwm.edu
gopher.cic.net
gopher.oise.on.ca
porpoise.oise.on.ca 70
nstn.ns.ca
gopher.ed.gov
gopher.mde.state.mi.us
gopher.cse.ucls.edu
cwis.usc.edu
gopher.briarwood.com port 70
```

Excursion 17.3. International K-12 Activity

As you might expect, other nations are also actively putting the Internet to its best educational uses. Canada's SchoolNet project has already been mentioned, but the Best of K-12 of the Internet listing (shown previously) can take you to other countries as well.

You can reach the Best of K-12 Gopher directly at `tiesnet.ties.k12.mn.us`. Once here, selecting the Best of K-12 line yields this menu:

```
1.  Current k-12 Information (postings from select Ed. Listservs)/
2.  Russian Far East Exchange/
3.  The Space Science and Engineering Center (Global Satellite Images)/
4.  WOLF STUDY PROJECT/
5.  Bosnian / Croatian Exchange Project/
-----------------------------------------------------
7.  Selected PICTURES, QUICKTIME MOVIES AND SOUNDS
8.  CNN Newsroom Classroom Guide/
9.  Project Central America/
-----------------------------------------------------
11. Africatrek!/
```

Several internationally based items present themselves, including the Russian Far East Exchange, the Bosnian/Croatian Exchange Project, and Project Central America. Let's look briefly at each of these.

The Russian Far East Exchange is primarily concerned with Kamchatka, and yields the following menu of items:

```
1.  KAMCHATKA: A Live Satellite Telecast Tuesday, March 15, 1994 .
2.  KAMCHATKA BROADCAST PROGRAM GUIDE, MARCH 15, 1994.
3.  Archives from Kamchatka's first English Newspaper: NEW GENERATIONS/
4.  Ivitation for E-mail exchange from Termalny, Kamchatka, Russia.
5.  Journal of a Russian Particapant the August Seminar.
6.  Proffesional Exchange Opportunity with Teachers in Kamchatka.
7.  *VICTORY! First School with Email in Kamchatka.
8.  Exchange Opportunity in Kamchatka.
9.  Hello and Introduction from Russian teachers.
10. Kamchatka Volcano Updates/
11. MAPS of Russian Far East/
12. Pictures:Chukotka,Russia/
13. Pictures:Kamchatka,Russia/
14. Publish student essays in Russian Newspaper.
15. Welcome to Kamchatka, Russia!.
```

While all are intriguing, we'll look at only two. First, a welcome message from a Kamchatkan teacher, who, in the remainder of this lengthy file, explains the land and the online project:

```
The following is an overview of Kamchatka written by Irina Ivanova,
English teacher from school #15 in Petropavlask, Kamchatka Russia

* * * * * * * * * * * * * * * * * * * * * * * * * * * * * * * * * * * * * *
                    Welcome to Kamchatka!


Planning to visit Kamchatka?
You are welcome! Any idea why our land is called  Kamchatka?
To tell you the truth, we do not know  for  sure  ourselves,
though the guides might offer you quite a few versions.  One
of them says that our land owes  its  name  to  the  Russian
Cossack Ivan Kamchaty, one of the first explorers here.
```

Next, some information about the Kamchatka exchange itself. While this is clearly oriented toward Minnesota students, it might well be an idea worth exploring for your own school district.

```
E-mail offers Minnesota students a bridge to Kamchatka
Our connections with the folks in the Russian Far East are expanding to
the Kamchatka Peninsula.  The Kamchatka Association of Greens (KAG) is
ready to provide an opportunity for all interested students to send and
receive letters through e-mail to penpals in this unique part of Russia.
Students in Kamchatka are eager to correspond with foreign sister schools.

To make the e-mail "conversation" possible, Minnesota students interested
in sending a letter to any school in Petropavlovsk-Kamchatsky can send an
introduction to KAG's e-mail address.  KAG has a weekly TV program, called
Green Marathon TV, which they will use to publicize the opportunity for
penpal correspondence.  Their program usually consists of one or two
reports on local problems (15-20 minutes) and a documentary provided by
one of the western TV companies.
KAG will forward the Minnesota student's letters to interested students in
" Petro"  When Russian students have prepared their letters, KAG will send
the letters to Minnesota through their e-mail.  As part of the initial
contact, Sergey Solovyov (Chairman, Kamchatka Association of Greens) says
they will tell a little about the state of Minnesota and explain the plan
to attract more people to this sister school penpal program.
```

From the Bosnian/Croatian Exchange (also through Minnesota), we find a small but fascinating group of items. Among them are letters such as the following, which can't help but demonstrate the need for this kind of collaborative activity:

```
Last May, Aida Bajric, a 16-year-old teenage refugee from Bosnia-
Herzegovina, sent the following message This message prompted TIES to
work with CARNet (the Croatian Academic and Resaerch Network) to
establish an E-mail vehicle for teens

***************************************************

           Dear lady and gentleman!

      First I would like to introduce myself to you. My name,
  is Aida and I'm 16. 10 month ago because of the war
  I had to leave my country Bosnia and Hercegovina and I'm
  now spending my time as a refugee in Povlja's hotel "Galeb"
  (it is now refugee camp) on the island Brac in Croatia. The
  town I come from is Banja Luka (NW Bosnia). My father is
  still there (he is doctor of Mechanical Engeneering and has
  been lecturing the Computer aided design - CAD). Banja
  Luka is the capital of Serbian republic and Serbs don't allow
  him to get out. My mother (she is electronic engineer) and
  my sister Elma (she is 17) are with me in this hotel. My
  sister and me go in the school in Bol which is 31 kilometer
  far from Pavlja.
      On Saturday 20th of March in hotel "Galeb" came Mr.Ted
  Pratt with idea for publishing the news for Bosnian teen
```

```
refugees. We have talked a lot about that. He said that
you would be able to finance organization and publishing
and we shall really appreciate if you decide to help us.
```

The first paragraph of Project Central America's description reads as follows:

```
Recent distance learning expeditions have included an educational
component: explorer turned educator.  Project Central America
capitalizes on teacher turned explorer to pull students beyond their
classroom walls and into the world around them.  Project Central America
provides an opportunity to involve and connect learners in an adventure-
driven distance learning project.  Teacher-student interaction is an
integral part of the project and not simply a component.  The team of
teachers turned explorers will cycle throughout Central America in the
spring of 1994.
```

The idea is to have the cyclists send back information as they make their way through Central America, and to use these technologies to communicate with schools throughout Central America as well. One journal entry, from Nicaragua, follows:

```
Nicaragua has been hit by so many natural disasters it's incredible.  The
capitol city, Managua, is mostly toppled buildings from a massive
earthquake in 1972.  The country's lengthy war has left it with little or
no money to rebuild, therefore hundreds of thousands of people live in the
ruins of Managua.

In 1992, a volcano, Cerro Negro, erupted spewing ash for 50 miles.  It was
so heavy in Leon the ash collapsed buildings.  Because the ash was hot
every animal covered was killed and whole herds of cattle bones are still
lying in the fields.  People had to cover their heads and faces as the ash
would easily burn and choke them.

As if that wasn't enough, the volcano's eruption caused a shift in the
earth which in turn caused a tidal wave (they think).  Anyway, this
country has been hard hit, added are the years of war which really ended
in "92.  The country seems to be in a desperate state.
```

Questions from students are filed in the Gopher as well, complete with answers from the touring staff.

Admittedly, these projects demonstrate U.S. applications of Internet resources, but nowhere else has the K-12 community been as focused on making best use of the technology. Still, these are the types of projects that will bring other nations onto the Net, at which point they will inevitably develop their own internal applications.

Excursion 17.4. Using WAIS and ERIC To Search Educational Resource Databases

Gopher systems are great; but, as you can see, they are not necessarily very focused. At times you want to be able to find information in a very short period of time.

A relatively quick and simple solution to this problem is the use of WAIS (Wide Area Information Servers) databases available on the Internet. Using WAIS enables you to search through databases of information for a particular topic. After you select WAIS (and you can do so through a Gopher server), your screen may look something like this:

```
1.   About Wide Area Information Servers (WAIS)/
2.   Subject Sorted WAIS databases from Sweden/
3.   WAIS (through Think Com) <TEL>
4.   WAIS (through University of Minnesota)/
5.   WAIS Sources from Arizona State University/
```

Any one of items 2 through 5 will set you up with databases available for searching. I always start by trying the one closest to my geographical area, although that is no guarantee of an easier, quicker connection. Needless to say, the furthest, Sweden, was the easiest for me to connect to. Choosing item 2, then, gives this screen:

```
1.   About "Experiment with Automatic Classification" (README)
2.   All WAIS databases in alphabetic (gopher) order/
3.   Subject tree (based on UDC)/
```

Selecting item 2, then scrolling down through the letter *A,* we come to the AskERIC Lesson Plans search heading. We have seen ERIC (Educational Resources Information Center) searches within the two Gopher systems earlier explored. Getting to the ERIC searchers through WAIS, however, is far easier and quicker. After AskERIC Lesson Plans is chosen, you are asked to type in a word that will be searched in this database.

In my case, I typed the word **`literature`**, pressed Enter, and the results of my search appeared on the screen. Numerous options appeared, and I simply surfed through the various files.

Some of the lesson plans I found valuable and consequently mailed to my own e-mail address included a teaching lesson (complete with objectives and goals) on preparing students to study for a final exam, a writing process lesson, a media lesson analyzing and deconstructing junk mail, a lesson in improving students' independent listening skills, and a literature lesson on Shakespeare's *Macbeth*. I have listed some excerpts from two of these lesson plan files:

```
Title: The Junk Mail Explosion: Why You Buy and How Ads Persuade
Author: Marcia Nichols, Daly Middle School, Lakeview, OR
Grade Level / Subject: 7-10 / English Mass Media Unit
Overview / Purpose: In 1990, 63.7 billion pieces of the third-class
bulk mail found their way into mailboxes across the nation. This
activity is designed to increase student awareness of persuasion tactics
in "junk mail" advertising.

Objectives: The students will be able to:
1. read direct mail advertising critically
2. identify persuasion techniques
3. employ intellectual defenses against persuasive techniques
4. neatly label and orgainize junk mail into a term paper folder

Resources / Materials...
Activites and Procedures...
Tying It All Together...
The Junk Mail Explosion Project...
Evaluation Scheme...
```

And another example:

```
Title: Literature Review
Author: Linda Burton, Condon Elementary, OR
Grade Level / Subject: 10-12 (adaptable to 7-9)); language arts.
Overview: This lesson is designed to review a literary work or unit
before an exam. Students should have already read and discussed the
literature. They need to understand in advance that a knowledge question
simply involves recalling a fact from the literature. An interpretation question
involves expanding the facts and offering some insight and / or explanations.
A judgement question calls for an ...
```

As you can surmise, using the WAIS to search an educational resources database is a quick way to find information if you have a specific topic that you want researched. Using any of the other ERIC databases follows the same procedure but enables you to search for other educational topics. If you need information to instruct other teachers in your department or school on a topic such as outcomes-based learning, benchmarks, or any current trend in education, you can use the ERIC archive to search for articles on these topics.

Excursion 17.5. Mailing Lists and Newsgroups

One other area that many teachers find useful is mailing lists. Mailing lists can connect you with other educators who are interested in specific topics. You will receive, along with everyone else subscribed to the list, a copy of all mail messages sent by subscribers of the group.

Mailing lists usually are moderated—that is, someone (usually the creator of the list) reads all the messages to make sure they remain professional and focused. In order to receive the mail messages from any of these groups, you need to subscribe to them by sending an e-mail message to their e-mail address. For example (using the standard Pine mailer):

```
To: GS-NET@earanpe.br
Cc:
Attachment:
Subject:
Message:
-- Message Area ----
SUBSCRIBE GS-NET Carol DeVrieze
```

This particular mailing list—GS-Net—is relatively new, but it connects you with other educators to discuss various concerns. So far, most of the mail messages have been from teachers and classes who are looking for pen pals for their students with other classes from various parts of the world. The following example is typical of a plea for a class connection:

```
We are a rural elementary school in upstate New York and would
like to communicate with another class anywhere in the country or
worldwide. If you are interested please contact us.
```

Another interesting mailing list is called APENGLISH. This list contains teachers who teach Advanced Placement English courses in high school. These teachers share lesson plans, e-texts, curriculum concerns, and approaches to new works of literature. Some teachers send copies of their course outline and summer reading list. This excerpt is taken from a message sent by a teacher of this special program containing a partial alphabetical list of suggested authors for course readings in Advanced Placement English:

```
Suggested New Titles
Achebe, Chinua. Things Fall Apart is probably taught world wide now. It's a
Nigerian novel about change and adjustment to change from a tribal culture
to conquest.
Allende, Isabelle.
Atwood, Margaret. Handmaid's Tale is a book I strongly advocate that
every person read although I'm not sure that it could be assigned or required
because of its content.
```

Two other mailing lists I became involved in are entitled Literacy and Learner. These groups have some really interesting discussions on many topics related to new learners of reading and to literacy issues. Bibliographies on research in this field are traded, comments on software for use with new readers is discussed, pen pal requests by new readers and writers are submitted, among many other discussion topics.

Following are the e-mail addresses for these mailing lists. To subscribe to one, just type **subscribe *Listname Yourname***—for example, **subscribe literacy Joe Smith**—in the body of the message.

```
LITERACY@nysernet.ORG
LEARNER@nysernet.ORG
GS-NET@ear.anpe.br
APENGLISH-L-REQUEST@adler.nec.mass.edu
```

Tip: To locate mailing lists of interest to K-12 educators, Gopher to rain.psg.com and select the item School Computing (mostly K-12). Here you'll find four extremely helpful files, one dealing with mailing lists and the others with FTP and Telnet sites, among other issues. Mail these to yourself and peruse them at your leisure.

There also are any number of Usenet newsgroups, as might be expected. In fact, there is an entire newsgroup hierarchy devoted to K-12 users! These range from k12.chat.teacher through k12.ed.math, as you can determine by activating a search in your newsgroup software (see Day 4 for details). Some of these groups are worthwhile, but because most are unmoderated they tend to be overly informal and rambling (which is typical for newsgroups, of course). My best advice is to search for and subscribe to a few of them, and then decide after a week or so which you want to keep. You may even decide to start one of your own, if the subject matter warrants.

Even though using the Internet has not made me feel less overwhelmed by all of the information being written about education today, I know that I have benefited greatly in many ways by making the connection. I know where I can go to search for information related to things that are important to me as an educator, whether they be new lesson-plan ideas, recent articles on educational research and trends, new ways to involve my students so that they become more responsible for their own learning, or just keeping in touch with other educators who are facing the same issues and concerns that I face as a teacher every day in my classroom.

Excursion 17.6. K-12 Information on the World Wide Web

Quite appropriately, Carol restricted her searches for K-12 information primarily to Gophers. I say quite appropriately because that's where the bulk of the action is taking place. In addition, you can use Gophers to access both ERIC and WAIS searches, and to download appropriate files.

Not a great deal of this information has appeared on the World Wide Web, except of course through the Web-as-Gopher interface. Figure 17.1 shows a portion of the Gopher servers that can be accessed through Mosaic or Cello, as taken from Brown University's WWW-based Gopher list at the address shown in the figure's Document URL box.

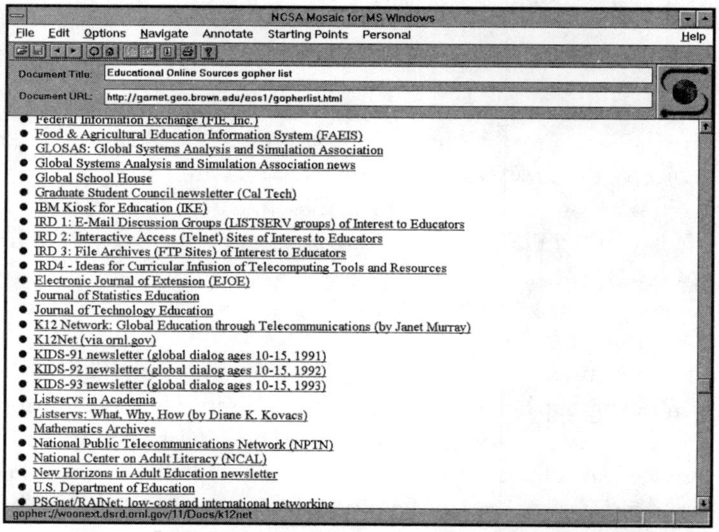

Figure 17.1. *Mosaic screen showing education Gopher list.*

A useful place to begin a search for K-12 Web material (or anything else on the Web, for that matter) is the CUI W3 Catalog. This is a search engine for WWW materials, and Figure 17.2 shows the results of a search for education.

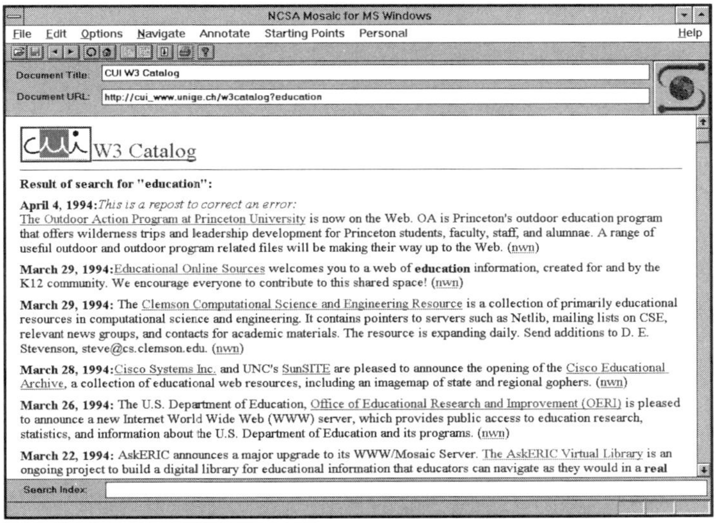

Figure 17.2. *Results of W3 Catalog search.*

Scrolling through that screen, one of the hypertext links leads to the specific section on Education Pages displayed in Figure 17.3. The number of clickable resources here will keep any educator busy for a few hours.

Another excellent starting point (and one referenced from the CUI page and other sources) is Cisco Systems Incorporated Educational Archive. From this colorful page (see Figure 17.4) you can access the AskERIC Virtual Library, and you can scroll down the page for access links to a number of other interesting Web and Gopher resources (see Figure 17.5).

One of the links in Figure 17.5 was to a 5th-grade World Wide Web page at Grand River Elementary School in Michigan. Now, one of the most certain ways of realizing how far out of touch you are is to learn that 5th-graders are creating WWW pages with hypertext links, an especially panicky feeling if you're a 5th-grade educator yourself (I'm not, but I can easily imagine…). The following are the 5th-grade page from Grand River (see Figure 17.6) and a 6th-grade page out of Hillside Elementary School in Minnesota (see Figure 17.7). Notice that the latter has a page done by 3rd-graders as well, probably as a ploy to make everyone on the planet feel technologically challenged.

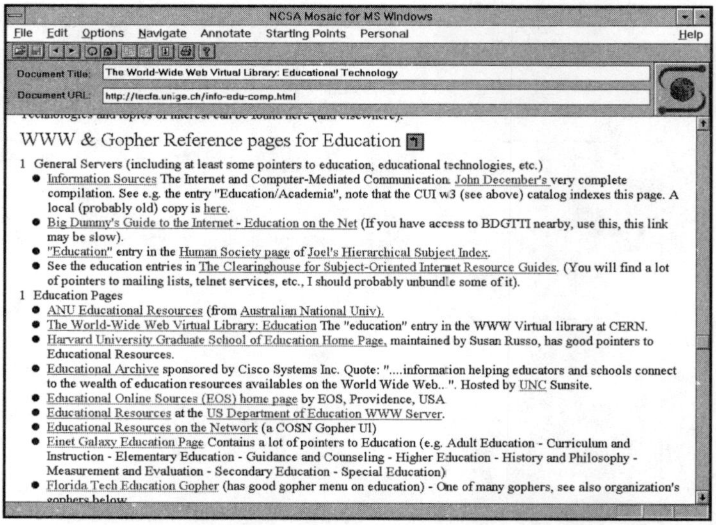

Figure 17.3. *Virtual Library screen showing educational resources.*

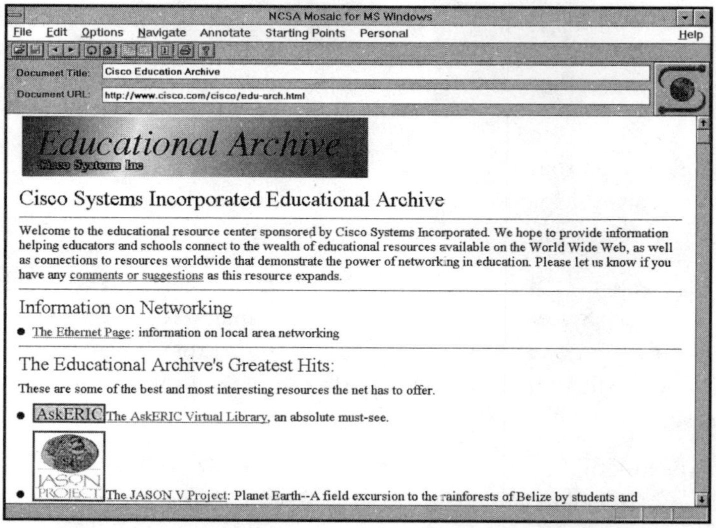

Figure 17.4. *Educational Archive from Cisco Systems International.*

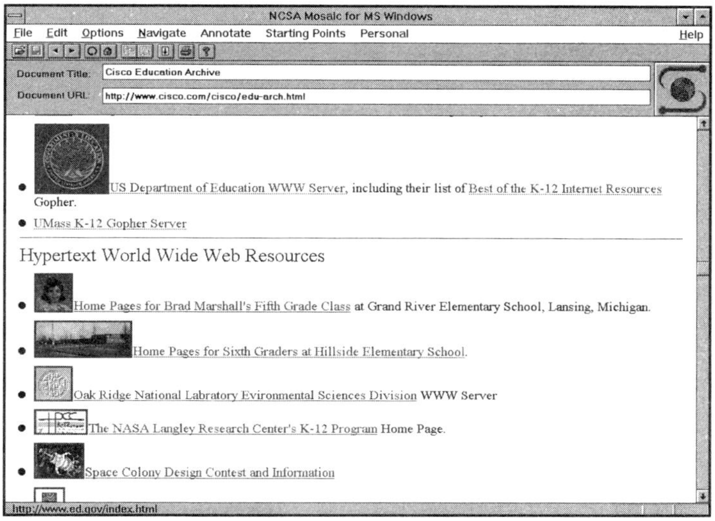

Figure 17.5. *More from Cisco's Educational Archive.*

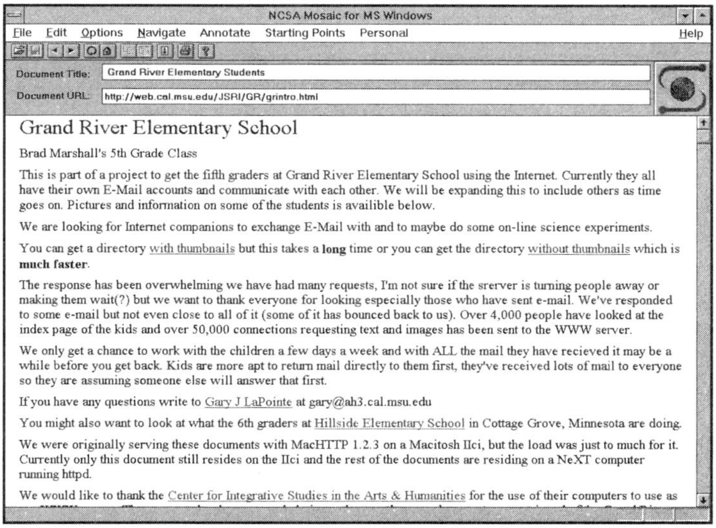

Figure 17.6. *World Wide Web page done by fifth-graders.*

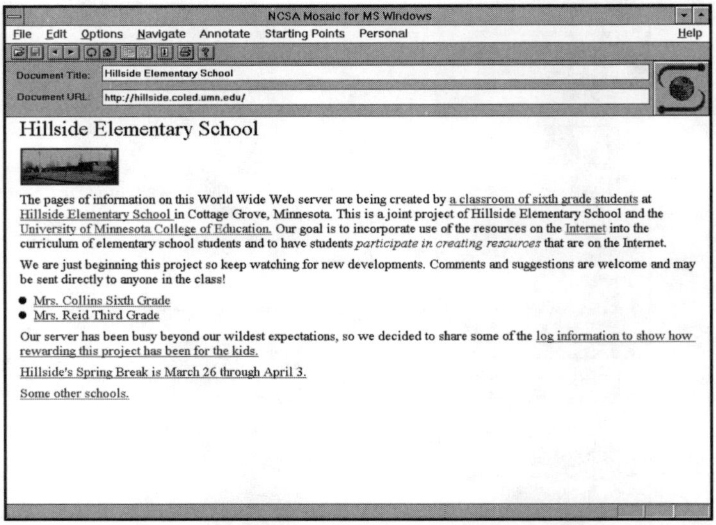

Figure 17.7. *World Wide Web page produced by sixth-graders.*

And, impressively, an even more complete WWW page is in preparation by Lincoln Elementary School in Iowa (see Figure 17.8). Not all the links worked when I accessed this page the first time, but it promises to be an excellent demonstration of the interaction between student and technology.

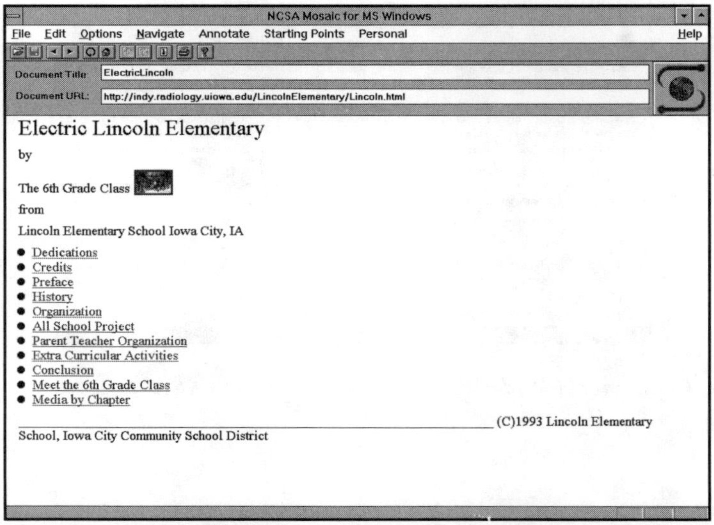

Figure 17.8. *Lincoln Elementary School home page.*

Of course, we should hardly expect the high schools to be outdone by all this grade-school activity. A few secondary schools had made the Web leap as this chapter was being completed, but the most advanced (and probably not surprisingly) was the page sequence from the Illinois Mathematics and Science Academy. Figure 17.9 is the home page for that group, whereas Figure 17.10 shows one of the group's online publications.

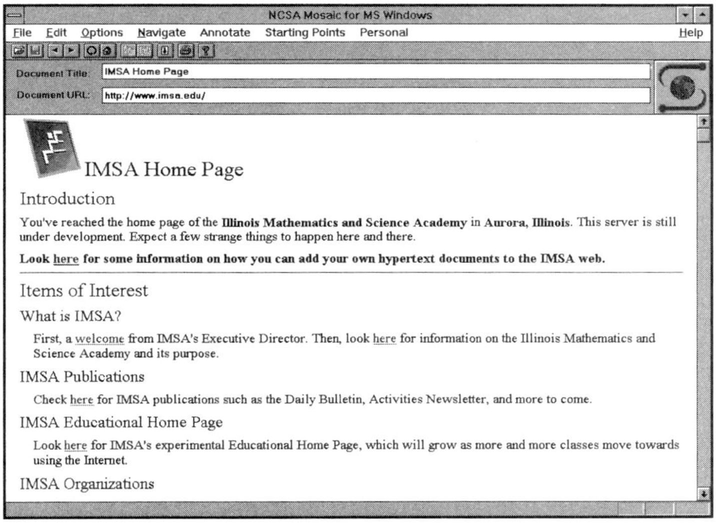

Figure 17.9. *Home page for Illinois Mathematics and Science Academy.*

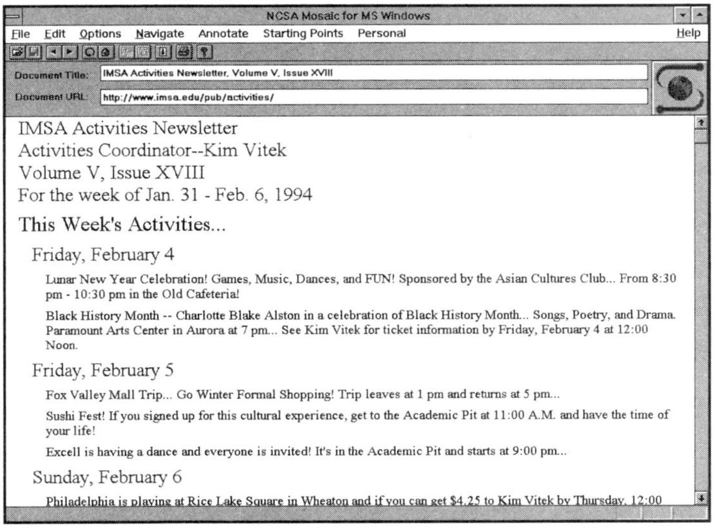

Figure 17.10. *IMSA Activities Newsletter page (Mosaic).*

Summary

There's no lack of K-12 educational material on the Internet. Most of it is available through a constantly and quickly growing number of Gopher servers; and because the equipment requirements for Gopher access are less than those for World Wide Web access, this fact is likely to remain. The amount of information available to educators is staggering in itself, but equally fascinating is the number of pedagogical possibilities that stem from using the Net as a classroom tool. Schools are only beginning to experiment with these ideas, but the next few years will almost certainly demonstrate the natural creativity of educators the world over.

Task Review

In this chapter, you learned the following tasks:

- ☐ How to use Gopher to access the growing number of information servers in the K-12 arena.
- ☐ How to consult WAIS to conduct a search for K-12 documents and information.
- ☐ Where to start joining mailing lists to keep abreast of new developments in education and educational technology.
- ☐ Where to find educational information on the World Wide Web.

Q&A

Q Will we ever see K-12 courses conducted over the Internet?

A Yes. Internet-based courses already have been done, albeit primarily by people teaching about the Internet itself. Keep watching the what's-new lists discussed in Day 2 to find out about them. Usually, these courses combine Gophers and e-mail, but some have experimented with MUDs and the World Wide Web. The main purpose of such courses for K-12 wouldn't be to improve distance education (as it is for other groups), but rather to take advantage of global connectivity to allow students from different parts of the country or even the world to work together on projects, and to let teachers team-teach where applicable. Anyone with e-mail access can already make this happen, and if you have WWW capabilities, and the time to develop the pages, any number of exciting possibilities present themselves.

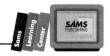

Q Are government agencies using some of their resources to help spread Internet use among K-12 classes?

A Apart from funding itself, several government agencies are getting involved. Education faculties in some universities are working with local schools on Internet-based programs, and even if your local university or college doesn't have such a faculty you'll likely find someone who'd be willing to help with specific projects. Furthermore, as Figure 17.11 shows, the U.S. Department of Education has Gopher and WWW access to a number of documents and activities, and state activity is increasing in this regard as well.

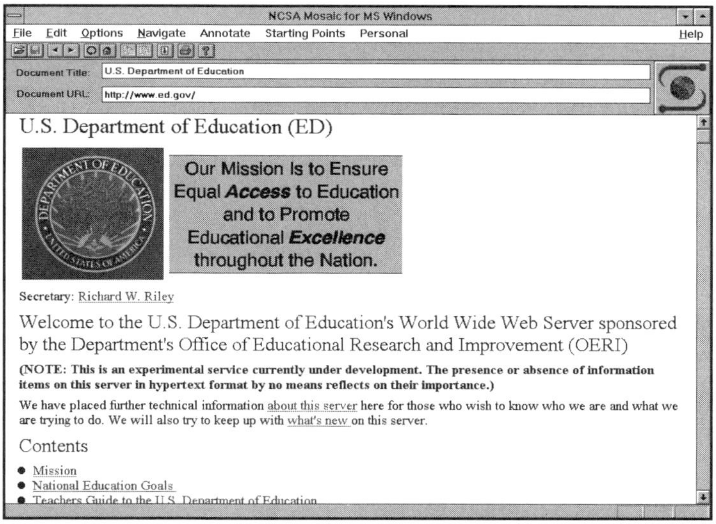

Figure 17.11. *U.S. Department of Education home page.*

To finish this answer, let's look at a particularly enticing project undertaken through NASA. Called The JASON Project, it attempts to draw school-aged children into the world of science and technology. Figure 17.12 outlines the mission of the JASON project, and hyperlinks to several stages in the project itself.

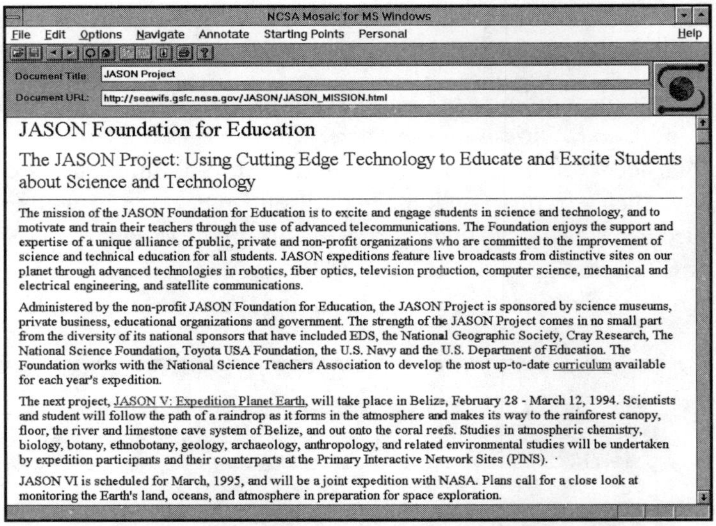

Figure 17.12. *The mission of the JASON Project.*

From Figure 17.13, we can see how the project works. The idea in this particular project was to follow a raindrop through the sky and into the rain forest, and you can click any one of these areas for more information and a look at the results. There's also an intriguing section called Letters from the Rainforest shown elsewhere, but I'll let you find these for yourself.

As a final note, the Greek Jason was, of course, an Argonaut, and the current buzzword for an Internet explorer just happens to be Internaut. Coincidence? You decide.

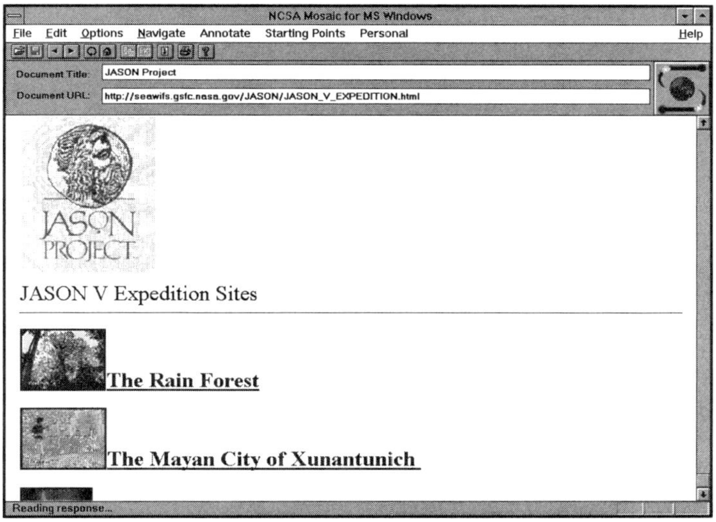

Figure 17.13. *Information from the JASON Project.*

18

WEEK
3

Education 201: The Internet and Continuing Education

On Day 18, you'll explore the Internet for information and discussions about continuing education in its variety of forms. First you'll look at the topic from the standpoint of continuing education professionals, and then you'll turn to the Net from the standpoint of the recipient (that is, the student) of continuing education, especially education while on the job.

Today you will do the following:

- ☐ Explore mailing lists and electronic journals devoted to continuing education.
- ☐ Search for newsgroups and mailing lists dealing with job-specific information.
- ☐ Perform Archie, Veronica, and WAIS searches for job-oriented material.

Exploring Continuing Education

Continuing education (often called *adult education*) means different things to different people. It is, first of all, a topic area within the education field itself, an item in the pre-school, K-12, and post-secondary educational lines. Here, it often has to do with the continuation of formal education, usually on a part-time basis (and including distance education).

Second, it incorporates specialized education such as English as a Second Language (ESL), as long as the students are out of the formal educational system.

Third, it deals with part-time courses taken purely for interest, such as the Tuesday evening "How to be More Assertive" course. Next, it encompasses the broad range of job-related education furtherance, except perhaps the issue of job training itself.

And finally, continuing education takes in the whole area of voluntary do-it-yourself learning, the kind the Internet is more than capable of providing.

So which one(s) did I decide to exclude in Day 18? None, really. In the spirit of the Internet itself, which seems to be all-inclusive, I simply let the task take over. What follows is this:

- ☐ A look at formal continuing education through Mailing Lists
- ☐ A walk-through of a job-related continuing education search
- ☐ A quick peek at the idea of using the Net for personal continuing education

Let's get going.

Formal Continuing Education

Formal continuing education usually refers to the kind conducted through established schools and toward recognized diplomas or degrees. There are many types, and the Internet covers a wide range of them. Here's how to find information.

Mailing Lists

The best place to follow continuing education issues is through mailing lists. (See Day 4 for how to subscribe to such lists.) Following is an abbreviated look at the various lists and what they cover:

ADLTED-L	Canadian Adult Education Network (`listserv@uregina1.bitnet`), covering a full range of continuing education discussions (not restricted to Canadian issues)
AEDNET	Adult Education Network (`listserv@alpha.acast.nova.edu`), with a strong international following and covering many topics
CAUCE-L	Canadian Association for University Continuing Education (`listserv@uregina1.bitnet`), which, unlike ADLTED, is focused on continuing education at the university level
CREAD	Latin American & Caribbean Distance & Continuing Education (`listserv@yorkvm1.bitnet`), as its name suggests, focusing on continuing education in Latin American and Caribbean countries
DEOS-L	International Discussion Forum for Distance Learning (`listserv@psuvm.bitnet`), with more than a thousand subscribers from dozens of nations, and a broad range of topics
EDNET	Education Net (`listserv@nic.umass.edu`), covering topics of interest dealing with the Internet as educational tool, subscribed by K-12 teachers through continuing education students
HILAT-L	Higher Education in Latin America (`listserv@bruspvm.bitnet`), dealing with post-secondary education in Latin American countries, and encouraging Spanish and Portuguese contributions
NEWEDU-L	New Paradigms in Education List (`listserv@uscvm.bitnet`), with discussions of many educational topics, including new technologies and distance education

Electronic Journals

In addition, several electronic journals are available for subscription, some of which provide excellent commentary on a variety of issues related to continuing education:

DEOSNEWS	The Distance Education Online Symposium (listserv@psuvm.bitnet), correlated with DEOS-L, but containing full-length articles.
DISTED	Journal of Distance Education and Communication (listserv@uwavm.bitnet), with broad issues in education, including continuing and distance education
EUITNEWS	Educational Uses of Information Technology(listserv@bitnic.educom.edu), which, as its name suggests, covers technology and education, including tutorials and self-directed learning
HORIZONS	New Horizons in Adult Education, (listserv@alpha.acast.nova.edu), distributed to subscribers in AEDNET mailing list

These are subscribed to as if they were mailing lists. Subscribe to three or four of these lists and to one or two journals, and you'll begin to see the size of the continuing education community on the Net. If you're in the position of teaching or designing continuing or distance education, you owe it to yourself to join some of these excellent discussions.

International Continuing Education

As you discovered on Day 17, the vast majority of the Internet's educational resources are concentrated in North America, and especially in the United States. It's good to see, there, a distance education resource such as the Gopher at the University of Southern Australia's Centre for University Teaching and Learning. The main menu is shown here:

```
1.  Information about this server
2.  University of South Australia
3.  Centre for University Teaching and Learning
4.  Distance Education Centre
5.  Information Technology Unit
6.  Connection to Other Information Servers
7.  The Internet
8.  Contributions to this Gopher
9.  Weather Information
10. Any Comments?
11. InfoTrain Electronic Journal
```

While the Distance Education Centre (item 4) lists only a few documents at this point, and the InfoTrain Electronic Journal item is just getting started, it's clear that the Centre plans to develop this Gopher substantially. It promises to become an important resource for distance education sources in Australia and the Pacific.

Job-Related Continuing Education

One of the most intriguing potentials the Internet holds is discovering information and forums devoted to specific professional activities. This is particularly true for those with careers that demand a constant focus on keeping up with what's new, something that usually demands attending workshops, seminars, conferences, and other time-consuming and often cost-ineffective activities.

This is not to suggest, in any way, that the Internet be used as the sole means of furthering a professional education. There is no substitute for the kind of face-to-face encounters and exchanges that only a meeting of a professional society or some other job-related organization can provide. The Internet shines in its capability to keep professionals instantly updated and to let them communicate with one another quickly, efficiently, and while sitting at their desks.

To offer an idea of the Net's potential in this regard, I asked Craig Miller, a technical communications professional with AT&T Global Information Solutions, to offer the results of his search for information.

About the Contributor

Craig Miller has graduated from his university's professional writing program recently, and as a result is still very much aware of the need for continual upgrading of his education in the field. He knows that other professionals out there have encountered challenges similar to his, and that the Internet may well provide a forum for tackling some of the issues cooperatively.

Note: Astute readers will have noticed by now that Craig's search, like Jim Hartling's in Day 8, deals with technical communication. This was partly coincidental—I know more technical communicators than astrophysicists—but it was partly planned as well. Because technical communications has nowhere near the scientific or technological prestige of many of the professions and sites on the Internet, the profession provides a very good example of finding unexpected areas of interest as well as those that would seem obvious. And the point is, after all, that Craig's and Jim's experiences are easily translated into any profession, whether it be teaching, nursing, or landscaping.

In Search of Higher Learning

by Craig Miller

While the Internet can provide entertainment and aesthetic pleasures, it is also a valuable resource of information relating to continuing education. By continuing education, I mean gaining academic or job-related knowledge through independent research. For example, if someone is interested in learning to program in C, writing a novel, or becoming current in the field of microbiology, the Internet can provide some very useful sources.

Since my field is technical and professional communications, especially technical documentation, I wanted to learn more about what's happening in that field so that I can apply it to my job—moving the information contained in books, such as user manuals, to online help screens. However, what is covered here should not in any way be perceived as limited to this field. The Internet covers topics so diverse and extensive that a similar search could be made for almost any field. In fact, I found more information on other professions than on my own, but I decided to stick to what I actually do.

Warning: It is extremely easy, when using the Internet for job-related material, to get distracted into other areas. The grass-is-always-greener syndrome kicks as soon as you see information about a profession you once considered, or wish you might have pursued. As with any job-oriented activity, the trick is to stay on topic and focused.

The goal of my search was to locate sources of information on the Internet that discuss how to design and write online help for computer applications. This is a fairly wide-ranging area, but any hints or tips I could get about converting information from paper documents to online text would be useful to me for my job.

> **Note:** My only equipment for spelunking the Internet is an account on a UNIX server at the local university. Although this interface isn't as attractive as Mosaic or Cello running on a PC or Mac or X Windows box, it does permit me to connect to other servers around the world and retrieve all—or nearly all—the material that is available.

My account provides me with access to the following Internet tools:

- Usenet newsgroups
- Gopher (which provides access to Archie, Veronica, and WAIS)
- FTP
- E-mail

Others are available as well, of course, but these are the tools I used in my search to further my professional education.

> **Warning:** As you will quickly see, the early searches were almost entirely futile. I've dispensed with some of the grisly details, but I don't want to eliminate the three main points:
>
> - Early activities on the Net are often frustrating.
> - Nothing you do on the Net is ever completely wasted, because eventually you'll be able to make use of it.
> - The trick, as always, is to use the various tools in conjunction with one another.

Excursion 18.1. It's News to Me

Usenet news is a fantastic resource with which to begin. Searching the newsgroups and talking with people with common interests and goals is probably the fastest and most efficient way of learning what is available on the Net. Also, the newsgroups are accessible to almost everyone with an account on a network server, which means you can gain the perspectives of a variety of people.

Tip: It's possible that, out of an often realistic fear that they will cut into productivity, your systems administrators have blocked access to newsgroups. If you know of a viable newsgroup for your job, one that is oriented toward furthering your education or training, you might want to obtain a private Internet account and try it out. Then, based on the material you've found, propose to your firm that access be allowed.

Because my subject of interest is technical communication in all its various forms, I started by jotting down some related terms that might make searching the list of newsgroups easier. These terms included *documentation*, *help*, *online help*, *technical*, and *writ* (which would cover writing and writer, or whatever a derivative could be).

Tip: When searching newsgroups for a specific subject, you can save time by doing a little brainstorming beforehand and jotting down related terms and subjects.

Of my subjects, *writ* was the most successful. It included the following groups:

Completely unsubscribed newsgroups:

```
misc.writing
rec.arts.sf.written
sdnet.writing
```

Of these, I decided to try misc.writing because it might incorporate technical writing. A scan of the subject headers turned up the following abbreviated list of subjects:

```
10510 Re: NEWSGROUP: Welcome to misc.writing
10511 NEWSGROUP: Newsweeding
10656 the Internet Writer Resource Guide
10680 2nd CFV: misc.creativity
10718 Re: rerererererewriting
10720 Macintosh writers can talk now, type later
10721 SURVEY: Short Fiction Collections— PLEASE RESPOND!
10722 How does a writer get an agent?
10727 Re: female detectives by female authors
10733 Re: Searching for...just the right word
10734 RECOMMEND: Short Fiction...
```

As I found, these subjects dealt with writing fiction rather than discussing issues related to technical writing. This was something I learned quickly on the Net: what is obvious to you may not be obvious to others. Try to expand the scope of what you're looking for to cover all the variations.

My other searches turned up similar red (and pickled) herrings. Though I was sure there was a newsgroup that covered my area of interest, I couldn't guess what kind of abbreviated name it was given. I suppose I could do a general list on the newsgroups (by entering **l** at the `what next?` prompt), but I figured I might do just as well making use of other Internet services. I'd experimented with the Gopher tool before, so I thought I'd give it a try.

We'll return to newsgroups in Excursion 18.6.

Excursion 18.2. Peering into the Gopher Hole

In a UNIX environment, Gopher is the access point to other Internet tools (such as WAIS and Veronica), which means Gopher is a good tool to turn to next after the newsgroups. I entered **gopher** at the UNIX prompt to enter the Gopher hole.

My first excursions were uneventful. I did manage to find the following reading list in an item called Reading and Writing Scientific and Technical Literature. (Only the first three items are reproduced here.) I thought I was on my way.

```
                    TECHNICAL WRITING

The purpose of technical or job-related writing is to communicate clearly informa-
tion such as instructions, results, or new proposals.  The following is a selected
list of sources on technical writing.

Alvarez, Joseph A.  The Elements of Technical Writing.
     T11.A38 1980 Davis.

Booth, Vernon.  Communicating in Science:  Writing and Speaking.
     Q223.B665 1985 Davis.

Chandler, Harry E.  Technical Writer's Handbook.
     T11.C45 1983 Davis.
```

These books looked like a good source of information about technical writing but seemed directed more at writing for the paper medium. Remember, I was looking for information about converting paper documentation to on-screen material. Also, the copyrights indicated that they were somewhat dated. I needed current information about what a person can do with today's technology to make the most of the online medium.

Excursion 18.3. Archie

Archie's greatest asset is also its weakest. Although Archie enabled me to search archives all over the world, I found it difficult to know what to search for unless I knew the names of the files. Trying to track down technical writing sources using Archie was tricky because I wasn't really sure how the name would be abbreviated to match a filename. In many cases, and not just for technical writing, a name of a file was quite unlike the information contained in that file. This made it difficult to guess what someone may have called the file. Still, I gave Archie a try.

To get to Archie, I found the Archie menu on my local Gopher server (`uwinfo.uwaterloo.ca`):

```
1.        Archie Guide.
2.        Archie Instructions.
3.        localarchie.html.
4.        About archie (Search FTP archives)/
5.        Archie (Search FTP archives)/
6.        Archie servers world-wide/
```

Note: Most Gophers have a link or sublink to Archie servers. See Day 2, or almost any other chapter in this book, for sample addresses.

I selected Archie servers world-wide to get the most comprehensive search and was presented with the following list of Archie servers:

```
1.  McGill School of Computer Science Archive Server.
2.  McGill School of Computer Science Archive Server <TEL>
3.  InterNIC Directory and Database Server.
4.  InterNIC Directory and Database Server <TEL>
5.  Server at SURAnet.
6.  Server at SURAnet <TEL>
7.  Rutgers University Archive Server.
8.  Rutgers University Archive Server <TEL>
9.  University of Nebraska, Lincoln.
10. University of Nebraska, Lincoln <TEL>
11. Advanced Network & Services, Inc.
12. Advanced Network & Services, Inc <TEL>
13. Imperial College, London, England.
14. University of Lulea (Sweden).
15. Technische Hochschule Darmstadt.
```

```
16. Finnish University and Research Network Server.
17. Deakin (Australia) File Server.
18. Victoria University, Wellington.
```

I was successful at connecting to the University of Nebraska, Lincoln <TEL> (via Telnet), where I performed a `find` for technical writing:

```
unl-archie> find technical writing
```

Tip: When performing Archie searches, be sure to do a screen capture to catch all the information. I used a UNIX command called `script`. (Check your UNIX man pages for more information on how to use script, by typing **`man script`** at the UNIX prompt.) This copied all the text displayed on the screen to file. Afterwards, I could refer to the file whenever I wanted to get the FTP or Telnet address of a particular site.

18

My Archie search for technical writing returned a huge list of files and their FTP locations. Here are a few of the results:

```
# Search type: sub.
# Your queue position: 1
# Estimated time for completion: 00:17
working...  # Your queue position: 1
# Estimated time for completion: 00:20
¦

>> technical

Host ftp.wustl.edu    (128.252.135.4)
Last updated 10:08 25 Dec 1993

    Location: /languages/ada/AJPO/asis/ASISWG
      FILE    -r--r--r--    14754 bytes  08:53 13 Aug 1993
9210-ASISWG-Technical-subgroup

>> writing

Host uceng.uc.edu    (129.137.189.1)
Last updated 13:04 14 Apr 1994

    Location: /pub/wuarchive/doc/EFF/CAF/faq
      FILE    -r--r--r--    7170 bytes  18:40 25 Jan 1994  netnews.writing.Z
```

This kind of search turned up a number of FTP sites, which I hoped would prove to be useful. To find out what the files contained, I exited Gopher to use the FTP tool.

Excursion 18.4. FTP

At the UNIX prompt, I used FTP to check out the results of my Gopher search. Some of the sites were the following:

```
maggie.telcom.arizona.edu
csus.edu
ftp.csc.nscu.edu
ftp.apple.com
```

Tip: If you are using the FTP command from a UNIX account and you locate an FTP site to which you wish to connect to frequently, there is a short cut. Add a file to your root directory (the one where you land when you first log in) called `.netrc`. Use whichever UNIX editor you want and add the following line to the file:

```
ftp.address login anonymous password userid@your.internet.address
```

where *`ftp.address`* is the name of the FTP site that you are connecting to, and *`userid@your.internet.address`* is your e-mail address.

Now when you make a connection to that FTP site, you don't have to enter a login or password. The system will do it automatically for you.

For each of these sites, I logged in as `anonymous`, with my e-mail address as the password. I tracked down the files from the Gopher directory and downloaded them into my account. I then viewed each file with `vi`.

Most of the files containing anything to do with writing were creative writings, writings for the Internet, collections of writing, and programming code. So I turned to Veronica for help.

Excursion 18.5. Veronica

On my UNIX account, Veronica is also accessed through Gopher; so I entered `gopher` at the prompt.

> **Tip:** As with Archie, Veronica searches can be conducted through any Gopher you find. Gopher Jewels or the University of Minnesota Gophers are, as always, good starting points. (See Day 2.) You can, however, get to a Veronica item from a huge number of locations.

The Veronica servers with which I had the most success were both universities: Manitoba and Cologne:

```
6.  Search gopherspace at University of Cologne <?>
12. University of Manitoba Veronica server <?>
```

I started with the University of Cologne and performed the following search. (I only provided `writ` so that the search would include writers, writing, or anything related):

```
—>Searching Text...Index word(s) to search for: technical writ
```

> **Tip:** When performing searches on subjects, leave out as many letters as you can in order to include all varieties of the word. I found that although the Net is expansive, spellings and terminology are rarely consistent.

My search for technical writ proved to be successful in providing me with a list of technical writing sources. A partial result of this search includes the following subjects:

```
1.  185. Technical Writing for Computer Engineers. W.
2.  Technical Writing Internship Program.
3.  Technical Writing Assistance for Martin Marietta Energy Systems I.
4.  ENGL 3764 TECHNICAL WRITING.
7.  Technical Writing/
9.  E80 EP 310 TECHNICAL WRITING..
10. BUSINESS AND TECHNICAL REPORT WRITING.
11. 105F\G   Technical Writing.
12. Technical Writing Program/
13. Technical and Professional Writing Program, UG.
15. Interdisciplinary Technical Writing.
16. bit.listserv.techwr-l    Technical Writing List./
17. technical-writing/
```

Some of these subjects were descriptions of credit courses in technical writing that are available at different institutions. One that I found interesting was item 3, Technical Writing Assistance for Martin Marietta Energy Systems I:

```
TITLE:
Technical Writing Assistance for Martin Marietta Energy Systems, Inc.;
Remideial Action Program
```

Item number 10, BUSINESS AND TECHNICAL REPORT WRITING, read as follows:

```
A Quick Course for Business and Technical Report Writers.

Designed specifically for business and technical writers, this four-session workshop
focuses on proven strategies for managing the report-writing process.  Participants
will learn practical tips to help them:
*  Compose documents that exhibit a keen sense of audience and purpose.
*  Develop and revise flexible outlines, parallel headings, and tables of contents.
*  Present "reader-friendly" definitions and descriptions.
*  Achieve a writing style appropriate to the writing situation.
*  Enliven the notoriously "boring" prose  that often accompanies formal business and
   technical writing.
*  Edit drafts for correct grammar and effective punctuation.
*  Prepare concise but informative abstracts and meaningful executive summaries.
```

Another similar course was a four-day tutorial offering private or public hands-on training for people wanting to know more about technical writing:

```
EFFECTIVE TECHNICAL WRITING: MAKING INFORMATION WORK FOR YOUR CUSTOMER (N1683)

4 days Hands-on Labs
Public, Private
This course teaches the fundamental skills needed by people whose job is to
develop technical information. By understanding concepts for clear, concise,
and effective writing, students learn how to identify their intended audience
and how to evaluate different styles and organizational choices relating to
that audience. The instruction primarily addresses these concepts as they
apply to technical communication and stresses clarity by focusing on a simple
"say what you mean" principle. The course takes students from the preparation
process through the rewriting and final proofreading of their work. Throughout
the training students receive constructive feedback from the instructor and
from other students.
```

Although these courses seemed worthwhile ventures, I was looking for a source of information on the Net where I could participate with questions and comments in my spare time without spending money on course fees or tuition. I already knew of workshops and seminars I could attend.

Then I came across the following subdirectory. (Note that names have been changed.)

```
1.  The Document Writing Project.
2.  Note From Donna Marriot.
3.  Opportunity Knocks For Donna's Students.
4.  Glad This Forum Is Here.
5.  Search Keyword and Title Word Index
<?>Press ? for Help, q to Quit, u to go up a menu                  Page: 1/1
Receiving Information...    The Document Writing Project              03/19/93
```

This turned out to be a forum for discussing online technical writing that came out of a document-writing project. In this forum, students participating in Donna Marriott's project discussed issues such as how to best convert the information contained on paper documents to online text. Some of the subjects discussed in this forum included the following:

18

```
1.  Informality Allows Some To Feel More Comfortable.
2.  Citing The Internet/APA Style.
3.  Re: Citing The Internet/APA Style.
5.  Elements Of E-Text Style.
6.  L1-A Style Crash In AutoCAD 12c3.
7.  Re: L1-A Style Crash In AutoCAD 12c3.
8.  Quality And Style Guide.
9.  Re: Quality And Style Guide.
13. JSC Shenanigans (Was Re: Quality And Style Guide).
```

The good point about this source was that it discussed the problems and issues I was interested in. However, I was limited because I could not participate in the discussions. I could only read about the experiences of others.

Another search turned up the following subject:

```
bit.listserv.techwr-l     Technical Writing List.
```

This turned out to be an Internet newsgroup as well as a Listserv (which is discussed later), so I decided to head back to the newsgroups.

Excursion 18.6. News Strikes Back

This time, with my second visit to newsgroups, I had the benefit of knowing what I was looking for. I had already seen a reference to a newsgroup that seemed promising. So after entering `rn` to start the news reader, I would look for `bit.listserv.techwr-l`:

```
******  64 unread articles in uw.talks — read now? [ynq] g bit.listserv.techwr-l
Newsgroup bit.listserv.techwr-l not in .newsrc — subscribe? [ynYN] y

Put newsgroup where? [$^.Lq]

******  82 unread articles in bit.listserv.techwr-l — read now? [ynq] y
```

This newsgroup contained the following subject headers:

```
 5700 Re: "dummy" books to...
 5701 Lowering monitor height
 5702 Re: (Was Glossaries etc.)
 5703 Lowering monitor height
 5706 Information retrieval systems for online Doc
 5707 Syntax conventions
 5709 Ergonomics and modular furniture
 5710 Re: "dummy" books to...
 5712 Re: (Was Glossaries etc.)
 5713 Re: It ain't Pacman
 5714 Glossaries....Again ;-(
 5715 Information retrieval systems for online Doc
 5716 Re: Glossaries....Again ;-(
 5717 reply to Jane re: modular furniture
 5718 Re: It ain't Pacman
 5719 Re: Ergonomics and modular furniture
 5720 Lenses, eyestrain
 5721 Re: Lenses, eyestrain
 5722 Re: marginal :-) definit...
[Type space to continue]
```

This was exactly the type of thing I was looking for. Here, the subscribers discussed topics such as tools for creating online help, style guides for presenting on-screen information, and even how to set up computer equipment to make computers work easier.

Because this was my first chance to voice some input on technical writing, I decided to take advantage of this opportunity and ask around for other sources of information about technical writing on the Internet. I entered the **postnews** command at the UNIX command and prepared this message:

```
postnews
Is this message in response to some other message? n
Subject: Technical writing on the Internet?
Keywords:
Newsgroups (enter one at a time, end with a blank line):

The most relevant newsgroup should be the first, you should
add others only if your article really MUST be read by people
who choose not to read the appropriate group for your article.
But DO use multiple newsgroups rather than posting many times.

For a list of newsgroups, type ?
> bit.listserv.techwr-l
>
Distribution (default='world', '?' for help) :

Hi.
I'm trying to look for resources on the net (WAIS, WWW, Gopher sites, etc.) that
deal with technical writing issues (such as the problems, tricks, and tips of
writing for the screen instead of the printed page).

This news/listserv group is one example of such a resource. Can anyone tell/show
me of any others out there?

Thanks.
Craig
(csmiller@watarts.uwaterloo.ca)

What now?  [send, edit, list, quit, write] send
Posting article...
Article posted successfully.
```

With my message posted successfully, I decided to check out the Listservs.

Excursion 18.7. Listserv Mailing Lists

To find out if there were any mailing lists related to technical writing, I sent away for the current list of BINET Listservs. This consisted of a mail message addressed to LISTSERV@BITNIC.BITNET with the following line:

```
list global
```

A reply was quickly forthcoming: a huge list of Listservs. (Fortunately, the vi editor was able to handle the file's size.) I made a quick search of all the Listservs that contained writ. Following is the result:

```
ACW-L           ACW-L@TTUVM1       Alliance For Computers and Writing
AWR-L           AWR-L@TTUVM1       A WRITER'S REPERTOIRE
BACW-L          BACW-L@TTUVM1      Alliance For Computers and Writing
```

```
CCCCC-L       CCCCC-L@TTUVM1     INTERCLASS COMPUTERS & WRITING
COMICW-L      COMICW-L@UNLVM     COMIC Writers Workshop
CREWRT-L      CREWRT-L@MIZZOU1   Creative Writing in Education for
CWC94-L       CWC94-L@MIZZOU1    MU's 94 Computers and Writing
DARGON-L      DARGON-L@BROWNVM   Dargon Project Writers Forum
ENG213        ENG213@UMSLVMA     ENG213-TECHNICAL WRITING
FICTION       FICTION@PSUVM      Fiction Writers Workshop
ICWAW         ICWAW@INDYCMS      Intercampus Committee on Writing and Writing
NOVELS-L      NOVELS-L@PSUVM     Novel Writers Workshop
PURTOPOI      PURTOPOI@PURCCVM   Rhetoric, Language, Prof Writing
RCWPMSU       RCWPMSU@MSU        Red Cedar Writing Project
RHETNT-L      RHETNT-L@MIZZOU1   CyberJournal for Rhetoric and Writing
SCRIB-L       SCRIB-L@HEARN      SCRIB-L Handwriting Production,
TECHCOMM      TECHWR-L@OSUVM1    Technical Writers List; for all
TESLMW-L      TESLMW-L@CUNYVM    TESLMW-L: Materials Writers Sub-list
WAC-L         WAC-L@UIUCVMD      WAC-L Writing Across the Curriculum
WIOLE-L       WIOLE-L@MIZZOU1    Writing Intensive Online Learning
WORKS-L       WORKS-L@NDSUVM1    WRITERS List Works Archives
WRITERS       WRITERS@NDSUVM1    WRITERS
WRITING       WRITING@PSUVM      Fiction Writers Workshop Writing
WWP-L         WWP-L@BROWNVM      Brown University Women Writers Project
ZWSUG         ZWSUG@MARIST       Marist Zwriter Users Group
```

This list took me by surprise because it seemed to contain everything I was looking for. Several lists dealt with the sort of technical writing I was interested in. I resisted the urge to subscribe to everything that looked interesting and just selected two at random: `TECHCOMM` and `RHETNT-L`.

Within a day, I received two mail messages from Brad Mehlenbacher, the list owner of TECHCOMM, and a professor of technical communication at North Carolina State University. One was a welcome and introduction to the Listserv, explaining its objectives and intent.

In addition to being a forum for discussing technical communication, the Listserv supports an archive of articles and papers that can be downloaded via FTP. The second message was a collection of Listservs that Brad anticipated might be of interest to subscribers.

As with the newsgroup, the list permitted a forum for dealing with topics rather than a simple download of material. For my particular subject of interest, this two-way communication seemed more useful than simply downloading texts because I could bring up issues relating specifically to my situation.

Excursion 18.8. Another Descent into the Gopher Hole

As a result of my posting on `bit.listserv.techwr-l`, I learned that a good source of information on technical writing was at a Gopher site at Carnegie Mellon, at their menu item The English Server. Under this Gopher heading, I found Technical communications/, which held the following information:

```
Internet Gopher Information Client v1.03
Technical Communications

1.  Problems.in.tech.comm (2k).
2.  Technical Communication Dropoff/
3.  University of Washington, Technical Communication Department/
4.  Welcome (1k).
5.  [Washington-Technical Communic] (1k) <HQX>

Press ? for Help, q to Quit, u to go up a menu:                Page: 1/1
```

This list contains some small overview material about technical writing in general, and it supports an archive of papers dealing with writing issues. I also found another subject to search for: communication. Previously, I had limited my searches to technical writing alone, but now I would extend my search to include communication. Later, though, while I was still in Gopher, I thought I'd check out the WAIS tool.

Excursion 18.9. WAIS

The first main WAIS list I received was a multiscreen list that began as follows:

```
1.  AAS_jobs: American Astronomical Society Job Register Listings <?>
2.  AAS_meeting: Abstracts, current American Astronomical Society mee <?>
3.  AAS_meeting_Summer92: Abstracts, June 92 American Astronomical So <?>
6.  ADC_documents: Astronomical Data Center on-line docs <?>
7.  ANU-ACT-Stat-L:  <?>
8.  ANU-Aboriginal-EconPolicies:  <?>
9.  ANU-Aboriginal-Studies: ASEDA, the Aboriginal Studies Electronic  <?>
10. ANU-Ancient-DNA-L:  <?>
11. ANU-Ancient-DNA-Studies:  <?>
12. ANU-Asian-Computing:   <?>
13. ANU-Asian-Religions: Bibliographic references to selected (mainly <?>
14. ANU-AustPhilosophyForum-L:  <?>
```

Although it was easy to eliminate some of the subjects, I found it difficult to decrypt what some of the other ones indicated. In addition, because I was on screen number 1 of a possible 38, I didn't want to have to track through each one of them. By screen number 11, I was about to call it quits when I noticed item 190, SGML: <?>.

```
185. RPMS-pathology:  <?>
186. RSInetwork:    <?>
187. Research-in-Surgery:   <?>
188. SDSU-directory-of-servers:  <?>
189. SDSU_PhoneBook: San Diego State University Faculty and Staff Dire <?>
190. SGML:  <?>
191. SIGHyper: Special Interest Group on Hypertext and Multimedia (SIG <?>
192. SPACEWARN: NASA SPACE-WARN bulletins <?>
193. STAR-Data:  <?>
194. STAR-NIPO-Data:  <?>
```

I remembered that this was discussed on the `techwr-l` newsgroup. Standard Generalized Markup Language (SGML) is a way of encoding text with formatting commands so the text can be more easily manipulated by computer programs. Because SGML is most closely associated with online text development, I decided I would try it. This led me to the `TEI-L` documents, which are a series of publications that, among many other things, defines SGML styles for formatting different kinds of texts—everything from plays to dictionaries. After skimming through some of the articles, I decided that this did fit my quest for online-related materials.

```
1.  bibliography     /local/ftp/pub/SGML/.
2.  TEI-L.LOG9010    /local/ftp/pub/SGML/TEI/.
3.  P2DR.DOC   /local/ftp/pub/SGML/TEI/.
4.  TEI-L.LOG9102    /local/ftp/pub/SGML/TEI/.
5.  TEI-L.LOG9203    /local/ftp/pub/SGML/TEI/.
6.  P2CO.DOC   /local/ftp/pub/SGML/TEI/.
7.  P2CO.PS   /local/ftp/pub/SGML/TEI/.
8.  P2DR.PS   /local/ftp/pub/SGML/TEI/.
9.  TEI-L.LOG9201    /local/ftp/pub/SGML/TEI/.
10. sgml_soa.sit     /local/ftp/pub/SGML/DTD/CAPS/.
11. TEI-L.LOG9305    /local/ftp/pub/SGML/TEI/.
12. P2WD.PS   /local/ftp/pub/SGML/TEI/.
13. futstrat.sit     /local/ftp/pub/SGML/DTD/CAPS/.
14. sgml_int.sit     /local/ftp/pub/SGML/DTD/CAPS/.
15. P2CO.P2X   /local/ftp/pub/SGML/TEI/.
16. evaluat.sit     /local/ftp/pub/SGML/DTD/CAPS/.
17. P221.PS   /local/ftp/pub/SGML/TEI/.
18. P2SG.DOC   /local/ftp/pub/SGML/TEI/.
```

All right. It was time to head back to the newsgroups.

Excursion 18.10. Old News as New News

The next time I returned to news, I searched for two new terms: `commun` (for communication, communicators, and so on) and `sgml`. Because SGML fit under online documentation as a process of presenting information, I decided to go back to the newsgroups to see if any SGML groups existed. Nothing turned up for communication, but a newsgroup called comp.text.sgml, dealt with SGML. Here is a partial listing of subjects in this newsgroup:

```
 3096 Re: Rules to detect ambiguity in content models (A System to do so)
 3097 Re: New Edition of Practical SGML Book?
 3098 Re: [Help] RTF Spec, parser, reader, converter needed
 3102 Real, true uses of SGML Real, true uses of SGML
 3107 Technical Documentation DTD and LaTeX Generator?
 3108 SGML sample files needed
 3109 Re: Technical Documentation DTD and LaTeX Gener
 3110 Survey on graphics
 3111 Re: [4375] SW Opinions wanted
 3112 Re: Real, true uses of SGML
 3113 First Intl. HyTime Conference
 3114 ATOS-MILB Conversion
 3115 DTD's....
 3117 embedding elements as attributes
 3122 Using Web Browser & Wais, Search & Index Local Files
 3123 Re: Survey on graphics
 3124 Real, true uses of SGML
 3125 Indexing HTML
 3129 SGML software?
 3130 ISO12083 to HTML
 3132 Bibliography for SGML-Databases (uncomplete, not only SGML)
 3134 Comparision between SGML and ODA ?
 3135 FAQ location?
End of article 3099 (of 3136) — what next? [^Nnpq]
```

Although many of the topics in this newsgroup were more technically oriented—implementing SGML text into existing computer applications—some topics covered issues such as the importance of formatting online text and the value of style over content. Some articles were even cross-posted both here and to the techwr-l newsgroup.

One topic that came up in the SGML newsgroup was hypertext, so I decided to check if there were any newsgroups devoted to this. Sure enough, there were:

```
Newsgroup alt.hypertext not in .newsrc — subscribe? [ynYN] y

Put newsgroup where? [$^.Lq]

******  24 unread articles in alt.hypertext — read now? [ynq]

 2789 Re: ANNOUNCING: UNIX HTML WYWSIWYG editor prerelease
 2790 Hypertext-Tools?
 2792 Mosaic 2.4 binaries with fish search
 2793 Re: UNIX and PC hypertext help
 2794 Unix html browser??
```

```
2795 design of hypertext-systems
2796 StorySpace - Help.
2797 Re: StorySpace - Help.
2805 html help
2806 Indexing HTML
2807 Testing package...
2809 April 19 Online SIG Meeting: 1993 Online Pubs Competition Review
2810 Hypertext for MAC
2811 Dexter Z-specification
```

As I have found, Internet tools are very interrelated, and it is difficult to simply use one tool in isolation from others. Instead, I constantly moved from one tool to another, where one search gave way to another. Instead of a linear search from the general to the specific, I kept jumping from specific to general, back to specific, and so on.

Summary

Day 18 was devoted to the idea of using the Internet for continuing education. I began by showing you the range of mailing lists and electronic journals dedicated to formal or semiformal continuing education and distance education. I then showed an extended example of using a variety of Internet tools to discover resources and discussion groups dealing with job-oriented continuing education. The World Wide Web was of minimal help in the area at this stage, but newsgroups and mailing lists provided discussion points, and Gopher pointed to a range of materials.

Task Review

On Day 18, you did the following:

- ☐ Discovered mailing lists and electronic journals devoted to continuing education.
- ☐ Used newsgroups to access job-specific issues.
- ☐ Accessed mailing lists for job-related education.
- ☐ Performed Archie, Veronica, and WAIS searches for job-oriented material.

Q&A

Q The Internet seems like a natural for distance education. Has this happened yet?

A It's just starting. Follow the education mailing lists and such information sources as the net-happenings list (see Day 12 for details), and you'll learn about events such as full online courses. The problem lies not in the technology but in the restricted access. At this stage in the life of the Internet, its access is not sufficiently open to make the Net a viable place to offer the sole version of an online course. Until that happens, few people will offer such courses. Nobody wants to develop several versions of the same course and deal with the complexities of multiple means of submitting assignments, offering tutorials, and so forth.

But, yes, the Net is a natural for distance education, and it's only a matter of time until Net-based courses happen. The Internet offers interactivity that no other form of distance course can possibly offer, including tutorials and demonstrations. E-mail and dedicated mailing lists could keep students in touch with one another, and assignments could be easily archived for use by future students. If you're interested, by all means, start making it happen.

18

Q Sesame Street has been criticized for teaching children about the medium of television itself rather than about the topics it offered in each show. Isn't an Internet-only distance education course in danger of doing the same thing?

A Yes. If you offer a course on Psychology over the Internet, make sure it's about Psychology, not about how to access Gopher and the World Wide Web—although those must be included. The content of a course, however, is never completely isolated from the medium in which it's presented. Students are taught how to read books every time they take a course with a textbook, for instance. So this criticism may be a bit of a red herring. Still, it's worth taking up with a group of interested people, so why not post it to a mailing list?

19

WEEK 3

Social Issues 101: Finding Information About Social Concerns on the Internet

Day 19 explores the growing coverage of social issues on the Internet. This coverage has grown as the Internet has expanded to include areas of interest beyond the scientific and the technological, and as the social sciences and the humanities have begun to find their particular niches on the Net. With its basis as a global communications medium, the Internet offers capabilities for world-wide sharing of information about any number of social issues, to the extent that the Net now provides a strong basis for research in these areas.

On Day 19, you will do the following:

- ☐ Search Gophers for information about AIDS and HIV.
- ☐ Explore the World Wide Web for material on world hunger.
- ☐ Explore a number of Internet sites for information about women's issues.

The Internet as Source for Issues of Social Concern

The Internet is a world-wide technology, and its users continually demonstrate a truly global range of concerns. Newsgroups have always shown a tendency toward becoming forums for a variety of social issues, but recently socially-conscious users have developed Gophers and World Wide Web sites dealing with these issues as well. Through a wide range of resources, Internetters have formed communities of socially-aware and -active participants, using the new technologies as a new way of fighting their battles.

Day 19 takes a look at a small percentage of the social concerns covered on the Internet. We'll begin with a look at the resources devoted to AIDS and HIV, and we'll take a brief look at resources on world hunger. Finally, we'll turn to an extensive exploration of women's issues. If you're the kind of person who likes to get involved, the Net can be an excellent place to start.

I'll start things off with a brief exploration of two particular social issues, then turn the chapter over to Charlotte Montenegro and Celine Latulipe, who will guide you through the Net's resources for women.

About the Contributors

Charlotte Montenegro is a graduate student at the University of Waterloo, Canada. She originally began her exploration searching for information on parenting, but shortly after, she realized that she was finding much more about women's issues instead. Because this information was of at least equivalent interest, it was only natural that she turn her attention to it, conduct a detailed search, and then report the results.

Celine Latulipe is the contributing author for Chapters 10 and 15 of this book. See those chapters for a short biography.

AIDS and HIV Information via Gopher

To be sure, the Internet houses a great number of newsgroups and mailing lists related to social concerns. In fact, one of the Usenet hierarchies is `.soc`, which refers to society and social issues. But there's such a huge range of such resources that the best approach is to search the list of lists resources via Gopher at `gopher.coloradu.edu`, in the path Other Gophers (by subject), then List of Lists Resources. That way, you'll be able to locate the newsgroups and mailing lists that pertain most closely to your topic.

In this section, we'll concentrate on Gophers that deal with social concerns, and even then there's room for only a few.

Excursion 19.1. The World Health Organization Gopher

The World Health Organization Gopher is located at `gopher.who.ch`. You'll find links to a range of health issues here, as the following listing demonstrates (found under the WHO's Major Programmes item from the main Gopher menu):

```
1.  Office of Information (INF) (WHO Press Releases, etc.)...
2.  Communicable Diseases (CDS)...
3.  Action Programme on Essential Drugs (DAP)...
4.  Programme for the Promotion of Environmental Health (EHE)...
5.  Food and Nutrition (FNU)...
```

```
6.  Global Programme on AIDS (GPA)...
7.  Global Programme on Vaccines (GPV)...
8.  Library and Health Literature Services (HLT)...
9.  Human Reproduction Programme (HRP)...
10. WHOSIS - The WHO Statistical Information System (HST)...
11. Noncommunicable Diseases (NCD)...
12. Programme for the Promotion of Chemical Safety (PCS)...
13. Strengthening of Health Services (SHS)...
14. Task Force on Health Economics (TFHE)...
15. Tropical Diseases Research (TDR)...
16. Technical Terminology Service (TER)...
17. WHO BBS Bulletin Boards (experimental)...
```

Obviously, this is a Gopher worth paying attention to. Several of the menu items are incomplete, but others show strong signs of developing well. The WHO BBS Bulletin Boards item, for example, takes you via Telnet to a site with documents about health futures studies (`telnet bbs.who.ch`, login as `bbs`).

Excursion 19.2. AIDS and HIVNET

There's probably no social issue in the world that's received as much press in the past few years as AIDS. Not surprisingly, the Internet has developed its share of Internet resources as well. First, from the World Health Organization Gopher, under the Global Programme on AIDS (GPA) menu, we find the following list:

```
1.  GPA Docbase...
2.  AIDS Frequently asked questions (SCI.MED.AIDS)...
3.  AIDS Related BBS and Internet resources...
4.  AIDS information from NIH...
5.  AIDS information from HIVNET...
```

From the GPA Docbase you have access to hundreds of text files on any number of AIDS and HIV topics, and the AIDS Frequently asked questions item offers a great deal of useful information as well. Furthermore, the Gopher offers a link to HIVNET, which houses an enormous store of material.

Located in the Netherlands (at `gopher.hivnet.org`), HIVNET is one of the primary archives for AIDS-related information, as the main menu shows:

```
1.  README
2.  HIVNET Info
3.  NEWS
4.  HIV Text Files 1
5.  HIV Text Files 2
6.  HIV Text Files 3
7.  Magazines, Periodicals and Libraries
8.  GENA Mailing List Archives
```

The last item on this menu, GENA Mailing List Archives, offers an extremely useful archive of information collected from newsgroups. Select this item and you'll get the following (partial) list:

```
1.  hiv-aids-arc
2.  hiv-aids-data
3.  hiv-aids-de
4.  hiv-aids-denews
5.  hiv-aids-dialogue
6.  hiv-aids-drugs
7.  hiv-aids-fr
8.  hiv-aids-hiv
```

There's so much information here that the second item only, hiv-aids-data, contained 1092 text files at the time of this writing. Roughly 150 additional text files can be found under the HIV Text Files items in the main HIVNET menu, and if you select Magazines, Periodicals and Libraries you get the following list, which contains almost 30 additional directories.

```
ATN Plus (Nederlands)
Abstracts
Aids Info (Nederlands)
Aids Information Library
Aids Link / ECAETC
Aids News Service (Veterans Administration)
Aids Related Law Review & Journal articles
Aids Treatment News
Being Alive
Body Positive Newsletter (UK)
Body Positive Online Magazine
CDC Aids Daily Summaries
Centers for Disease Control
Community Aids Treatment Exchange
Critical Path Aids Project
```

```
EuroCaso Newsletter
FOCUS : A Guide to Research and Counseling
Focus
Gay Mens Health Crisis Treatment Issues
Health Info Comm Newsletter
HivNieuws (Nederlands)
Nachrichten Deutsche Aidshilfe
Pediatrics
Project Inform Perspectives
STEP Perspectives
Searchlight
```

A superb Gopher dealing with AIDS and HIV information resides at `gopher.colorado.edu`. The main listing below displays even more material than we've seen so far:

```
1.  Ben Gardiner's AIDS BBS database - Via RiceInfo (Rice University CWIS)
2.  CHAT (AIDS database)
3.  E-Serials on AIDS - CICNet
4.  HIVNET (Global Electronic Network for AIDS, Europe) Gopher
5.  Mary Washington College - AIDS and HIV Information
6.  National Institute of Health - AIDS Related Information
7.  PennInfo - AIDS Information System for 3rd World
8.  The National Library of Medicine (NLM) - AIDS Publications
9.  UC Davis Campus AIDS Network
10. Welch Medical Library, John Hopkins University - Caring for patients
11. World Health Organization (Geneva) Gopher - Global Programme on AIDS
12. Yale biomedical gopher
```

Each of these items offers an extensive range of information, enough to satisfy all but the most ardent researcher. There's no lack of AIDS and HIV information on the Net, and it's only one of a range of social issues represented.

World Hunger Information on the World Wide Web

Lately, the World Wide Web has shown signs of moving towards issues of social concern. Here we'll explore some of the most useful and interesting sites, all of which point to other resources as well. In this short section, we'll look briefly at only one issue, world hunger, realizing that others are beginning to make their appearance.

Excursion 19.3. Hunger Web

Located at `http://www.brown.edu/hungerweb/`, Hunger Web deals with a broad range of issues related to world hunger. Figure 19.1 shows the extremely well-designed home page for Hunger Web, and further down this page you'll find links to a large number of related sites.

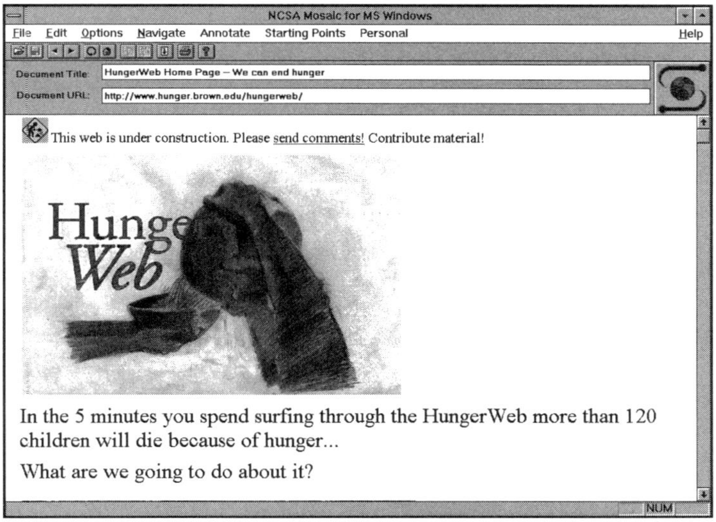

Figure 19.1. *Hunger Web home page.*

Linked to the home page is a WWW form encouraging you to become actively involved by sending a message about the problem of hunger to the White House. Figure 19.2 shows this page, complete with Clinton and Gore's e-mail addresses and a plea not to abuse them.

Among the more interesting offerings on the Hunger Web site (and the most sobering, once you try it), is the Hunger Quiz shown in Figure 19.3.

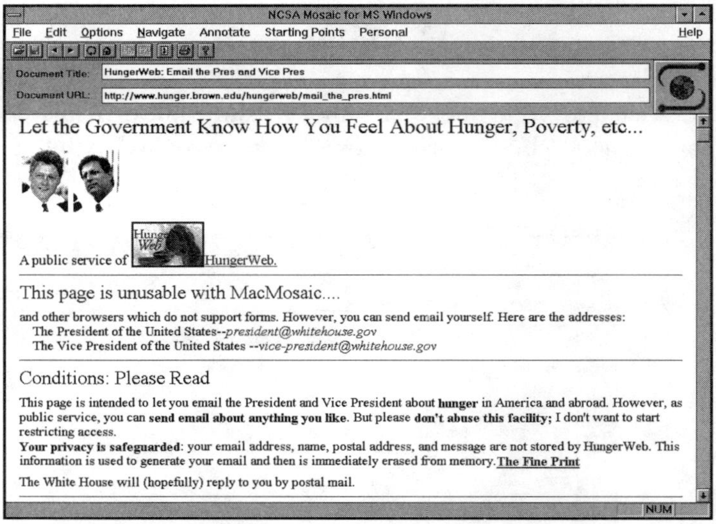

Figure 19.2. *Hunger Web form for e-mailing the White House.*

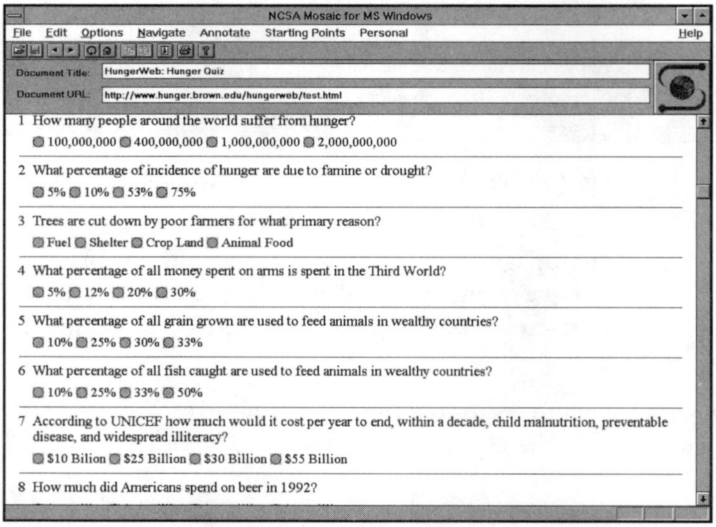

Figure 19.3. *Hunger Quiz from Hunger Web.*

First, you answer the questions by clicking on the appropriate circle (if you don't have a browser that supports forms, an alternative page is available). Then you click on the button at the bottom of the page (not shown here) to submit your answers for electronic grading. The results are returned, and if you're like me you're not likely to be pleased with how little you know about all this.

Obviously, there's much more to be researched than HIV and World Hunger. But we'll spend the remainder of this chapter on another major social topic of the '90s, women's issues. Charlotte Montenegro offers her observations first, and then Celine Latulipe closes the chapter off.

Women's Issues on the Internet

by Charlotte Montenegro

In this section, you will go with me on my tour of the Internet. My goal was to find anything that might pertain to the issues that are important in women's lives. I didn't start out with any particular focus, but as I continued surfing, I realized the most heavily debated and researched issues relate directly to the topic "Women on the Net" itself. Women are exploring their place on the Net and within electronic/computer media in general. I decided to surf these issues to see what I could find.

Mailing Lists and Newsgroups

Excursion 19.4. Listserv Mailing Lists

Listserv turned out to be a useful Internet tool. I received several requests for help on a particular area of research that someone was undertaking. One woman was interested in information on the implications of new computer technology for feminism. She wanted to know if anyone else knew of information pertaining to the issue. What an efficient way to get access to information. Even with my limited time on the Net, I quickly realized that people with a great deal of knowledge on a many women's issues also read the list and if I needed help in finding information all I had to do was ask.

I found a very interesting women's network called WOMEN'S WIRE (Worldwide Information Resource and Exchange). It's a new computer network serving the information and networking needs of women.

Note: For information on joining WOMEN'S WIRE, send an e-mail message to `info@wwire.net`.

If WOMEN'S WIRE doesn't interest you, there are many others. Here is a short list:

- ☐ BIFEM-L: moderated list for bisexual women. Send subscriptions requests to `LISTSERV@BROWNVM.BROWN.EDU` (Internet).
- ☐ EDUCOM-W: moderated list of technology and education that are of interest to women. Send requests to `LISTSERV@BITNIC.EDUCOM.EDU` (Internet).
- ☐ FEMAIL: open to all male and female feminists. Send requests to `FEMAILREQUEST@LUCERNE.ENG.SUN.COM` (Internet).
- ☐ GENDER: moderated list devoted to issues of gender and communication. Send requests to `COMSERV@VM.ITS.RPI.EDU` (Internet).
- ☐ GEOGFEM: gender issues in geography. Send requests to `LISTSERV@UKCC.UKY.EDU` (Internet).
- ☐ KOL-ISHA: moderated list for halachic questions and issues on women's roles in Judaism. Send requests to `LISTSERV@ISRAEL.NYSERNET.ORG` (Internet).
- ☐ MEDFEM-L: list for female medievalists. Send requests to `LISTSERV@INDYCMS.IUPUI.EDU` (Internet).
- ☐ SASH: (Sociologists Against Sexual Harassment) moderated list focusing on sexual harassment. Send requests to `AZPX@ASUVM.INRE.ASU.EDU` (Internet).
- ☐ WON: the Women's On-line Network. Electronic political group for women who want to distribute information and aid in political action. Send requests to `CARMELA@ECHONYC.COM` or `HORN@ECHONYC.COM` (Internet).
- ☐ WOW: Women on the Well, for women only. Send requests to `well.sf.ca.us.vice`: 415-332-4335.

Excursion 19.5. Newsgroups

Many newsgroups pertain to women's issues. For example, `alt.feminism`, `alt.abortion`, `alt.inequality`, `alt.adoption`, `alt.child.support`, and `alt.sexual.abuse.recovery`, are just a few of the many groups that give you access to varied amounts of information.

Two groups directly related to women's issues are `soc.feminism` and `soc.women`. The first, `soc.feminism`, deals with a variety of issues related to men and women, relationships and problems. It is a moderated group, and as such its postings tend to be more serious than in many newsgroups. The second newsgroup, `soc.women`, deals with relatively the same issues as `soc.feminism`, but it's far chattier. The `soc.feminism` newsgroup does not allow abortion and rape topics. The moderators say they do this because `talk.rape` and `talk.abortion` already exist to deal specifically with these issues and also because the topics are extremely volatile. Readers who objected to `soc.feminism`'s moderated format created the unmoderated group `alt.feminism` in the summer of 1992.

Gopher

As usual, Gophers provided a wide variety of relevant resources. I examined several, but those outlined following proved the most important.

Excursion 19.6. The Electronic Newsstand: *internet.com*

My first Gopher search was at `internet.com`, where I found the Electronic Newsstand. Item 12 in the ENews main Gopher allowed a search of all the available articles by keyword. Selecting this gave me the following search box, in which I typed the keyword, **`women`**:

```
       1.  Introduction to the Electronic Newsstand/
       2.  Notice of Copyright and General Disclaimer -- Please Read.
       3.  Sweepstakes -- Win Two Round-trip Air Tickets to Europe!/
       4.  Best of the Newsstand/
  |---------- Search All Electronic Newsstand Articles by Keyword -----------|
  |                                                                          |
  | Words to search for  women                                               |
  |                                                                          |
  |                                       [Cancel ^G] [Accept - Enter]       |
  |                                                                          |
  |--------------------------------------------------------------------------|
       12. Search All Electronic Newsstand Articles by Keyword  <?>
```

Note: The Electronic Newsstand is essentially a subscription service for magazines. Through the Newsstand you can browse a variety of publications, subscribing to the ones you like best. The archives give you an idea of what each publication features.

The search resulted in an extensive list of relevant articles—more than a hundred, in fact, and many which looked interesting. It was immediately apparent than several of the articles weren't really about women's issues *per se*, so I began the process of selecting and browsing those that looked most pertinent. This is the first portion of that list:

```
1.  June 1994 -- Bootlegging Mothers and Drinking Daughters: Gender an...
2.  November 29, 1993 -- ARE OPINIONS MALE?.
3.  December 1993 -- "The Hand of Refined Taste" .
4.  Fall 1992 -- Women of Valor.
5.  August 2, 1993 -- THE BOOK OF RUTH by Jeffrey Rosen.
6.  March 1994 -- Antinuclear Antibodies and Breast Implants.
7.  Fall 1993, Number 66 -- CULTURAL ASSAULT.
8.  January 10, 1994 -- WOMEN SCIENTISTS' GROUP LAUNCHES EFFORT TO PRO...
9.  August 2, 1993 -- Gender Benders by David Norbrook.
10. September/October 1993 -- SISTER AGAINST SISTER by Brenda Peterson.
11. January 1994 -- What Do People Desire In A Mate?.
12. May/June 1994 -- Blood Sisters.
13. January 3, 1994 -- SEDUCTION AND BETRAYAL.
14. October 18, 1993 -- Obsession By Richard A. Posner.
15. March 25, 1994 -- Equal, But Different.
16. November 1, 1993 -- THE FOUR BABY BOOMS.
17. December 20, 1993 -- DEMOCRACY AND HOMOSEXUALITY.
18. November 15, 1993 -- Of Arms and the Woman, By Michael Lind.
19. April 1994 -- The Nature Of Romantic Love.
20. February 1994 -- Salt 'N Pepa: Rap's Real Queens.
21. August 23, 1993 -- They Had a Dream by Tom Bethell.
22. January 3, 1994 -- GOOD SOLDIERS.
23. December 1993 -- Giving and Getting.
24. March 1994 -- Alcohol & Breast Cancer.
25. Fall 1993, Number 66 -- YOUR HONEY OR YOUR LIFE.
26. March 7, 1994 -- Report: Gender, Ethnic Diversity Coming Slowly To...
```

I browsed many of the articles for information related to women in the workplace. I received articles such as "Women of Valor," regarding the women of Israel who have always held positions in the Israeli army. I also found articles entitled "Japanese Women Lack Equality" and "Birth of Newborn Triggers Stress only After Mother Quits Work."

Because I quickly received many articles on women in the workplace, I envisioned my research going in that specific direction. However, I found more heated debates in other areas.

Excursion 19.7. A Veronica Search Through Gopher

Through the Australian National University Gopher at `life.anu.edu`, I conducted a Veronica search (I could have done it from any Gopher with a Veronica menu item, of course). Knowing I'd had luck using the University of Cologne before, I selected Search all items in GopherSpace: Veronica (U.Cologne, Germany), to start my search. When the search box appeared, I typed **women** and pressed Enter:

```
1.  # Email additions to this menu to coombspapers@coombs.anu.edu.au #.
      2.  About using the Veronica databases.
      3.  About using the Jughead databases.
      4.  Search all items in GopherSpace: Veronica (AARNet,Australia) <?>
 lqqqqqqqSearch all items in GopherSpace: Veronica (U.Cologne,Germany)qqqqqqqqk
 x                                                                             x
 x Words to search for  women                                                  x
 x                                                                             x
 x                                        [Cancel ^G] [Accept - Enter]         x
 x                                                                             x
 mqqqqqqqqqqqqqqqqqqqqqqqqqqqqqqqqqqqqqqqqqqqqqqqqqqqqqqqqqqqqqqqqqqqqqqqqqqqqqj
      12. Search all items in GopherSpace: Veronica (U.Bergen,Norway) <?>
 -->  13. Search all items in GopherSpace: Veronica (U.Cologne,Germany) <?>
      14. Search all items in GopherSpace: Veronica (U.Manitoba,Canada) <?>
      15. Search all items in GopherSpace: Veronica (U.Nevada,USA) <?>
      16. Search all items in GopherSpace: Veronica (U.Pisa,Italy) <?>
```

The result was an extremely long list consisting of several consecutive screens. Rather than page through them all, I pressed the slash (/) key to initiate a search and then typed **women's studies** in the search box. This took me several screens down and gave me the menu shown after the Tip.

Tip: Although the Gopher screen doesn't show it anywhere, you can search the items in any Gopher list for a keyword. Press the slash key (/), and Gopher will pop up a dialog box. Enter the keywords and press Enter. You'll be taken to the first menu item with that keyword. This is extremely handy for menus exceeding three or four screens in length.

```
109. Women's Studies.
     110. Women's Studies in Religion Program.
     111. Women's Studies.
     112. Women's Studies.
     113. Women's and Children's Health.
     114. WOMEN_S STUDIES.
     115. WMST-L (Women's Studies).
     116. Women's Studies: Reference Guide for the UCSB Library.
     117. Listservs in Women's Studies.
     118. Women's Commission.
     119. Women's Studies/
     120. Women.
     121. WOW: Women's group update.
```

```
122. Program in Women's Studies.
123. Women's Studies.
124. Women in Western Political Thought. S.M. Okin..
125. Women's Suffrage and Social Politics in the French Third Republic....
126. Women Writers and Poetic Identity: Dorothy Wordsworth, Emily Bront...
```

The only clear choice was item 119, because it was the only directory on the page (the rest were documents). The result was (in part) as follows:

```
4.  Listservs in Women's Studies.
5.  Listservs:  What, Why, How.
6.  SOC.FEMINISM: Organizations, Publications, Lists, Bookstores.
7.  Women (from Institute for Global Communications)/
8.  Women's Studies (University of Maryland)/
9.  Women's Studies: Reference Guide for the UCSB Library.
```

Selecting the item Women (from Institute for Global Communications), brought me to another directory, from which I selected Other Sources of Women's Information. Following is the resulting screen, which leads to valuable information on WOMEN'S WIRE, FEMISA, women's health issues, bibliographies, book reviews, and papers on gender and electronic communication:

```
1.  Women's Studies at University of Maryland/
2.  Gender and Electronic Networking (CPSR)/
3.  Women's Studies on the Internet (Univ of Michigan Fall 93).
4.  Internet/BITNET Women's Studies Resources (Murdoch Univ Sept 92).
5.  Women's Wire Gopher/
6.  Women of Color Resource Center (WCRC).
7.  Femisa/
8.  Women's Bibliographies and Other Information/
9.  Women and The Law (UNDER CONSTRUCTION)/
10. Pacifica Radio.
```

More Resources for Women

by Celine Latulipe

Excursion 19.8. More Mailing Lists

On various Internet surfing sessions, I have noticed items here and there that pertain to women. I've never paid much formal attention to women's issues, so I didn't really pay much attention to the items I came across. But this time, I decided to look closely at what was available and determine for myself what I wanted to pursue.

I decided that checking for feminist-related newsgroups and mailing lists (Listservs) was as good a way as any to start my investigation. I went into Winsock Gopher, got into a Veronica search through the University of Minnesota, and used `women list` as my search terms. I got exactly what I wanted—a directory that contained information of female-related Listservs. Some of them didn't interest me at all, but I found a few that definitely did. The first, femecon, is a Listserv for women in economics. It may sound boring to you, but it's my major, so I thought it was fantastic! Like any other Listserv, I subscribed by sending an e-mail to the specified address, `listserv@bucknell.edu`. I left the subject line blank and then typed **`sub femecon Celine Latulipe`**.

I received confirmation of my subscription within a few hours. The traffic on this Listserv is moderate; I've received an average of six messages a day. And I've found some really interesting discussion and research going on.

I also joined a Listserv called femail, a general Listserv for male and female feminists at `femail-request@lucerne.eng.sun.com`. However, to join this Listserv, the moderator requests that you include full name, Internet address, and gender in the body of the message. Because the moderator obviously takes care of subscriptions manually, it takes awhile to actually be put on the list. I still hadn't received confirmation or messages five days after subscribing.

Excursion 19.9. Women and The World Wide Web

I began my World Wide Web search in LII Cello, at the LII Home Page for Cornell Law School (`http://www.law.cornell.edu`). Right away I found something of interest to the female gender—a hypertext link to a page on Supreme Court Justice Ruth Ginsburg. Upon investigating the link, I found the page contained a full biography, including family, education, work experience and interests. There was also a further hypertext link to Recent Supreme Court decisions, by Justice Ginsburg. I looked at a few of these decisions and found them interesting, although I didn't necessarily understand all the legal language. The decisions didn't haven't anything to do with women's issues directly, but the delivery of the decisions were written by Justice Ginsburg. It is nice to read the reasoning behind the rulings, knowing that they come from a fellow female. It's fascinating to see the work of and get a glimpse into the mind of one of America's most intelligent and successful women.

Note: The Supreme Court home page and information about Justice Ginsburg is featured in Day 20.

Back to the Cornell Home Page and then on to a subpage through the Topical Fields link, I found a page on Feminist Jurisprudence, with a link for the Feminist Curricular Resource Clearinghouse. This contained a number of links that looked as though they led to promising sites: Feminist Jurisprudence, Women and The Law, and Index of Contributors. Unfortunately, the message at the top of this page, which warns that the site is under construction and links may not be functioning, is quite correct. Of those three links, the only one which I was able to connect with was the Index of Contributors. However, it is good to know that the other items will be available at some point in the near future. Figure 19.4 is a screen shot showing the Resource Clearinghouse page. Notice the URL address: `http://www.law.indiana.edu:80/fcrc/fcrc.html`.

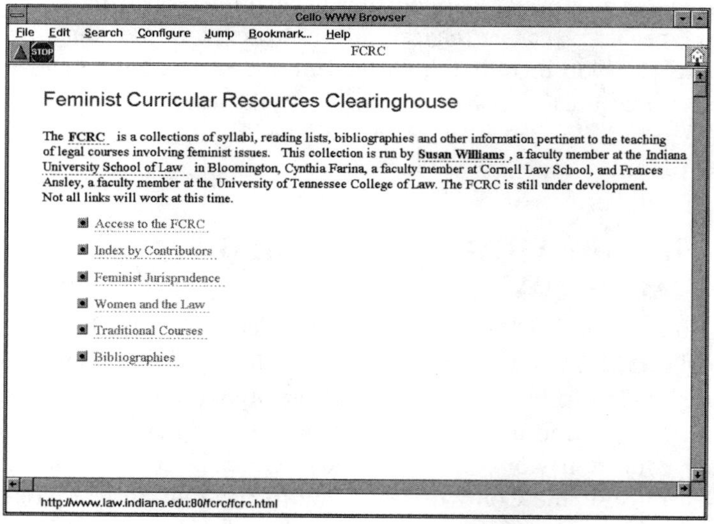

Figure 19.4. *The Feminist Curricular Resource Clearinghouse WWW page.*

I examined the link for Index of Contributors and found two links to female contributors: one for Cynthia Grant Bowman and one for Amy Kastely. Ms. Brown teaches, among other topics, Feminist Legal Theory, and her link leads the user to a lengthy and very complete reading list on legal issues relating to women. There is also a course description for her Feminist Legal Theory Course at the University School of Law. Under Amy Kastely, I found three items, all obviously course descriptions. The first two were Feminist Theory Reading Group Fall 1990 and Feminist Theory Reading Group Fall 1991. I looked at one of these and found a course description and list of reading resources. The third item was much the same, although it sounded very different—Directed Study Group on Storytelling. It was a course offered by Ms. Kastely and encourages and teaches the impact of promoting feminist jurisprudence through telling stories using a feminist voice.

Another indirect link from the LII Home Page, which I investigated for women's issues was The Whole Internet Catalog, obtained through the link to the Global Network Navigator. Within the Current Affairs subheading was the Gender & Sexuality Listing. Figure 19.5 depicts this part of the Whole Internet Catalog page.

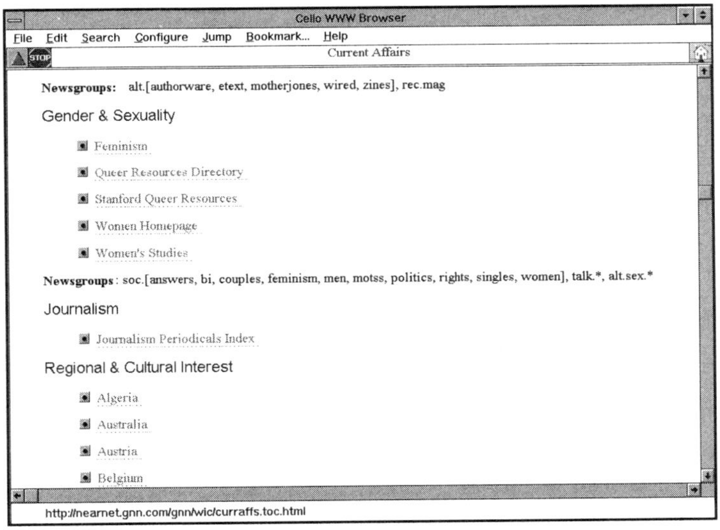

Figure 19.5. *Whole Internet Catalog—Gender and Sexuality.*

There were five page links here, and I began with the first one, Feminism. This turned out to be an archive of information drawn from the newsgroup `soc.feminism`. However, it is not the archive of the newsgroup, just useful information taken from it. There is a description of the newsgroup and its origins, a call for more moderators, and a list of on- and offline resources for feminism (including Listservs, e-mail networks, and newsgroups) and subtopics within feminism.

The next page I linked to was called Women Homepage, and here I found a wealth of resources and interesting connections. This is by far the best WWW page for women that I have seen. Of course I bookmarked it, using Cello's excellent bookmark feature. Part of the page is shown in Figure 19.6.

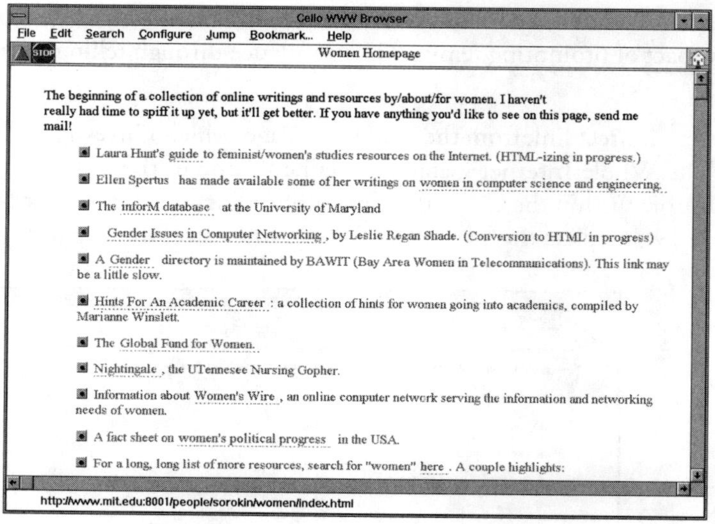

Figure 19.6. *The Women Homepage.*

The thing that is different about this homepage is that it really concentrates on connecting the user to sites where the information is not just referenced, but actually available online. This is a definite plus in my opinion, because there is nothing worse than finding an FTP or Gopher filename that sounds like it is exactly what you want and then opening it to find that it is a reference to a book published on another topic completely.

One of the more interesting things I found was a link to a page containing information and hints for women going into academic careers. I found information on tenuring, teaching, getting published, finding a job, and getting the right classes. It was a very informative page, and I didn't even have to download anything, unless I wanted to. I obviously made sure to bookmark this site.

There were a number of other directories on the Women Homepage, and I checked out a few more. One directory is the InforM directory of women's resources at the University of Maryland. This is an FTP site with a number of different hypertext links that looked promising, including one on Film Reviews and one on Gender Issues. Being the curious person that I am, and not incidentally a big fan of film, I investigated the film reviews section. It consisted of film reviews by a feminist at the University of Maryland, and the reviews are actually transcripts from a radio show called The Women's Show on WMNF-FM, on which Linda Lopez McAlister is a regular.

Almost all the most popular films of the last three years are listed, as well as a file containing her favorites from 1992 and 1993, and a number of less-known films dealing with feminism throughout history and in the 1990s. (Just to partially satisfy your curiosity, a few of her favorite films from 1993 include *Like Water For Chocolate*, *Orlando*, and *The Piano*.) The reviews are well-written and provide a different viewpoint than many reviews found in today's newspapers and magazines. I really enjoyed reading these reviews because the author really does her homework and lets you know about the people involved in the movie, the historical basis of the original novel or screen-play, and gives a list of other related movies.

Another directory within the InforM page I checked into was the Gender Issues page. Here I found links to pages on Women's Health, Violence & Women, and a directory on the Glass Ceiling issue. Figure 19.7 shows some of the directories available.

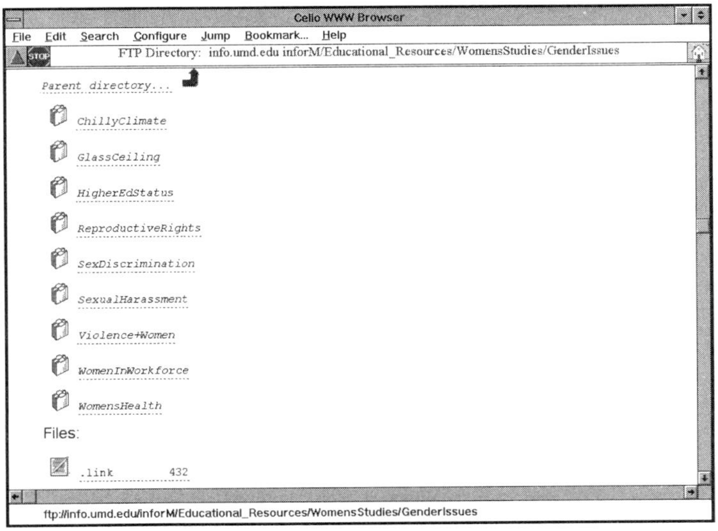

Figure 19.7. *Gender Issue's FTP site.*

My first impression of the Web was that it was not a great source for women's issues. But as I delved deeper, I found that I was wrong, and that the Web is a great place to find items of interest to women. Granted, a lot of the links that I found led me to women's studies courses at all sorts of different institutions, which wasn't what I was looking for. But that's okay, because that may be exactly what you're looking for. All I have to say is go for it. Explore, have fun, and learn.

Summary

In Day 19, we've explored Internet resources on AIDS, world hunger, and women's issues. These topics are only three among a large and growing number of resources available for the researcher, the activist, or simply the concerned. The point of the chapter has been to demonstrate that there's a great deal of collaborative activity about the world's problems taking place on the Internet constantly, and to offer you a sense of where you might turn to get involved. I invite you to do so.

Task Review

On Day 19, you performed the following tasks:

- ☐ Searched Gophers for information about AIDS and HIV.
- ☐ Examined the World Wide Web for material dealing with world hunger.
- ☐ Explored newsgroups and mailing lists devoted to women's issues.
- ☐ Explored the World Wide Web for information about women's issues.

Q&A

Q What advantages does the Internet offer for people interested in social issues or social reform?

A First, it offers the chance to meet. True, commercial services like CompuServe, GEnie, Prodigy, and America Online offer these as well, but most of the members of these services are U.S.-based. The Internet is also dominated by U.S. membership, but as we've seen throughout this book there's a important and growing non-U.S. population. What this means is that people from around the world can collaborate on ideas and topics of common social interest.

Second, the Internet provides a number of different methods of collaboration. Groups can establish newsgroups and mailing lists, and they can also jointly develop and maintain Gophers, with material added from any number of different locations. The same goes for the World Wide Web, with the added benefits of attractive appearance and multimedia technologies. And unlike magazine ads and television, information on the Net changes constantly. Internetters actively concerned about a topic can check out the Internet sites daily to see what has changed, rekindling his or her interest as he or she does. These are important advantages.

20

WEEK 3

Government and Law 101: Finding Information on the World's Governments and Courts

In Day 20, we'll examine the growing wealth of material available on the Internet concerning the policies and decisions of governments and courts. We'll focus on the White House and the U.S. Supreme Court, but we'll also discover resources from Mexico and Canada as well. By the time you've completed the chapter, you'll know where to look for the latest in government publications and court decisions, along with materials that will help you understand those important institutions.

Today you will learn how to do the following:

- ☐ Explore U.S. government Gophers.
- ☐ Use these Gophers to discover available information about the House of Representatives, the 1995 U.S. Budget, the National Information Infrastructure, and White House papers.
- ☐ View, mail, and save text documents from these Gophers.
- ☐ Examine the primary Gophers for accessing legal information.
- ☐ Explore the growing number of law-related World Wide Web sites.
- ☐ Find and read Supreme Court decisions.
- ☐ Locate a wide range of other legal information.

Government Information on the Internet

If there's been one crucial question surrounding the accessibility of information on the Internet, it's had to do with the willingness of governments to make their own information readily available. It's true, after all (in democratic nations, at least) that governments are public institutions, but it hasn't always been easy or convenient collecting material about their doings. Sometimes the reason has been security; usually, it's because we either don't know where to look, or because getting what we need requires too much effort.

To a significant degree, the Internet has changed all this. Don't expect classified documents to start appearing in your local Gopher site, but do expect to be pleasantly surprised when you discover the wealth of governmental and legal resources available. While the Internet is still no substitute for a well-stocked government bookstore, the indications are that it might be, quite soon. Attribute this change to Vice President Gore's information superhighway, if you will, but whatever the case, there's never been a time like the present for learning what your government or your Supreme Court is up to (at least, the things they're willing to make public).

This information is especially useful if you're engaged in a project that requires up-to-date research on a specific government or legal topic, or if part of a presentation you're making depends on the timeliness of your institutional data. It's extremely useful material for journalists and teachers as well.

Note: Most of the tasks performed in this chapter are Gopher menu selections. That's because, so far at least, Gopher is the Internet tool most institutions seem to understand best. While it's certainly possible for each government agency to offer an FTP site (many do, in fact), and to build a series of hypertext-linked World Wide Web pages, Gophers have become the early medium of choice. This is for very good reasons: Gophers are easy to access and even easier to move around in, while FTP is still too *computery* for many people. Web pages are beginning to appear, but too few people have access to the necessary connections and software. You can expect to see Gophers proliferating for the next few years.

Government 101: What the White House Has Made Available

Given President Bush's signing of the High Performance Computing Act in 1991, and the Clinton-Gore pushing of the Internet and the information superhighway, it's not surprising that the White House has been reasonably hard at work developing Internet-based access to documents and files. But that still may not prepare you for the sheer amount of White House information now available. In short, the White House demonstrates quite clearly, to governments the world over, how to use the Internet to make its actions known—not every action, maybe, but certainly a large number and a wide variety.

Excursion 20.1. Around the U.S. Government Gophers

Our first stop for government sources is the same as the first stop for any number of interesting items on the Internet: Gopher Jewels. This exceptionally strong Gopher, highlighted way back in Day 2, offers a wide range of information, arranged conveniently by subject.

Note: Gopher Jewels is available from many, many Gophers, but you can access it for certain through by typing `gopher cwis.usc.edu` and maneuvering through the Other Gophers and Information Servers menu item.

Note: In all Gopher examples, the selected menu item is shown in **boldfaced** type.

Let's take a quick look at how Gopher Jewels will help us with our search for government and court information:

```
Gopher-Jewels

1.  About Gopher Jewels.
2.  A List Of Gophers With Subject Trees/
3.  AIDS and HIV Information/
4.  Agriculture and Forestry/
5.  Anthropology and Archaeology/
6.  Architecture/
7.  Arts and Humanities/
8.  Astronomy and Astrophysics/
9.  Biology and Biosciences/
10. Books, Journals, Magazines, Newsletters, Technical Reports and Pub../
11. Botany/
12. Chemistry/
13. Computer Related/
14. Disability Information/
15. Economics and Business/
16. Education and Research (Includes K-12)/
17. Employment Opportunities and Resume Postings/
18. Engineering/
19. Environment/
20. Federal Agency and Related Gopher Sites/
21. Free-Nets And Other Community Or State Gophers/
22. Fun Stuff & Multimedia/
23. General Reference Resources/
24. Geography/
25. Geology and Oceanography/
26. Global or World-Wide Topics/
27. Grants/
28. History/
29. Internet Cyberspace related/
30. Internet Resources by Type (Gopher, Phone, USENET, WAIS, Other)//
31. Language/
32. Legal or Law related/
```

```
33. Library Information and Catalogs/
34. List of Lists Resources/
35. Manufacturing/
36. Math Sciences/
37. Medical Related/
38. Military/
39. Miscellaneous Items/
40. Museums, Exhibits and Special Collections/
41. News Related Services/
42. Patents and Copy Rights/
43. Photonics/
44. Physics/
45. Political and Government/
46. Products and Services - Store Fronts/
47. Psychology/
48. Religion and Philosophy/
49. Social Science/
50. Weather
```

At the very least, items 20 and 32 promise to help us. We'll leave the Legal or Law related section until later, when we explore the goings-on with the courts. For now, let's try Federal Agency and Related Gopher Sites and see what it brings us.

As the following list shows, the answer is simple: There's a huge amount, if we're willing to explore it.

```
Federal Agency and Related Gopher Sites

1.  A Collection of US Government Gophers via UC Irvine/
2.  Brookhaven National Laboratory Protein Data Bank/
3.  Bureau of Labor Statistics, US Dept of Labor (via ftp)/
4.  Climate and Radiation Server at Goddard Space Flight Center/
5.  Commerce Business Daily - Vai CNS, Inc Gopher/
6.  Department of Energy Office of Nuclear Safety (Federal Gov. Info.)/
7.  Dept. of Labor Occupational Outlook Handbook 1992-93 - U. Minn./
8.  EGIS (Electronic Government Information Service)/
9.  Extension Service USDA Information/
10. F.B.I. Gopher at NASA Network Applications and Information Center/
11. FedWorld (NTIS Gateway to Federal Bulletin Boards) <TEL>
12. Federal Info. Exchange (FEDIX)/
13. Lawrence Berkeley Laboratory (LBL)/
14. Library of Congress (LC MARVEL)/
15. Los Alamos National Laboratory/
16. Los Alamos National Laboratory, T-2 Nuclear Information Service/
17. Martin Marietta Energy Systems/
18. NASA (Goddard Space Flight Center), Gopher Gateway /
19. NASA (netgopher.lerc.nasa.gov)/
20. NASA COSMIC's gopher server - NASA Software/
21. NASA Goddard Space Flight Center/
22. NASA Mid-Continent Technology Transfer Center/
```

```
23. NASA Network Applications and Information Center (NAIC)/
24. NASA Office of Life and Microgravity Sciences and Applications/
25. NASA Shuttle Small Payloads Info/
26. NASA, Center for Aerospace Information/
27. NASA, High Energy Astrophysics Science Archive Research Center/
28. NASA, Johnson Space Center, Space Mechanisms Gopher/
29. NASA, Lab for Terrestrial Physics Gopher/
30. NASA, Langley Research Center/
31. NIST Gopher, Boulder, Colorado/
32. NOAA National Geophysical Data Center (NGDC)/
33. NSF Center for Biological Timing/
34. National Aeronautics and Space Administration/
35. National Center for Atmospheric Research (NCAR)/
36. National Coordination Office for HPCC (NCO/HPCC) Gopher/
37. National Institute of Allergy and Infectious Disease (NIAID)/
38. National Institute of Environmental Health Sciences (NIEHS)/
39. National Institute of Standards and Technology (NIST)/
40. National Institutes of Health (NIH) Gopher/
41. National Library of Medicine (National Institutes of Health)/
42. Oak Ridge National Lab, Center for Computational Sciences/
43. Oak Ridge National Laboratory ESD Gopher/
44. Occupational Safety & Health Gopher (OSHA regulations)/
45. U.S. Bureau of Mines Gopher/
46. U.S. Bureau of the Census Gopher/
47. U.S. Department of Energy, Headquarters Gopher/
48. U.S. Department of State Gopher/
49. U.S. Dept. of Commerce Economic Conversion Information Exchange/
50. U.S. Dept. of Education/
51. U.S. Dept. of Energy, Environment, Safety & Health, Tech. Info. Se../
52. U.S. Dept. of Energy, Environmental Guidance Memos/
53. U.S. Environmental Protection Agency/
54. U.S. Environmental Protection Agency, GLNPO Gopher/
55. U.S. Geological Survey (USGS)/
56. U.S. Senate Gopher/
57. USA Environmental Protection Agency (Future Studies Group
```

Wow! Where do we start? No question, the F.B.I. Gopher at NASA Network Applications and Information Center looks interesting, as does the National Institute of Environmental Health Sciences. Then again, how can we avoid the Climate and Radiation Server at Goddard Space Flight Center? Later, of course, we'll be absolutely certain to go through all these Gophers in detail (sort of like that pile of unread books sitting on the study shelf), but in the meantime an almost depressing item makes itself instantly apparent.

Gopher item 1 is entitled A Collection of US Government Gophers via UC Irvine. That means that there's even more available than this 57-item Gopher already shows, or at least so it seems. It's time to dig ourselves in even further.

Warning: Just because a Gopher listing appears to offer additional resources through one of its items, don't necessarily get your hopes up. Often a Gopher site will point to a different Gopher site that, in fact, is practically the same as the one you're already in. Gophers are developed individually by any number of institutions, and their menu items point to other Gophers without taking into account that the information may well be repeated.

```
A Collection of US Government Gophers via UC Irvine

1.  Call for assistance....
2.  POLITICS and GOVERNMENT/
3.  Definition of a "United States Government Gopher".
4.  Federal Government Information (via Library of Congress)/
5.  LEGI-SLATE Gopher Service (via UMN)/ /
6.  AVES: Bird Related Information/
7.  Americans Communicating Electronically/
8.  Arkansas-Red River Forecast Center (NOAA)/
9.  AskERIC - (Educational Resources Information Center)/
10. CYFERNet USDA Children Youth Family Education Research Network/
11. Co-operative Human Linkage Center (CHLC) Gopher/
12. Comprehensive Epidemiological Data Resource (CEDR) Gopher/
13. Defense Technical Information Center Public Gopher/
14. ERIC Clearinghouse for Science, Math, Environmental (OSU)/
15. ERIC Clearinghouse on Assessment and Evaluation/
16. ESnet Information Services Gopher/
17. Electronic Government Information Service/
18. Environment, Safety & Health (USDE) Gopher/
19. Environmental Protection Agency/
20. Environmental Protection Agency/
21. Environmental Protection Agency Great Lakes National Program Offi../
22. Extension Service, USDA/
23. Federal Communications Commission Gopher/
24. Federal Info Exchange (FEDIX)/
25. Federal Register (via Internet.COM)/
26. Federal Register - Sample access/
27. GrainGenes (USDA) Gopher/
28. Information Infrastructure Task Force (DoC) Gopher/
29. LANL Advanced Computing Laboratory/
30. LANL Gopher Gateway /
31. LANL Nonlinear Science Information Service/
32. LANL Physics Information Service/
33. LANL T-2 Nuclear Information Service Gopher/
34. LANL Weather Machine/
35. LTERnet (Long-Term Ecological Research Network)/
36. Lawrence Berkeley Laboratory (LBL)/
37. Library of Congress MARVEL Information System/
38. Los Alamos National Laboratory/
39. NASA Ames Research Center K-12 Gopher/
```

```
40. NASA Center for Aerospace Information/
41. NASA Center for Computational Sciences/
42. NASA Goddard Space Flight Center/
43. NASA High Energy Astrophysics Science Archive Research Center/
44. NASA Laboratory for Terrestrial Physics Gopher/
45. NASA Langley Research Center /
46. NASA LeRC Telecommunications and Networking Gopher/
47. NASA Lewis Research Center (LeRC)/
48. NASA Library X at Johnson Space Center/
49. NASA Mid-Continent Technology Transfer Center/
50. NASA Minority University Space Interdisciplinary Network/
51. NASA Network Application and Information Center (NAIC)/
52. NASA Office of Life and Microgravity Sciences and Applications/
53. NASA Scientific and Technical Information/
54. NASA Shuttle Small Payloads Information/
55. NASA Space Medicine and Life Sciences/
56. NASA Telnet Sites/
57. NIST Computer Security/
58. NOAA Environmental Services Gopher/
59. NOAA National Geophysical Data Center (NGDC)/
60. NOAA National Oceanographic Data Center (NODC) Gopher/
61. National Agricultural Library Genome Gopher/
62. National Archives Gopher/
63. National Cancer Institute/
64. National Center for Atmospheric Research (NCAR) Gopher/
65. National Center for Biotechnology Information (NCBI) Gopher/
66. National Center for Education Statistics/
67. National Center for Research on Evaluation, Standards/
68. National Center for Supercomputing Applications/
69. National Coordination Office for High Performance Computing and Co../
70. National Geophysical Data Center (NOAA)/
71. National Institute of Allergy and Infectious Disease (NIAID)/
72. National Institute of Environmental Health Sciences (NIEHS) Gopher/
73. National Institute of Mental Health (NIMH) Gopher/
74. National Institute of Standards and Technology (NIST)/
75. National Institutes of Health (NIH)/
76. National Library of Medicine /
77. National Library of Medicine TOXNET Gopher/
78. National Oceanographic Data Center (NODC) Gopher/
79. National Science Foundation (STIS)/
80. National Science Foundation Center for Biological Timing/
81. National Science Foundation Metacenter/
82. National Toxicology Program (NTP) NIEHS-NIH/
83. Naval Ocean System Center (NRaD) Gopher/
84. Naval Research Laboratory/
85. Naval Research Laboratory Central Computing Facility/
86. Oak Ridge National Laboratory Center for Computational Sciences/
87. Oak Ridge National Laboratory ESD Gopher/
88. Protein Data Bank - Brookhaven National Lab/
89. STIS (Science and Technology Information System-NSF)/
90. Smithsonian Institution Natural History Gopher/
91. U.S. Agency for International Development Gopher/
92. U.S. Bureau of Mines Gopher/
93. U.S. Bureau of the Census Gopher/
94. U.S. Dept Agriculture ARS GRIN National Genetic Resources Program/
```

```
95. U.S. Dept Agriculture Children Youth Family Education Research Net../
96. U.S. Dept Agriculture Economics and Statistics/
97. U.S. Dept Agriculture Extension Service/
98. U.S. Dept Agriculture National Agricultural Library Plant Genome/
99. U.S. Dept Commerce Information Infrastructure Task Force/
100. U.S. Dept Commerce Economic Conversion Information Exchange/
101. U.S. Dept Education/
102. U.S. Dept Energy /
103. U.S. Dept Energy Environment, Safety & Health Gopher/
104. U.S. Dept Energy Office of Nuclear Safety/
105. U.S. Environmental Protection Agency/
106. U.S. Environmental Protection Agency Futures Group/
107. U.S. Environmental Protection Agency Great Lakes National Program ../
108. U.S. Geological Survey (USGS)/
109. U.S. Geological Survey Atlantic Marine Geology/
110. U.S. House of Representatives Gopher/
111. U.S. Military Academy Gopher/
112. U.S. National Information Service for Earthquake Engineering/
113. U.S. Naval Observatory Satellite Information/
114. U.S. Navy Naval Ocean System Center NRaD Gopher/
115. U.S. Senate Gopher/
116. Voice of America (Radio)/
117. PEG, a Peripatetic, Eclectic Gopher/
```

Note: Throughout this book, Gophers have normally been abbreviated. In this case, reproducing the entire listing is important. It demonstrates, even more than the Gopher Jewels list, the enormous range of governmental material available for browsing, perusing, downloading, and so forth. Not surprisingly, given the importance placed on telecommunications by the Clinton administration, the United States has led the way in making its information publicly available, but a list like this one can take even the most jaded cynic aback. There seems to be no end to it all, and it's growing weekly.

Obviously, we aren't about to read everything that's available. Americans Communicating Electronically is a must-browse at some point in the next few sessions, as is the Cooperative Human Linkage Center. Even the Federal Communications Commission has a Gopher offering, and that too would seem to be worth checking out. That's not even counting all the NASA material that's spawning itself all over the Net. Undoubtedly, the NASA sites will offer graphics available for download, maybe even the Voyager photographs.

Excursion 20.2. The U.S. House of Representatives

At this point, we know that the range of possibilities is enormous. Any student of the U.S. government probably has enough material in these various Gophers for primary research for any number of high school or early college essays, and anyone doing a research presentation can make equally good use of the material. It seems nearly endless.

Right now, though, we have to make a choice. Let's focus on material that discusses governmental activities themselves, starting with—because we have to start somewhere—the U.S. House of Representatives Gopher:

```
U.S. House of Representatives Gopher

1.  About the US House Gopher/
2.  Congressional Information/
3.  House Committee Information/
4.  House Directories/
5.  Other Internet Resources/
6.  Visitor Information/
```

Good. It's short. Maybe we've finally found something we can get a handle on. Starting at the top, we'll begin with some information about this Gopher site by choosing item 1. The following even shorter menu results:

```
About the US House Gopher

1.  Welcome to the US House Gopher.
2.  Welcome.au <)
3.  Internet Etiquette.
```

Note: Remember the rule about Gophers in general. Any menu item with a slash (`/`) on the end represents a subdirectory; items without the slash are files. If you choose a file, it will be retrieved and displayed. For text files, this isn't a problem: the Gopher software will display it easily. For other files, however, you must set up the appropriate viewers to see or hear them. Files with extensions such as `.gif`, `.pcx`, `.jpg`, and the like are graphics files. Files with `.au`, `.wav`, or `.mid` extensions are sound files.

Because there's no slash (/) at the end of the lines, we know that all three of these items are files rather than further subdirectories. Because we don't have sound hardware installed, choosing the .au file won't to any good (it's a Sun audio sound file), and we know enough about Internet etiquette not to worry about it. Let's see what the welcome message has to say, by choosing item 1:

```
                         WELCOME TO
              THE U.S. HOUSE OF REPRESENTATIVES'
                        GOPHER SERVICE

        The U.S. House of Representatives' Gopher service
provides access to information about Members and Committees of
the House and to other U.S. government information resources.
This Gopher serves staff of the U.S. House of Representatives
and constituents throughout the world. It was built using the
Gopher software from the University of Minnesota. Maintaining
the menus on this Gopher server is coordinated by the House
Administration Committee Internet Working Group in cooperation
with service units and divisions throughout the House of
Representatives. Posting and maintaining information in Member
and Committee folders is the responsibility of the individual
Members and Committees.

        This gopher server does not provide anonymous FTP.

         If you have suggestions or comments regarding the U.S.
House of Representatives' Gopher service or if you need to
report operational difficulties with the system, please contact
the House Internet Working Group at the Internet address:

               househlp@hr.house.gov

        Thank you for your interest.

        *** Last update March 24, 1994 (daa) ***


Press <RETURN> to continue,
   <m> to mail, <D> to download, <s> to save, or <p> to print:
```

Well, things are starting to cook (at least a little). Here we have at least one agency asking for feedback on its Internet offering. Of course, the name househlp@hr.house.gov doesn't sound overly personal, but at least it's something. Also comforting, for those who care about such things, is that the Gopher's title (The House of Representatives' Gopher Server) actually contains the proper punctuation—an apostrophe in the right place.

Pressing Enter to get back to the Gopher menu, then the u key to get back to the original House menu, we find ourselves at this familiar-looking menu:

```
1.  About the US House Gopher/
2.  Congressional Information/
3.  House Committee Information/
4.  House Directories/
5.  Other Internet Resources/
6.  Visitor Information
```

This time, let's give item 2 a try. What we find is this:

```
Congressional Information

1.  About Congressional Information.
2.  Educational Resources/
3.  General Information/
4.  House Schedules/
5.  Legislative Resources
```

Recalling that the information screen for the previous Gopher offered some useful material, we assume we'll find something similar here as well. A quick look at Educational Resources yields a Gopher menu "under construction," so we'll go down the list and try General Information instead. Here, the material starts to expand, and from the following menu we select the document in item 2, House Email Addresses:

```
General Information

1.  95 Budget (cyfer.esusda.gov USDA)/
2.  House Email Addresses.
3.  US and World Politics (Sunsite UNC


            UNITED STATES HOUSE OF REPRESENTATIVES
              CONSTITUENT ELECTRONIC MAIL SYSTEM

        We welcome your inquiry to the House of Representatives
Constituent Electronic Mail System. Currently, eighteen Members of
the U.S. House of Representatives have been assigned public
electronic mailboxes that may be accessed by their constituents.
The results of the six month public mail pilot have been very
encouraging. The nature and character of the incoming electronic
mail has demonstrated that this capability will be an invaluable
source of information on constituent opinion. We are now in the
process of expanding the project to other Members of Congress, as
technical, budgetary and staffing constraints allow.
```

```
        A number of House committees have also been assigned public
electronic mailboxes. The names and electronic mailbox addresses
of these committees are listed below after the information about
participating Representatives.

        Please review the list of participating Representatives
below, and if the Congressional District in which you reside is
listed, follow the instructions below to begin communicating by
electronic mail with your Representative. If your Representative
is not yet on-line, please be patient.

        U.S. REPRESENTATIVES PARTICIPATING IN THE CONSTITUENT
                     ELECTRONIC MAIL SYSTEM.

Hon. Dave Camp
4th Congressional District, Michigan
Rm. 137 Cannon House Office Building
Washington, DC 20515
DAVECAMP@HR.HOUSE.GOV

Hon. Maria Cantwell
1st Congressional District, Washington
Rm. 1520 Longworth House Office Building
Washington, DC 20515
CANTWELL@HR.HOUSE.GOV

Hon. John Conyers, Jr.
14th Congressional District, Michigan
Rm. 2426 Rayburn House Office Building
Washington, DC 20515
JCONYERS@HR.HOUSE.GOV

Hon. Sam Coppersmith
1st Congressional District, Arizona
1607 Longworth House Office Building
Washington, DC 20515
SAMAZ01@HR.HOUSE.GOV

Hon. Peter Deutsch
20th Congressional District, Florida
Rm. 425 Cannon House Office Building
Washington, DC 20515
PDEUTSCH@HR.HOUSE.GOV
```

Several more names follow, but this is enough to get the general idea. This is substantiated proof that the government is becoming Internet-savvy, with all these Representatives establishing e-mail addresses and partipating in this project. Immediately following, however, is a note that dampens enthusiasm a mite:

```
                    INSTRUCTIONS FOR CONSTITUENTS

     The list above includes the electronic mail addresses of
members who are participating in the program. However, if
your Representative is taking part in the project, we
request that you send a letter or postcard by U.S. Mail to that
Representative at the address listed above with your name and
internet address, followed by your postal (geographical) address.
The primary goal of this program is to allow Members to
better serve their CONSTITUENTS, and this postal contact is the
only sure method currently available of verifying that a user is a
resident of a particular congressional district.

        In addition, constituents who communicate with their
Representative by electronic mail should be aware that Members
will sometimes respond to their messages by way of the U.S. Postal
Service. This method of reply will help to ensure
confidentiality, a concern that is of upmost importance to the
House of Representatives.
```

Excursion 20.3. The 1995 U.S. Budget

General information is fine, but as its name suggests, it's merely general information. At this stage we're getting a bit impatient for some real material, something useful and maybe worth getting angry about (that's what government information is for, isn't it?). Back at the previous menu, we select the first item, the '95 Budget. The budget is always of interest, but the next menu shows that there may well be more available than we're actually interested in:

```
95 Budget (cyfer.esusda.gov USDA)

1.  95 Budget Table of Contents.
2.  94-02-07 The Budget Message of the President.
3.  Chapter 1 -- Where We Started.
4.  Chapter 2 -- What We Have Accomplished: The Clinton Economic Plan.
5.  Chapter 3a -- Prosperity and Jobs .
6.  Chapter 3b -- Investing for Productivity and Prosperity.
7.  Chapter 3c -- Delivering a Government that Works Better and Costs ...
8.  Chapter 4 -- Reforming the Nation's Health Care System .
9.  Historical Tables/
10. Information on the electronic version of the Budget.
11. Introduction -- An Overview of the 1995 Budget.
12. Lists of Charts and Tables.
13. National Defense and International Affairs.
14. Personal Security: Crime, Illegal Immigration, and Drug Control.
15. Summary Tables..
16. The 1995 Proposed Federal Budget.
17. charts-95budget-tiff/
```

The Table of Contents can't possibly be very interesting, but the president's message might be. Besides, knowing where it is will be useful if there's ever a need to study the actual speeches related to such a controversial topic. Selecting item 2, we get a transcript of the entire speech.

Let's see what else this Gopher has to offer about the budget:

```
3.  Chapter 1 -- Where We Started.
4.  Chapter 2 -- What We Have Accomplished: The Clinton Economic Plan.
5.  Chapter 3a -- Prosperity and Jobs .
6.  Chapter 3b -- Investing for Productivity and Prosperity.
7.  Chapter 3c -- Delivering a Government that Works Better and Costs ...
8.  Chapter 4 -- Reforming the Nation's Health Care System .
```

It's hard not to be interested in prosperity and jobs, so let's check in with item 5. Clearly, it's another rather long text file:

```
Title:Chapter 3a -- Prosperity and Jobs
Author:The White House
Document-date:94-02-07
Content-Type: text/ascii charset=US ASCII


                         3A. PROSPERITY AND JOBS

                          THE ECONOMIC PROGRAM

  At the time of the 1992 election, the U.S. economy was caught in a
destructive cycle of weak investment in household durables (with
unsatisfactory growth in business plant and equipment as well),
adverse consumer sentiment, and stagnant employment. To break out of
that cycle, the economy needed jobs--to add to household incomes, and
to give families the confidence to make commitments for housing and
other big-ticket consumer goods that, in turn, stimulate investment in
the business sector and build momentum for the economy as a whole.

  The jobs picture was not encouraging. The unemployment rate had
risen, predictably, with the recession that began in mid-1990.
Surprisingly, however, employment remained stagnant--and the
unemployment rate continued rising--for a year after the recession
technically ended. Breaking this pattern of sluggish employment
growth would be essential to energize the recovery.

  The same prescription would help toward the ultimate goal of the
President's vision for economic renewal: increasing prosperity for all
Americans. In the long run, even if every qualified job seeker can
find work with just a limited search, living standards depend upon the
```

```
factories, machines, and technology available to make our workers
productive (as well as the skills of the workers themselves).
Increased demand for big-ticket items, and hence investment goods,
would begin the process of building for the future.

  The greatest resistance to this economic takeoff--the major source
of inertia--was the burden of debt service in all sectors of the
economy. With interest rates stubbornly high, much of current income
was absorbed in meeting past commitments; and future commitments for
major purchases appeared dauntingly expensive. This Administration
recognized that cutting interest rates would be crucial to stimulate
the economic recovery.


  Insert chart: CHRT3A_1
```

Hmmm…a chart. Going back up a couple of menus, we discover that the charts are contained in the final menu item, charts-95budget-tiff. These are downloadable graphics files in .TIF format, which we can retrieve if we want to construct the document in its entirety.

For now, though, there's no need to keep reading. We'd like easy access to the document, though, so why not save it to disk or mail it to ourselves? In this case, I was using the Gopher while in an account I don't commonly use, so I decided to use the short menu that appears after every retrieved file to mail it to my normal account.

```
Press <RETURN> to continue,
   <m> to mail, <D> to download, <s> to save, or <p> to print:m

1.  95 Budget Table of Contents.
2.  94-02-07 The Budget Message of the President.
3.  Chapter 1 -- Where We Started.
4.  Chapter 2 -- What We Have Accomplished: The Clinton Economic Plan.
+-----------------------------------------------------------------------+
|                                                                       |
|                                                                       |
|     Mail current document to:  nrandall@watserv1.uwaterloo.ca         |
|                                                                       |
|                                                                       |
|     [Cancel ^G]   [Accept - Enter]                                    |
|                                                                       |
|                                                                       |
+-----------------------------------------------------------------------+

12. Lists of Charts and Tables.
13. National Defense and International Affairs.
14. Personal Security: Crime, Illegal Immigration, and Drug Control.
15. Summary Tables..
16. The 1995 Proposed Federal Budget.
17. charts-95budget-tiff/
```

Excursion 20.4. The National Information Infrastructure (NII)

This time, it's back up several menus to the US and World Politics (Sunsite UNC) menu, from which we'll choose item 1, which deals with the National Information Infrastructure, better known as the information superhighway. Because Vice President Gore has been trumpeting the information superhighway for months now, and because of the superhighway's potential impact on the Internet, any information about it promises to be especially interesting.

```
National Information Infrastructure Information

1.  National Information Infrastructure by Section /
2.  Boucher-Bill-to-change-NSFnet-funding (HR 1757).
3.  National Information Infrastructure - Agenda for Action (full).
4.  Technology for Economic Growth: President's Progress Report
```

Item 1 yields the following menu of documents:

```
National Information Infrastructure by Section

1.  Table of Contents.
2.  Executive Summary.
3.  Agenda for Action.
4.  Benefits and Application Examples.
5.  Information Infrastructure Task Force.
6.  U.S. Advisory Council on the NII.
7.  NII Accomplishments to Date.
8.  Key Contacts
```

20

Because the interesting part to date is how the superhighway will come into being, the Agenda for Action sounds like the best place to start. Choosing 3, we get the following:

```
                THE NATIONAL INFORMATION INFRASTRUCTURE:
                          AGENDA FOR ACTION

                          EXECUTIVE SUMMARY

        All Americans have a stake in the construction of an
advanced National Information Infrastructure (NII), a seamless
web of communications networks, computers, databases, and
```

```
consumer electronics that will put vast amounts of information at
users' fingertips. Development of the NII can help unleash an
information revolution that will change forever the way people
live, work, and interact with each other:

o       People could live almost anywhere they wanted, without
        foregoing opportunities for useful and fulfilling
        employment, by "telecommuting" to their offices through an
        electronic highway;

o       The best schools, teachers, and courses would be available
        to all students, without regard to geography, distance,
        resources, or disability;

o       Services that improve America's health care system and
        respond to other important social needs could be available
        on-line, without waiting in line, when and where you needed
        them.

*************************************

        The benefits of the NII for the nation are immense. An
advanced information infrastructure will enable U.S. firms to
compete and win in the global economy, generating good jobs for
the American people and economic growth for the nation. As
importantly, the NII can transform the lives of the American
people -- ameliorating the constraints of geography, disability,
and economic status -- giving all Americans a fair opportunity to
go as far as their talents and ambitions will take them.
```

Lots here, but again no need to read it online. This time, instead of mailing the file, we'll save it as a text file by choosing the s command.

```
Press <RETURN> to continue,
   <m> to mail, <D> to download, <s> to save, or <p> to print:s

4.  Benefits and Application Examples.
5.  Information Infrastructure Task Force.
6.  U.S. Advisory Council on the NII.
7.  NII Accomplishments to Date.
8.  Key Contacts
+--------------------------------------------------------------------+
|                                                                    |
|          Save in file: Executive-Summary                           |
|                                                                    |
+--------------------------------------------------------------------+
```

Warning: If you're using a desktop PC as a terminal on a UNIX system, choosing Gopher's save command saves the file on the UNIX system's hard disk, not your own. If you want the file for personal use, you'll have to use a command such as XModem or Kermit to download it to your PC. Or, with the most recent versions of Gopher, you can use the download command directly, for which you must press Shift+D (not just d).

The only other item on the NII Gopher we want to see at this time is Key Contacts. Maybe, in the list, we'll find someone who might be interested in hearing of concerns and other comments:

```
ADMINISTRATION NII INFORMATION SOURCES


To submit comments on "The National Information Infrastructure:
Agenda for Action" or to request additional copies of this
package:

      Write:                  NTIA NII Office
                        15th Street and Constitution Avenue
                        Washington, D.C.  20230
      Call:                   202-482-1840
      Fax:              202-482-1635
      Internet:         nii@ntia.doc.gov

To obtain copies of this package electronically see instructions
on next page.

Key Administration Contacts:

Ronald H. Brown, Secretary of Commerce
Chair, Information Infrastructure Task Force
15th Street and Constitution Avenue, NW
Washington, D.C.   20230
phone:            202-482-3934
fax:              202-482-4576
internet:         nii@ntia.doc.gov

Larry Irving, Assisant Secretary for Communications and
Information, Director, National Telecommunications and
Information Administration, Chair, IITF Telecommuni-cations
Policy Committee
15th Street and Constitution Avenue, NW
Washington, D.C.   20230
phone:            202-482-1840
fax:              202-482-1635
internet:         li@ntia.doc.gov
```

```
Arati Prabhakar, Director, National Institute of Standards and
Technology, Chair, IITF Applications Committee
NIST, Administration Building, Room A1134
Gaithersburg, MD.   20899_[K
phone:          301-975-2300
fax:            301-869-8972
internet:       arati@micf.nist.gov
```

More names follow, but the general idea is clear. There are people in the government to contact, each of whom has an Internet address. Of course, whether they respond is an entirely separate issue, so it might be wiser, at this stage, to write letters rather than e-mail messages.

Near the bottom of the Key Contacts section is another interesting list. Here we're given Gopher and FTP addresses for retrieving the NII Agenda package, as well as bulletin boards that also carry it.

Not that we're distrustful, but let's load some FTP software and find out if the file is where it's supposed to be. Figure 20.1 shows Winsock FTP (a Microsoft Windows-based FTP package) connected to `ftp.ntia.doc.gov` as suggested. The filename isn't what the Gopher item said it would be, but because there's only one file listed it won't be hard to check out. Using Winsock FTP's View command, we load the file into an ASCII editor. Sure enough, it's the same information we've been reading here.

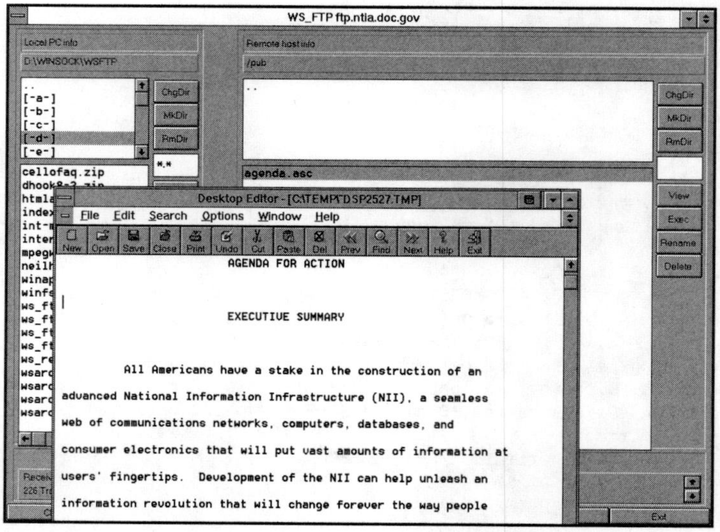

Figure 20.1. *FTP screen showing NII Agenda for Action.*

Excursion 20.5. The White House Papers

We're almost at the end of our all-too-brief dalliance with material concerning the U.S. federal government. We haven't even begun to explore the Gophers or FTP sites of state or municipal governments, but keep in mind that an increasing number of government levels are adding such sites. Watch your Gopher and WWW announcements over the next year; you're certain to see a wide proliferation of government-related information, especially (once again) given the importance placed on the issue by the White House and its telecommunications policies.

Our last excursion takes us back to the US and World Politics Gopher, where we'll look at the enticing item called Browse White House Papers. Here, supposedly, we'll find all kinds of officially presented government information. The first three menus look like this, with the selected menu item once again boldfaced:

```
US and World Politics (Sunsite UNC)

1.  National Information Infrastructure Information/
2.  1992 US Presidential Campaign/
3.  Browse  White House Papers/
4.  Community_Idea_Net   proposals on how on-line databases can help l../
5.  Federal Information Resources/
6.  International Affairs/

Browse  White House Papers

1.  1993/
2.  1994/

1994
1.  Apr/
2.  Feb/
3.  Jan/
4.  Mar/
```

No matter how many online documents we might have been expecting, the following (truncated) list is almost certain to surprise. Also, remember, it's only for one month, March 1994:

```
Mar

1.  1994-02-28-President-Remarks-Welcoming-PM-John-Major-in-Pittsburgh.
2.  1994-02-28-Presidents-Public-Schedule.
3.  1994-02-28-Presidents-Remarks-in-Photo-OP-with-PM-John-Major.
```

```
4.   1994-03-01-Background-Economic-Briefing-on-4th-Quarter-GDP-and-Exp...
5.   1994-03-01-Briefing-on-Crime-Initiative-by-VP-Gore-and-AG-Reno.
6.   1994-03-01-President-Nominates-Chong-to-FCC.
7.   1994-03-01-President-Remarks-to-Dallas-Cowboys-Football-Team.
8.   1994-03-01-Presidents-Remarks-at-Wright-Junior-College-in-Chicago.
9.   1994-03-01-Presidents-Remarks-in-Photo-Op-with-House-Budget-Commit...
10.  1994-03-01-Presidents-Statement-on-Bosnian-Croat-Peace-Agreement.
150. 1994-03-25-President-Nominates-8-to-National-Council-on-Arts.
151. 1994-03-25-Presidents-Remarks-Upon-Departure-to-North-Carolina.
152. 1994-03-25-Proclamation-for-Greek-Independence-Day.
153. 1994-03-25-Statement-on-Public-Access-to-NSC-Records.
154. 1994-03-25-Statement-on-Subpoena-for-Staff-Secretary-Podesta.
155. 1994-03-28-Presidents-Statement-on-Tornado-Losses-in-the-South.
156. 1994-03-28-Statement-on-President-Conversation-with-PM-Hosokawa.
157. 1994-3-19-ABC-Childrens-Questions-with-the-President.
158. 1994-3-7-Presidents-Press-Conference-with-Chairman-Shevardnadze.
159. Presidents-Schedule-32294.
```

To get an idea of the sheer amount of information available from this one Gopher menu, here is a short excerpt from item 157, the `ABC-Childrens-Questions-with-the-President`:

```
                         THE WHITE HOUSE

                   Office of the Press Secretary
_____________________________________________________________________
For Immediate Release                                   March 19, 1994


                     REMARKS BY THE PRESIDENT
           IN ABC SPECIAL "ANSWERING CHILDREN'S QUESTIONS"


                          The East Room



11:30 A.M. EST


         MR. JENNINGS:  Let's get right to it.  Kevin, how about
you.

         Q  My first question is for those children who wish to
pursue a college education, what are you going to do to guarantee
that there are jobs for them when they get out of college? Today,
```

```
many adults have graduate degrees, bachelors -- they have a hard time
finding jobs. They have as good a chance as those who are straight
out of high school. What are you going to do to guarantee that when
I get out of college, I have a job waiting for me?

          THE PRESIDENT:  I don't know that I can guarantee it,
but I think we can make it more likely. But perhaps the main reason
I ran for president was to try to restore the economic health of the
country. And what I am trying to do is to follow policies that will
generate more jobs in America. I have tried to bring our deficit
down, get interest rates down, to create more jobs. I've tried to
open more markets to our products, and sell more American products
overseas. I've tried to train people to do the jobs of tomorrow, and
I've tried to take the technologies that we developed when we had a
big defense budget and turn them into jobs in the peacetime economy.
And in the last 13 months, since we had this meeting last, we created
over 2 million new jobs in this economy.

          And let me also say, I know it's tough for college
graduates, but let me tell everyone of you one thing:  Your chances
of getting a good job are still much, much better if you first
graduate from high school, then get at least two years of further
training, and, finally, if you get college degree. The unemployment
rate in America for college graduates is 3.5 percent. The
unemployment rate for high school dropouts is 11.5 percent.

          MR. JENNINGS:  So the answer is, stay in school.

          THE PRESIDENT:  So the answer is, even though it's
tougher than it has been for college graduates, you still have a much
better chance if you stay in school to have higher incomes and to
have a job.
```

Rather than read the rest at this point, why not just mail the entire file to ourselves for perusing later? That's what I decided to do:

```
Press <RETURN> to continue,
   <m> to mail, <D> to download, <s> to save, or <p> to print:m

 ---------------------------------------------------------------
|                                                               |
|                                                               |
|    Mail current document to: nrandall@watserv1.uwaterloo.ca  |
|                                                               |
 ---------------------------------------------------------------
```

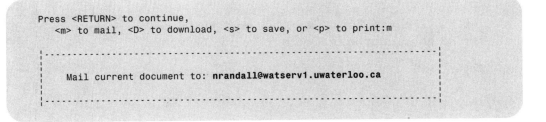

Law 101: Legal Information at Your Fingertips

Excursion 20.6. The Supreme Court Decisions

Obviously, we could spend days exploring the government Gophers. But the day is getting on, and we want to spend some time with the courts as well. So it's back to the main Gopher Jewels menu again, and this time into the Legal and Law related section.

Note: For the rest of the excursions in this chapter, I've switched to graphical Gopher software. As explained in Day 2, while several such programs are available for X Windows, the Macintosh, and Microsoft Windows, I regularly use Winsock Gopher (available free from many FTP sites) and WinGopher (a commercially available package) on my 486 with Microsoft Windows. Both are pictured here, with the emphasis on Winsock Gopher. Also included are several screens from the two major World Wide Web browsers for Microsoft Windows, NCSA Mosaic and LII Cello, both of which offer excellent access to Gophers. Note that most screens here use Cello, which seems appropriate in a section on law (Cello was developed by the Legal Information Institute at Cornell University).

The cascading menus in Figure 20.2 clearly show the path taken to arrive at the texts of the Supreme Court decisions for the 1994 term.

Note that the path went through the University of Chicago Law School, which is only one of several routes that will bring you to this same Gopher menu. Each of the listed decisions is a text file that can be downloaded, mailed, or any other Gopher option.

Supreme Court decisions can also be ordered. Figure 20.3 is a screen from Mosaic showing the hypertext ordering system offered by the World Wide Web site at Cornell.

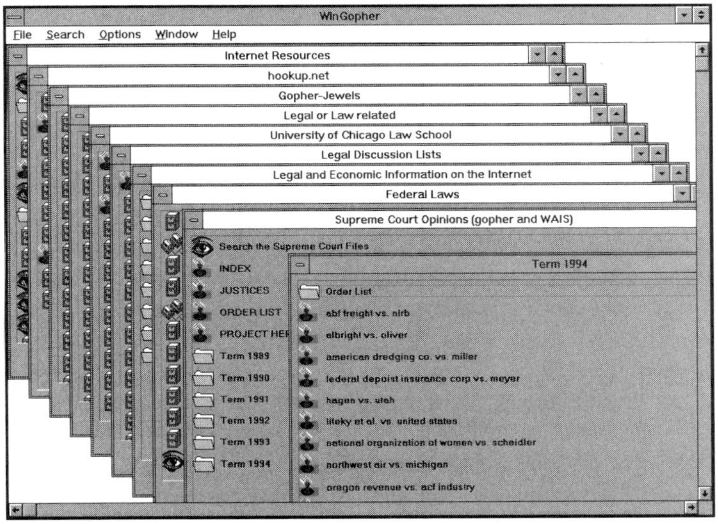

Figure 20.2. *Gopher path to Supreme Court decisions.*

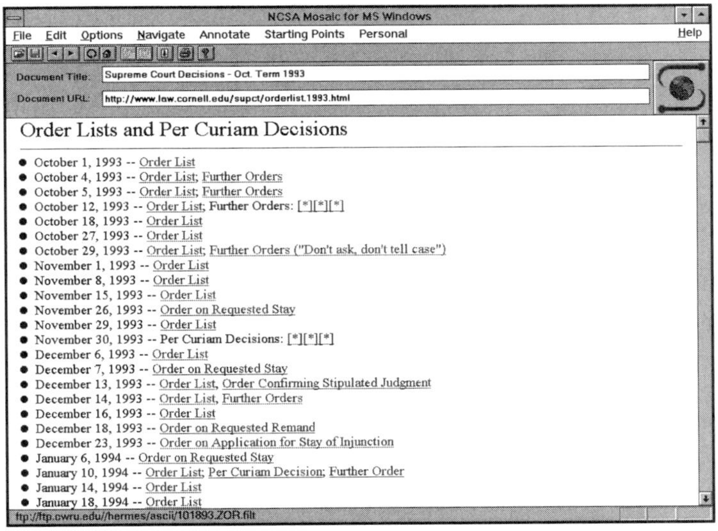

Figure 20.3. *Mosaic screen showing ordering system for Supreme Court documents.*

The point about these Internet-published decisions is that they're available on the day the decision is made. Often, in fact, if you're following a particular case, you can read the decision less than four hours after it's rendered. For anyone whose job or research depends on knowing such things as they occur, this is obviously an extremely valuable service.

Excursion 20.7. Other U.S. Legal Matters

The Supreme Court's decisions aren't the only legal resources available on the Internet. Far from it, in fact. In this excursion, we'll explore a small sampling of other material that's out there, and from this sample you can get an idea of where you might want to turn.

One of the best-maintained Internet sites for law-related material is Cornell Law School's Legal Information Institute. The LII keeps an active and growing Gopher, and they've developed a well-organized series of World Wide Web pages as well. They're so committed to their Web offerings, in fact, that they've released a Web browser, Cello, to make sure these pages are accessible for Microsoft Windows users (who make up the largest percentage of graphical-interface users).

Figure 20.4 shows a path through the LII Gopher to a separate section about the Americans with Disabilities Act. One of the parts of the act deals with employment, under which we find a text file (Section 102) regarding discrimination. Accessing this file, we see the following:

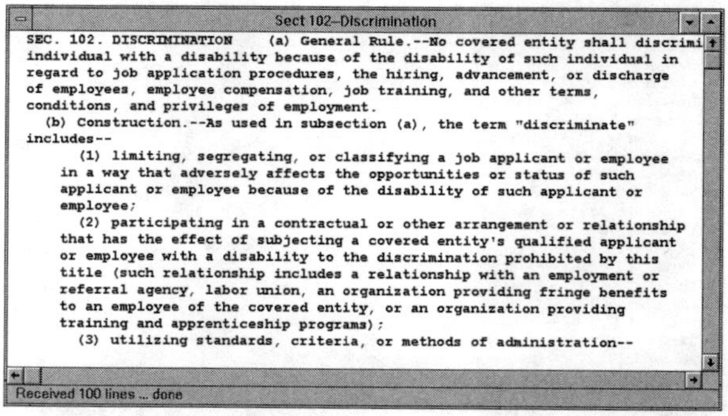

Figure 20.4. *Gopher screen showing a portion of the Americans with Disabilities Act.*

The LII's Web server is equally useful for documentary information. Figure 20.5 is a list of accessible files about copyright law, as taken from the `http:` address shown at the bottom of the screen. In Cello, clicking any of these documents will download it for reading.

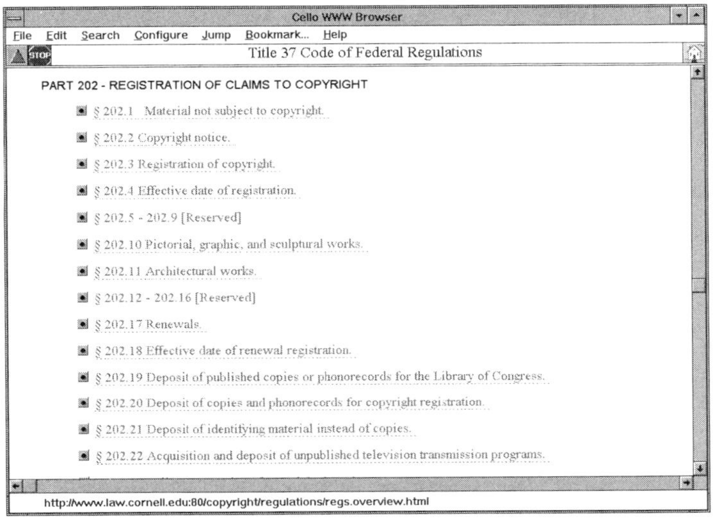

Figure 20.5. *Downloadable files regarding copyright law.*

Also prominent on the LII's home page is an item dealing with new happenings in the courts. Here, Justice Ruth Bader Ginsburg, the most recently appointed Supreme Court justice, is featured. We could read her most recent decisions from the screen shown in Figure 20.6.

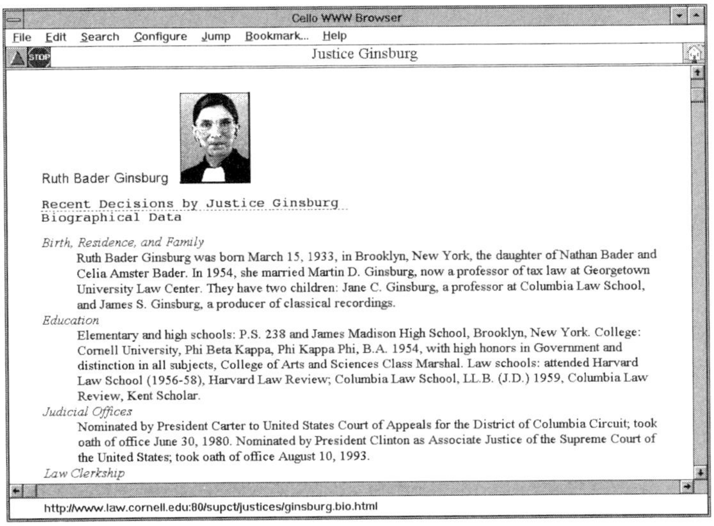

Figure 20.6. *Legal Information Institute page about Justice Ginsburg.*

Cornell isn't the only law school working to establish useful World Wide Web sites. As shown in Figure 20.7, Indiana University's schools of law in Bloomington and Indianapolis have begun a service called LawTalk, featuring audio files explaining important legal issues.

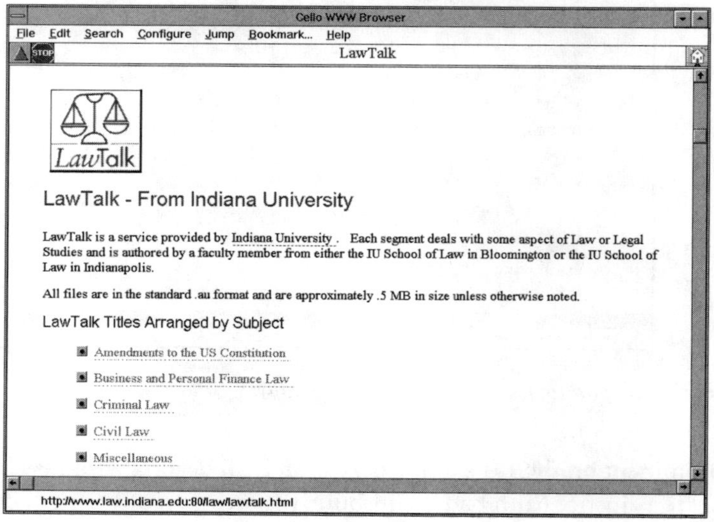

Figure 20.7. *Indiana University's LawTalk audio files.*

As this home page states, all files are in `.au` format (the standard sound format for Internet audio files), and you'll need appropriate software and hardware for your computer to play them. At only a half-megabyte each, however, they're well worth downloading and hearing. Every one I've listened to is informative and well presented.

Inevitably, legal issues give way to taxation issues, and there's a broad range of taxation information available on the Net. Among the most useful, apart from the tax laws themselves which can be found in the law school servers, is the set of WWW pages shown in Figures 20.8 and 20.9, available at the `http:` addresses shown at the bottom of the page. Developed by the S-Cubed group at Maxwell Labs, these two pages offer the majority of IRS forms in a number of different file formats.

Now, for Canadian readers. Note that these forms are primarily in Microsoft Excel format.

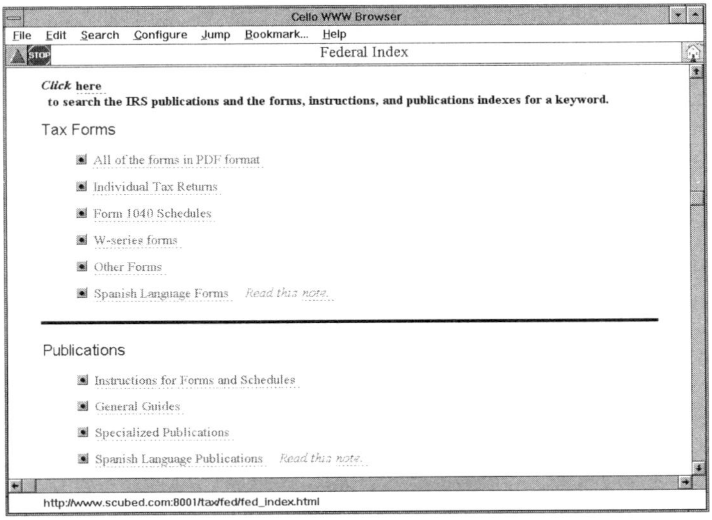

Figure 20.8. *Information on tax laws from S-Cubed.*

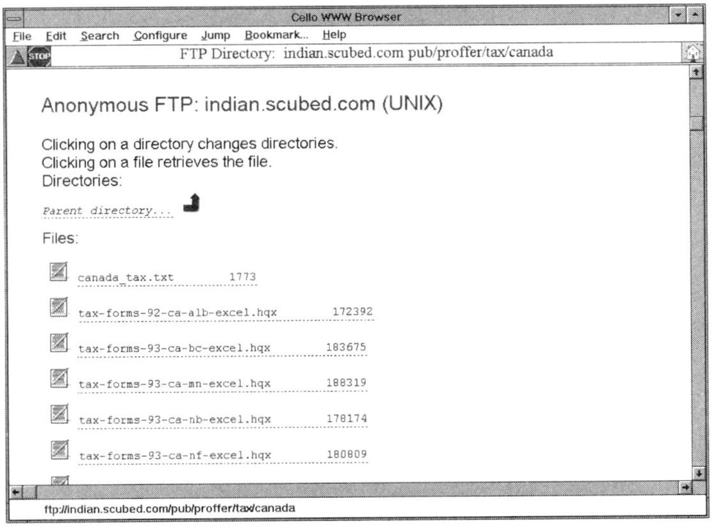

Figure 20.9. *S-Cubed's information on Canadian tax laws.*

Although this excursion could go on for days, we have to start somewhere. Of particular interest to many Internet users is the role of the Federal Communications Commission in establishing the telecommunications regulations for the future of the information superhighway (of which the Internet is an integral part). Fortunately for us, the Indiana University School of Law at Bloomington, along with the Federal Communications Bar Association, have developed an online journal available on the World Wide Web. Entitled Federal Communications Law Journal, it promises to deal with a wide range of aspects regarding FCC practices and laws. Figure 20.10 shows the Web page for issue 1.

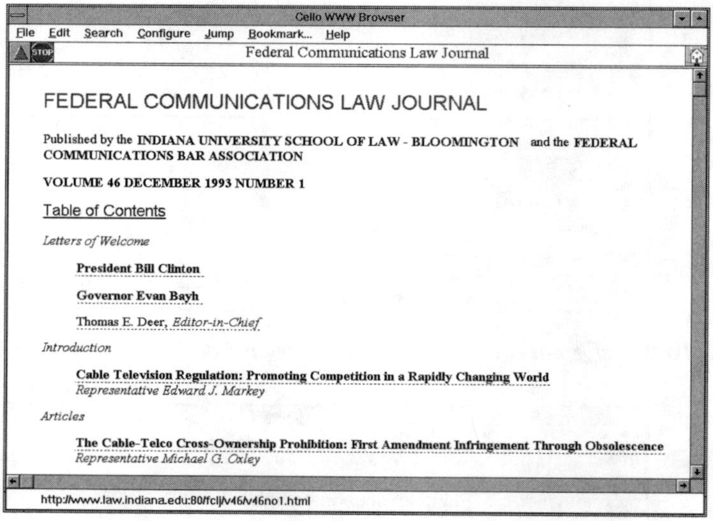

Figure 20.10. *Cello screen showing Federal Communications Law Journal.*

Summary

Government and legal resources on the Internet are plentiful now and growing almost daily. Expect even more accessible information as the White House develops its commitment to the information superhighway, and watch for Gopher and World Wide Web servers from governments of other nations around the world as well. In addition, with law a central focus of societies the world over as we move to the new century, expect hordes of legal documents, court decisions, and even trial news to become almost instantly accessible.

Task Review

Today you've learned how to do the following:

- ☐ Explore U.S. government Gophers.
- ☐ Use these Gophers to discover available information about the House of Representatives, the 1995 U.S. budget, the National Information Infrastructure, and White House papers.
- ☐ View, mail, and save text documents from these Gophers.
- ☐ Examine the primary Gophers for accessing legal information.
- ☐ Explore the growing number of law-related World Wide Web sites.
- ☐ Find and read Supreme Court decisions.
- ☐ Locate a wide range of other legal information.

Q&A

Q Do state and municipal governments maintain Internet sites as well as the federal government?

A Not to the same degree, but many are starting and some are quite far along. Of particular interest are new Gopher and Web sites developed by governments in Texas, North Carolina, and, in particular, California. New York State has some well-developed resources, as do a growing number of other states. Some municipalities are appearing online as well, with Palo Alto, California among the most interestingly presented. Often, however, community Internet access doesn't incorporate government issues *per se.*

All these Gophers sites can be accessed through the University of Minnesota's main Gopher, which in turn is almost always available as a menu item on your local Gopher. As for Web pages, keep watching the NCSA What's New Page (see Day 6 for details on how to access it); any interesting Web developments are noted here.

Q Will we ever see trials online?

A Who knows? Technologically it's certainly possible, but what the legal aspects might be I really don't know. In all likelihood, any trial that can be televised could also be done over the Net, and it's not hard to see what the benefits might be. A well-designed World Wide Web session or Gopher could include a wide range of background material, all of it accessible while you're watching the full-motion live video of the trial (live multimedia, in other words). More likely for the time being will be transcripts from trials, or perhaps even audio files, almost immediately downloadable. Questions of the legality of such accessibility still take precedence, however.

Q On Day 6, we saw an example of casting votes over the World Wide Web. Will we ever be able to vote for our politicians this way?

A To be honest, I've never quite understood why there isn't a high-tech way of voting even without the Internet. Every night of the week I can pick up my phone and punch in my favorite song of the day, then have my vote tabulated with all the other listeners to determine the top 10 playlist for that evening. Why isn't this possible at election time, albeit under much more rigorous conditions?

Maybe the Internet can provide an answer. Election Gophers and Web pages could be an excellent source of background on the politicians, the issues, the platforms, and everything else that makes up a candidacy. On election day, using a variety of forms or automatic e-mail or what have you, we could cast votes, using a password drawn from our Social Security numbers. Given enough development, it could quite probably work, and it would likely solve the problem of low voter turnout. (Or maybe I'm completely missing something.)

Q Is a list of Internet government resources available on the Internet itself?

A Yes. Among the best anonymous FTP sites for such material is `una.hh.lib.umich.edu`, in the directory `inetdirsstacks`. Start with the file `government:gumprecht`, an excellent list compiled by Blake Gumprecht, Documents Librarian at Temple University. Several other excellent files are available here as well.

Extra Credit: International Government and Law

There's no question that, up to this point, the U.S. government has put more information online than any other government in the world. That's only understandable; the Internet was begun by the U.S. military and has been maintained by a series of U.S. government institutions (most recently the National Science Foundation) since its inception. It would only stand to reason that government departments would make use of a service they had already put in place. Then, too, there's the fact that the United States has traditionally made its records more accessible than most other countries. Sure, there are hordes of classified documents, but it's always possible to be flooded with official government information if you wanted to be.

Excursion 20.8. International Governments and the Internet

That's not to say, however, that you can use the Internet to study only U.S. domestic law. Cornell's Legal Information Institute, for example, offers a Gopher menu called Foreign and International Law (`gopher.law.cornell.edu`), well worth exploring if your interests are global rather than domestic or local. Included here, as Figure 20.11 shows, are legal documents from Australia, Hong Kong, Canada, Germany, the United Nations, and so on. Also available here are files pertaining to the North American Free Trade Agreement (NAFTA), which by definition is international rather than national. Figure 20.11 shows part of Article 1302 of NAFTA, which deals with telecommunications issues.

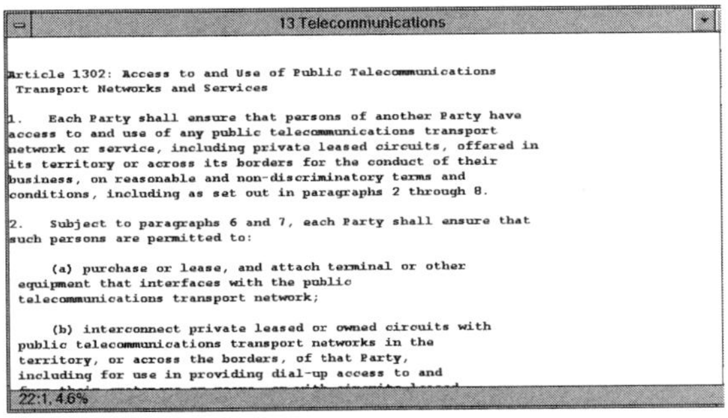

13 Telecommunications

Article 1302: Access to and Use of Public Telecommunications Transport Networks and Services

1. Each Party shall ensure that persons of another Party have access to and use of any public telecommunications transport network or service, including private leased circuits, offered in its territory or across its borders for the conduct of their business, on reasonable and non-discriminatory terms and conditions, including as set out in paragraphs 2 through 8.

2. Subject to paragraphs 6 and 7, each Party shall ensure that such persons are permitted to:

(a) purchase or lease, and attach terminal or other equipment that interfaces with the public telecommunications transport network;

(b) interconnect private leased or owned circuits with public telecommunications transport networks in the territory, or across the borders, of that Party, including for use in providing dial-up access to and

22:1, 4.6%

Figure 20.11. *Telecommunications section of North American Free Trade Agreement.*

Of course, the whole point about NAFTA is that its documents revolve around two other nations as well: Canada and Mexico. Further down that NAFTA Gopher menu are files discussing Canadian and Mexican agreements and timetables, as partially shown in Figure 20.12. Also in 20.12 is part of a document dealing with Mexican issues, appropriately enough in Spanish.

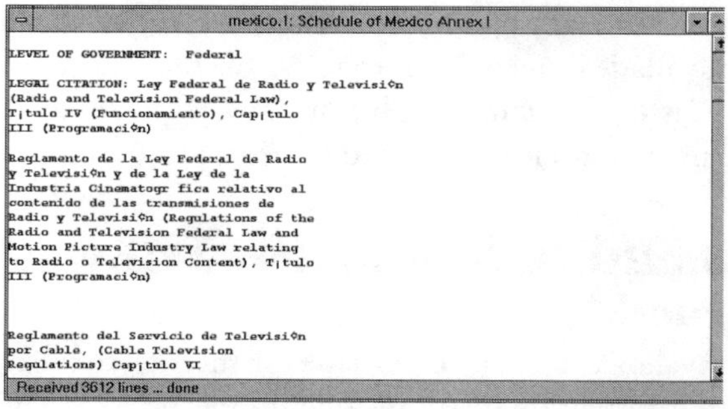

Figure 20.12. *Gopher screen showing Mexican issues in NAFTA.*

NAFTA is one element of international law, but far from the only one. The LII Gopher also carries the texts of a wide range of international agreements, primarily those of which the United States is a part. In Figure 20.13, we see the first page of the 1973 Convention on the International Trade in Endangered Species of Wild Fauna and Flora. If you have an interest in international environmental agreements and efforts, you'll find much to start with here.

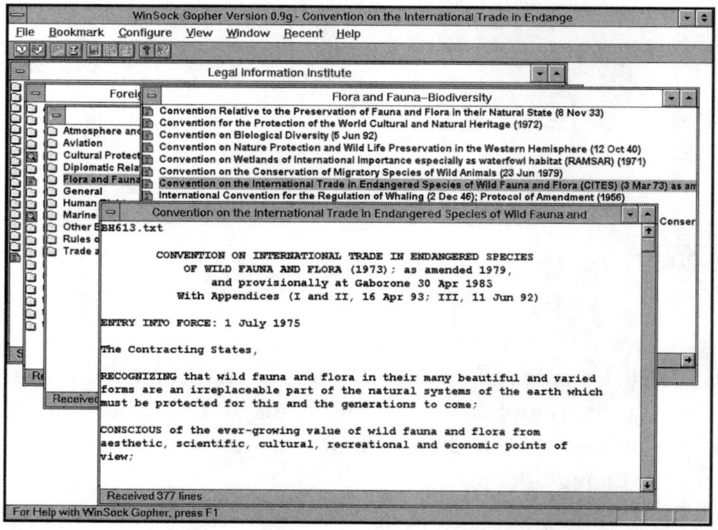

Figure 20.13. *Gopher path to international agreement on fauna and flora.*

There are also the multilateral treaties. These things have proliferated over the years, agreements between and among nations as developed through the United Nations, through other organizations, or independently. One glance at Figure 20.14 is enough to get a sense of how many documents are available for perusal. Again, this screen is part of LII's superb collection. (I didn't even know there was a multilateral agreement on the rescue and return of astronauts.)

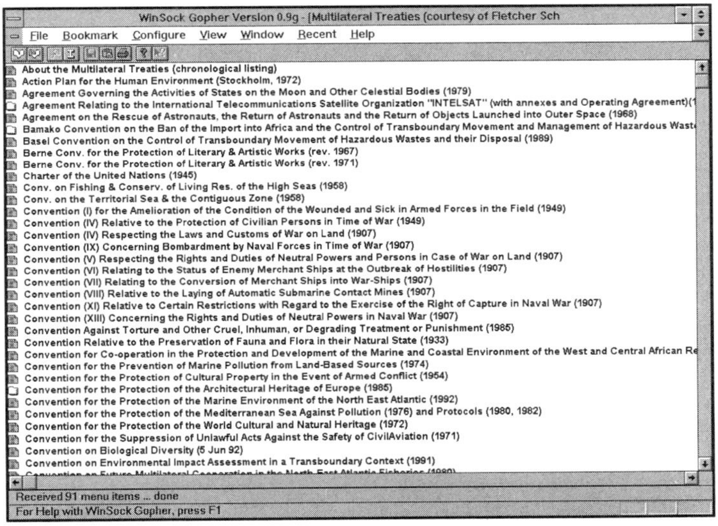

Figure 20.14. *Legal Information Institute gopher menu showing multilateral agreements.*

Back in Excursion 20.4, we looked at the resources describing the National Information Infrastructure. Canada has taken on the issue of developing their own version of the information superhighway, one that will closely link to the U.S. model. One key difference is the means of getting the first pavement in place. Unlike the U.S., Canada has developed a government-led consortium to see that the country doesn't fall behind. Figure 20.15, through the Communications Canada Gopher available from several Canadian Gophers, shows a text file explaining the mission of CANARIE, the nickname for this consortium.

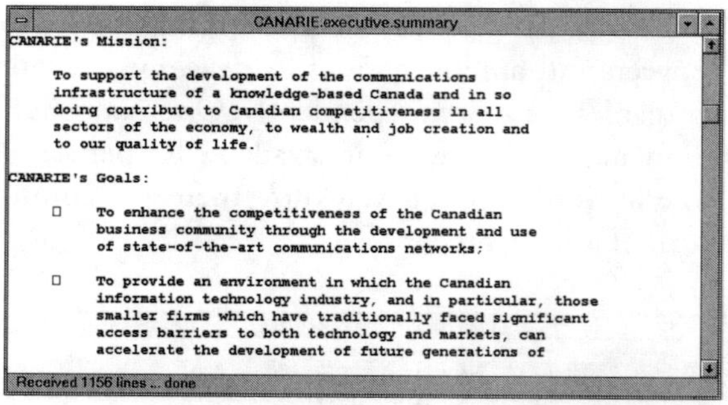

Figure 20.15. *Gopher screen showing mission of Canada's information superhighway consortium.*

One of the best-developed government Gophers outside the United States resides in Israel. Figure 20.16 shows the path to this Gopher through the University of Minnesota's main Gopher server. On the screen are documents related to the February 1994 Hebron massacre; if you want to understand the Israeli viewpoint on this important international crisis, in a way the news sources in North America didn't even begin to explore, this is an extremely good starting point. Even without this New Material - Latest Developments section, however, the Gopher is a capable guide to Israeli governmental resources.

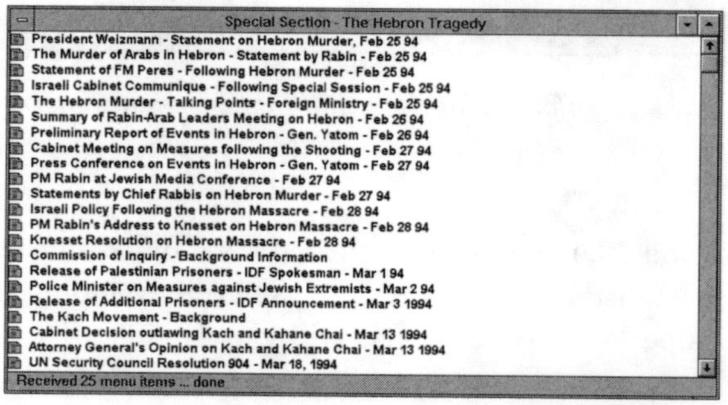

Figure 20.16. *Israeli Information Service—files about the Hebron tragedy.*

As any business student knows, International Trade is an important and growing field today. Not surprisingly, International Trade Law is also growing as well. Ananse is a Norwegian organization that has constructed a World Wide Web page (see Figure 20.17) pointing to several international trade resources on the Internet. Some links are European-based, while others simply point back to the LII pages at Cornell. From here it's possible to discover a considerable amount about the European Maastricht Treaty and many aspects about the European Economic Community, a very important concern for Europe's future.

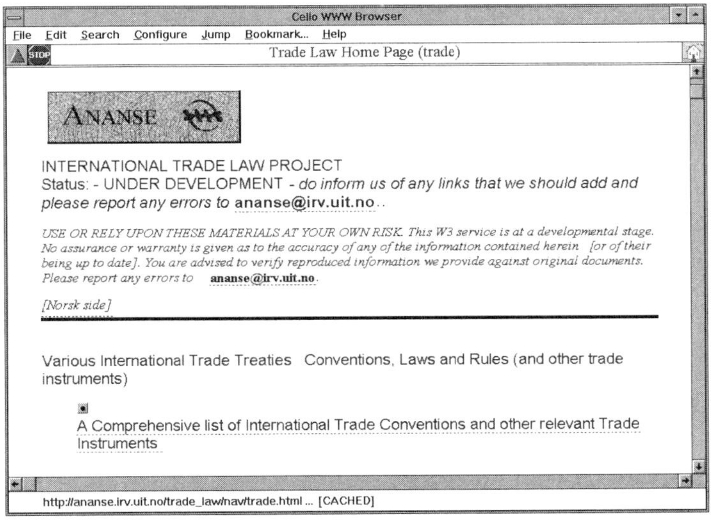

Figure 20.17. *Gopher screen showing Maastricht Treaty information.*

21

WEEK
3

Science 101: Discovering Science Research Projects Around the World

The Internet offers vast amounts of information about science research projects under way around the globe. Depending on the quality of the Gopher, FTP, or World Wide Web site, you can acquire a significant introduction to these projects through nothing but the Net itself. In some cases, tutorials and demonstrations take you further inside the project's workings. Day 21 concludes our journey around the world of the Internet by demonstrating some of the most advanced applications of Internet technology for the purpose of disseminating information.

On Day 21, you will do ther following:

- ☐ Use search tools to discover projects in science.
- ☐ Use the World Wide Web to access these projects.
- ☐ Examine projects taking place in locations around the world.

Science on the Internet

It's hardly surprising that the scientists and technologists have established a commanding presence on the Internet. From its beginnings, the Net was oriented toward the scientific and computing communities, for two predominant reasons. The first was that scientific researchers saw the potential and the need for collaborative activity, something that only a wide-area network could provide. Second, the computing specialists were needed to make the thing work and to conduct research into standards and enhancements. It wasn't until electronic mail became a fully workable application that research communities from other areas found the Internet useful.

Even knowing this, however, the sheer amount of scientific information available for the diligent searcher is almost staggering. All the major disciplines are represented—physics, chemistry, biology, astronomy—and several more specialized sources are accessible as well. Gophers and FTP sites abound, and increasingly the world of science and technology research is being demonstrated and disseminated on the World Wide Web. Use of the Web is also easy to understand. Multimedia is at the focus of contemporary computing (the computing perspective), and a greater need than ever exists for scientific research to be made publicly accessible (the scientific perspective).

What's also apparent is that the scientific and computing communities are leading Internet activity outside the U.S. and Canada as well. A quick look at the Web sites in Europe, Asia, Australia, the Middle East, and South America (as seen through SUNY Buffalo's Virtual Tourist display) reveals that by far the majority of WWW activity in these places is tied to scientific research in the universities. It's no exaggeration to suggest that, just as science and technology drove the development of the Internet in the United States in the first place, so it is driving the adoption of the Net in the world's other leading research centers.

On Day 1, we went on a quick tour of the world. On Day 21, we take a tour of the world as well. This time, though, the tour is of some of the science centers that are pushing the Internet's capabilities, with a goal of learning how to discover what's happening in the world of research. We'll focus on the World Wide Web, because that seems to be where much of this activity is showing up.

> **Note:** The list of scientific disciplines explored here is anything but complete or exhaustive, nor should this chapter be seen as anything beyond the smallest sampling of what's available. If I've omitted your favorite discipline or WWW site, it's because I had to stop somewhere.

Starting Points

As you're well aware by now, the Internet has many, many starting points. For subject-oriented searches on the World Wide Web, let's turn to two of the best sources: the EINet Galaxy and the WWW Virtual Library.

The EINet Galaxy

Figure 21.1 shows a portion of the home page for the EINet Galaxy (`http://www.einet.net/galaxy.html`).

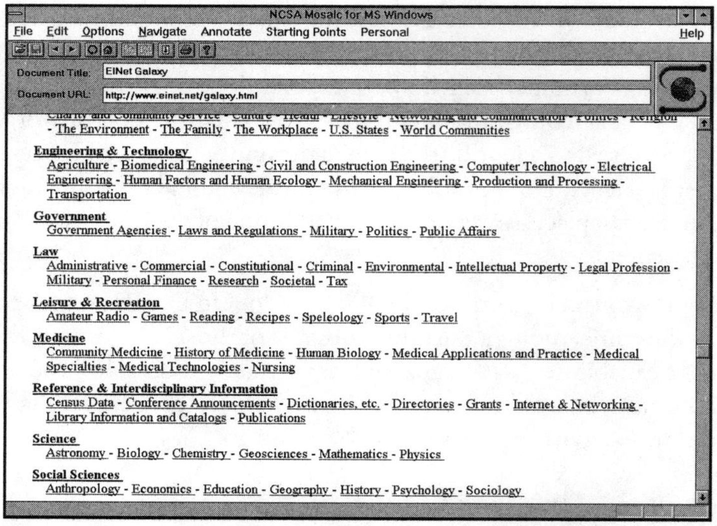

Figure 21.1. *The EINet Galaxy subject categories.*

Clearly, this is an excellent place to start. Near the top of the screen we find Engineering and Technology issues, while at the bottom the subject list shows the Sciences. It's hard to go wrong from here.

The WWW Virtual Library

A different search tool is shown in Figure 21.2.

The WWW Virtual Library (`http://info.cern.ch/hypertext/DataSources/bySubject/Overview.html`) offers a subject list that is a little less conveniently designed than EINet's, but it's still extremely useful. Shown here are categories such as Astronomy, the BioSciences, and Chemistry; the others we need can be found by scrolling down the screen.

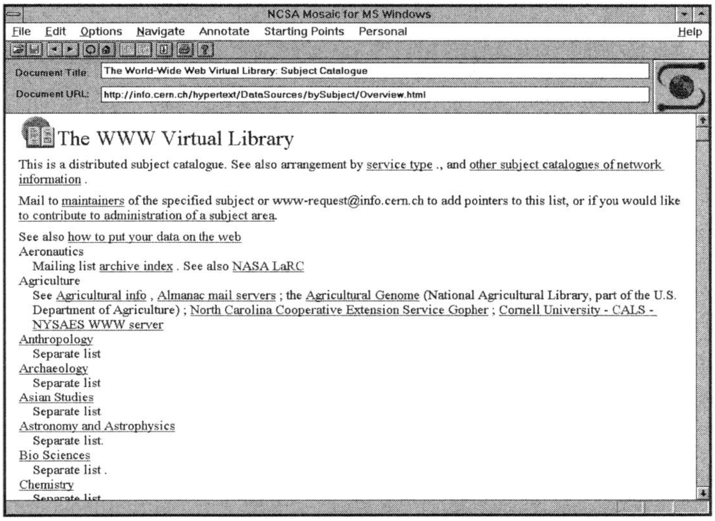

Figure 21.2. *The WWW Virtual Library subject list.*

Astronomy

A couple of screens inside the EINet Galaxy's Astronomy listing, we arrive at this screen showing a huge array of resources (see Figure 21.3).

As the address on the status bar at the bottom of the Mosaic screen shows, some of these are FTP sites. You can retrieve the files from within Mosaic or Cello, or through your favorite Gopher or FTP program. For now, though, let's go for the two most obvious sites, shown at the top of the page: the National Aeronautics and Space Administration (NASA) and the European Space Information System (ESIS).

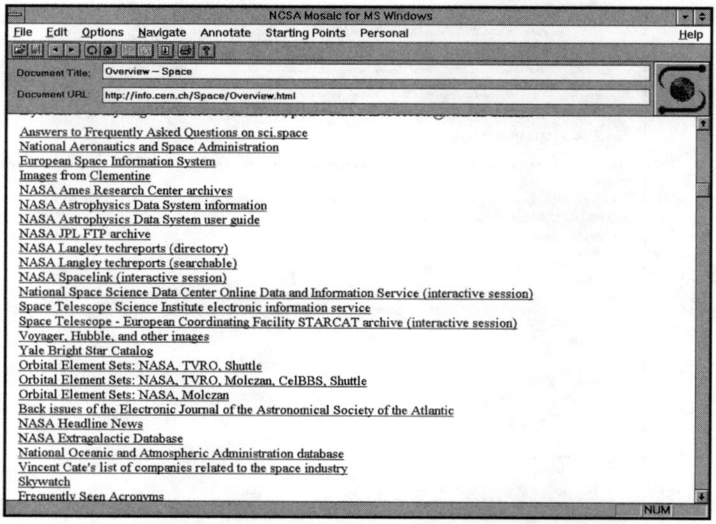

Figure 21.3. *List of astronomy-related Gopher, Telnet, FTP, and Web sites.*

Excursion 21.1. NASA

As we might expect, NASA's World Wide Web involvement is exemplary. Figure 21.4 shows the agency's fully developed home page (`http://hypatia.gsfc.nasa.gov/NASA_homepage.html`), complete with clickable map of home pages for the various NASA centers.

Obviously, we could spend hour upon hour searching through all this information, but let's just take a sampling, because we have many more sites to explore.

The temptation is to start with the Kennedy Space Center (if only because it's drawn most of the glory over the years), but this is an examination of research into astronomy, so let's give the Langley Research Center a try (`http://mosaic.larc.nasa.gov/larc.html`). See Figure 21.5.

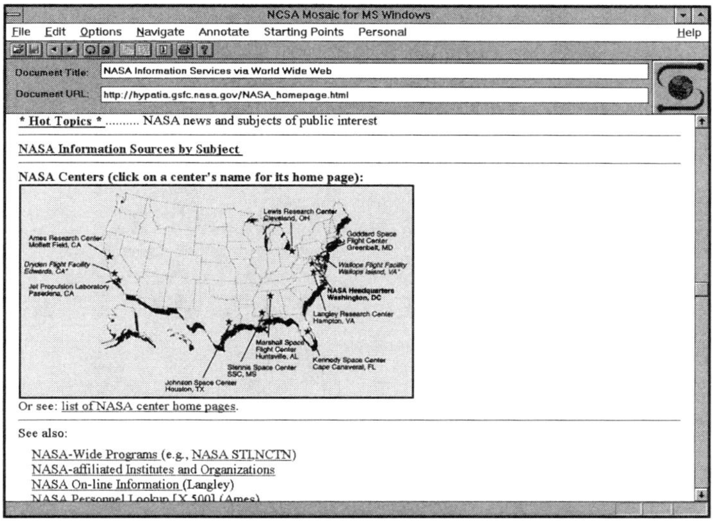

Figure 21.4. *NASA's WWW home page.*

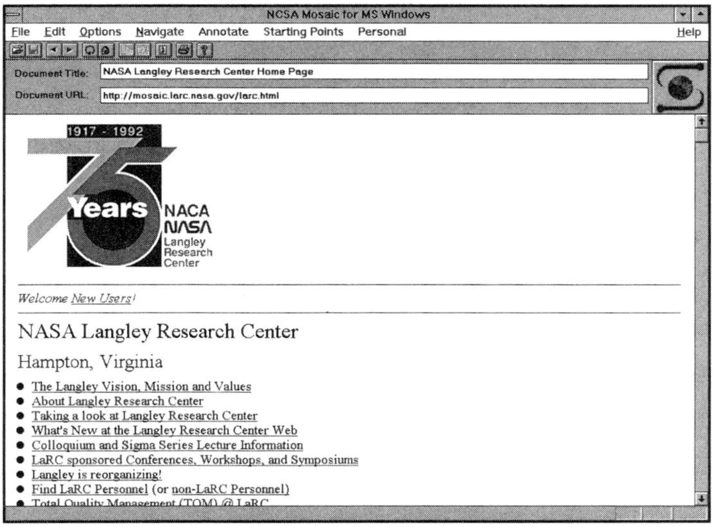

Figure 21.5. *The Langley Research Center's home page.*

Where this page becomes especially useful from a research standpoint is further down. The Langley Technical Reports link takes us to a page with reports categorized by year, and clicking on the 1994 link yields Figure 21.6 (`http://mosaic.larc.nasa.gov/ltrs/1994.html`).

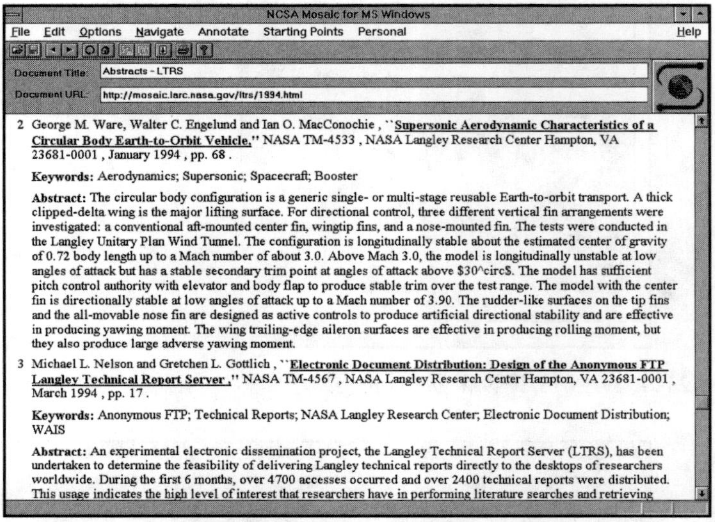
NCSA Mosaic for MS Windows
File Edit Options Navigate Annotate Starting Points Personal Help
Document Title: Abstracts - LTRS
Document URL: http://mosaic.larc.nasa.gov/ltrs/1994.html

2 George M. Ware, Walter C. Engelund and Ian O. MacConochie , ``**Supersonic Aerodynamic Characteristics of a Circular Body Earth-to-Orbit Vehicle.**'' NASA TM-4533 , NASA Langley Research Center Hampton, VA 23681-0001 , January 1994 , pp. 68 .

Keywords: Aerodynamics; Supersonic; Spacecraft; Booster

Abstract: The circular body configuration is a generic single- or multi-stage reusable Earth-to-orbit transport. A thick clipped-delta wing is the major lifting surface. For directional control, three different vertical fin arrangements were investigated: a conventional aft-mounted center fin, wingtip fins, and a nose-mounted fin. The tests were conducted in the Langley Unitary Plan Wind Tunnel. The configuration is longitudinally stable about the estimated center of gravity of 0.72 body length up to a Mach number of about 3.0. Above Mach 3.0, the model is longitudinally unstable at low angles of attack but has a stable secondary trim point at angles of attack above 30^circ. The model has sufficient pitch control authority with elevator and body flap to produce stable trim over the test range. The model with the center fin is directionally stable at low angles of attack up to a Mach number of 3.90. The rudder-like surfaces on the tip fins and the all-movable nose fin are designed as active controls to produce artificial directional stability and are effective in producing yawing moment. The wing trailing-edge aileron surfaces are effective in producing rolling moment, but they also produce large adverse yawing moment.

3 Michael L. Nelson and Gretchen L. Gottlich , ``**Electronic Document Distribution: Design of the Anonymous FTP Langley Technical Report Server .**'' NASA TM-4567 , NASA Langley Research Center Hampton, VA 23681-0001 , March 1994 , pp. 17 .

Keywords: Anonymous FTP; Technical Reports; NASA Langley Research Center; Electronic Document Distribution; WAIS

Abstract: An experimental electronic dissemination project, the Langley Technical Report Server (LTRS), has been undertaken to determine the feasibility of delivering Langley technical reports directly to the desktops of researchers worldwide. During the first 6 months, over 4700 accesses occurred and over 2400 technical reports were distributed. This usage indicates the high level of interest that researchers have in performing literature searches and retrieving

Figure 21.6. *The Langley Technical Reports Series—1994 Abstracts.*

Here we see the abstract for an obviously advanced discussion regarding a circular body earth-to-orbit vehicle. By clicking on the article's title, we can retrieve a PostScript file of the entire article. This is only one of three possible downloads from the 1994 series, and many, many more are available from 1993 back through 1988. Again, the sheer amount of information is overwhelming.

Excursion 21.2. ESIS

Our look at NASA's resources came nowhere near to completeness, but more research beckons. This time, it's the European Space Information System, accessible once again through the Space Science page shown in Figure 21.3.

Figure 21.7 shows the ESIS home page (`http://mesis.esrin.esa.it/html/esis.html`). The two main links are ESIS for Astronomers and ESIS for Space Physicists, of which the former is of more interest to us right now. Clicking on it, and then on the fascinatingly titled ESIS Walkthru, brings us to Figure 21.8 (`http://mesis.esrin.esa.it/html/demo/session.html`).

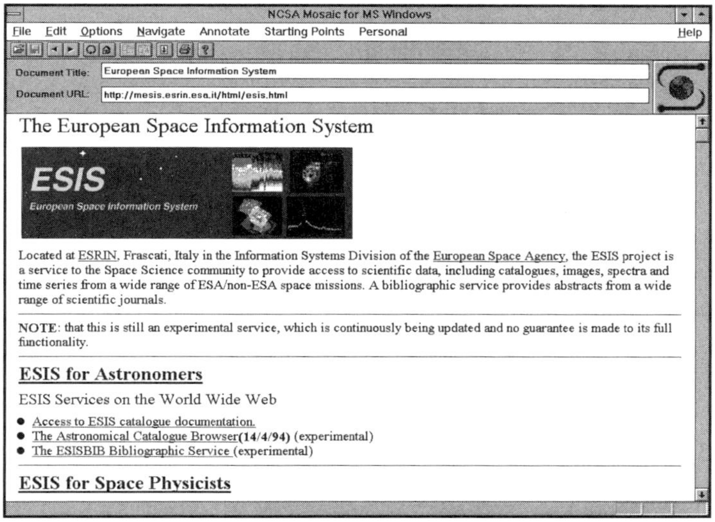

Figure 21.7. *The European Space Information System home page.*

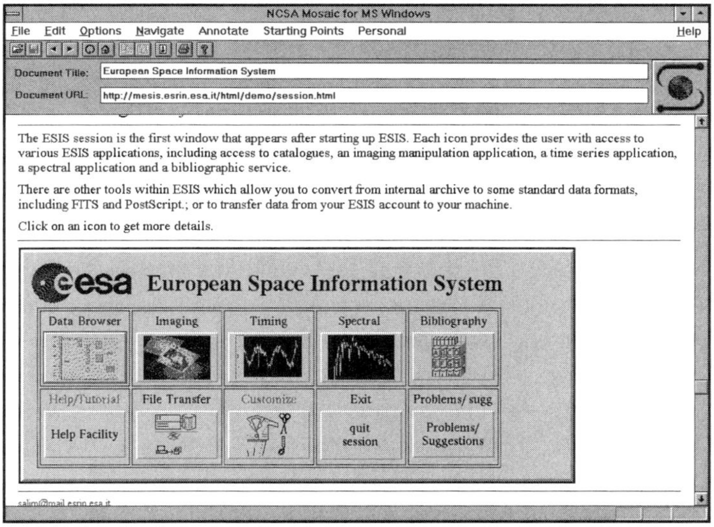

Figure 21.8. *The ESIS Walkthru—graphical, push-button searching.*

This intriguing interface lets us decide what we want to look at, and, in fact, how deeply we wish to search. Actually, this system is designed for X Windows systems, but even in a Mac or Windows environment it's at least of some use. Clicking on one of the examples of an Imaging interaction yields Figure 21.9, including a portion of the downloaded .GIF file.

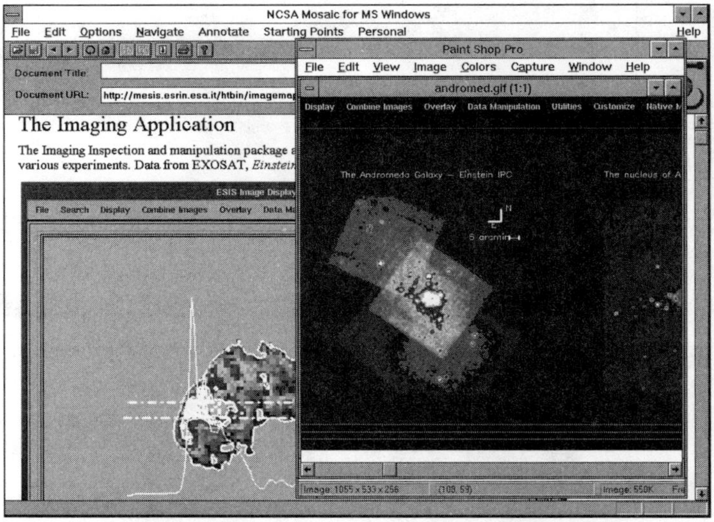

Figure 21.9. *The ESIS Imaging Database—one pictorial example.*

Excursion 21.3. The Hubble Telescope

A quick look at the various databases and Web pages accessible through ESIS reveals still a greater archive of data. However, a wide range of other astronomy projects are on the Web, and at this stage we'll take a look at one, the Hubble Telescope. This expensive piece of equipment, you may remember, was launched with a promise of changing the nature of telescope viewing, but it immediately ran into problems and required a daring and exciting rescue mission.

The Hubble's details are available on the WWW through the Space Telescope Science Institute (`http://stsci.edu/top.html`). One view of the telescope is presented in Figure 21.10.

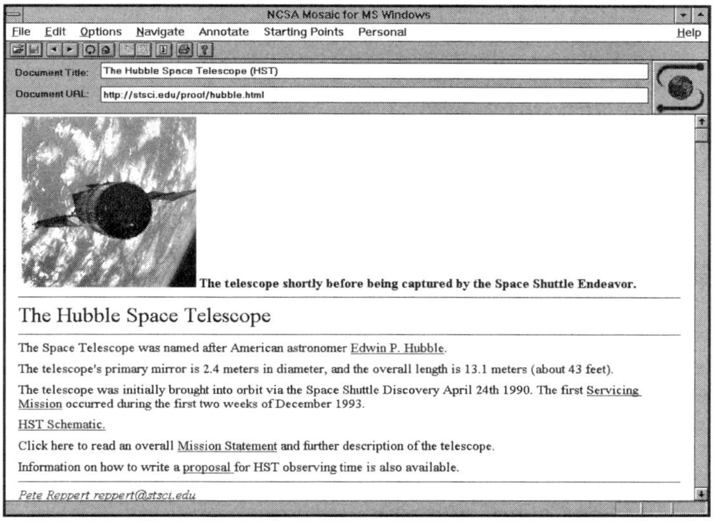

Figure 21.10. *The Hubble Telescope—general details.*

The capabilities of the Hubble are demonstrated to a small degree in Figure 21.11. Here we see the far greater clarity in image detail through a technology called COSTAR.

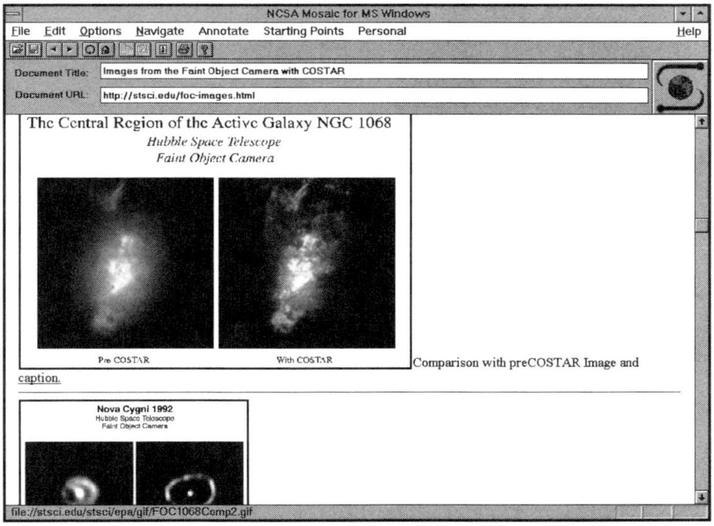

Figure 21.11. *The Hubble Telescope—the need for new technologies.*

Biology

To begin our search for biology projects, we turn to the CUI W3 Catalog. A search for the term `biology` yields a list of results partly shown in Figure 21.12.

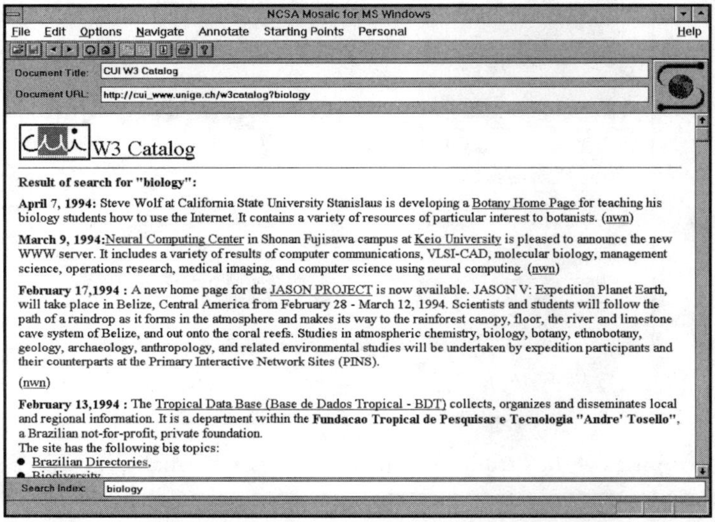

Figure 21.12. *CUI W3 Catalog—results of search for the term biology.*

Excursion 21.4. Biodiversity in Brazil

The immediately irresistible item on this page is the Brazilian Biodiversity link. Clicking it and then a subsequent link, we come to the Microbiology page (`http://www.ftpt.br/structure/microbiology.html`).

Most of this page consists of searchable databases. Also available is information about catalogs such as the American Type Culture Collection, whose details are shown in Figure 21.13.

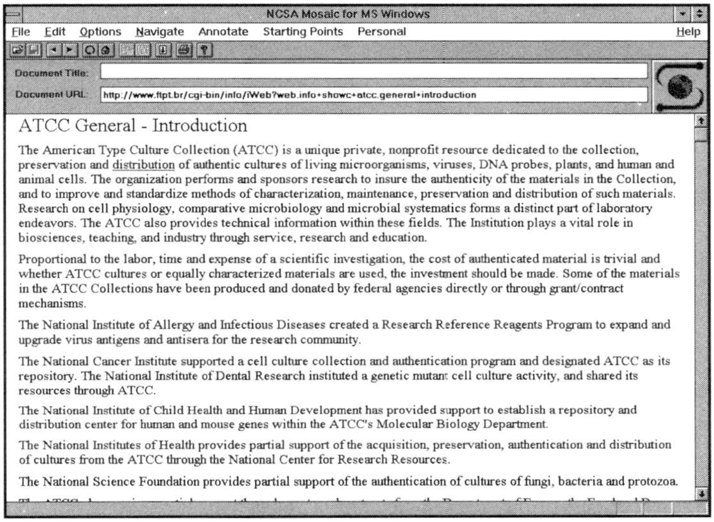

Figure 21.13. *The Brazilian Biodiversity—American Type Culture Collection page.*

Excursion 21.5. Bioinformatics in Australia

From Brazil we head to Australia, where the Australian National University maintains an extremely useful Bioinformatics home page. Figure 21.14 displays this page (`http://life.anu.edu.au/`), which offers several enticing links.

From this page it's easy to see where further searches might lead us, but in fact, it's deceptive. As Figure 21.15 shows, clicking on a topic as open-ended as Molecular Biology from the ANU home page brings up a page (`http://life.anu.edu.au/molbio.html`) with a significant number of additional choices.

> **Note:** As you've discovered by now, this is one of the charms and the frustrations of the World Wide Web—even more, perhaps, than Gopher. Just when you think you have a bit of a handle on things, you click and encounter another array of selections. It can be overwhelming at times, especially if you're not searching for one specific item.

21

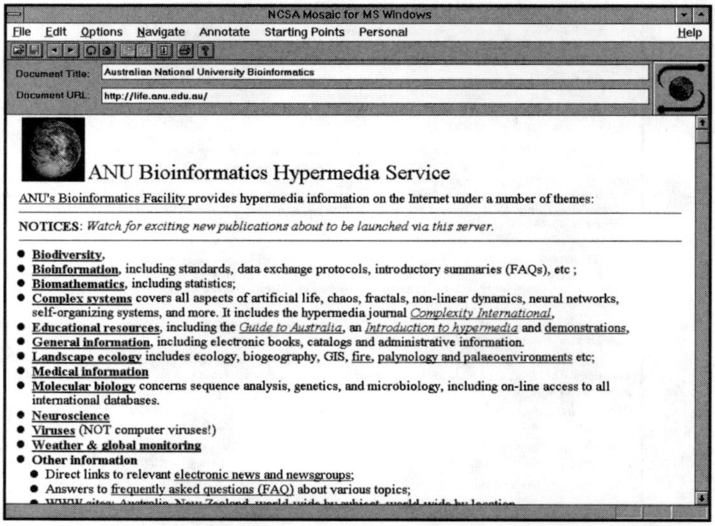

Figure 21.14. *The Australian National University—Bioinformatics home page.*

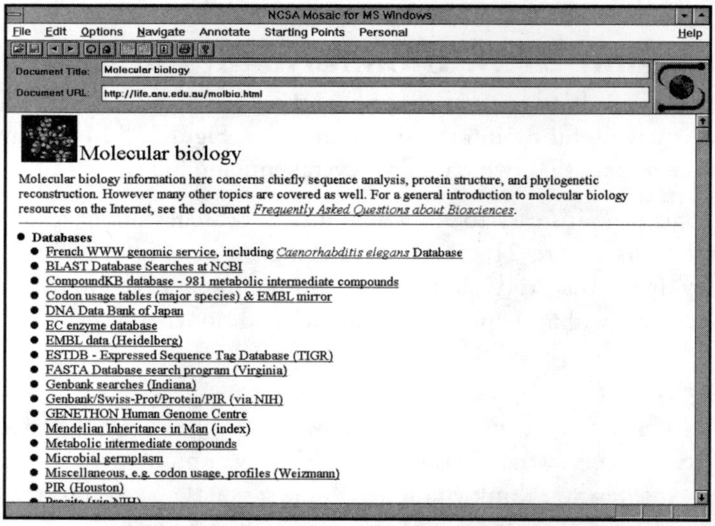

Figure 21.15. *The ANU: Molecular Biology resources page.*

From here, we could perform searches for the information we needed. Of course, because we're just discovering all the possibilities, we don't really need those data. The point, as with astronomy, has become very clear that there's a great deal of information for biologists to be found on the Web as well. There's more, however, as the home pages clearly show, found in Gopher sites in all parts of the Internet world.

End of biology. Time for chemistry. This is beginning to seem like a survey course.

Chemistry

Once again, a quick click on the Chemistry item in the WWW Virtual Library reveals more resources than we can possibly visit. Unlike the Biology sources, moreover, the screen in Figure 21.16 shows primarily World Wide Web sites (`http://www.chem.ucla.edu/chempointers.html`). For our purposes, that means a wealth of graphically rich information.

> **Tip:** If you're trying to determine from within Mosaic whether the site is a WWW or Gopher server, position the cursor over an item and glance at the status bar at the bottom of the screen. If the location begins with `gopher://`, it's a Gopher site; `http://`, a WWW site. You might also see `ftp://`, `telnet://`, and `WAIS://`, which point to these types of sites. In Cello, the best way is to hold the Ctrl key while you click on the highlight. This is called peek mode, which loads only the first 4KB of the destination file. If you want the whole file, select Reload Document from Cello's File menu.

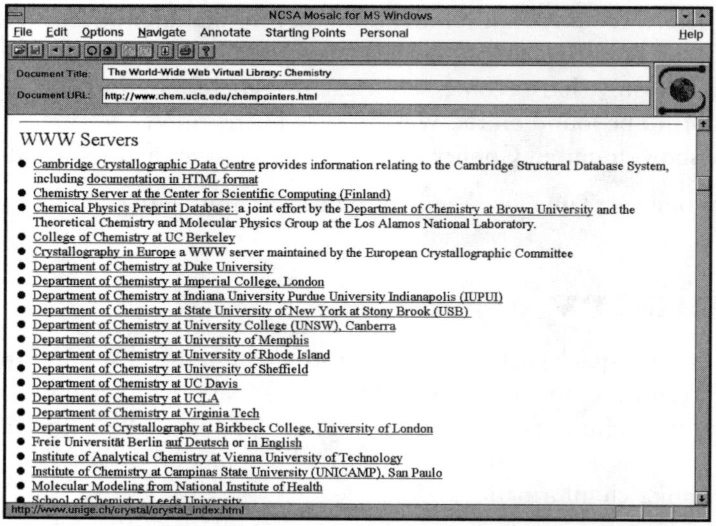

Figure 21.16. *WWW Virtual Library—chemistry-related sites.*

A quick scan through this list shows several items from Europe, including some from the U.K. So from France at the end of our biology excursion, it's off to the U.K. for a look at chemistry-related activities there.

Excursion 21.6. Imperial College of Science and Technology

The home page for the Department of Chemistry at Imperial College in London (see Figure 21.17—`http://www.ch.ic.ac.uk/`) shows a tendency among European home pages toward graphics domination, as opposed to a more hypertext or simply list appearance of many North American pages.

Clicking on the topmost icon, we come to the nicely designed Figure 21.18, which offers a graphic of the researchers within the department from which we can get information about ongoing research.

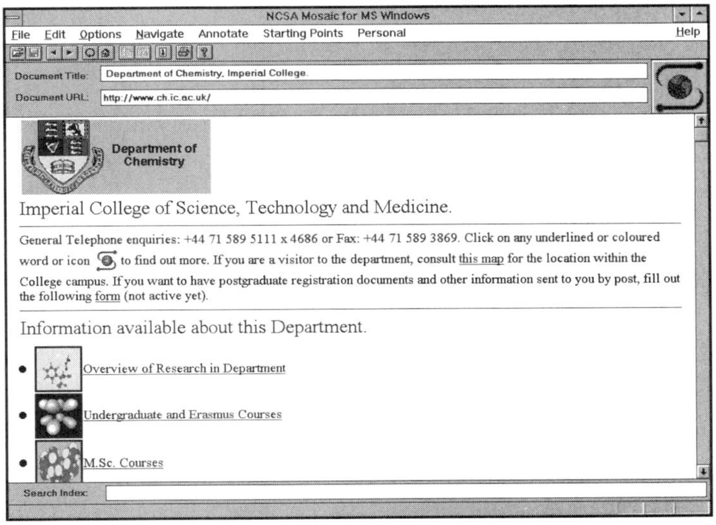

Figure 21.17. *Imperial College, Department of Chemistry home page.*

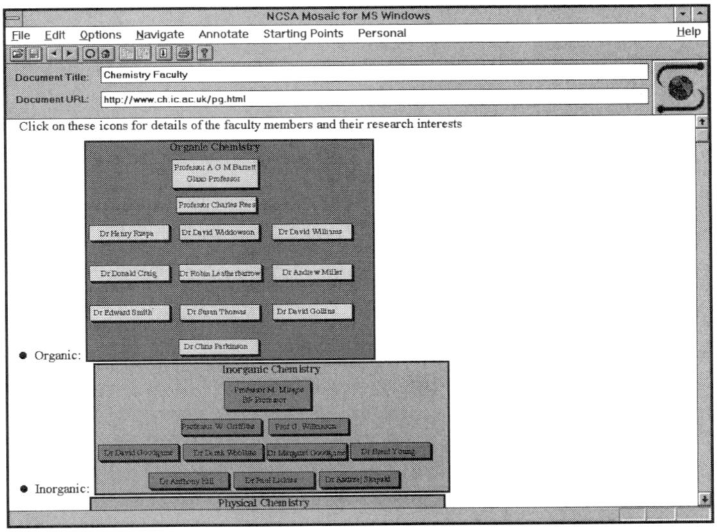

Figure 21.18. *Imperial College, list of researchers in Organic Chemistry.*

Excursion 21.7. Department of Chemistry, University of Sheffield

Another U.K. site, the University of Sheffield, offers a feature called WebElements, as Figure 21.19 (`http://www2.shef.ac.uk/chemistry/chemistry-home.html`) demonstrates.

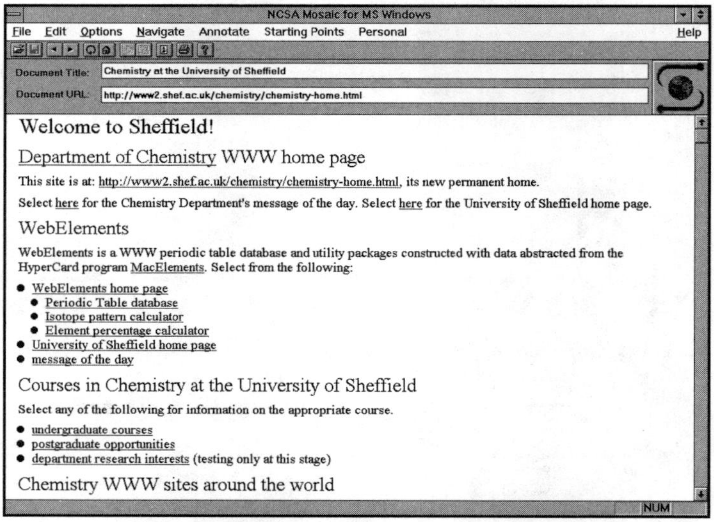

Figure 21.19. *University of Sheffield, Department of Chemistry home page.*

Clicking on the WebElements Home Page item offers a Periodic Table Database, an Isotope Pattern Calculator, and an Element Percentage Calculator. By selecting the first of these, the Periodic Table Database, we arrive at Figure 21.20.

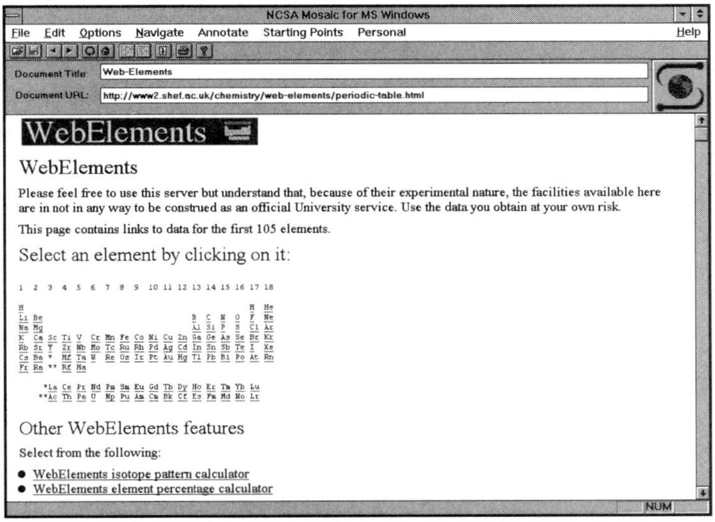

Figure 21.20. *WebElements Periodic Table Database.*

Now for the fun part. Choose a favorite element, click on it, and get a wealth of information. I've always been partial to sodium (it has to do with an old potato chip obsession), and clicking on `Na` yields the data.

Physics

Back to the WWW Virtual Library, and this time into the separate list entitled Physics. Figure 21.21 shows part of the resulting page (`http://info.cern.ch/hypertext/DataSources/bySubject/Physics/Overview.html`), with several tempting sites to explore. For openers, though, it's impossible to resist the last item in the Specialized Fields section, Experiments Online.

We were right not to resist, as Figure 21.22 clearly points out (`http://slacvm.slac.stanford.edu/find/explist.html`). With links to places as disparate as Beijing and Amsterdam, this might be the only browsing page we need.

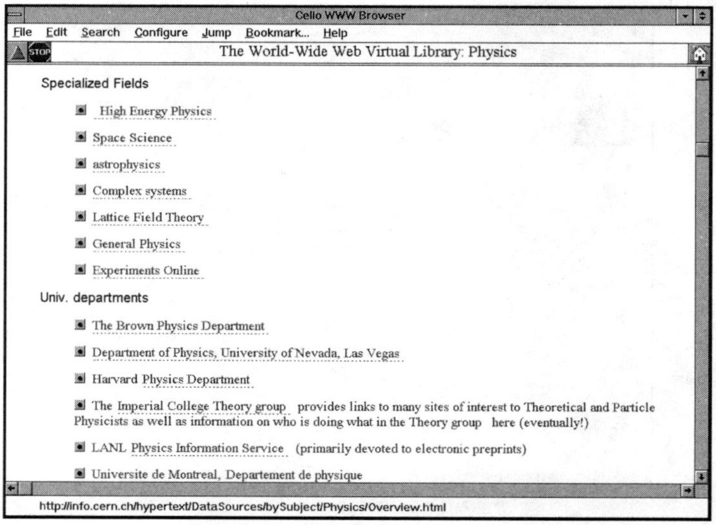
Cello WWW Browser
File Edit Search Configure Jump Bookmark... Help
The World-Wide Web Virtual Library: Physics

Specialized Fields

- High Energy Physics
- Space Science
- astrophysics
- Complex systems
- Lattice Field Theory
- General Physics
- Experiments Online

Univ. departments

- The Brown Physics Department
- Department of Physics, University of Nevada, Las Vegas
- Harvard Physics Department
- The Imperial College Theory group provides links to many sites of interest to Theoretical and Particle Physicists as well as information on who is doing what in the Theory group here (eventually!)
- LANL Physics Information Service (primarily devoted to electronic preprints)
- Universite de Montreal, Departement de physique

http://info.cern.ch/hypertext/DataSources/bySubject/Physics/Overview.html

Figure 21.21. *Cello—WWW Virtual Library Physics page.*

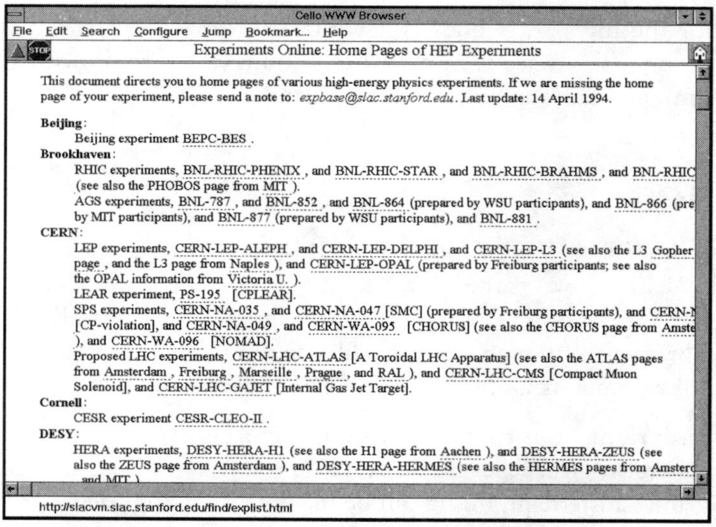
Cello WWW Browser
File Edit Search Configure Jump Bookmark... Help
Experiments Online: Home Pages of HEP Experiments

This document directs you to home pages of various high-energy physics experiments. If we are missing the home page of your experiment, please send a note to: *expbase@slac.stanford.edu*. Last update: 14 April 1994.

Beijing:
Beijing experiment BEPC-BES .
Brookhaven:
RHIC experiments, BNL-RHIC-PHENIX , and BNL-RHIC-STAR , and BNL-RHIC-BRAHMS , and BNL-RHIC (see also the PHOBOS page from MIT).
AGS experiments, BNL-787 , and BNL-852 , and BNL-864 (prepared by WSU participants), and BNL-866 (pre by MIT participants), and BNL-877 (prepared by WSU participants), and BNL-881 .
CERN:
LEP experiments, CERN-LEP-ALEPH , and CERN-LEP-DELPHI , and CERN-LEP-L3 (see also the L3 Gopher page , and the L3 page from Naples), and CERN-LEP-OPAL (prepared by Freiburg participants; see also the OPAL information from Victoria U.).
LEAR experiment, PS-195 [CPLEAR].
SPS experiments, CERN-NA-035 , and CERN-NA-047 [SMC] (prepared by Freiburg participants), and CERN-N [CP-violation], and CERN-NA-049 , and CERN-WA-095 [CHORUS] (see also the CHORUS page from Amste), and CERN-WA-096 [NOMAD].
Proposed LHC experiments, CERN-LHC-ATLAS [A Toroidal LHC Apparatus] (see also the ATLAS pages from Amsterdam , Freiburg , Marseille , Prague , and RAL), and CERN-LHC-CMS [Compact Muon Solenoid], and CERN-LHC-GAJET [Internal Gas Jet Target].
Cornell:
CESR experiment CESR-CLEO-II .
DESY:
HERA experiments, DESY-HERA-H1 (see also the H1 page from Aachen), and DESY-HERA-ZEUS (see also the ZEUS page from Amsterdam), and DESY-HERA-HERMES (see also the HERMES pages from Amster and MIT)

http://slacvm.slac.stanford.edu/find/explist.html

Figure 21.22. *Home page of High Energy Physics Experiments Online.*

Excursion 21.8. The OPAL Experiment—Germany

We haven't been to Germany yet, so why not now? From the University of Freiburg comes information about the OPAL experiment, as shown in the home page in Figure 21.23 (`http://hpfrs6.physik.uni-freiburg.de/opal/opal_allgemein.html`).

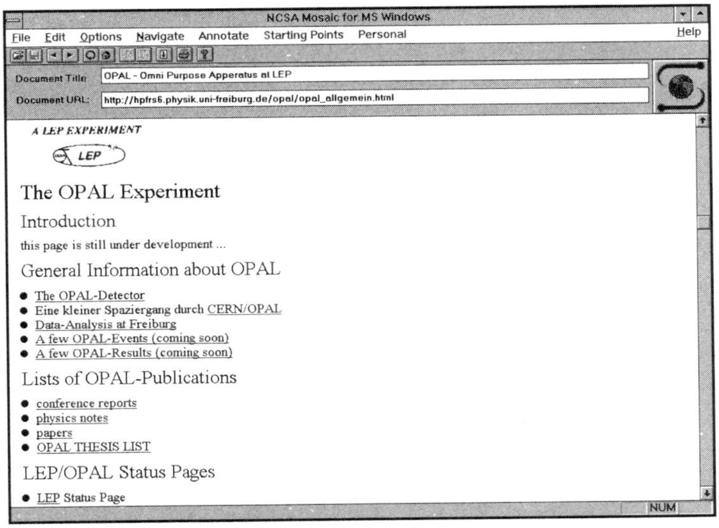

Figure 21.23. *Germany—the OPAL experiment home page.*

Clicking on The OPAL Detector item yields Figure 21.24, an extremely well-designed WWW page with accessible explanatory text supplemented by inline graphics. From here we can learn the basis of the OPAL project, as well as a list of the 24 institutions collaborating with Freiburg. This is clearly an impressive project and one well-articulated on the Net.

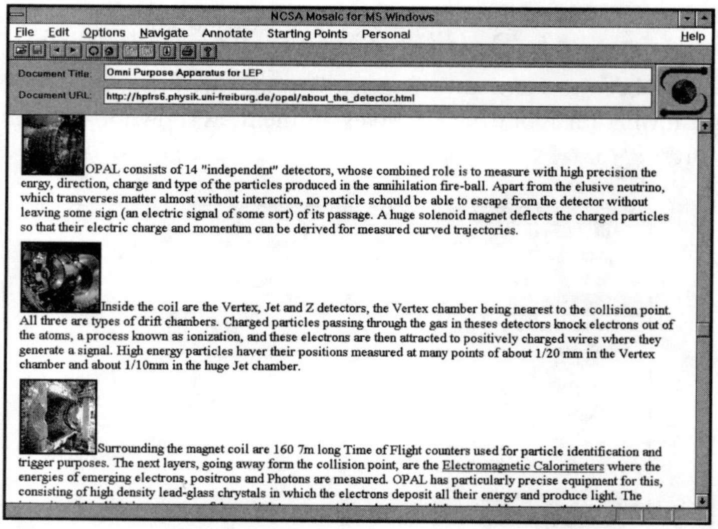
NCSA Mosaic for MS Windows
File Edit Options Navigate Annotate Starting Points Personal Help
Document Title: Omni Purpose Apparatus for LEP
Document URL: http://hpfrs6.physik.uni-freiburg.de/opal/about_the_detector.html
OPAL consists of 14 "independent" detectors, whose combined role is to measure with high precision the enrgy, direction, charge and type of the particles produced in the annihilation fire-ball. Apart from the elusive neutrino, which transverses matter almost without interaction, no particle schould be able to escape from the detector without leaving some sign (an electric signal of some sort) of its passage. A huge solenoid magnet deflects the charged particles so that their electric charge and momentum can be derived for measured curved trajectories.
Inside the coil are the Vertex, Jet and Z detectors, the Vertex chamber being nearest to the collision point. All three are types of drift chambers. Charged particles passing through the gas in theses detectors knock electrons out of the atoms, a process known as ionization, and these electrons are then attracted to positively charged wires where they generate a signal. High energy particles haver their positions measured at many points of about 1/20 mm in the Vertex chamber and about 1/10mm in the huge Jet chamber.
Surrounding the magnet coil are 160 7m long Time of Flight counters used for particle identification and trigger purposes. The next layers, going away form the collision point, are the Electromagnetic Calorimeters where the energies of emerging electrons, positrons and Photons are measured. OPAL has particularly precise equipment for this, consisting of high density lead-glass chrystals in which the electrons deposit all their energy and produce light. The

Figure 21.24. *Germany—details about the OPAL project.*

That's it. We've toured the world of science. Not that there isn't another 30-40 chapters of material left to get, but for now we have at least some idea of the vast quantity of material that's out there waiting for us to access it. There's scarcely any excuse left for not knowing the kind of scientific work that's being done all over the world.

Summary

Day 21 provided an introduction to the projects in science being conducted throughout the world and available for perusal over the World Wide Web. There's a wealth of material and knowledge offered for access and download, information that professionals in the fields, or followers (for whatever reason) of a particular branch of science can scarcely be without if they wish to consider themselves up-to-date. A great deal of collaborative research is starting to appear on the Internet, and the World Wide Web offers an excellent way for this work to be made accessible to the public. Much more of this activity is certain to find its way onto the Web as the months go by. Keeping up is going to be challenging, but that's the way it should be.

Task Review

On Day 21, you learned how to

- Use a variety of starting points to access scientific research information.
- Explore research centers and projects on the World Wide Web.
- Learn of the wealth of information available to anyone with scientific interests, either professional or personal.

Q&A

Q All of the information explored in this chapter is available through Gopher or FTP as well, isn't it?

A See the Extra Credit section, following, for a hint of what's available through Gopher browsing. In fact, much of what we found on the World Wide Web is indeed accessible through Gopher, as many of the linked sites were Gopher rather than WWW sites. However, some information is *not* available through anything except the Web. The WWW is the only means thus far on the Internet of conveying the graphics information, and the easily browsed hypertext screens, displayed in several of the resources throughout this chapter. In other words, even though much of the raw data is accessible elsewhere, the presentation of that data, and often the introduction to that data, is available only through the Web's multimedia capacity. For experts in the field, FTP sites alone are likely the only source necessary, but for nonscientific professionals, the Web offers the most enjoyable and educational entry points.

Q Isn't there a problem in that we see only the successful research, not the failures?

A Dissemination of research information has always been problematic in this regard. Research is funded, after all, and the funding agencies want to know everything that's going on, but for obvious reasons nobody wants to report a continuing string of failures. Research results made available for public consumption on the Internet have already been screened, except of course for other researchers on the project, who have the information available through FTP in password-protected directories and sites. This is no more a problem than is the suppression of any scientific research results, and perhaps the Internet makes things a bit less suppressible. If research initiatives are announced over the Net, after all, and given their own WWW home pages and Gopher sites, then at least we can find out that they're taking place. If we're interested, we can follow their progress, and if for some reason that progress stops (or the sites disappear), we may want to follow up and find out why. Without the Internet, there isn't an easy way of even determining what kinds of projects are under way.

Q Is the Internet all I need to keep abreast of project developments?

A No, not at all. It's not even all you need to figure out which projects are being developed. There are other resources for that, and for the presentation of results. The Internet can help you locate projects and institutions about which you might want to learn much more. All centers offer packages of materials detailing their activities, and through the Net you can find out how to get these packages. They will also offer information about how to follow the results.

Extra Credit: Gopher Access to Projects in Science

The World Wide Web is not, of course, the only way to get information about projects and archives in the world of science. In fact, it's not even the primary method. Most of the information resides, first and foremost, in FTP and Gopher sites. In this Extra Credit section, we'll examine some Gopher sites very briefly to give an idea of the data that awaits you.

> **Note:** As always, many of the Gopher sites offer links to FTP sites. In most cases, you can FTP directly to the site if you prefer using FTP software. As we've seen throughout this book, however, FTPing through Gopher or WWW is significantly easier, as is finding the site itself.

Excursion 21.9. The University of Chicago Gopher

Instead of Gopher Jewels, let's start at the well-constructed Gopher at the University of Chicago (`gopher.uic.edu`). We first see the introductory menu:

```
1.       Gopher at UIC/ADN/
2.       What's New (1 Mar 1994).
3.       Search the UIC Campus and Beyond/
4.       The Administrator/
5.       The Campus/
6.       The Classroom/
7.       The Community/
8.       The Computer/
9.       The Library/
10.      The Researcher/
11.      The World/
```

Several items are of interest, but for our purposes we'll access item 10, The Researcher. The result is the following menu:

```
The Researcher
   1.       About The Researcher Menu.
   2.       UIC Office of the Vice Chancellor for Research/
   3.       Grants and Opportunities/
   4.       Veronica: Netwide Gopher Menu Search/
   5.       Aerospace/
   6.       Agriculture and Forestry/
   7.       Anthropology and Culture/
   8.       Arts/
   9.       Astronomy and Astrophysics/
   10.      Biology/
   11.      Chemistry/
   12.      Computing and Computer Networks/
   13.      Economics/
   14.      Education/
   15.      Environment and Ecology/
   16.      Geography/
   17.      Geology and Geophysics/
   18.      Government, Political Science and Law/
   19.      History/
   20.      Language and Linguistics/
   21.      Library and Information Science/
   22.      Literature, Electronic Books and Journals/
   23.      Mathematics/
   24.      Medicine and Health/
   25.      News and Journalism/
   26.      Oceanography/
   27.      Paleontology/
   28.      Physics/
   29.      Reference/
   30.      Religion and Philosophy/
   31.      Sociology and Psychology/
   32.      Weather, Climate and Meteorology/
```

Lots to choose from, and several scientific disciplines. Let's revisit Biology, to see if the resources here are as strong as those on the Web. As the next menu shows, they are

```
1.     About this directory.
2.     *= Global Biological Information Servers by Topic =*/
3.     *= Grant Abstracts Searching: NSF, NIH, DOE and USDA =*/
4.     *= Search BOING (Bio Oriented INternet Gophers) =* <?>
5.     A Biologist's Guide to the Internet/
6.     A Caenorhabditis elegans Database (ACEDB) <?>
7.     AAtDB, An Arabidopsis thaliana Database <?>
8.     ACEDB BioSci Electronic Conference <?>
9.     ACEDB, A Caenorhabditis elegans Database (1-21) <?>
10.    APIS/
11.    ATCC - The American Type Culture Collection/
12.    About Genbank.
13.    About LiMB.
14.    About Multiple Database Search.
15.    About PIR.
16.    About PROSITE.
17.    About Protein Data Bank (PDB).
18.    About SWISS-PROT.
19.    About Transcription Factor Database (TFD).
20.    American Physiological Society/
21.    Arabidopsis/
22.    Arabidopsis Research Companion, Mass Gen Hospital/Harvard/
23.    Archive of BIOSCI mailing lists and newsgroups <?>
24.    Artificial Intelligence in Systematic Biology, 1990.
25.    Association of Systematics Collections/
26.    Australian Herbaria Specimen Data Standards/
27.    Australian National Botanic Gardens (ANBG)/
28.    Australian National University Bioinformatics/
29.    BIOSCI/bionet biology newsgroups server/
30.    Base de Dados Tropical (Tropical Data Base), Campinas, Brasil/
31.    Baylor College of Medicine Genome Center/
32.    Beanbag/
33.    BioBit Archive, Oxford/
34.    BioInformatics gopher server: Weizmann Institute of Science, Israe../
35.    BioMOO, the biologists' virtual meeting place <TEL>
36.    BioSci Arabidopsis Genome Electronic Conference Archive <?>
37.    BioSci Archive, IntelliGenetics/
38.    BioSci and Other Electronic Publications/
39.    BioSci documents <?>
40.    Biodatabases from SERC Daresbury UK FTP Archive/
41.    Biodiversity Resources/
42.    Biodiversity and Biological Collections Gopher at Harvard/
43.    Bioinformatics Resource Gopher/
44.    Bioline Publications/
45.    Biological Sciences Directorate Reports/
46.    Biology FTP Archive for Macintosh (MacSciTech USA)/
47.    Biology Gopher at OSU (BCC)/
48.    Biology Journal Contents <?>
49.    Biomedical_Shareware/
```

```
    50.       Bionet Newsgroups <?>
    51.       Biotechnet Buyers Guide - Online Catalogues for Biology <TEL>
    52.       Blocks Database (FHCRC)/
    53.       Botanical Electronic News/
    54.       Botanical Information/
Press ? for Help, q to Quit, u to go up a menu Page: 3/17
```

The bottom right of the screen tells us that these 54 items comprise a mere three of the 17 pages. We're barely a sixth of the way through the list. One area we examined on the WWW was Biodiversity, shown here in items 41 and 42. Selecting item 42, we arrive at the following menu:

```
Biodiversity and Biological Collections Gopher at Harvard
    1.        About the Biodiversity and Biological Collections Gopher.
    2.        Museum, Herbarium and Arboretum Collection Catalogs/
    3.        Biodiversity Information Resources/
    4.        Directories of Biologists/
    5.        Biodiversity Journals and Newsletters/
    6.        Curation & Management of Biological Collections/
    7.        Standards Organizations and Reports/
    8.        Software/
    9.        Biological Images/
    10.       Taxacom Services/
    11.       Other Biological Gophers/
    12.       Other Gopher and Information Servers (mirrored from U.Minnesota)/
    13.       Top Ten Items at the Biodiversity Gopher/
```

In the spirit of both Dick Clark and David Letterman, the most interesting choice here simply has to be item 13, the Top Ten Items at the Biodiversity Gopher. Selecting it, we're offered the menu below:

```
Top Ten Items at the Biodiversity Gopher
    1.        Harvard Gray Herbarium Index of New World Plants/
    2.        Image files/
    3.        Biodiversity Authority Files/
    4.        Catalogs/Search by Discipline/
    5.        Biodiversity Authority Files/Botany/
    6.        About this Biology Image Archive.
    7.        Biodiversity Database and Software Development Projects/
    8.        Flora Online: Journal for Collections-Oriented Botanical Research/
    9.        Collection Catalogs/Botany/
    10.       Collection Catalogs/Institution/
```

Several places to go here, but let's assume we've been looking for images to download. Clearly, item 2 should have something to offer, and as the following menu shows, it does.

```
Image files
   1.        hbia0001.jpg <Picture>
   2.        hbia0002.jpg <Picture>
   3.        hbia0003.jpg <Picture>
   4.        hbia0004.jpg <Picture>
   5.        hbia0005.jpg <Picture>
   6.        hbia0006.jpg <Picture>
   7.        hbia0007.jpg <Picture>
   8.        hbia0008.jpg <Picture>
   9.        hbia0009.jpg <Picture>
   10.       hbia0010.jpg <Picture>
   11.       hbia0011.jpg <Picture>
   12.       hbia0012.jpg <Picture>
   13.       hbia0013.jpg <Picture>
   14.       hbia0014.jpg <Picture>
   15.       hbia0015.jpg <Picture>
   16.       hbia0016.jpg <Picture>
   17.       hbia0017.jpg <Picture>
   18.       hbia0018.jpg <Picture>
Press ? for Help, q to Quit, u to go up a menu Page: 1/21
```

Eighteen files are shown here, all in .JPG format. Again, however, look at the bottom right of the menu. This is only page 1 of a 21-page list, which means we have access to well over 300 files. Choosing item 17 on this list (for no reason other than it's the highest prime number here—okay, I didn't say anything about a *good* reason), we download it to our account. The result of the download is Figure 21.25.

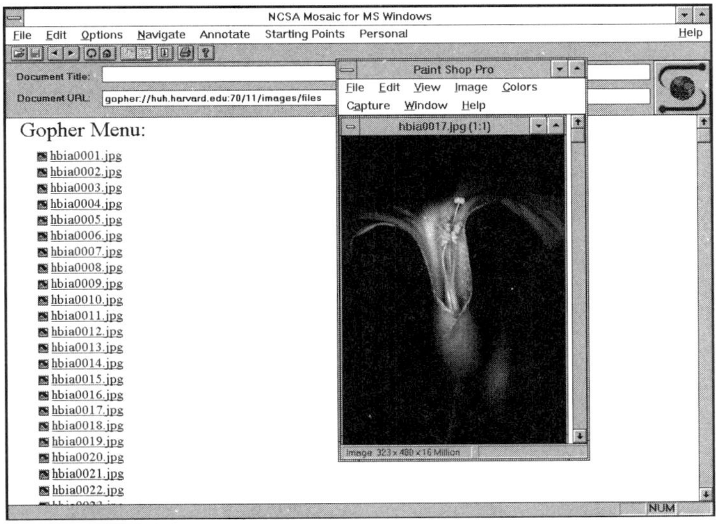

Figure 21.25. *Downloaded .JPG picture from Image files Gopher menu.*

The thing to keep in mind, as with our WWW searches in the main part of this chapter, is that this is but one graphic from one menu from a host of possible menus on one topic from one Gopher. It wouldn't take much for a diligent Gopher browser to compile a huge amount of information on the latest topics in scientific research. What you do with it, of course, remains up to you. It's there, and it's easily accessible.

A

Internet Access Providers

This appendix lists companies and organizations that provide dial-up access to Internet services for individuals. For more information on different types of Internet access and what to look for in an access provider, see Day 2, "Into the Breach: Getting Started on the Net."

Area Code Summary: US/Canadian Providers

This is a listing of North American provider names arranged by the telephone area code the provider services. Details and contact information for each provider follow in the next section.

202	CAPCON Library Network
	Clarknet
204	MBnet
205	Nuance Network Service
206	Eskimo North
	Netcom
	Olympus
	Teleport
212	Echo
	Maestro Information Service
	Mindvox
	Netcom
	Panix
	Pipeline
213	CRL
214	Netcom
	Texas Metronet
301	CAPCON Library Network
	ClarkNet
	Digital Express Group (Digex)
303	CNS
	Colorado SuperNet
	Netcom
305	CyberGate
	Gateway to the World
310	CERFnet
	CRL

	Netcom
312	CICNet
	InterAccess Co.
	Netcom
313	Msen
314	Neosoft
403	Alberta SuperNet Inc.
	CCI Networks
404	CRL
	Netcom
408	a2i Communications
	Netcom
	Portal
410	CAPCON Library Network
	ClarkNet
	Digital Express Group (Digex)
412	Telerama
415	CERFnet
	CRL
	Institute for Global Communications (IGC)
	Netcom
	The WELL
416	Internet Online Inc.
	UUNorth Incorporated
503	Agora
	Netcom
	Teleport
504	Neosoft
508	The World
510	CCnet Communications
	CERFnet
	CRL
	HoloNet
	Netcom
512	Netcom
513	Freelance Systems Programming
514	Communications Accessibles Montreal, Inc.
516	Panix
519	Data Tech Canada
	Hookup Communication Corporation

602	CRL
	Data Basix
	Evergreen Internet
603	MV Communications, Inc.
604	Cyberstore Systems Inc.
	DataFlux Systems Limited
	Wimsey Information Services
609	Digital Express Group (Digex)
	Global Enterprise Services, Inc.
614	OARNet
617	Delphi
	Netcom
	North Shore Access
	The World
619	CERFnet
	CTS Network Services
	Netcom
702	Evergreen Internet
703	CAPCON Library Network
	ClarkNet
	Digital Express Group (Digex)
	Meta Network
	Netcom
704	Interpath
	Northcoast Internet
	Internet Access, Inc.
707	CRL
708	CICNet
	InterAccess Co.
	XNet Information Systems
713	Neosoft
714	CERFnet
	Digital Express Group (Digex)
	Netcom
718	Echo
	Mindvox
719	CNS
	Colorado SuperNet
800	CERFnet

	CICNet
	CNS
	CRL
	Global Enterprise Services, Inc.
	Msen
	Neosoft
801	Evergreen Internet
810	Msen
815	InterAccess Co.
817	Texas Metronet
818	CERFnet
	Netcom
908	Digital Express Group (Digex)
909	Digital Express Group (Digex)
910	Interpath
916	Netcom
919	Interpath
CompuServe Packet Network	The WELL
	The World
PSINet	HoloNet
SprintNet	Delphi
	Meta Network
	Neosoft
	Portal
Tymnet	Delphi
	Holonet

Providers in the United States and Canada

a2i Communications

Area code	408
Voice phone	408-293-8078
E-mail address	`info@rahul.net`
Dialup number	408-293-9010, login as `guest`
Services provided	Shell, Usenet, e-mail, Internet access, including Telnet and FTP

Agora

Area code	503
E-mail address	`info@agora.rain.com`
Dialup number	503-293-1772
Services provided	Shell, Usenet, FTP, Telnet, Gopher, Lynx, IRC, mail, SLIP/PPP coming

Alberta SuperNet Inc.

Area code	403
Voice phone	403-441-3663
E-mail address	`info@supernet.ab.ca`
Services provided	Shell, e-mail, Usenet, FTP, Telnet, Gopher, SLIP/PPP

CAPCON Library Network

Area codes	202, 301, 410, 703
Voice phone	202-331-5771
E-mail address	`capcon@capcon.net`
Services provided	Menu, FTP, Archie, e-mail, FTP, Gopher, Telnet, WAIS, Whois, training

CCI Networks

Area code	403
Voice phone	403-450-6787
E-mail address	`info@ccinet.ab.ca`
Services provided	Shell, e-mail, Usenet, FTP, Telnet, Gopher, WAIS, WWW, IRC, Hytelnet, SLIP/PPP

CCnet Communications

Area code	510
Voice phone	510-988-0680
E-mail address	`info@ccnet.com`
Dialup number	510-988-7140, login as `guest`
Services provided	Shell, SLIP/PPP, Telnet, e-mail, FTP, Usenet, IRC, WWW

CERFnet

Area codes	619, 510, 415, 818, 714, 310, 800
Voice phone	800-876-2373
E-mail address	`sales@cerf.net`
Services provided	Full range of Internet services

CICNet

Area codes	312, 708, 800
Voice phone	800-947-4754 or 313-998-6703
E-mail address	`info@cic.net`
Services provided	SLIP, FTP, Telnet, Gopher, e-mail, Usenet

ClarkNet (Clark Internet Services, Inc.)

Area codes	410, 301, 202, 703
Voice phone	800-735-2258, ask for extension 410-730-9764
E-mail address	`info@clark.net`
Dialup number	301-596-1626, login as `guest`, no password
Services provided	Shell/optional menu, FTP, Gopher, Telnet, IRC, news, Mosaic, Lynx, MUD, SLIP/PPP/CSLIP, and much more

CNS

Area codes	303, 719, 800
Voice phone	800-748-1200
E-mail address	`service@cscns.com`
Dialup number	719-520-1700, 303-758-2656
Services provided	Shell/menu, e-mail, FTP, Telnet, all newsgroups, IRC, 4m, Gopher, WAIS, SLIP, and more

Colorado SuperNet

Area codes	303, 719
Voice phone	303-273-3471
E-mail address	`info@csn.org` or `help@csn.org`
Services provided	Shell, e-mail, Usenet news, Telnet, FTP, SLIP/PPP, and other Internet tools

Communications Accessibles Montreal, Inc.

Area code	514
Voice phone	514-931-0749
E-mail address	`info@cam.org`
Dialup number	514-596-2255
Services provided	Shell, FTP, Telnet, Gopher, WAIS, WWW, IRC, Hytelnet, SLIP/CSLIP/PPP, news

CRL

Area codes	213, 310, 404, 415, 510, 602, 707, 800
Voice phone	415-837-5300
E-mail address	`support@crl.com`
Dialup number	415-705-6060, login as `newuser`, no password
Services provided	Shell, e-mail, Usenet, UUCP, FTP, Telnet, SLIP/PPP, and more

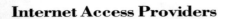

CTS Network Services (CTSNet)

Area code	619
Voice phone	619-637-3737
E-mail address	`support@cts.com`
Dialup number	619-637-3660
Services provided	Shell, e-mail, Usenet, FTP, Telnet, Gopher, IRC, MUD, SLIP/PPP, and more

CyberGate

Area code	305
Voice phone	305-428-4283
E-mail address	`sales@gate.net`
Services provided	Shell, e-mail, Usenet, FTP, Telnet, Gopher, Lynx, IRC, SLIP/PPP

Cyberstore Systems Inc.

Area code	604
Voice phone	604-526-3373
E-mail address	`info@cyberstore.ca`
Dialup number	604-526-3676, login as `guest`
Services provided	E-mail, Usenet, FTP, Telnet, Gopher, WAIS, WWW, IRC, SLIP/PPP

DataFlux Systems Limited

Area code	604
Voice phone	604-744-4553
E-mail address	`info@dataflux.bc.ca`
Services provided	Shell, e-mail, Usenet, FTP, Telnet, Gopher, WAIS, WWW, IRC, SLIP/PPP

Data Basix

Area code	602
Voice phone	602-721-1988
E-mail address	`info@data.basix.com`
Services provided	Shell, Usenet, FTP, Telnet

Data Tech Canada

Area code	519
Voice phone	519-473-5694
E-mail address	`info@dt-can.com`
Dialup number	519-473-7685
Services provided	Shell, e-mail, Usenet, FTP, Telnet, Gopher, WAIS, WWW

Delphi

Area codes	617, SprintNet, Tymnet
Voice phone	617-491-3393
E-mail address	`info@delphi.com`
Dialup number	617-492-9600
Services provided	Gopher, FTP, e-mail, Usenet, Telnet

Digital Express Group (Digex)

Area codes	301, 410, 609, 703, 714, 908, 909
Voice phone	800-969-9090
E-mail address	`info@digex.net`
Dialup number	301-220-0258, 410-605-2700, 609-348-6203, 703-281-7997, 714-261-5201, 908-937-9481, 909-222-2204, login as `new`
Services provided	Shell, SLIP/PPP, e-mail, newsgroups, Telnet, FTP, IRC, Gopher, WAIS, and more

Echo

Area codes	212, 718
Voice phone	212-255-3839
E-mail address	`info@echonyc.com`
Dialup number	212-989-3382
Services provided	Conferencing, e-mail, Shell, complete Internet access including Telnet, FTP, SLIP/PPP

Eskimo North

Area code	206
E-mail address	`nanook@eskimo.com`
Dialup number	206-367-3837
Services provided	Shell, Telnet, FTP, IRC, Archie, Gopher, Hytelnet, WWW, Lynx, and more.

Evergreen Internet

Area codes	602, 702, 801
Voice phone	602-230-9339
E-mail address	`evergreen@libre.com`
Services provided	Shell, FTP, Telnet, SLIP, PPP, others

Freelance Systems Programming

Area code	513
Voice phone	513-254-7246
E-mail address	`fsp@dayton.fsp.com`
Dialup number	513-258-7745
Services provided	Telnet, FTP, FSP, Lynx, WWW, Archie, Gopher, Usenet, e-mail, and more.

Gateway to the World

Area code	305
Voice phone	305-670-2930
E-mail address	`m.jansen@gate.com`
Dialup number	305-670-2929
Services provided	Dial-up Internet access

Global Enterprise Services, Inc.

Area codes	609, 800
Voice phone	800-358-4437
E-mail address	`market@jvnc.net`
Services provided	Dial-in Internet access

HoloNet

Area codes	510, PSINet, Tymnet
Voice phone	510-704-0160
E-mail address	support@holonet.net
Dialup number	510-704-1058
Services provided	Complete Internet access

Hookup Communication Corporation

Area codes	519, Canada-wide
Voice phone	800-363-0400
E-mail address	info@hookup.net
Services provided	Shell, e-mail, Usenet, FTP, Telnet, Gopher, WAIS, WWW, IRC, Hytelnet, Archie, SLIP/PPP

Institute for Global Communications (IGC)

Area code	415
Voice phone	415-442-0220
E-mail address	support@igc.apc.org
Dialup number	415-322-0284
Services provided	E-mail, Telnet, FTP, Gopher, Archie, Veronica, WAIS, SLIP/PPP

InterAccess Co.

Area codes	312, 708, 815
Voice phone	800-967-1580
E-mail address	info@interaccess.com
Dialup number	708-671-0237
Services provided	Shell, FTP, Telnet, SLIP, PPP, and more.

Internet Online Inc.

Area code	416
Voice phone	416-363-8676

E-mail address	`vid@io.org`
Dialup number	416-363-3783, login as `new`
Services provided	Shell, e-mail, Usenet, FTP, Telnet, Gopher, IRC, Archie, Hytelnet

Interpath

Area codes	919, 910, 704
Voice phone	800-849-6305
E-mail address	`info@infopath.net`
Services provided	Full shell for UNIX, and SLIP and PPP

Maestro Information Service

Area code	212
Voice phone	212-240-9600
E-mail address	`info@maestro.com`
Dialup number	212-240-9700, login as `newuser`
Services provided	Shell, e-mail, Usenet, Telnet, FTP, Archie, IRC

MBnet

Area code	204
Voice phone	204-474-9590
E-mail address	`info@mbnet.mb.ca`
Dialup number	204-275-6132, login as `mbnet` with password `guest`
Services provided	Shell, e-mail, Usenet, FTP, Telnet, Gopher, WAIS, WWW, IRC, Archie, Hytelnet, SLIP/PPP

Meta Network

Area codes	703, SprintNet
Voice phone	703-243-6622
E-mail address	`info@tmn.com`
Services provided	Shell, e-mail, FTP, Telnet, conferencing

Mindvox

Area codes	212, 718
Voice phone	212-989-2418
E-mail address	`info@phantom.com`
Dialup number	212-989-1550
Services provided	Shell, e-mail, Usenet, FTP, Telnet, Gopher, Archie, IRC, conferencing

Msen

Area codes	313, 810, 800
Voice phone	313-998-4562
E-mail address	`info-request@msen.com`
Services provided	Shell, e-mail, Telnet, FTP, Usenet, Gopher, IRC, WAIS, SLIP/PPP

MV Communications, Inc.

Area code	603
Voice phone	603-429-2223
E-mail address	`info@mv.mv.com`
Dialup number	603-424-7428
Services provided	Shell, Usenet, FTP, Telnet, Gopher, WAIS, SLIP/PPP

Neosoft

Area codes	713, 504, 314, 800, SprintNet
Voice phone	713-684-5969
E-mail address	`info@neosoft.com`
Services provided	Shell, Usenet, FTP, Telnet, Gopher, SLIP/PPP, and more.

Netcom On-Line Communications Services

Area codes	206, 212, 214, 303, 310, 312, 404, 408, 415, 503, 510, 512, 617, 619, 703, 714, 818, 916
Voice phone	800-501-8649

E-mail address	`info@netcom.com`
Dialup number	206-547-5992, 212-354-3870, 214-753-0045, 303-758-0101, 310-842-8835, 312-380-0340, 404-303-9765, 408-261-4700, 408-459-9851, 415-328-9940, 415-985-5650, 503-626-6833, 510-274-2900, 510-426-6610, 510-865-9004, 512-206-4950, 617-237-8600, 619-234-0524, 703-255-5951, 714-708-3800, 818-585-3400, 916-965-1371; login as `guest`
Services provided	Shell, e-mail, Usenet, FTP, Telnet, Gopher, IRC, WAIS, SLIP/PPP

North Shore Access

Area code	617
Voice phone	617-593-3110
E-mail address	`info@shore.net`
Dialup number	617-593-4557, login as `new`
Services provided	Shell, FTP, Telnet, Gopher, Archie, SLIP/PPP

Northcoast Internet

Area code	707
Voice phone	707-444-1913
Services provided	Shell, FTP, Telnet, Gopher, SLIP/PPP

Nuance Network Services

Area code	205
Voice phone	205-533-4296
E-mail address	`info@nuance.com`
Services provided	Shell, Usenet, FTP, Telnet, Gopher, SLIP/PPP

OARNet

Area code	614
Voice phone	800-627-8101
E-mail address	`info@oar.net`
Services provided	Shell, SLIP/PPP

Olympus

Area code	206
Voice phone	206-385-0464
E-mail address	`ifo@olympus.net`
Services provided	Shell, FTP, Telnet, Gopher

Panix Public Access UNIX and Internet

Area codes	212, 516
Voice phone	212-787-6160
E-mail address	`info@panix.com`
Dialup number	212-787-3100, 516-626-7863, login as `newuser`
Services provided	Shell, Usenet, FTP, Telnet, Gopher, Archie, WWW, WAIS, SLIP/PPP

Pipeline

Area code	212
Voice phone	212-267-3636
E-mail address	`infobot@pipeline.com`
Dialup number	212-267-6432, login as `guest`
Services provided	Pipeline for Windows software, e-mail, Usenet, Gopher, Telnet, Archie, FTP, WAIS

Portal Communications Company

Area codes	408, SprintNet
Voice phone	408-973-9111
E-mail address	`info@portal.com`
Services provided	Shell, e-mail, Usenet, FTP, Telnet, Gopher, IRC, SLIP/PPP

PSI

Area codes	North America, Europe and Pacific Basin; send e-mail to `numbers-info@psi.com` for list
Voice phone	703-709-0300

E-mail address	`all-info@psi.com`
Services provided	Complete Internet services

Teleport

Area codes	503, 206
Voice phone	503-223-4245
E-mail address	`info@teleport.com`
Dialup number	503-220-1016
Services provided	Shell, e-mail, Usenet, FTP, Telnet, Gopher, SLIP/PPP

Telerama

Area code	412
Voice phone	412-481-3505
E-mail address	`sysop@telerama.lm.com`
Dialup number	412-481-4644
Services provided	Shell, e-mail, Telnet, Usenet, FTP, Telnet, Gopher, IRC, SLIP/PPP

Texas Metronet

Area codes	214, 817
Voice phone	214-705-2900
E-mail address	`info@metronet.com`
Dialup number	214-705-2901, 817-261-1127; login as `info`, with password `info`
Services provided	Shell, e-mail, Usenet, FTP, Telnet, Gopher, IRC, SLIP/PPP

UUNorth Incorporated

Area code	416
Voice phone	416-225-8649
E-mail address	`uunorth@north.net`
Dialup number	416-221-0200, login as `new`
Services provided	E-mail, Usenet, FTP, Telnet, Gopher, WAIS, WWW, IRC, Archie, SLIP/PPP

VNet Internet Access, Inc.

Area codes	704, public data network
Voice phone	800-377-3282
E-mail address	`info@vnet.net`
Dialup number	704-347-8839, login as `new`
Services provided	Shell, e-mail, Usenet, FTP, Telnet, Gopher, IRC, SLIP/PPP, UUCP

The WELL

Area codes	415, CompuServe Packet Network
Voice phone	415-332-4335
E-mail address	`info@well.sf.ca.us`
Dialup number	415-332-6106, login as `newuser`
Services provided	Shell, e-mail, Usenet, FTP, Telnet, conferencing

Wimsey Information Services

Area code	604
Voice phone	604-936-8649
E-mail address	`admin@wimsey.com`
Services provided	Shell, e-mail, Usenet, FTP, Telnet, Gopher, WAIS, WWW, IRC, Archie, SLIP/PPP

The World

Area codes	508, 617, CompuServe Packet Network
Voice phone	617-739-0202
E-mail address	`office@world.std.com`
Dialup number	617-739-9753, login as `new`
Services provided	Shell, e-mail, Usenet, FTP, Telnet, Gopher, WAIS, WWW, IRC

XNet Information Systems

Area code	708
Voice phone	708-983-6064
E-mail address	`info@xnet.com`

Dialup number	708-983-6435, 708-882-1101
Services provided	Shell, e-mail, Usenet, FTP, Telnet, Gopher, Archie, IRC, SLIP/PPP, UUCP

Australia

Aarnet

Voice phone	+61 6-249-3385
E-mail address	`aarnet@aarnet.edu.au`

Connect.com.au P/L

Areas serviced	Major Australian capital cities (2, 3, 6, 7, 8, 9)
Voice phone	1 800 818 262 or +61 3 528 2239
E-mail address	`connect@connect.com.au`
Services provided	Shell, SLIP/PPP, UUCP

Germany

Contributed Software

Voice phone	+49 30-694-69-07
E-mail address	`info@contrib.de`
Dialup number	+49 30-694-60-55, login as `guest` or `gast`

Individual Network e.V.

Area serviced	All of Germany
Voice phone	+49 0441 9808556
E-mail address	`in-info@individual.net`
Dialup number	02238 15071, login as `info`
Services provided	UUCP throughout Germany; FTP, SLIP, Telnet and other services in some major cities

Inter Networking System (INS)

Voice phone	+49 2305 356505
E-mail address	`info@ins.net`

Netherlands

Knoware

E-mail address	info@knoware.nl
Dialup number	030 896775

NetLand

Voice phone	020 6943664
E-mail address	Info@netland.nl
Dialup number	020 6940350, login as new or info

Simplex

E-mail address	simplex@simplex.nl
Dialup number	020 6653388, login as new or info

New Zealand

Actrix

Voice phone	(04) 389-6316
E-mail address	john@actrix.gen.nz

Switzerland

SWITCH - Swiss Academic and Research Network

Voice phone	+41 1 268 1515
E-mail address	postmaster@switch.ch

United Kingdom

Almac

Voice phone	+44 0324-665371
E-mail address	alastair.mcintyre@almac.co.uk

Cix

Voice phone	+44 49 2641 961
E-mail address	`cixadmin@cix.compulink.co.uk`

Demon Internet Limited

Voice phone	081-349-0063 (London)
	031-552-0344 (Edinburgh)
E-mail address	`internet@demon.net`
Services provided	SLIP/PPP accounts

The Direct Connection (UK)

Voice phone	+44 (0)81 317 0100
E-mail address	`helpdesk@dircon.cu.uk`
Dialup number	+44 (0)81 317 2222

B

Glossary

B

Glossary

account Your account at the bank gives you space and tools to work with your money; your account on a network gives you space and tools to work with files and data. The same idea, really.

address The string of characters that identifies you or an Internet file or site. My address is `nrandall@watserv1.uwaterloo.ca`, for instance; yours will be in the form *`username@host.name.type`*. A Gopher site has an address such as `cwis.usc.edu`, while a World Wide Web address is in the form of a URL (see *URL*).

Archie A search system that lets you locate files you can then download via anonymous FTP (see *FTP*).

ASCII The major standard for files that users on various machines can share, abbreviated as ASC. Also known as text files, which is what most ASCII files are.

binary A file containing codes and characters that can only be used by specific kinds of software. Program files, graphic files, and formatted documents are the most common.

Cello A graphical World Wide Web browser for Microsoft Windows; a competitor to Mosaic.

dial-up access As the name suggests, connecting to the Internet by dialing through a modem.

direct access Internet access that makes your computer a separate Internet node. SLIP and PPP (see both) effectively simulate direct access. See also *indirect access.*

discussion list Another name for mailing list. See *mailing list.*

e-mail An abbreviation for electronic mail, e-mail has become the single most used function of the Internet. It is essentially a messaging system, although it incorporates file transfer as well.

emoticon Pretentious name for smileys (see *smiley*), which really don't merit that much thought.

FAQ (Frequently Asked Question) A list of common questions and answers about some specific topic. They're designed to keep users from asking the same questions constantly.

finger A program that lets you determine if a specific user is currently online, or, instead, which users are currently online at a specific site. Not to be freely used in conversation at non-techie parties.

flame To be nasty, vicious, or insulting over the Net, usually in response to an e-mail or newsgroup message that the flamer didn't like. Usually a bad idea.

freeware Software available at no cost from FTP sites.

FTP (File Transfer Protocol) An extremely important tool that enables you to transfer files between remote computers. Its most popular Internet use is "anonymous FTP," where you log in to a remote system using the login name "anonymous" and typing your full address as the password. With anonymous FTP you don't need an account on the remote machine in order to access certain files. Note: You can perform FTP through Gopher and the World Wide Web, or directly from the command line.

Gopher The most popular Internet browser by far, Gopher displays files and directories in a conveniently accessed list. You can perform many functions from Gopher, including Telnet (see *Telnet*), FTP (see *FTP*), and searches of various kinds.

header The top portion of an e-mail message, showing the route taken by the message across the various networks. Unreadable by all but the most technologically unchallenged.

HTML (Hypertext Markup Language) The coding applied to text files that allows them to appear as formatted pages on the World Wide Web.

indirect access Internet access in which your computer is simply a terminal on a host computer, which is in turn directly connected to the Net (see *direct access*). Only the host computer is a separate node on the Net.

Internaut An Internet browser, usually ranging toward the expert.

Internet The global network of networks that are all intercommunicable.

Internetter An Internet user, whether expert or novice.

IP address The Internet Protocol address is the numeric address of a computer on the Internet. If you have an IP address, you're essentially a separate Internet node.

Kermit Common protocol (and program) that lets you transfer files between your personal computer and the host computer (see host). See also *XModem* and *FTP*.

Listserv A program that allows for the creation and distribution of mailing lists. See *mailing list*.

login The process of getting connected to a networked computer. As a verb it's two words: *log in*.

login name Your account name, to be typed when logging in to a computer (see *login*). Usually the login name is the first portion of your full Internet address (see *address*).

Lynx A character-based World Wide Web browser for UNIX systems.

mailing list An automated message service, often moderated by an "owner," where subscribers receive postings from other subscribers on a given topic. See also *discussion list* and *newsgroup.*

Mosaic A graphical World Wide Web browser for X Windows, Macintosh, Microsoft Windows, and Amiga systems; often used synonymously with the term World Wide Web, but that's incorrect.

MUD (Multiuser Dialog or Dimension) Formerly called Multiuser Dungeon, a MUD is an interactive role-playing game played on the Internet. Players join the game from anywhere on the Internet by telnetting into the system where the game is stored, then interact with each other as they play.

netiquette Internet etiquette, consisting of things like not replying to everyone in the group when you have something to say to only one, and not dragging files from an FTP site in Mongolia when the university next door has the same stuff.

newsgroup An automated message area, usually operated through Usenet (see *Usenet*), in which subscribers post messages to the entire group on specific topics. See also *mailing list.*

password The secret string of characters assigned to your individual login name on that particular system. Typically, you're assigned a password at the same time you're given your login name, and you're expected to change the password often. It's the thing that keeps other people from accessing your account, and you from accessing theirs.

PPP (Point-to-Point Protocol) Like SLIP (see *SLIP*), a method for tranferring information through serial links. The dominant protocol for Macintosh dial-up users.

protocol The codes and procedures that make it possible for one computer to exchange data with another.

shareware Software available as a trial at no cost from FTP sites. After the trial period, users are required to register (that is, pay up), which usually gets them more features.

shell The software that lets you interact with the UNIX operating system. Actually, there are DOS shells and other shells as well, but "UNIX shell" is a more common expression.

signature The personalized identification at the end of an e-mail message, automatically loaded by the e-mail program.

SLIP (Serial Line Internet Protocol) Protocol that lets IP (see *IP*) run over telephone circuits and through modems. Essential for anyone connecting through Microsoft Windows.

smiley Dumb little line graphics consisting of a collection of keyboard characters that sort of look like a face with an expression on it when you turn your head to the appropriate angle and subsequently spill your coffee on your mouse. See also *emoticon*.

subject line The line on the e-mail message that tells you what it's about. When used well, it's indispensable. When never changed or simply ignored, it's a terrible thing.

surf To move (virtually) from computer to computer on the Internet, usually without staying too long in any one place.

TCP/IP (Transfer Control Protocol/Internet Protocol) The combination of protocols that let computers on the Internet exchange data among them. TCP/IP is the *sine qua non* of the Internet today, although replacements have recently been proposed.

Telnet Important tool enabling you to log in (see *login*) to a remote computer from the one you're sitting at. Note: You can perform Telnet from Gopher or the World Wide Web, or directly from the command line.

UNIX Operating system specializing in customizability and multiuser capabilities. The software backbone of the Internet.

URL (Universal Resource Locator) A standard addressing system for Internet files and functions, especially apparent on the World Wide Web.

Usenet A networking system, linked to the Internet, that houses the popular newsgroups.

Veronica Search tool that provides keyword-based searches of Gopher directories and files.

WAIS (Wide Area Information Servers) A sophisticated search system designed to make searching user-friendly, efficient, and cumulative.

Winsock The necessary "sockets" for using the Internet through Microsoft Windows over a modem. You must have the Winsock software to use Windows programs such as Mosaic, Cello, Winsock Gopher, Eudora, and so on.

World Wide Web Hypertext-based interface to the Internet, consisting of HTML documents (see *HTML*) with built-in links to other resources. The most popular WWW browser is Mosaic.

XModem Very common protocol (and program) that enables you to transfer files between your personal computer and the host computer (see *host*). In general terms, you FTP files from one UNIX system to another, but if you want the file on your PC or Mac, you use XModem to get it there. See also *FTP* and *Kermit*.

Index

Symbols

A

B

D

E

H

I

J

K

L

M

N

O–P

Q–R

S

T

U

V

W

X–Z